EAST OF THE
S·U·N
OF THE

EAST OF THE SUN

Barbara Bickmore

BALLANTINE BOOKS

NEW YORK

Grateful acknowledgment is made to Liveright Publishing Corporation
for permission to reprint an excerpt from the poem "it is so long since
my heart has been with yours." Reprinted from IS 5 poems by E.E.
Cummings, by permission of Liveright Publishing Corporation. Copyright © 1985 by E.E. Cummings Trust. Copyright 1926 by Horace
Liveright. Copyright 1954 by E.E. Cummings. Copyright © 1985 by
George James Firmage.

Library of Congress Catalog Card Number: 87-91636
ISBN: 0-345-34259-3

Cover design by James R. Harris
Illustration by Jim Griffin
Text design by Mary A. Wirth

Manufactured in the United States of America
First Edition: July 1988
10 9 8 7 6 5 4 3 2 1

ACKNOWLEDGMENTS

▼

I wish to thank:

Dr. Jeffrey Beckwith, a dear friend, who helped me with all of the medical scenes.

Con Sellers, a great teacher and friend, who told me I had talent and opened doors for me.

Walt Davis

Dr. Munir Katul

Diane Browning

and

Meg Ruley, who made a dream come true. Certainly the greatest of agents, she forced me to stretch to places I didn't know were within me.

Ann La Farge, an editor par excellence, who buoyed me up, had faith in me, and made criticism easy to digest.

Frank Clapp for "Animal Birds."

Drs. Stephen and Alison Jennison—whom I met on a train in Guilin, China, and with whom we spent wonderful days. They were young doctors, married, who had taken a six-month leave from their hospital in Cape Town to travel around the world. I have always compared South Africa's racial policy to Nazism, but two more personable, friendly, and intelligent representatives of a country there aren't. These two showed us that South Africa isn't all evil. I learned part of their story on the long train ride, and more in the time we spent together in Kunming. I thought about them a great deal after we parted and began to imagine—fictionalize, if you will—the details that had necessarily remained blank in such a short acquaintance. This novel started out to be what I imagined their story was. However, my agent, Meg Ruley, forced me to a much larger canvas. So this is not their story, after all, though much that I know of Cape Town is from them and their letters. Though they will probably not approve of my view of their country, I want to thank them for letting me into a small part of their lives, for setting my imagination to work, and for the time we spent together. It changed my life.

"Thus do I take possession of thee, O Africa."

—CAESAR, LANDING AT ARDRUMETUM

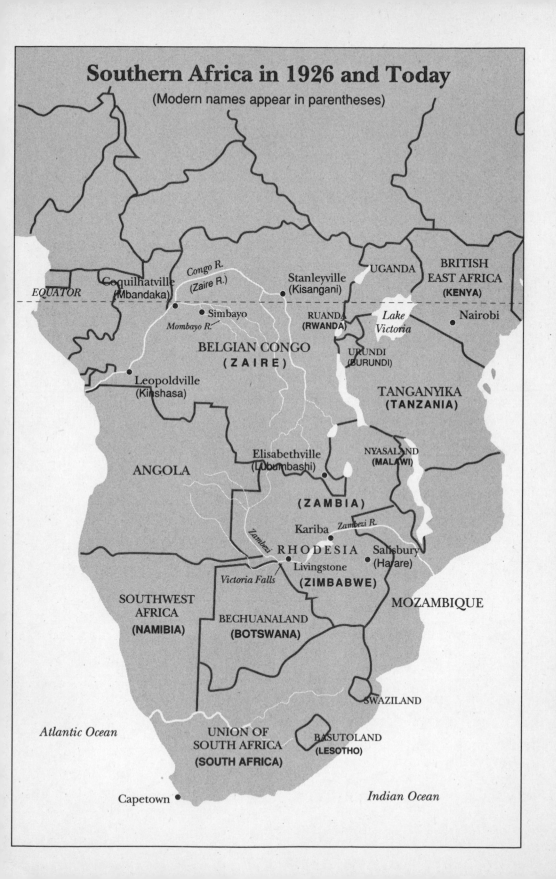

Southern Africa in 1926 and Today
(Modern names appear in parentheses)

EQUATOR

Coquilhatville
(Mbandaka)

Congo R.
(Zaire R.)

Stanleyville
(Kisangani)

UGANDA

BRITISH
EAST AFRICA
(KENYA)

• Simbayo

RUANDA
(RWANDA)

Lake
Victoria

• Nairobi

Mombayo R.

BELGIAN CONGO
(Z A I R E)

URUNDI
(BURUNDI)

Leopoldville
(Kinshasa)

TANGANYIKA
(TANZANIA)

ANGOLA

Elisabethville
(Lubumbashi)

NYASALAND
(MALAWI)

(Z A M B I A)

Zambezi R.

Kariba

Salisbury
(Harare)

Zambezi

R H O D E S I A

SOUTHWEST
AFRICA
(NAMIBIA)

Victoria Falls

Livingstone

(ZIMBABWE)

MOZAMBIQUE

BECHUANALAND
(BOTSWANA)

SWAZILAND

Atlantic Ocean

UNION OF
SOUTH AFRICA

BASUTOLAND
(LESOTHO)

(SOUTH AFRICA)

Capetown •

Indian Ocean

PART ONE

▼

1926
TO
1931

CHAPTER 1

▼

PEELING PAINT CRUMBLED ON HER FINGERS AS LILIANE RAN HER hand along the railing of the old wooden boat, which still chugged up the swollen river. She patted herself with a soggy handkerchief to keep the perspiration from dripping down her forehead into her eyes and blinked as the salt stung. Her pale dress hung damply on her body. She sat staring at where they'd come from, listening to the soft, erratic murmur of the engine, looking at the tall, green-black trees that overhung the river. She felt they would reach out and grab her if she got too near them; she shivered despite the sultry heat. By the banks of the sluggish river, where sunshine dappled through the heavy leaves, crocodiles snapped in the muddy water. The denseness of the trees, the encroaching jungle, and the strange echoing animal noises seemed to pull her ever deeper into Africa.

A solid woman in her midthirties, her manner brisker by far than Liliane's, even though her clothes were as damp, sat fanning herself with a handkerchief. Perspiration glowed on her upper lip. "It gets easier," she said.

Liliane smiled but said nothing. She wondered if she'd ever feel energetic again. The humidity wafted around her like an invisible sea, the heat and dampness palpable. Waves shimmered in the air above the water. Nothing, except the crocodiles and an occasional hippopotamus, seemed to move. There wasn't a breath of air. Even when she inhaled, Liliane felt as though she were fighting for breath.

Parrots cawed and monkeys screeched in the trees overhead.

The river smelled of decay. All through the last eleven days on this slow-moving river, which wound through the heart of Africa, Liliane had peered at the monotonous wall of green that unrolled before her eyes. She did not tire of looking at it; it mesmerized her.

Now and then, far apart, there were river villages, huddles of huts crowded beside a bank along which naked children ran, waving, laughing, and calling out in high-pitched voices. Unchanging,

3

▼

seemingly unending, the green impenetrable wall wove on. Where trees overhung the river, it was gloomy, but when the river was wide enough for sunlight to pour down, the sky was cobalt. In the late afternoon, long shadows formed, spreading out ahead of them on the water. Clouds hung, fixed, in the sky, large white balls accentuating the blueness behind them. As evening came, the clouds grew denser. Darkness descended quickly in the tropics.

Then, as if by magic, the boat would pull up to a village dock, where there was always wood for sale. As the natives carried the wood onto the boat, fires began to flicker into life along the shore, and voices, filled with laughter, carried into the evening. As Liliane and the crew ate, so did the villagers; the air was filled with pungent aromas.

As the fires died down, so did the voices. Then the utter quietness of the tropical jungle descended.

The only sound at night was the buzzing of mosquitoes.

Then dawn—the unbelievable Congo dawn. With the night air still damp against her face, she would awake when the ship's engines began to hum and the boat lurched back into the current. The dawn burst over the jungle treetops. There is no sunrise on earth like this, she thought, and watched it from the railing, day after day after day.

Liliane came out of her reverie as the older woman pulled up a dirty, torn deck chair and sat down. She wore a white sun helmet and a short-sleeved white dress—white, just as Dr. Hathaway had worn. Liliane had read somewhere that white deflected heat.

"How long have you been here?" she asked Rose Eversham.

"Six years. I came out with the doctor." Her voice faded, almost whispering. "Six wonderful years."

"Why did you come?"

"Oh, probably the same reason you did." She patted Liliane's arm. "I wanted to help people who mightn't be helped if it weren't for me. I wanted to show backward people how to find God. I wanted to be important." She laughed. "And I didn't want a man to be at the center of my life."

You didn't? thought Liliane. Not at all? Not ever? The image of Baxter Hathaway filtered through her consciousness.

Miss Eversham continued. "So I came to the heart of Africa to find my life ruled completely by a man." Her soft smile indicated that she did not resent this. "Sticky wicket, what?"

Is she in love with him? wondered Liliane, waving her damp handkerchief as a fan. It helped not at all.

"What's Simbayo like?" she asked.

"Wait till you see what he's done. He's cleared away the jungle almost single-handedly. Built the hospital himself. Cut down the trees himself. Raised money for all the instruments, the supplies, the drugs, the furniture. Designed the dormitories. Everything . . . every bed, every stick of furniture, every pin, every space cleared of trees, every trained helper, every pirogue, the leper colony, the conquering of malaria, the low infant mortality rate . . . are all due to Dr. Hathaway." Her voice held awe, devotion.

Tension fluttered across Liliane's chest: Leper colony.

Staring into the dark jungle, watching the wake of the boat as it chugged up the river, listening to the drone of insects that buzzed around her head, Liliane murmured, "You love him, don't you?"

Miss Eversham laughed. "Oh, m'dear. You'll soon see." She reached out and touched Liliane's arm. "It's much deeper and less complex than that. Of course I love him or I'd never have stayed here so long. I love and respect him more than anyone I've ever known, but his mind is on a much higher level than romance. As it is, I'm allowed to serve him, God, and humanity, all at the same time."

"The best of all possible worlds?" Liliane asked softly.

"Exactly," Miss Eversham said. "I have the most rewarding life imaginable." She chuckled. "Except for the heat, the interminable enervating omnipresent humidity. But it's worse for you, coming new to it. You'll get used to it."

Would she? Liliane had spent nineteen days on a crowded paddle wheeler coming up the Congo itself before these last eleven on the Mombayo. It had been over two months since she had left home.

Home. Her mind drifted back to the moment, over a year ago, that had given direction to her life.

She was nineteen in that golden year of 1926, in that age of innocence. She danced the Charleston and wanted to be like Irene Castle and had recently bobbed her hair, much to her father's disapproval.

They lived in Buffalo, New York, a dirty, dreary city, but Liliane had nothing with which to compare it; she had had a happy childhood. Her father, the minister of All Souls' Church, was a kind, soft-spoken man; the only time he got really angry with Liliane was when she said "damn" within his hearing.

Her mother was the most beautiful person she'd ever seen—

long, soft brown hair, big brown eyes, a constant smile on her face. Lucinda Wentworth enjoyed being the wife of a minister and the mother of three children. Liliane grew up with the smell of home-made bread and freshly baked cookies greeting her when she came home from school. Her parents hoped she would become a teacher rather than a nurse because nurses had to handle dirty things and look at people's bodies, but Liliane wanted to help alleviate suffering. She wanted to help mankind.

She also wanted to have fun. She went to dances and parties every weekend and flirted outrageously, but except for a mad infatuation in the tenth grade, she had never been in love. She'd see Clara Bow and Greta Garbo in the movies and she longed to suffer as they did, all for love, but none of the boys she knew affected her that way. The boys she knew all seemed the same to her. They were all well groomed, and they were all studying to be businessmen or lawyers or something very practical. They were interested in how much money they'd earn and how soon they could afford a car. Liliane wanted more out of life than that. She didn't want money to be her criterion for success. She wanted her life to have meaning.

Two or three times a year missionaries on home leave came through Buffalo to show flickery homemade movies and to tell what their lives were like and how many souls they were saving. Collections were taken to help their missions. Liliane liked to listen to their stories. She heard missionaries from China and India and Africa—all heathen countries where the natives didn't believe in *her* God. Sometimes she'd wonder what it would be like to go to China and help save those pagan souls, show them the *true* God, but she wasn't really sure who or what the real God was.

A year ago, when Liliane was in her second year of nursing school at the university, one of the world's most noted missionaries came through Buffalo and stayed with the Wentworths in their big, old three-story parsonage on Euclid Avenue right next to the church.

Her mother told her that Baxter Hathaway had been a Broadway actor and then a movie star. At thirty-four, at the height of his fame, he had renounced his acting career, studied medicine at Stanford University, and given away all of his possessions.

Heading for Africa in 1920, at the age of forty, as a medical missionary, he wanted to heal bodies and to save souls. What he wrought out of a God-forsaken jungle along a tributary of the Congo River had become an inspiration to practicing Christians everywhere. Dr. Hathaway was marveled at and revered. This great work of compassion, by a famous and successful person, appealed to Americans; writers and politicians and famous churchmen made pilgrimages to Simbayo. By the time he came to visit the Wentworths in Buffalo, Baxter Hathaway was one of the most famous missionaries of his time.

Liliane remembered the day clearly. Even then she had suspected it would change her life.

Baxter Hathaway was forty-six years old when he stood in the Wentworth doorway; he had to stoop to enter the room. It was summer and he was dressed all in white; he carried a white sun helmet. Liliane had been watering a fern; she turned her face toward the door and nearly dropped the watering can. As her mother and father greeted him, welcoming him to their home, Liliane stared, immobilized.

Dr. Hathaway had a ruddy face, tanned from years in Africa, eyes so blue they cut through her, chestnut-brown hair graying at the temples, and big hands with long, slender fingers—the hands of a surgeon. He wore a white short-sleeved shirt that day, and his arms were laced with muscles that showed he was used to hard physical labor. He was the most impressive man she'd ever seen.

"Lili," her mother called. She must have called several times from the tone of her voice. "Liliane!"

And he stood there—so tall, filling the doorway, stooped a bit so he could fit through it—looking at her, smiling down at her.

He moved into the house and the center of the room changed: It followed him.

She heard his voice.

He held out his hand and took hers in it, putting his other hand over their combined hands, and smiled into her eyes. She thought perhaps she was in a dream, the world moving slowly, everything seen through gauze. His hands were dry and warm. Then she heard the rich timbre of his voice, but now, as she tried to relive the moment, she couldn't remember what he had said.

"Here, m'dear. A spot of tea." The clipped British voice interrupted Liliane's musings. Rose handed her a cup and saucer.

"I can't tell you how glad I am to be . . . Oh, dear, sounds so funny. Glad to be coming home," she said.

She was returning from a six months' leave in her native England. She told Liliane that it was the longest six months she had known. She had wanted to be back in Simbayo the whole time. That was her home now. She had felt a stranger in England.

"I feel so . . . unprepared." Liliane's voice was low. She felt wilted. Bright ringlets of damp hair curled uncontrollably around her face. Her perspiration-soaked dress clung to her body, accentuating the thin figure that would have been boyish had it not been for her lovely, curving breasts. She knew she looked worn out rather than appealing. She noticed her own paleness next to Miss Eversham's rosy, healthy glow, though Rose had no waist and her legs were as straight as a piano's. Her arms were muscular. Liliane was afraid that she could not cope with Africa the way Miss Eversham could; the older woman was a picture of solidity and health.

"M'dear, don't worry. Everyone will be patient. The doctor is only impatient with himself; he's really quite unaware of his surroundings and what's going on most of the time. He leaves the daily business to us." Liliane wondered who "us" was. "His mind is on other things. He'll give you much time to learn. He'll hardly even be aware of you. If he doesn't talk to you, don't take it personally. He's solving important problems . . . far weightier things than what you and I are concerned with."

What shall *I* be concerned with? wondered Liliane, leaning over the railing, staring into the jungle and hearing its dissonance of strange sounds.

Liliane fanned herself; the silence stretched into hours. The heavy languorous midday, when a hush fell over the river, brought drowsiness, detachment from reality. Liliane's senses were drugged by the humidity, by the enormous silence, broken now and then by the screeching of monkeys running through the treetops or of birds calling harshly.

Miss Eversham got up and stood at the rail of the old boat.

"We're almost there!" she said breathlessly. Liliane wondered how she could tell. It all looked alike.

"Oh, yes, here's Simbayo!" Rose cried.

And there, around a bend in the river, was Liliane's future home. Abruptly, the jungle ended. Not even stumps remained. She saw low white buildings; the longest one must be the hospital. They looked trim and cozy, shaded by immense overhanging trees. Around them was bright sunlight and openness. She could already hear voices calling, chickens squawking, muted as the boat rolled across the water. She could see natives walking; two men in loincloths tugged at a huge pig. A woman, wearing only a bright yellow skirt and bangles around her ankles, carried a water jar on her turbanned head. Her breasts bounced as she strode along. Three naked children chased a dog in a circle, their laughter floating down the river, making Liliane smile. All dashed toward the dock when the ship's whistle blasted.

From this distance the compound gave the false impression of tidiness. No grass grew on the hard-packed earth; wherever someone walked, dust rose in small, flurrying circles before settling again, lending the compound a miragelike quality. The screened windows surprised her; below nearly every window was a small fire, apparently coming from clay pots.

"The relatives of the sick person," Miss Eversham explained. "They come and cook for the patient. They are from varying tribes, each of whom thinks another tribe might try to poison him. So members of the family do the cooking to safeguard him. Or her."

"Do they stay in the hospital, too?" asked Liliane.

"No, they sleep on the ground, by the pots. They don't go off into the jungle for fear of animals."

The air was like steam coming out of a prehistoric mist.

"What kind of animals?" asked Liliane, a thrill surging through her.

"Gorillas, elephants, a leopard now and then, pythons—that sort."

Liliane tried to ignore the gooseflesh rising on her arm.

"From dark until dawn"—Miss Eversham smiled—"we have curfew. No pirogues."

"What is a pirogue again?"

Rose laughed. "A dugout canoe. At night one can't see the crocs or the hippos that could easily tip over a pirogue, so the doctor has a rule: No travel after dark."

Liliane looked at the large clearing that had been hewn out of the tropical forest, which hovered behind it as though waiting to pounce and reclaim its land. Strangely, the jungle seemed to hold no hint of danger. She tried to brush away the mosquitoes that circled her head, buzzing into her ears.

Waiting at the dock was a short, plump woman with braids wound around her head, holding the ubiquitous white sun helmet. There was no sign of Dr. Hathaway.

"That's Heidi. Heidi Schmitt," Miss Eversham said, waving joyously. She turned back to Liliane. "Up until now, she and I have been the only two nurses. She manages everything. If Heidi can't get it, it can't be gotten. Any organization here is due to Heidi." Rose's voice betrayed her growing excitement. "Everyone will make you most welcome here," she said. "Your help will be appreciated. And a new face will add variety and diversion for us all."

The boat pulled into the dock, ropes were tossed to half-naked men ashore. As soon as the boat was securely tied, Miss Eversham jumped down and embraced Heidi.

Liliane stood at the rail, watching as boatmen began to lift down the many bales and wooden crates. The wharf was filled with activity, sharp staccato calls in a strange, high-pitched language. Liliane thought she would never learn to decipher it. She stood there, feeling helpless, abandoned, until Miss Eversham turned to her and indicated that she should jump down. She did, landing squarely in front of the German nurse.

Rose put her arm through Liliane's. "Heidi," her voice came in little rushes, "this is our new nurse, Liliane. Liliane, my dear and good friend, Heidi."

Heidi's face was not cordial. In her thick German accent, all she said was, "The doctor said you were coming. We didn't know when." Her eyes never left Miss Eversham, who was instructing a laborer to be gentle with her boxes.

"I've brought you presents, Heidi!" Rose said. "Oh, you don't know how I missed you, how glad I am to be back. Six months is too long for a leave!" She chattered as she waved her hands, indicating where her boxes should go. Liliane's boxes were stacked in a corner, and Heidi told two natives to take them to the dormitory.

Although it was late afternoon, a heavy mist, reeling along the river, began to dim the relentless sunshine. It felt damper than ever.

As the two nurses led the way to the dormitory, Liliane's first impression of tidiness was quickly dispelled. The community was unkempt, with garbage tossed carelessly around. Liliane saw someone emptying a slop jar from a window into an open drain. She shuddered. Broken crockery was everywhere and dirty bandages rolled by in little balls. Liliane nearly tripped over a large tree root.

None of the natives stared at her; as she neared, they cast their eyes to the ground after greeting Rose with grins and words of what Liliane surmised were welcome. Rose nodded her head and spoke unintelligible staccato sounds to each person she passed. All those bare breasts discombobulated Liliane; once in a great while she had stared at her own in her dresser mirror but had vaguely felt she should hurry into a chemise. The black glistening skins made her feel pallid by comparison.

Voices droned lazily from the hospital building, and she wondered what the other buildings were. There had to be a dining room, Dr. Hathaway's office, storage buildings, dormitories. Though the buildings were all simple rectangles, there was a grace about them. They had not been built without thought.

When they came to the dormitory it was clean. Miss Eversham showed Liliane to her room, where her baggage had preceded her and was piled high in a corner. The cross ventilation helped to cool her, and the screened windows were shaded. There was a narrow iron bed, with clean though wrinkled sheets, and a kerosene lamp on a small table next to a wicker chair. A washstand stood on the table next to the bed. There was no closet. The room was spartan but looked surprisingly comfortable. The door opened onto a shady verandah that ran the length of the building. A bright green and yellow parrot flew past her window.

Despite the dampness and the terrible heat, despite the lethargy the humidity created, Liliane now felt excitement flow through her. Rose spoke sharply to one of the blacks, who ambled off, returning shortly with a pail of water, which he poured into Liliane's washstand.

Heidi stood looking at them, saying nothing, staring at Liliane with unblinking eyes.

Miss Eversham smiled and said, "You'll want to rest and wash. We'll leave you alone. But dinner will be in about an hour and a half. You'll hear the bell." Walking to the door, she pointed, through a grove of trees, along a cleared path. "The dining hall is over there. We dine at six o'clock."

Then she turned to Heidi, who broke into a beatific smile and put her hand through Rose's arm; they walked away together.

Liliane took off her damp clothes and unpacked only enough to find another dress, which was wrinkled already. She sponged herself off in the cool water and then, dampening the towel, lay down and put it across her head. In a few minutes she'd examine her room, look out at her surroundings, orient herself to this new existence. She was aware of a stab of disappointment. She had waited a year to reach this destination. Now that she was here, momentary depression settled around her. A nagging awareness of why she was depressed circled in her consciousness: Baxter Hathaway had not come to meet her. She had carried the memory of him within her every day since that first time she'd met him.

She lay down and closed her eyes, remembering.

That Saturday just over a year ago, he had arrived at the Wentworths' at noon. The Ladies' Aid Society had planned a social for him that evening, but Liliane was going to a dance, not the social. She had long ago started living her own life. Her parents realized their interests didn't have to be hers. And how else would she find a suitable husband if she didn't go out to parties where nice young men were? She was going to the dance with Gilbert Phipps, with whom she'd been friends since childhood.

But once Baxter Hathaway walked through her front door, she was lost.

He kept her parents mesmerized while he told them of tribal rites, of baboons, of snakes, and of crocodiles. He told them of poor, uneducated Africans who needed medicine and food, of lepers with no toes and stumps for arms and empty sockets for noses. Liliane shivered, even though it was nearly one hundred degrees that July evening, picturing people walking around without fingers. He told of little purple flowers and oranges as big as grapefruit. He told them of torrential rain and of how he had brought God to the jungle: He was saving bodies so that God could save souls.

The rich melody of his voice magnetized them, and his handsome face engraved itself upon Liliane's mind. She watched the way he swallowed and the way his hand lay on the table. She saw him smile with his mouth but not with his eyes. Once, however, when he looked directly at her, his eyes twinkled, and she felt they were sharing some secret, though she didn't know what it was.

They were still sitting around the dinner table listening to his stories when Gil rang the doorbell. Liliane had forgotten all about him. And instead of rushing to get dressed and go with Gil, she just told him she couldn't go to the dance. She didn't even give an excuse; she just told him she couldn't go. Gil stood on the stoop, waiting for an explanation, and she closed the door in his face and went back to sit across from Dr. Hathaway and listen to his stories about black people and exotic animals in the Congo.

She followed him around all evening, and all the next day, too, sitting enraptured while he preached the sermon, his thunderous voice filling the big church. To him she must have seemed a smitten schoolgirl. After all, he was twenty-six years older than she was.

All the time Baxter Hathaway was in Buffalo, all forty-four hours, Liliane had a chill. Gooseflesh never left her, and she wondered if she were catching some dread disease that he might have brought with him from black Africa.

She was. But it was nothing medicine could cure.

Liliane told herself that it was souls that she, too, wanted to save.

The dinner bell pulled her out of her reverie. At first she couldn't remember where she was.

Rushing into her clothes, hardly stopping to smooth her hair, she dashed along the hard-packed dirt path under the tall okoume trees. Breathless when she arrived at the dining hall, she opened the screen door and saw, down the length of the room, the two nurses, and Dr. Hathaway at the head of the long table. The three were sitting there in silence, waiting for her. The doctor gave no greeting, other than nodding his head to acknowledge her.

"I'm sorry," she apologized about her lateness, "but I fell asleep."

When she sat down next to Miss Eversham, Dr. Hathaway bowed his head and said grace, his resonant voice flowing out into the jungle. Heidi clapped her hands and boys began walking in with platters of food.

There was food in abundance. A large bowl of a thick vegetable soup and a mountain of rice, carrots, small new onions, and steamed bananas. She was to find steamed bananas at every meal. Everyone helped themselves, and Rose and Heidi giggled and gossiped like schoolgirls. Dr. Hathaway smiled several times but did not talk. Liliane heard the mosquitoes buzzing outside the windows, the sharp slap of bare feet on the earthen floor as platters were brought in or taken away, and food being chewed.

She was too hot to eat much and marveled at the others' appetites. She glanced at the silent doctor.

He wore a wrinkled but clean white shirt; the muscles in his arms rippled below his short sleeves. His face looked even more authoritative, stronger, and handsomer than when she'd first seen him; the gray at his temples was more pronounced. She'd forgotten what clear blue eyes, what a forceful chin, he had; what a big man he was. His fingers clasped around his fork were strong and sensitive; his hands eloquent.

When dinner was finished, Dr. Hathaway stood, said, "We will sing hymn one sixty-seven," and handed them each a hymnbook. Walking to the end of the room, he picked up an old, scratched guitar, handling it as if it were a jewel. Music poured forth, richer in timbre than Liliane had ever heard from a guitar. The clear, crystal voices of the two nurses blended in perfect harmony. Dr. Hathaway's voice was a beautiful baritone. Liliane's soprano was drowned out.

He returned to his place at the table, picked up a well-worn Bible, and read a brief passage.

Then he and the nurses stood. At last he looked at Liliane. "Would you like a tour of our establishment?" It was the first time he had spoken to her.

"Oh, yes," she said, her chair falling behind her as she scrambled to rise.

Miss Eversham and Heidi exchanged looks and stood behind their chairs, waiting for Liliane and the doctor to walk the length of the dining hall. He opened the screen door and touched her elbow as she went down the solitary step.

"I'm sorry not to have met you at the boat," he said, his voice resonant yet quiet. "I didn't know you would be here today. I trust your trip was without catastrophe."

Liliane laughed lightly. "Well, it was an adventure!"

She suddenly felt light-headed, as though the last month in Africa, perhaps even the whole scary time since she'd left Buffalo, had fallen away from her. This big, silent man beside her gave her a feeling of safety.

They walked away from the buildings toward the jungle. Natives roamed the compound or squatted by small fires, eating bananas. "They get eight bananas a day as food rations," Dr. Hathaway explained. Liliane wondered if that was all they got.

Everyone was so black! And so undressed. At the same time that it was like nothing Liliane had ever experienced, it was almost exactly as she'd imagined. But dirtier. The indecipherable chatter of the natives, the jungle surrounding them, the screeches of the baboons—it seemed as though she had been prepared for it all. Except for the slowness; everyone moved so slowly, and to a Buffalo, New York, girl this was frustrating. The humidity slowed her down, she knew, but she took for granted that, with time, her blood would become used to that and she would begin to function efficiently. Perspiration dripped down her forehead. No wonder the natives wore so few clothes. Though seminudity was embarrassing to an American Episcopalian, it nevertheless seemed sensible.

"I want to show you my zoo," he explained. Chickens squawked and picked in the dirt. A pig, tied to a tree, snorted and pawed at the earth. Liliane saw an ostrich through the leaves. The zoo was behind a wire fence; in little paddocks were dozens of animals, all making shrill, deafening noises when they saw Dr. Hathaway.

They walked beside the animals, all of whom tried to nuzzle

Dr. Hathaway through the wire. He gave them tidbits of food and related the history of each. His particular pet was the antelope, whom he called Zulu.

"Africa's animals are its jewels," he said, rubbing Zulu's nose. "These have all been brought in injured. Sometimes I let them go when they're well. Sometimes I keep them—I get attached and I like to think I'm keeping these from being hunted."

Liliane didn't ask if that was preferable to the lack of freedom.

He turned to look directly at her, the first time he had done so. "I imagine you'd like to see the hospital. After all, that's what you came to do, work." They walked back toward the compound, where natives were strolling back and forth. Several who passed had gentian violet on their hands or feet. Neither they nor the doctor looked at each other. Most of them looked at Liliane out of the corners of their eyes.

Noticing this, he laughed. "Be prepared to be stared at. I imagine they didn't know white ladies could be so pretty. They've not seen any other than Heidi and Rose."

The hospital was cleaner than the compound, but not by much. Sanitary conditions left much to be desired. Each room was dark and narrow; the patients lay on mats on the floor. Only one room had a bed.

"This," he explained, indicating the white man lying on the bed, "is for Europeans. They're not used to sleeping on the floor." Liliane noticed that this room was swept and even the walls looked as though they might have been washed. Dr. Hathaway continued, "Africans are frightened of beds, afraid they'll fall off onto the floor."

"How did a European get out here and become sick?"

"Malaria," he said. "We get them often from the logging camps. It's either malaria or accidents caused by saws. Once in a while a tree falls on a novice. Nasty, that."

The white man sat up, leaning on his elbow. He was unshaven and unkempt. "I think I've died and gone to heaven," he said in what she thought must be an Irish accent.

"You see," the doctor said to Liliane, "already your presence is working miracles."

The operating room was the only room in Simbayo that had electricity. Bare forty-watt bulbs hung down in four places from the center of the ceiling. As soon as they walked in, Liliane could tell that this was the doctor's domain. Fire lit his eyes as he explained, with wide gestures, what was accomplished here. There were four operating tables—could he possibly perform four operations in the same room with no sterilization in between?

"What illnesses are here?" she asked.

He sighed heavily. "Sickness," he said, "is the archvillain of Africa. Long ago some bishop said that 'one is not born into Africa, but doomed into it.' They stand little chance of ever being well. Sickness is a condition of life with them. They don't even know what it would be like to feel well, most of them.

"Yaws, worms, sleeping sickness, malaria, bilharziasis, tuberculosis," he answered. His voice went on. Energy emanated from him as he strode around the room. His deep voice flowed through her; it caressed, vibrated, reached inside her. No wonder women had dreamed of him, yearned for him. In this light his eyes looked like molten steel. His body was like a panther's: lean, graceful, ready to overpower.

Suddenly she was aware that he had stopped talking. She hadn't even heard what he had said. Prickliness covered her body.

Dr. Hathaway looked at her for a long time where she stood in the center of the room, illuminated, as the quick darkness of the tropics descended.

He stared at her for so long that the silence became pronounced, and she guessed what she must have known all along: That it was chemistry as well as God that had brought her to this remote outpost.

Even though she was tired from the trip, even though the equatorial weather enervated her more than she'd thought possible, blood surged through her. The doctor seemed to be looking not only at her but into her, as though her thin veneer of clothing fell away until she stood in that strange Congo twilight, naked in soul as well as body.

Then he was walking across the room toward her, his large body framed against the last dying light of day. He stopped inches from her, looking down at her, the darkness making his eyes unreadable. She could feel his breathing.

"Come observe tomorrow," he said, his voice low. For a minute she thought he might reach out to touch her. But his voice remained impersonal. "You might as well throw yourself into it right away. We can use all the help we're offered." He added, "You must be tired."

She didn't want to go to bed yet. She wanted to sit up and talk, to look at him, to hear him explain Simbayo, to hear his voice talk about anything.

He began to walk from the room, out into the night that was alive with the sounds of jabbering animals. She followed him.

Darkness had fallen as it had every night for the last month, as it had every night for the last millennium in this primeval land. Quickly. There was no lingering light, no streaks in the sky, no prolonged twilight.

At the door to her room, he said, "As you find things you may need or have questions you want answered, make a list and Heidi or Rose will help. I hope"—he paused—"that you will not be sorry you came. I hope that we do not disappoint you. It's a very quiet life here. There are no entertainments, few pleasures. It is a far cry from American comforts."

"I didn't come for comfort," she responded. "I came to be of service."

That's not totally true, she thought. I came to be near you.

"There's no place I know where God is nearer," he said, his voice hollow, and, turning, walked off into the night. She stared after him as he faded from view.

CHAPTER 2

▼

THE ONE TIME THEY HAD BEEN ALONE, RIGHT BEFORE DINNER THAT Sunday afternoon over a year ago in Buffalo, she had wanted to know everything about him, about Africa.

"Where *is* Simbayo?" she asked.

He smiled down at her; he was sitting in the big overstuffed chair, and she was curled on a pillow on the floor.

"Let's see," he answered, talking to her as he would a child. "What do you know about Africa?"

"It's hot, and there are jungles and deserts, and the people are colored. It's primitive and savage; there are poisonous snakes—"

His laughter stopped her. "That's all true," he admitted, "but woefully inadequate. Africa is also a state of mind."

"What do you mean?"

"I call it Simbayo because that means East of the Sun. . . ."

Liliane smiled. "There is no such place as east of the sun." He must be teasing her.

"Oh, but that's where I live. See, it's a mental state. All those places that society relegates to 'God-forsaken place,' where no normal white person could imagine living, are East of the Sun. . . . Simbayo is such a place."

Liliane looked up at the powerful figure, trying to understand what he was saying. "But, really, where *is* it?"

She thought his smile was tinged with sadness.

"It's over one thousand miles up the Congo River, and beyond that two hundred or so miles as the crow flies, but many hundreds of miles as the Mombayo River winds, down the very heart of the Belgian Congo jungle."

"Belgian Congo?"

"It's an enormous country in the middle of Africa that Belgium thinks it owns. Which is a step better than being owned by its king, which was the case for many years."

"You mean one man owned a country?"

Baxter Hathaway nodded. "Or tried to. All of the inhabitants were his personal possessions, and he made a fortune selling or enslaving them."

"How dreadful," cried Liliane.

"That's no longer true, of course. But the government doesn't bother us. I suspect it's either glad to have us in such a remote spot or unaware of our existence. It encourages missionaries and hospitals."

"The whole world must know of *your* existence."

Just then her father had announced that the chicken and dumplings were ready.

East of the Sun . . .

AND IT WAS SO STRANGE, IT WAS SO LONELY, IT WAS SO . . . SHE TRIED to capture it in a letter to her parents.

It's not frightening, really, but it's unlike anything or anyplace I've ever known. I feel cut off from life since I'm only able to communicate with Dr. Hathaway, who does not invite conversation, and with Rose, who is a dear soul and always helpful, but she is about a dozen years older than I, and I am afraid we have nothing at all in common. She is terribly British, so, despite her friendliness, she exhibits a certain reserve. She seems not to abide foolishness and is very efficient. Unless we're talking about medical cases, we have little to share. And so far I feel terribly inadequate as a nurse. She and Heidi are so experienced and so familiar with the ailments here. Heidi, whose thick German accent often renders her English incomprehensible to me, never cracks a smile or initiates any conversation with me, though she and Rose chatter endlessly. She seems to suffer me. I very much doubt that these women and I will develop any kind of closeness.

The natives and I eye each other with friendly smiles and a complete lack of understanding. I am sure that even were I to try I could never understand their language. Dr. H. never even tries. Rose has mastered it a little. It's not a language, I think, in which English-speaking people could *ever* become proficient. It doesn't even sound like it has words. I don't know how to explain what it does sound like. They don't know how to talk quietly—they speak shrilly and loudly and sound as if they're ready to argue most of the time, even when they're helpful and smiling.

They are eager to please. I tried to move a heavy bench into the shade yesterday and immediately four natives rushed to help. They are not suspicious but implicitly trust us and "white man's medicine."

I'm not sorry I made this journey—at least, not yet. It's certainly not a place where I'd want to spend my life, not even very many years, but it is an adventure and I feel brave and proud that I've dared to undertake it.

Oh, how I miss you. Mother, I miss the long talks right before bed, and I miss the fun of shopping with you. There's no one here to giggle with over the silly things that have always amused you and me. There's no smell of warm apple pie, or laughter around the dining table. At night, as I lie in bed after a busy day, but one where I feel I haven't really mattered to anyone, I remember the Friday nights when the three of us used to go to the movies, and I'd sit between the two of you, holding hands with both of you. At the time it just seemed safe, but now it's one of my most treasured memories.

I look around Simbayo and try to imagine how you'd view it. Daddy, I think you'd view it as a place ripe for God's presence.

She stopped and thought for a moment. Wasn't God supposed to be everywhere?

I already feel different, and I've barely been here two weeks. Where's the girl who stood in front of her mirror putting on dress after dress trying to decide which to wear to the Saturday-night dance? The only mirror I have here is the hand mirror I brought with me, and that scarcely reflects half my face. One tends to forget one's looks here, anyhow.

Yet I am so aware of how everyone else looks. Rose and Heidi both look so solid, so purposeful. Rose seems older than thirty-five. Her hair is mouse-brown, cut very short and straight. She wears thick glasses, which magnify her quite pretty gray eyes, and she has a beautiful English complexion. Neither she nor Heidi has one whit of style; they wear housedresses that are wrinkled and look as though someone cast them off from too much wear. Probably sent over by some church's missionary society. Clothes are utilitarian and not for enhancement.

Heidi always has a severe countenance, even when she is being gentle with a native. Her dark blond hair is wound in thick braids around her head. I think if she ever laughed or softened her judgmental look, she might be attractive in a Teutonic or Wagnerian manner. She intimidates me a little. I know, Daddy, that surprises you. You never think anything or anyone daunts me, do you? Well, I'm always on my best and most ladylike behavior when Heidi's around. Good, you'll say. She must be a good influence. Ha! Oh— dear—how I miss you. As I wrote this last, I could see the two of you smiling.

Yet I'm not sorry I left home and came halfway around the world.

Black people *smell* different. Dr. Hathaway says it has to do with diet. They think *we* smell. Well, sometimes we do, even to ourselves. I long for a bath, even a shower. And a hole in the ground is a far cry from a flush toilet. It takes some getting used to.

Dr. Hathaway is a god here. I think he likes the role. He is aloof (yes, even with his staff) and sometimes I think he forgets we're here. He has prodigious energy, and I wonder if he ever sleeps. He seldom indulges in small talk and

never appears to relax. He's always busy, as though driven
to accomplish all that he can in this lifetime. The vitality he
injects into this community, his complete selflessness, his
dedication to what he calls his black children is truly what
Christianity must be about. I'm not afraid of him (or even
intimidated by him, as I am of Heidi), but he doesn't seem
quite human. He's on a far grander scale.

I am often lonely in the evenings. One can't take walks
in the jungle alone, and there are few books here (do send
me some—anything!), and no radio, of course. I wonder,
if I were troubled, to whom I would turn. Maybe I would
have to come home to you.

Do keep my letters safe. When I return, I'd like a record
of my months (or years) here. (I wonder if I can stick it out
the two years I promised? Right now two years here seems
like forever.)

As the weeks became months, Liliane slipped into the rhythm
of Simbayo. Heidi still intimidated her, but Liliane relaxed more
in her presence. When she initiated conversation with Dr. Hathaway, he responded, sometimes even prolonging the conversation.
She fell into the habit, as did Rose and Heidi, of napping after
lunch, during the worst heat of the day. The heat reminded her of
summers in Buffalo, when people would sit on front-porch swings,
fanning themselves, the swings and the lightning bugs the only
things moving. Liliane found the Congo heat no more debilitating
than Buffalo in its humid heat spells. The major difference was that
after a while Buffalo's weather changed. The Congo's never did.

Nor did the scenery. Always green, so dense as to be nearly
black; foliage whose leaves dropped big beads of water; so thick
and luxuriant as to be impenetrable.

There were narrow, well-worn paths leading into the jungle,
and periodically Liliane saw people using them. To where? From
where? There was nothing out there—only more jungle.

The smell of decay hung in the air. Replenishing itself daily,
the jungle died nightly and sent the aroma of death throughout the
land. Yet it was filled with life. Monkeys swung through treetops,
screeching loudly. Wild, gaudily painted birds swept by in long
arcs and nibbled crumbs from the ground, unfrightened by the
people.

There was much that Liliane found distasteful. The sanitary
conditions revolted her. Animals defecated all over the compound.

No one bothered to clean it up. Apparently, Xhoso was supposed to, but he somehow never got around to it. Human excrement was dumped out of windows into ditches that had been dug for that purpose. The ubiquitous smell was of urine. Liliane wondered if no one else smelled it; the others seemed oblivious of it. With all this waste, flies were everywhere. Mosquitoes were peskier, but screens helped with that, and the beds were surrounded by mosquito netting so that only their buzzing was irritating.

All water had to be boiled, so there was little to drink or to wash with. One could not wear clean clothes daily, not even clean underwear. Heidi and Rose wore sturdy stockings even in this climate, but Liliane abandoned hers the second day.

She slept poorly, the humidity awakening her when she found her pillow so wet she stuck to it. But that was no different from a Buffalo summer.

A redeeming feature was the food. Dr. Hathaway prided himself on his garden. The garden space he had cleared years ago had four rotating vegetable beds, and as soon as one began to bear forth, he planted seeds in another section. Early morning, before the others were up, he would be on his knees in his garden. That and the zoo were his passions. When he slept, she couldn't fathom. The routine, though not rigid, followed a pattern. At 6:30, a series of musical bells pealed forth. Every day of the week Liliane looked out her window at that hour, while the bells were ringing, and saw Dr. Hathaway gardening on his knees. It seemed symbolic; this was his thanksgiving every day. He was the first person she saw every morning.

Breakfast, cooked by a gnarled black man named Lubuto who had been trained by Heidi, consisted of great quantities of tea for the two nurses and coffee for the doctor and Liliane. There was a toasted bread, quite unlike any Liliane had ever known but altogether delicious, and pots of jam made from the local fruit. There were always soft-boiled eggs and bananas. Often there were plump, squashy, ambrosial grapefruits, more succulent and sweeter than any she'd ever tasted. Sometimes there were small juicy oranges with soft skin that peeled easily. Mangoes and papayas, which she had never tasted before, became new delights to her.

Then, if there were operations to be performed and no emergencies, she and Rose took turns assisting the doctor. The first week Rose hovered over her shoulder, but when she saw Liliane's competence, she was satisfied. Sometimes the operations were on animals; Dr. Hathaway thought they were just as important as people. They wandered around, even in the operating room. A gray dog reclined in the corner, scratching, and an orange cat lay on the table beside the doctor's operating instruments. The operating room was also the recovery room. Sometimes two or three patients would be recuperating there while a fourth was being operated on. There were hernias, broken legs, cut-off fingers, and people with distended stomachs, victims of malnutrition. Liliane gained more operating-room experience in her first month at Simbayo than she would have in six months in Buffalo.

All of the natives who worked for Dr. Hathaway were given a daily ration of eight bananas. That was their entire food supply, unless they had other sources. Once in a while leftover rice was meted out, but that was usually given to the pets first. The people on banana rations, however, never evidenced malnutrition or any other deficiency related to nutrition. Liliane began to have great respect for what seemed to be the perfect food.

On her second day Liliane had asked Rose why so many natives had gentian violet painted on their fingers or toes. Her back had crawled with gooseflesh when the nurse replied, "Oh, they're the lepers."

The leper colony was on an island. The less unsightly lepers came over daily to work in the compound. "Just don't touch what they've touched. Wash it off first." Don't touch what they've touched! How did she know what they'd touched? What would happen to her if she did? How was she to wash it off when there was so little water?

One day she saw one of the native women, one who did sewing, splash some water inadvertently. After lunch she saw her walking, cowed, from the doctor's office. This was the hour when he reprimanded those he felt should be scolded, meted out punishment to those he thought needed it. He treated the natives as though they were naughty children. When he punished, it was for the good of the community so that whatever happened would not happen again. His heavy eyebrows drawn together, frown lines across his forehead, he sat erect at his desk, meting out justice like a god. Oh, thought Liliane, I would not like to come before him like that. But he never did that to the nurses. When she or Rose or Heidi did something he did not approve of, he simply stopped talking to them. He never explained what was wrong. They had to figure it out for themselves, feeling guilty all the while, wondering what rule, what ethic they had transgressed. Eventually he either forgot or forgave.

When the day came that he stopped talking to Liliane, she suffered pangs of anguish. What had she done to deserve the silent treatment? She asked Rose, who simply said, "Oh, m'dear, I've no idea what you could have done." She never did divine what rule she had transgressed, and after four days he talked to her again.

Heidi was courteous to her, but she never smiled at her, never invited confidences, never made small talk. Yet both Heidi and Rose were beloved by the patients. Their intelligent fingers were quick, kind, gentle. They each had learned what the doctor never did—some of the black people's words. The natives had learned enough English so that between the nurses' minimal vocabulary and theirs, they managed to communicate. Dr. Hathaway, on the other hand, always spoke to them in English. He'd prod them, gently, trying to figure out where the pain was and why. "Have to be a veterinarian to figure out what's wrong with these people," he was fond of saying.

Yet he was marvelously kind to patients. His blue eyes softened; he smiled—a marvelous electric smile—and was reassuring. With babies, he seemed to have an innate knack.

"Too bad you never had any of your own," Liliane commented one morning.

He looked up at her, his hair flopping over his forehead. "These are all my children."

And so they seemed. He was the benevolent, though stern, father.

Liliane decided to stop trying to figure him out, though she could not stop reacting physically when she was near him. She lay in bed at night, his face a mirage on the ceiling above her.

He was often silent. When others took naps, he wrote. When Heidi and Rose and Liliane sat around after dinner, talking, playing simple games, sewing, rolling bandages from threadbare, too-often-washed gauze, he studied. He thought. He wrote articles that were published all over the world, adding to the fame and prestige of Simbayo. He studied the medical journals that arrived monthly, though sometimes they were months old.

Once in a while he joined the conversation after dinner, and then it was jolly. There was laughter, and Rose and Heidi flirted with him. But Liliane didn't. She'd spent a lifetime in Buffalo flirting with boys, but Dr. Hathaway was not a boy, not someone she could flirt with.

One night she said, "It would be really nice if we could create a bathing pool."

The nurses looked at her as though she'd lost her mind. Dr. Hathaway, his eyes alight, smiled at her. "What exactly do you have in mind?"

"It would be so nice to cool off at night, to take baths without being afraid of crocs." She had learned the local lingo. "I saw all that chicken wire in one of the sheds the other day. I don't see why we couldn't fence off that little inlet of the river over by the palm trees that makes a little lagoon. We could stretch wire across underwater and have ourselves a safe place to cool off, get clean, wash clothes."

Heidi and Rose looked at the doctor to see what his reaction would be.

"A croc or a hippo could easily smash through that wire," he pronounced, though she could tell he was interested.

"Oh," she said, disappointed.

But the next morning, as she left her room for breakfast, he was still in his garden. As he rose from his knees, he called out to her. "Liliane." It was so unexpected that she wasn't sure she had heard him.

He called again and gestured to her.

His hands and knees were covered with dirt. As he brushed his hands together, he said, "Walk down to the river with me. Breakfast will wait for us. I've been thinking of your idea all night."

Her heart pounded. Was it that he had listened to her and taken her seriously, or the unexpected nearness of him, or his calling to her, or his breaking his breakfast routine? She didn't know.

As they walked in the early-morning mist to the river, he asked, "Are you happy here?"

It was a question she hadn't allowed herself to ask. Everything was still so strange. No one but Rose really talked to her, and there were so many long hours. Evenings when all there was to do was sit around the kerosene lantern and read the tattered magazines and old books, or to darn, or to play Parcheesi with Rose and Heidi, or word games, in which they seemed to take such great delight. They liked, too, to read aloud to each other, and Liliane hated that. They read in such monotones! She far preferred to read to herself. And they read such long books. Dickens was their favorite. Even though they knew his novels almost verbatim, they read and reread them.

Liliane felt useless much of the time. She was given no responsibilities; she just followed orders. Sometimes she felt like a servant, and she didn't seem to have anything in common with any-one. Though the natives now nodded and smiled at her whenever she encountered them, they were still alien to her. She couldn't get used to seeing just loincloths on the men and the women's lips, in which bracelets had been inserted when they were children, ex-panded out of all proportion. Yet even the fiercest-looking men— the ones with hideous bones stuck through their noses and elaborate tattoos over their bodies—were gentle.

She didn't know how to answer the doctor's question.

Her hesitation must have been answer enough. Stopping, he turned her to him, his garden dirt rubbing off onto the shoulders of her dress. The heat from his hands flowed into her. He reached down and took her hands in his. "My dear, it takes time."

"I know," she replied, trying not to let her voice tremble, trying not to let her frustrations show. "Tell me, are *you* happy here?"

Abruptly, he dropped her hands and began again to walk toward the river.

"No one's ever asked *me* that," he answered. "I don't think I know what the word means."

They reached the indentation in the river where she had envi-sioned her pool.

"See," she said, rushing to the point that jutted out into the river and created a small lagoon, an eddy past which the river flowed. "I thought if we stretched wire from here to there, it would enclose all of this area for bathing. It would make such a differ-ence."

He stared at her across the expanse of water. "Would it help to make you happy?"

"Oh, yes!" she cried.

He leaned his back against the palm tree and crossed his arms.

"If I solve this, will you understand that we are happy to have you here? You are, you know, a breath of spring to us."

Oh, no. No, she didn't know that. She didn't even know if anyone was aware of her. If anyone even cared.

She walked slowly toward him, her untameable auburn hair curling in damp ringlets framing her face, her turquoise eyes look-ing squarely into his.

He stared back at her. She felt hypnotized, walking toward him as though in slow motion, being drawn closer to him than she had ever dared go. She was so close she could feel his breath.

His eyes left hers, went to her slightly parted lips, his hand rising to touch the ends of her hair and to curl around a tendril.

In a soft voice, he answered, "I'm happier now than I've been in a long time."

Blood rushed to her face; heat seemed to cascade down her cheeks, across her breast, down her arms.

"Oh, there you are," Heidi called, her accent more guttural than usual. "We began to worry. You are never late for breakfast!"

The doctor's hand shot down to his side, and he smiled at the approaching nurses. Liliane's heart beat like a drum.

They walked back toward the dining hall, the two older nurses surrounding him like moths around a flame, Liliane trailing behind.

CHAPTER 3

▼

LATER THAT DAY, SHORTLY BEFORE THE DINNER HOUR, WHEN LILIANE was returning to her room after hospital rounds, Dr. Hathaway came bounding along the path, his clothes dripping wet, his hair plastered tight to his head, a huge smile on his face.

"I think we can do it!" he shouted, although he was not far from her. "I just dove down to investigate." He did not stop, but strode on, carrying his shoes and sun helmet.

Liliane turned to watch him as he headed toward his room. Smiling to herself, feeling happiness curl itself around her, she walked to her room and found a tall ebony woman waiting by the screen door. The woman had a regal bearing; her black hair was coiled high on her head. Six brilliantly colored bracelets were banded around her neck, and she wore a bright yellow skirt. Above her bare feet more bracelets wound around her ankles. Her full, pointed breasts jutted straight out; Liliane tried not to look. Bare breasts still made her uncomfortable.

Why would someone be waiting here for her? The wife of a sick patient, perhaps? She smiled encouragingly at the woman. "May I help you?" she asked.

Silently, the woman held out her hand, palm up. It was swollen badly. Liliane took the offered hand and studied it. A large splinter had lodged itself there and had become severely infected.

"Why didn't you come to the hospital?" she asked the woman, who stared at her uncomprehendingly.

Liliane took the woman's arm and began to lead her toward the hospital. The woman wouldn't budge. "I have to get some instruments," Liliane tried to explain.

The woman shook her head and squatted, resting on her heels, her knees drawn up, in that position in which natives seem to be able to stay forever and which white men scarcely attempt. Her eyes implored Liliane as she continued to hold out her hand.

"What's your name?" Liliane asked, not expecting an answer.

"Naldani," the woman answered, in a voice of such deep resonance and beauty that Liliane scarcely believed she'd heard it. Whether it was an answer to her question or a word indicating something else, she didn't know. She stooped down and spoke slowly, trying to enunciate each word clearly. "I must go to the hospital to get tweezers, a knife, and some alcohol. I shall be right back. You wait here."

The woman stared into her eyes.

Liliane started toward the hospital, looking back to make sure the woman was still squatting there. She began to run.

When she returned, the woman was in the same position, resting on her heels. Liliane knelt next to her and took up the inflamed, puffy hand. She would have to cut it open, she saw, and let the pus run out.

"This will hurt," she warned the woman, knowing full well she couldn't understand. How to tell her, how to make her realize she was not trying to hurt her? Liliane held the small, sharp knife before her and squeezed her face into a grimace.

The black woman nodded. She never made a sound. She stared at the whole operation, breathing a heavy sigh when Liliane removed the large wooden splinter, watching the pus ooze onto the ground. She blinked hard when she felt the alcohol; tears formed in the corners of her eyes, but no sound escaped her.

Liliane bandaged the hand. "Do not get this wet."

The woman said, "Naldani not get wet."

Their eyes met, Naldani's big, round black ones and Liliane's bright blue-green ones; a bond formed. For the first time since she'd left Buffalo, Liliane felt close to someone. Not someone she could communicate with, not someone with whom she had anything in common, not someone she had known fifteen minutes before. They smiled at each other, an inner warmth palpable in the humid air.

Liliane pointed at the other woman. "You, Naldani; me, Liliane." She then pointed to herself.

Naldani's eyes lit up. She struggled to repeat Liliane. But what she kept coming up with was "Lili."

"I like that," Liliane said. And to herself she thought, Let it be Lili. I have just made myself a friend.

As Naldani rose gracefully from her squatting position and walked away, Liliane opened the door to her room and wondered if she would ever see the woman again.

The next day she saw not only Naldani but also the beginning of "Liliane's swimming pool." Across the area she had indicated, the doctor was building a barrier of corrugated metal sheeting, with holes punctured to allow the flow of water in and out of the lagoon. Late every afternoon she would see him down by the palm grove supervising four of the natives, sometimes jumping into the water himself, with all his clothes on, to show them what to do. The pool was ready within a week.

After lunch the doctor smiled at his harem of three and announced, "Liliane's swimming pool is ready. Shall we go see it?"

Although Rose had wandered down to the river with Liliane to look at the progress, Heidi had not gone near it. Now all three followed the doctor to the palm grove. It was indeed a lovely place for bathing.

As the women oohed and ahed, the doctor eyed Liliane. "I was thinking," he said, "that we ought to have hours here. Perhaps you ladies can decide what time you would like to come here. Now that it's built, I could certainly use a bath now and then."

"Oh"—Liliane sighed with pleasure—"I would like to come after lunch instead of sleeping. Or after dinner."

"Fine," he said, not waiting to hear from the other women. "I'll find other times."

Turning on his heel, he left. Heidi and Rose looked at Liliane. "Isn't it delightful." She laughed, beginning to take her blouse off. "Oh, how perfectly wonderful!"

Heidi stood and watched. Unself-consciously, Liliane began to peel off her clothes and stood in her chemise in the sunlight. She looked around as though to assure herself of privacy. Then, with great delight, she jumped in. The warm water flowed over her, cooling her like nothing had since her arrival so many months ago. She pushed herself under the water, feeling it ripple through her hair. Oh, God, she thought, smiling underwater, this may be as close as I'll get to heaven.

When she surfaced, Rose had waded in up to her knees, still wearing all of her undergarments. On the shore, Heidi was sitting in her slip and taking off her stockings. Stolidly, she stood up and marched to the water. She looked at Liliane and at Rose and then jumped in, making a great splash that showered them both. They laughed. Heidi laughed, too. It was the first time Liliane had heard Heidi laugh when Dr. Hathaway wasn't around.

When she returned to her room after an hour of frolicking with Rose and Heidi, she discovered, by her door, a neat pile of her clothes, freshly laundered.

AT TEN EVERY MORNING, AFTER THE OPERATIONS WERE OVER, THE doctor took care of the outpatients. A line began to form at dawn. Sometimes there were as few as fifty patients. Usually, there were over one hundred, and once in a while close to two hundred. Hardly anyone ever came alone. Groups kept arriving. The sick came with relatives and friends, some making journeys of days or weeks. Their progress was slow. Food had to be carried with them, and their water gourds, cooking pots, and charms.

Some could not walk and either had to be carried in on the backs of their wives or in a hunting net tied to a pole and slung between the shoulders of two friends. A woman could carry a man or another woman, but a man would never carry a woman. Many came down the river by canoe.

They had yaws, with its sickening yellow pus, sleeping sickness and venereal disease, tropical ulcers and hernias, broken bones, bad teeth, and a thousand horrid skin conditions. They were infested with worms. They had chicken bones caught in their throats. They'd been mangled by crocodiles or bitten by snakes or clawed by leopards. They had dysentery, indigestion, and lice. And they had cut each other up with knives.

They all smelled terrible. Liliane wondered if any of them had ever taken a bath or brushed their teeth. The odor of a hundred Congolese was overwhelming.

Liliane stopped gagging after the third month.

Due to the lack of a common language, there was little or no talking with the doctor, so the line moved quickly. At lunchtime, the doctor simply left the line and returned after eating.

The nurses took turns helping him. After Liliane arrived, Heidi, then Rose, and then she would take turns. At first, Liliane helped only on Wednesdays, but gradually, Heidi did less and less, moving more and more into the arena of management, and Liliane began to assist with patients every Monday, Wednesday, and Friday. It was her favorite part of her life at Simbayo. Mainly, she stood by and handed the doctor instruments or medication, and she loved studying the natives. From the very first, she had been determined to communicate with them and had implored Rose to teach her the little of the language she knew. To her delight, the sounds had come easily to her.

She sought Naldani out. How to thank her for the clean clothes? By that time-old way, with hands, with gestures, with smiles, she communicated to Naldani that she wished to speak her language. So, little by little, she was accumulating the words that led to communication, that broke barriers. There was no written way to study the language, so Liliane listened. When she heard a word repeated over and over, she asked what it meant.

By the time she'd been in the Congo five months, she was able to communicate on a basic level. At least she could tell the doctor where the patient hurt. The first time she did that the doctor stared at her. Though he said nothing, when the next patient approached the outdoor table where he saw all of his patients, he glanced up at her questioningly. She translated.

She had grown used to the lepers who wandered around the compound, with their brightly painted purple fingers and toes. It was not until she had been there for many months that she saw a man with no nose. He walked out of the jungle with a woman and three small children. He had stubs for fingers and he limped on feet that had lost several toes.

Despite herself, she recoiled with horror. They had come, she later learned, from a village many miles away. Ostracized by their tribe, they had but two choices: face certain death in the jungle by themselves, or find their way to the leper colony, where—though their lives might not be lengthened—they could live with others like themselves and not be completely shunned. The more disfigured cases were relegated to the island. Their women, or their men, could either visit them there or live with them on the island and care for them, continuing to share their lives, but unless children were infected, they were not allowed on the island. They had to stay on this side of the river in an encampment just for the children of lepers. They were examined monthly, and had playmates; two extremely large native women of indeterminate age mothered them. The doctor supplied all the food and their housing. Liliane thought there ought to be a school for the children, but when she argued for this, Dr. Hathaway dismissed her idea with a shrug.

"Educate them for what?"

In his pirogue, the doctor visited the leper island weekly. He never took any of the nurses with him. It was only acts of extreme courage and love that led the uninfected to live on the island with their mates. The courageous ones were usually women, who cared for and took care of their men. However, sometimes a man followed his wife there, staying no matter how gruesome the leper became, bound by ties so strong that Liliane decided no word had been invented for that degree of love.

Liliane thought of the island with horror. She imagined it peopled with deformed, noseless, earless, fingerless, toeless creatures, so ugly as to defy description, all painted purple. Sometimes she dreamed of the leper colony, her imagination casting fear into her. She felt apprehensive when she came into contact with a leper, although the doctor tried to explain that her chances of contracting the disease were about nil. Then how, she wondered, did all these others get it? How did Father Damien contract it on Molokai if not from close contact?

Liliane remembered reading about Father Damien, that selfless Belgian priest who had condemned himself to spend the last sixteen years of his life trying to make a civilized, hopeful community out of the cesspool of savage humanity that the island of Molokai had become. Back in the late 1880s any Hawaiian with leprosy was torn from family and society and sent by ship to the Hawaiian island leper colony. They were thrown overboard and forced to swim ashore. Many drowned. Sometimes food was thrown overboard, to float around in wooden casks. More often the inmates were forgotten—until Father Damien arrived and taught them to live out their remaining days with self-pride and brotherly love. In one of the incomprehensible ironies of God's ways, this good Belgian priest contracted the dread disease and died hideously among his beloved lepers. By then he had accomplished the near impossible—world awareness of impossible conditions. If Father Damien had gotten the dread disease, might not she?

She became used to dealing with malnutrition, with worms, with raw, running sores, with malaria, with the myriad illnesses typical of the humid tropics, but she was unprepared for the most gruesome thing she had ever seen. One day, seemingly out of nowhere, a wrinkled, bent-over man entered the compound bearing a crude wheelbarrow in front of him. Liliane first saw him from the back. He walked painfully, slowly, gingerly placing one foot before the other, his hands never leaving the handles of the wheelbarrow.

It was midafternoon, the hour of rest, and Liliane had just come from a swim. Heidi and Rose had left the bathing early, in time to take naps, but she had stayed at the pool, lingering in the water, then lying wet in the shade of the palm trees.

The man and his wheelbarrow moved toward her as she walked to her bungalow. As she crossed in front of him, she gasped. His testicles lay in the wheelbarrow, grown so enormous and ponderous they looked like withered watermelons, too heavy to move without support.

Instead of moving to help the poor man, she fled. She ran to the doctor's office, where she found him writing. "Come quickly!"

Laying down his pen, the doctor rose and dashed out the door with her. As they approached the man, still coming toward them at a slow pace with his wheelbarrow, Liliane tried to avert her eyes but was hypnotized by the terrible sight.

"Oh," said the doctor. His hand shot out and grabbed Liliane's arm. "I'll take care of this. Don't stay. Tell Rose I need her."

Grateful but disgusted with herself, Liliane ran to her room. Lying on her bed, she closed her eyes, trying to put the picture out of her mind. Her teeth chattered.

After dinner that night—and Liliane had eaten very little—the doctor said to her, "Liliane, come to my office for a few minutes."

Heidi shot a glance at Rose. Unless the doctor stayed in the dining hall in the evening, he spent his time in solitude. He never invited anyone into his office at night. Not even visitors. During the daytime, yes, but no one had ever been invited there in the evening.

Though it was not yet dark, the doctor lit a kerosene lantern and gestured Liliane to the chair opposite his desk. His office was lined with books. There were magazines in piles all over the floor. A microscope tottered on the edge of his desk. He leaned back in his chair and put his fingers together, making a pyramid with them.

"It's elephantiasis," he said.

Liliane looked around. "What is?" In the lamplight, her hair looked like newly burnished copper.

"The man with the wheelbarrow," he said kindly. "I've never seen it in such an advanced degree before. Usually it hits the legs. It's caused by nematode worms that attack vertebrates. Probably fifty million Africans have some form or other of filariasis.

"I think the genesis of what makes Africans lethargic and slothful is disease. They're riddled with sickness. Sometimes they spend their whole lives with a low fever and anemia. If malaria or sleeping sickness or bilharziasis or leprosy or TB don't do away with them, their general health and often their brains are attacked by malnutrition or worms. Sometimes I feel whatever I'm doing is water down a drain."

He had been looking out the window, and now he turned to her. "I'm sorry you had to see that. Did it frighten you?"

She looked at him. There were lines at the corners of his eyes, and despite his always wearing his white helmet outdoors, his face had a swarthiness to it. His hair, which Rose cut infrequently, curled over his ears and fell gently onto his neck. Liliane had an overwhelming urge to lean over and touch it; to touch the nape of his neck, feel a tendril of his thick, wavy hair, sprinkled with gray. His blue eyes looked straight into her, as though he knew what her soul looked like. The veins in his hands stood out. He emanated power and, at this moment, kindness.

She was so caught up with looking at him that she had forgotten he had asked her a question. He repeated it.

"Yes," she admitted. "How terrible for that man. How can he be helped? Can anything be done?"

"Someday maybe some drug will help. But for now, an operation. I operated this afternoon. He'll probably weigh sixty pounds less. Testicle elephantiasis is really rather common here."

Liliane was embarrassed. Anatomy lectures were the only places where she had heard these terms used. She had never sat and talked about sexual anatomy with anyone. She looked away from him.

"Am I embarrassing you?"

She wanted dreadfully to say no, of course not. Instead, she remained silent.

The buzzing of mosquitoes around the lantern broke the quiet; darkness descended in one dramatic gesture.

She was conscious of this being his room; she smelled the odors that made it his, indefinable male smells that pulled at her.

"You know," he said, his voice tinged with sadness, "sometimes I feel lonely. I'm Dr. Hathaway to everyone. I haven't even heard my first name spoken since I left America well over a year ago." His eyes narrowed. "Do you think you could force yourself to call me Baxter? I'm not a god, after all."

Oh, thought Liliane, Baxter.

"Say it!" he urged. "Say my name aloud."

She turned her face from the window, looking across his desk at him in the flickering light.

"Baxter," she whispered, her voice wrapping itself around his name.

"Thank you." He smiled, his face lighting up, his intense eyes drilling into her. He arose and walked around the desk and stood towering above her. "That wasn't so difficult, was it?" He reached down and touched her chin, raising her head so that she looked up at him. He let his hand remain on her chin. Then it moved to push back a wisp of hair.

"Don't be sorry you're here, Liliane Wentworth," he said, his voice thick. "I'm not."

She found herself trembling despite the heat. He must have felt it.

"Do you want to return to the dining hall?"

She wanted to be alone, not to gossip with Rose and Heidi. She wanted to hold tonight in her heart and wind it around herself. "No," she answered, her voice smothered. "I'll go back to my room."

"Sometimes," his voice was soft, "at this hour I see you coming up the path from bathing."

So he had noticed her.

"Yes," she said with a nod. "It's my favorite time. It cools me off so that I can sleep. Rose and Heidi never seem to want to go down after dinner. I'm alone then and it's peaceful. I can't thank you enough. It makes such a difference to me."

"I don't know why I never thought of it before," he said, smiling. "I like it, too."

"Oh." Liliane had never seen him there. "I didn't know you used it."

"Before you get up in the morning. I'd go in the evening, too, but I don't want to disturb you."

Liliane didn't answer. He hadn't moved away. He was just inches from her. As she turned to go, they brushed against each other. She wondered if he were as aware of it as she was. Their bare arms touched, and electricity shot down her arm.

I'm being a fool, she thought. Just because he asked me to call him Baxter.

As she reached the door, he said, "Good night." It felt like a caress.

She didn't respond but walked languidly into the dusk, listening to the silence that surrounded her.

She sat in the dark for a long time, gazing out into the velvet night. She didn't know whether the incessant rhythmic beating was her heart or drums in the night.

When she went to bed, she lay staring into nothingness. She imagined holding Baxter in her arms. When she fell asleep, she dreamed of Baxter Hathaway swimming naked in the moonlight in her pool.

CHAPTER 4

▼

IT BECAME LILIANE'S HABIT, LATE IN THE AFTERNOON AFTER HOSPITAL rounds were over and before the dinner hour, to spend time with Naldani. They met in what Liliane jokingly called "the village square," an area of hard-packed earth under the okoume trees where there were crude wooden benches and chairs. It was the area where the women who sewed worked during the early part of the day and where people sat to eat bananas, to gossip, to carve wooden objects, to roll bandages. There were always washed bandages to make smooth and roll into balls. Liliane had long gotten over being repulsed by nonsterile bandages.

Sometimes, waiting for Naldani, she would sit on one of the benches and think back on her day, try to sort things out, ponder the problems faced here, problems unlike any known in America. What she saw mostly were diseases and ailments she had never heard of. At the University of Buffalo there had been no courses in tropical medicine.

Malaria was the chief threat to health. Though not often fatal, it did render its victims susceptible to many other diseases. By itself, it created what seemed like eternal lethargy. Most cases were chronic. In fact, the natives did not come to the hospital for these symptoms. They took for granted that this was how life was lived. A low fever continually sapped their energy, but they didn't even know they had a fever. Mainly it was children who were brought in with the severe anemia and the loss of appetite and weight so characteristic of the disease. The adults had mostly built up immunity or learned to live a generally debilitated life, unaware that anything was wrong with them. Baxter told her that at least one third of all deaths in Africa were due to malaria.

Liliane never feared it.

She did fear sleeping sickness, caused by the tsetse fly. It was not dying from it that she feared, but the aftermath of prolonged sleep, the almost certain insanity, the idiocy that resulted from massive brain damage.

For each disease, there was a separate building, insofar as it was possible—one for malaria, one for sleeping sickness, one for bilharziasis, one for tuberculosis. These, along with leprosy, were the African illnesses that meant permanent infirmity. Permanent, of course, could mean a matter of months or limitless years. It did mean that someone else had to care for the diseased.

As Liliane adjusted to the rhythm of life in Simbayo the thought of leprosy never really left her mind. Wild animals, encroaching jungle, enormous pythons, loneliness—none of these cast the specter leprosy did. Though the lepers she had seen were not all that ghastly, they did have fingers and toes missing. She knew that once they became more unsightly they were sent to the island.

In her imagination, the island loomed large as a place of untold terror, of deformed, faceless people. In her nightmares, lepers had sunken faces, and where their noses should have been, their bones showed through. Rose, sensing her terror, had tried to reassure her, telling her that leprosy was usually the result of overcrowding and filth. She did not mention that it was overcrowding in hot, humid areas, but Liliane knew that. She knew the incubation period was long and nightly searched herself or felt her arms and legs to see if there were spots without feeling.

Must I do this for the next ten years? she wondered. Her fear had no rationale, and she knew it. Yet she could not conquer it.

Her friendship with Naldani grew. Each afternoon they schooled themselves in each other's language until they were able to communicate on more than a rudimentary level. Naldani learned English almost as quickly as Liliane learned Bantu.

Shortly after arriving, Liliane had noticed that there were no newborn infants at the compound, nor any births. Rose had told her that one of the unbreakable taboos was that men were not allowed to be around when babies were born. No matter what the difficulty, a woman in labor would never consider coming to the hospital, where the doctor would deliver her child. Liliane had wondered if they might come if she or Rose or Heidi were to perform the deliveries, but it was an unheard-of idea. Birthing was just a part of life, a hard part of life. Infant mortality was phenomenal, and many women died in childbirth.

Liliane asked Naldani if she could witness a native birthing some time. Several weeks later, Naldani appeared late in the afternoon and indicated that a woman in the neighboring village, which consisted of no more than a hundred natives, was in labor. If Liliane wished to come, she could.

The woman had been taken from her home by other women, and the husband had to pretend he didn't even notice his wife was gone. She had been taken down a path leading into the jungle, just on the outskirts of the village, where a clearing had been hacked to form an open space about eight feet in diameter. The woman in labor squatted over a mat, a woman on each side of her holding her arms so that she could not sit or lie on the mat, which had sharp edges of palm fronds sticking out of it and was incredibly filthy.

Five naked women, most of them quite old, kept mumbling to themselves. They looked up when Naldani and Liliane entered the clearing but paid little attention. Obviously, Naldani had made arrangements with them. Two of the wrinkled women moved so that there was space for the newcomers. The pregnant woman gasped; she never let out a cry, though she was obviously in great distress, but kept sighing, longer and heavier gasps as time went on. Liliane already knew that native women did not voice pain.

When the women holding her tired, two others replaced them, holding her up in the squatting position even when her legs gave way.

Suddenly, the baby burst forth onto the mat. The women made no move to touch the infant, who lay in mucus while the afterbirth slowly followed. A conditioned reflex in Liliane made her start forward, but she felt Naldani's hand on her wrist and stayed where she was. When the delivery was complete, one of the women gathered up the placenta and disappeared with it. Another removed a dirty palm-frond knife from her hair and cut the cord, not bothering to tie it.

The baby, who had not cried, was not touched until this was all accomplished. Then one of the women took a gourd and sloshed cold water on the baby, who immediately began to scream.

The new mother had not been allowed to sit or to rest in any way or to hold her child. Now the women helped her to stand up, and the small procession, with two women still supporting the mother by holding her under the arms, left the clearing. The only noise, in the dark of the forest, was the whimpering of the baby and the murmuring of incantations by the two oldest women.

Naldani and Liliane trailed behind. When they reached the woman's hut, she went inside and chased her husband out. He pretended not to be aware of what had happened and disappeared into the night. The women laid the mother down on a dirty blanket and lit a fire. The room was small, there was no ventilation, and eight women in the room with a fire almost made Liliane pass out. Dizziness swept through her, but she blinked and inhaled the fetid odor of the hut, swallowing hard. When the water had boiled, a woman reached in the corner and brought forth a small broom, dipped it into the boiling water, and rained hot drops onto the mother's stomach. The woman twitched but made no sound. The unwashed baby was then put into the mother's arms, and the women filed out of the hut, an older one staying to watch over the newborn and the mother.

Liliane did not wonder at the high mortality rate.

Someday, she thought, as she stared out her window into the moonlight later that night, I shall do something about it. I shall make it easier and safer. In the distance she heard the insistent beat of the tom-toms.

SHE AND NALDANI SAT IN THE SHADE OF THE OKOUME TREES ON HOT afternoons. Naldani wore a bright wraparound skirt, with bracelets around her neck and ankles; her glistening dark breasts swelled proudly, her great, round eyes were bright in her almost purple-black face, and her short, tight black hair haloed her long, regal head. Naldani's face should have graced a coin, Liliane thought. Her thick Negroid lips and her broad, almost flat nose might give a white person, accustomed to Caucasian standards of beauty, the impression that Naldani was ugly. Whether Naldani's inner beauty shone through or Liliane was becoming accustomed to the African features, it was not long before she realized how beautiful Naldani was. It gave her pleasure to look at her new friend.

Liliane always sat opposite her on the bench, in a light dress, her bare feet in sandals, the ubiquitous sun helmet that Baxter demanded they all wear failing to hide her unruly auburn hair, her alabaster skin lightly freckled. She and Naldani leaned toward each other, their hands often touching. Liliane was trying to write down the sounds on a note pad so that she could study them when she was alone. Naldani was trying to decipher the figures on the paper, amazed that the words she said looked the way Liliane drew them. Every day she practiced writing her name.

They spoke a mixture of each other's language, laughing together, their eyes and hands doing the rest.

One late afternoon, they heard the sharp, penetrating whistle of a boat. Such an unusual occurrence brought everyone running to the dock. Even transient visitors became events of major proportions. To people who have never lived in isolated parts of the world there are no words to express the joy, the anticipation, and the delight that a visitor or the mail brings. Any visitor, any mail.

Like all the boats that plied the river, its paint was peeling and it looked grimy. Steering it into the dock, and pulling the whistle at the same time, was an unshaven, medium-sized man wearing baggy pants. Heidi and Rose began to jump up and down, waving and crying, "Oh, Jack!" at this disreputable-looking man.

He waved back at everyone, a jagged grin covering his stubbled face and showing a gap where a tooth was missing.

As soon as his boat, its name—*My Gal Sal*—part of the peeling paint, was tied to the dock, he jumped down and headed immediately to Heidi and Rose, hugging each of them, telling them they'd grown more beautiful since the last time. They giggled and acted as though Jack were one of the delights of their lives.

Actually, he was.

Even Baxter had sauntered down to the dock.

"Hi, there, Doc," Jack shouted, in a gravelly voice, his watery, pale blue eyes in sharp contrast to Baxter's. For a moment, Liliane thought the two of them were going to embrace, but they just shook hands.

Then Jack turned toward her. "And who's gonna introduce me to the new lady? I swear, Doc, when you get women here, you really got an eye for looks." He had a decided cockney accent.

Rose made the introductions. "Oh, Jack, this is Liliane. She's been with us for about six months now. Liliane, this is Cap'n Jack."

In his filthy cutoff pants, wrinkled open-neck shirt, sailor's cap, and laceless sneakers, he was certainly seedy-looking.

"Well, now, miss," he said, walking over to her. "It's a pleasure, I'm sure." His grin was infectious. He must have been in his late forties.

There had been several visitors to Simbayo since Liliane had arrived—important churchmen from various countries, a reporter from London and one from Berlin—but none had been accorded the welcome that this unkempt-looking man engendered.

He turned to the group on the dock. "I tried to time it to get here for dinner. Tell me I succeeded."

He had. Before they all headed toward the compound, Jack reached into his boat and brought out a bottle of whiskey.

Uh-oh, thought Liliane, not in this group. But she was wrong.

He grabbed Heidi and Rose by an arm each, and the trio headed toward the dormitory, laughing loudly.

By dinnertime he looked a different person. He had bathed and shaved, and his clothes were clean. Rose explained, "He leaves a set of clothes here so that we know he'll come back. He has his own room, which no one else ever uses, even though he comes by only once or twice a year."

"Once," Heidi said, "he arrived in the rainy season and he stayed and stayed."

"Oh, yes," cried Rose, "remember that, Jack?"

"I do indeed." His voice sounded like rusty nails, a raspy twang to it. He turned to Liliane. "I stayed for damn well close to three months. Happiest three months since I came to this country . . . 'cept I ran outa gin."

They all laughed. And he brought out the bottle.

Liliane couldn't decide whether drinking the whiskey was akin to a confessional rite or a holy moment, waiting to toast the success in finding the Holy Grail. With a jolt, she realized that she hadn't thought of God in months despite Baxter's nightly ritual of reading from the Bible and singing a hymn. She responded to Baxter's theatrical voice as he read from the Bible, to the magical sound that he coaxed from the old guitar when the hymn was sung. She never even thought of God at such times, but of Baxter. She had come, she thought, to bring God to the Congo, and she had forgotten Him!

There was a brief Sunday morning service whenever a visiting missionary or minister came, but that was rare. Baxter did insist on silence between eleven and noon on Sunday. They gathered in "the village square"—she and Baxter, and Rose, Heidi, and a handful of Africans—and meditated. Then they sang hymns. The natives had high-pitched voices and they didn't understand the words they had memorized; it sounded both weird and beautiful. Liliane's meditations were never about God. They were about the trees, or the things she was learning, or how to overcome her fear of leprosy, or repeating new words she was learning, or of Baxter.

It filled her with neither guilt nor distress that God had disappeared from her thoughts. What did shock her was her thought: If there is a God, I'm sure He thinks I'm living a Christian life, helping people. *If* there is a God! She had come to Africa to do His will, but she was discovering that she was doing it for herself.

Brought back to reality by Jack's handing her a partly filled glass, she heard him say, as he raised his in a toast, "Well, what'll we toast this time?"

Rose and Heidi looked at him with expectant eyes, glowing with excitement. Jack charged energy into them.

Amusement danced in Baxter's smile.

"To health, happiness, and a rollickin' good time," shouted Jack, and downed his whiskey. Liliane had never tasted it before. It burned going down, but within a few minutes it felt golden.

Jack dominated the dinner conversation. He told them there was a big celebration up the river; some chief had invited everyone for miles around. There had to be more than three hundred people up there, just about an hour upriver, at what was normally a tiny village. The celebration had been planned for the full moon, which meant dancing every night. He warned them that he would accept no excuses, and he'd even wash the boat tomorrow. They were all going to the celebration tomorrow night. Liliane was sure there would be excuses: that they couldn't leave the hospital unattended, that dancing was not exactly Baxter's or Rose's or Heidi's cup of tea. But oh, my, she realized, how long it had been since she'd danced, been to a party. She hoped they'd let her go.

To her amazement, there was unanimous pleasure.

Jack then told them the gossip from up and down the river; he told Baxter he'd brought him some books. And, turning to the older nurses, he said, "And do I have some new authors for you!"

He apologized to Liliane. "I didn't know you was here, ma'am. Next time I can bring you some, if you tell me what you like. Though I've a couple on *Sal* I never heard of. You can look at 'em." She would have thought, from the way he used the English language, that he had never heard of or read very many books. She didn't dare tell him she liked Ernest Hemingway; after all, he wasn't the sort to appeal to young women. She did say she liked Mark Twain but didn't add that she enjoyed stories of love and how it could ennoble. She told him she'd enjoy books about Africa—there was so much she didn't know. She could barely figure out where she was on a map. And she'd like a book about the stars.

She was wrong about Jack. He was probably the best-read person in the Belgian Congo. He could quote lines upon lines from *Moby Dick,* his favorite. He didn't have much use for Mr. Dickens, "my apologies to you ladies." Never did he visit that he didn't bring books and tattered magazines, such rare treats in this place. He also brought rarities like spices, coffee, flashlight batteries, old copies of newspapers, nails, and a motley collection of other junk he'd accumulated in his trading up and down the river.

This time he'd brought an old typewriter with a faded ribbon, which the doctor immediately commandeered.

He regaled them with stories of what was happening in the outside world, at least as recently as two months ago when he'd been in Léopoldville.

Jack looked as though he would have drunk all night had it not been for the Christianizing influence of the present company, but he made no effort to have more than a second drink and sat amusing them for hours. Baxter made no move to leave. Jack did not participate in the hymn singing, but afterward he led them in singing "A Bicycle Built for Two" and "Harvest Moon."

It was a festive evening. Liliane had more fun than she could remember having. Despite his disreputable looks, Jack was delightful company. His uninhibited conversation was liberally sprinkled with "damn" and "hell," but no one seemed to take offense. Liliane looked at her companions the first few times Jack used these words and saw them take it all in stride.

It was nearly eleven when Heidi stood. "Jack, you got me laughing so much I like to die." Her face was so animated, so full of color that she looked almost pretty in the lamplight. Her stocky body had come alive in Jack's presence. "But instead I think I go to bed."

The party was over.

"Well, not often do I get to walk three pretty ladies to their rooms at night, I'll tell you that," sang Jack, as he picked up one of the lanterns.

Baxter smiled. "Jack, much as I like to see you, I'm not often envious of you. But I am right now." He looked at Liliane as he said this, and when the party emerged from the dining hall, Baxter stood and watched as Jack walked the women to the dormitory, singing at the top of his lungs, "Let Me Call You Sweetheart, I'm in Love with You."

Liliane's room was at one end of the dormitory, with open windows on three sides. Heidi and Rose had rooms next to each other in the middle. There were two empty rooms between theirs and Liliane's. Jack's room was beyond Rose's. He bid the two older nurses good night, patting each one lightly on the behind, and walked Liliane to her room.

"It's a joy seein' what you've done to the doc," he said.

"What I've done? I don't know what you mean."

"Well, maybe you don't," said Jack. "But it's a joy anyhow." He held up his bottle. "I don't suppose I could talk you into a wee one before bed?"

She nodded her head. "No, but thanks."

"Well, if you change your mind, I'll be up another hour or so," he said. "You know where my room is."

When she was alone, she marveled at the reactions of her co-workers to this slovenly man with his "he don'ts" and his "hells" and his whiskey. Yet he was a perfect gentleman, and more amusing and irreverent, in a reverent way, than anyone she'd met in Africa. Or maybe any place.

What did he mean, she wondered, by what she'd "done" to the doc?

She lit her kerosene lantern and sat on the edge of her bed. What had she done to him? How was he different? What did Jack mean? She sat pondering this for a few minutes and then decided to make a bold move. She would go have a drink with him. After all, this was not Buffalo. Going to a man's room in the Congo was not the same as doing it at home. She felt quite safe with Jack.

After blowing out her lantern, she walked out into the inky night. She had never been outside at midnight alone here. She just had to walk down the verandah, quietly so as not to disturb Rose and Heidi or to scandalize them. She laughed to herself. As she neared Rose's room, she saw that the nurse had her lantern still burning dimly. She would be quiet so as not to call attention to herself. She didn't want Rose to think she was doing something indecent!

Then she stopped, riveted to the spot. Heidi was in there with Rose, and they were both naked. Rose stood, her hands on Heidi's head, looking down at her tenderly. Heidi was kneeling on the bed in front of Rose, her hands cupping Rose's breasts, and she was kissing them, her mouth moving from one to the other.

Liliane put her hand over her mouth so as not to let out a cry. She wanted to move her feet and flee from the scene, but she could not.

Heidi's tongue darted out and made circles around Rose's nipples; her head slid down Rose's stomach, her tongue tracing patterns there. Rose moaned, spreading her legs wider apart.

Liliane turned and ran back to her own room, gasping.

She shivered. Gooseflesh crept up her arms, and she found herself shaking. She put her hands over her eyes, pushing against her eyeballs. Oh, God! she thought. I can't have seen what I thought I just saw. But she knew she had.

Rose doing that with Heidi. She knew that men and women . . . But women together?

When she had lain in bed nights and thought of Baxter, his face floating near her ceiling, she had imagined his kissing her breasts, his hand gliding down . . . But Rose and Heidi!

It was after three o'clock before she fell asleep. She slept so deeply and so dreamlessly that she would have totally missed breakfast had Rose not come to her room and gently shaken her.

"Wake up, dear," she said softly.

Rose looked just the same.

CHAPTER 5

▼

JACK'S PRESENCE BROKE THE ROUTINE. HE BARKED ORDERS AT them and they loved it, even Baxter, who went around with a smile all day. It was, Liliane realized, the first time she'd ever seen him happy. She even heard him whistling.

Jack told them to hurry through their work "or leave it 'til tomorra, nothin's going to be different. The same patients'll be in line, and the earth's not gonna have folded up." He spent the day washing down *My Gal Sal* "so it'll be ready for real-live princesses."

Rose and Heidi were almost pretty that day. Their cheeks had a bloom to them, their eyes sparkled; they looked as though the weight of the world had been lifted from their shoulders.

Liliane looked at the two women all day long. How could they do what she had seen them doing? How could they do that, and now act just like other people acted? How could they flirt with Jack so outrageously?

Rose and Heidi and Jack bubbled with excitement, but Liliane was listless. The memory of what she had seen last night dulled her senses.

I'll think about it later, she told herself, eager to participate in the excitement Jack engendered. He had ordered a picnic supper to be packed, and they would cruise leisurely down the river to the celebrating village. "It sounds like a circus," he volunteered.

To the four who made Simbayo their home, whose break in routine was seldom more than a mail call or visiting clergy who made demands of them and took up their time, Jack's visit was a celebration.

Early in the morning he had said, "Doc, I gotta have a tooth out or I'm not gonna go another day."

Baxter had cut him off. "Heidi's the dentist. It'll give her a thrill to work on a tooth that hasn't been filed to a sharp point."

So Heidi had extracted Jack's tooth. Though he had let out a wild yell, he had refused any of his own whiskey because, he said, "I gotta keep my wits sharp all day. I wouldn't wanna miss that party tonight."

He had rubbed his chin after the extraction and grinned wickedly at Heidi. Saying "Migod, woman, it's better already," he had swung her into the air and planted a kiss on her cheek. She had giggled happily.

By four o'clock what hadn't gotten done wasn't going to. The women dressed as though they were going to a high tea. They wore dresses that had lain long in trunks, wrinkled and pale, made of lawn and meant for parties. Rose's was a pale gold, accentuating the faint rust of her hair, and Heidi's was green, with soft folds, looking so unlike the Heidi that Liliane knew. Liliane's was pink, a soft chiffon that clung to her breasts and swirled gracefully around her legs. As always, Baxter was dressed in white, looking quite as he had when she first saw him. Liliane wanted to reach her arms out to him, wanted to hear a waltz playing; she wanted Baxter to hold her in his arms and dance her around a brightly lit room.

The picnic basket, as Rose called the crate that contained their supper, was carted onto *Sal* and Jack chugged the motor into life. It was the first time in six months that Liliane had left this small patch of land.

Only those who have lived off the beaten path, lived isolated from the rest of the world, can realize the excitement such a trip brought. Having been shut off from outside contacts for so long, one tended to forget that the rest of the world existed. What a thrill it was to be gliding along, even if the water was coffee-colored, even if one could not see beyond the impenetrable wall of jungle. The river flowed between solid banks of greenery; there was never a break. The tall trees, with climbing vines trailing over their massive trunks, grew to the river's edge, where crocodiles sunned themselves on logs and hippopotamuses lay submerged. The vegetation was rank, the ubiquitous smell of decay invading the nostrils. Yet there was excitement and enthusiasm aboard *My Gal Sal,* a camaraderie Liliane had not felt before. This down-at-the-heel, paint-peeling antique boat on a minor tributary of the Congo seemed like an excursion ship of first-class proportions.

In his raspy voice, Jack amused them with stories—he was a born raconteur. No one believed any of his tales. For the first time in six months, Liliane felt the sense of responsibility slip away; she was a girl again.

While Rose and Heidi and Jack laughed together, she glanced at Baxter, who sat across from her in a crooked chair that threatened to collapse under him. He was staring at her. When she smiled, he did not return it but kept his eyes riveted on her. Perhaps his mind is somewhere else, she thought, and he really doesn't see me. But she could tell that that was not true. His glance traveled slowly down her body and came back to her face. Their eyes locked. He didn't even blink but gazed at her and, it seemed, into her. What does he see? she wondered. I can't be pretty anymore. She realized that it had been weeks since she'd even looked in a mirror. In the constant humidity she had no control over her hair; it curled in tight ringlets around her head. She had taken scissors and whacked it off one afternoon when it had hung damply on her neck. She could imagine how she must look: as though the jungle had gotten hold of her. All vestiges of the proper Liliane Wentworth were long gone. She never wore stockings, only sandals. Her dresses were clean, but never pressed. Ever since she had taken care of Naldani's hand, she found her clothes freshly laundered on a table by her bed every day. It was a luxury she enjoyed. But sometimes she would wear the same dress for days in a row, she had become so unconscious of her looks. It seemed as though it were another world, another lifetime when she had stood in front of a closet and debated what to wear, when she had spent time in front of a mirror combing her hair and pinching her cheeks to add color, when she had begun—to her father's distress—to wear lipstick.

She looked at Jack, in shorts, and wondered if she couldn't wear them, too. Who would care? All sense of femininity had disappeared from Liliane in just six months. Yet Baxter sat across from her, staring as though she were all woman. Why did he never touch her? Why did he never say anything personal to her? Why did he do kind things for her yet remain so aloof?

The boat's whistle brought her out of her reverie. It was nearly five o'clock, and she began to hear noises: the incessant beat of the drums that pervaded all of Africa, horns blown—ones that sounded like English hunting horns, gongs that could have been struck in ancient China, and bells that would have sounded at home on the mountainsides of Switzerland. Together it was an unbelievable dissonance.

They rounded a bend and the sight was something to behold.

The jungle had been cleared here, too, and there were about forty thatched-roof huts in a large semicircle. There were fires everywhere and hundreds of people. There were men of impor-tance—chiefs, obviously—with breechcloths and skin belts, wear-ing necklaces of leopard's teeth and monkey-fur caps; their bodies gleamed with wild colors and raffish streaks of clay.

The women, their bodies glistening with oil and decorated with bizarre designs of phosphorescent colors, wore what could only be called G-strings, with feathered bustles on their derrieres.

The younger women were glorious. The bodies of women in this part of Africa gave them a twisting sort of walk, and their ample hips were prominent. By wearing bustles, they deliberately accentuated the movement of their buttocks and swayed as they moved. Liliane thought they had a soft, velvet beauty; they were graceful, lithe, and sleek. She envied them their flamboyant sexual-ity. The unmarried ones flaunted themselves shamelessly.

Liliane already knew that their time was fleeting. By thirty, women were old; by forty, they were considered hags. Even their personalities tended to reflect the change in their looks. But to-night even the older women laughed and shouted. There was only one decibel of speaking—as loud as possible, and as fast.

As Jack pulled up to the dock, a dozen natives came running, catching the lines he tossed out and making them secure.

He turned to his guests. "Now, we got choices. They'd be happy to have you come eat with them, but it's awful stuff. I'd suggest eatin' here, when they do, after it's dark. And then if we want, we can go join the celebration. Whatever we decide, we can see all their fun from the deck here. It's gonna be a wild night." He bared his teeth in what looked like a snarl but was really a pinched grin.

He bowed to Rose and then to Heidi. "And I'm warnin' you, ladies, I'm not takin' you back till you've danced with me."

What about me? wondered Liliane. Doesn't he want to dance with me? Aren't I going to be a part of it?

Then she realized that Jack was arbitrarily putting her and Baxter together. He was treating them as though she was already Baxter's. Finding herself embarrassed, she felt a blush creep up her cheeks and was irritated with herself. Then she was angry at Jack. Would she sit on the boat all evening while he and Rose and Heidi danced and sang? Baxter was never going to . . . Or was he? She looked over at him.

He was smiling, surveying the spectacle. "I feel like I've just gone back two thousand years," he murmured. "They've been doing this same thing for millennia."

Liliane looked at him, so handsome with his dark hair curling, his suntanned face accentuating the deep blue of his eyes, his aristocratic nose. A twentieth-century scientist framed before the panoply of primitive, wildly dressed Congolese. She said, "This must feel like a scene from one of your movies."

He turned to her and said lightly, "You're too young to remember any of my movies."

"I know," she said, moving over to the railing next to him, looking out at the splendor of the scene, "but it does seem that it should be in a movie. It can't be real. I can't be here." She laughed. "I feel like a trespasser."

He nodded. "They've been here forever. Cooking the same simple food, lighting the same kinds of fires, living in the same kinds of huts, hunting the same kinds of animals since—since long before Christ. Nothing's changed for them. How we must perplex them."

The sun began its quick descent, sinking behind the treetops. The bewitching hour of the Congo had arrived. The sultry heat of the day was replaced by gentle night breezes that riffled through the leaves.

As the darkness deepened and settled over the primeval forest, the small, aboriginal village flamed with life. Heidi brought out the "picnic supper" as natives on shore crowded around their big clay pots of manioc whose bitter smell wafted through the air. The horns, the cowbells, the gongs all stopped.

The little group on *My Gal Sal* sat in a circle, on two beat-up chairs and on crates, and gorged themselves on a tropical feast. Though grapefruit was not usually grown in this part of Africa, Baxter prided himself on the trees he had planted long ago that were now bearing remarkable fruit. They dined on roasted ears of corn wrapped in cassava leaves, on carrots as small as fingers freshly picked from the garden, on onions as tender and sweet as though sugared, on flatbread that Rose herself had baked over an open fire early in the morning. The pièce de résistance was stringy chicken—there was no other kind—that had been stewed for so long it was tender. It had been smothered in coconut and cooked in the juices. Liliane was sure she had never eaten a more divine meal.

Jack proclaimed it was worth traveling over a thousand miles for.

Then he brought out a bottle of cognac. Everyone had some, including Baxter. Jack toasted "the greatest group of people in the Congo"; Heidi toasted "Jack's coming out of the mist"; Rose toasted "friendship"; and, trying anxiously to think of what she could add, Liliane toasted "life unlike anything I ever expected." They all turned to Baxter, waiting to see what he might say. He held up his glass and looked at each of them in turn, his gaze resting finally on Liliane. "To that most elusive of feelings—happiness." He continued to stare at her as he finished his brandy.

"You know," said Jack, "the natives don't drink much, but tonight they'll get drunk. Lemme warn you about their booze. It's made outa their homemade sugarcane and palm nuts. It has a kick like nothin' you ever knew. So be careful when they offer you some. Unless"—he grinned his toothy smile—"that appeals to you. Then have fun. After all, I'm the one drivin'."

The full moon rose, more slowly than the sun had set, swimming above the trees. With it, the drums again began to beat. To one who has never heard the drums of Africa, it is difficult to describe what they do to a person's soul. They began tentatively, with irregular light taps, almost casual.

Little vaporous clouds of fog, like spirit wraiths, drifted from the river to disappear into the jungle, to mingle with the other ghosts that Congolese think inhabit the forests.

The drums began to beat regularly, gaining momentum and rhythm. Their persistence called to the people, lured dancers to the center of the semicircle. Liliane felt tenseness in her chest; the tom-toms unsettled her, awoke in her an urgency she didn't understand. Nor did she try to. She let her body flow to the beat, to the insistent staccato sounds that ripped through the night.

Women danced first, only the young women. They danced gracefully, lightly, and they laughed as they wove their hands in the air and undulated their hips. Their glistening bare breasts jiggled in the firelight. Liliane couldn't help wondering if breasts were erotic to Congolese men. They were always in view, never hidden. Did Congolese men look at these women and yearn to touch their breasts, so pointed, so voluptuous? Did they kiss them when making love? Did Baxter look at their breasts and yearn to touch them? Yearn to run his lips across them?

She turned to look at him and saw beads of sweat on his forehead.

The drumbeats accelerated, and the women, bowing down, danced backward, withdrawing into the crowd, while the men moved forward to replace them.

The dancers all wore leopard's teeth necklaces, which swayed brightly in the night, accentuating the primitive ferocity. Around their left ankles they wore ivory bracelets; boar's tusks that had been carefully and brutally trained to grow back into the boar's mouth, forming a circle, causing excruciating pain to the wild pig. Their bodies were rubbed with oil that made them shimmer; aside from their jewelry, they wore only loincloths.

The men around Simbayo wore tight breechcloths, so these men who, for all practical purposes, were naked, embarrassed Liliane. Their bodies vibrated to the quickening drumbeats; they stomped the ground and waved their spears in circles around their heads. They, and the audience, let out high-pitched, haunting cries that echoed through the night. The faster the tom-toms sounded, the louder the audience began to chant, clapping in unison as they did so. They, too, swayed to the erotic rhythm.

The moon, high now, threw its light into the circle, as if by magic.

The dancers began to wail and moan as they jumped back and forth, kicking their feet into the earth. The taut tones of the drums invaded Liliane's body, and she swayed with the music, clutching the rail tightly.

Abruptly, the drumbeats ceased. The silence came as a shock. No one moved. No one made a sound. Then the women dancers walked out of the darkness and faced the men.

Slowly, very slowly, insistently, the beat began again. The fires at the circle's edge flamed brightly. The dancers moved as in an erotic dream. They shrugged their shoulders at the men, beckoning them on. They swayed their hips back and forth, and the men stayed still. They wove music into the air with their hands, and the men were motionless. They ran their hands over their breasts, lifting them up to the men, who remained unmoving. Sweat poured from gleaming bodies; the women leaped in arcs, the regular rhythm increasing in tempo. Their hips began to move suggestively, while their shoulders, their breasts, their arms stayed still. Their hips then moved in circles, back and forth, gyrating with self-imposed frenzy.

Then, in one unanimous motion, the men responded, each partnering the nearest woman, lifting her high into the air, seemingly possessed. Their frenetic energies burst forth in the jungle night, screams rent the air, and all the people began to dance, their cries echoing and reechoing from the forest walls. Magic was in that sound; its reverberations shot through the night.

Jack turned to the nurses. "Ladies," he said, bowing gallantly, "it's time for us to participate."

Rose and Heidi looked at each other, then over at Baxter. Jack grabbed each of them by an arm and said, "Come on. I guarantee your safety."

They followed him onto the dock, turning to look questioningly at Baxter.

"Well," he said to Liliane, and there was a throb in his voice, "shall we join them?"

He jumped over the side of the boat and reached for Liliane's hand. He held it as they walked toward the delirious dancers; he held it tightly—caught up, too, in the frenzy of the moment, in the rhythmic beat in the night, in the shadows dancing wildly, in the musky smells that emanated from the crowd.

Jack shoved a coconut shell filled with liquid at each of them and, looking over the rims at each other, they drank deeply. The noise of hundreds of dancers pounded into Liliane's blood; the wine pulsed into her veins; the drumbeats pummeled into her core.

Whipped by rhythms beyond their control, she and Baxter, facing each other, began to move. Perspiration ran between her breasts; she felt the touch of Baxter's hands on her shoulders, saw his hips moving, swaying with the music. Back and forth, back and forth, the movements broke like waves upon her consciousness.

It was a dream, the same one she had dreamed for months: Baxter holding her, wanting her, moving to her. Baxter staring into her eyes, at her partly open mouth, at her breasts. Baxter moving with the agile grace of a panther, pulling her to him so that her body melded along his. Their bodies undulating to the music, brushing against each other, backing off, touching again. Baxter's eyes intense and fiery, dark in the flickering shadows of many fires;

a pulse throbbing in his throat, matching the beat of the tom-toms. His look never leaving her, ramming his soul into her.

He pulled her to him and she felt her breasts crushed against his chest, felt his heartbeat through their shirts, heard his breathing in her ear. His lips brushed her ear and she thought he moaned.

They were alone. The thunderous noise around them faded; the hundreds of wildly clapping, stomping dancers disappeared. Only she and Baxter existed. His lips sought hers; urgent, yearning lips that had no gentleness in them, lips that parted hers. His hand slid up her back; he cradled her head in his hand, pulling her tightly into him, releasing passion in her that she had only suspected was there. They were one; the hammering of the blood in her veins kept tempo with the drums.

He whispered in her ear, "I want you! Oh, God, how I want you. I've wanted you since the day I first saw you."

His lips covered hers again, his tongue meeting hers, his arms crushing her into him as though he would never let her go.

CHAPTER 6

▼

ANOKA CAME OUT OF THE JUNGLE ONE AFTERNOON.

He did not come out as most of them did—limping or covered with sores or being carried. He did not come out nervous or sick or with a toothache or pleading for help. He walked out of the forest with self-confidence, erect and tall. He was slender and very black, with wide lips, thin hips, and a ready smile. He was the handsomest Congolese that Liliane had yet seen.

He wore a breechcloth, a gold bracelet around an ankle, and a single leopard's tooth on a leather thong around his neck. A monkey followed him, jumping from branch to branch or leaping to the ground and running on all fours. The monkey made funny sounds and, when they came into the compound, reached its hand up and put it into Anoka's. It took three quick steps for every one of Anoka's and looked around furtively.

When Anoka reached the center of the clearing, he stopped. Only then did he look around. Very slowly he turned a full circle and then stood waiting. He didn't move. The monkey jumped up into his arms.

Nearly everyone was napping during the hottest part of the day, but Liliane saw him from the bathing pool. She saw him standing there, all alone except for his monkey and the few chickens that ran around at every hour of the day. When he realized that no one was around, he raised his right foot and, storklike, brought it to rest on his left knee, standing the way natives do throughout Africa, in a position that apparently never tires; a waiting position that not one white person can mimic for more than a few minutes. Natives stand like that for hours.

In a few minutes Baxter emerged from his office and walked over to the man. From her vantage point, Liliane looked at the tableau. The black man, as tall as the white man, planted both legs firmly on the ground and talked; Baxter shook his head. The monkey ran around in a circle. More interested in the monkey than in the man, Baxter leaned down and patted the animal, who jumped up on his shoulders and then to the top of his head. She saw Baxter laugh and reach his hand up to let the monkey know it was all right. But he kept shaking his head.

Curiosity took second place to the emotion she felt whenever she saw Baxter. That night still tucked itself around her mind, never letting go. Why had he acted with such passion and then pretended nothing had happened? She could still remember the heat of his breath, the sweat generated by the frenzied dancing, the feel of his body next to hers, his lips against hers with such urgency. She could still feel his arms around her, could still hear the beat of the tom-toms surging through her blood, could still see the fierce desire in his eyes as his face came close to hers.

That night they had all slept on the deck of the *Sal*; she had lain under the stars, only a few feet away from Baxter, staring into the heavens, listening to his even breathing, knowing that he, too, was awake. Once, in the darkness, his hand reached out. He did not hold hers, only brushed it.

In the morning, at the first tinge of dawn as Jack chugged the engine into life, her eyes fluttered open to look over at Baxter, but he was not there. She saw him leaning against the railing, staring into the dim distance.

She had gone to stand next to him, her heart filled with joy but too unsure of herself to touch his arm, which she wanted to do. Her eyes were warm with happiness, but he did not respond, even after she'd said "Good morning" twice. He had walked away from her, to the front of the boat, and stood talking with Jack, seemingly oblivious of her. With tears stinging her eyes, she watched him until Rose and Heidi stirred themselves, and then she hid her heartbreak and dismay by hypnotizing herself, watching the wake of the boat.

Baxter never mentioned the kiss, never hinted about the frenzied dancing that followed, never met her questioning, hurt eyes. From then on he acted as though he scarcely knew her.

When they worked together, his coolly impersonal voice spoke simply as a doctor would to a nurse; no personal look, no warmth. He disowned that night, that passion. And in so doing, rejected Liliane.

Had he just been caught up in the music, in the wildness of the ceremony, in the unaccustomed cognac?

She looked at him there in the clearing with the black man and his monkey, his shoulders slightly hunched over, his sun helmet askew, and knew that his clear blue eyes were denying the native whatever it was he wanted. He pulled the monkey off his head and into his arms, stroking it for a moment before giving it back to Anoka. Then he turned and went back to his office.

The black man stood there for a minute, then looked around. He walked toward the dormitory building, in the shade of the overhanging trees, and squatted on his haunches outside Liliane's door. The monkey squinted at him, then jumped up on his shoulder. The two stayed there, immobile.

When Liliane came across the clearing, shaking water from herself, the man rose. He smiled at her, a most ingratiating smile. His black eyes were intelligent; his teeth were unfiled; his manner was friendly.

"I am Anoka," he said, introducing himself. He spoke with a British accent. "I have come here to learn."

Before she realized what she was doing, she held out her hand. "I am Liliane. I work here."

He looked at her hand a minute and then grasped it, a beatific smile covering his entire face. He shook it up and down with great vigor. Liliane realized it was the first time she had ever shaken hands with a native. She wondered why.

"I will, too," he said, his English enunciated clearly.

Not knowing what else to say, she entered her room. She had never had anyone stand outside her window and didn't know how to get dressed. Should she ask him to move? Should she ignore him? But his head disappeared from view as he slid down into a sitting position. The monkey, however, watched her from the windowsill, chattering at her as she pulled on her dress.

When she walked to the hospital, she was conscious of an extra heartbeat as she approached Baxter. I've got to follow his lead, she told herself. Doctor to nurse, nothing more. Professional yet friendly.

Baxter's eyes barely flickered as she entered the room. Damn him, she thought.

"What is Anoka going to do?" she asked.

"Anoka?"

"The native who just arrived. He said he is going to work here."

Baxter shrugged his shoulders, his voice irritated. "Nonsense. I told him he couldn't."

"What does he want to do?" she asked as she took the pulse of a man who was recovering from a hernia.

"I'm not sure." Baxter's curtness conveyed his lack of interest.

After a silence, Liliane pursued. "His English is remarkable."

"Yes."

It was like pulling teeth.

"Where's he from?" she asked.

"The Lombato mission. Says he went to school there."

"Well, he certainly went to school somewhere."

Baxter did not respond. Instead, he left the room.

Partly because Anoka was not like anyone else she had met, she was fascinated. She knew no natives who spoke English, except for a sort of pidgin, none who were so straight and tall, none who carried themselves as he did. When she finished her afternoon rounds, he was still sitting outside her room. It was nearly dinnertime.

"Do you have anything to eat?" she asked him.

He smiled and shook his head back and forth. "God will provide," he answered.

Yes, she thought, doesn't he always?

She brought him three bananas. He thanked her. He gave one to the monkey and ate the other two quickly.

"What do you want?" she asked.

He stood up and faced her. "I want to save my people."

Oh, my God, she thought. She didn't know what to say.

"Is that not what you are doing?" he asked in his formal way, in deep, round tones.

"It sounds like such a big task," she said.

He nodded solemnly. "I want to learn to be doctor."

"Oh, dear." She hadn't realized she had said it aloud until she saw the look on his face.

"It's not impossible." The firmness in his voice attested to his faith.

Liliane reached out a hand to touch his arm. "No, no, of course not."

"The famous doctor thinks it is not possible."

Liliane had no response.

"But I am patient. He will see."

As she walked to the dining hall, Liliane smiled. I will help this man, she thought. I will show Baxter Hathaway that he is wrong.

At dinner, she brought Anoka into the conversation. "Why don't you want him to learn?"

Every time Liliane disputed the doctor's motives or was ready to argue with him, Rose and Heidi clammed up. They seemed to think it was sacrilegious to question him.

Baxter showed impatience. "Oh, come, Liliane. Have you ever known a native who could learn the complicated techniques of medicine? I've never even known one who could master an abstraction. They don't know how to think beyond today."

"That doesn't mean they're all like that," she argued. "Couldn't you give the man a chance?"

"A chance to what? Fail?"

"Don't we all have that right?" she countered. "If we don't take the chance to fail, how can we ever succeed?"

"Oh, Liliane." Exasperation filled Baxter's voice. "We've had thousands of years of mental training. They still have millennia to catch up with us. They're still on the level of children. Don't tempt them."

"Tempt them!" she cried. "Don't let them grow is what you mean. How can you possibly think that way? We all come into the world knowing nothing. Do you mean to say that because their skin is darker than ours their brain is smaller? Does it go together, is that what you're trying to tell me?"

He looked at her. Directly at her, his eyes meeting hers for the first time since that night. "I am trying to tell you that."

"Oh, Christ!" she cried, standing up.

Rose and Heidi gasped in unison.

She hadn't felt this angry in years, certainly not since her arrival in Africa. Was she really angry at his attitude toward the natives, or was this her way of releasing frustration at him for the way he treated her?

Patience emanated from Baxter. "Sit down, Liliane. Calm yourself. An African does not think the way we think."

"I know that." Her voice was still loud. "Does that mean they *can't* think? Does that mean they *can't* learn what we can learn?"

"Maybe in a thousand years," he continued, "maybe even in a couple of hundred, they can begin to think as we do. Then perhaps we can train them to assist doctors."

"To assist?" she wanted to scream. Instead, she said sarcastically, "But only those who were rescued and brought to America as slaves? Having been brought up in the white man's culture and taught in our schools, I suppose, they stand more chance of their brains becoming enlarged? How do you measure intelligence? By how well they speak English?" She remained standing.

Baxter picked up his fork and speared a carrot. "Or French," he murmured.

"Oh." Her voice sounded strangled. "The wonderful Dr. Hathaway who brings white Christianity to the jungle but doesn't know the meaning of brotherly love and faith in his fellow human beings! You don't even think they are human beings, do you? They're not even on a par with your precious animals, are they?"

She knew she was shouting.

Baxter spoke, his voice calm. "Liliane, if you want to try to educate him, do so."

She looked down at him, tranquilly eating his dinner. The nurses hadn't taken a bite since she'd started her tirade. Maybe they hadn't even breathed.

Anger swept through her.

She turned quickly and walked the length of the room, slamming the screen door as she left.

THE NEXT MORNING, WHEN BAXTER CAME TO THE LINE OF LONG-waiting patients, Liliane was at her usual place, at the table next to his chair, where she would be near his right shoulder with the medical supplies and a notebook. Positioned next to where his left shoulder would be was Anoka.

When Baxter appeared, his glance flickered over the black man, but he said nothing. He ignored him. Anoka stood there all morning. Liliane repeated all of the symptoms of each patient and the medication given, slowly, enunciating clearly. Twice Baxter looked up at her with obvious irritation, but he still said nothing. As she stood there, beginning to educate this Congolese, she thought, Why not Naldani, too?

God helps those who help themselves, she reminded herself. Isn't it my Christian duty, then, to help them help themselves? Or am I just trying to show Baxter he's wrong, to get even with him?

Whether or not her motives were pure became unimportant. She liked the idea. True, the Congolese attitude toward time was exasperating. They had nothing *but* time. They were never in a hurry. If something wasn't done today, there was always tomorrow, except they never quite got around to tomorrow. They lived and thought in today. Their worries were never of the future. Their worries were of the spirits that haunted the forest, or of how to satisfy their in-laws, or of other matters of immediacy. They were not a happy, carefree people, but a people always frightened of the darkness in which they lived yet never doing anything about it. They had no ambitions, because ambition had to do with tomorrow or next year, abstract concepts seemingly beyond native comprehension. They were, however, good at memorizing and solving concrete problems.

But, Liliane reasoned, they knew no better. They had lived like this from time immemorial, with nothing ever changing. If things changed, wouldn't their thinking change? How could they think differently if no doors were ever opened, no light shone in? White missionaries shouldn't give them glimpses of change and then refuse to show them *how* to change.

In the course of her conversations with Anoka, Liliane learned that he had lived down the Solenga River, where a mission school had operated for years. Once, there had been a doctor, but not for several years now. Anoka had been so impressed with the wonders the doctor had worked that he had decided he, too, had to be a healer. A teacher at the school had told him of Simbayo. He didn't know how long he had been traveling, but he thought it must be nearly a year as white men measured time. Much later, Liliane flew over the Solenga and realized that, measured in a straight line, his mission school was not quite two hundred miles from Simbayo. With no maps, no roads, and little knowledge of geography, it was a marvel that Anoka had found them at all.

Certainly men like Booker T. Washington and George Washington Carver had shown the world that black people had the same capabilities as whites. She would prove to Baxter that he was wrong! She would teach Naldani how to read English as well as to speak it, and she would see how much of her medical knowledge she could pass on to Anoka. Joy surged through her. A sense of mission had entered her life.

CHAPTER 7

▼

ON SATURDAYS, THE NURSES RAN SIMBAYO. THERE WERE NO OPERA-tions, and Baxter was never at breakfast. He seldom appeared for dinner and, if he did, he was always silent. Saturday was the day he rowed himself over to the leper island.

He asked no one to go with him. It was never discussed. Several times, when she had awakened early, just as the darkness was becoming day, Liliane saw Baxter at the dock, untying the rope that held his pirogue, jumping into it and casting off, rowing himself into the invisible wall of fog.

A shudder always passed through her. Even though he had repeatedly explained to her that leprosy was not highly contagious, she did not believe him.

Can they really be helped? she'd ask.

No, he'd answer, if you mean cured. But they can be helped in other ways.

What other ways?

He shrugged off further conversation.

Maybe she was still trying to prove things to him: that by ignoring her he was missing a woman who was his equal; that he was not the only altruist, not the only selfless person, not the only hero; that she was courageous; that . . . What? Maybe, after all, she was really trying to prove these things to herself. Whatever her motives, and they were still unclear to her, she knew on Friday that she was going to go with him the next day. Perhaps she knew before then, but on Friday she was unable to eat dinner, and she wondered if it were the last day of her life that she would live without leprosy. She told herself that she knew what she would see. She reminded herself not to touch anything, hardened her stomach into a knot, and straightened her shoulders.

When the first faint sounds of the forest responding to the approaching dawn came, she woke with a start, sitting straight up. To her relief, it was still dark; Baxter would not have left yet. She pulled her clothes on without lighting the lamp, and when the gray streaked the sky, she felt her way along the path to the river.

She was waiting for him when he arrived. Sitting in the pirogue as straight as she could, surrounded by the mountains of bananas he had stowed aboard, she tried not to shake. He came bounding onto the dock and stopped abruptly.

He looked at her for a full minute and then asked, his voice impatient and gruff, "What do you think you're doing?"

"I'd like to come with you."

"Why?" was all he asked, his voice belligerent.

She hesitated a moment. "I don't know."

"Get out," he ordered roughly, his stance angry.

"No," she said, "I think not."

Hands on hips, he stood looking at her. Then he reached down and picked up the box of medicine, threw it into the canoe, and untied the ropes. He jumped in and pushed away from the dock, paddling in cold silence.

She looked at him; his brow was furrowed, his eyes stormy. His lips were set tightly, and she noticed, with surprise, that the gray at his temples was more pronounced than when she'd first met him over two years ago. His face was no less handsome because of its present rigidity. She thought him quite the most beautiful person she'd ever seen. Looking at him gave her pleasure. His nearness always gave her a heightened sense of life.

Neither of them said anything. Another pirogue, coming from the island, appeared silently out of the haze. Five women paddled in unison.

"Who are they?" Liliane broke the silence.

Baxter turned from his rowing to look behind him. "Wives of some on the island. They go over there every night to be with their husbands. The healthy children aren't allowed, as you know. They're in a camp down the river, looked after by two women whose husbands died of leprosy long ago. But these"—he gestured with a shoulder toward the approaching canoe—"work at the camp and choose to come over to the island every night to be with their husbands."

As the boat came closer, Liliane saw Naldani.

Her mind swirled. Naldani, over here every night? Was it possible? She had never asked Naldani if she had a family, where she slept at night. She had touched Naldani! Her clothes were washed by Naldani.

Inadvertently, her hand came up, waving her fingers at the black woman as they passed in the gray dawn. Naldani smiled, then her face was drawn in puzzlement. She turned to look back at Liliane as the boats pulled apart.

Within minutes they reached the jungle island.

The beach was filled with jabbering children, who stretched out skinny, festered arms to grab the ropes Baxter thrust out at them and pulled the boat onto the beach. Baxter became a different person. His voice thundered jokingly at them, a grin covering his face, and then he jumped, with great vivacity, out of the pirogue and onto the sand. The children clustered around him, their faces raised, their arms banding around his long legs, reaching up to him.

Welts covered their naked bodies and some of their faces. One little boy had only two toes. Their large shining eyes, like brilliant pieces of coal, laughed with Baxter, their voices high-pitched and demanding. They fought over who would carry his box; they stared at Liliane shyly as she sat in the back of the canoe.

She waited for Baxter to offer her a hand, but he ignored her. As he started up a path, surrounded by the little children, he glanced back at her and smiled—as though laughing at her—as she clambered onto the sandy beach, running to catch up with them.

A large grove under palm trees had been cleared close to the river's edge. Here, sitting or lying listlessly, were dozens of Congolese in varying degrees of deformity. Baxter and the chattering children strode into the clearing, but Liliane stayed on the path, partly hidden, peeking at them.

What she saw broke her heart. Echoes of what had once been people crawled along on all fours, having lost faces, noses, toes, or hands. Some had only eyes, their lips and noses having long gone—eyes with pleading voices. The fetid smell of disease was everywhere. She heard coughing and spitting and recognized the sounds of pneumonia and TB: illness compounded.

While some moved around more easily and some were not yet deformed, all of them were in advanced stages of the disease. She saw Baxter talking to a woman, a young woman who would have been handsome and desirable but her hands had fallen away, so she gestured with arms that ended at her wrists. She could not hold anything. Liliane winced with the realization that before too long the woman's entire body would be riddled with the disease: sores would cover her body and her other extremities would also disintegrate.

She vomited into the edge of the jungle.

When she looked up again, a little girl was staring at her.

The child had welts of sickly white patches covering her body. Her luminous eyes looked shyly at Liliane crouching in the forest, vomiting up her fear and horror. Liliane noted that the little girl had just three toes on one foot.

No, there can be no God, Liliane thought. Not and let this exist, unless He is the Old Testament God of wrath. I cannot love a God like that.

The child reached out her hand, still intact, and touched Liliane's arm. Liliane shrank from her as the little girl ran her finger up and down Liliane's white skin. Looking into the bright questioning eyes, Liliane fought down the temptation to jerk her arm away. I don't want to catch this, she cried to herself, but neither could she brush the child away. The little girl continued to stare at her and then said something. She repeated it over and over, in a small, diffident voice.

"Here," she heard Baxter's voice saying, "let me help you," and he reached out a strong, firm hand and pulled Liliane up. He must have felt her trembling, but he said nothing. Instead, still holding her hand—just as he had that night so many weeks ago— he pulled her along the path, striding through the center of the circle, where all eyes stared at them, and onto another path into the forest. She heard the dripping of water. Around a curve in the path, splattering over large boulders, was an iridescent feather of a waterfall.

Baxter finally let her hand go. "Here, wash your face." he said. "You'll feel better. Rinse your mouth. The water is uncontaminated. It's perfectly safe."

How did he know? she wondered. She hated it when people told her, "It's going to be all right." How did he know? Empty words of comfort. She stood there.

So Baxter took her hand again and, as though she were a child, led her to the dripping water. Cupping his hands under it, he caught some water and splashed it on Liliane.

She awoke as if from a trance.

"There." His stern face gentled.

He suggested she drink from the stream that captured silver in the sunlight. Immediately she felt better.

His voice was slow and firm. "You must not let them see your revulsion. You have chosen to come here, and you must find the strength to face it."

Numbly, she nodded.

"Can you do it?" he asked, his voice kind, concerned.

Before she could answer, Baxter put his hands on her trembling shoulders and held them tight. "Liliane, stop!"

She stopped.

"If you want," he said, and his voice became less personal, colder, "you can spend the day in the boat. But I am not going to be hurried because you decided to be heroic—or foolish."

He started to leave her, to wend his way back along the path toward the clearing of lepers. "Stay here as long as you like," he said. "I won't be far away." He disappeared around the bend.

Only the splashing of the water broke the enormous silence. The screech of a parrot only accentuated it. She forced herself to breathe deeply. The cold water on her face felt good. She inhaled again.

As she did so, she felt something soft creep into her hand. It did not frighten her, for it felt comforting and . . . human. She looked down.

The little girl with the sores had reached up and put her small hand into Liliane's larger one. The hand felt and looked like an ordinary little girl's hand. Her solemn eyes stared up at Liliane. There was no way to resist this child.

Liliane stooped. She pointed at herself. "Lili," she said. And again.

The little girl stared with wide, lonely eyes and pointed at herself. "Mbula," she said in a voice that was scarcely a whisper.

Holding each other's hands, they walked down the path toward the lepers.

Liliane was not sick again. She followed Baxter as he washed sores, as he smiled and joked with each leper, though neither understood the other's language. Once, she jumped into the exchange and translated for Baxter when an old man was complaining. Many of the complaints had nothing to do with leprosy. In weakened condition and living in the open without shelter against the elements, the lepers were prone to TB and pneumonia and malaria. Baxter dispensed much quinine.

At noon, resting under the trees, they ate bananas. Baxter asked Liliane, "Are you holding up better than you thought you would?"

Mbula had curled up next to her, on the sand, and fallen asleep. "Where's Mbula's mother?"

Baxter shrugged, as he always did when he had no answer. "The little girl appeared in the camp about two years ago, with lesions that told us what she had. We had to bring her over here last year."

"If they're not contagious, why are they isolated?"

"I never said they weren't contagious. I said not highly so. We don't understand leprosy. It germinates in the tropics. There are very few cases in the States, and those are always from Louisiana or Texas or warm, humid places like that. Of course, it was rampant in Hawaii and still is in the Philippines. They have an entire island devoted to lepers from all over the world. We don't know the genesis of the disease. We know that you and I are very unlikely to get it." He laughed roughly, but with a touch of gentle irony. "I more so, perhaps, because I touch their sores."

"Doesn't it frighten you?" she asked.

"Not really."

"Have you ever wondered what would happen if you did get it?"

"At first. But death hasn't bothered me in years." He paused and stared up into the trees, where sunlight filtered through the leaves. "Not until lately." A shadow brushed across his cheek.

"Why lately?"

Baxter was silent for a while, letting sand sift through his fingers.

"Life," he said, as though speaking to himself, "has become different. Suddenly dying has become important. I don't want to. I find myself worried about things that never used to worry me. I find myself thinking of things I haven't thought of for years. I find myself . . ."

The pause lengthened.

Finally, Liliane asked, "You find yourself . . . ?"

He jerked to attention, as though his mind had been somewhere else. "Huh? Oh, I find myself . . . a part of . . ." He stopped and stood. "See what you've done. You do it all the time."

What had she done? Gotten him to talk a little. To drop a wall, even if just for a second. "What?" she asked. "What did I do?"

He looked down at her with a mixture of what she could only describe as amusement and irritation, if such were possible. "Get under my skin."

He walked off, disappearing down a jungle path.

Here, on this leper island, happiness welled up in her.

Mbula stirred and sat up, rubbing sleep from her eyes. Without realizing what she was doing, Liliane hugged the scarred little girl to her.

As she did so, she heard a long, agonized cry, like that of a wounded animal. A cry so drawn out, so full of pain and despair that she jumped up. It had come from beyond, up the path where she had not yet been.

Without hesitation, she let go of Mbula's hand and ran up the path into the darkness of the jungle. Here, away from the light, there was no dense undergrowth; the flowers were pale and the hush enormous. To the right she heard the voice of a woman moaning, yet she knew Congolese women never cried in pain.

Parting the thick hedge of greenery, she entered a labor area. Three women, in varying stages of leprosy, held a fourth, who was covered with warts and badly deformed. Her legs dangled, her knees barely touched the ground while the women held her. They would not let her lie down. Long, low moans escaped her. Her eyes, agonized, stared at Liliane. Liliane could tell the woman, covered with sweat, was on the verge of delirium.

In her limited Bantu, Liliane tried to explain that she was a nurse. The word had no meaning. She tried doctor. Yes. That they understood. White doctor magic. It took her about half an hour, but they finally allowed her to lay the woman down and examine her. She was aghast to discover that the baby was lying sideways in the woman's abdomen. Oh, God, she thought, there's no hope at all. I couldn't even turn it around.

Urging them to leave the woman lying there, she rushed out of the jungle and back down the path, searching for Baxter. She nearly stumbled over the waiting Mbula, who stood sucking her finger and staring into the forest where Liliane had disappeared.

She found him a quarter of a mile away, ministering to an old, toothless man who waved his handless arms in the air. Baxter turned as she ran breathlessly up to him, her face flushed, her eyes frantic.

"There's a woman," she gasped, trying to catch her breath, "in labor—not even a breech, the baby's sideways. The other women say she's been like that for more than a day. She's nearly unconscious. Come quickly."

He automatically stooped and picked up his bag, already two steps ahead of her by the time she realized he was coming with her. As they ran down the path, he called over his shoulder, "You know they won't let me near her?"

Liliane had forgotten that.

"And she'll die anyway."

"We can save the baby."

Baxter stopped and turned, looking down at her. His eyes had a peculiar expression. "At least we can ease her pain," he said, and continued on.

When they came to the waterfall, Baxter said, "Let's wash here." With a jolt, Liliane realized this pure cold water was the closest they could come to sterilization here. And there was no soap. Her shoulders sagged.

Baxter saw this. His large hand touched her shoulder, and with kindness in his voice, he said softly, "We'll do what we can. Life can ask no more of us than that."

As they neared the small clearing the women had hacked out of the forest, they heard the woman vomiting.

"Go in to them," Baxter said, "and examine her. See if they'll trust you to do that."

Liliane nodded. They had already shown her that much trust.

"It has to be a cesarean, you know that. See if they'll let you cut into her."

"Let *me* cut into her? Oh, Baxter! I've never—"

He covered her mouth with his hand. "Just go look, then come back out here." He stood in the center of the path, a tall, intense figure in white, like a ray of light in that dark place.

The older crones had allowed the woman to lie down while she vomited. Liliane saw the sweat, the glazed look in her eyes. Touching her, she felt the fever within the woman. Obviously, she had been in labor far too long. There was no hope of anything but pain and delirium before death without a cesarean. But could she? She had seen one back in nursing school, but that was so long ago. She had never cut anyone open, never operated on anyone.

But without help the woman was doomed to a long, agonizing death. She felt the woman's belly; she winced at any touch, though her eyes stared up blankly into the trees. The baby was still alive.

Liliane explained that she would be back. They nodded, welcoming her help, trusting her because she had white man's magic.

Baxter waited where she'd left him.

"She's losing consciousness."

"Thank goodness for that."

"Her water's broken; she's dry. It's still alive, but there's no way that baby will come out."

She started to cry.

"Don't be a fool," Baxter said, grasping her arm. "You can do it. Of course you can. Your only other alternative is to watch her die, slowly and painfully. What kind of nurse are you?" He knew what kind of nurse she was. "I'll stand out of sight here where they can't see me. I'll lead you through it."

"But what about instruments? Sterility?"

"I have alcohol in my bag—and a knife."

"What about anesthesia? I can't do it without that."

"I have chloroform."

Liliane looked up at him. His eyes were fierce, demanding, confident.

"Now, look," he ordered, pulling up his own shirt. He pointed at his stomach with his finger, said, "Here's where you'll make the incision," and traced, on his own belly, the direction and place where Liliane would cut.

He handed her the knife, alcohol, and choloroform.

Her hands shaking, a flutter in her chest increasing, Liliane returned to the circle where the three women were again holding the weakened woman upright. She had lost consciousness.

Like naughty schoolgirls, they let go of the woman, who sank onto the mat they had prepared. They stood by silently and suspiciously as Liliane looked around and finally tore a strip from her skirt, soaking it with chloroform and laying it over the ill woman's face. Her breathing eased. The women stood at the edge of the circle and nothing Liliane did could make them leave.

"Now," Baxter's voice called from outside the clearing, "take the knife and . . ." Sweat poured down her face. She had to brush the stinging salt from her eyes. She forced her hands to stop shaking. Poising the knife, she shut out everything except Baxter's voice and the woman's distended stomach.

"Now," his voice was calm and reassuring, as though he had complete faith in her, "trace where you're going to make the incision with your finger so you know the place. Can you see exactly where you're going to do it?"

A rivulet of perspiration crept down her cheek. Her breathing came hard. "Yes," she whispered back. Then, knowing he couldn't hear, she called louder, "Yes."

"All right. Now we're going to do this very slowly. Liliane, listen to me. You can do it. You're one of the best nurses I've ever seen. Do you understand? You're going to do it slowly and carefully. Now, first, you'll make an eight-inch cut low in the belly, the incision starting near the navel and going toward the pubic bone. Are you ready?"

"Yes," she said clearly, feeling strength surge through her, necessity replacing fear.

"Okay, let's start. The cut starts low in the belly, and it's going to go through several layers. First the skin layer, then about an inch of slippery fat with some oozing blood vessels . . ." He waited while Liliane followed his directions, too caught up in the enormity of what she was doing to think for herself. "Then you're going to go through a layer of fascia, of thick gristle; it's about one-eighth-inch thick and—don't get scared—it makes a sort of sharp tearing sound when cut."

It did.

"Then comes a thick muscle layer, which you'll cut straight down the middle in between the rectus muscles. Now, these long rectus muscles can be pulled apart and will reveal the last layers of fat—now, slowly, surely—and peritoneum before getting into the belly.

"The next layer will be the uterus itself—it's a smooth, bluish organ. The bladder will be poking up right on top of the uterus. Push it down in the muscles and peritoneum and fat and pull it away to get a clear view of the uterus."

He waited for her to follow his directions. "Now, cut into the uterus very slowly—you don't want to hit the baby or cut into it. Make slices—very gentle slices—until there is a leak of amniotic fluid . . ."

Liliane forced herself not to jump at the gush of liquid that splattered her.

"The fluid is surrounding the baby. Now, don't be scared. Insert two fingers into the uterus and, with the knife, cut upward in between the two fingers. The fingers are providing a buffer between the baby and the knife. Now, Liliane, figure out where the head is. Take your time."

Liliane knelt with her hands deep within the woman, blood up to her elbows and spattered over her dress, amniotic fluid spurting onto her face, a knife in one hand. She searched for the baby's head.

"Have you located it?" Baxter asked, his voice calm and encouraging. "Now, put your hand behind the head and very slowly pull it upward into the wound. You're going to deliver the baby headfirst through the surgical incision."

Liliane struggled through the slipperiness to turn the baby so that its head would face her.

Baxter understood her silence and said, through the trees, "Reach up to the top of the belly and push from there with one hand and then gently pull with your other hand."

With her left hand, Liliane pushed, and with her right, she felt the head sliding into position as she gently tugged on it. A *whoosh,* and there was the head!

"It's here," she exclaimed, "the head's here!"

The old women looked at her.

There was a smile in Baxter's voice. "Good girl. Good girl. Now, after you pull the head out, remove the shoulders in the same way, by pressure from above. Then, when a shoulder comes out, grab into the axilla—a couple of fingers into the armpit will help to pull the baby out farther. Gently! Gently!"

"It's out," she cried, holding the infant in the air. The joy she felt when she took the wet pink-brown baby from his mother's stomach was unutterable. She always felt intense pleasure at delivery, at seeing a new human being come into the world, but to have delivered this baby by cesarean herself was a marvel.

The new mother lay motionless.

"It's a boy," she called to Baxter.

"Lay it between the mother's legs," Baxter continued. "You'll have to tie off and cut the umbilical cord."

Liliane laid the baby down.

"Now, wait for the placenta to loosen and help to separate it so it comes out of the uterus, by gently pulling the cord."

The old women made no motion to reach for the baby, but stood in fascination. Perhaps they had never made the connection that a baby came out of a belly.

Gently, Liliane pulled on the cord, and the placenta oozed out of the uterus.

There was blood everywhere. Liliane's clothes were sticking to her through sweat and the sticky blood that covered her.

"What do I do to sew her back up?" she called.

She knew that without instruments or clamps the bleeding was a terrible problem.

There was silence from Baxter.

When he spoke, she could sense his hopelessness. "You might squeeze the bleeding edges and massage the uterus, trying to get it to cramp down and shut off the bleeding on its own. . . . Liliane . . ." She heard a catch in his voice. "Let her die."

Let her die? Mustn't I try to save her? At least try?

"Listen to me, Liliane." Baxter's voice was gentle as it floated, disembodied, through the air. "This woman is in the painful last stages of leprosy. She won't last much longer anyway. She can't nurse the baby. She probably couldn't recuperate from a cesarean under the most sterile and best of conditions. She's unconscious now. Let her die that way."

Liliane's chest pained her. It was hard to breathe. Let her die? Wasn't that the same as killing her?

"For God's sake get rid of those women and let me in there."

"I can't do it, Baxter. I have to help her to live."

"For what?" His voice was gruff. "Pain? Despair? Misery?"

Oh, she thought, I wish I could say, "Oh, God."

Tears welled in her eyes. The three women continued to stare. She knew perfectly well that infection would set in, knew that after the misery she had just gone through, this woman—alone out here, away from doctors and help—would die slowly, painfully. More quickly than if she had not had an operation, and that was probably merciful, but a death racked by the raging infection and compounded by her leprosy. In her mind's eye, she saw this woman regaining consciousness, lying weak and in pain where she was and no one rescuing her. No one able to help her. She heard the cries in the night, the plea for release.

Slowly turning to the three women, she spread her hands helplessly in front of her. She murmured the Bantu word for death.

With no visible emotion, one of the women picked up the baby and the three women and the baby left the circle. Liliane broke into tears. Then Baxter was there. While Liliane sobbed uncontrollably, he took the chloroform, emptied the bottle onto the rag, and laid it back over the woman's face.

Then he turned and took Liliane in his arms, letting her cry herself out, stroking her hair, whispering in a soft voice, "There, there."

She put her arms around him and cried some more, her body racked by sobs.

As she regained control of herself, Baxter pulled back, extricating himself from her embrace.

He looked at the dying woman lying on the ground. "You did a fine job." His voice was clinical again. "A fine job, Liliane."

"At least we saved the baby."

"She could have gone on for hours in that agony," Baxter tried to console her. "Part of being a doctor"—then he looked at her and amended—"of being a healer is not just to prolong life, but to ease pain. Pain that has no end."

On the path, Mbula was waiting. Without thinking, Liliane reached down and brought the girl up into her arms, and that's how they walked back.

Already, coming from the opposite direction were natives going to claim the body for burial. In this climate, burial needed to be immediate.

When they were ready to go, Liliane turned to Baxter and asked, "Can we take the baby?"

He just stared at her.

Didn't he want to give this child a chance? Couldn't he see how much better the baby's chance for life was on the mainland, being fed and cared for rather than left here with dying men and women who could hardly take care of themselves, who were dying as much from malaria and pneumonia as from leprosy? Couldn't he see that the baby must be taken from this island of sickness? Certainly he could help give life to this small creature that, together, they had brought into the world?

Her eyes pleaded with him.

"They'll have buried the baby with the mother."

She looked at him uncomprehendingly. "Buried? He's alive. They can't bury a baby alive." Her tongue was dry.

Baxter sat her on a nurselog, that giant trunk that had fallen hundreds of years ago and now gave life to other tall, thin trees, to lichen that covered its rotting hulk, to a pale lavender flower that would be gone tomorrow.

He knelt down next to her and took her hands in his.

"It's dead."

"Dead?" There was numbness in her voice.

Baxter held her hands tightly, his gaze level. "Whenever a mother dies in childbirth, her baby is buried with her. There are too many children as it is; there's no one to care for the baby. The father never raises a child. It is always done, Liliane. In this case, of course, there's no one at all." Sadness sank into his body. "This sounds cruel, but—in the end—it may be better. When a woman dies in childbirth, it means there is no one to care for the baby. No way to feed it, to care for it."

"I . . . I don't understand. Where *is* the baby? I know he's not dead."

"They buried the woman immediately. They buried the baby with her."

Liliane stared at him. "Alive?" she whispered. Then, grabbing Baxter by the arms, she screamed, *"Alive?"*

Her eyes were glazed, and she said thickly, "I could take care of him. I'll be his mother."

"Liliane, don't try to change their ways."

"Baxter"—her voice was beyond control—"it's murder. They're murdering an innocent, helpless baby."

He stood. "It's too late, I'm sure."

"Where? Where are they?" Her eyes were frenzied and her tongue stuck in her mouth.

He turned and marched quickly; she followed. The late-afternoon heat made rivulets of sweat trickle down her neck. When they reached a clearing, the women who had taken the baby and several others stood in a semicircle while two men shoveled loose dirt into a shallow hole.

"Stop!" Liliane screamed, breaking into the funeral. Baxter did not try to stop her, but he did not help either. She wrestled a shovel away from one of the men. The other stopped, his home-made shovel in midair. Liliane sank to her knees and began clawing at the earth with her hands. It was only a matter of inches before her nails raked soft flesh. Rigor mortis had not yet set in.

She dug frenziedly, throwing earth aside with abandon. Her audience watched, bewildered, unmoving. Her breath came in short gasps. The baby lay in the crook of the mother's arm, dead, his body still warm—smothered by the earth clinging to his nostrils. An involuntary moan escaped Liliane, a sound that rose to a high wail as though she, herself, were in pain. She clutched the baby, jerking him from the earth, putting her mouth over his, trying desperately to breathe life into the small body.

She felt a hand on her shoulder, knew without looking that it was Baxter's. At the same time, she knew he was trying to comfort her. She also knew he was telling her to stop. Enough, his touch said.

She laid the baby on the ground, tears clouding her vision. Leaning over, she placed him within his mother's arm. Gently, Baxter pulled her up.

Out of control, she began to beat him with her fists. "You knew they were going to do that!" she shouted. "You let me deliver that baby and didn't tell me. You didn't give him or me a chance. I could have taken care of him!"

She cried, raining her fists on him. "Damn you. God damn you for doing this to me!" Great gulping sobs enveloped her.

He grabbed her wrists and looked down at her. "Liliane, you did not come here to change the way they have lived for all these centuries."

"Oh," she cried, "why not? Why not, if I see things that are so wrong?"

"If you can replace them with something better, fine. But don't take tradition away from them and leave them with nothing. Or force them to live like Americans. They're not ready for that. Their values are not ours. If you are to live in their country, you must learn that."

THE TRIP BACK, GLIDING OVER THE RIVER IN THE NEAR DARK, WAS silent. Liliane was bent over, her arms clasped around her stomach, staring straight ahead into nothing. When they docked at Simbayo, she sat there, unaware that they had stopped. Baxter touched her shoulder. She climbed out of the pirogue like a somnambulist and stood on the rotting wood of the dock, seeing only emptiness.

He took her hand and led her to the dormitory, opened her door and took her in, led her to her bed. After lighting the lamp, he sat beside her, taking her hand in his.

"You were very brave, Liliane."

She didn't answer.

"I don't know anyone braver," he said.

He left her sitting like that, staring into the void of a blacker night.

CHAPTER 8

▼

FOR THE NEXT THREE DAYS, LILIANE LIVED IN A STUPOR. SHE PARtook only marginally in conversation; she carried out her duties in a perfunctory manner. Her dazed eyes and her slow, subdued movements gave her the appearance of an automaton.

Then, on Wednesday, she appeared at breakfast alert and charged with energy and ambition; her purposeful step commanded attention. As though continuing a conversation with Baxter, she demanded, "Why don't you do more for them?"

She seated herself at the table.

Rose interjected, "More for whom?"

"And what," asked Baxter, with his mouth full, "do you suggest? I do supply them with enough food and take care of their medical needs."

Liliane hoped he was not merely speaking defensively, that he really wanted an answer.

"Keep the rain off them for one thing. That would reduce TB and pneumonia. Get roofs over their heads."

Baxter peeled a banana. "Not so easy. No one from the mainland will go over there. And they certainly can't do it themselves."

"I think they can. Some of them still have fingers and energy. And what about the wives and husbands who go over there every night? Can't they help rather than just stand around waiting for death?"

He looked at her with patience. "Dear Liliane," he said, his voice holding warmth, "wanting to save the world."

She couldn't tell whether or not he was making fun of her, treating her like a naïve, idealistic child. Yet Baxter lived his life each day as though it made a difference to the world.

There was an edge to her voice. "Well, at least this part of the world." She would not be dissuaded. "They need to have a reason for living, not just lie around waiting to die. They might as well be already dead. Let's help them find a reason for going on, let's make their lives still worth living." Her voice grew loud with enthusiasm.

Rose caught a little of her fever. "What do you want to do?" she asked.

Liliane turned to her with gratitude. "Oh, Rose, come out with us. Come see it. Come help."

Baxter tilted his chair back, never taking his eyes from Liliane's face. "What do you have in mind?" he asked.

"I want them to build something with roofs over their heads. It can be done so easily. I've seen pictures of houses built in the South Seas. We can cut down some trees and use them as beams and corner poles, and the lepers themselves can thatch palm leaves to use as roofing. They're out there now with no protection from the weather! We can try to get more blankets for them. We can teach them hygiene. Don't tell me the way these people live, their lack of sanitation, has nothing to do with leprosy! If these people in all the villages didn't live in airless huts, if they weren't crowded in together, if they took baths, if they washed utensils, if they didn't step in . . ." She ran out of breath.

Heidi nodded her head up and down. "I always suspected leprosy comes from filth," she said.

"I can see I'm outnumbered," Baxter said with a thin smile. "However, I don't want Heidi or Rose to go. I want them to stay here. I want to know Simbayo is in their hands."

Okay, thought Liliane. I'll find people. There are others who can help.

NALDANI CAME TO MIND. NALDANI SPENT EVERY NIGHT ON THE island. She would have no qualms about working there. And Anoka. Maybe she could talk him into it. Maybe he could enlist others and eventually . . .

When Liliane approached her, Naldani agreed to stay on the island Saturday, meeting her and Baxter and Anoka at the boat landing. Anoka had not hesitated to agree to accompany them.

Liliane was amazed at herself. She realized she was not doing this for altruistic reasons only—it wasn't simply that she had to ease lives of pain and anguish, though certainly that was a large part of it; she also had to prove something to herself. Scared and revolted as she was, she had to prove she could conquer her fright. It was the first time, in what was to become a lifetime habit, that she would do something because she feared it.

How I've changed, she thought. That girl from Buffalo, who thrived on parties and boys, has disappeared, hasn't she? She liked herself better now. She liked the self-disciplined woman of direction she was becoming, leaving behind the lighthearted young girl.

That first Saturday was difficult. Work was something the lepers had not done since their banishment. Disease had sapped their energies and their interest in life had so dissipated that at first little enthusiasm could be engendered, but with Liliane's direction, Anoka's patient teaching, and Naldani's encouragement, they began to react like schoolchildren who trust the teacher if not the process. Anoka and Liliane showed them how to chop down trees. Some of the men were already familiar with the process and demonstrated to others, including the abler women, just how to stand—two on either side of a tall, straight tree whose trunk was no more than eight inches in diameter—and take turns hacking it.

When the tree began to fall, they ran from it, but they ran smiling. It had been a long time since any of them had done constructive work. Liliane set them to work peeling the bark off the fallen trees, not an easy task with no tools and fingers that were none too nimble. But no one complained.

The ensuing weeks saw marvels. On Saturdays, the forest was filled with the thud of axes chopping, with the thunder of falling trees, with laughing conversation as the men and women sat in rows beside the tall trees, tearing the bark away, smoothing the wood with their hands. Anoka and those most able dug postholes while the less able sat plaiting palm fronds for the roofs. They were the ones who taught Liliane. The nimbler men climbed high into the palm trees, tossing down leaves until there were piles of them. Then, sitting cross-legged, those whose fingers could work deftly braided the leaves into large squares. They built ladders out of slender trees, and the younger men climbed the ladders, criss-crossing the rough-hewn beams with the plaited fronds.

Late one afternoon, Naldani began to sing, her contralto soaring into the air. Liliane looked up in astonishment at the rich sound. Though she understood only a few words, her friend's voice sent a thrill through her. Gradually, others joined her, harmonizing in an atonal dissonance that introduced Liliane to the tribal singing of Africa. The music haunted her with its strange beauty.

Naldani's husband, Bmeno, stared at her, love and pride written across his dreadful face.

He hobbled along on feet that had no toes, and his hands had no fingers. His nose was being eaten away, yet Naldani treated him with warmth and kindness, deferring to his opinions. Once Liliane came upon them in a private moment. Bmeno had reached up and was touching Naldani with the stump of his hand, brushing love along the curve of her cheek. A tear gathered in Naldani's eye, and she cupped his face in her capable hands.

At first, Liliane had wondered how Naldani could love this deformed man, why she would voluntarily come to this island every night. But her Saturdays on this island taught her a lesson she should have learned long ago: that looks have nothing to do with love. A far cry from the movies of her youth, where a hot glance from Theda Bara made strong men weak and beauty was the core of attraction and passion.

When she saw the compassion with which Naldani treated her husband and knew her eagerness and ability to learn, Liliane knew that Naldani could be taught nursing, along with Anoka. Then Naldani could nurse those lepers who needed help.

When she asked Naldani if she would like to learn "white man's medicine," the native woman's eyes lit up.

"Oh, yes," she said, her regal face breaking into an eager smile. "I would like to help my women in childbirth. Too many die. Too many hurt."

"No," countered Liliane, "I thought you could stay out on the leper island and nurse those out there. No one else will do it."

Naldani looked at Liliane with consternation. She said nothing. She looked away, then back at Liliane. In her eyes, joy gradually changed to fear.

"You mean live out there *all the time*?"

Oh, how stupid I am, Liliane moaned to herself. What could I have been thinking of? Relegate her voluntarily to that way of life? When Bmeno dies, she probably will never want to see the place again.

She looked into the eyes of her friend. No, she could not wish that on her. She knew if she asked Naldani to stay there, she would, but the look in the woman's eyes told Liliane that she couldn't ask it. Let it be enough that she stayed to help on Saturdays and that she did what she could every night.

Liliane reached out and touched Naldani's hand.

"I like your idea better. Yes, that's good. We shall save babies and women, and you will lead your women to a better life."

In assuaging Naldani's worries, she had no idea of the prophecy of her words.

Naldani brightened. "I have long wished to learn white doctor magic."

"Why didn't you ask before?"

Naldani lowered her eyes. Humbleness did not become such a magnificent creature.

Liliane put her arms around her friend. "Naldani, I have faith in you." Her head came to Naldani's shoulder. "This afternoon, after my swim, you and Anoka and I will meet under the okoume tree—no, I shall set up tables as desks and create a school at one end of the dining room."

She thought of inviting Naldani to swim with her but knew she needed that time for herself. She had come to resent it when Rose or Heidi came at that hour. It was her alone time, the time she needed to replenish her soul, to gather the strength she needed to keep on giving.

At dinner that night, Rose's long face broke into crinkles of approval. "It looks like you're starting a school."

Baxter's head turned to her. "A school?"

"Well, Anoka is learning nursing techniques so well. I can't seem to teach him fast enough. And now I'm going to teach Naldani, too. It seems she would like to learn midwifery. And I will teach them both English. Not only to speak it but to read it also."

"Ach," said Heidi. It never ceased to surprise Liliane when Heidi bobbed into a conversation. "That is good. These women never let a man near them. One of their own women—that is good." Her round head, encircled by her golden braids, nodded approvingly.

"A black woman?" Baxter blurted out.

All three nurses stared at him. Liliane smiled to herself. A year ago, when she was new here, Rose and Heidi would never have reacted as they did now. She felt supported.

"Well, Anoka is learning, you must admit. So that proves blacks can learn." She refused, absolutely refused, to say anything about a woman's intellectual capabilities compared with a man's.

Later, Liliane had to admit that Naldani did not take to book learning with the ease that Anoka did, but the facility with which she learned in the operating room or out in the bush, when Liliane was called to childbirths, was amazing.

HAPPINESS FLOODED LILIANE WHEN HER MOTHER WROTE THAT THEY were planning to visit her this summer.

> Your father hasn't taken a vacation—a real vacation—in so many years that I've forgotten what it's like. But not seeing our only daughter for nearly two years has given us the excuse to take not only a prolonged vacation but to see parts of the world we never dreamed of seeing. He's been granted a six-month sabbatical. We figure it will take us three months altogether just to get up the Congo to Simbayo and back.

Liliane felt a pang of happiness; she would see her parents again!

> I don't know how long the boat trip to the Congo will take. The Congo! It sounds so exotic. I can hardly believe

we're coming, much less that you have been there so long. Our friends are all worried for us, but I tell them you think it a most safe place.

Oh, my darling, I can hardly wait to see you, to put faces to all the people you write about, and to see how you truly live your life. Your father joins me in sending love and is as full of exhilaration as I am.

Liliane put the letter down and sighed happily. She had received a total of five letters in this month's mail and had learned to discipline herself to open one a day so that the excitement would last. Sometimes she went for days without thinking of her parents. That life seemed so long ago, so far away. Yet nightly she wrote down the happenings of the day, her thoughts, the people she met, her dreams. And when a month had passed, she jammed all of the loose sheets of paper into a large envelope and sent it out on the mail boat. Someday, she'd have a journal of her Africa years—her mother was keeping the letters in a shoebox "so that you can remember when you come home and Africa becomes a long time ago."

All week she carried the happiness within her. How would her parents react to Simbayo, to the way she now lived, to bare breasts, to leprosy? Would they think life here appalling, or would they be able to see how it magnetized her? Would they like Rose and Heidi? Would they be able to accept Anoka and Naldani? Would her mother be able to stay for a month without plumbing? She walked around all week trying to view life here through her parents' eyes.

She laughed as she opened each letter that week, knowing no news could equal that of the first letter. The fifth was from her aunt, who usually wrote the most boring of letters.

She stared at the spidery writing until it blurred on the page, the words running together. Bright, blinding shafts of light came between her and the paper, stabbing her head like daggers.

No, she thought. That's not what it said. But it was.

She tried to think. It was now April. When had her mother's letter been written? The end of February. And on March 6, her parents, driving home through a blinding blizzard from the Wednesday night prayer meeting, collided head-on with a truck. Her mother was thrown through the windshield, and her father's car door was smashed in as the car slithered out of control. They were killed instantly.

The memory made her double over in pain—pain that she would never see them again. Pain at the enormous loss. Her arms hugged her stomach trying to clutch at the pain.

Their deaths made her feel stranded, rootless. With them gone there was no place to call home, no one to whom she was so beloved, no one to give her security. There was no one to love unequivocally, no one who understood her so completely, no one.

She burst into tears.

She was twenty-three years old and did not like her first taste of tragedy.

A LONE INSECT'S INSISTENT BUZZ WAS THE ONLY SOUND THAT BROKE the after-dinner quiet in the dining hall. Rose and Heidi were playing their favorite Parcheesi at the far end of the room; Liliane was mending a tear in a skirt. Yet Baxter made no move to leave as he usually did. Instead, he sat in companionable silence, though every time Liliane looked up from her needle and thread, he was studying her.

"Do you know," he finally ventured, "how grateful I am that you came to Simbayo?"

"Not really." He was trying to cheer her up, she knew.

His voice was gentle and a smile crinkled the corners of his eyes. "You do almost as much around here as I do. I walked past the window here this afternoon. No, what I really did is eavesdropped. I stood outside listening to you and those two. Maybe teaching is your forte. No, don't misinterpret. Teaching is *one* of your fortes. Is there anything you don't do well?"

She laughed self-consciously. "What I do, I try to do as well as possible. There's so much I wouldn't even begin to undertake."

"When you first came out, I thought you might last three months. But I thought a pretty face would be welcome for even that length of time. I never thought . . ."

Oh, don't stop now, she pleaded silently. But he did.

"You never thought what?" she urged.

"Nothing." Abruptly, he stood up, towering over her. The smile had disappeared. "Good night." He strode from the room.

Bewildered, she stared at the empty space his presence had left. He hadn't even tried to fill the void in her life.

CHAPTER 9

▼

THE MANAGING EDITOR OF *THE TIMES OF LONDON* HAD SENT FOR Marshall Compson.

It was not like sending for another one of his reporters and waiting a matter of minutes. It might be hours, or even days, before Marsh appeared. It was one of the reasons that, at age twenty-eight, Marshall Compson was *The Times'* most famous reporter.

Now, Phillip Clapton had a relatively unexciting but nevertheless interesting assignment. And who else to do it but Marsh Compson?

Clapton sat at his enormous desk near a window that overlooked Trafalgar Square, wiping his glasses clean with a handkerchief. Just thinking of Marsh Compton made him smile.

The daring of that young man, combined with his flamboyant writing style, sold millions of newspapers. Armchair travelers the world over followed Marshall Compson on his journeys. But Marsh had recently married—one of the biggest society events of the year—and Clapton wondered if the new groom would accept an assignment that would involve months in the heart of Africa. Well, he'd soon find out.

MARSHALL COMPSON HAD SPENT THE DAY GROUSE SHOOTING AT HIS father-in-law's estate when he received word that Phillip Clapton wanted him. Adrenaline began to flow through him when the butler said "of *The Times.*" With suddenness, Marsh realized he was bored. It was not just living the life of a gentleman; it also had to do with his marriage.

He walked out of the bathroom, still wet from his shower, and looked at his wife. She sat at her dressing table; the myriad jars she dabbed into amazed him. He thought her so beautiful that she needed none of them. Looking at her now, he remembered the first time he had seen her, nearly two years ago, in the interim between a sojourn through China and his taking off for the Solomons. He saw her first across the drawing room at the prime minister's, dressed in a green velvet gown that revealed her alabaster shoulders. Her black hair was twisted high on her head, and her eyes appeared regally purple from that distance. Entranced, and speaking to no one in particular, he informed a total stranger, "That's the woman I'm going to marry."

Through his charm and wiles, he twice obtained invitations to affairs Riana attended. At the second one, he managed to meet her and later he led her from the party. He found her clever and witty *and* familiar with his exploits. He hated to leave her.

While staring at stars high above the Pacific islands, he saw Riana's face. When he returned to England, he asked her to marry him. She did. She liked being Mrs. Marshall Compson, wife of the famous explorer and journalist, wife of the man whose name was recognized wherever newspapers were read.

He walked over to her now, his towel still tucked around his waist, and leaned over to kiss her bare shoulder.

"Don't get me wet," she said, pulling away from him while continuing to apply her mascara.

All the more reason to go down to London tomorrow and see what Phillip Clapton had in mind.

PHILLIP CLAPTON HAD SIMBAYO IN MIND.

"Simbayo?" exclaimed Marsh. "What're you trying to do, convert me, sending me to a missionary outpost?"

Phillip leaned his elbows on his desk and made a temple of his fingers. "It's much more than that. But just what, I don't know. I want the real story. I want you to be suspicious of everything. Is something going on there?"

"Something?"

"Something more than meets the eye. What makes a movie idol chuck it all and take himself to one of the world's most remote savage places? What's with the women there? There are several nurses—two or three, I think. What's up? God's work or a harem? If it's on the up-and-up, I want the whys explored. What makes people do this?

"From what I hear," Clapton continued, "it's not a Sunday school–conversion type of operation. What kind of people find satisfaction in giving up decent living standards and a normal life and martyring themselves in a godforsaken jungle? Are they women who couldn't get men? Does Hathaway have some hold over them?

"If it isn't on the up-and-up, I want an exposé. But, whatever you do, don't write about the great white doctor, the humanitarian, the ex–movie star. No sainthood. Nothing like what we've read about half a dozen times. A big story. Something that'll interest the whole world."

Well, thought Marsh, why not? It might lack the sense of adventure that climbing the Ruwenzoris had—those mystical, ice-laden mountains on the equator in Uganda; it certainly would lack the challenge that tracing the silk route from Sian in central China westward through Urumchi and Kashgar to Afghanistan had offered. It couldn't compare with flying over the Himalayas or spending six months with the aborigines of Borneo and the Solomons. Simbayo would seem tame after that, but then it *was* in the very heart of Africa, in territory not yet explored. And taking a personal as well as a geographical slant would be different, would force him to look at life differently. Maybe it was about time for him to begin studying people as well as the planet.

He went home to pack: one ditty bag, his typewriter, a camera and a tripod, and three boxes. Riana did not seem dismayed. She had never considered accompanying him on his travels. Not for her a life of inconvenience and dirt and slithering animals. And, he was sad to discover, not for her either a life of intimacy. There was always her golf game or guests or a party.

Her cool lips brushed his as he bid her good-bye.

"I don't know how long I'll be gone," he told her. "Three to four months."

Riana smiled her Mona Lisa smile. "I'm sure you'll be a great success," she said. "You're taking along enough charm to melt the Blarney Stone."

Marsh was pleased; she so seldom flattered him. He reached out to pull her to him, but her hand went to her hat and she murmured, "Not here. Not in public."

Not in private either, he thought.

THIS, THEN, WAS THE NEXT VISITOR TO ARRIVE AT SIMBAYO.

Visitors were always welcome. There were occasional passengers, on their way upriver to the logging camps, who stopped for dinner and stayed overnight, and there were those on their way out from the logging camps, too. In the years Liliane had been at Simbayo, had also been a Boston reporter from the *Christian Herald* whose article about Simbayo made the *New York Herald*

Tribune as well as other lesser newspapers around the world. He had stayed three days. There had been a bishop, assigned by the mission board to tour the remote missions of the Congo. He had stayed two weeks and decided that Dr. Hathaway was the church's resident saint, but Bishop Peterson had been uncomfortable the whole time he'd been in Simbayo. The unrelenting humidity, the mosquito-ridden nights, the ubiquitous beat of drums all unnerved him. The filth of the natives revolted him. He concluded that anyone who voluntarily chose to live in this "hellhole of heathens" must be a saint. The fact that Rose, Heidi, and Liliane also labored here skipped his notice.

The mailboat always brought old newspapers, which were devoured—every word absorbed by all four of the whites at Simbayo—but welcome as the reading matter was, it was no comparison for real-live visitors, even when they did not speak English. A visitor not only broke the routine but brought news of the outside world, even if that were only five miles up or downriver. There were a large number of Germans, and Heidi served as translator. There were Belgians and French, with whom both Dr. Hathaway and Heidi could communicate. Liliane and Rose knew only English and various dialects of Bantu.

Whether she could communicate in their language or not, Liliane never failed to charm visitors. Disembarking from the creaky riverboat, expecting the formidable Dr. Hathaway, anticipating undressed savages (both titillating and scarifying), a newcomer did not expect to see a red-haired beauty whose green eyes wove themselves into the visitor's heart. Her smile brightened their lives; she had the knack of making anyone she spoke with feel like the most interesting person in the world, that there was no one with whom she would rather talk. She laughed easily—and who would not be enchanted by laughter deep and resonant as a bell? But one was also aware that here was a serious woman, one who did not take life lightly. The perspiration that constantly made wild ringlets of her copper hair never affected the cool dryness of her hands. Her touch soothed.

Having devoured every word of any book, magazine, or old newspaper in camp, she was conversant about world affairs if they hadn't happened too recently. She had none of the Teutonic solidity and rigidity of Heidi, none of the British reserve of Rose, and none of Baxter's superciliousness, which alternated with the charm he could call forth. She was outgoing, unreserved, and always delighted to see new faces.

Typically, visitors went away raving about what Baxter accomplished in the middle of the dark continent, but it was Liliane they remembered long afterward. Even the bishop found himself dreaming of her, dreaming of her as he never dreamed of his wife. Every visitor who stopped at Simbayo, however briefly, was captivated by Liliane.

When the *Oregon* sounded her whistle, it was late afternoon. The *Oregon* brought the mail. The Simbayans knew when to expect it. Not that it operated like clockwork; nothing in this part of the world did. When a month had passed, they knew it was time to hear from the outside world again. Unconsciously, they listened for the familiar whine of the *Oregon*'s horn. When it sounded, they hurried to the dock.

Heidi not only looked for mail but for supplies she had ordered; they all looked for reading material. None of the women received much personal mail; Baxter always got bags full. Liliane devoured letters from her Buffalo friends who wrote of parties they attended, dress styles, their babies. It seemed such an alien world to her now, yet she read and reread letters from friends she hadn't seen in so long. They were getting more and more infrequent, she realized. None of her old friends could begin to understand the world she now inhabited. They were caught up in the routines of their lives and wrote less and less often.

No one was prepared for the tall, lanky man who leaped over the side of the *Oregon*. Though all of them—even in this remote outpost—had read something by Marshall Compson, none of them identified their guest by sight when he disembarked from the riverboat. A lock of dark hair falling over his forehead, handsome—oh, he is so exceedingly good-looking, whoever he is, thought Liliane—his eyes nearly black, his long, bare legs below his khaki shorts. His wrinkled short-sleeved cotton shirt accentuated his tanned, muscular arms; his Australian bush hat was cocked at a jaunty angle. He surveyed the group gathered at the dock; his glance stopped when it rested on Liliane and his eyebrows went up. A moment later, his glance moved to the doctor.

With an ingratiating grin, he strode over to Baxter and held out his hand. "Dr. Hathaway, I presume?"

Baxter shook his hand stiffly, showing little warmth. Liliane always wondered at Baxter's reserve with visitors, for she knew he enjoyed them.

"I'm Marsh Compson," said the stranger, "from *The Times of London*."

Rose poked her elbow into Liliane's ribs. She looked flustered. "My goodness. Do you know who he is?"

Liliane had to think for a minute. Of course, that English reporter who traveled all over the world. What could he be doing in Simbayo? This was no Everest to climb or an unexplored point on the map. She had so assimilated herself to Simbayo that she had quite forgotten she was living in uncharted territory, that magazines and newspapers and Fox Pathé News considered this part of the world one of the remote areas of savagery and mystery.

"I hope," Marsh told Baxter at dinner, "that it won't inconvenience you if I stay for a month."

Baxter smiled. "We welcome any visitors. We get rather inbred here and find someone from the outside refreshing. But I suspect you may get bored within a month. We lead busy lives medically, but sedentary otherwise. There is very little to amuse you."

Marsh looked directly at Liliane. She felt herself blushing. She stared into his dark eyes. They danced in the light from the lanterns. "I don't think that will be a problem," he said. Then he returned Baxter's smile. "Besides, I didn't come to be amused." Turning to Rose and Heidi, he added, "Dr. Hathaway is certainly not the only person who makes this place run. I'd like to talk with all of you."

Baxter said, "Well, then, Mr. Compson, you must give us something, too."

"Please, it's Marsh. And whatever I have . . ."

"Oh, it's simple." Baxter smiled, his lips curving, but his eyes remaining aloof. "Just a breath of the outside world. You must tell us of your trips, and what is happening in the world now, and of new books. . . ."

"That's easy. You'll find I like to talk. But I want to see everything here. May I watch you treat patients?"

"You may"—Baxter glanced over at Liliane—"do whatever you want to do."

Marsh followed his line of vision. Liliane saw his eyes linger on her, meeting her level gaze. His glance touched her softly, like a warm breeze. She liked the feeling.

It was after ten when they left the dining hall. They had sat around singing to the accompaniment of Baxter's guitar, songs Liliane had never before heard him play: "It's Three O'Clock in the Morning," "Casey Would Waltz with the Strawberry Blonde . . . ," and "A Bicycle Built for Two."

When the group left Baxter and walked together toward the dormitory, Marsh asked, "Don't you usually play hymns?"

Liliane answered with amusement, "You mean, isn't everything religious around here? No. I suspect the most religious thing you'll find is our attitude; we believe in brotherly love. But we don't push Christianity down people's throats."

"Not even the natives?"

"Especially not the natives," Rose added. "There are no conditions for medical treatment."

"Then," asked Marsh, "how do you show them God?"

Liliane hadn't thought about that for a long time. "By our actions, I guess," she said, realizing it herself for the first time. "But we don't think that way. Our job is not to teach about God."

"Then why are you out here?"

They had reached the dormitory.

He had been assigned the room next to Liliane's.

Rose answered, "To heal. To help. To do God's work."

She held out her hand, saying good night. Marsh shook it pleasantly and smiled. Heidi followed suit, and the two nurses headed toward their rooms.

"Breakfast's at six-thirty," Rose called over her shoulder.

Marsh leaned against Liliane's door. "Don't go in yet," he urged. "Stay and talk with me."

She was aware of his body. She could not see clearly in the darkness, yet she imagined the muscles rippling in his arms. She remembered his slim waist, his long legs. Then she caught herself.

"We have a month for that," she said, pleased at the anticipation she felt. "But I'm really tired. Maybe if I didn't have to get up at six tomorrow I'd be willing to. But catch me some time before ten at night."

She intuitively knew he wanted to touch her. She gave him her hand. Instead of shaking it, as he had the other nurses', he held it and pulled it to his lips. In the continental manner, his lips brushed across the back of her hand. A warm tingle fluttered up her arm. Then he turned her hand, palm up, and more slowly brushed his lips across her palm. This time the warmth did not stop at her arm but ran down her side and spread through her body.

Even in the darkness she could see the light in his eyes.

He moved aside so she could enter her room. She knew he was still standing out there even after she closed the door. She knew he was still standing there as she slid out of her dress. She stood in the darkness, naked, and slid her hands down her hips, then across her breasts. She cupped her hands under them. She knew he was standing outside her room in the night.

Setting aside her nightgown, she lay on her bed, letting the warmth of the night air caress her naked body. Soon she heard sounds in the next room. Lying there, listening, with a heightened awareness of her nude body, she heard a soft knock penetrating the wall next to her head.

Her hands touched her hard nipples.

THE NEXT MORNING, MARSH WAS UNCOMMUNICATIVE, A FAR CRY FROM the ebullient man who had gotten off the boat. He responded monosyllabically at breakfast and drank at least ten cups of coffee. It was not until he had sat in the shade and watched Baxter and Liliane dispense advice and medicine for over an hour that he came to life.

Baxter talked loudly and slowly to the natives, hoping irrationally that it would enable them to understand his English. He now routinely relied on Liliane to interpret. He never showed any evidence of having acquainted himself with Bantu in spite of the many years he had heard it spoken.

Marsh watched the natives patiently standing in line or being supported by others. He saw the distended stomachs of malnutrition. One woman stood in line for hours; when it was her turn, they saw that her baby had been burned and was lying with its eyes staring blankly, its breathing shallow, its body racked by relentless pain, though it made no sound. There was more anguish in the mother's eyes than in the baby's.

Baxter jumped up in anger. "Good God, woman! Why didn't you push forward? Why didn't you come in last night?" Of course she understood not at all. He nodded to Liliane, who quickly ushered the woman and her baby into the operating room. The wounds were a filmy white and flies stuck to the pus that oozed from them. Liliane elicited from the woman that the baby had fallen into a fire two days ago. They had been traveling ever since to the "white doctor magic." The agony the child must have felt was horrible to think about. It made no noise as Baxter and Liliane laid it on the table. Neither could help grimacing at the areas of charred skin hardened like black leather.

Liliane could imagine the baby's pain, despite the vacuous look in its eyes.

The less severely burned areas were red and swelling; draining pus dripped from them; insects clung to the wounds.

Baxter said, to himself as much as to anyone else, "The areas of black eschar aren't as sensitive to pain or touch as the reddened, infected areas. They must be pretty damn painful." It was the first time she'd ever heard him say damn.

Marsh leaned over to look, gulped loudly, and left the room.

At lunch he asked, "Will that baby live?"

As usual when he had no definitive answer, Baxter shrugged his shoulders.

"Yes," said Liliane.

She was willing it to live. It would live and run and feel, if she had anything to say about it. She was beginning to see that will had as much to do with living and dying as anything else.

After lunch Rose and Heidi indicated they were going to nap. Marsh turned to Baxter and Liliane. "Does everyone do that in the afternoon?"

Baxter shook his head. "I usually write. If you like, at about three I can talk with you."

Marsh said he would like that. He was eager to start interviewing as well as observing. He turned to Liliane. "And you?"

Baxter answered for her, glancing at her sideways as he spoke. "She usually swims."

Glee jumped from Marsh's voice. "I could do with a splash. May I join you?"

No man had ever accompanied her at her pool. How would she swim with him there? Though long ago her mother had sent her a bathing suit, she still felt undressed in it. Only Rose or Heidi ever swam with her. Once or twice she thought she had seen Baxter's face through the curtains of his office, but somehow she hadn't minded that. She liked to think that he wanted to see her, that he cared enough to peek through curtains, that he yearned for her. But Marsh—swimming with her? A stranger? She remembered her feelings of last night.

She looked across the table at him, his eyes excited, warm. It would be nice to see his chest, to look at his shoulders, to see him look at her.

Baxter pushed back his chair and stood. "I'll leave you two young people"—he accentuated the "young"—"to plan your afternoon."

As the screen door slammed, Marsh said, "I sense hesitation. Is there?"

Liliane answered, "I'd really like to have company, but I'm not used to swimming with a man." Yet she remembered the beaches along Lake Erie, and she had never felt shy then.

Marsh's eyes danced. "That won't bother me."

She smiled.

Marsh was delighted with the pool. The palm trees kept the sun out of it at this time of the afternoon, and though it was not cool, it was shady. She could see Marsh watching her as she waded into the clear pool.

"This is the most comfortable I've been since I came to the Congo," he volunteered as he swam across the pond.

Her fears evaporated. Marsh made no innuendos. He kept up a running conversation as they swam back and forth. When they had finished their swim, they sat together, under the palm tree, wrapped in their wet towels, hair plastered to their heads.

"Why are you out here?" he asked.

"It seems rather obvious, doesn't it?" she asked, shaking her wet hair, running her fingers through it. She couldn't help noticing there was very little hair on his chest.

The sun danced through the palm fronds, throwing dappled shadows across them.

"Oh." Marsh leaned back on his elbow and stared out at the river. "God's work. Serving society. Are those your answers? Isn't that every missionary's answer? Are you here to serve God?"

She thought, I've tried not to ask that of myself. "I think," she replied slowly, thinking her way through to an answer, "that I originally came with that in mind. It sounded so romantic and heroic. But . . ."

"But that's not why you stay?" He was lying on his back, staring up at the trees, his hands under his head. She studied his sharp profile. The aquiline shape of his nose, his high cheekbones, the firm jaw—all spoke of strength. The fine sensual lips, the jagged dark eyebrows indicated the most tantalizing combination of tenderness and passion.

He turned to look at her when she failed to answer. She had been absorbed in staring at him and started at his glance.

"I don't think so," she finally responded. "I'm not sure God has anything to do with it."

Nodding his head in the direction of the compound, Marsh asked, "Does *he*?"

"You mean Dr. Hathaway?"

"Sure."

"I don't know. He's certainly a shining example of courage and altruism."

"That's not quite what I mean. Are you . . . under his spell?"

Liliane stiffened and raised her chin. She looked directly at him, her cheeks hot. "I really don't think that's any of your business, Mr. Compson. It has nothing to do with anything you're trying to find out." A note of resentment had entered her voice.

Marsh remained unruffled, still staring up through the palm fronds. "Sure it does. I want to know why you're all here. Why you stay here. Why a woman as beautiful as you would choose to hibernate in this remote outpost. What keeps you going?" He paused. "I agree"—he turned to face her—"that it may be none of my business—yet. But I suspect it is going to be, before too long."

She looked at him. "What about the rest?" she asked. "Why don't you ask them why they stay?"

"I intend to," he said. "This is the first of thirty days, after all. I'm most interested in why *you* stay."

"Why me? Baxter's the famous one."

"Ah," his voice was soft, "but Baxter is not the one I am likely to dream about, nor do I lie in bed knowing he's but feet away from me, or wonder if he is sleeping in the raw, or if the moonlight is playing over his body."

Oh, my God, she thought.

Sand sifted through her fingers, and she asked, remembering how much fun it could be to flirt, "And you're likely to do those things about me?"

"There was no moonlight last night, but I've already experienced the rest."

She laughed out loud. Then she said, "Maybe we don't know why we're here. Or why we stay. Maybe it's not really to help people. Maybe it's not really to make ourselves feel better. Maybe it's not our destiny. How *do* we know why we're here or why we stay?"

"Have you ever thought of leaving?"

"Not really. No, not once."

"Are you going to stay here forever? Do without men and children and love and a normal life?"

"How do I know what I'm going to do with the rest of my life?" She had asked herself these questions many times. "I'm

twenty-three. I really don't think I have answers to much of anything."

"What did you think when you came out?"

She was able to laugh at that one. "That I was going to save
the world. That I was being noble and unselfish."

"You don't think so anymore?"

She sighed and sat up. "The limits of my world have narrowed
considerably. I do think I make a difference in this world. I like that
feeling. But I do not feel noble or unselfish anymore. Not," she
added, "that I feel selfish. I do feel that every day I do something
that makes life a little easier for someone. I go to bed at night with
a free conscience."

"God, are you lucky!"

"I am. I think I'm amazingly lucky. Now, what about you?
What's made you . . . you?"

He looked at her and then, with his hands under his head,
closed his eyes. "I was a brat as a child, I'm afraid. My father was
in the diplomatic service, and I was born in Cape Town, of all
places. We'd go 'home'—to London, that is—every two years, but
I've never felt England was home. I felt more at home wherever
my father was stationed. Istanbul, Athens . . .

"'When I was fourteen and my father was appointed attaché in
Cairo, my parents left me at Eton. I'd been enrolled there since
birth, of course, but they actually left me there this time. I resented
and hated it. Three months of that and I jumped on a freighter
bound for Egypt. For two months no one knew where I was."

Liliane lay down again and turned over on her stomach, resting her chin on her hands so that she could look at Marsh as he
talked. He was watching the palm fronds above them, but she knew
he wasn't seeing them.

"You did other aggravating things?" she encouraged him.

"I went back, several times. I'd take just as much of rigid
routine as I could and then I had to take off again. The Middle East
fascinated me. I wanted to experience living in the desert, I wanted
to see Mecca and go down the Nile to Khartoum. I did all those
things—dressed in native robes so as not to be conspicuous. My
parents never knew where I was. My father gave up worrying by
the time I was seventeen, expecting I'd show up in my own good
time. But I don't think my mother ever relaxed about my frequent
absences."

"How did you ever manage to graduate from school?"

"I never have," he admitted. "But I like to think that hasn't stopped me from getting educated.

"When I was in school, I must have been insufferable—always arguing with my teachers. The only subjects I liked were geography and literature. I spent my youth poring over maps and reading."

"How in the world," Liliane asked, "did you get to be one of the world's most famous reporters?"

Marsh's eyes had been focused on the mesmerizing swaying of the palms. Now he sat up and stared at the slow-moving river as it flowed past the pool and the storks in the rapids on the other bank. He looked at her, reaching out to brush back the unruly curls that had flopped over her eyes. He smiled at her, a warm, boyish smile. "I don't want to bore you all at once. Let me save some of it until later. Besides, it must be time for me to interview the famous Dr. Hathaway."

He stood and reached down to pull her up.

"Liliane Wentworth, I think I'm going to like you."

They started to walk back toward the dormitory. "Had you thought you weren't going to?" She was not exactly flirting.

"I don't think I thought about it. I knew the minute I saw you I was going to desire you." Oh, what a nice thing to hear. Then she hadn't deteriorated in the jungle. Or was it because they were in the jungle and there was no other choice that he felt that way? "I have an antenna that reacts to beautiful women, but I hardly ever wonder if they're going to be nice."

"And I'm nice?"

He laughed. "You are that."

She gave him a challenging look. "Does that mean your antenna stops working?"

"Not for a moment." He grinned. "You probably don't even know it, though somehow I always thought beautiful women did. But even dripping wet, even with a shapeless towel draped around you, you are incredibly beautiful."

They were at her door. "I like hearing that," she said. "I wasn't sure what I looked like anymore."

She closed the screen door and he pressed his face against it. His expression was serious. "Let me tell you something. I'm married."

That he was married bothered her not at all. For she would not leave here, and he would not stay. And she was in love with

Baxter Hathaway. But she was ready to be kissed. She might even need to be kissed.

She wondered what it would be like to be kissed by Marshall Compson.

CHAPTER 10

▼

FOR HUNDREDS OF YEARS BARE FEET HAD PADDED ALONG THIS PATH. The hard-packed dirt had been worn smooth as marble. Back here, under a canopy of trees, the light slanted, like constant twilight; here the jungle was transformed to true forest. The trees towered high above like giant emerald umbrellas. Here, too, in ever-green-light shadows were but darker shades. For Liliane, space was the pervasive sensation. The dense, seemingly impenetrable jungle had given way at the outer boundary of dusk. Back this far from the river and sunlight, one could understand how Africa was named "the dark continent."

Four native carriers, two ahead and two bringing up the rear, wound along the path with Liliane and Marsh.

"You know," Liliane called over her shoulder, her voice echoing in the vast gloom, "I'd never have been allowed to do this if you weren't here to accompany me."

"I'm glad you think I'm of some use!" responded Marsh.

For many months Liliane had been urging Baxter to extend the medical services beyond the Simbayo compound, but he had resisted; on this he had been obdurate. "We can't save the whole world," he had told her. "The sick manage to get to the compound if there's hope. We're too busy here to take time to go rustling through the jungle. What would our Simbayo patients do if we left for days? I leave only in emergencies."

In the back of her mind an idea had been growing for a long time. If only, somehow, they could make rounds to the villages, perhaps they could save those who were too sick or too scared to be carried to Simbayo, not to mention those who were not quite sick enough to bother with such a trip. The natives would feel more comfortable in their own villages, and Simbayo would be freed of those whose needs were minor. How much more humane it would be to treat those with low-grade malaria or with incipient diseases; to advise those with hernias to come to Simbayo for operations. And, possibly most important, going to the villages would give her an opportunity to teach sanitation and to practice preventive medicine. If she could see what kinds of problems were rampant in the backland, ward off infection, dispense quinine, and suggest that water be boiled, wouldn't that make a difference? Liliane was convinced it would.

Yet she understood Baxter's reaction. They were busy enough as it was. "No one here is dispensable," he muttered.

"I am." He looked up from the dinner table at her. "Heidi," said Liliane, "spends most of her time organizing, supervising . . ." She turned to the German nurse. "Heidi, would you mind going back to actual nursing for three weeks?"

The usually taciturn woman nodded. "Sometimes," she said, "I do wish for patient contact. I like what I do, I like bossing, but once in a while, I like to stay in touch. To see patients."

"For heaven's sake, Liliane," Baxter growled, "a white woman can't go out there alone. You don't even know how to use a gun."

"I'm not afraid," she responded. "If you think I need a gun to ward off dangerous animals, then what I really need is someone who knows how to shoot."

Baxter knew how but refused to touch a gun. None of the nurses knew anything about guns, and the natives had no access to them.

In the silence that hung there, Marsh volunteered, "I can shoot."

Everyone knew that.

Baxter looked sideways at Liliane.

She turned to Marsh. "But you're leaving next week. Maybe," she said softly, "before you go, you could teach me how to use a gun."

It was as though no one else was in the room with them. Their eyes held each other's across the table in the lamplight. She saw a vein pulsing in his temple.

She felt like laughing. What she desired might actually come to pass. How wonderful to feel like a woman again, to exert the power that, as a woman, she could wield. To know, with absolute certainty, that Marsh would delay his departure to go into the jungle with her.

Baxter would have to capitulate. He didn't rule her, after all.

She was breaking down the barriers he had set up: Heidi would do more nursing. Marsh would protect her. She would use this man, if need be, to get what she wanted. He would be her avenue to circumvent Baxter's authority.

And, she had to admit, she had enjoyed Marsh's company this past month. Perhaps she was also purposely throwing herself together with him. Baxter was always so aloof with her. Every night he and Marsh philosophized or played chess. Once in a while, they even condescended to play Parcheesi with the women. Baxter was obviously stimulated by Marsh's company, but he had withdrawn even more from Liliane. Not, of course, that he'd ever expressed closeness. She wondered if he remembered that kiss so many months ago?

I'm twenty-three, she thought. I can't help it if I find two men attractive. I can't help it if I like to hear that a man enjoys looking at me. I can't even help it that I want to be kissed. Maybe I'd let any man kiss me.

Yet she knew that wasn't quite true, but both Baxter and Marsh had awakened desire in her. She wanted Baxter to talk with her. Not just *to* her, but *with* her. She wanted to see not only admiration and respect in his eyes, but also desire. She wanted to walk so close together that they touched. She wanted to get into his mind, to know how he thought. She wanted to swim naked across the pool with him. She wanted him to touch her breasts. She found herself blushing as she thought about Baxter and looked across the table into Marsh's eyes.

She was surprised to note amusement in them. Maybe he sensed the game she was playing.

So now, when Marsh should have been leaving, they were winding through jungle paths to outlying villages, places where no white woman and few white men had ventured before.

Though it was cooler back here, with no sunlight filtering through the trees, the air was oppressive. There was little breeze and high humidity. The canopy of trees kept the atmosphere still and stagnant. Nothing, thought Liliane, can make one feel so insignificant as being in a Congo forest. It's lonely and frightening and marvelous. There was a remarkable hush to the forest, only an occasional *whir* of wings or snap of twig to indicate life, and always the continuous hum of myriad mosquitoes. Once in a while they heard the scold of a monkey from the treetops, and they could look up to see a troop of them swinging in a line through the tree branches.

She was surrounded by the musty odor of decaying leaves and logs. A moist green scent mingled with it. Spreading far overhead, the tree limbs were festooned with climbing vines. Now and then a single shaft of sunlight found its way through the interlacing leaves and shimmered there like a translucent bar of gold. Flowers were rare, pale, and well hidden in the underbrush.

Thunder suddenly jolted the air, and the earth trembled.

"Elephants!" cried one of the carriers.

Liliane had yet to see one, and here they were so close to Simbayo. They hadn't been gone a day from the compound and already there were elephants. She was gripped with excitement.

The lead carrier, Nbundo, gestured for them to move off the path. They followed him a hundred yards into the forest and stood waiting.

Approaching from the opposite direction came three elephants, their enormous feet precisely following the narrow footpath. The beasts were wondrous to behold. From the great gray bulks of their heads, their trunks drooped toward the ground, their small, alert eyes concentrating on the path ahead. They lumbered along gracefully, with an agility that contradicted their large mass. The front elephant raised its trunk and stopped abruptly. The second and third ones nearly slammed into it. The lead elephant raised its trunk, swinging it in the air, and let loose a loud, trumpeting blast. Nbundo held a finger to his lips; they must be silent, for the elephants sensed their presence.

The three majestic animals stood for minutes. When no sound was heard, no sight seen, no danger evidenced, they proceeded onward, their small tails waving, their massive bulks, like great gray rolling waves, merging into the green-gray background of the forest.

With heightened awareness, Liliane knew the grandeur of what she had just witnessed. Marsh's elbow touched hers, and she could see that he, too, had felt it.

It was late afternoon when they came upon the first clearing, a village of native huts. It looked abandoned at first. A tiny village, perhaps thirty small huts made of leaves: circular and hexagonal-shaped dwellings, with low doors and conical-pitched roofs. A dry dustiness engulfed the village. The earth was barren of vegetation.

Scattered here and there sat an elder, cross-legged, plaiting reeds. Nbundo explained that soon it would be dinnertime, and the women would return from their gardens. They left early in the morning, with all of the children, while the men went hunting or fishing. This ritual was followed every day of every month of every year of every century of every millennium. The pattern had not changed in thousands of years.

White people were not unknown to the people of this village. Some of the natives had even been to Simbayo, but the villagers returning from the fields or the hunt reacted with great shyness, standing on first one foot and then the other, holding their hands over their mouths, grinning self-consciously, then welcoming Liliane and Marsh, wanting "white man's medicine" for their myriad physical ailments.

Liliane explained in her still limited Bantu that she would see patients tomorrow; she was tired tonight.

Although the villagers tried to insist that Liliane and Marsh accept their hospitality and use the guest huts, Liliane couldn't stand to sleep in one of their hot, airless huts. She and Marsh pitched their tents near the periphery of the village. Everyone watched the tents being erected. They touched the canvas and crawled in and out of the tents. They stood up inside them, giggling. They marveled at the cots and asked if one didn't fall off them while asleep.

When darkness descended and only the sound of chirping insects and the distant erratic beat of drums could be heard, Marsh and Liliane sat on an old log, watching the flickering fires around the circle of huts—fires left burning to ward off leopards that might wander into the village at night and to keep jungle spirits at bay.

"You're amazing," he said.

She laughed. "Well, compared to other American girls, I'm certainly different. But I can't even envision living any differently."

"Don't you ever long for a hot bath? For comfort? For those things girls grow up wanting? What about a home? A husband? Children?"

"There's plenty of time," Liliane responded. "I'm still young."

She couldn't pretend she hadn't thought about these things, even occasionally longed for them.

"What about love?" Marsh asked. "Don't you want love? What about a man?"

Liliane sighed.

"He's old enough to be your father," said Marsh in the darkness.

She couldn't be so false as to ask "Who?" so she remained silent.

"He can't give on a personal level. You must see that. He either doesn't know how to or is scared."

"I don't know," she murmured, as if talking to herself. "Maybe I keep thinking that, with time . . ."

"With time? You've been out here nearly two years! How much time does it take for a man to show interest?"

"Oh, Marsh, it's not that simple. It's not just him. My life has meaning out here."

"Don't you get tired of always giving? I look at you every day and you're the giver. Don't you ever want to be given to?"

She laughed softly in the night. "I've thought about that a lot. I've decided there's no justice in the world. Givers aren't necessarily given to. But then I don't think givers give in order to get a return. I think people who give just have to give. *That's* how they get. Their pleasure is in making life easier or better. They get by knowing that what they give is important. Givers don't have a choice."

They were quiet for a while, listening to the night sing.

"Are you going to stay here forever?"

"How do I know what I'm going to do forever? You're asking questions that I don't have answers for."

"Are you in love with him?"

Had he irritated her? He couldn't see her eyes in the darkness. Finally he heard her breathing.

"Sometimes I am," she answered slowly. "He's difficult. He's opinionated. He's narrow. He's also marvelous." She paused. "He's more noble than anyone I've ever known." She thought about his noble qualities, about his skills as a doctor, a scholar, a builder. Baxter can do anything, she thought. "He's kind," she said, more to herself than Marsh.

"And how do *you* feel?"

"I thought I came out here to serve God, but somehow I seem to get further and further away from Him. If there's a god, I don't think he's the God that Baxter and Rose and Heidi know. I don't think he's the God I was brought up to believe in."

They were silent again.

"What about you?" she asked. "We're always talking about me or Baxter. What's your life been like? You never told me how you became a writer."

"Luck. Gall. Despite spending more time out of school than in, I passed Oxford's entrance exam and did attend for two unbroken years. A record for me. But then I read Stanley's accounts of searching for Dr. Livingstone and decided to trace his footsteps, fifty years later, to see if Africa was the same. I hopped a freighter again and traveled through the Suez, landing at Dar es Salaam in Tanganyika. I cabled *The Times* and asked if they wanted the story. I was heading west from the Indian Ocean across the African continent to Léopoldville. I'd be the first to follow Stanley."

"Obviously, they answered yes," Liliane said.

"The rest was easy."

"What's it been like?" she asked. "Hasn't it been frightening?"

"I haven't been frightened," he answered, "but I've been everything else. I've gone without a lot. I've camped in some of the more remote reaches of the world. Without comfort. Without cleanliness. Without edible food. With beetles and snakes. With heat and humidity. With food of unknown origins. With skies bluer and clearer than most civilized men have ever seen. With cannibals. With people who had never seen a white man or a camera. With stars that were low enough to touch. With maps that were more often erroneous than not. With the roar of a lion ringing in my ears as I fell asleep by a campfire. With loneliness."

He was silent for a long time.

"You know," he murmured, "this will be the farthest I've slept from you since we've met."

Liliane turned toward him and looked into his eyes. "That's only geographically," she said softly. "I've shared more of myself with you than I have with anyone."

As she lay on the edge of sleep, she heard Marsh's voice call through the night, "Damn you, Liliane Wentworth."

She stretched like a lazy cat and called back, "Damn you, too, Marshall Compson." But she smiled as she said it.

IN THE MORNING, BEFORE IT WAS COMPLETELY LIGHT, LILIANE WAS awakened by the sound of voices. Looking out of her tent flap, she saw a line of people, maybe forty or fifty of them. Most of them held babies in their arms, and she realized they were waiting for the magic of the white medicine to cure their ills. What a responsibility, she thought as she brushed her hair out of her eyes. Yet she was also aware of the adrenaline flowing through her at the thought.

She had barely pulled on her clothes when Marsh walked through the flap. "Good morning," he said, a smile spreading from the corners of his eyes. "As you can see, your adoring public awaits you. I thought you might need some coffee before tackling the day."

He held out a mug to her. "See what Africa has done for me? Changed me into an early riser."

She sipped the hot coffee, felt it awakening her. "I am amazed," she said. "A month ago you were hardly awake by ten."

"But a month ago I didn't know I wanted to share every waking minute I could with you."

"Oh, come on, Marsh, you *are* a married man." Yet she enjoyed hearing it.

"Have I told you I'm only married because I hadn't yet met you?" He smiled a slow, lazy grin.

God almighty, she thought, don't let me get involved with a married man just because I'm out in the middle of nowhere. It could only spell trouble.

Stoically, she walked out of the tent to face her workday.

THEY TRAVELED TO NINE VILLAGES IN THE THREE WEEKS THEY'D allotted themselves. They spent their evenings talking in the dark—of his travels, of Liliane's childhood in Buffalo. And he talked of books and politics, a topic that had never been of interest to Liliane.

"My God, woman. Politics affects your whole life."

"Politics has nothing at all to do with me," she answered serenely. "What happens in other parts of the world doesn't concern me."

"Oh, poor naïve Liliane." Marsh's voice was condescending. "Someday you will discover that even in this remote pocket of nowhere, what happens in the world will affect you personally."

"Tell me," she said, changing the topic to one of more interest to her, "what's she like, your wife?"

He was quiet, and she couldn't see his face in the night. "She's very beautiful," he answered eventually.

When he said no more, Liliane plunged on. "Surely there's more."

"I've been married less than a year. I'm told the first two are the hardest."

"Is it hard?"

"Oh, Liliane, I don't want to talk about my wife. I don't even know what I think about her. I know I wasn't sorry to leave her for this trip. I know I've never talked with her as you and I talk. I know I never . . ." His voice died out.

"Maybe marriage is one of those rigid conventions you rebel against."

"I've wondered that. Yet it's not that I feel tied down. Riana doesn't seem to care whether I'm there or not. She likes introducing me to her friends as *the* Marshall Compson, but I often think it stops there."

Liliane reached out in the dark to touch his hand.

HER DREAMS AFFECTED HER WAKING HOURS. SHE FELT A BURDEN OF guilt. She felt emotionally superficial. She had dared to leave her homeland, dared to come to one of the world's remotest regions, dared . . . because the vision of Baxter haunted her thoughts and her reality. Now, here she was, but days from him, and another man constantly surged into her dreams and her fantasies.

She found herself watching Marsh all the time. She watched him as he fussed with his camera. She watched him build a splint for a native with a broken leg. She observed him going fishing with villagers and looked for him returning from a hunt with them. She studied his hands and the way his long legs looked as he strode around in shorts. She noticed how his face crinkled when he smiled. She noticed a brooding faraway look. And she saw him studying her, too.

She felt his breath when he was near her, was aware of longing when he came close.

She looked away from him only when he listened to her. He had a knack for pulling out of her thoughts she had not shared with anyone before. Not that they were so private she didn't want to share them; there simply had been no one with whom to explore them.

He engaged her in new ideas. Not his, necessarily, but new ways of thinking, new thoughts to fathom, sparks that would ignite long after he had gone.

"I don't believe in your Baxter's God either," he said one night. "I don't think there's any meaning to life except what one gives it."

"No meaning to life? Then why do we do all the things we do? Are you suggesting that my life is meaningless?"

"No. *Au contraire.* I didn't say life is meaningless; I said it has no meaning until you give it meaning. If you don't think your life has meaning, then it hasn't. All of you out here at Simbayo have meaningful lives. You think your lives matter, so they do."

"You don't think God sent me here?"

He laughed, and his eyes shone with amusement. "Of course not. You did."

"What about all the people who live everyday lives? Do their lives have meaning?"

"Only if they think so."

"Do you believe in life after death?"

"You mean in the Christian sense of heaven?" He looked down at her, one foot perched on the bench next to her.

"I guess so."

"No."

"No immortality?"

"No physical life after death, unless I mingle with the earth or the atmosphere. With luck, I'll have immortality. I think Jesus and Herman Melville and Shakespeare and Buddha are immortal. Parents, through their children, have intimations of immortality. What we do in this life that affects others will remain after we die."

"But what of when *they* die?"

"They may, in some form or other, pass on whatever you or I have done to influence *them*. But it doesn't really matter. Though the most immortal ones influence the world forever."

"Then what makes you, or anyone, behave morally?"

Marsh sat down on the bench next to her. He reached over and took her hand. "Ah, we go from immortality to immorality. A good question." He traced invisible designs on her palm and he stared into her eyes. "You know, what you really need"—his voice became soft—"is to be loved. You need to be tumbled on the grass and kissed and told how beautiful you are and made passionate love to. I don't want you to miss that in life."

It sounded lovely. "Would that give my life meaning?" She hoped she sounded flippant.

He let go of her hand and laughed loudly. "Well, at least it might make you think so."

He started to walk away. With a mixture of relief and disappointment, she ran to catch up with him. They returned to their chores, to the healing they had come to do.

Marsh had been fantastic help. As well as being curious about everything, he had learned a few words of Bantu that he heard repeated over and over. He had sampled village food wherever they went. He had made splints and helped her as she cauterized wounds or scraped out infections. His charm overcame the language barrier. He smoked what must have been marijuana with the natives; he drank palm wine and suffered such a hangover that he vowed never to do it again.

In one village they encountered, they could hear the wailing before they saw the huts. A child's racking sobs. As they approached, a frantic mother and her tear-stained, screaming four-year-old came up to them. The mother dragged the child behind her. His face was streaked with the salt trails of tears and his eyes lit with fright when he saw the white strangers. He hid behind his mother's skirt and became momentarily silent.

He had been like this for over two days, the desperate mother told Liliane. Was he dying? Had spirits taken hold of him? His screams were driving the whole village to distraction, especially as the people generally suffered in silence. Nothing the mother did consoled her son. He screamed incessantly. She pushed him toward Liliane.

He was not very feverish. His eyes, however, raged with pain. As she touched him, he quieted, more from fear than anything else. He refused to open his mouth for her. She automatically looked at his ears. And there it was: a large abscess had formed deep in the ear and would have to be lanced.

By now a crowd of natives thronged around Liliane and the child.

"I have to sterilize a long needle," she said to Marsh. "Do you want to do that, or do you want to convince him and his mother he'll live?"

Marsh sterilized the needle. When the little boy saw the long needle coming toward him, he began to pull away, screaming wildly. Liliane said to his mother, "Hold him. Hold him so tight he cannot move. Here, Marsh, you hold his head still and don't let him move an inch!"

Carefully, and with perfect aim, she lanced the abscess. Immediately, pus poured out of his ear. The screaming stopped.

In less than a minute, the boy was hugging his mother and looking shyly at Liliane. As soon as Liliane had swabbed his ear with alcohol and quinine powder, he ran off to play.

The villagers who had gathered in a semicircle looked at Liliane as though she were a witch.

In the last village they visited, Liliane was aghast to discover a twelve-year-old boy's head sticking up out of the ground beside the path in the center of the village. People came up and talked to it, and it blinked. The boy was very much alive, buried neck-deep in the ground. His eyes were scared and pained. The mother of the boy sat not far from him, three other children clinging to her. Once in a while she stood and filled a gourd with water and ladled it gently into the boy's mouth.

Liliane put her hand over her mouth to muffle her horror.

"Jesus Christ!" muttered Marsh.

He wanted to dig the boy up, but Liliane restrained him with a hand on his arm. "No," she said softly, "let me find out what's happening. If a medicine man is in charge, we better not defy him. If I offend any of them, they'll make sure that no one cooperates with me."

They were welcomed to the village; this was true every place they'd been. As villagers stood around watching them put up the tents, Liliane learned that the buried boy had fallen from a tree during his "rite of passage"—the process of becoming a man—and must have broken his back and an arm. The medicine man was working magic; the boy had been buried for three days.

She waited all afternoon, knowing the medicine man would come to see the patient some time before dark.

In early evening he appeared out of the jungle in full-dress regalia. He was smeared with vivid paint and wore a many-feathered headdress. He had a ring through his nose. This was no ordinary native doctor, but a man of obvious importance and wealth. His teeth were filed sharp and gleamed whitely against his black-velvet skin. Around his waist he wore a circle of feathers. His genitals were painted bright white.

From a distance Liliane watched him kneel and make some incantations over the boy, who blinked hard and nodded the only visible part of him. The medicine man danced around the boy's head, hopping from one foot to another. He beat softly on a calabash and chanted atonally. By the time he was finished, most of the village had gathered around to watch.

When it was time for dinner, Liliane sought out the chief of the village and asked him if she could meet the medicine man. It was not until dark that he sent for her. Marsh accompanied her as far as the witch doctor's hut. She entered it alone, crawling through the door not only because it was so low but also to prostrate herself before the medicine man to show her respect.

He was courteous when Liliane explained who she was, and condescending about her interest in his treatment of the boy, but he did not deign to treat her as an equal. He intimated that he would talk with Marsh, but not to her—she could not possibly understand.

She crawled out of the hot, airless hut. The stench had been overwhelming and she was glad of the fresh air. She told Marsh, "He'll talk with you. Try to find out what he expects and what he did."

An hour later Marsh crawled out of the hut, pallid even in the dark, not from what he had heard but from smoking an herbal pipe with the medicine man. In distress, he walked to the edge of the forest and threw up. Beads of sweat covered him. Liliane led him back to their tents and sponged him off with cool water until he felt better and could recite what he had learned.

"Who knows whether the boy really broke his back or whether it was just severely injured. Whatever, he couldn't stand up straight and his left arm dangled uselessly. So the medicine man dug a long flat pit, horizontal to the ground. He laid the boy in it himself and would let no one else touch him. Then he packed in around the boy a mixture of earth and leaves."

Liliane asked, "What kind of leaves?"

Marsh shrugged. "I don't know. Do you think it matters? He piled the dirt on so that only what you see, the boy's head and neck, are aboveground. God, Lili, do you realize how painful that position must be to the boy? He's been there three days! Then the medicine man piled dry leaves and small bits of wood on top of the earth and set it afire!"

Liliane said nothing, but her stomach knotted. If only she could bring modern medicine to this place. If only the boy were in traction, he might stand a chance.

Marsh continued. "He kept the fire going for four hours. Four hours; he emphasized the importance of that time element. Then he dug the boy out and applied water as hot as the boy could tolerate. He did that for an hour, but no one was allowed to watch. Then he poured hot water over leaves, covered the boy's body with these steaming hot poultices, and packed the earth back around him.

"The boy was told not to make a sound. This process is to continue for five days. On the fifth day he will be dug out and will supposedly be able to stand straight and use his arm again. We are invited to the digging out, but not to watching him bathed with hot leaves."

Liliane was filled with impatience. It won't work, she told herself. The poor child will have been put through hell, compounded with suffering in silence, and be crippled for life.

For the next two days she went through the routine of offering "white man's magic," as she waited to see the boy released from the dirt. She cleansed wounds, pulled teeth, dispensed quinine.

In the early afternoon the whole village gathered around. Liliane and Marsh were accorded places where they could see clearly. In full regalia again, the witch doctor danced and chanted. He beat loudly on his multitude of gourds, hopping with a frenzy induced, perhaps, by the herbs he smoked. Then he threw his arms to the heavens and all noise stopped. He began, with his hands, to dig the dirt away from the boy's body. Visions of grave robbers flared through Liliane's mind. When he reached the boy's frail body, he lifted him up as though his weight were nothing and turned him around, laying him on his stomach. Then, with a sharp knife, he slashed shallow skin wounds along the boy's spine and above his elbow. He rubbed herbs and ground up leaves into the wounds. Applying steaming hot leaves to these wounds, he told the boy not to move for five hours. Liliane and Marsh stayed to watch until dark. The boy never moved a muscle. Maybe he slept.

Flares had been lit in the village so they could observe the resurrection in the dancing light. When the witch doctor returned, he wore only his headdress. He stood naked but for the gaudy feathers that protruded from his kinky hair. Kneeling next to the immobile body, he murmured something to the boy. Then he spread his arms wide and reached over and picked up the child. He stood him up.

After five days of immobility, the boy's legs were stiff. The witch doctor knelt to massage the legs, working blood circulation back into them, then he gently rubbed the boy's arm. In the flickering glow, strength perceptibly crept back into the boy.

The doctor then walked backward from the boy, ten feet, twenty feet. Raising his arms in a beckoning gesture, he ordered the boy to walk toward him.

"He's going to fall flat on his face," Liliane whispered.

Marsh reached down and took her hand.

But the boy didn't fall. Very deliberately, one foot carefully placed in front of the other, the boy walked haltingly toward the medicine man. He walked erect and seemingly without pain. When he reached the healer, he turned around to face the villagers and triumphantly raised his left arm, holding it out straight. A big grin spread over his face as a roar went up from the villagers.

Liliane looked at the medicine man with awe.

▼

LATER, AFTER THEY HAD SPOKEN OF THIS MIRACLE, LILIANE SAT ON AN old log; Marsh sat on the ground beside her. It was, they both realized with a certain sadness, the last night they'd be alone.

He leaned against a tree, one leg stretched out in front of him, his hands resting loosely on his raised knee.

He sighed loudly. "Oh, Liliane, my lovely Liliane." He looked at her for a very long time and she met his gaze.

Marsh reached out and took her hand in his, just holding it as they watched the river flow past them. "Who would have dreamed," he said. He traced his finger along her cheek.

Liliane looked up at the leaves overhead. Marsh leaned over her. His lips brushed her cheek; gently he kissed her nose and her eyes, and she felt his tongue in her ear. She reached for him and felt his kisses cross her neck. His quickened breathing joined hers and then his lips touched hers hungrily. His body pressed against hers as his tongue tasted her lips, as he gently urged her lips apart. She felt the warmth of his mouth, the touch of his tongue against hers. She moved her body close against his and held him tightly with her arms.

Everything else disappeared. Only she and he existed. She wanted this never to end; she wanted him to kiss her and kiss her and kiss her.

He did.

CHAPTER 11

▼

TWO DAYS AFTER THEY RETURNED TO SIMBAYO, THE *OREGON* CAME downriver on its way to Coquilhatville. Marsh was packed and ready to go.

He would be missed. Baxter would have no one with whom to play chess or to discuss literature. The women's horizons would again be limited—no stories of the outside world, no gargantuan laughter, no excitement of having a worldly man pay attention to them. No more kisses, thought Liliane. No flirting. No feeling beautiful. No being treated as an equal by a man. No heightened sense of her body as she swam. No sense of electricity as she lay in bed knowing he was but inches from her on the other side of the wall.

Anoka would miss him, too. Marsh had sat with Anoka for hours, teaching him, talking with him, forcing him beyond the limits he had always known. Marsh had walked into the heart of Simbayo and his leaving was no easy thing for any of them.

"I'm torn, you know," he said after dinner on his last night at Simbayo. "You have given me something I've never known before. I leave a part of myself here forever."

Rose blew her nose. Liliane hoped she wouldn't cry.

Trying to make light of it, Marsh smiled. "I shall not miss your humidity. I admire your unflagging energy under such conditions. But"—his voice choked a little—"I shall miss you. I shall carry you all with me back to merry England. And remember you always."

"You can write to us," Liliane suggested.

He looked across the table at her. "Yes," he said. "I can."

Later, when everyone else had gone to bed, Liliane and Marsh sat on the bench under the okoume tree, unable to say good-bye.

"You know," he said to her, "I have mixed feelings about going. I couldn't stand to live in this climate or to be as isolated as this, but, my God, Liliane, I hadn't expected to find you here."

"Yes," she said. "I shall miss you, too. Thank you for taking the trip with me."

"I tell myself you dreamed it up so that I would stay, so that we would have time together."

"Maybe I did, but I didn't know it at the time. And if I'd known what it would be like, I *would* have dreamed it up. You've given me something I've never had before."

"I'd like to give you more, but I don't know how fair it would be to either of us."

Leaves rustled in the darkness.

"What are you going to do about Baxter?" he asked.

"Do? There's nothing *to* do."

"Do you want him?"

She had known the answer two months ago.

"How about some advice? If you want him, go after him. I see the way he looks at you, even if you don't. He doesn't know what to do about you, Liliane. Learn to play chess. Make him teach you. Get him to share his books with you—not just medicine. He has wonderful books."

Even in the dark she knew that Marsh was smiling. "Why the

hell am I giving you advice on how to get that man?"

"Because we'll never see each other again." Her eyes glistened with tears.

There was silence. Then Marsh reached for her hand. "Liliane," he said softly, "just because you're in the most remote place in the world doesn't mean you won't see or hear from me again. Even if you think you're in love with Baxter Hathaway."

I am in love with Baxter Hathaway, she told herself. Yet Marsh was here and now, and his hand rested on her knee.

He pulled her to him, his lips seeking hers in the night, and his hand touched her breast, fondling it gently yet urgently. A sigh escaped her. She felt his tongue against hers and damned the Puritan God who controlled her universe.

LIFE RETURNED TO ITS PREVIOUS ROUTINE, EXCEPT LILIANE KNEW, now, that there should be more.

She decided it was up to her, as Marsh had suggested, to create that more.

One evening, after dinner, after Marsh had been gone a week, when Baxter started for his office, Liliane asked, "Are you patient enough to teach me chess?"

"You want to learn how to play chess?" he asked, surprised.

"I think so." She smiled.

He stood looking down at her, finally said, "Come on, then," and strode out of the dining room.

She followed him to his office. It was, as usual, littered with papers and books. He walked through it into his bedroom. When she stood, waiting, in the office, he called, "Come in here."

His bedroom was neat and uncluttered. Books lined the walls; on his bedtable were two books and a flashlight. A card table was set up, and on this he put the chess set that he took from a bookcase. He drew up a chair and got another from his office.

"You couldn't learn chess with those two women talking," he said. "One needs utter quiet for concentration."

He sat down and indicated that she should sit, too.

He was a patient teacher. After two hours, he called a halt. "I must do some work," he apologized. "But I'd be glad to continue tomorrow." His voice was impersonal.

"I'd like that."

The next afternoon, though, a man was brought in with an infected wound on the length of his arm. At first the nurses wondered if it was gangrenous and if amputation would be necessary. The man, Ikido, was feverish. Baxter sat up with him all night. By the next afternoon it was obvious that Ikido would pull through. He ate a little and sat up.

After dinner, Baxter asked, "Another chess lesson?"

The chess pieces were where they had left them two nights ago.

That night, Liliane really began to understand the game.

In the morning they all rejoiced at the progress Ikido was making. But shortly after lunch, before Liliane went swimming, she heard a scream and went running to his room.

Ikido's eyes were round with fright. He shook. He babbled. Nothing he said made sense. "I saw Mkimo," he muttered, terror in his voice.

During the course of the next hour of careful listening, Liliane learned that Ikido had fallen in love with a woman who loved Mkimo. Mkimo, however, did not have enough goats with which to buy her. Ikido did. He married her and they lived in apparent happiness; his wife never mentioned Mkimo, never looked at him as he passed. They had two children and Ikido began to forget about Mkimo. However, as he lay on his sickbed, he saw Mkimo outside the window, pointing a finger at him and laughing. A spell had been cast; Ikido knew that Mkimo was willing his death.

After he told Liliane the story, he lay down and stared at the ceiling. The fright had passed, and he resigned himself to death. That night he would not eat. He lay staring at the ceiling.

After dinner, Baxter asked, "Chess?" Liliane nodded, though her mind was on Ikido.

"Will he die?" she asked Baxter as they walked to his room.

"I expect so," he answered. "No rational reason, but then rationality does not rule Africa. We'll do what we can, but he has accepted his death already. He'll put his face to the wall and die."

"Oh, what waste!" Liliane cried.

"We have our own superstitions," Baxter commented as they entered his room.

Though he was a healthy man, Ikido died on the sixth day.

Liliane commenced, in earnest, to attack the reserve with which Baxter protected himself. As she left his room after an evening of chess, she asked, "May I borrow your *The Brothers Karamazov?*"

"Hardly a book I'd think would interest you," he said.

"Why? What's it about?"

"What all worthwhile books are about. Good and evil. God or not."

"Why wouldn't I like it?"

He shrugged. "Well, it doesn't seem like a book a woman would enjoy."

"May I decide for myself?"

"Of course." He took it from the shelf.

She read until very late. Dostoyevski certainly danced circles around Dickens. She wondered how Baxter could relate to this novel, filled as it was with unbridled passion and emotion. It also made her question how Baxter, the actor, had been able to sweep passion and emotion into his soul and portray it to an audience. When she first met him she had seen it under the surface, held in tight rein, but since coming to Simbayo, she had come to think that Baxter had no personal emotions. His compassion was for his impersonal relationships; his passion was for ideas.

Chess became a regular event. In fact, near the end of dinner, his eyes would begin to light, and every night he said, as though he never took it for granted, "Chess?"

Gradually, as she came to understand strategy, Liliane began to enjoy the game. Once in a great while Baxter would say, "Good move, Liliane." He seemed to like rolling her name on his tongue.

As if accidentally, Liliane brushed her leg along his under the table.

One night he asked, "Aren't you ready for a furlough?"

"Are you trying to get rid of me?" she asked, half seriously.

He didn't answer, but his eyes burned into hers, as though trying to find an answer to an unasked question. The light from the oil lamp flickered, the reflection shimmering on his arms.

"What would I do, Baxter? I have no home in America anymore. I have no desire to go look up old acquaintances and hear about their babies and their husbands' jobs and . . ."

"What about your life? Wouldn't you like a baby?"

It was the first intimate question he had asked her in her two years here. "I don't know," she responded. "I don't think about it too often. I do think"—she raised her eyes to look levelly at him—"that I would like love."

His eyes held hers. "You could go to England."

Is that what you want? she asked silently. Are you trying to push me into the arms of a married man?

"My home is here."

Her hand touched his wrist, ran featherlike along it. He did not move his hand. And his eyes did not leave hers. She noticed a muscle in his arm twitch.

"You're needed here," he said. "I hear what they've begun to call you, those natives who come in from the jungle."

"What do they call me?" She let her fingers rest on his wrist.

"They're calling you Mother Lili."

"Mother?" She laughed, pleased. "Then see, they are all my children."

"But don't you want a life of your own?"

"*Are* you trying to get rid of me?" she teased, her eyes shining.

He grabbed her wrist, and with great intensity, with fire in his eyes, he said, "Don't you see? You're needed here. You've become a part of this place."

"Then don't," she said, her voice low, "try to send me away."

"Send you away? I thought maybe you wanted . . ." He let go of her and stood up. Pacing to the window, staring out into the night, he said, "You're a part of me, too."

He paused and collected himself. Then he said, more calmly, still with his gaze into the darkness, "I'm going upriver for two days. A logging camp called for me. I'll be back Friday. Take care of the place."

On that impersonal note, she realized, she was being dismissed.

But she did not sleep. She lay in bed wondering if she could ever transfer her feelings and desires from one man to another. She had not really been a part of Marsh. She had been attracted to him because he was young and handsome and wanted her and made her feel beautiful, and because no man had paid attention to her for two years. She had responded to Marsh because he gave her what she wanted from Baxter. He was a substitute, and she knew it all along. Except when he kissed her. Then she was only aware of the moment, of the lovely feeling of touching, of closeness. He had been a prelude. He had given her assurance, courage to begin playing chess.

There were more strategies to the game of chess than she had counted on. She laughed to herself. Heavens, at home in Buffalo I'd sit and wait by the phone, I'd wait for a man to make the moves. That's what's held me up all this time. I hadn't grasped that a woman could take the initiative. I hadn't realized that seduction involves more than something physical, that it includes the mind and the heart. The heart . . . Ah, that's what she really wanted of Baxter, wasn't it? She wanted him to love her. Her real desire was for him to share himself with her, to unfold like a flower. But what was it Marsh had said?

"Beware of watering dead flowers," he'd advised. "You may think that all they need is sunshine and a little water to flower luxuriously. You spend time and energy and heart on caring for them, only to discover later that you've been watering dead flowers."

She wasn't convinced Baxter was a dead flower. A dormant one, perhaps, in need of proper nurturing to bloom but with sturdy roots yet. "You're a part of me, too," he had said.

He returned on Friday with a broken arm. He was in minimal pain because he had led Anoka through setting it and splinting it. Anoka beamed when Baxter said, "It's as good as I could have done." High praise, indeed, from a man little given to praise.

Though Baxter never admitted he'd been wrong about Anoka, he did accept him into the medical nucleus of Simbayo. Whenever he left camp for a few days, he took Anoka with him. When in camp, although he relied on Rose and Liliane for medical help, he increasingly gave Anoka responsibilities. He set up a cot in the infirmary for Anoka and assigned him night calls, though he was not to treat night patients directly. Rather, he was to alert Baxter to the need for help. Nevertheless, it was a step in a direction Liliane had never thought he'd take.

Anoka was a born healer. When Liliane remarked on it to Baxter one morning, he looked up from suturing a patient's wound and smiled at her. "That makes two of you, then, doesn't it?" He was beginning to smile more frequently.

However, frustration with his broken arm made his temper short. "How will I perform surgery?" he barked.

Rose answered, "You seem to forget that you have three rather capable nurses here."

That night over chess, Baxter said to Liliane, "Well, you managed a cesarean; are you ready to try a hernia?" Hernias were the most common operation they performed.

"Oh, you did that just so I wouldn't concentrate on my move!" Liliane accused him.

He laughed.

It was not a sound she heard often. It actually sounded happy. "Well?"

"Of course," she answered. She'd seen enough of them, assisted in at least a hundred. She was ready to do one herself. She would be nervous, at first, but she knew she could do it, especially with Baxter across the operating table leading her through it. "But don't you think you ought to ask Rose first?"

"If I wanted to ask Rose first, I would have," he said, his hand sliding across the table to make a fist over hers tentatively. He had reached out to touch her! Her belly tightened. She turned her hand palm-up. Baxter stood up self-consciously.

"We'll do the operation right after breakfast," he said. Then, "Good night."

She dreamed that night, reliving the moment when Baxter's hand slowly reached out across the table to enfold hers, yet when she looked up into his eyes, they were Marsh's. When, in her dream, he leaned across the table to kiss her, it was Marsh's kiss she felt, Marsh's kiss that reverberated through her body.

As morning mist disappears in sunlight, her dream dissipated with the day. Liliane became caught up in the intricacy of her first hernia operation.

Baxter led her through it. "Cut here." His gloved finger traced the area where she would make the incision. "Then, between these layers of muscle. Cut into the peritoneum. There, you're doing beautifully."

She was surprised at her lack of nervousness. Whether it was because she'd assisted at so many or because she knew Baxter would let her make no mistakes, she felt calm and capable.

"Release that sac," he said, "the one that's constricting that bowel." The bowel should have blanched white and then turned pink when pressed, but it was dark and swollen.

Baxter told her, "Clamp off the normal bowel from the infected one." He handed her the clamps. She did as he told her. She made a sharp incision on either side. "Now, extract the infected section."

When that was done, he helped, with his one good hand, with the irrigation. "With small sutures, tie the ends together," he said, nodding his head in approval. "If you have it—and we do—the inner stitches should be catgut and the outer ones of silk."

They kept irrigating the intestines with sterile water until Baxter was satisfied that all of the bacteria had been removed.

"Fine," he said, and she could tell he was pleased. "Sprinkle this antiseptic in the incision and sew it back up." He watched her

adept fingers, not having to tell her the necessary steps. She knew
how to make a strong hernia closure.

Automatically she reached for the patient's pulse and then
smiled at Baxter.

He commented, "Perhaps you should have been a doctor,
Liliane."

She was thinking, I am, but said nothing.

For the second time since Marsh had been gone, the mailboat
arrived that afternoon. A slim package arrived from him post-
marked Kunming, China. He had sent her a bright turquoise silk
scarf, along with a brief note in dark, sprawling ink.

> This reminds me of your eyes. On my way to French
> Indochina via the Mekong River. Am in this beautiful Chi-
> nese city of Kunming, near the Burmese border. Shall go
> west beyond Tali and find the Mekong (called the Lan-
> cang here in China). It originates in the Himalayas and
> trickles down to a pretty good size stream by the time it
> gets to the China-Burma border. From there, by foot and
> sampan, I shall trace it south, going along the Siamese-
> Laotian border, through Cambodia and eventually to its
> delta in French Indochina. Wonder why these hot, humid
> countries magnetize me when I tolerate humidity so
> poorly? I'll end up in Saigon, which is supposed to be a
> fascinating city. Plan on the trip taking four months or so.
> I'm glad to get away from London and all that was there.
> I think of you daily. You are with me every night. I won-
> der if you would like this kind of trip. I wonder why we
> did not make love.

Then it was signed, in a large splashy scrawl, "Marsh."

This is the softest thing I've ever touched, she thought as she
drew the scarf along her cheek.

In the next six weeks she performed operations daily, standing
across the operating table from Baxter, learning the finer intrica-
cies of surgery. Baxter was infinitely patient, and she could tell
from the tone of his voice and the look in his eyes that he was
beginning to consider her a colleague, not merely a helper. Now,
over evening chess, he would discuss surgical procedures with her
and even ask her opinion on cases. She had never been so happy.

Their relationship ascended to a new level when, one evening, he pulled *Moby Dick* off his bookshelf and handed it to her. "This is probably the greatest book ever written," he said.

"It's about a whale, isn't it?" Liliane asked, taking the well-worn book that he offered her.

"It's not about a whale at all," Baxter said. "It's about whether or not there is a God, and about the soul. It plumbs the innermost recesses of man's mind and heart. I think you'll appreciate it."

She was satisfied that he was beginning to appreciate her intellect, too. He had already begun to appreciate her healing skills. Now, if only he desired her body! She'd hoped he would yearn for her. He was nearly fifty. Maybe he was too old to have physical desires. He wasn't too old to build buildings, to oversee this large complex, to trek through the jungle, to exist on four hours of sleep each night. Nor was he too old to keep a schedule that would exhaust men half his age. Maybe his marriage had turned him away from women, maybe . . .

To hell with the maybes, she thought. I want Baxter to desire me. I wish he would hold me. When he watches me across a room, I want him to want me. I want him to kiss me. I want to know he's happier when he's with me than without me.

Oh, God, she thought. I'm my own worst enemy. Why do I think like this? It doesn't do me any good, it just frustrates me.

She sat up in bed.

"It's the terrible moonlight," she said aloud. Her room was flooded with a creamy glow. The scent of hibiscus wafted into the room. The night was strangely silent, and the midnight illumination moved like a vestige of some vague spirit world. It danced around her, holding her at its core. She rose from bed like a somnambulist and, as in a dream, opened her door and walked into the brightness of the night. The tall trees cast dark shadows across the compound, but she could see even into their depths.

The moon is pulling me, she thought, just as it does the tides. A waltz played in her brain as she began to dance gracefully with the white orb, turning in slow circles, humming as her hands waved in the air.

In the moonlight she danced to her pool, which was brightly lit. She pulled her nightgown over her head and threw it off so forcefully it floated through the air. Slowly she waded into the water. The pool accepted her like a caressing hand. It drew her into it. She sang with the melody that played in her head. She lay on her back, her hair fanning out, and let the moon have its way with her. It kissed her eyelids and her breasts, while the warm water washed rhythmically over her. The moon's eye stared down at her white, naked body. She felt it pull at her as if it called to all of her silken smoothness, all of her quivering yearning, all of her restless need.

Some sixth sense forced her eyes open, and she looked over toward the palm tree. There was a man standing in the shadow of the tree. She could see only his silhouette.

She swam toward the tree.

He stood still, his face hidden. Slowly Liliane surfaced. She walked deliberately out of the water and stood in the moonlight with her feet apart. Her body shining with the wet, she walked toward Baxter, slowly, tantalizingly, offering herself to him.

His face was still in darkness though she could see the light of his eyes.

Reaching out, she took his hands and laid them on her breasts. She began to unbutton his shirt. He stood quite still, his eyes on hers. His hands came alive to her body. Then the years of pent-up desire burst forth like rockets and he slid out of his clothes, pulling her close to him so that her breasts met his chest. His mouth crushed hers as his arms surrounded her.

She felt his body awaken with an intensity of passion she had not thought possible. His hands returned to her breasts, holding them so fiercely they hurt. Bending her backward, he kissed her breasts, rushing from one to the other, his tongue devouring her nipples. Oh, she thought, I didn't know it would be like this. Each nerve ending was alive, and every time his tongue touched her nipples she felt fire between her legs.

He raised his lips to her and kissed her roughly, his tongue exploring her mouth. His hands ventured over her body, digging into her shoulders, clawing at her. He picked her up and laid her on the ground, covering her with his body, rocking back and forth, back and forth. She felt him between her legs and spread herself wide for him. She loved the feel of it, his strength and power. His fingers teased her thighs. In one swift thrust he was inside her. He kissed her breasts and plunged deep within her, stopping only for a moment when he heard her soft cry.

Then he moved his lips to hers. His tongue softly caressed her lips as he moved back and forth, in and out, with the force and rhythm of drums that beat into the night. Finally he sobbed, pushing into her, his face at her neck. "Oh God!" he moaned.

CHAPTER 12

▼

SHE THREW THE BED SHEET ASIDE AND LOOKED DOWN AT HER NAKED body, remembering his touch. He had kissed her as though he were starved. He had entered her as though he were desperate and could wait no longer. The memory of his shuddering release brought a smile of pleasure to her face.

So this is what it was all about. Why, she wondered, was such a high value placed on virginity? Why would anyone want to be a virgin when they could have *this*?

As she gently stroked her hands over her body, she anticipated seeing Baxter this morning. She imagined a sparkle in his eyes, a new tenderness now that a love was openly admitted. A sigh of happiness escaped her lips.

He had held her as though he would never let her go. Well, he would not have to. Delicious thoughts drifted through her mind: how it would feel to sleep beside him every night, to feel his body next to hers, to lie drowsing in the curve of his arm.

FROM AFAR, THE BANGING OF POTS TOLD HER THE COOK WAS beginning breakfast. How could she keep from throwing her arms around him in front of Rose and Heidi? Well, she'd have to control herself until they were alone. But surely their eyes would give them away.

She very nearly missed breakfast. Opening the screen door to the dining hall, she found only the two nurses there. She had not seen Baxter in the garden, either.

As she sat down at the table, she saw that a peeled banana skin was at his place. Answering her unasked question, Rose said, "The doctor had already eaten and gone by the time we got here." How strange. That had never happened before. But then, neither had last night. Her heart continued to sing as she ate breakfast and talked mindlessly with her friends, scarcely able to follow the conversation, so bursting was she with her own joy.

She tried not to rush through the meal, forcing herself to keep the slow pace with Rose and Heidi. Heidi, in fact, was unusually verbal, relating a dream she'd had. "It was strange," she said, though Liliane did not listen enough to understand what was.

She made herself walk with Rose toward Baxter's office, where they would get ready for the stream of patients that was already forming. Surely they could not avoid sharing knowing smiles, finding ways to brush against one another.

Baxter was nowhere in sight. Rose and Liliane, with Anoka, began to set up the tables, to move the chairs outside, to wheel the medicine carts, to get things in order. Rose did not seem to think anything was amiss; she chattered as usual, saying she would start on rounds of the sick. She invited Anoka to go with her, which pleased him. He responded happily when any of them included him, but his great joy was in Liliane. Nothing she asked of him was too much; he worshipped her. Rose once said, "I don't know whether he's in love with learning medicine or does it mainly to please you."

Every afternoon, when her classes with him and Naldani were finished, Liliane was pleased to see them study together. He was far ahead of Naldani, but this seemed to bother neither of them. Naldani could read and write English as well as Anoka, but she had difficulty grasping abstract concepts. She was remarkable at memorization, though, as were most of the natives.

Baxter suddenly appeared out of the forest, very businesslike, even brisk. He scarcely glanced at Liliane but nodded in his usual manner and sat down. He avoided looking at her as he reached for his stethoscope. She handed it to him, touching his hand as she did so. His eyes flickered upward to her, the warmth in them veiled immediately. But she saw the warmth, saw what he was hiding.

He said no personal word to her all day. Her heart slowly flattened. She didn't understand. Of course they were surrounded by people all day. There was no time to be alone, but she thought that could have been managed.

In the afternoon it rained. Torrents converted the earth to mush. Water poured down in great slanting lashes; the sky opened in giant bolts of lightning, followed by crashing thunder that ruptured a hole in the universe.

Even though they were in the midst of a rain forest, it usually did not rain like this. The thunder and great slashing rain reminded Liliane that it was November. April and November were the rainy months. Otherwise she forgot what month it was, for there were no seasons here, except for the two months of rain.

Days had a way of marching by that rendered calendars meaning-less. Hours had a way of losing meaning. She awoke with the sun and knew that mealtimes would regulate her day. Mail took months, so it did not matter what day it was. If chores were not done one day, they would be done the next, or perhaps next month—or next year. There was no hurry, no rigid schedule, though the days all followed a similar pattern. Saturday was the only day the routine was broken and that, in itself, was routine; somehow she always knew when leper day arrived. A calendar was unnecessary.

The rain stopped at dinnertime and probably would not start again until nearly dawn. The land smelled freshly washed. Frogs surfaced, the river swelled, and the aroma of hibiscus and bougain-villea filled the air. But Liliane was little aware of these. In the afternoon, unable to swim, she sat in her room wondering if Baxter were purposely ignoring her. There was a tightness in her chest.

Baxter seemed in no hurry to leave the dining room after dinner, and Liliane began to fear he was going to ignore chess. But after he played two hymns and chatted briefly with the nurses, he turned to Liliane, his eyes as blank as she had ever seen them, and asked, "A game of chess?"

Now, her nerves frayed, she didn't know how to respond. She followed him to his room, stood by the door as he moved toward the table. He turned to face her, and she saw that his eyes had become tender. The mask fell away.

"Come here," he ordered.

She moved toward him, slowly, walking into his outstretched arms, which encircled her and held her so tightly she was crushed into him. He breathed in her ear, "Oh, Liliane. My dear Liliane," and moved his lips to hers.

Desire, pent-up for over two years, assaulted them, and their lovemaking spent itself quickly. Liliane didn't want it to be over so fast. She wanted Baxter to touch her everywhere, to explore her body with his lips and hands. She craved to run her tongue over his chest, to taste his stomach, and to nibble his navel. She wanted to proceed slowly, to feel every touch with total awareness, to savor the exaltation. She knew men were ready more easily than women; yet she had felt ready all day. She had wanted to make love since dawn. She wished Baxter would tell her he loved her. She wanted . . .

She was ashamed of herself. Baxter *was* telling her he loved her. The tingling she felt when he kissed her, when their tongues touched, when he fingered her breasts, awakened a desire that was not easily quenched by his rapid thrust into her. It seemed over far too quickly. Maybe, she thought, I'm just a wanton. Maybe I should not want more. Should ladies feel this way? Everything she had ever read, and the tentative conversations with girls back in school, indicated that ladies didn't really like sex. They enjoyed the romance, not the physical part.

Afterward she would have liked to lie next to Baxter, to idly trace her fingernails across his chest, to put her head on his shoulder, and to have him stroke her hair. She would have enjoyed listening to them breathe in unison, lying with their legs entangled and passion spent—his, if not hers. And then she would have liked to talk. Talk of whatever it is lovers talk about: how long they'd loved each other, how beautiful it was now, their hopes for the future—the thoughts they shared with no one else.

But Baxter would not lie in bed. He jumped up and said, "Well, now to chess."

While they played, looks of love crossed the table; he put his hand around hers and smiled at her.

They did not make love every night, but even when they did, Baxter always asked her to leave afterward. "I must do my writing" or "studying," he'd say.

One night he said, "You know I'm much too old for you." She crossed to him, kneeling beside him, putting her head in his lap. "Please, never say that again," she urged. His hand ran through her curly hair.

After returning from the leper colony, on Saturday nights, they never made love. Other times, when they played chess, the tension of being together built up and they touched legs beneath the table, leaning across to touch each other, kissing little kisses until they were no longer able to control themselves. Then, they tore at their clothes, throwing themselves on his bed. Occasionally, Liliane felt her body begin to quiver as if she were reaching a magical mountain summit, but she never quite made it over the edge of that height.

She wanted, desperately, to say, "Baxter, I love you," but was afraid to.

Never, during the day, did he look at her in a different manner than he looked at Rose or Heidi, yet she became aware of subtle changes. He relied on her more and more; he asked her opinion frequently; he listened to her suggestions; he watched her relentlessly even if he did mask his feelings. She noticed that he began to give her authority—he treated her more as a colleague than in previous months. He taught her more complex surgery. And she understood what one had to do with the other. This was his way of saying "I love you."

At night, he was no more talkative. He held her face in his hands and combed his long fingers through her hair. His eyes probed hers and he said only, "Liliane, oh, Liliane."

Later, before she left to walk through the dark to her room, he kissed her, then stood in his doorway watching her as she disappeared into the black night. He never came with her and he never asked her to stay.

A year slipped by. Liliane's feelings alternated between happiness greater than she had ever known and frustration at Baxter's lack of communication. Why would he not declare his love? Why would he never talk about it? Sometimes Liliane thought she didn't know Baxter at all. Other times she thought she knew him better than he knew himself.

One inky night, walking back to her room on the path she now knew by heart, she stepped on a twig that snapped. Its end flew up and struck her on the calf of her leg. She started, then laughed in relief. Strange, she thought, that a stick would fly so high. By the time she reached her room her ankle hurt sharply. She lit her lantern and looked at her leg. Two small holes had punctured the skin above her calf.

She screamed.

A snake! Oh, dear God, it must have been a viper. She yelled again. She couldn't stop screaming. In less than a minute Rose appeared in her room. Liliane pointed at the puncture wounds, shaking, her ankle already throbbing and beginning to swell. It felt like the stings of dozens of maddened hornets.

Baxter hurtled into the room not far behind Rose. He took one quick look and said, "Try to calm yourself." He turned to Rose. "Calm her down so the venom won't circulate through her. I'll get the snake serum. A viper's sting can kill in a couple of hours." Before he ran from the room, he reached out and grabbed a towel that lay on the chair. He wound it around her leg above the two tiny holes that had perforated her skin. Looking around wildly, he saw a pencil and inserted it through his makeshift bandage, twisting it to make a tourniquet so that no blood could pass up or down.

"Here," he said to Rose, "hold this until I get back."

Rose held the tourniquet in place.

Heidi appeared in the doorway. Right after her was Anoka. He rolled his eyes in fright when he understood what had happened.

Liliane heard the thumping of her heart.

Baxter seemed to be gone for ages. When he returned, pale and out of breath, he yelled, "Quick! Where's the snake serum? I've turned the dispensary upside down, but I can't find it."

They all stared at Heidi when they heard her intake of breath. "Oh, Gott in Himmel!" she whispered. "None came on the last boat. We have none. We are out of it!"

Baxter whipped a scalpel out of his pocket, held it over the lamp's flame, and wiped it in alcohol he had brought with him, working swiftly and silently.

Liliane turned her head so she would not see the knife plunge into her flesh. But it scarcely pained her. The tourniquet had so successfully cut off the flow of blood that she couldn't feel anything below it. Baxter raised her leg and put his lips to the bleeding wound, sucking deeply, stopping every few seconds to spit the venom and blood onto the floor. After a minute, he signaled to Rose, who took over the job. Then Heidi took a turn. Baxter was about to repeat the procedure when Anoka moved into the room, shouldering Baxter aside, and reached for Liliane's leg. They took turns, she knew, so that none of them would get too much poison into their stomachs.

After fifteen or twenty minutes, which seemed like hours, Baxter loosened the tourniquet and Liliane felt the blood literally rush into her ankle and foot. Sharp, piercing prickles, like a foot awakening from sleep, only more piercing, made her wince.

Baxter ordered Anoka to get water and bandages. When he returned, Baxter put a wet bandage over the wound.

He murmured something to Rose and Heidi, then he and Anoka disappeared. The two nurses undressed Liliane and put her to bed. She seemed unable to move and let their gentle hands drape her nightgown around her, plump her pillow, and pull the sheet over her.

When Baxter came back to the room, he carried a hypodermic. "Liliane," he said softly, "I'm going to give you a sedative. You're going to be all right. You won't feel well for a week or so, but I promise you, you're going to be all right." He plunged the needle into her arm.

Of the next few days Liliane had but dim memories. Whenever she was conscious, she saw Baxter's face. Anoka, Rose, and Heidi were there, too, and she thought once or twice she recognized

Naldani. Their faces were filled with tenderness and compassion. Baxter's was always filled with anguish. She thought she heard him murmur, over and over, "It's my fault. I should never have let you walk alone out there in the dark."

Or she thought she heard him say, "My Liliane," with his face pressed against her cheek. Or once, "Oh, my darling!"

When she fully regained consciousness, she was not allowed out of bed for four more days. For the first time in her three years at Simbayo, she felt sorry for herself. She knew it was only because she was idle, because she had nothing to do but think. The rain compounded it—the rainy season again. And that was what did it.

She thought of the season. It was Thanksgiving at home. Not that she cared that much for Thanksgiving, but that was when her family would start to get ready for Christmas. She'd spent three Christmases in the Congo and never let herself feel homesick. They'd celebrated with Baxter's reading of Dickens's "A Christmas Carol" in his resonant voice. Though Liliane could listen to him talk all day, she tired of the repetition of the piece. Rose and Heidi enjoyed the ritual for its own sake and pretended it was a new suspense story each year. Liliane had taught Naldani Christmas carols, which Naldani had taught to others who worked in the compound. Each year they sang them over and over again, their beautiful voices carrying into the jungle, the words strangely out of place in this green land. In December the rains stopped, and the temperature was comfortably in the mid-eighties. Spotty cumulus clouds hardly disturbed the bright sunlight, chasing each other across a sapphire sky.

But lying in bed, recuperating, Liliane had time to remember.... She remembered happy childhood Christmases, snow-covered streets when she and her friends caught risky rides on their sleds, gripping onto the backs of slow-moving cars. She remembered the colored lights on Christmas trees and leaving a dish of cookies for Santa Claus. She heard the roar of buses making slush of powdery snow. She saw the shop windows decorated with tinsel and silver ribbons and the streets adorned with green and red lights stretched on wires. She remembered how shoppers would hunch over, their arms full, fighting the biting winds off Lake Erie. Christmas Eve and the clink of glasses, the carols sung in the parsonage, decorating the tree! Happy anticipation and goodwill about everything. A sense of common purpose and connection with all people. Christmas Day brought parishioners dropping in all day long, their arms laden with gaily wrapped packages, always a gift for "little

Liliane." It was the one day of the year her father allowed spirits in the house, brandy in the eggnog. Liliane got tipsy on it the Christmas she was seven, but her parents blamed it on her stuffing herself with too much turkey.

In those days, in those years, she was wrapped in a cocoon of safety and love. As she lay in bed now, she longed for her mother.

Heidi found her crying one afternoon when she came to bring her tea and to massage her leg. Liliane was astonished when the German woman leaned over and kissed her forehead, patting her gently on the shoulder.

Perhaps she could talk them into really celebrating Christmas this year. Maybe she could make some gifts. They could make a game of it.

But Jack's sudden appearance put an end to that dream.

FOR THREE MORE NIGHTS LILIANE LAY IN BED RECUPERATING. ROSE and Heidi came to her room from the dining hall directly after dinner, but they left as soon as Baxter appeared with a book tucked under his arm. He read to her.

"You saved my life, you know." Liliane smiled, reaching out to touch his arm.

"If I hadn't," he said, "mine would have been worth nothing."

Closing the book, he looked at her, taking her hand in his. He had openly shown tenderness toward her ever since her snake bite.

"Tomorrow I'll let you get up, but I don't want you to work yet."

"My goodness"—she smiled softly at him—"I feel pampered."

He slid off his chair and knelt by her bed. Framing her head in his large hands, he ran his tongue over her lips and whispered, "Lili . . ."

She moved over and whispered into his ear, "Come to bed with me."

He jerked his head back. "Here? Now?"

She leaned over and blew out the lamp. "Here. Now." She threw the covers back and heard him silently undressing in the dark.

After he left, she lay smiling, her heart filled with happiness. Though he consistently refused to say it, she knew he loved her, more than ever now. Tomorrow she would talk with him about Christmas, entice him to exchange presents with her even if it was something they made themselves. Entreat him to share something tangible with her.

SHE FELL ASLEEP WITH HER HAND ON THE PILLOW NEXT TO THE imprint of Baxter's head.

In the morning, Liliane got up. She felt wobbly after nearly a week in bed. Though she did not assist Baxter, she wandered through the infirmary, talking to patients. Naldani followed her like a shadow. She had sat, afternoons, in Liliane's room, studying her English, asking questions, recalling her marriage before leprosy threw its specter into her life. Naldani had a drive that few of the native women displayed. Using Liliane as her model, she was determined that her husband's disease, and eventual death, would not limit her. She was allowing herself to grow in ways that would have been impossible had Liliane not entered her life.

As Liliane was tiring, well before noon, they heard the sound of Jack's boat. Nothing else in the world sounded like that whistle. Oh, Liliane thought immediately, maybe we can talk him into staying for a couple of weeks. Maybe he'll stay for Christmas.

Even though she felt weak, she was the first one to reach the dock.

Jack looked even more disreputable than usual. He hadn't shaved in days, and though his eyes were not bleary from alcohol, they were tired and bloodshot.

Liliane ran onto the dock as he was throwing the rope. Catching it, she handed it to one of the natives. Jack jumped off his boat, and Liliane threw her arms around him.

"Oh, what perfect timing," she cried. It had been far too long.

"Oh, what a sight you are for sore eyes," he said, keeping an arm around her waist. Rose appeared, out of breath, followed quickly by Heidi.

The three women encircled him as they walked toward the dining hall. "You just knew when it was lunchtime, didn't you?" teased Rose.

Baxter loped down the path, extending his arm, grabbing for Jack's hand—shaking it with one hand while throwing an arm around his shoulder with the other.

"Let me have a bath first," begged Jack, "and then a decent meal."

They were prepared for a joyous lunch, but their spirits were soon dampened by his news. "I'm not here for a visit," said Jack, spearing his fish and eating it off his knife. "Though I wish I could kidnap your cook. I'm here on an errand of mercy."

They looked at him expectantly.

"Upriver 'bout one hundred miles, on the other side of Boleko, there's a smallpox epidemic. It's outa control."

In the silence, all of them stared at Jack.

"Good Lord," muttered Baxter.

"Can something be done?" he pleaded, though he had not stopped eating for a second. "They're dying like flies."

"Nothing can be done for those already stricken," said Baxter, "but others can be innoculated."

"Oh," said Rose, "don't say nothing can be done. You mean it can't be helped whether they die or not."

Baxter nodded. "Yes, yes, that's what I meant. Those who are going to survive can be given comfort."

"Well," said Jack with his mouth full, "you got some serum? Something to give them?"

Heidi nodded. "Yes. We have a good deal. We can help. Who can give it?"

Jack jabbed a fork into the air. "I was hoping one of you would come back with me. Certainly you've all been vaccinated. I have, too."

There was silence as the four looked at each other.

One person won't be enough to stem an epidemic, thought Liliane. Maybe he'll take me. Maybe Baxter and I can go. A thrill ran through her.

"Doc," rasped Jack, finally laying down his knife and fork. "I figure you can teach me to give a shot. Or whatever it is that's gotta be done. Maybe I'm not smart enough to be a doctor, but I gotta be smart enough to vaccinate someone."

Baxter smiled at him. "Jack, my good friend, I have no doubts at all about your ability to do so. We'll need another one to go with us, too. I'll take Anoka."

Liliane felt her heart sink.

"I'd like to go, too," she said.

Baxter looked at her. "You three ladies will run Simbayo," he said, and Liliane realized there was no use arguing. "However," he said to Liliane, "you can find Anoka and show him how to give vaccinations and make sure he has one, too. Jack, it will take me until tomorrow morning to get everything ready. Can you wait?"

"I was hoping one day wouldn't make that much difference,"

admitted Jack. "If I'm having company, I gotta wash my boat, and I got to enjoy these ladies. And this food. We better take some of it with us. Who knows how long this is gonna be. It takes six days to get there."

The rest of the day was spent in a flurry of regular jobs compounded with getting Baxter and Anoka ready for the trip. Liliane's adrenaline pumped. At the same time, she yearned to be going and already felt the loss Baxter's absence would bring to her heart.

After dinner, because of Jack's presence, there was no chess. It had been a busy day and everyone retired early. Liliane lay in bed, knowing she had to go to Baxter. He could not leave her for several weeks without a private good-bye.

When she walked into the darkness of his bedroom, he sensed her presence. "I hoped you'd come," he whispered. "Snakes or not." He was lying in bed naked, waiting for her.

After their lovemaking, they clung together, and she said softly, into his neck, "I shall miss you so."

"Don't worry. I'll be back."

She kissed his neck and ran her hand over his chest. "I shall miss you, anyway. Oh, Baxter, do you have any idea how much I love you? I've loved you from the day I first saw you!"

There—she had finally said it. Now was his chance, too. They could vow their love to each other, they could leave each other with the spoken words of love to console them.

But she heard no words; instead, just a strangled sigh.

After a while he said, "I thank God every night for that. Your presence in my life proves God to me every day that I live."

Dammit, thought Liliane, that's so formal. Cast caution to the winds and just admit you love me!

She stayed next to him until nearly dawn.

CHAPTER 13

▼

"WELL," SAID ROSE, HER EYES TWINKLING, "ANOTHER MINOR triumph." They had just stitched a deep, even gash on the leg of a young hunter.

There was a keen vitality about the responsibility cast upon them by Baxter's absence.

On Saturdays, Liliane went to the island and met Naldani; together they tended to the lepers. Naldani's husband had lost all of his toes and fingers; his nose was nearly eaten away and looked no more than an empty socket. Never once did Naldani indicate she thought him gruesome. Liliane's stomach never stopped flip-flopping at the sight of him and others like him. She wondered if she could ever love anyone enough to accept such cruel disfig-urement.

"Ah," responded Naldani when Liliane spoke of it, "but you didn't know him when he was well. You don't see the man beneath the skin. He is the same man."

Naldani was young. She wasn't much older than Liliane her-self. Though Africans reckoned time by different standards than westerners did, she and Naldani one day figured that—in linear time—Naldani must have been wedded at thirteen or fourteen and had been married for the same number of years. Bmeno, according to their calculations, was thirty-two. He looked as ancient as any elder at Simbayo. It was now necessary for Naldani to lift him, for he was unable even to hobble around. His eyes followed his wife wherever she moved, always with love and pride. As pride in one's wife was not traditional, Liliane was pleased that Bmeno recog-nized Naldani's worth; he was indeed fortunate. Many on this island had been abandoned by their spouses. Liliane and Naldani attempted to instill a spirit of comradeship on the island in an effort to dispel the utter loneliness that characterized the last years or months or days of most of the lepers.

Heidi, in her implacable yet unobtrusive way, ran the business part of Simbayo smoothly. She saw that medical supplies and food were ordered, that all of the compound's inhabitants were fed, and she oversaw all of the employees—the cook and the women who sewed and washed. She trained the aides. She held the purse strings and warned Baxter when they needed more money; then he churned out several articles or wrote letters to the home office of the mission. She sterilized the medical instruments and taught the cook how to prepare food that the westerners enjoyed. She bought meat from hunters when it was available, and sterilized old bandages for recycling. She was always busy. She liked to keep her hand in at nursing, too, so she usually made rounds after lunch, before her nap.

Liliane and Rose shared the medical work in harmony. They

helped each other and each made decisions, yet it was clear that Rose preferred to follow. When an operation was called for, they would discuss whether or not they felt capable of performing it and, if so, it was Liliane who did the actual surgery while Rose assisted and acted as backup.

Sweat broke out on each of their foreheads, but their hands were steady. After each successful operation, they smiled at each other with accomplishment, pride, and a little relief. Through the intensity of their efforts together, these two very different women deepened their bonds of friendship.

One morning, they finished with the line of patients early and were relaxing together in the office. Rose said, "You know, I think I'm actually glad the doctor was called away."

Liliane glanced over at her. She missed Baxter. The independence and the decision-making helped to offset her loneliness. In his absence she realized her own strength. Is that what Rose meant?

"No," answered Rose, wiping a smear off her glasses, "I mean because of you and me. I know we're different. You're more daring and I know you don't like the routine things that give Heidi and me a sense of security. You and I have always liked and respected each other, but now I feel close in a new way. Now I'm more aware of our similarities than of our differences." She reached out and put a hand on Liliane's shoulder. Then she asked, "You know, don't you?"

Liliane didn't have to ask "Know what?" She nodded her head. "Yes. I have, for years."

Rose looked up in surprise. "For years? And you haven't judged?"

Liliane smiled reassuringly. "Oh, I did at first. It took me a long time not to think—"

"We are evil."

"Well, I don't know if that's exactly the word."

Rose's lips curved in a narrow smile. She nodded her head. "Yes, it took us a long time to accept that, too. I don't know, if we were back in civilization . . . but we're not. Do you think the doctor knows?"

Liliane shrugged. "I have no idea. We don't talk about personal things."

Rose was silent for a minute as if analyzing a new risk. Tentatively, she began, "I took for granted that you and the doctor had found what Heidi and I . . . what we share. That you and he . . ."

"Yes. But we never talk about anything personal." Her distressed tone surprised even her.

"Oh, my dear!" Rose responded with compassion.

"I know." Tears filled Liliane's eyes. "I love him so much, but he never opens up. He never shares himself. Sometimes I wonder if there's anything to share. I wonder if . . ." She began to sob and walked into Rose's consoling arms.

Rose patted her as she cried. "It's not you, Lili," she murmured. "Something happened, we think, a long time ago. Some personal failure or tragic event, something about his past life compels him to hide from himself. Heidi and I used to wonder about his aloofness. But since you . . . We thought maybe he'd changed. . . . You do know he loves you, don't you?"

Liliane wiped the tears away and emerged from Rose's maternal arms. "Oh, yes, I know that. But I don't know if he knows it."

"I've often wondered," said Rose, her long face thoughtful, "if loving or being loved is more important. We spend so much of our lives wondering if someone will love us. The ideal, of course, is mutual love, but I do think that if we can only have one, then the ability to love is more important. Certainly you are happier than the doctor is. Almost everyone is loved at some time, but not everyone is capable of loving."

Liliane looked at Rose with astonishment. Rose had become increasingly real to her. For the first time, she realized she loved Rose.

Their conversation was interrupted by the strangest assortment of people Liliane could remember seeing. An ancient crone, the shortest woman Liliane had ever seen, led a strange group into the infirmary. Her shriveled breasts sagged on her wrinkled chest. Her grimace displayed a mouthful of gaps. Her teeth were as spare as the thin hair on her scalp. Following her were a man, equally short of stature but certainly more handsome, a little girl of about three, and a tall, thin young man who carried a baby.

The old woman planted herself before the two nurses and stared at each of them in turn. Pointing her finger at Liliane, she jerked her head at the younger man, who then held out the baby.

Liliane and Rose glanced at each other while Liliane accepted the baby. She held it close to her, protectively. In Bantu, she asked what was wrong. The strange crew stared back at her in silence.

Rose tried. In vain.

"Well," said Liliane, "I guess we'll have to find out for ourselves what's wrong."

Laying the little boy on the examining table, she and Rose hovered over him. Except for the little girl, the natives stood in stoic silence. The three-year-old, however, jumped up and down. She wanted to see what was happening. Pointing her finger at the baby, she sobbed. The adults ignored her.

"He can't be more than six months old," said Rose. "And he can't move his right leg."

"What do you suppose is wrong?" Liliane wondered.

The baby fussed, not crying exactly, but it was a restless sound. He balled his fingers into little fists and rolled them in the air, and his left leg moved up and down in a cycling motion. But the right leg lay unmoving.

"I'll get Naldani and see if she can interpret," said Liliane, starting for the door. But the old woman, arms folded over her drooping breasts, moved to stand in the doorway. She adamantly refused to let Liliane pass.

Instead, she pointed to Rose.

"Okay," said Liliane, "*you* go find Naldani."

The old woman let Rose pass.

While they were waiting, Liliane examined the baby. He's the color of cocoa, she thought, looking at the plump little boy.

The three-year-old still hopped around, shifting from foot to foot. Was she afraid that Liliane might harm her little brother? The girl was so frightened that she urinated on the floor. No one paid any attention.

Rose returned with Naldani, who could understand the strangers to a limited extent. The mother had died three days ago, when paralysis had set in. Liliane and Rose looked at each other with sudden realization.

"It's polio, isn't it?" Liliane asked.

Rose shook her head. "I'm afraid so." They looked at each other helplessly. There was absolutely nothing to do. The disease would have to run its course.

"I wish Baxter were here," Liliane murmured. She asked Naldani to tell the grandparents, or whoever they were, that they would watch over the baby. The old woman nodded her head. They had brought blankets and cooking utensils and were prepared to wait until the "white doctor magic" could be wrought.

"If only he doesn't die," Rose said, looking down at the baby. By evening, the baby was no worse; the paralysis had not spread beyond the leg. "I don't think there are likely to be further complications," she said. "I think the disease has run its course."

He will be crippled, thought Liliane, but other parts of his body will not be affected. Heidi volunteered to stay up all night with a regime of hot baths and massages.

That night, when sleep did come to her, Liliane had a strange dream. At first she thought the dream was of Marsh, but when she awoke, she knew it was more than that. She relived, in her dream, the three weeks she and Marsh had traveled through the jungle to outlying villages. And in the dream she saw the boy's head buried in the path.

She lay for a few minutes in that drugged state of consciousness, waking from deep sleep. Then she sat straight up, as though shocked with electricity. "That's it," she said aloud. It was not yet dawn, so she crept out of bed. Dressing quickly in the darkness, she walked in silence to the hospital, where a lamp was burning, even though Heidi had gone to bed and Rose, hovering over the baby, had fallen asleep on the floor beside him, her arm flung next to him. Liliane awoke them.

"I have an idea I want to try," she said, her voice low but trembling with excitement. "Remember a couple of years ago when Marsh and I went on that trip to villages? Remember I told you about the boy who had fallen from a tree and was buried in the ground? Let's try that with this baby."

"Oh, no," Rose cried. "We can't bury him. He won't want to stay still. He's too little."

Liliane turned to her. "He'll either stay still for this or for the rest of his life."

"How do you know it will work?" Heidi asked.

"I don't know. What other choice do we have?"

Since it was only his leg that was paralyzed, Liliane saw no sense in burying the baby up to his neck. The three women dug a pit in the earth outside of Heidi's room, deep enough so that the baby could be placed upright in it. Rose held him while Liliane threw the loose earth back in, covering him up to his armpits. She and Heidi firmed the dirt around him by stamping on it, as one does with newly planted roses. The baby cried and held out his hands. "I imagine we'll have to be with him constantly," said Liliane. "We'll do it in shifts."

"No matter how tired he becomes"—she struggled to recall exactly what the witch doctor had done to that boy—"we make him

stay that way for four hours." Yes, she was sure it was four hours.
"Then, we'll dig him out and bathe him in water as hot as he can
stand. Then four hours in this again. We must do this for"—oh,
what was it?—"five days."

"It sounds like torture," cried Rose.

"Yes, it does. Yet I saw it work." But she had seen it work on
a boy with what seemed to be a broken back, not a paralyzed leg.
And the medicine man there used herbs and set the dirt on fire.
We'll pour hot water on instead, she thought. It must be the heat,
not the leaves, that's important.

Half buried in the ground, the baby's frightened sobs were
soothed by Heidi's rubbing his shoulders.

When Naldani heard about it, she said, "I have heard that the
Mboodu do that."

"Do you know, then," Liliane wondered aloud, "what herbs
they use?"

Naldani did not know.

The baby was the best patient they had ever had. He stopped
crying and seemed to listen to the voices of the women who spoke
soothingly to him. He slept much of the time. They dug him out
every four hours and bathed him in hot water, massaging his leg.
They all swore it had more flexibility. He cried when they returned
him to his hole, but stopped as soon as the dirt was repacked and
hot water poured over it.

When they took him out of the pit that last time, sponging him
off with warm water, massaging his leg, they were relieved to notice
that the leg had not shrunk. They gently moved it back and forth
and then watched as he kicked it, back and forth, in tandem with
the other leg. Rose swore he smiled at them.

"The wonders of modern science," Liliane murmured, enormously pleased at their success. Perhaps I am learning more than
I teach, she thought.

They took turns with the baby all day long, and when they
were satisfied that he would not be crippled, that his illness was
over, they returned him to the strange entourage.

When the little band left, all of the nurses were aware of how
much they missed the baby. They had opened their hearts, and in
finding love they also found emptiness. But as they sat around,
smugly congratulating themselves on their miracle cure, Rose said,
"It's Christmas Eve."

▼

THE NEXT DAY BEGAN AS PERFECT AS ANY LILIANE COULD ASK FOR—
blue skies and a temperature of eighty-five degrees. The day was
filled with newfound happiness for the three nurses.

Just before noon, down the river came two dugout canoes.
Each was paddled by six natives, who stood, with long-handled
oars whose blades were shaped like palm leaves. Out of the center
of the first one stepped a white man in khaki shorts, calling loudly,
"Merry Christmas!"

The nurses looked out the screened windows and then at each
other. Who in the world would arrive by dugout? Oh, not another
logging accident. No, *they* came by motor launch, not by pirogue,
and they came from upriver, not down.

"Maybe it's Santa Claus." Liliane laughed. She headed toward
the dock.

From a distance he looked familiar. She paused as the identity
of the guest became clear, then stared, overcome with both pleasure and dismay, her feet rooted to the ground.

He loped toward her, calling.

"D'YOU KNOW HOW I HAD TO PUSH THESE MEN TO GET HERE ON
Christmas? I've been on that damn river ten days. Tell me"—
Marsh planted himself in front of her—"are you married?"

She couldn't help but smile. "No." She laughed nervously.

"Well, then." He reached out to her, pulling her to him,
kissing her in the bright Christmas sunlight. He felt her pull back
and released her.

"Your letters all caught up with me at once. After reading all
nine of them in one day I had to come back and see you." His
ebullience was contagious. As always with Marsh, she felt the energy he radiated flow into her. His dark eyes danced with excitement.

He had brought them all presents but wouldn't let them open
any of them until after dinner. He asked Heidi to round up candles,
and he took from a tin a plum pudding for Christmas dessert.
Before he let them enjoy the sweet, he said, "It's time to open
presents. Don't look. Give me a minute."

The women sat, their eyes closed, filled with pleasurable anticipation. A festive air predominated. They heard a light thud and
then scratchiness, and out into the Christmas night, in that remote
corner of the world, they heard the rich voice of the famous tenor
Enrico Caruso singing "Silent Night."

Marsh sat down again, smiling smugly. The eyes of all three women were round with delight. One by one they began to sing along with the famous tenor. Heidi's "Stille Nacht" was in her own German. Liliane felt her eyes glisten.

There wasn't a dry eye when it was finished.

"Oh, that's not all," Marsh said, grinning, when the carol ended. He, too, was affected by the emotion of the moment. "I brought you forty records. Hey, that's no small thing to cart down these rivers. Weighs a ton!"

The women pawed through the records to see what songs he had brought. Music. What a difference it would make! No present could have been more welcome.

Yet there were more.

He was sorry, he said, that he couldn't deliver the typewriter and an entire case of ribbons to Baxter himself, and a dictionary, a biology textbook, and a shirt to Anoka.

"You have to open them one by one," he commanded, "and you have to promise to ooh and ah at every one. I spent a long time shopping, and I want my reward."

He gave Heidi a small box, wrapped in shiny blue paper. She took forever opening it, savoring every fold of the paper, every moment of suspense. Inside was a music box. A ballet dancer twirled as the music played "Brahms' Lullaby."

"The music comes on things that look like ribbons." Marsh was like an excited boy as he explained. "There are several more, and"—he looked into Heidi's face—"they're all German songs!" He handed her another box.

Heidi was speechless. She turned the little key and watched the ballerina whirl round and round.

To Rose, he apologized, "I'm afraid yours isn't nearly as romantic. But I heard you gripe over and over again, 'If only I had . . .' so I brought you something very practical."

Hers was a much larger box, so large it looked like a piece of furniture. In her excitement, she tore the paper and gasped when she saw what it was. "Oh," she said, her eyes filling again with tears, her hand flying to her mouth. "Oh!" It was a treadle sewing machine.

Marsh threw bolts of fabric on the dining table. "These are for everyone," he said, his voice loud and happy. "Take your choice. Except that yellow one, that's for Naldani. Of course," he continued, "that's going on the assumption Rose will let you use her Singer."

"Oh, will I!" Rose cried with glee. "Marsh, it is so wonderful!"
Liliane fingered the fabric with pleasure.

So, it was to be Marsh and not Baxter who gave her a Christmas present! She wondered what hers would be.

Marsh finally turned to her and said, "You were more difficult. I wanted to buy the world for you." He was unembarrassed by his declaration.

The box, covered in red paper, contained several packages. The top one contained a pair of "shorts," Marsh told her. "Women in America are beginning to wear them. I thought they'd be just perfect for your treks into the bush. Your skirt kept getting in your way," he explained. "And the next one"—he helped her with the paper—"is because those old sandals of yours must be wearing thin."

She opened another of the small packages and found a jade hand mirror. "You're always saying you forget what you look like," he said, watching for her approval. "When I found this in China, I knew you had to have it."

She held it up to her face. How happy I look, she thought. This is a wonderful Christmas.

"There are more," he urged her on.

The next package held a jeweled comb for her hair. It curved like the crescent of a moon. The blue, red, and green stones sparkled in the light from the lamp. It was not until many years later that she learned its monetary value.

"Here," he said, coming over to her, "let me fix it. I've known ever since I saw it in Saigon just how it should look in your hair." He smoothed it into her curls. "Now, look in the mirror," he said, smiling, "and never again doubt how beautiful you are."

Then he himself opened the largest and heaviest carton. Out on the floor spilled books. And more books. There were dozens.

"This should last you for the next year." He was, indeed, Santa Claus incarnate.

They sat in the dining room, late into Christmas night, singing Christmas carols, admiring their presents, and hearing about the outside world. Marsh had returned to England from the Orient by traveling across the United States, "a country of varied marvels," he told them.

He was on his way, now, to interview Tafari, King of Ethiopia. Then he hoped to meet up with Martin and Osa Johnson and their big-game photography expedition, but his detour to Simbayo might prevent that.

It was late when Rose touched Heidi and, standing up, said, "It's late. We'll see you tomorrow." Liliane knew Rose was giving her time alone with Marsh. She wasn't sure she wanted it.

When the two nurses had gone, he looked at her for a long time. Then he walked around the room, with that graceful panther-like gait of his, turning off all but one of the lamps.

When he sat down again, he crossed his legs carefully. His dark eyes grew serious. He leaned toward her and said, "Riana and I have separated."

Maybe she had known that.

"There hasn't been a day since I left here that I haven't thought of you. I've carried you around the world with me. You've been"—his black eyes smiled—"to places you've never even heard of."

Liliane held up a hand trying to ward off his words. "Marsh . . ."

"No, Liliane, please don't shrink away. I have come back to get you, in one way or another, and I won't leave until I have a part of you, at the very least."

"But I'm in love with Baxter."

"Does he give you what you want? what you need?"

"I don't even know what I need. I do know I'm happy here."

He rose from his chair and walked over to her, reaching down and pulling her up. He rested his hands on her shoulders. His eyes searched hers. "Are you able to say that, despite your attraction for the good doctor, you feel nothing for me?"

Before she could answer, his lips were on hers and his arms crushed her to him. She tried to stand unmoving, her arms at her sides, but the vitality he injected into her would not let her remain so. Her arms wound around him; her mouth opened to receive his kisses; her heart pounded in her ears.

"Oh, my love," he whispered in her ear.

She disentangled herself from his embrace.

"Marsh, wait. I wasn't prepared for this."

"I leave in one week," he said. "I've traveled a world and a half to find you and I won't leave you gracefully."

His vitality excited her, but she said, "Give me time, Marsh. Please."

SHE WAS STIMULATED BY THE GIVE-AND-TAKE MARSH OFFERED. SHE enjoyed arguing with him; she found herself challenged by his viewpoints. She also discovered herself watching the vein in his temple, his long, slender fingers, the lines of his mouth. She wanted to be kissed again, but he had not even tried since his first evening at the camp despite the burning looks he sent her way.

On the fifth night, however, when he walked her to her quarters, he held the door of her room closed so she could not enter.

"The time has come," he said.

"The walrus said," she added.

"To talk of many things . . ."

"Of cabbages and kings . . ."

"And love."

"Does one talk of making love?"

"Ah-ha," he whispered. "Are you thinking of making love?"

He couldn't see her blush in the darkness, but she felt her face flame.

"Doesn't that take excitement away?"

"I'll let you be the judge of that."

They were silent in the darkness. Her back was flat against the door. His hands pressed the door on either side of her, and he leaned over to kiss her. Only his lips touched her; the air between them pulsed with an electric charge.

Then she felt his chest next to hers, burning her. His legs pressed into hers.

He took her in his arms in a strong embrace. One hand moved to her chin, tilting her head back, and his mouth moved down on hers in a long, slow, lingering kiss.

She stood as though paralyzed, arms at her sides. With her mouth, she responded to his warmth and power. There was an urgency to his kisses.

His arms still around her, he bent his head to her neck and kissed her throat. Involuntarily, she moaned, her arms circling his neck. Her breasts pressed against him. The full length of their bodies came together.

Their mouths sought one another. Their tongues touched, first gently, and then, ripe with passion, thrusting into each other, around and around, exploring.

"You electrify me," Marsh murmured. He laid his chin on top of her head, holding her tenderly, tightly. "I want you as I've never wanted anything."

"Oh, Marsh," she breathed against him, kissing his shirt; she felt the warmth of his skin beneath it. Clinging to him, her hands pressed against his chest; she moved her body close to his as though she lacked control over it. She slid her arms around his neck.

He lightly kissed the end of her nose; his tongue gently touched her eyelids; he cascaded kisses down the side of her cheek, running his tongue slowly toward her ear, into it, breathing softly. His knees urged her legs apart; they stood swaying, touching.

Marsh took Liliane's face in his hands. Slowly, his mouth moved across her cheek to her lips. He touched her breast lightly, fondling it ever so gently, rhythmically. She tasted coffee on his tongue, felt the hot wetness of his mouth. No longer in control of herself, she curled her fingers into his dark hair, pressing his head toward her to intensify the kiss, wanting to crush him into her.

She was impelled onward in a dream, savoring each touch, each kiss.

He touched a button on her blouse, started to unfasten it, then stopped. She herself unbuttoned her top; He stopped for a moment, as she stood half naked in the night, murmuring, "I want to see you."

She reached out to unbutton his shirt. She heard the tempo of his breathing increase. His fingers were on her nipples, then his tongue. Her body was afire.

With one hand, he opened the door to her room and they moved inside. He pulled the rest of her clothes off and, picking her up, carried her to the bed. She heard his clothes slip to the floor. Against the night outside her window, she saw his silhouette above her, saw him kneel beside the bed and touch her naked body.

His hands slowly crossed her stomach and, cupping her breasts, he said softly, "I love you." His tongue caressed one breast while his hand gently massaged the other one. She felt his teeth tease her nipples as they became erect. Her body trembled.

CHAPTER 14

▼

"I DIDN'T KNOW IT COULD BE LIKE THIS," LILIANE MURMURED AS Marsh lay with his head in her lap. They were sitting under the palm trees around the bend in the river, out of sight of the compound. Marsh had talked Liliane into a picnic lunch. Today was carefree, her responsibilities having been assumed by Rose.

She ignored the twinges of guilt that began to assault her. Making love with Marsh was a symphony of the senses. Crescendos climaxed through her, her blood pulsing to the beat of drums in the night. She had never experienced such exquisite pleasure.

Today Marsh had taken her down by the river so, he said, "I can see you. I want to devour your body with my eyes. I want to study you, touch you, see sunlight dance upon your skin. I want to see my body next to yours." His words alone brought her body alive.

Her face flushed as she recalled the last two nights. A lust she had never experienced had overwhelmed her.

Marsh did not make love quickly. He stretched it out until the exquisite pleasure became torment, every nerve ending pulsating and raw.

The turbulence of his lovemaking was like waves crashing against rocks. His hands were dedicated to exploring her body; his tongue discovered what delighted her. He was intent on pleasure, and his passion was limitless.

His hands played music on her body, and her whole being quivered to the symphony he created. Cataclysmic shudders, beginning deep within her, sent shock waves of heat throughout her body. She had cried out in the night.

He did that to her again.

And again . . . stopping only when he, too, shuddered, holding her tightly in a viselike grip.

"We are one," he had whispered. Their passion spent, they lay in each other's arms.

Sex had become ecstasy. The exquisite pleasure, the sensual, insistent wildness jarred her into a kaleidoscope of abandon.

Marsh's body was hard and lean and beautiful. . . . She enjoyed watching what happened to her body as well as to his. She had never felt so alive. She liked the taste of his mouth, the odor of his body, the touch of his tongue. His talk heightened her senses, the gravelly resonance of his voice so unlike the deep timbre of Baxter's. Maybe what she loved the most was his laughter and the way he made her laugh. She gazed at him in the daylight.

"Lili," Marsh said, looking up at her. "How can I leave you tomorrow? How can I ever leave you?"

She didn't want him to leave, either. She had just gotten dressed, but her insatiable desire returned as she watched him. She wanted him to keep touching her, to feel him desire her, to feel him inside her and keep him there. That's what she *really* wanted. Yet these feelings for him frightened her.

"Come with me tomorrow."

"Oh, Marsh!" Why was he forcing reality into this? "You know I can't."

"You mean," he suggested, his eyes holding hers, "you don't want to."

"All right," she said, "I don't want to. You've always known that."

"You're not even tempted?" His voice cracked.

"No." She knew it hurt him. "I'm not even tempted." But she was. This wildness had captured her. A life with no responsibilities, roaming with careless ease around the world, always to the danger zones. Not ever the civilized cities, never the safety of the suburbs. Always the unexplored. Never living by rules. A life unchained. A life of wild nights, of sensual days . . . Oh, Marsh, I am tempted!

"You wouldn't like this to go on forever?"

"Yes," she answered. "I'd like this kind of loving to go on and on. I'd like to pretend, now and then, that I had no responsibilities. I'd like to feel loved and beautiful and special every day of my life."

"I promise you all of that for the rest of your life if you'll come away with me. Lili, we can see the world together. We can live enchanted lives."

"No," she said. "*You* can live an enchanted life. I would be merely your shadow. I would be following *your* dream, not mine. It's not for me. I don't know how to be a fairy princess."

It might be fun to try, though, she thought. Not ever to worry. No sickness, no poverty, no death. Marsh's mouth on my breast every night.

Marsh sat up. "Lili, it's not a fairy tale. It's real."

She clenched her teeth with firm determination. "You don't even know what real is. You've never lived in an everyday world. Your life is a canvas that's larger than reality. You think tearing off to China and America, wandering through India . . ."

"I haven't done that," he objected. "And you're not telling me that your life here in the Congo is 'everyday,' are you?"

"Marsh, don't you see? Even this is not reality. One doesn't stop in for a quick week in the Congo."

"Well, I do, and it's real enough for me. And for your information, by the time I get in and out of this place, it's closer to six weeks."

"Even that is a fantasy to me. Not many can take six weeks out of their lives to satisfy an impulse."

"Impulse? Is that all you think you are to me?" His voice held anger.

"No, but sometimes I do feel like a figment of your imagination. You don't even listen to me." That was unfair. She knew it wasn't true. "You don't seem to hear me when I say I want to justify my life by helping people, that I like feeling important, I like to feel worthwhile, I want to save lives. I wouldn't be happy doing anything else."

Or would I? I haven't laughed so much in years, I've never thought about so much. I haven't felt as cherished. I haven't been so awake, so alive!

"How do you know?" His pleas were useless.

"I know, that's all. And as I've told you all along, I'm in love with Baxter." I am, she told herself. I know I am. Oh, then how can I do this with Marsh? I don't know how. Or why. I don't know what I'll think of myself later.

"You can't love him as much as you think and be this way with me."

"I *am* bewildered," she admitted. She leaned over and nibbled his ear. He held on to her, his hands gliding down her body as his tongue sought hers. When his hand caressed her thigh, she opened her legs. Oh, she thought, what kind of woman have I become? I can't keep myself away from this man.

WHEN HE LEFT AT DAWN, LILIANE STOOD ON THE DOCK WATCHING THE pirogue disappear into the mist. His voice was muffled in the fog as he called out, "I shall be back. I won't take no for a final answer."

As she walked back to the compound, she told herself that she had been living in a dream and had known it all week.

Rose and Heidi were at breakfast when she entered the dining room. I've been so preoccupied with Marsh, I don't even know what's happened here the past week, she thought.

Rose's eyes met hers. I wonder what they think, she asked herself. They can't help but know. And I once thought *they* were immoral!

The emptiness she was feeling was a big hole. She wished she could talk with someone, expiate her sins.

As they performed their medical duties and dined together

during the following days, Liliane saw Rose closely observing her. Once Rose started to say something, but refrained. What would she say? Would she censure her? As though Rose were her own conscience, Liliane read into Rose's inexpressive glances her own confused longing and guilt.

When they heard the *Sal*'s whistle, Marsh had been gone for five days.

She was slow to go greet Baxter and Jack. What bothered her most was how little she was plagued by actual guilt. And yet she felt judged. If she had done wrong, would she not feel guilt? She had sinned, hadn't she? Her acts were immoral, weren't they?

Now that she thought about it, by those same standards, she had been immoral for more than a year. She slept with Baxter without benefit of marriage. Wasn't she compounding her immorality by making love with Marsh, too? Having sex with a man she didn't love? Was that more sinful than having an affair with a man she did love?

Her true guilt, she realized, lay in experiencing no remorse. What kind of woman am I? she wondered. Am I immoral in the eyes of God as well as in the eyes of society? Must these be the same? And here, in Simbayo, what society judges me?

And how do I judge myself? She was unsure. She had not yet decided exactly how she felt about herself.

At that moment, *My Gal Sal* came around the river's bend and sputtered into sight.

Jack and Baxter, at the railing, looked like river bums. They had not shaved in a month, since they'd left. Their eyes were bloodshot, their clothes were dirty and rumpled. Liliane thought a beard became Baxter; Jack *always* looked as though he needed a shave—he never quite had a beard, but neither was he clean-shaven.

Baxter's tired eyes met hers and a sliver of a smile caught her. Oh, he's exhausted, she realized. I've been having a lovely time and he's been . . .

As the boat pulled up to the dock, Baxter climbed over the side of the boat, and in a voice that could barely be heard, he said, "It's good to be home."

She noticed the slump of his shoulders.

He turned to Jack, who was tying the boat to the dock. The two of them made the boat secure. Jack was unnaturally quiet. They were both thinner than when she'd last seen them.

"Hi there, princess," rasped Jack, as though it were too much of an effort to talk more.

They walked slowly, as if they might not make it, to Baxter's office. "I think we each need a bath," he said. "Will you ask the cook to rustle up something to eat?"

Though the three nurses sat with them as they ate in the middle of the afternoon, neither Jack nor Baxter had the energy to talk about their journey. Baxter ate slowly; Jack wolfed his food down. When they were through, Liliane suggested they needed sleep. Neither objected to a nap.

They hadn't yet awakened at dinnertime.

Nor even when the women prepared for bed. Liliane lay wondering if Baxter were awake and expecting her. Should she go to him? She'd have to some time. Could he tell she'd been with Marsh? Were there telltale marks?

He and Jack were both at the breakfast table when she arrived. They looked more rested, but Baxter's eyes were still haunted by something. Starved, Jack shoveled endless quantities of food into his mouth.

When Liliane sat down beside Baxter, she was surprised to feel his leg press against hers and remain there. She would have liked to meet his eyes in silent acknowledgment of the hidden affection, but she couldn't. At that moment, Rose and Heidi entered.

Their chattering erased Liliane's discomfort.

"Was it perfectly terrible?" asked Rose.

"Yeah," sputtered Jack with a mouthful. "You could say that."

"What we did was but a drop in the bucket," was all Baxter would say. Liliane asked him about it later, when they were alone, and he said, "I don't want to talk about it." Here was a pattern, she realized. When things really mattered to him, he was unable to talk about them.

He immediately returned to the regular routine, but he was lacking his usual energy.

Together briefly before lunch, he said, "I missed you," and put a hand on Liliane's shoulder. Their eyes met, and she thought, I do love you.

By evening, Baxter looked as if he wouldn't last through dinner. Jack had had the luxury of an afternoon nap and was recuperating more quickly than Baxter, but then Jack had no responsibilities at Simbayo.

As soon as dinner was over, Baxter shoved back his chair and turned to Liliane. "I don't know if I even remember how to play. Want a quick game of chess?"

"But you must be tired," she exclaimed. She didn't know whether she was quite ready for him. What kind of woman went directly from one man to another? And did she want to be that kind of woman?

"I am tired," he admitted. "But I'd like a quick game to let me know I'm back in civilization." He gave Liliane a knowing look.

"Civilization?" Rose laughed. "How the rest of the world would laugh hearing what we think of ourselves." Her eyes were kind as she watched Liliane. Liliane wondered, Is she trying to give me comfort?

As they walked toward Baxter's rooms, he reached out and took her hand. He had never done that before. As he closed the door to his office, he took her in his arms.

The urgency in his embrace, in his searching kisses, was new. He tilted her head back and looked long into her eyes. Is he searching for fidelity? Liliane asked herself. Whatever he found there reassured him. He picked her up in his arms and carried her to his bed. A month of abstinence rushed him. His passion hurt her. When she cried out, he paused.

"I'm sorry," he apologized. "I want you too much." And he continued until his shuddering climax.

Liliane lay there in the dark, unable to help comparing him with Marsh . . . There was a tenderness in the time Marsh took, in his words of endearment. Marsh's explorations led unrelentingly to the shattering fireworks that exploded within her body when he made love to her.

"When I heard Marsh had been here," Baxter began, as he lay beside her, "when I saw the typewriter, I'm amazed to find you still here."

She sat up in bed. "Baxter, I love *you*. Marsh asked me to leave with him, he even wanted me to marry him. I wasn't even tempted. He's a glamorous man, but I love you." She'd wanted him to say it first. "I am already married, I told him. To Simbayo. I don't want anything or anyone else."

Baxter reached up for her, pulling her down across his chest. "Oh, Liliane, sweet Liliane."

Then he was asleep.

Life resumed its routine at the compound with one major change: Baxter allowed his affection to surface. He never mentioned the word *love,* but he showed his feelings more openly and did not hide them from Rose or Heidi or Jack, who stayed three weeks. He reached out to touch Liliane's hand at the dinner table. He gazed at her fondly. He swam with her in the afternoons.

Jack made a party out of daily life. But he was also often the harbinger of any bad news from the outside world. From the invisible network he carried wherever he went, he was the first to hear that cholera was flaring up in the interior, to the east this time, away from the river.

"If it's not one thing, it's another," grunted Heidi. "That's why we came." It was true. More and more often, disease called them away from camp. Liliane's dream was still to establish camps "out there," to practice preventive medicine and to perceive the first sign of outbreaks and thereby control them more quickly. Whenever she mentioned this to Baxter, he said only, "We're already stretched too thin."

Liliane, who seldom felt ill, wondered what she had eaten when, handing Baxter a scalpel one Wednesday, she was overcome with nausea. She fought it down and felt better within a few minutes. The next day it happened again. Walking down the infirmary hallway, she saw the walls began to swirl, circling faster and faster until she could no longer see them. When they slowed down, she was sprawled in the hallway, slumped against the wall. The sensation passed, but the incident worried Liliane.

The next morning, Naldani had called her to assist in a difficult childbirth. They walked along the forest path together. The world suddenly went dark and she was disappearing into its vortex. She reached out to grab her friend for support. In the void, she felt her friend's arms encircle her and hold her upright. That moment passed, too. She saw the concerned look on Naldani's face.

The next morning the moment she saw the bananas on the breakfast table her stomach turned. Naldani found her, shivering, hunched over, vomiting into the jungle's edge. The native woman knelt down next to her, her hand on Liliane's shoulder. Reflected in her eyes was a smile—a secret smile.

"I, too, am with child." She grinned, her teeth a dazzling white next to the nearly purple-black of her velvet skin.

"With child? Is that what this is? Oh, God, oh, God!" she moaned in her agony. "What have I done?"

Liliane looked at her squatting friend and was momentarily distracted from her own problem. That meant that Naldani and

Bmeno . . . Oh, God! In her mind's eye, she saw the empty spot where his nose should have been, the toeless stumps, the hands with fingers that ended at the first knuckle. She saw Naldani lifting him because he could not move. Oh, Naldani, she cried to herself, how could you? In disgust, she vomited into the ferns again.

She reached for her friend's hand and held it. The bond was cemented. They would bear children together. It was a reassuring thought.

Liliane went to her room and lay down. She would have to tell Baxter. How would he react? With fury? They'd never mentioned children. True, they had taken no precautions. How could one, out in the jungle? Would he be angry with her? How could she have let this happen? It was, of course, his fault as much as hers, but nevertheless would the idea of a child anger him so that he would take it out on her? Would she have to leave Simbayo? Would he rise above such scandal? Would he send her away?

Would he consider marrying her? It was the right thing for him to do. Would she want him to marry her only because she was carrying his child? Of course not. She wanted no ties that reeked of obligation. Then what to do?

Do I want to marry him?

She had always wanted to marry Baxter Hathaway. She wanted him to love her enough to desire marriage without being trapped into it.

She would wait to tell him; she would try to get through this period of sickness. Once she recognized what was causing her distress, she built a fortress around it. When she felt sick or dizzy, she immediately absented herself from Baxter or Rose or Heidi. The feeling always passed within minutes.

But Rose was not fooled. One afternoon, when Liliane was swimming, Rose came down to the river. She sat on the bank but made no move to join Liliane. She waited for Liliane to emerge, then patted the sandy bank next to her.

Liliane sat down, towel-drying her hair.

"You're pregnant." Rose wasted no words. "Does he know?"

Liliane dropped her gaze and shook her head.

"He must be very obtuse not to have noticed. You have to tell him."

"Oh, Rose, what if it angers him? What if he sends me away?"

Rose shook her head and showed impatience. "It never ceases to amaze me how you two have lived together in this place for three years, have loved each other all that time, and know each other so little. You know Marshall Compson better than you know Baxter Hathaway."

"Marsh lets me know him, begs me to. Baxter is so reticent. He's never even told me he loves me."

"Oh, Liliane." Rose sighed with disgust. "You are so smart about other people and so blind about yourself. Well, anyway . . . you have to tell him. He's going to find out soon enough. Better it's from you than someone else. You have to face the music."

"Face the music?" Liliane repeated bitterly. "Does that mean you think what we've done is wrong?"

"Who am I to judge you? But if I were, no, of course I don't think what you've done is wrong. Indulgent, perhaps. Careless, I think. But wrong—of course not. A man and woman—out here away from any other humans for four years . . . Liliane, it's normal. It's not wrong. Heidi and I have been happy for you. We love you, Liliane. We want you to be happy, too. We also love the doctor. Marry him. Have the baby that will bring joy to everyone here."

"Easy to say, marry him. What if he doesn't want that?"

"Don't you think it's time to find out?"

"What do I do? Say 'Baxter, I'm pregnant and I need you to marry me now'?"

"Not unless you have to. He's not completely blind. Well"— she permitted herself a laugh—"I guess he is where his heart is concerned. He refuses to admit he has one. Help him face himself, Liliane."

Rose stood and reached down a hand to pull Liliane up.

Baxter wasn't at dinner. He'd been called upriver to amputate a logger's leg. The logger was caught under a tree and there was no way to move him.

Liliane retired early that evening. She lay on her bed in the quiet of the gathering darkness and thought. She had to make plans, had to find answers to her own questions. She fell asleep with nothing resolved.

She was awakened later by the sound of her door opening. A whisper said, "Don't be alarmed. It's me."

She could see Baxter's outline. It was the first time he had ever come to her. He stood beside the bed, showering his clothes onto the floor. Still drugged with sleep, she felt herself tingling. As he lowered himself to the bed, she reached up and drew her fingers across his chest. As he slid next to her, she bit one of his nipples and buried her head against him, tracing designs with her tongue. She heard the tempo of his breathing increase.

Pushing the sheet away from her, she turned over, moving on top of him. Setting a slow pace, she led him to the rhythms she had learned satisfied her. With their torsos meshed, she leaned over him, rubbing her breasts along his lips. She sat on top of him, sliding up and down until she heard him moan. She stopped. Now it was his turn. She would not let him hurry tonight.

And he didn't They made love as they never had before. Their passion soared, and they became one. Over and over again. Their sexual energies exhausted, they lay and talked. For the first time, they spoke about themselves. They exchanged words of love.

"I first knew I loved you the moment I saw you, watering a fern, in Buffalo. . . ."

"I did, too."

"I was afraid . . . I was too old for you."

It was still dark when she lit the lamp. She wanted to see his eyes when she told him.

Silently, he gave her the answer she yearned for. Tears welled in his eyes. He reached out for her, more tenderly than she could have imagined, and held her tightly.

"Why have you never before told me you loved me?" she asked.

"Before I answer that, I want to tell you again I love you. It's been much too long in coming, I know. But I do love you. I thought you knew it. I thought you've known it all along."

"Oh, I guess I've suspected—even assumed. But I wasn't sure. I needed you to proclaim it to me. I've never understood why you keep so much of yourself from me."

He sighed and lay silent for a long time. Then he pulled her to him again, her head on his chest, his arm around her shoulders.

He said, "I'll tell you a story."

CHAPTER 15

▼

I'LL HAVE TO TELL YOU ABOUT THE ACCIDENT.

Doug Fairbanks and I insisted on doing our own stunts. *We* weren't going to have stand-ins. Perhaps we were trying to convince ourselves that we were the characters we played on the screen. We weren't, of course. But we didn't admit that then.

It's easy to get caught up in believing what the studio publicity department writes about you.

My story really starts before the accident. I won't bore you by going all the way back . . . There's so much to tell. But other things can come later. Oh, my love. How wonderful to say it. We have a lifetime for details, don't we? Let me fill you in on this episode of my past—you'll understand me better.

Her name was Naomi. She was the most beautiful woman in the Ziegfeld Follies. She couldn't sing or dance, but she didn't have to. She just had to walk down those stairs and every man in the audience was breathless.

She didn't give me the time of day. I used to stand in the wings staring at her, but she didn't even know I was alive. Then the leading man, Roger Cheatham, suffered an attack of appendicitis.

I'd detoured from my original goal of studying medicine the year before. I was a senior at Northwestern when the acting bug caught me. My parents, of course, were dismayed that I gave up medical school and decided to try my luck on Broadway. Immediately, though, I landed a part as understudy to Roger. He was a mediocre actor, but he was provokingly handsome and had a beautiful voice. One didn't have to act to be in the Follies. One had to be able to sing or dance or to look so beautiful nothing else mattered.

When it was discovered Roger would be out of the show for three weeks, I was called to take over.

That first night, Alexander Devine was in the audience. You're not too young to remember him, are you? He was, and still is, one of the giants of the industry. He was filming, then, across the Hudson River in Passaic. None of us thought movies would last. The theater was where respectable actors stayed.

Well, Mr. Devine asked me to make a screen test. I had no desire to be in movies, but I did the test anyway.

Roger was still recuperating and I was playing the lead and loving every minute of it. The New York papers were kind to me; I felt sure I was on my way. People who had never noticed me now invited me to parties. One night after the show, I felt someone press against me and turned right into Naomi Tasmand. She looked up at me . . . I'd never seen such long eyelashes! Her hair was like midnight, and her eyes were the blue of a robin's egg. She told me she was on her way to a party and did I want to come along?

Naomi Tasmand inviting me to a party? All night she hung on to my arm, danced with me in ways I'd never experienced in college. She sang slightly off-key with her head on my shoulder as we rode in a horse-drawn cab through Central Park. It was the most romantic evening of my life.

The next morning, Alexander Devine called and asked me to drop in at his office. He was, he told me, moving his company to California, where the sun shone all year long, making more days of filming possible. In 1904, California seemed as far away as New Zealand or . . . the Congo! He invited me to come along and star in his next movie.

Star? I laughed at the offer.

"Don't laugh," he said, a cigar sticking out of the side of his mouth. "I can make you rich."

"I'm not interested in rich," I said. "I'm interested in acting."

It was his turn to laugh. "Listen, kid," he said. "I'll make you famous. I'll make you a household word. This picture is gonna be about pirates, and every woman in the country'll fall in love with you."

I doubted it. I started to leave, but he called me back.

"Wait a minute. Whatcha makin' as Roger's stand in?"

I was earning twenty-five dollars a week, but I told him it was forty. Most of the fellows I'd graduated from Northwestern with were making about forty now, just a little over a year out of school.

Forty dollars? He laughed. It was more of a snarl. "Listen, kid. Tell you what. I'll give you one thousand dollars a week. If I like you in this flick, I'll make it two thousand a week in the next one. If we sign a contract, I'll go up to five thousand a week in a year."

I sat down. That would get me rich in a hurry. I thought of Naomi.

Mr. Devine cut through my thoughts. "I'll give you three months to get to Los Angeles. By then we'll be ready to shoot. When you get out there, ask for the Devine Studios. We're gonna be big, kid."

I could hardly wait to get to the theater that night and tell her. I thought I was the luckiest man in the world. I really thought the madcap Naomi had fallen in love me, the bookish, unsophisticated ex–med student.

Naomi Tasmand, the toast of New York, the life of every party, the spontaneous center of attraction wherever she went, decided *we* should drive her car across the country. And what a drive it was!

We left every small town in a state of shock. Naomi danced on tables, Naomi dined dressed in glittering sequins in third-rate diners, Naomi flirted with accountants and farmers. They didn't even know who she was. She'd say to me, "See that man at the bar? Watch."

And half an hour later she'd have him so befuddled he couldn't think straight. I'd sit there and laugh, knowing that soon she'd come over and put her arm through mine and show everyone who she *really* wanted to be with.

When she'd see kids swinging on playgrounds, we had to stop the car and she'd run over and swing with them. When she saw those midwesterners playing baseball, she'd slam on the brakes of that long car of hers and go bat a ball. The temperature soared over one hundred degrees and it was someplace in Nebraska that she complained, which she rarely did, of the heat. She made a game of everything. When you were with Naomi, you laughed a lot. But this one hot day we passed a pond in a farmer's field. She brought the car to a jolting halt and jumped out, running to that pond. She stood there on the bank and pulled all her clothes off and jumped in.

I stared at her. I knew she was beautiful, but I'd never seen a naked woman before. I found myself shaking.

Come on, she cried. It's wonderful.

It was, too. She swam over to me and put her arms around me and I felt that great, wonderful body of hers next to mine, felt her legs encircle my hips, and I was lost. From then on, we shared the same hotel room.

I didn't want to reach Hollywood. I didn't want this to end.

I asked her to marry me. Funny, even now, all these years later, I can see her face that day. She was wearing a yellow dress and a blue ribbon that matched her eyes wound through her hair.

With narrowed eyes, she looked at me and laughed.

"I'll marry you on two conditions," she said, as though she'd already thought it out. "I'll marry you if this movie is a success. And if you tell Mr. Devine you want me to play the countess."

The countess wasn't even the lead. It was easy to talk him into that. But her dream wasn't what I thought it was.

California was bizarre. I'd never seen so much sunshine. I found an apartment that had a lemon tree outside the window. Naomi rented a house. I threw all my energies into that picture, wanting it to succeed so Naomi would marry me.

She threw crazy parties that lasted till dawn. I'd go from one of them to a full day of shooting and wonder why I was tired all the time.

The Normandy Pirate was a success. Naomi did marry me, and we bought a big house. She never made another movie. She never had a desire to. What Naomi wanted was money and power.

I went from one movie to another. When one ended, another began. In two years I never had a day off. I was twenty-six years old, already famous and rich, and had no time to do anything I wanted. What did I want? The reading public would have thought I wanted to be at parties, that I wanted to hobnob with the Gold-wyns and the Griffiths, and spend my time at Pickfair. I did enjoy the latter—oh, not so much the formality that went with Pickfair, but I really liked Doug Fairbanks. We were able to make fun of ourselves, but, at the same time, we believed we were really capa-ble of those exploits we performed on the screen. We were men playing at boys' games and didn't know it. We thought it made us men.

I found myself too tired to stay awake during the dinners Naomi always gave. She never complained, but it didn't slow her down. She continued her wild social life—she became famous for jumping into swimming pools with her clothes on. She'd rent a sailboat and take a party out to Catalina on the spur of the mo-ment. She'd call people up at midnight and get a party going.

She had her tender moments, too. She always knew when people's birthdays were and when their children were ill. People loved Naomi. She was wild yet compassionate, and certainly one of the most interesting people in Hollywood. I thought she was the most exciting person in the world.

But I couldn't keep up with her.

I couldn't keep up with myself! Wherever we went, we were mobbed. Naomi would stand back, looking beautiful in her long, white fox coat, and smile while I signed autographs. We couldn't go to the beach or to the movies or shopping, or drive out into the desert, without people surrounding us.

After five years of nonstop picture-making I told Mr. Devine I needed a vacation. Of course, he said, come to Europe with us. Isabel and I are going there next month. Come with us—it'll be on me. We're going to Paris and Athens and Rome.

I didn't want that. I wanted to go to the back country of Wyoming or down to Baja. I wanted to get away from people. And I didn't want to be with the Devines, though he was never anything but kind to me. Whatever I asked for, I got. But even when he threw an arm around my shoulder, there was a wall. I think now that maybe it was my fault. I was never convivial. I've always had the temperament of a college professor more than an actor and I never felt at ease with Naomi's high jinks. I didn't realize I was going on this vacation only to please her. I wondered why I wasn't having as much fun as everyone else.

When we returned, I churned out more movies. Devine was now taking longer to make each movie—and being more careful. We no longer rushed through filming in six or eight weeks. But the weeks began to seem like years, and the years rolled by so fast that when I try to recall those years, they just slide by.

Naomi became pregnant, to what I thought was our great delight, but she soon miscarried. She miscarried three times. Though she was wonderful with children, I don't think she wanted to be tied down. She was too busy living Naomi's life. I've wondered, since then, if they really were miscarriages.

I didn't even know what she did most of the time. She was there when I came home to dinner and when I crept out of bed before dawn. But when I went to bed early, she went partying.

I told myself I shouldn't complain. I was one of the most famous men in America; I lived in a mansion with sixteen servants. Can you imagine sixteen servants for two people? The most beautiful woman in the world was my wife, though we no longer talked, it seemed, except to plan what to wear to a party or who to invite to one. I felt I didn't know her anymore.

Naomi, on the other hand, knew everyone in Hollywood. It wasn't just the important producers and directors and stars she knew; she also knew cameramen and extras and the gatekeeper on the lot. She'd sweep in to have lunch with me and Mr. Devine, and everyone on the set paid more attention to her than they did to the stars. People came alive when she entered a room. And she knew how to listen. I thought she listened to everybody but me.

But then I had little to say except how the picture was going. I think I had the typical Hollywood syndrome; my life centered around me. And I was gradually beginning to think that person was empty.

The catalyst was the fall I took. Doug and I said we wanted audiences to believe our capers; in reality we loved the danger and excitement, the look of fear in the eyes of those watching the filming. It made us feel like the heroes we were portraying. In trying to show myself as well as the unseen audience what a man

I was, I insisted on jumping across a narrow gorge. But I tripped over the cape I was wearing and plunged down the escarpment, injuring my back and legs so that it was doubtful I would ever walk again.

I underwent three operations in five months, lying prone in a hospital, unable to do more than wiggle my hands.

It was a national event. Every day more flowers than could fit in my room arrived. Daily reports on the state of my health made the newspapers. People I'd never met sneaked into the hospital. At first I felt important, but then I realized it wasn't *me* they cared about. It was the parts I played, the shell that surrounded the real me. And I had no idea who the real me was anymore.

Then Dr. Geoffrey Drew walked into my life. He sauntered into my room the evening before the first operation—a tall string-bean of a man, looking more like a boy than an experienced doctor. He had red hair and wore a bow tie. His gray-blue eyes were solemn, and in his quiet voice he said, "Well, Mr. Hathaway, we're going through this together."

He proceeded to examine me, making notes on his chart. "Trying to be a hero, huh?" he asked. Then, his eyes piercing me, he asked, "Do you believe in God?"

"Of course," I answered, though I had never thought much about it. I took for granted that everyone believed in God. He was out there ruling the universe while I played so heedlessly in it. I thought Dr. Drew was suggesting I pray before the operation.

"That wouldn't hurt," he said with a smile, "but I'm not convinced a plea is necessary. He's very aware of you as it is."

That's all he said that night. But, as I lay there the next few months, recuperating from operation after operation, wondering if I'd ever walk again, this man became the most profound influence of my life.

Never once did he let me give up. Never once did he doubt that I'd walk again. He'd come into my hospital room and force me to do exercises that I swore were impossible to do. I'd cry. For the only time in my life I cried. The pain was incredible. Never once did he offer sympathy, yet his compassion was infinite.

One day about five months after he'd entered my life—on his way to saving it—he sat down in the chair next to my bed. It was April, and California breathed spring into the room. I still remember it. The late-afternoon light spread gold into the room and I swore a halo surrounded Dr. Drew. I knew it was my imagination, probably helped by the pain medication, but the moment was, nevertheless, sacred. He looked at me for a while and then leaned forward.

"Baxter," he said. "You're not an ordinary person. You exude some kind of magic. That's what's made you a big star. You may not know what it is, but it's there. I'm talking about the inner you that projects itself bigger than life." He paused. Then, "Do you know you nearly died?"

No, I hadn't known that.

"And even I wondered whether or not you'd walk. Now I need your help. We are going to begin such a regimen of exercise that you will often feel discouraged and defeated. I've never gone this far with anyone before. The exercises will stretch you physically *and* mentally. You *have* to cooperate. Baxter"—and his voice grew soft, so low I had to strain to hear him—"I am convinced God has saved you for a purpose. We must find that purpose. I believe, really believe"—he seemed to be talking to himself—"that God has singled you out, that He has things planned for you. You must make Him proud of you. You are not like other men."

Of course he scared me. I had no idea what he meant. Nor, do I think, did he.

He left, and I lay in that golden afternoon, with the scent of roses in the air, staring at the ceiling. God had plans for me? That seemed pretty ludicrous. I did not believe in predestination. I thought I had some control over my fate. Why would God have plans for *me*? Was this doctor just a fanatic?

But he had made me begin to question, begin to think. I began to question everything, not just the concept of God. I questioned the life I had been living. I questioned my marriage, my work, my friends—everything. I began to read books that dealt with the universal problems of life.

When I was not reading, I was studying the world around me. Geoff, as I'd begun to call him, would personally take me through my exercises; though he didn't speak of God again for a long time, he did talk to me of his patients and of medicine. Now and then he took me, via wheelchair, on his hospital rounds with him.

"Give the patients a thrill," he'd say. "They've never met a real-live movie star."

Time and again I wanted to give up those exercises. The pain stretched into torment. He never let me abandon them. I failed to perceive why this man cared so much about one person's learning to walk again.

One day, he left a book on my bed. It was an elementary

medical textbook. I couldn't even understand it. I read the entire first chapter and nothing in it made sense to me.

When Geoff returned the next afternoon, he didn't ask if I'd read it. He knew I had.

"Now"—he smiled that serious smile of his—"if you'd like, I'll help you begin to understand. You've shown so much interest in everything here at the hospital, I thought you might want to continue the education you abandoned for the theater."

He had created a reason for me to go on with my life. Instead of following shadows on the ceiling, I began to study. I found myself more and more bored and impatient during visiting hours when Naomi and her friends would drop by on their way to a party, acting solicitous, laughing raucously. Never once in all those months did Naomi and I have a conversation about anything that mattered.

I thought it was because she was shallow, but I know now that it was also my fault. I didn't know how to share my new interest. I was afraid she'd make fun of me. I realized that I'd always been afraid to share anything important. I was afraid that others would convince me that what I thought was insignificant. Rather than take that chance or find the courage to stand up for my ideas, I hid them.

The more involved I became with Geoff Drew and medicine, the more I wondered if God *had* saved me for a purpose. I decided to test Him. If God let me walk again, I'd know that He had done so for a reason. And if that were true, I had to find that reason.

I did walk again. I walked nine months after my accident. A new birth, said Geoff. A new life to dedicate. I not only walked again but went back to doing movie stunts. I knew, though, that *this* couldn't be what God had in store for me.

I continued making movies for another three years, though I no longer participated in Naomi's frenetic life. We had become strangers to each other. We had nothing to talk about.

Finally, Geoff and I talked it over. "I've thought all along," he said, "that God sees you as a healer. I've thought He wants you to do His work."

His work? I asked Geoff if *he* was doing God's work.

"Not entirely," he answered. "If I were, I wouldn't be making so much money. I wouldn't be operating in Hollywood but in the Ozarks or in ghettos or in Brazilian jungles. I think I *do* make a difference, but not the way you will."

He believed so fervently in what he was saying that I was

touched. Whether what he was saying was true or not, I knew I had to give up acting. I wanted to study medicine. With or without God, I *had* to do what I could to help.

Geoff warned me, though. "If you dedicate your life to other people," he said, his eyes solemn and sad, "everyone close to you will suffer. You can't give equally to a cause and a family. Whether you want it or not, your loved ones will come second. Nothing worthwhile is ever achieved without loss."

I made up my mind. I'd been on a glamorous treadmill. It was time to get off.

The only way to be alone with Naomi, I decided, was to invite her to dinner—just the two of us. I told her we were going to Luigi's, a wonderful little Italian restaurant we liked, and I rented the whole restaurant. There was a band, and we danced, and she said, "Oh, it's like old times, isn't it? I thought we'd lost each other."

But it wasn't like old times, I told her. I wanted to quit the movies. I had hoped the romantic atmosphere would soften the blow.

She looked at me, her fork poised in midair. Her eyes took on a sapphire hardness. "I suppose you're going to become a doctor," she said. "I've seen those books you've been reading. My God, do you know how old you are? You can't start studying medicine at your age."

"I'm thirty-four," I said. "And I can do anything I want."

"What kind of doctor do you think you'll be?" she asked.

I think she was pleading with me more than being sarcastic. "Doctors have to relate to people, have to feel compassion," she said. "I'm not questioning your intellect, but you don't know how to think about anything except yourself."

I thought, then, how little she knew me. Now I realize she probably knew me very well.

"Knowing you, you'll be one of the richest of doctors, of course. But it can't compare with what you earn acting. Have you really thought about what you'd be giving up?"

"We have enough money to last for years. Sell the big house, have a few lean years while I go through medical school and . . . "

"We? You can't be serious. Not we. That's not why I married you. My dear"—and she reached across the table and took my hand into hers, spattered with diamonds—"when you give up films, you also give me up."

If it was a threat, it failed to dismay me. Naomi and I hadn't done more than eat together and sleep in the same house for years. We hadn't made love in months.

"What will you do?" I asked.

She put down her fork and called for champagne. When it came, she raised her glass and smiled. "I think I'll marry Alexander Devine," she said.

Marry . . . I choked. "What about Isabel?"

"Oh, you poor naïve darling," she said. "Did you think I wasn't getting any love just because you and I . . . ?"

I thought of the black cigar that always drooped out of the side of his mouth, of his balding head, of the fact he was shorter than Naomi, of his Brooklyn accent. . . .

Naomi, of course, thought of the power he wielded as head of one of the world's great studios, of the millions of dollars he had amassed, and maybe of the way he made love. Who knows.

Geoff hoped I wouldn't mourn. "Now you're free to do what you were born to do," he said.

That was 1914.

I went to Stanford med school and Naomi married my producer. Funny, even when he and I shook hands at the end, I called him Mr. Devine.

I still didn't know what God had saved me for, but I was convinced that becoming a doctor was the avenue He wanted. I never questioned that. I believe it now as much as I did then. It wasn't until my last year at Stanford that I read a book about Africa. I read that this particular part of the Congo was "God forsaken."

How, I wondered, could any place be God forsaken? He doesn't forsake anyone. I read everything I could get my hands on about this part of the world, and the constant, recurrent phrase was "God forsaken." I knew then what God wanted of me: I was to show that He had forsaken no part of the world.

IT WAS STILL DARK WHEN BAXTER CONCLUDED HIS STORY, THOUGH Liliane could tell by the chirping of the birds that dawn would soon lighten the sky.

Baxter lay on his back, his hands under his head, and stared straight up. The telling had worn him out.

But he was not finished talking. She put her arms around his neck. As she started to speak, he put his finger on her lips.

"Let me finish," he said. He was quiet for a long time. Then he turned on his elbow to face her. A tired smile lit up his face.

"I vowed never to let anyone tempt me away from my destined role in life. Here, in this remote outpost of Africa, I knew I was safe. And then you! When I saw you back in Buffalo, I thought I was repeating my life. Falling in love with a beautiful woman. When you wrote that you wanted to come to Simbayo, I was torn. You were beautiful and young enough to be the daughter I've never had, but that wasn't what I felt for you. You were Danger and I knew I had to stay away from you.

"I thought you'd last three months and I'd be safe again. But you've never been what I thought you'd be. Even after I knew you were here to stay, I was afraid you'd take me away from God's work. I thought you'd want to go back to America and have a family and live a normal life. Then I'd think you couldn't possibly love me. I'm too old. And I remembered what Geoff said: 'It's your family that will be sacrificed.' I didn't want to do that to you. You deserve more than that.

"But you didn't play the role I assigned to you. You kept creeping into my work, sharing my dreams."

"I didn't know," she whispered.

"I haven't known how to tell you. When I hold you in my arms, I want to tell you that you've become a part of the dream. I want you to know you help prove God to me. You are my reward and my partner. You were sent to make this life bearable.

"But for years I was afraid you were the temptation to test me. It has not been hard for me to keep myself from you because I've never learned how to share. But oh, how I wished I were different. How I have yearned for you—in all ways." A tear glistened in the corner of his eye.

Liliane leaned down to kiss it away.

She heard him murmur into her neck. "Teach me. I have loved you since the minute I first saw you. I have longed to share my thoughts and hopes with you. I *have* learned to share my work."

"You have shared more than that." She leaned back so that she could look at him.

"Marry me, Lili," he pleaded. "Let us share our lives."

"Oh, Baxter!" She threw her arms around him.

"As soon as I come back," he said, "we'll be married. And we'll have a family, and . . . Oh, Lili, do you know how I've yearned for a child? I thought I was destined never to have one. If it's a son, I'd like to call him Geoffrey. Oh, my dear. My darling!"

What she had heard was "as soon as I come back."

She sat upright. "Come back? Come back from where?"

"I have to go to the cholera outbreak. I'm taking Anoka. We're leaving in the morning."

"In the morning? That's in a few hours!"

"Yes." He sighed.

"Oh, damn you, Baxter. You *do* have so much to learn about sharing! Why didn't you tell me?" She didn't wait for an answer. She knew there was none.

He reached for her, enfolding her in his arms. Her head lay on his shoulder and they breathed in unison.

CHAPTER 16

▼

THEY BURIED BMENO ON A THURSDAY NIGHT. NALDANI LEFT THE island, with her few belongings, the next morning and refused to ever return. Liliane felt the loss of Naldani's unflagging help on Saturdays, but she understood.

Though she really wanted Baxter's approval, she wasn't willing to wait for it. She ordered three of the boys to build Naldani a hut at the edge of the compound. She insisted, against tradition, that it have a window and that the doorway be tall enough to stand in.

Naldani could hardly believe it. "All to myself?" she asked, the luxury incomprehensible to her.

"You'll need space for the baby, too," answered Liliane, delighted with the pleasure her friend evidenced. A far cry from the way she had been living these past few years. Or maybe forever. "After all, Naldani, you are part of Simbayo. You *are* our chief midwife."

Her hand touched her belly when she felt life kicking faintly. Smiling with happiness, she thought she must be the luckiest woman alive.

Everything was perfect. She'd seen the look in Baxter's eyes as he turned around at the edge of the jungle when he left. She'd seen love there. And happiness, too. Rose had hugged Liliane, happy for her and Baxter when she'd announced they were going to wed. Heidi's eyes had even smiled, and she'd said, "At last!" and put her hand on Liliane's arm, squeezing it affectionately. Liliane hugged herself and headed toward the infirmary, humming. She had never been happier in her life. She smiled to herself. Mrs. Baxter Hathaway. Liliane Hathaway. Geoffrey Hathaway. Mr. and Mrs. Baxter Hathaway and son. She was so happy she was afraid she would burst with sheer joy.

She missed Anoka, too. She so often took him for granted that it came as a surprise to realize she missed him. She was used to his taking care of patients during the nights, to his sleeping in the room next to the dispensary. And why isn't he married? All the natives are married. Maybe he's too busy to find a wife.

She dreamed of Anoka that night, dreamed that he stood in ceremonial robes, arms raised high, chanting.

When she awoke in the morning, she knew she'd see him that day. She knew it! That meant Baxter and he were coming home. She and Baxter could begin life together. They'd send for the priest downriver and she'd become Mrs. Baxter Hathaway. Liliane Hathaway. She giggled to herself.

Could a priest marry people who weren't Catholic? Would they have to wait until the Methodist missionary came through? Maybe they'd have to take the *Oregon* all the way down to Coquil-hatville and get married there. That might be nice. Three weeks of laziness on the river. Possibly buy a few trinkets in town. See people. She'd suggest it to Baxter. She wondered what she could possibly wear to get married in. Oh, silly, she told herself. That doesn't matter. You're not back in America.

Could the *Oregon*'s captain marry them? Didn't ship captains do that? She'd have to ask him. He was due any time now.

She glanced out the screen and noticed Naldani standing in the sun, talking to—Anoka.

Oh, she laughed, I was right, and raced out the door.

Anoka and Naldani looked up when they heard the screen door slam and started toward her. Something was wrong, she sensed. It was in the slope of Anoka's shoulders and the look in Naldani's eyes.

"What is it?" she cried. Maybe he'd come back for more medicine. Maybe they needed more help. Maybe . . .

Naldani reached her and put her hands on Liliane's shoulders to stop her headlong dash.

"I knew you were coming home today," Liliane said in a burst.

Something was wrong.

"I dreamed about you last night, Anoka, and . . . Where's the doctor?"

A haggard Anoka stood in front of her, while Naldani's arm went around her shoulders.

"He's still out there, isn't he?" Fear was spreading through her. "He needs help. He—"

Anoka's deep voice interrupted her. "The doctor is dead."

There wasn't a sound. Not the whir of an insect's wings, not the call of a bird, no clatter in the compound, no slight breeze to rustle the leaves, no voices, nothing. There was total, complete, unbearable silence.

The sun rolled itself into one giant ball and thrust itself behind her eyes, the jagged brightness blinding her before it exploded.

Her fists pummeled Anoka's chest. "No, that's not true. That can't be true," she cried. "It can't be!"

Before she knew it, she was crying into his chest. He stood awkwardly. Naldani moved to gather Liliane in her arms.

Rose ran out of the dispensary, hearing the commotion.

Anoka repeated, "The doctor is dead," his quiet voice shaken. Liliane hated him.

She heard Rose let out a high, long moan. She heard deep gasps and sobbing. But all she saw were bright, jagged edges of light.

"What is it?" The urgent questioning of Heidi.

Again, "The doctor is dead."

Anoka. Damn him. She'd get rid of him. She'd tell Baxter about him.

She heard Heidi's solemn voice ask, "How?"

They had started home, Anoka related, over a week ago. Three days ago Anoka had awakened at their campsite, hearing Baxter crying out to him. He jumped up to see a python wound around Baxter, crawling in circles up his body. It had slid down from the overhanging trees and wrapped itself around Baxter while he was asleep and now had him in its clutches so that he could not move. Adrenaline shooting through him, Anoka ran and barehandedly tried to pull the python away from Baxter. The more he pulled, the tighter the snake wound around Baxter. The only knife was in Baxter's hip pocket. Anoka tried to wrestle with the snake as it slithered up Baxter's body, crushing life out of him as it wound itself tightly around him. He saw the fright and the terrible pain in Baxter's eyes. He heard the crunch of bones. As the snake circled Baxter's neck, Anoka saw life leave him. He heard the rattling gasp, and ran.

He ran for the entire first day. And then he slept, he didn't know for how long, but it was dark again when he awoke. He had been walking ever since. No, he had not slept since that one time.

Liliane screamed. She slid to the ground, the yellow sunlight crashing into her eyeballs, a knife stabbing into her brain. She yelled. She howled like a banshee, rending the forest with her anguish.

Arms encircled her, and Rose lay next to her, shaking, wrapping her arms around Liliane's inert figure, sobbing with her, crying her anger and loss.

Only Heidi made no noise. She sat down cross-legged in the dusty earth, staring into space.

"He was the only man," she said, "who ever let me feel important. He was the only man I ever loved."

Her eyes stared into a vacuum.

LILIANE INSISTED ON A FORMAL BURIAL.

She and Anoka, with two natives, walked back into the jungle for Baxter's body. In this climate, it was already well into decomposition, but Liliane would not leave it unburied. He did not look like the Baxter she had known. He had shrunk out of his skin; maggots were already gnawing at him. Ants crawled around his neck.

Liliane sank to the ground, sobbing uncontrollably. She realized they could not carry the disintegrating body back to Simbayo. They would have to bury him here, away from his beloved Simbayo, out here where he would be alone forever, a place she could not glance at every day, a place that meant nothing to either Baxter or her.

Leaning over a Baxter she had never known, smelling the horrid smell of death and decay, she emptied his pockets and gave Anoka the army knife Baxter had always carried, the knife that might have saved him. She placed it in Anoka's hand and saw that he, too, wept for this man who had so long ago tried to reject him. And she realized these two men had come to love each other. So many people had loved Baxter. He had made a difference in so many lives.

Within her, the baby kicked. She thought, He has given this life to me.

Taking a deep breath, she forced a halt to her tears. Standing, she ordered the native bearers to dig a grave for the body. It was not easy. Roots of trees hundreds of years old crisscrossed each other. It was hours before even a shallow grave was hacked out of the jungle's earth.

Why had this happened, she wondered, when we had just begun?

LIFE AT SIMBAYO CAME TO A STANDSTILL. SILENCE HUNG OVER THE jungle like a stormcloud. At the end of the second week, the *Oregon* hove into view.

"I guess," the captain said, standing first on one foot and then the other, "you'll be packin' up to go. Need help, I can get it for you. I can pick you up when I come downriver in 'bout ten days."

Liliane looked up at him, her eyes like empty sockets, devoid of feeling. Pack up? Go where?

She put her hand on her belly; what is to become of us, she silently asked her baby. Go back to America and . . . and what? Yet what other choice was there?

She heard Rose say, "I have nowhere to go."

Liliane looked over at her friend, who sat slumped over, her arms flung over her knees, palms out, her shoulders sagging. Heidi walked over to Rose and put a hand on her shoulder, patting it.

Oh, no, Liliane thought, trying to reject the idea that had filtered into her consciousness. Impossible.

But was it?

She . . . Three women couldn't do that. And what of the baby? She couldn't have a baby alone out here in the jungle.

Why not? She'd planned to, if Baxter were here. They were going to make a home here, be a family. Why couldn't she anyhow?

She must be mad, thinking such things. Three women couldn't cope with life out here alone.

For the first time since she had learned of Baxter's death, life rippled through Liliane. "We have no intention of leaving," she said. "Simbayo will go on."

Heidi and Rose raised their eyes to her. "But," Rose said, "Liliane, I don't know that I can work for someone the mission sends out. I—"

"Nonsense," Liliane said sharply. "We'll run it. We're perfectly capable. Baxter would want Simbayo to continue as it is. We don't want a stranger to take it over."

Heidi waved a hand in the air, whether to dismiss her idea or to encourage her, Liliane couldn't tell. "Women? Women run a hospital?"

Energy soared through Liliane. "Heidi, you've been running the business end for years. There's no reason in the world we can't run it."

Rose's hopeless look irritated Liliane. She became aware that she, herself, was returning to life. To two lives, she amended, as she felt her baby kicking. Liliane walked over and knelt by Rose, urging, "Let's try, Rose. How do we know what we can do until we try? I'm sure we can do it."

She turned to the captain, framed in the doorway, and stood. "We shall be staying."

Baxter had created Simbayo and she would keep it going, as a monument to the man she had loved. Simbayo would not die with him. As long as Simbayo lived, a part of Baxter lived, too, just as part of him lived within her, with the life she felt growing stronger each day.

Heidi's eyes showed feeling for the first time in days. "Yes, Lili, we can do it! Nothing can stop us! You are right." With pride, she turned to the captain. "Is this all the mail?" She indicated the small package in his hand.

"No," he said, "there's much more on the boat, but this is to Miss Liliane and it's marked 'Fragile.'"

"Come, then." Heidi gathered up energy and proceeded him out the door. "We shall get supplies and mail."

With purpose for the first time in nearly two weeks, she started for the dock.

When they were alone, Rose reached out a hand to touch Liliane's arm. In a faint voice, she asked, "Can we really, Liliane? I've been thinking my life was over. I've been mourning for myself as well, thinking I had to return to England. I don't want to leave. I want to stay here. It's the only life I know. The only happiness I've ever known. Dr. Hathaway, and you, and . . . Heidi."

"Don't forget the natives." Liliane was talking to herself as well. "This is our world, Rose. This will keep Baxter alive. I want his baby to be born here."

A faint smile crept across Rose's face. "I've wanted so much to ask. May I be its godmother?"

Liliane threw her arms around the older woman. "Oh, Rose, of course. I'd be so pleased. I know he would be, too."

She picked up the slender package wrapped in brown paper and saw that the postmark was New York. She recognized Marsh's handwriting. She would open it later. Now was not a time for Marsh.

After the *Oregon* had sailed on, Liliane went to Baxter's office to put things in order, to touch the things that he had treasured, to . . . "to live in it," she said aloud. "That's what I'm going to do. I'm going to move over here."

She looked at the medical books lining the shelves of his office and thought, This will be my library. I will read every one of those books.

At dinner that night, the first meal any of them had really eaten in those long days, she asked, "Would you mind if I moved to Baxter's room? If I take over the office?"

Rose's look of compassion settled it. "I think it quite fitting," she said. "I'll do whatever you want me to, Liliane. But you must tell me what you want."

Dear Rose. Afraid to lead but always lending strength.

That night, as she lay in Baxter's bed for the first time without him, Liliane told herself that this was the last time she'd let herself cry. Starting tomorrow, another world would begin. But tonight, she let herself miss what might have been and cried until the pillow was wet with her tears.

If only he hadn't died in such a grisly way. When she thought of his suffering and pain as he died, when she imagined how frightened he had been, when she heard the crunch of his bones, when she saw the maggots burrowing in his body . . .

She awoke before dawn and walked into the office. The microscope tottered on the edge of his worktable. She picked it up lovingly, rubbing its smooth metal. Then she put it down in the center of the table. Absentmindedly she fingered the pencils, the little sharp knife, the petrie dish. They were so—so Baxter. She slumped down in the chair, her hands touching his belongings. She closed the book that lay open there. When her reverie ended, it was no longer Baxter's worktable. Though still filled with the scientific paraphernalia that had belonged to him, it was Liliane's. It was neat and in order.

Oh, she thought, I didn't mean to.

But she had looked at the desk, littered with magazines, papers scattered every which way. Boxes were tossed around the room, forcing her to walk carefully. Without thinking, she automatically began to straighten it up. By breakfast time, though she had not decided where everything would go, she had some sort of organization begun and the room was looking less like a storeroom that had been hit by a hurricane and more like an office.

As she left for breakfast, she glanced around the room. She felt a guilty satisfaction. She would live from now on constantly surrounded by Baxter's possessions. She would teach herself from Baxter's extensive medical library; she would carry on Baxter's work, but she would do it her way.

That she would lie in bed at night yearning for what could have been, remembering the timbre of Baxter's voice, remembering the way he had looked at her when he left that last time, remembering their last night of lovemaking—this was beyond her control.

But she would manage. And so would Rose. And Heidi. This would be their memorial to the man they had all loved. They would keep him alive. She realized that by so doing they would keep themselves alive, too.

That afternoon, before a very brief swim, she moved her belongings to her new quarters. She asked for no help. It was important that she do it herself. She didn't change the bed sheet, for she wanted to sleep where Baxter had lain, she wanted that which had touched his skin to touch hers.

She tossed the still-wrapped package marked "Fragile" on the table next to the bed. And waited to open it until she was nearly asleep that night. It wasn't fragile at all. It was a slender volume of poetry. On the flyleaf, in Marsh's sprawling black handwriting, he had written:

I'm in the Plaza Hotel overlooking Central Park in New York City. It is late, past midnight, and it is like looking *down* at stars, to see all the city's lights. I have been reading this wonderful book of poems by a new poet (new to me, anyhow) and feel I must share them with you. They are strange and wonderful and irreverent about everything except love. And with love he is very reverent. That is why I am going to mark this package "Fragile." If I could write like this e. e. cummings, the poems about love would be yours. He captures what my heart feels for you. I miss you. I miss you every day and every hour and every minute. ILY, Marsh.

The book fell open at a poem that began:

it is so long since my heart has been with yours

shut by our mingling arms through
a darkness where new lights begin and
increase,
since your mind has walked into
my kiss as a stranger . . .

and ended with the couplet:

—after which our separating selves become museums
filled with skilfully stuffed memories

The book lay on her swelling belly as she stared into space. Marsh's book of poetry brought Baxter back to her.

IT WAS ROSE WHO TOOK CARE OF WHAT COULD HAVE BEEN THEIR first potential problem before it even developed.

Liliane no longer stayed in the dining room after dinner to chat idly with Rose and Heidi. She took herself to the office and sat studying the medical texts and journals there. There was so much to learn! Since she found herself falling asleep trying to absorb all of the information, she got in the habit of getting up at five and studying while she was awake and alert. Though she was constantly tired, she realized she could exist quite well on five and a half or six hours of sleep a night.

It was after dinner one evening when Rose said, "I want to ask you something, Lili."

Liliane halted and sat down again, waiting.

"One of the great pleasures here is the way we eat," Rose began.

"That's true." Liliane smiled, wondering where this was leading.

"We do get the little meat we eat from hunters, but all of our wonderful vegetables—succulent, I might say"—and she smiled as she rolled the word on her tongue—"come from Baxter's garden. Close your eyes a minute."

Both Liliane and Heidi did so. "Now try to visualize," Rose continued, "life without tender new carrots, without those little

onions that taste like sugar, without golden sweet potatoes, without those tiny sweet beets, without—"

"Stop," cried Heidi in mock horror, flashing her eyes open.
A sense of humor had begun surfacing in this dour German. "What
do you want?"

"I've always thought," Rose answered, "that I'd like to garden. I guess I was thinking of English tea roses. But I like eating
well enough"—she patted her stomach—"to think I could learn to
garden here. There must be gardening books in the doctor's library. Of course," she apologized, "I don't have his stamina, so I'd
like to recruit some of the native women to help me. Heidi, you
must have records of where he sent for seeds. I'd like to take over
the doctor's gardening. I think it would be quite a nice project for
me." Her eyes shone as she thought of the task ahead.

Liliane got up to hug Rose. "Let's go to the office and see what
books we can find on gardening," she said.

The next major trial also failed to materialize. Again, Rose
came to her aid.

The Methodist missionary came to offer condolences. Liliane
had never really taken to him. He lacked any sense of humor or
warmth, he believed in a God of wrath, and his moral code was
narrow and rigid. She always felt depressed when he visited.

"Certainly you're not staying on?" he asked with disapproval.
"Three women alone in the Congo?"

Liliane forced herself to smile at him. "Do you really think that
something bad will happen to the three of us that one man could
deter?" She would put herself against him any day in a match for
survival.

"It doesn't look right. Three women alone . . ."

"Oh, my dear Mr. Thompson, what do you think we can possibly do that wouldn't be acceptable?"

He didn't answer.

"Are you afraid we'll be raped?"

"Oh, my dear Miss Wentworth!"

"Mrs. Hathaway," she interjected, very aware of the size of her
belly.

"Oh, Mrs. . . . Mrs. Hathaway? I had no idea."

"Yes." She glanced over at Rose. Rose nodded imperceptibly.

"Our only problem is money. But I've written to the mission,
and I'm sure they'll help before long."

But before any response came from the mission board, Liliane began to worry. How long could they hold out? How long could they afford to buy the vital medicine? How long could they continue to order canned milk and flour and coffee? There was close to a thousand dollars in the cigar box where Baxter had kept the money. How long would it last? She began to pore over Heidi's account books as well as the medical texts.

The baby, she calculated, was due in mid to late October. She wished she had someone with whom to share her questions and worries and her joy, too. Naldani seemed to have no questions or worries, and though each of them had delivered untold numbers of babies, Liliane found herself nervous about going through it alone. But she had no qualms about sending Rose and Heidi upriver to the logging camp when malaria broke out at the end of September.

"You just have to stay a week or so," she assured the two nurses, who had never gone out in the jungle before despite all their years at Simbayo. "I can't go in my condition. The baby's not due for another four or five weeks, and even if it comes early, no one's better at delivering babies than Naldani."

With a sense of fear and adventure, the two older nurses set off in the logging camp's motor launch. "If the baby's born while we're away, I'll never forgive myself," said Rose.

Three days later, Liliane woke in the middle of the night in labor. She lay there quietly, regulating her breathing, timing her contractions. It was not yet time to call Naldani. Liliane felt no fright; euphoria and exaltation surged through her. Each spasm sent joy as well as discomfort. By dawn, her water had broken. Why, she wondered, did I not have the sense to get up so my bed wouldn't be wet? Her contractions were now less than two minutes apart.

Any suffering is bearable, she told herself, when you know it's going to be over soon. She slid her feet into her sandals and went to get Naldani. Once, she doubled over, clutching her belly, a pain so sharp she could not stand erect.

Without knocking, she entered Naldani's hut. In the still-dim light she saw Anoka lying on the mat next to Naldani. One arm circled Naldani, whose head lay in the crook of his arm.

Liliane silently backed out of the hut, her surprise tempered with pleasure. She backed away about ten feet before calling out, "Naldani!"

She appeared in a minute, tucking a skirt around her waist; her breasts, pendulous with pregnancy, swayed. She walked in that awkward gait of pregnant women, though more graceful than Liliane at this time.

Liliane explained how frequently her contractions were coming.

"Do you feel like you have a grapefruit sitting in your rectum?" asked Naldani, showing her newfound medical terminology.

"No." Liliane shook her head as they began to walk back to the office.

"When you do, that is the time for the baby."

Two hours later, Liliane gripped the side of her bed, her hands cold and sweaty. Damn, she thought, I didn't know pain could be this bad.

Naldani stood framed between her legs at the foot of the bed. Her eloquent hands reached up to massage Liliane's stomach. As she smiled reassuringly, Liliane saw her wince.

"Is everything all right?" Liliane gasped, her breath now coming in short spurts.

Naldani nodded. "You are fine. The baby is in the right position. Push hard, again. You are having a very easy time, for a white woman."

Liliane laughed in spite of herself. "What do you know about white women having babies?"

Naldani laughed, too. "You are my first, it is true. But I hear they have much harder times."

"Harder? Oh!" She pushed.

"I see the top of the head. Push, push." Liliane felt Naldani's soothing hands as an excruciating pain blackened her world for a minute.

"Shh," she heard Naldani whisper.

I must have screamed, Liliane thought. I didn't hear it, though. Native women don't yell. Dear God, don't let me scream. Let them see I can do it their way. She clenched her teeth as another pain assaulted her.

Naldani made comforting little sounds as though already talking to the baby.

Oh.

Oh.

Oh. Oh. Oh.

Liliane's hands formed hard fists; her eyes closed tightly. I'm creating a new life, she told herself. Of course it takes pain. . . .

Oh.

Oh.

She heard a scream rend the air.

And then a smaller one, more like a gurgle.

She opened her eyes. Naldani held a wet, pink creature by its ankles. Its head was covered with tufts of white hair. Its lusty cry made the native woman grin widely.

She walked around the side of the bed and put the newborn in the cradle of Liliane's arm. "A girl," she said.

Oh, why am I so glad it's a girl? Liliane wondered as she looked down at her new daughter.

"Push," she heard Naldani order.

Oh, yes, the afterbirth. She pushed as her lips touched the crown of blond fuzz.

Naldani busied herself cleaning up. Liliane noticed, though, that she did it very slowly, stopping occasionally, turning her back to Liliane.

"Naldani, look at me!" The woman turned to face her friend. "You're having a baby today, too, aren't you?"

Naldani nodded, her smile broken by her own pain.

Tiredness and joy rippled through Liliane, but she realized she could not yet relax and enjoy newfound motherhood, could not lie in bed long, cuddling her daughter.

"How long, do you think," she asked Naldani, her voice weak from her exertions, "before your time?"

Naldani shrugged her shoulders.

Oh, Liliane almost cried, that's what Baxter always did when he didn't know an answer.

"Maybe tonight," said Naldani, her voice calm. "I want it in my home. I want it there."

"Will you come to get me?" pleaded Liliane. It mattered a great deal that she should do for her friend what had just been done for her.

"I will stay with you until my own time comes," answered her friend, washing the baby with a cool cloth.

The little girl reminded Liliane of a chipmunk. She's not beautiful at all, thought the new mother, as the miracle of creation surged through her. This human being, she thought, gazing with awe at the tiny thing, came out of me. What a marvel. She examined the baby's fingers and toes.

Then she fell asleep. When she awakened, Naldani was holding the baby, rocking back and forth, crooning softly.

The black woman laid the child next to Liliane and said, "I think I must go back to my home. My time has come."

"I will come right over." Liliane's voice was not as weak as she felt. Would she be able to get as far as Naldani's hut? "Put the baby in that box," she said, indicating the makeshift bassinet Heidi had prepared.

She wondered, as she pulled on clothes, what the date was. She held on to the side of the bed as she stood up straight. Her legs did not give out under her, though the walls swirled. She sat down on the bed again and waited a minute. "It's October 1, 1930."

OCTOBER 1, 1930, WAS NOT ONLY THE DATE OF CAROLYN HATHAWAY'S birth, but of Naldani's Petelo, the Bantu equivalent of Peter. The only strange thing about either of the births was that for the first time in memory, a Bantu man attended a woman's birth.

Naldani informed Liliane that Anoka was going to stay and watch her childbirth. They had talked it over and felt free of the superstitions of most Africans, at least in regard to medical matters. How could he learn to be a doctor if he did not participate in this?

Liliane looked at the sweat pouring down his face and thought, How blind I am! Bmeno's not the father of this baby. Anoka is!

PART TWO

▼

1932
TO
1940

CHAPTER 17

▼

AT NIGHT, AFTER CAROLYN WAS TUCKED INTO BED AND LILIANE FOUND herself alone, she felt compelled to study Baxter's numerous books. She knew she desperately needed more medical knowledge to keep Simbayo viable as a medical community. For years she had been existing on less than six hours' sleep a night. There were spells when she felt quite driven and others when she felt over-whelmed with the task, tense and even resentful.

There had been few visitors since Baxter's death over two years ago. Liliane's sense of isolation was compounded by her withdrawal into her studies. Visitors had always been a welcome change, but now they also represented precious time taken from her work.

The strain of responsibility weighed heavily upon her. She thought often of Baxter, of whether he would approve of the way she was continuing Simbayo. She asked herself questions about him that had no answers. How she missed him!

Yet, in spite of an abstract sort of loneliness, Liliane was also aware that she was more content than she had ever dreamed possi-ble. Funny, wasn't it, to find life so fulfilling, when she had been brought up to believe that a woman was only truly alive when she was sharing her life with a man. Here she was in remote Africa, her only companions a child, two middle-aged women who were in love with each other, and two black people whose cultural differ-ences from her own were as wide as the Atlantic Ocean she had crossed.

She smiled to herself. Life certainly was strange. Listening to the even breathing of Carolyn in her makeshift crib, Liliane sighed happily.

She hadn't allowed herself to dwell upon thoughts of Marsh in months, but lately he had begun to creep into her fantasies as she drifted off to sleep. His lopsided smile danced before her eyes. She sometimes dreamed of him.

She had not heard from him for nearly two years, not since his brief letter saying he had read of Baxter's death. He was sorry. It was quite impersonal. She reread the volume of poetry he had sent.

Not that she consciously longed for him. He came into her mind unbidden, projecting himself into her life at the oddest times. He stood in line one morning with the natives, queued up for treatment. Waiting patiently behind a squat woman with an infected shoulder—a leopard had clawed her. He smiled at Liliane, as though to say, "I'll wait for you."

One night as she lay in bed reading, he stepped magically out of the page as she turned it. His bush hat cocked at a jaunty angle, he approached her with his pantherlike lope until he stood beside her bed; in a gravelly voice he claimed, "Next time you're not getting away."

Then mists surrounded him as she drifted off in sleep. But as she dreamed, he took her into the mountains to a place where they could view the ocean. It was cool, lovely, tempting.

She awoke in the dark, startled. Nothing should tempt her from Simbayo!

Liliane disclosed her imaginings to no one, herself half embarrassed by them. Her life was full, but her dreams and fantasies made her aware of an emptiness she could no longer deny—a small, gnawing loneliness.

At night, when all the children were asleep, Naldani and Anoka and Rose and Heidi could lie talking into the night, laughing at shared nothings, making plans and dreaming dreams together. This was the hour when, for the first time in many years, Liliane's loneliness would surface and cast its specter over her. How she longed for someone to share her fears, her dreams—and yes, her body, too. For, as the veil of grief over Baxter's death and the subsequent threats to Simbayo slowly lifted from the forefront of her life, emotional openness and physical desire returned. She was healing.

She recognized the happiness that flowed through her. And she recognized, too, the emptiness. However, much as she had loved him, her newfound sense of responsibility made her realize that she did not, again, want what she'd had with Baxter. She did not want anyone to dominate her.

She wanted to share. Heidi and Rose share, she told herself. Anoka and Naldani share. Yet the possibilities of finding a true partner for a lone twenty-six-year-old white woman in the midst of Africa were nil. The white visitors who came down the Mombayo were not people to whom she wanted to commit any part of herself. And she understood it was only a *part* of herself, now, that she was willing to commit to anyone. There were too many things she wished to accomplish; she couldn't devote her life and all her thoughts to another person.

She was restless. There were no crises. The children were well and happy, yet everything had an edge to it. It was as though her very recognition of the incompleteness of her life was self-fulfilling; she felt her tranquillity threatened.

She had taught Carolyn and Petelo how to swim before they were able to walk. Now that they were at the toddler stage, they were already good swimmers. She and Naldani looked forward to their time together each afternoon, when the four of them swam together in the lagoon, the children full of exuberant play, she and Naldani unreservedly admiring their own children and gossiping about the day's events.

Despite her closeness to Rose and Heidi, it was Naldani from whom Liliane drew her emotional support. Not that the other woman could understand Liliane's dream of expanding Simbayo, but the deep bond that had begun between them so long ago had only grown stronger, tied now by what Liliane laughingly called "our twins."

Carolyn was a study in contrast to Petelo. Her fair hair was more white than blond, and her skin seemed bleached until the Simbayo sun, in its own democratic manner, eventually converted this pallid baby to a toasty tan color. It was not only her pale blond hair but her startling turquoise eyes, so like her mother's, that continued to set her apart from her young playmate. Her eyes were the only visible quality she inherited from Liliane. Liliane had looked often in her hand mirror and at her daughter. She saw little of herself reflected there. Her daughter's lips were thinner than her own, which Marsh had once told her looked ripe for kissing. Carolyn had prominent cheekbones, which Liliane thought were beautiful, giving her a sculptured look. She had no broad forehead, no slanted eyebrows like her mother's. One could tell from birth that she was never destined to have her mother's voluptuousness, but would always look more fragile. She seemed like a porcelain doll, particularly next to the sturdiness of Petelo.

Liliane could not bear for Carolyn to be out of her sight, except at nap time or when she was operating. She had carried her as a baby to the dispensary and wondered why all of the patients in long lines did not exclaim at the beauty of her daughter.

Simbayo had been a matriarchal commune since Baxter's death. As soon as one of the babies cried, it was picked up, if not by one of the mothers, then by Rose or Heidi. Carolyn and Petelo never knew loneliness or a lack of love. Liliane read to them and they were mesmerized by the sounds even before they had any understanding of the content. First, she read from adult books. She sent away for children's books, which—when they arrived— the three nurses enjoyed more than the children did at that early age. They all fell in love with the new series of Winnie the Pooh books. It brought England back to Rose, and childhood revisited them all.

Liliane did leave Carolyn in Heidi's and Rose's charge on Saturdays, for she insisted on continuing work on the leper island. She constantly missed Naldani's help on the island, but Anoka never missed a Saturday. It was as though he had volunteered to be her surrogate. After Petelo was born, Anoka and Naldani married themselves to each other. Whenever Naldani passed Anoka, he smiled at her. He no longer tried to relate to her in the impersonal way that the other native men treated their wives. To them, wives were property. But Anoka admired and liked Naldani; together they wanted to help save their people. They wanted to jump into the twentieth century, and Liliane was their passport.

On the leper island, most of the older patients, who had been there when she arrived over five years before, were dead by now, and the new patients were accustomed to their shelters and ready to follow the new life-style and Liliane's rules for cleanliness. Her dream was to build a leprosarium, a building where medicine and love would be dispensed, where hope would be centered, where both physical and emotional comfort would be available. That took money and staff, though, and neither was in sight. But neither was the island recognizable as the same one she had first seen. Though doomed, the lepers no longer despaired to the degree of hopelessness they had when Liliane first met them. At her instigation, they had cleared a space and were growing their own vegetables. Liliane talked to them in their own language and urged them to take care of themselves and each other. She swore that some even appeared improved, but doubted that was possible, though it was obvious a few were in remission. The quality, if not the length, of life had improved considerably.

But she was not thinking of these things as she and the children played in her pool. She had trained herself to let no thought of responsibility interrupt her afternoon idyll. Even the *Oregon*'s whistle could not lure her today. Rose and Heidi could take care of any deliveries; the boat would still be in dock by the time they'd finished cavorting in the water. She was again telling Naldani of her dream, the one she still harbored of setting up medical outposts and training the Congolese to sanitation. She thought many diseases could be prevented. She knew, though, that putting shoes on Africans was impractical. But she could educate them: explain to them the demons of sewage; suggest they use care about where they stepped; even better, urge them to use restricted areas for waste. That simple practice alone would eradicate a common but sometimes fatal problem—jiggers that clung to the toes and worked their way into the bloodstream, carrying with them an infectious host with myriad bacterial possibilities. So many of Africa's dreadful diseases could be wiped out with sanitation and education.

It was good to have such a dream. How to accomplish it, she had only vague ideas, but that did not dissuade her from the hope of its eventual reality.

Naldani had heard it many times over the years. She and Liliane swam in tandem, with long, slow strokes across the lagoon, in water so clear they could see the sandy bottom. Petelo and Carolyn ran in and out of the water, screeching and splashing each other, filled with their own shared laughter.

Suddenly, Naldani pointed. Liliane looked beyond the palm trees toward the compound. With the sun at his back, one could not see the man's face, but the graceful lope, the slant of the shoulders, the Australian bush hat . . .

"Marsh!" exclaimed Liliane with a great intake of breath. She stopped swimming and stood, the water above her waist. Without thinking, as though by conditioned reflex, she rushed toward shore, running when no longer impeded by the water. Marsh had stopped, watching her. For swimming, she had adopted the native *pareau,* a cotton sarong-type clothing that now clung wetly to her.

Sand kicked up as she ran toward him; if he had wondered at his reception, there was no longer doubt. He began to run toward her. They stopped only when their arms wound around each other and she cried, "Oh, Marsh."

"Darling," he whispered as his lips met hers.

When they came apart, she smiled, looking at him. He was tanner than she remembered and not as thin. His tall frame had filled out, his features had become more rugged, though his cheekbones were still prominent. A lock of dark hair fell over his forehead.

He reached out and took her hand, his eyes never leaving hers.

She felt a heavy weight begin to slip from her shoulders. Marsh had reached out to her.

She reached up to kiss him again. Oh, no one in the world kissed like Marsh did. His arms around her felt good. His lips touching hers awakened long-dormant desires.

"I didn't even know if you'd still be here. You might have been back in Buffalo by now. I haven't heard from you since I was here last." He spoke softly into her ear, still holding her tightly, but his eyes focused on the children.

Liliane noticed his startled look. Petelo and Carolyn stood by the water's edge, staring at them. Liliane turned and beckoned for the children to come. Smiling at Marsh, she said, "This is Carolyn." Carolyn stared at him as her thin fingers grabbed at her mother's skirt.

"Carolyn?" Marsh was silent for a minute. Then, "Yours?"

Liliane smiled with pride.

"I had no idea." A veil fell over his eyes. "So you finally married your doctor."

Liliane looked straight at him. "I'm Liliane Hathaway."

Naldani greeted Marsh in the shy way she had with white people she didn't know well. Taking Petelo's hand, she said, "It's time for his nap."

Still looking at Carolyn, Marsh said, "I could use a swim."

"Let me put Caro down for her nap, too," Liliane said, unwilling to leave him. "And I'll be right back."

Carolyn had her finger in her mouth, staring suspiciously at this stranger who had won her mother's affection. Liliane scooped her up and carried her back to their room. For the first time, she neither sang nor read Carolyn to sleep, but ran back to her pool. Marsh was swimming across it.

I wonder, thought Liliane, if he's really that beautiful or if I'm just glad to see him. She sat on the sand and watched him, enjoying the easy grace with which he swam. He came to her and, sitting down, began to claw in the sand. A soft breeze sprang up. "I've a mad urge," he said to explain his digging.

He knelt down by the water's edge and, grabbing a handful of sand, scooped out the earth beneath it. Water seeped quickly into the hole, and he began building a sand castle.

Liliane observed him curiously.

He looked up at her, the crow's-feet at the side of his eyes crinkling. With surprise, she realized his eyes seldom smiled despite his great warmth.

"Marshall Compson, you know what? I like you. I really really like you."

He pulled her down to join him in the sand. She laughed as she hadn't in many months.

They laughed out loud and grinned at each other as they proceeded with the castle. It took glorious shape. Marsh was a far more meticulous builder than was Liliane. Each time a beautiful portion was accomplished, they looked at each other with shared excitement and approval. Their eyes sparkled with fun.

When it was nearly finished, Marsh said in somber tones, "You know, this is all going to disappear by tomorrow."

Liliane nodded acknowledgment, but she wasn't sad. Her pleasure lay in being with him.

When they had finished, Marsh sat back, examining their effort with pride.

"Now, that," he said smugly, "is a castle worth calling a castle."

"You're right." Liliane stretched. "Oh, Marsh, I haven't done that since I was a child. What fun."

He sat cross-legged, in the lotus position, his hands resting casually on his knees.

"I feel sorry for so much of the world," he exclaimed, looking with fond satisfaction at the result of their efforts.

"Why?"

"They don't know how to enjoy themselves. There's the majority who are asses. Jerks. Care too much what the neighbors think and try to behave so no one can criticize. They don't know how to be themselves or to act with spontaneity. They simply exist, never daring, never risking, never playing."

"And," quizzed Liliane, "the others?"

"Not any better. Haven't grown up. Behave irresponsibly. Still live for class reunions. Think practical jokes are the ultimate in life. Always need to be amused by some external force."

Liliane had never heard him so cynical.

"You know, I think there are too many childish adults in this world," he intoned. "But, on the other hand"—and he pointed at their castle—"I have no use for adults with none of the child in them."

Liliane leaned over to wash the sand off her hands.

"Do you know the difference?" he asked.

"Of course. And you're one of the latter. You live as you feel. One of the things I like most about you is your charm. I read someplace that all charming people have a bit of the innocent child about them."

Even his brown eyes laughed this time. "Oh, am I so charming, then?"

"I'd have thought you'd be tired of hearing of your charm and charisma."

"Never!" His voice sounded delighted. "Especially from you." He reached out a toe and touched her foot. "Now, tell me. Why do you look as though the weight of the world is on your shoulders?"

"I suppose because it is," she answered. Marsh always did this to her. He hadn't been here two hours and already he was inside her heart, her thoughts. "Marsh, there are so many things I'm responsible for and don't know answers to. But can't they wait? Let me enjoy you first. Let me forget my responsibilities for a while."

At dinner Marsh regaled his hostesses with stories of his latest adventures. He told the delighted nurses that this time he had not spent nearly as long getting to Simbayo. "The Mombayo trip still took ten days—I didn't push them as I did that Christmas," he said, his eyes sparkling. "But I flew into Coquilhatville. That saved me nearly a month. I flew from Nairobi."

"What were you doing in British East Africa?" asked Rose.

"Trying to get here." He smiled in reply. "I had to cover George Eastman's trip into the back country, to Lake Paradise. He and the *National Geographic* arranged for me to go with him into elephant country. While there I became fascinated with the Masai. When we were through there, I had to prove to myself I could do anything the Masai do." Marsh was always able to poke fun at himself. "So I talked them into taking me on a lion hunt. Mr. Eastman was more intelligent. He stayed in the camp with the Johnsons. I, on the other hand, fell out of a tree trying to see a herd of elephants. But not until after I'd shot my lion and been inducted into the Masai tribe." There was pride in his voice.

"You're a Masai now?" asked Liliane, her eyes shining. What an exciting man Marsh was.

"Well, yes, but there was something even more difficult for me than shooting the lion." His eyes took on a faraway look. He was silent for a moment. "I found I didn't like it, shooting the lion. After it was dead I looked at it. Its mane was like a halo surrounding the majestic cat. I felt like a criminal. To appease my ego, I had killed this animal that I really only loved as a living thing. I looked at it, lying there dead, and knew that I had also killed a part of myself." His voice was distant, back in the high country with his memory. "To the Masai, however, I had proven my manhood. They insisted I partake in the celebratory feast. They had immediately bled the lion. All who had participated in the hunt drank of the warm blood, to absorb the lion's power. As the one who had shot him, I had the honor of the first drink."

"Ugh." Liliane shivered.

Rose made an indecipherible gagging sound.

"Yes, it took some intestinal fortitude," admitted Marsh. Then more seriously, "To drink his blood was only a different way of facing that lion. In English, right out loud before the whole tribe, I asked of the lion's power forgiveness for my senseless killing. Then I drank deeply, for I wanted to be truly connected to this regal beast."

There followed a long, respectful pause. Finally, Heidi spoke. "So what about your arm?" she asked, wanting Marsh to continue his storytelling, but indicating the way he gingerly favored his left arm.

"A herd of elephants was sighted on the horizon and I sought a panoramic view. I climbed up a tree. And broke my arm coming down sooner than I expected! For a long time I suspected it was retribution for killing that lion. The injury is why I wasn't here sooner."

One of Marsh's charms, thought Liliane, was that he was unafraid to admit weakness or error, never afraid to admit he wasn't what others thought he should be. His fear never stopped him from trying. These were qualities they had in common.

After dinner Marsh followed her and Carolyn to their rooms and waited while she put Carolyn to bed.

"Is she too young for a bedtime story?" he asked.

"Oh, no," answered Liliane, kneeling beside the crib. "I've been reading to the children for a long time."

"I'm a storyteller without equal," he volunteered, one eyebrow cocked.

"May I listen, too?" She smiled.

He pulled a chair next to the crib and sat next to Carolyn, who stared at him with her blue-green eyes, wondering whether or not to like him.

By the time he had finished his story, he had begun to win Carolyn over. She slept, her tiny fist clutched around Marsh's thumb.

Marsh, Liliane thought, it is so good to be with you again.

They sat up late, talking, pulling chairs from the office out into the night, listening to the muffled sounds the jungle sent forth. She told him of her fears about money, about help. She thought the dreams could wait until later.

"How long are you staying this time?" she asked.

He reached out and took her hand. A silver wedge of moon appeared above the tall trees; a puff of cloud raced across it and disappeared. "That depends on you," he answered.

She pulled his hand to her mouth and kissed it. "A while would be nice," she said softly.

"A while it will be." He squeezed her hand.

They sat in silence, listening to the frogs. "Tell me about it," he urged.

She was surprised to find no pain in the telling. But then, over two years had elapsed since Baxter's death. She told him of Carolyn and Petelo sharing birthdays, of how difficult it had been at first, three nurses alone to carry on in spite of their grief.

"I'm sorry," Marsh whispered. "I had no way of knowing." Their eyes met.

After a pause he added, "Nights are seldom this silent." But for Liliane there was nothing silent about it. Her heart pounded in her ears with the force of a hundred native jungle drums.

His hand touched her leg, his fingers pressing gently. He stood and pulled her to him. "I've waited so long for you, Lili. I may never leave." His mouth crushed hers, the heat from his body enveloped her, and she felt his hands over her body, giving life to desire, before he picked her up and carried her to the bed, where they made love next to Carolyn's even breathing.

WHEN LILIANE AWOKE IN THE MORNING, CAROLYN WAS NOT IN HER crib. Marsh leaned in the doorway to the office, that cockeyed grin covering his face, a cup of coffee in one hand. He walked over to her.

"I could watch you sleep forever," he said, kissing her lightly on the nose. "But I'm glad you're awake. Carolyn and I have been out walking, getting to know each other."

She sipped from his cup. "You never used to be a morning person," she remembered.

"Oh, much about me has changed," he said, his eyes warm with affection. "I hope you'll be delighted to discover."

"But I liked the old Marsh." She plopped back on the pillow.

"Ah, how sad to never grow," he teased. "Now, get up. I am brimming with ideas that need sharing."

Happiness washed over her and made her wonder why, in her dreams, she had equated Marsh with a dangerous temptation that threatened her life at Simbayo. Ah, but dreams can be crazy. Marsh was going to stay for a while, and he made her feel good. Good? Wonderful! The feel of last night lingered: his tongue touching her in places she had forgotten existed, his kisses on her neck, the way his lips parted hers, his words of endearment whispered in her ears. She would rather have reached out her arms and said, "Come back to bed," but knew that wasn't possible. So she arose. There was medical work to be done.

He watched her and Rose attend to the line of patients all morning. At noon he regaled the children, as well as the women, with unlikely stories he fabricated on the spot. After lunch each child took a turn lying on his back, clutching him around the neck, as he swam across the lagoon. Their squeals of delight rewarded him. He helped put Carolyn down for her nap and promised to read to her after dinner.

Then he followed Liliane into her office.

"What's Carolyn's birthdate?" he asked casually.

"October first," Liliane answered, riffling through some papers that she really didn't want to cope with now. "Not quite time for a birthday party, if that's what you're thinking."

"It's not what I'm thinking," he said seriously, sitting in a chair and facing her. "Sit down and talk to me."

Liliane grew suddenly tense.

"Has it not dawned on you that Carolyn could be my daughter?" Marsh queried.

Liliane stared at him. She did not sit down.

"No." She was defensive. "I know the very night she was conceived. It was the last night before Baxt . left."

He leaned toward her, his eyes intense. "Think, Lili," he commanded, "you were with me the week after Christmas."

Oh, she thought, averting her gaze, the idea's been there. I just haven't let myself think it. I wanted Baxter to have a memorial. I wanted proof of Baxter's love. I wanted the world to think I'm Mrs. Baxter Hathaway . . . it gives me more credibility here. And finally: I don't want to think I'm the kind of woman who doesn't know who the father of her baby is.

Her eyes were cold when she turned to answer him. "It is a possibility. But I don't think so."

He reached for her hand, pulling her, bringing her close to him. "Lili, of course it's a possibility. I've had an eerie feeling since I first saw her. And when I woke up this morning and lay looking at her, asleep, I thought how much she looks like my mother. And it hit me!"

Liliane's eyes misted. "Marsh . . ."

He stood beside her, putting his arms around her. "It's all right, Lili. All I ask for is the possibility that I could be—can be her father. Lili, it's unimportant to me if the world thinks Baxter is her father. I *could* be. I've looked at her all day and, Lili, deep inside me, I know Carolyn is mine! Ours." His eyes shone. "Oh, Lili. Would it be such a tragedy for me to be her father?"

It's wishful thinking, she thought. But, in truth, she finally admitted to herself, she didn't know who Carolyn's father was. She had buried that fact so deeply that she had never allowed herself to think it. Yet as soon as Marsh suggested it, she knew it might be the truth.

"I don't have to tell anyone," he reassured her, "not even Carolyn. It's immaterial to me what others think. But I know here"—he tapped his shirt-covered chest where his heart was—"and that's what's important."

He took Liliane's chin in his hands and kissed her eyes, her cheeks, her nose. "She's the tie that binds," he suggested. "She is what will make us always a part of each other."

CHAPTER 18

▼

"I'VE BEEN THINKING," MARSH SAID AT DINNER. "HOW ABOUT IF I settle in?"

"How lovely," chirped Rose. "A man comes in so handy."

Marsh smiled; he enjoyed her teasing. He knew that Rose was fond of him. He looked for Liliane's reaction.

Why had he chosen dinnertime to make such an announcement instead of telling her in private? Was he afraid she'd reject the idea? Actually, the thought of his staying warmed her. It would be wonderful to have Marsh around. He always made her happier.

And if he wanted to be Caro's father, well, let him. Maybe, just maybe, he *was* her father.

"I have decided to solve your financial woes," he announced. Heidi and Liliane always worried about money.

"How?" she asked. She never knew whether to take Marsh seriously.

"I'm going to write about you. Not my usual newspaper stuff, but a long magazine article. There won't be a dry eye in the place, and they'll rush to put their money in envelopes to send to Simbayo. You'll be solvent for years. We'll circumvent that old mission of yours!"

Several times a year the mission sent boxes of discarded clothes: woolen coats, high-heeled shoes, warm sweaters, even a bowler hat once. Threadbare blankets, surprisingly, were useful, as were cans of food, though they were seldom what Heidi would have liked. Medical supplies were ordered directly, rather than through the mission, so they did receive what they ordered, but there was a limit to how much they could order. The mission gave them a monthly quota. Shortages were a part of the way of life in Simbayo.

"Oh, Marsh." Liliane realized he *could* do it. "Why have I never thought of that?"

"Because," he suggested, "you don't see yourself as a heroine. I'm going to make you one. An international heroine." He glanced at Heidi and Rose. "Heroines."

Heidi harrumphed, but Rose's eyes shone. "A heroine, how nice. I think I could fancy that rather well."

They all laughed.

MARSH HAD MOVED HIS BELONGINGS INTO HIS OLD ROOM IN THE dormitory. He would stay indefinitely.

"You know what I think I'll do?" he said one evening as he and Liliane sat in her office. "That little hill right beyond the river's bend is just waiting to be built on. I think I'll build me a house there."

"A house?" Liliane didn't mask her surprise.

"Yes," he answered. "A house."

She smiled. Marsh made her happy.

"Do you think," he asked, "that some of the men might help me build a house when I get it designed?"

"Designed? That sounds pretty fancy."

"I know what I want," he said. "Basically simple, but to meet my needs."

"Ask Anoka. He'll find some help."

"I'd like to pay them for their labor. What would be right?"

"Ask Anoka about that, too. He seems to know every-thing."

By afternoon, Marsh had his labor force. He told Liliane she couldn't come to see the house until it was finished, though he invited Rose to join him in overseeing the work and he took the children with him mornings. Hammering and the drone of a saw cut through the lazy afternoons.

Six weeks later, when the house was finished, he and Rose took off into the jungle one morning, warning everyone they would be gone all day. Rose was as excited as a child at Christmas, bursting with the importance of secrets and enjoying every moment of being part of the conspiracy.

They returned from the forest covered with dirt, lugging fat, bulging burlap sacks. They had collected all manner of flora with which to surround the new house. Rose spent the next week, in her free time, helping Marsh with his landscaping. Liliane thought she had never seen Rose so happy. Her eyes shone and her cheeks had a constant flush. How wonderful it is to feel important, thought Liliane.

When the house was ready, Marsh asked the cook to bake a cake. Though the only candles were large ones, he planted one in the center and invited them all to his housewarming. Liliane and Carolyn picked some tiny orchids at the edge of the jungle and put them in a jar. Carolyn carried them in her pudgy hands as they walked along the river.

It was charming. He had chosen a hillock, so that from the long verandah one could watch a flock of long-legged storks stand-ing in a shallow eddy on the far shore. There was privacy because the compound was hidden by the river's bend, and toward the left there was the long expanse of river. Rose and Marsh had already tried to train the purple bougainvillea to climb up the porch railing and had it tied to the roof, hoping it would spread over that. Around the porch were also planted cape jasmine, gardenia, honeysuckle, and hibiscus. Though a thatched roof overhung the verandah, large bokungu trees shaded the house without obstruct-ing the view. It was the loveliest thing Liliane had seen since coming to the Congo.

"Pretty, pretty," voiced Carolyn, her eyes wide with delight.

Marsh stood on the porch, welcoming his guests, his eyes alive with pleasure.

He ushered them inside. There were three rooms, unheard of for this part of the world: first, there was what Marsh said would be "my living room, work area." It now held only his typewriter on a handmade table. There were two windows on one side and an immense one overlooking the porch, with a view of the river. It was a light, airy room that Liliane envied. Behind it was a small room, that, he announced to one and all, was Carolyn's. "I'm hoping she'll come stay overnight with me now and then."

Her long, narrow eyes grew as large and as round as they could. "What sleep on?" she asked, peering into the empty room.

"We'll have to do something about that," Marsh assured her.

"What about me?" Petelo asked.

"You can come, too," Marsh said. He turned to Petelo, the unasked question in the little boy's eyes. "What I really meant is that this is the children's room. I shall find a flag, a red flag, and when it is on the porch, you can come visit anytime."

"Will you tell stories?" asked Petelo, needing a reason for a visit.

Marsh's popularity at storytelling was unequaled.

"The bedroom." Marsh indicated the large room next to the children's room. It also overlooked the verandah and the river. His eyes met Liliane's. She read his mind and thought to herself, "Our" bedroom.

Everyone agreed it was lovely. Marsh lit the candle on the cake.

"IF THIS GODDAMN HUMIDITY DOESN'T DO ME IN," HE SAID TO LILIANE later that night, "I think you've got me on your hands. I have some plans."

They were sitting on his verandah, listening to the river's rush. The stars appeared low enough to touch. Liliane stretched up, pretending to grab one, and Marsh caught her hand, bringing her fingers to his lips.

"I feel so alive. Why am I not as tired now that you're here?" she wondered aloud.

"Among other things"—even in the dark she sensed the wickedness of his grin—"I inject energy into you." He leaned over and kissed her neck.

She put a hand on his knee, walking her fingers up his thigh.

"Careful," he murmured, "unless you want to be flat on your back on a hard wood floor."

Her fingers continued up his leg. He unbuttoned her blouse.

"Even in the dark, I can tell"—his voice was low—"you have the most beautiful breasts in the world."

"In the world?" She laughed, nibbling his ear, running her tongue along it, letting him pull her blouse off. What a wonderful feeling, she thought as she felt his mouth on her breast.

It was the last thought she had for an hour.

Later they lay, arms entwined, listening to the night sounds. A sigh of contentment escaped Liliane.

Marsh's arm tightened around her. "You know what I really want to do?" he asked. "But I've been afraid to try?"

"Tell me," she murmured into his chest.

"Perhaps I came here with a twofold purpose," he admitted.

"Not just me?" she said with mock disappointment.

"Yes, just you. But thinking I could also find the courage and the solitude to do what I think I must do."

She was silent, waiting for him to continue. "I want to write a novel. I want the courage to tell my newspaper that the article about you, which they *must* run in the Sunday magazine section, will be my last. I want to stay here, away from the pressures of life. . . ."

Liliane laughed to herself. This, she thought, was where the pressures of life were!

". . . and have no deadlines or demands on my time or expectations of high adventure, and concentrate and write a book. I don't just mean an ordinary book. I want to write a great book."

"Of course. You want to ask the great universal questions that have no answers and still have a best-seller."

He laughed and his hand tickled her arm. "Not quite. I'd like to make enough money so that I can spend the rest of my life writing. I think I've seen enough and heard enough and done enough that maybe at last I'm ready. I've always known that was what I wanted to do. I've known since I was nine years old that I wanted to be a writer."

"The idea frightens you," suggested Liliane, raising her head to try to look into his eyes. It was too dark.

"The idea," he said, "scares the hell out of me."

"You sound as if you have to do it anyway."

His lips brushed her forehead. "I want to be alone and away from *having* to do things, and I want to be with you. It looks like both can be accomplished here."

"Oh, Marsh." She raised herself on her elbow and kissed him. "It's a perfectly lovely idea."

"Why don't we get married?" he suggested.

She became immediately apprehensive. Married? Then when he left, would she have to go also? She would be trapped; she couldn't do what she wanted with her life. With Baxter it had been different. They both wanted the same thing; they wanted Simbayo. Marsh would want to leave someday. Marsh would get tired of the evenness of life at Simbayo. He would want city lights and social gaiety, friends and comfort, and he would not be content to live a lifetime in Simbayo. And this was where she *had* to spend her life.

"Marsh," she said, her voice soft, tinged with sadness. "We each *have* to do different things with our lives. And they don't always mix. Can't we find happiness in those times when our lives do mesh? Don't ask me to give up myself."

"Marriage isn't giving up yourself. It's adding another dimension."

"I can't give up Simbayo. I'm not ready, and don't think I ever will be, to live in England or to trek around the world. I am not willing to be just your wife and not do what I need to do with my own life. Here."

He was silent for a long while.

"I love you, Liliane. If you won't marry me, will you come live with me part of the time, will you share my house? Will you spend nights with me over here? And what about Carolyn? I want to be a father to her."

Liliane thought he would not want to be a father consistently. She could not imagine his settling down, performing the routine acts that made up day-to-day living. She thought he would do it only until it lost its novelty.

"I think people can stand all the love they can get. Be a father to Carolyn. Maybe you are her father, Marsh. I have no way of knowing. Love her in whatever way you can. Let's be happy that our lives are together right now."

"Goddamn it, Lili"—his laugh had a brittle edge to it—"I think you're always going to win. I don't think you're ever going to be mine."

"I am me, Marsh, and I'll share whatever of me I can with you.

Sometimes when I'm with you I want to share every bit of me, every thought, every dream, every action . . ." She sat up. "I'm happy you're here. Really I am. And I'm happy you feel as you do about Carolyn. I'm happy you've built this house and are going to stay and write. I'm happier than I can ever remember being. Let that be enough for now. You give me things I've never known. I do love you. But I love myself, too."

"Did I hear the word *love* spoken?" He made no attempt to hide his eagerness.

She laughed. "Oh, Marsh, of course." She tickled his belly button so that his laughter joined hers.

"Well, I have a few things to do before I settle down to writing."

HE WAS GONE FOR MOST OF THE NEXT DAY. HE APPEARED LATE IN THE afternoon, sweating and tired. He reacted poorly to the humidity of this part of the world. Though enervated by the activity of the day, he rallied his energies and announced at dinner, "About a quarter of a mile upriver there's a clearing that was used apparently to grow maize. The jungle is reclaiming it, but I think I'm going to get some of the boys to clear it out."

"Whatever for?" asked Rose, ready to approve anything that Marsh might suggest.

"Since I've built a house and put down some sort of roots, I don't feel too comfortable about leaving my plane in Coquilhatville."

"Oh." Liliane's eyes brightened. "I didn't know it was *your* plane."

"Well, it is." Marsh grinned. "I'd like to fly it down here. If I get that field cleared, it could serve as a landing strip."

"Just think," said Rose, laughing, "our own airport."

It took three weeks of backbreaking labor to make the field smooth enough for Marsh's purpose. Then he announced to Liliane, "I'm going to take the *Oregon* on its next trip downriver. I'll go to Coquilhatville and get the plane. And now that I have a house, there are a few necessities—or maybe they're luxuries—that I want. How about it? You haven't been away from here for almost six years. Wanna come?"

What fun! A change *would* be nice. For just a short time it would be wonderful to be carefree, to have no responsibilities.

"I'll buy you a new dress," offered Marsh. "Several, in fact. I bet you haven't had a new dress in all these years."

"It's true, I haven't," she said. "Does it show?"

He nodded his head, grinning. "My darling, if you looked like everyone else, maybe I wouldn't find you so irresistible."

"Then don't buy me a new dress." She sighed as he bent over to kiss her neck. "But I would love that. Yes, let's see if everyone thinks Simbayo can run without me for . . . for how long?"

"It takes about ten days to get downriver to town. It's about three hundred miles as the crow flies, but the river winds. The boat stops at every place. It would be fun to have several days . . ."

"In civilization?" volunteered Liliane.

Marsh couldn't help laughing at that. "This is what is known as the Compson interpretation of Einstein's theory of relativity. Coquilhatville may be civilization to you, but to the western world it's a backwater eddy."

"That may be, but I stayed in the hotel on my way here. And there was a European restaurant. And shops."

"Oh, my poor Lili." He reached out a hand to stroke her cheek. "Not a shop for these many years. Tell you what. We'll go into every one and I'll buy you whatever you want."

"What if I want lots and lots?"

"I shall, my darling, buy you whatever will make your heart content. You forget, I'm a relatively rich man."

"Is that Einstein's 'relatively'?"

"Approximately."

"Does your paper know where you are?"

"Approximately."

"Don't they wonder?"

"That's part of my excitement to them. They'll love me so much for the article I envision writing about you, telling the world how beautiful you are, and what wonderful breasts you have, and what it's like to kiss the back of your knee, and . . ."

"Come on." She giggled. "Let's go see if I can get leave and have a real vacation. Would you be disappointed if we left Carolyn here?"

"No," he answered. "We'll be back in two weeks, give or take a couple of days. I think you need relief from *all* responsibilities."

Anoka, Rose, and Heidi all encouraged her to take a vacation.

Rose had completely accepted Marsh as a romantic interest in Liliane's life. She had, in fact, told her that she knew Marsh gave her more than Baxter was able to. Heidi liked Marsh, too, but no one could replace Baxter in her life. She wondered how this carefree, jubilant spirit who came and left at will could capture Liliane's heart after she'd known Baxter.

The *Oregon* was due within the week, though they never knew exactly when. Liliane packed her few belongings so that she would be ready when the boat appeared.

"I feel like a child," she said. "I'm so excited at the thought of a trip. And to think I'm going to fly back in a plane."

But on Thursday night Carolyn developed a high fever, her throat was red with white blotches, and she cried all night. Whether it was merely a sore throat or the precursor of something more dreaded, there was no time to decide before the whistle of the *Oregon* was heard.

With pleading eyes, Liliane looked across the sick child at Marsh.

"I can't go," she said, her voice breaking. It would be another month before the boat would be going downriver again. She knew Marsh couldn't wait that long.

Disappointment flooded his eyes, but he reached across Carolyn's crib to put his hand on Liliane's. "I know." He didn't urge her. They looked at the now sleeping child, covered with perspiration, her skin flushed with fever. They listened to her erratic breathing.

Then Marsh strode out of the room.

An hour later he returned. "I hope you don't mind if I take Anoka. It's about time he saw a big town. Sees what's out in the great beyond. I asked him and he's so excited he can't talk."

So Marsh and Anoka sailed away from Simbayo, while the women stood on the dock and waved to them. Marsh stood still, leaning on the rail. But Anoka's hand jerked back and forth in rapid waves of excitement.

Liliane sensed that Marsh was not only going for his plane. He needed to get away from Simbayo. He could take it for just so long. Next time he left it would be for a longer time, and a colder clime, far from the heat and humidity that enervated him. Longer than the two years of last time?

She watched Anoka's hand swing like a metronome as the *Oregon* hove out of sight.

CHAPTER 19

▼

"I'VE BEEN SO GODDAMNED SICK I'D LIKE TO DIE," JACK RASPED.

He was so pale he looked bloodless.

He and the *Sal* appeared two days after Marsh's and Anoka's departure.

"Now, don't put me in that hospital of yours," he growled. "If you don't mind, I'll just lie down in *my* room." The very word *hospital* sent him into paroxysms of fright.

"Come on," he begged. "I ain't dying. I just feel lousy enough to."

Liliane looked at Heidi. "Your blood count," she said to Jack, "is so low we're going to have to give you a transfusion."

"Whata you mean 'a transfusion'?" His eyes darted with fear. "You talking blood?"

She and Heidi smiled at each other, seeking reassurance. They were concerned by Jack's condition.

Heidi stepped closer to Jack and put a comforting hand on his arm. "Yes, Jack. But we've done many of them. It's nothing to worry about."

"We have to find out what your blood type is and then find someone to match."

"Whata you mean 'match'? I don't want blood from no one but you two or Rose."

"It depends on matching types of blood. It would be very dangerous," Liliane explained, "if a different blood type were transfused into yours. But don't be upset. There are always people around who are willing to give blood in return for favors. Or grateful patients who nervously repay us in this way." She laughed. "One thing we haven't run out of yet is blood." She wrapped a tourniquet around his upper arm. "I'm going to take some blood and study it under the microscope and then we'll find someone with your blood type."

"Can't you tell what I have without all this folderol?"

"We already know what you have. You have a bleeding ulcer."

"A . . . How the hell did that happen?"

"Drinking," mouthed Heidi with disapproval.

"Jesus!" he cried as Liliane stuck a needle in his arm. He began to tremble violently. They could hear his teeth chatter.

Heidi tried to reassure him. "I shake like that when I'm enclosed in a small space. Don't be embarrassed."

"Who's embarrassed?" He made a weak attempt at a smile. Then he turned his head and, seeing his blood fill the syringe, blanched.

"You're not going to bleed me!" he shouted as Liliane left the room. He turned to Heidi. "I don't want no one else's blood in me."

Too bad, thought Liliane, when she typed the blood. Anoka has this blood type, but he's not here. We'll have to find someone else. Wouldn't it be wonderful to find a way to preserve blood of different types and have it already saved, ready to transfuse?

She set about trying to find the same blood type. In the meantime, Jack's condition deteriorated. He was restless and frightened. He broke out in clammy sweats, and it was obvious he had lost a great deal of weight. His eyes were sunken and hollow. He vomited blood and it showed, too, in his black diarrhetic stools. Heidi tried to explain the reason for the transfusion.

"It won't cure you," she told him. "It will just keep you alive until we *can* cure you. We'll feed blood into you, but it will go right through you until the ulcer stops bleeding. And you have to help with that."

"How?" he asked through chattering teeth.

"Give up drinking. Give up smoking."

"Give up living?"

"That *is* the choice." Heidi was severe.

He shivered constantly, whether from fright or illness, they were uncertain. He told them it had taken him three weeks to get here, and he'd wondered every day if he were going to make it. Each day he became weaker. He had willed himself to maintain enough control to guide the *Sal* to Simbayo. Now he had no strength. They had to take turns feeding him, literally spooning bland food, such as rice, into his mouth, forcing him to chew it.

Fortunately, they had a goat for the children's milk, and they carefully fed him the boiled goat's milk. It was the best thing they could do for him.

He tossed and turned, in varying degrees of consciousness. Someone had to sit by him constantly, making sure he did not fall off the bed. To Rose and Heidi fell the responsibility of alternating the night shifts because Liliane couldn't leave Carolyn at night while she was sick.

Carolyn's fever had broken; Liliane was sure it was a streptococcal infection. Carolyn still coughed and was fussier than usual, but her throat was no longer red with white pustules. She was willing to sit and listen to stories but had shown no desire to go running off with Petelo. The boy ran screaming around the compound, trying to get Carolyn's attention, irked that he was not allowed into the sickroom. Liliane had not taken him swimming since Carolyn's illness began. The regular patients, Carolyn, and Jack absorbed more of her time than usual—she had no time for a leisurely swim. To compound the situation, Naldani was across the river delivering a baby that was fighting entrance into the world.

It took two days to locate the right blood type for Jack; and by that time, he had weakened considerably. When Liliane and Rose brought the transfusion apparatus into his room, he screamed, "I ain't gonna have none of that. I ain't gonna go crazy. Just let me die."

By patient questioning, they learned the source of his fear. He had known someone, back in Liverpool many years ago, who had submitted to a blood transfusion and within months was in the county sanitorium "crazy as a loon."

"Jack, that's an old wives' tale," Heidi said. "There's no truth to such a thing."

"I know it myself. I saw him before and after." Jack forced himself to sit up in bed and waved his arms at them. "Let me die in peace." Sweat covered his brow, and he collapsed on his pillow from weakness.

Heidi looked at Rose and Liliane. "Should we strap him down?"

In all her years here, Liliane had never had to do that to a patient. She shook her head. "No," she said, "we have to persuade him. He must agree to it."

"Let me try to explain," Rose said.

She drew the room's one straight-backed chair close to Jack's bed and sat down beside him.

"Jack, you know we love you, don't you?"

He eyed her suspiciously; his eyes closed then fluttered open again. He reached out a hand but couldn't quite touch her, even though she was so near. She wrapped her hand around his. "Jack, we don't want you to die. We want you to be around for many more years. Don't you know we wouldn't do anything that would be dangerous to you? Jack, we would do this to ourselves. You're part of us. Please, please, trust us."

"Jesus, Rose." His breath came in short bursts. "I guess I'd as soon die as disappoint *you*. You promise I won't go loony?"

"No loonier than you already are," she joked, trying to lighten the moment.

He clutched at Rose's hand and smiled weakly up at Liliane. "Okay. But no black blood."

The three women looked at each other in astonishment. Did he mean no blood from natives? He'd spent more than twenty years living among the black people up and down the Congo and its tributaries, and he was afraid of their blood? Jack had never evidenced a shred of racial superstition before.

Rose leaned closer to him. "Jack, God gave all human beings the same blood. Blood from natives and blood from whites are exactly the same."

"Yeah, well, they got different diseases from white men."

"That's because they live differently," Heidi said. "It has nothing to do with black or white."

"Well, I've lived here half my life and I've never gotten the godawful things they do."

"And you've been vaccinated, and you don't walk around with bare feet, and you take quinine, and you eat at least halfway decently."

"Then why am I sick now?"

"Because you drink too much. And, I imagine, there are times when you forget to eat and just drink." Heidi was not giving comfort. She was scolding him.

"Find some other blood." Jack was stubborn. "I don't want black blood."

"There is no other blood," Liliane said. "None of us has your type."

Rose raised his hand to her cheek. "Trust us, Jack. You always have."

He turned his frightened eyes to Liliane. "What would the doc have done?"

"Exactly what we want you to do."

"Goddamn," he muttered, and closed his eyes. "Goddamn it."

Over the next two days, they fed him four pints of blood. They also urged quantities of goat's milk into him. On the third day he asked for a cigarette.

They refused. Heidi had thrown out all his cigarettes. There wasn't one in the compound. "No more," she said. "And no more drinking. Except milk."

"Now where the hell am I gonna find milk up and down the river?"

"Oh," Liliane said serenely, "nearly every tribe has a goat or two. You'll manage."

"I hate milk. It's so white. It tastes like chalk sounds on a blackboard." This made the nurses laugh.

Carolyn was out and running around again, forgetting she'd ever been ill. After two weeks, Jack was up but spending a great deal of time sitting, staring off into space. He was able to join the nurses and children for meals, though he was never up in time for breakfast.

Marsh and Anoka still had not returned. By the time more than three weeks had passed, Liliane was having trouble suppressing the nervous tension that was surfacing. Where were they?

She found herself wondering where Marsh was as she put the saw down on the table. She shouldn't be thinking of anything other than the man on the operating table and the arm she'd just amputated above the elbow. A logger had been caught under a falling tree. Pinned to the ground for hours, his bones were crushed and circulation to his arm had been cut off. By the time a motor launch brought him, unconscious, to the hospital, there was no alternative to amputation.

Sometimes medicine could make one sick. She looked at the severed arm, still lying beside the man, as Rose clamped the end of the upper arm to stop the bleeding. Liliane reached for the needle and thread. She looked at Rose and their eyes met; Rose's face was as blanched as her own felt.

Leaning over, she pulled the layers of flesh close together. This will be ugly as long as he lives, she told herself, folding the skin carefully, making sure her stitches were not so tight that they puckered his skin. She didn't want to leave a permanent wrinkle.

She had entered nursing to be a healer, to help make bodies whole; it always constricted her stomach when she took from a body. She knew the man would never feel whole again, that some amount of bitterness would be a part of him for the rest of his life.

"Remove the clamp," she told Rose as she sewed neat little stitches.

Blood covered the man; it leaked from the dismembered arm; it soaked Rose's and Liliane's uniforms. When she finished tying the thread, the bleeding had stopped, but blood still dripped onto the floor from the dead arm, on which the fingers still jerked.

A shiver rolled down Liliane's spine. "I guess we can tell ourselves we saved his life."

"Of course," Rose concurred. But, understanding the cost, neither felt very good about it.

At that very moment they heard the distant *whir* of a plane's engine. It was a sound Liliane had not heard since she left the States.

Despite her haunted feelings of a moment before, her body relaxed; she literally felt the tension ease from her chest.

She tore off her surgical gloves and threw her cap onto a table. Flinging herself out the door, she called, "Caro!" and ran toward the cleared landing strip, without waiting for her daughter.

Not until that moment had she realized how much Marsh had come to mean to her. As she ran through the forest along the worn footpath, she realized with a jolt, I don't just love him. I've fallen in love with him. "Oh, Marsh!" she called out as she came to the cleared field, though the plane was just approaching its landing.

The silver metal shone in the sun and looked like a giant bird soaring gracefully toward the earth.

She waited where the path left the forest, her hand shading her eyes against the glare. It's beautiful, she thought. For a moment Marsh was forgotten in her appreciation of this remarkable machine. The plane glided smoothly onto the stubbled field, its engine purring, the propellor visibly slowing its whirring rotation.

Then Marsh jumped from the rear seat in the cockpit onto the wing, and she found herself rushing toward the plane. Marsh saw her, sprang to the ground, and stretched out his arms. She ran into them as Anoka lowered himself from the front seat. Marsh's strong embrace welcomed her and, even in front of Anoka, his lips touched hers. He and Anoka both looked happy.

Anoka, in fact, looked far more sophisticated than he had a month ago. What could have given him that look so quickly? Did going to a city and flying in a plane change one so? Was the experience that enlarging? Ah, his clothes were different. He wore pants that fit and a colorful shirt. His feet were encased in sandals.

"I was beginning to worry," Liliane said.

Marsh looked at Anoka, and they laughed. "We had lots to do," he said without further explanation.

At that moment Naldani ran out of the woods, followed by Carolyn and Petelo. They all stopped and stared at the plane. The children refused to move out onto the field despite the fact that Naldani slowly walked toward the plane. Her eyes were filled with distrust. She looked first at the plane and then at Anoka and didn't like what she saw. He was different. He had changed in that brief time, and she had not.

Marsh told Liliane that he had bought many things. They were gone so long because he and Anoka had flown into Léopoldville. Coquilhatville had been too small to buy all that he had wanted. They would have to wait until the *Oregon* arrived on its next trip to see everything he had purchased.

"TOO BAD I DON'T HAVE A DARKROOM," MARSH MUTTERED. "I NEVER know whether or not the movies I take are any good. If they're as good as I think this time, maybe we can get a travelogue into movie theaters. Frank Buck and the Johnsons do; I don't see any reason why women surviving in the midst of Africa wouldn't fascinate moviegoers. It would be a fine way to raise money."

Marsh still did not settle down to writing. But when the *Oregon* arrived two weeks later, it brought furniture for his new house: wicker chairs and a sofa, a desk, and a double bed. His smile challenged Liliane. "Now you'll have no excuse to spend the nights alone," he said.

She had never used an excuse. She loved sleeping close to him. She liked waking in the morning with his even breathing on her neck; she liked curling around him and tossing her legs over his; she liked his hands cupped over her breasts when he did the curling. She liked waking up knowing he was there. But it had always been in her single bed, in the room with Carolyn. They had to be quiet; they could not talk into the night. He had bought, too, a small bed for Carolyn so that both of them could spend nights in his house. He brought hurricane lamps and a generator.

"No," he admitted, "I don't know a thing about it. But one of these years we're going to have electricity. Until then it can sit. Can't you just see it in my article? These three valiant ladies deprived of sorely needed electricity because lack of knowledge allows a perfectly good generator to go to waste in their storeroom? An engineer in Cairo, in need of a vacation, jumps onto the next boat and appears here."

The nurses giggled. "Maybe they know something about generators at the logging camp," Heidi volunteered.

The pièce de résistance was hundreds of pieces of wood and metal, designed—when assembled—to be a water tower. Liliane could scarcely believe it. "This is what we went to Léopoldville for. I've had it in my mind since I was first here. You have to boil all the water for hospital use. It rains here enough so that this should fill easily. We can rig up some sort of primitive shower, and you won't have to haul water anymore. You'll have a supply of running water instead. Okay, am I nominated as the creative thinker of the year?"

He was.

"Hell," muttered Jack, who still spent most of his time sitting. "What I don't know about generators ain't worth knowing."

Four pair of eyes looked at him curiously. "Give me something to do while I'm recuperating."

Color was returning to his face, though he was still gaunt.

"It may take me a while, but I'll get Anoka to find me some boys and we'll work on it. Now, ain't this exciting!" His eyes came to life at the thought of the challenge and of how he could repay those who had saved his life. "Not," he noted daily, "that it's much of a life. No booze, no smoking, no eating anything with one iota of taste."

Marsh took great delight in the amenities of civilization that he'd brought, but refused to be hooked up to the electricity Jack was soon ready to generate. For him, the hurricane lamps.

Jack electrified the operating room, the office, the dining hall, and the kitchen. He alloted one forty-watt bulb each to the infirmary rooms, and in the evening it looked as though civilization had come to the remotest part of the dark continent.

Marsh pushed himself and the workers he hired. When the water tower was finished, he announced, "I am not going to do another lick of work here until I finish that article and make you all rich."

A red flag on Marsh's front porch indicated that anyone was welcome. Otherwise, he was not to be disturbed. When he skipped meals, Liliane or Rose slipped a plate of food onto his verandah, and he always thanked them but made no apologies for his withdrawal from their society.

His work did not interfere with their nights together. Liliane and Carolyn habitually slept at his house. The first few nights Carolyn had been afraid to sleep in a room by herself and had awakened screaming when she found herself alone. Both Marsh and Liliane had held her until she slept. Gradually she became used to the new arrangement, though at times she appeared to resent Marsh.

When he was not at Simbayo, she slept in the room with her mother. When he wasn't here, she had her mother's attention. Yet with him here, she was told stories, taken for walks, rocked on his lap. She alternated between delight in Marsh's company and resentment at his intrusion. Petelo had none of this ambivalence. He enjoyed Marsh. Marsh made up stories that included the children in the plots, and he made them see faraway places and people. He taught them about lions and cannibals and high buildings and snow.

One late afternoon, when the red flag was waving, Liliane headed toward the cottage for a respite before dinner. She heard the children giggling and urging, "More, more." When she appeared, they insisted he repeat the poem he had just recited for them.

"You really want to hear it?" Marsh asked. "My nurse used to read it to me."

"Of course. I've never heard you recite a poem."

"Well, now, it's called . . ."

" 'Animal Birds'!" shouted the children.

"Here's how it goes," Marsh said, gazing solemnly at the youngsters.

"Lions and tigers and bears, oh, my—
Supposing these animals all could fly!
How would we walk to our school each day?
And how could we ever go outside to play?

A lion or tiger or bear, you see,
Might nest out in back, in our biggest tree!

And my goodness, just think of the size of the nest,
Where Mamma and Papa and Baby could rest!

He would sing with a grunt or a growl or a roar,
And who would be brave to go out the door?

His wings would be huge just to lift his size,
And a very small flock would quite darken the skies!

Yes, lion-birds, tiger-birds, bear-birds seem strange,
But maybe as birds their whole natures would change!

With no teeth in their jaws, and no claws on their feet,
They might become cuddly, playful, and sweet!

A cuddly lion or tiger or bear
Whose soft, furry wings let him fly through the air,

Would love little children who treated them well,
And play with them gently by the trees where they dwell!"

Almost shyly, he looked for Liliane's reaction.

Her blue-green eyes smiled at him. "Maybe you better forget your novel and write children's books."

"I keep doing everything except write my novel." The dinner bell clanged. As they walked toward the dining hall, he said with apparent exasperation, "I build a house. I take off for civilization. I build a water tower. I write kids' poems. I finish my article. . . ."

"That's done?"

"Do you want to see it?"

"Of course."

He opened the door and the children ran in ahead of them. "If all goes as I fantasize it might, you're next in line for the Nobel Prize."

SHE WAS EMBARRASSED AT THE ARTICLE. "YOU EXAGGERATE HORRENdously," she exclaimed, when she read it later that night. "I think you've caught the spirit of Heidi and Rose, I like what you've done with Anoka and Naldani, though they're all a bit larger than life, but as for me . . . !"

"You mean the young widow carrying on the great Dr. Baxter Hathaway's dream?"

"Well, that part is mostly true, but, Marsh, your prejudice shows through."

He reached over and ran a finger through the tendril of hair that curled behind her ear. "I want the world to love you, too. Love you so much you won't have to worry about money for years."

"Is that really how you see me?" she asked, when they lay next to each other, surfeited with lovemaking, listening to the river. "It's not true, you know. I'm not noble."

"De gustibus non est disputandum," he said to the night.

"Huh?"

"Oh, everyone to his own taste, or beauty's in the eye of the beholder, or that may be how you see yourself, but not how I do."

"Maybe you're in love with a figment of your imagination. That's not the real me."

"It always amazes me"—Marsh's hand rested on her thigh—"that we think we know ourselves better than anyone else does, when in actuality we're quite blind to so much of ourselves."

"So you know me better than I do?"

"Oh, I won't go that far. But I know some things about you in ways you can't see yourself. I think that what we see of ourselves and what the outside world sees of us are quite different."

"Well, right now I'm glad the outside world isn't here."

Marsh reached up and drew her to him, her head on his chest. He kissed her hair. "Oh, Lili. We may possibly be the two luckiest people in the whole world."

CHAPTER 20

▼

"You know what i'd like for my birthday?" liliane asked as she slipped into her sandals.

"Hmm?" Marsh was not awake yet. He never awoke as gracefully, as ready to greet life as Liliane did. Once she was awake, she was ready to begin the day. She loved lying close to Marsh and talking long into the night, but she couldn't seem to stay in bed for long after she awoke in the morning.

"I know what I want for my birthday," she said.

Marsh's eyes shot open. "I don't even know when your birthday is."

"A situation I'm about to rectify." She leaned over and kissed his chin. "It's tomorrow."

"Tomorrow?" His voice cracked. "That doesn't give me very long. You could've warned me." He ran a finger down her spine as she straightened her skirt.

"Oh, this is enough warning for what I yearn for."

"Tell me it's my body." He pulled her to him, reaching for her breasts before she enclosed them in her bra.

Oh, she thought, if he starts that, I'll never get out of here. I'll want to stay here all morning with him.

"I want a ride in your plane," she said, fastening her bra and eluding his lips. Just in time, for Carolyn came sleepy-eyed into their bedroom, dragging her clothes with her. Marsh's eyes left Liliane and fastened on Carolyn. He patted the bed next to him, and she crawled up, curling herself into the curve of his arm. "It's nice somebody wants to cuddle in the morning," he said. Carolyn grinned and grabbed his hand.

"Please think about it," Liliane said. "Want me to dress you, honey?" she asked her daughter.

"No." Carolyn snuggled closer to Marsh and giggled. "Want to stay here."

Liliane's heart warmed at the sight of the two of them cuddling together. Marsh played the father role quite well—far better than she had imagined he would. He seemed to have settled into domesticity rather willingly. The wildness in him was sublimated. She wondered for how long.

As she walked to the dining hall in the early-morning mist, it suddenly dawned on her that she and Naldani weren't as close as they had been. Since Anoka had moved in with Naldani and Marsh had arrived to monopolize Liliane's time, they saw each other only during work. Naldani and Petelo still joined them for afternoon swims, but the long talks had stopped. Liliane missed the closeness she'd felt with Naldani, the times shared. Whenever she had free moments during the day now, she spent them with Carolyn; evenings were reserved for Marsh.

He never wrote at night. That broke a lifelong habit, he'd intimated, but if that was the only undivided time she had, then he would regulate his life to hers. He arose early, though not always willingly, and she scarcely saw him all day. More often than not, he didn't show up for lunch. Now and then she saw him sitting at the river's edge, at the bend beyond her pool, staring into the hypnotically flowing water.

She decided to try once more to persuade Anoka, Naldani, and Petelo to share mealtimes with them. She saw more of Anoka than of Naldani. He was on his way to becoming an acceptable surgeon. One day after she'd burned her left hand, it lost its mobility for a brief time. She hadn't realized it until he was assisting her in surgery and she couldn't move her fingers with agility.

"Anoka, come over to this side of the table," she'd said. "You're going to help me operate. Be my left hand." So, side by side, with her right hand and his left, they had finished the operation. He had puffed up with pride.

Ever since then she'd found ways to let him participate in the surgical aspects of their work. But she missed Naldani.

She used to soothe me, Liliane remembered. Just listening to her deep, rich singing relaxed me. Now the only time Liliane heard Naldani's voice raised in song was sometimes in the evenings, when it floated through the air of the compound.

When Anoka joined her and Rose with the line of patients that morning, she told him, "I'm going to urge you to join us for dinners. We really can talk over more ideas that way, and we *are* a family. Can't you talk Naldani into trying? We'll learn to eat some of the things you enjoy."

Ever since Marsh had taken him to Coquilhatville and Léopoldville, Anoka was determined to learn western ways. Here was an opportunity to participate in one more aspect of that way of life.

"I will talk to her. I am ready for this step. I would like to share meals with you and Marsh . . . Miss Rose and Miss Heidi, too, of course." He could not break the barrier of formality with the two older nurses. They had all given up trying to force him.

"Petelo will enjoy it, too," Liliane added.

"Naldani will, too, once she gets used to it. She needs more exposure to your ways." He meant white people's ways.

That evening they gathered around the dinner table together. Carolyn giggled with delight at having Petelo dine with them. The cook had sniffed at the idea of having to cook for ones like himself, but Heidi suggested they could always train another cook. Naldani, obviously ill at ease with silverware, had to be reassured that table manners were of no consequence. Hers were impeccable, however, for she used her fingers daintily. She and Anoka quickly noticed that one did not spit bones onto the floor, and for a while it looked as though she might swallow them rather than put them on her plate.

"It'll take time," Liliane said later to Marsh, who was delighted with the idea. At times he stole Anoka from his medical duties and they went fishing together. Marsh always treated Anoka as an equal, at the same time subtly instructing him not only in reading English, but in writing, carpentry, table manners, addition, and subtraction. He spent hours trying to make maps real to Anoka; he taught him geography and history.

"With time," agreed Marsh. He lay back on a pillow and watched Liliane. "You know, I never tire of watching you undress. Actually, I never tire of watching you, period."

"Funny, isn't it? I feel the same about you," she said as she came toward him.

He held his arms out to her, and she took his hands in hers, lowering herself on top of him. "Ah," he whispered, "do you have any idea of what the touch of you does to me?"

She kissed him silent.

"THAT WAS SO NICE," HE SAID LATER, "THAT I AM IMPELLED TO GIVE you what you want for your birthday."

IF EVER A MACHINE AND A HUMAN BEING WERE MEANT FOR EACH other, Liliane and Marsh's airplane, *Cleopatra,* were. From the moment she climbed into the front cockpit it became part of her. The wind riffling through her hair gave her a glorious sense of freedom. All that she could see below her were trees. A carpet of endless gray-green trees as far as the eye could see—into infinity, she thought. Occasionally the sun glinted on the ribbon of the Mombayo, which divided into two branches to the south. They flew in between what had become the Luilaka and the Lokolo, so that first she saw one on the left, and then the other on the right, shining in the sun's rays. Nothing else broke the terrain. It looked far more ominous from up here than it did from below. It looked so dense as to be impenetrable. Yet Liliane knew that that was not so. They flew toward the horizon over monochromatic and monotonous scenery that, nevertheless, fascinated Liliane. She had no idea that where she lived looked like this from the air.

The sky. It was bluer than any Liliane had ever seen. Once they flew right into a cloud and she could see nothing for a moment. She heard Marsh's laugh over the roar of the engine.

Her lungs felt different. She breathed more deeply, exhilarated. It was not only the excitement of flying, but the lack of humidity. She had forgotten what it was like to breathe air that wasn't damp.

"Hold on!" shouted Marsh, and began a dive. Without warning, the plane began to roll; it turned somersaults in the air. Marsh was trying to impress her.

How, she wondered, studying the lush vegetation as they evened out, could clearings be made so that she could attain her dream of outposts? Was this a way to achieve her dream? A team of nurses at the outposts to handle routine cases and to educate;

radios to inform Simbayo to send a plane for the really sick patients. A radio relay could keep the headquarters and the outposts in touch. A plane could tie them together. Epidemics could be stopped before they became rampant.

Liliane sighed. She wondered if she were incapable of sheer enjoyment, without thinking of work. Just once in a while, she thought, I'd like a beachcomber's mentality. I'd like to be able to simply and totally relax.

She forced her mind from dreams of the future and let her spirit soar along with the plane. She emptied her mind of thought. She was a bird flying above the world, a creature unchained. Looking down on the green world, she was uninvolved, removed from its toils and troubles; she was free.

Even from a distance she recognized the cleared patch of airstrip. It blatantly made its presence known; though here and there were occasional cleared fields, they were far smaller than the airfield. From the air, she could tell where home was.

Before they were even out of the plane, she turned to Marsh, her enthusiasm keen.

"Marsh, teach me to fly!"

He laughed, and his eyes danced as he helped her onto the wing. "Something we can share, huh?"

And it was. Liliane couldn't get enough of it. One fine day Marsh even talked her into taking a day off and at last she flew out of Simbayo. They left at dawn and flew to Coquilhatville, ostensibly to bring back a supply of gasoline, but also to get Liliane away from her jungle habitat for the first time in over seven years.

They could only spend two hours in the town if they were to return to Simbayo before dark, which Liliane insisted on. But to think that on the river it took ten days, and they had flown the distance in a little less than three hours. Since she was not far advanced in the art of navigation, despite the evenings she and Marsh spent poring over diagrams and books, she tried to follow the river when she saw it and knew that Marsh had them on a northwesterly course. He allowed her to pilot the plane over half the time, and the sense of power thrilled her.

Coquilhatville had grown in the years since she'd last seen it. Marsh insisted on buying her two dresses and some new underwear, hand made by Belgian nuns.

"I haven't thought it was diplomatic to mention it, but yours is in sad condition." He grinned as he led her along the street, stopping in each of the little shops. They picked up trinkets for the children.

Liliane was as agog as any tourist. "It's Einstein's theory of relativity again, isn't it?" she asked Marsh.

"You mean after Simbayo you think this rinky-dink town is cosmopolitan?"

"Exactly." She grabbed his arm and held it tightly. "You know, I feel like a girl again."

He put his hand over hers as they walked along. "You are pretty ancient. All of twenty-eight now."

"Well, I haven't felt this carefree in ages."

"I offer you the fountain of youth, then. Leave Simbayo and come away with me into the higher altitudes and cooler climates, where you can buy pretty dresses to your heart's content and—"

Her heart froze. "I don't need pretty dresses."

"It's true. You look beautiful in anything you wear. Or don't wear."

"And I wouldn't quite call Coquilhatville a cooler climate or higher altitude. It is *exactly* on the equator at sea level."

"You're not telling me anything I don't know." He wiped the sweat from his brow. "I don't know how people spend lifetimes in this humidity. No wonder the natives are thought lazy. It's the weather, not the nature. It's too hot to move. Let's go get a cold drink. All this talk about the heat knocks me out."

They had gin and tonics at the hotel and then headed back to the airport, which, like the town, was squalid and inefficient.

The sun was a golden ball sliding into the jagged edges of the treetops as Marsh and Liliane glided into Simbayo. It had been a refreshing day until Marsh spoke of leaving; ever since then Liliane had felt tentacles clutching her innards.

They were just in time for dinner, where Jack announced that he "needed to get going. I've been here three–four months, and I need to get going."

He had not gained back the weight the nurses would have liked him to, but he had not had a drink or a cigarette and he was now eating regular food. They knew they couldn't kidnap him or keep him against his will—even for his own protection.

Heidi admonished him, "If we pack you food, will you promise to eat right?"

Rose added, "Stop daily and get goat's milk from some village. Every tribe seems to have goats."

"And stay off that booze." Marsh was not to be outdone.

Jack seemed to have permanently lost his jubilant spirit. Later Liliane confided to Marsh, "I think he's leaving in order to prove to himself that he's all right. I don't think he really feels well enough to go."

"How long does it take to cure a bleeding ulcer?"

"He should be well by now, and it shouldn't recur if he disciplines himself. But I don't think he will. I don't know why he's not more like his old self than he is. He worries me."

As Jack left, the *Oregon* arrived, and with it came three large bundles of mail. They had not received that much mail all at once since Baxter died. Most of the letters were addressed to "Mother Lili, Simbayo, the Congo."

"Oh, Marsh, what if you were right, and there's money in them?" Rose and Heidi shared Liliane's excitement. They were sitting at the dining-room table with the three bags on the table.

"Well, open one," urged Marsh. "I want to see how influential I am in this world."

Each of the nurses took an envelope and opened it. A bank note and a letter fell out of the one in Liliane's hand. The letter was brief: "I read about you in the paper and think you are doing God's work. I'd like to help." There was money in Rose's and Heidi's letters, too.

They stared at each other, while Marsh grinned. He opened the letter to him from The *Times* and was satisfied at the size of the check. Then the three women tore into the pile of mail, whooping and hollering like silly schoolgirls. By the time they'd finished counting, they had the equivalent of $14,000. They looked at each other in disbelief.

"I suspect," Marsh said smugly, "that it's but the tip of the iceberg. The article hasn't yet had time to go round the world. You just wait."

Liliane was satisfied with the $14,000. That would last them for years if they were careful and the mission continued to supply most of the medicine.

"I think," said Rose, "it would be nice to read each of the letters, too. Can we afford postage to answer them all?"

"Or the time?" interjected Heidi, who was gathering the money up into one of the gray mail sacks.

"We must," said Liliane. "What a lovely thing to sit around and do after dinner each evening. But there are hundreds of them!" To herself, she thought, Maybe there is a God after all.

Or then, again, maybe it was Marsh.

In the morning, she looked in Carolyn's room and saw that her daughter had already gone out. Lately Carolyn had been asserting her independence. She seldom went into the jungle alone, always with Petelo, but she was becoming elusive, a natural fairylike creature of the forest. The children never went far, but they were expanding their horizons. Liliane wondered why she thought they were safe; they had never been warned away from the river or from the jungle paths. Perhaps, she thought, it's because they seem so much a part of this place. Her daughter was growing up like a Bantu child.

That morning, as she, Rose, and Anoka tended to the waiting line of patients, which seemed to grow increasingly larger each day, Anoka told her, "Bomatelo says he is going to leave."

Anoka had spent over a year training his assistant. His dream was to train as many natives as possible, to educate his people so that they could help others on the journey to the twentieth century.

Liliane looked at him. Did Bomatelo hope to go to another mission to practice what he'd been taught? Though she approved of the idea, she hated to think of losing their best helper.

"No," replied Anoka to her question. "He says he's going to Coquilhatville and away from here because he is having wife trouble."

"He's been having that for ages," responded Liliane, thinking of Bomatelo's wife, Malia, an extraordinary-looking woman by any standards. She carried herself regally, aware of the looks she garnered from every man in sight, knowing that once she passed by they would dream of her that night. Her face was smooth as chocolate cream, her eyes had a golden hue. Her breasts were voluptuous and jutted straight out in front of her, bouncing suggestively as she moved along in her feline stride, the feathers around her waist swaying. All work stopped when Malia walked by. She looked straight ahead until suddenly she turned a sidelong gaze at a man and smiled, a glorious invitation to follow her. It was said that many had.

She refused to work in the garden and would not cook for Bomatelo. He knew that he lost respect by being unable to control his wife, so he beat her in front of their hut. Congo women were used to beatings and suffered them in silence, but not Malia. Her wails rent the air. The more he beat her, the less work she would do. When he came home in the middle of the day, she was never there, and he was convinced she was lying out in the forest with someone.

Though he beat her often, and she infuriated him with her lack of obedience, he was so in love with her that it drove him crazy. He could scarcely bear to be away from her for more than a few hours at a stretch.

When she was not at home, he would search for her, examining all of the places he knew she would not be. He didn't know what he would do if he discovered her in the act of adultery. Yet the thought that she was giving herself to another man ate at him.

"He thinks he can get a good job in a town now that he is trained," Anoka said, "and can save some money. Malia refuses to cook for him. I don't know what else she refuses to do. He thinks if he leaves her, peace of mind will return to his life."

"Is there anything we can do to help?" Liliane asked.

Anoka shook his head. "I don't think so. But I regret his leaving. It will take a long time to train someone as able as he."

"I'm really glad"—Rose joined the conversation as she put ointment on a burn—"that I never married. Life is so much less complicated."

Liliane refrained from saying what she thought: You are married in a way. But yours is a good one. "Nevertheless I shall ask him," she said. Which she did that afternoon.

"Anoka tells me you are thinking of leaving," she said to him after lunch.

He nodded his head without looking at her.

"We would be very sorry to lose you, Bomatelo. We value you here. You are a good worker."

He nodded his head again.

"I must teach my wife a lesson. She will have no one to take care of her if I leave."

"How will that make you happy?"

He shrugged. "Then I can come back after many months and she will want to do as I say. She will see that other men do not give her what she will get as the wife of one who works here. She will change her ways."

Liliane put her hand on the assistant's arm. "Would you like me to talk with her?"

"No!" He shook his head furiously. "It is a matter only between her and me." His eyes brooded.

When he came to work the next day, he sat down often, complaining of dizziness.

"Maybe he's under a spell," suggested Marsh.

"Oh, come on. I think he's so bothered that it's upsetting his equilibrium."

Marsh's equilibrium also seemed to be upset. He became increasingly less communicative, absorbed in his imaginary world. He found it difficult to put his own thoughts out of his mind and to concentrate on the daily minutae of Simbayo.

"Bomatelo is acting very strangely," Anoka told Liliane several days later. "I made him lie down in one of the hospital rooms this morning. He had severe cramps and an attack of vomiting."

"I'll look in on him," Liliane said.

She performed a number of tests on Bomatelo but could find nothing wrong. He refused to stay in the hospital overnight and Anoka helped him home, where he immediately lay down and fell asleep. Malia was nowhere in sight.

When they were forced to hospitalize him, however, Malia came to see him every day. Her velvet body sashayed down the hospital corridor, and her catlike, sinuous walk drew everyone's attention. She was so used to being stared at that she took it as her due and paid scant attention to the glances.

Her eyes became slits when she entered Bomatelo's sickroom, and she hissed at him, "I have come to say good-bye." She did this every afternoon. When she saw the look of pained panic on his face, she smiled maliciously and walked over to touch his shoulder.

Maybe Bomatelo deserved it, Liliane thought. Maybe he beat her once too often. Or perhaps, with Malia, once was too often.

Bomatelo lost weight daily and had periods of unconsciousness. Three weeks later he died.

The funeral was filled with wailing and the beating of pots and pans; he had been a popular man. Most of the other men felt sorry for him, even the men he had suspected of cuckolding him. All of the men desired Malia, but none desired her as a wife.

Two days after the funeral Bomatelo's brother arrived from a village downriver. He had come to collect his sister-in-law, who, according to custom, automatically became one of his wives. Everyone pitied him. Malia fought him tooth and nail.

He tied a rope around her, tossed her into his pirogue, and sailed off down the river.

"The rumor says she poisoned him," Anoka told everyone at

dinner. "That's why she visited Bomatelo in the hospital every day. To continue to administer the poison."

"There's no way of knowing, though, is there?" asked Rose.

Naldani answered, "No. But that one is capable of it."

Several months later they heard that her brother-in-law had stripped her of her fancy clothes and forced her to work, though he would not let her cook. He permitted his first wife to treat Malia as a slave, and they tied a stake to the ground and put a chain around Malia's ankle so that she could not escape. She could not wash or strut proudly around, but was forced to weed the fields and do whatever the first wife made her do.

"This," said Anoka, "is how justice works in the Congo."

Perhaps it was not any crueler than the way it was meted out in other parts of the world, thought Liliane.

CHAPTER 21

▼

THE FOLLOWING MONTH'S MAIL BROUGHT $37,215. MANY OF THE letters were in languages that none of them could decipher.

"You know what I'm going to do," Liliane announced at dinner. "I'm going to advertise for a doctor and a couple of nurses."

Heidi and Rose looked at her in astonishment.

"No, no," she assured them. "Not to run Simbayo. To work *for* us. There's enough money to last us for years. I'm ready to try an outpost and see how it works. Just one, at first. At last I have a chance to see if my ideas might work."

"How many of these outposts do you envision?" asked Rose.

"Oh, ten, twenty." Liliane laughed. "But let's start off with one." Then, more seriously, "Are you with me in this?"

Rose and Heidi looked at each other, then back at Liliane. They nodded their support.

Liliane turned to Anoka. "Maybe we'll have to take a trip and see what we think of the geography."

He nodded, too, but it was apparent he was not comfortable.

"What is it, Anoka?" Liliane asked, concerned. But Anoka was silent.

In the morning, Liliane took him aside. "You're worried that a doctor will take over your duties, your position. You're afraid you'll no longer be needed here. Is that it?"

"It is true," he acknowledged, his deep voice solemn.

"That's not how I'd envisioned it," she reassured him. "I thought we'd start a doctor at an outpost to work with nurses until they could confidently take charge. Then have several doctors here. We're getting too busy to handle everything. You are more important to us here than any other doctor will ever be."

He responded to "any other doctor" as if she had included him as a physician, too. When she told Marsh about it later, he suggested they have a formal ceremony initiating Anoka into the realm of doctors.

Liliane giggled. "I can just see that! Three nurses officiating at his medical graduation."

One Sunday noon, with much ceremony, which the delighted Rose and Heidi had concocted, Anoka officially became Dr. Anoka and Naldani received her R.N. There was no one to disprove the legality.

"Now I am as you are," Naldani said to the women. She had been for a long time. No midwife could have a better record of birthing than Naldani had achieved. She seldom lost a patient in even the most difficult cases. And Liliane shared with her the new methods being practiced whenever a medical journal arrived.

Liliane knew that achieving her dream might bring other problems to this harmonious group, but it was a risk she needed to take.

"I think," she told Marsh after the little ceremony, "I'll circumvent the mission society. I think I'll advertise in a couple of medical journals."

"American ones?" Marsh asked.

"I hadn't thought about that. What do you think?"

"Well, don't limit yourself."

Liliane and Anoka spent days trying to decide where the first camp should be.

"It'll take a lot of work," she reported. "We must clear an area for the buildings and build housing and an infirmary. We must get radios that will put us in touch with the outpost. We must find a way to get food and supplies to it."

She and Anoka took an exploratory trip, five days up the river. Marsh decided, after all, that he needed a two-week vacation from his writing, though Liliane knew it was because he did not want to think of her out in the jungle without protection. What had happened to Baxter, even though it had been four years ago, still haunted them.

Up here, along the river, one could see why logging camps proliferated. Mahogany, oak, walnut, red cedar, and rubber trees grew to over two hundred feet. Moss and lichen hung from the tree branches like ghostly drapery. Giant orchids attached themselves to the tree trunks, and crocodiles glided in the ooze of the river's bank, their hooded eyes hypnotically watching the long-legged cranes and herons. Along the nearly deserted river, hippos and crocodiles sunned themselves on the silvery sandbanks.

In the midafternoon hush, Marsh said, "The stillness seems an implacable malignant force."

Liliane looked at him curiously. She had never felt that way about the jungle.

Day and night hordes of monkeys swung through the upper branches of the trees, letting loose hysterical screams.

They passed dugout canoes, whose standing tribesmen paddled in unison, their weird, high-pitched voices singing in time to their paddle strokes. The blades of their oars were shaped like magnificent palm leaves. They glided swiftly along the river carrying bunches of green bananas. Other pirogues trailed fishing nets, idling in the glassy waters of some quiet cove.

"This is your milieu, Lili," Marsh said, and Liliane was surprised to sense despair in his voice. "This silent humid gloom breeds all your dreadful diseases: malaria, bilharziasis, sleeping sickness, blackwater fever." He was talking more to himself than to her.

The fourth night, after seeing many river villages hardly worthy of the name, Liliane thought she had found the right place. It was an unusually large clearing; the land fell sharply to the water, and she could see that when they cleared the trees away, there would be a view far up and down the river. A small, clear-running stream fed into the river, shining silver in the sunlight. If any place would get a breeze, this would. The soil looked fertile enough to garden.

"Now," she asked, as much to herself as to her companions, "if we build here, where do we get lumber and workmen?"

Marsh was heating coffee over a campfire. "I am sure you will have that solved by the time we get back to Simbayo."

"What I really need before a doctor," she said thoughtfully, "is an engineer."

"Or a carpenter," suggested Anoka.

Liliane said, "We passed one of the logging camps on our way up here. Perhaps some of the men would have time to help build a place for us."

And indeed they would. Boredom ruled the logging camps, whose workers had ended up in this part of the world for reasons one didn't question. However, when they had been patients at Simbayo, they were unfailingly courteous. Most of them spoke English ungrammatically; most of them were of either French or Belgian background. To a man, they hated the Congo and could hardly wait to save enough money to grubstake their way to a new future. In their free time, of which there was much, they drank, told tall stories, and gambled with each other. They had few other pastimes. So when Liliane asked for help and said she was willing to pay them, a dozen or more responded.

She should tell them what kind of buildings she wanted and they would work on a plan. She saw energy galvanizing itself at the thought of something new to divert their attention and occupy their time.

Back at Simbayo, she bubbled with enthusiasm as she told Rose and Heidi and Naldani of their discovery and how the loggers would help.

"Can we afford them?" Heidi asked.

"Well, we didn't haggle over price. But I'm sure they'll be reasonable. Now, all we need is to send out some ads and wait."

"What if no one answers?" asked Marsh.

The nurses looked at each other. They hadn't even considered the possibility.

That night, as they lay listening to the river rush by, Marsh said, "You know, you get so excited about your ideas and so caught up in accomplishing things, that you leave Caro out of your life."

Her defenses went up. "I don't think so!" Her voice gave away her irritation. "What do you mean?"

"You gave her a perfunctory kiss when we landed and didn't answer her questions during dinner or pay any attention when she tugged at your dress."

"Oh, Marsh, for heaven's sake. There were important matters to discuss. Caro knows I love her."

"Did you ask what happened to her while we were away?"

"No," Liliane admitted. "What can happen to a three-year-old?"

She heard Marsh sigh. "Actually, you could manage rather

well without either of us, couldn't you? It wouldn't change your
way of life one bit."

She sat up in bed, in the dark.

"What a horrid thing to say. We're together all the time. You
and Caro are what make me happy."

"Not really," he said in a somber voice. "I do think we add to
it, but we're the icing on the cake. We're not *the* important part of
your life."

"Are you trying to make me feel guilty?"

"Oh, God, Lili, don't get that tone in your voice. I'm just
trying to point something out. A three-year-old child wants your
attention after you've been away, wants to tell you what she discovered and what she did while you were gone, wants to let you know
she missed you. You're so involved with your new plans you don't
seem to see her."

Liliane lay down again, staring at stars through the window.
She was silent for a long while.

"Am I that bad?"

"Well, it was really noticeable tonight. But I've noticed in the
last couple of months that Carolyn doesn't seem to be your num-
ber-one priority. Do you take walks with her? Or explain the flowers around here, or talk of the animals, or answer her 'why'
questions?"

"I'm so busy all the time."

"And you're inventing ways to become even busier."

"Are you asking that I give you more time?"

"You're not listening, Lili. We're not talking about you and
me. We're talking about Carolyn."

"I guess," she said after a few minutes, "I feel that Caro will
be all right. I'm not sure about the rest of the country."

"You can't take on the rest of the country. But you can take
care of Carolyn. I know this is a bit premature, but what are you
going to do when she needs school?"

Liliane had not let herself think that far in advance. But she
had a ready answer. "I'll start a school. When I advertise for a
doctor and nurses, I'll advertise for a teacher."

"And do what? Sentence Caro to twelve years of a one-room
school in Simbayo? Then what? Lili, use some sense. You can't do
that to our daughter."

"I'll teach her things the school doesn't."

"You don't have time for her now. What'll you do when you
have outposts everywhere? And do you think she'll really learn

enough here to stand her in good stead in the outside world?"

Does she have to go to the outside world? Liliane silently asked. I don't plan to. Can't Caro learn to be a doctor as Anoka has, as Naldani has, and just stay here and work with us?

Marsh was reading her thoughts, for he said, "Unless you plan to imprison her here for the rest of her life."

"You make it all sound so . . . so limiting. So awful."

"Jesus, Liliane! It *is* limiting. It's *awful.* Not only awful, but godawful. You don't even see how you're living. Maybe you can stand a lifetime of it, but it certainly isn't fair to Caro. Two more years, at most, and you *have* to do something. You *have* to let her experience civilization, to be educated!" Anger throbbed in his voice.

That sense of danger she had been so free of lately enveloped her. It swirled around her in the darkness, painting itself over her, choking her pores. She jumped up from the bed and walked out of the bedroom to the verandah, seeing the white water by starlight.

What was Marsh doing to her? What had prompted this? Just because she hadn't paid much attention to Carolyn today? Damn him!

Whether to the night air or to Marsh, she shouted into the dark, "Well, I've got two more years anyhow!"

She didn't go back to bed until she thought Marsh was asleep.

The next morning she resolved to pay more attention to Carolyn. It was partly Marsh's fault, she told herself. If he weren't here, she'd spend more time with Caro. She sat around with him evenings, stayed up late talking or making love. After lunch they all swam together, but she had to admit she swam around with Marsh more than she did with the children. Well, she would do something about that. In a way, she was glad Marsh had called it to her attention.

But Jack arrived, six months to the day after he'd left, and her good intentions were sidetracked.

My Gal Sal crept into the dock without so much as a whistle. It was Petelo who signaled them. "Uncle Jack's here," he shouted.

If Liliane hadn't recognized the boat, she wasn't sure she'd have recognized Jack. His face was so thin that his eyes seemed to bulge. He must have lost another twenty or thirty pounds. He could scarcely stand.

Liliane immediately called two natives to help him to his room. Heidi ran from the office to see him.

"It's that blood," Jack railed in his raspy voice, though they had to lean over to hear him. "I knew that blood would do me in." He collapsed, unconscious.

Marsh and Anoka carried him to his room. In examining him, Liliane noted that he was feverish, probably had been for days. The lymph nodes in his groin and armpits were swollen, as well as those under the jaw and in the back of his neck.

"They feel like movable marbles," she murmured to Rose and Anoka. Rose felt them and her alarmed eyes met Liliane's.

When Jack regained consciousness, they forced liquids into him and he told them he'd had night sweats, diarrhea, and fatigue for the last three months. He was hesitant about mentioning his bodily functions but admitted he had diarrhea more often than not.

"And my throat. Sometimes it gets so sore I can hardly swallow." Liliane noted that there were thick white patches on the hard and soft palates. She scraped some tissue and examined it later under the microscope. She stepped aside and told Anoka to look.

"What do you see?" she asked. She'd been training him this way for years.

"It looks like yeast thrush."

"Yes, doesn't it?" she responded, pleased at the rapidity of his diagnosis. "Only babies get that. How in the world does this middle-aged man have it?"

"It's that blood," Jack kept reiterating. "I knew it would do me in."

"Oh, nonsense," Heidi said. "Jaundice you might get from a blood transfusion, but nothing else."

"I got black blood in me now," Jack persevered.

"Then why are you so pale?" Liliane tried to joke.

"Jesus, Lili, am I dying?"

Rose answered for her. "Of course not. You don't think we'd let that happen, do you? And deprive ourselves of the light of our lives?"

Jack managed a weak smile.

Rose pressed his hand. He held it as he closed his eyes. She felt the weakness of his pulse.

His fever followed the pattern he had explained. It was erratic. It would last several days and then disappear. Then it would reappear.

"I can't figure what it is," Liliane said. "It doesn't fit into any of the patterns it should."

"It's certainly strange," Rose agreed.

"How do we cure it when we don't know what it is?" Heidi asked. They all noticed that Jack's lymph nodes changed in size with his fever. They swelled and obviously pained him. His tongue had a thick white coating. He often had great trouble swallowing.

Marsh kept the children away from him, and the nurses did the most they could to sterilize themselves when they left his room.

"Jack's dying, isn't he?" Marsh asked.

"I don't know," Liliane answered. "I feel defeated. I really don't know what to do." But they kept on trying.

Meanwhile, she went on with her plans. She talked Marsh into writing ads to submit to various medical journals and religious organizations. "Not that I care a whit whether or not someone believes in God," she told him. "It's just that religious people are more likely to devote their life to charity. At least with the money you've raised for us with your article we don't have to rely on the mission society and its edicts. Though it's left us wonderfully alone for nearly two years."

"Have I been here that long?" he asked aloud.

Oh, dear, she thought. One of these days it's going to have been too long. I wonder how close he is to finishing his book?

She didn't want to ask him. If she didn't know, she could fantasize about his staying forever.

Not that he'd ever said he would leave when his book was finished. But his constant complaints about the "goddamn humidity," the "closed-in feeling" the jungle gave him with "no horizons to free the soul," the long naps he sometimes took because the weather so enervated him, were clues to Liliane. She had always known it could not last.

"You give me such moral support," she said.

"I'd just as soon you'd think of it as immoral." He grinned, reaching over to her side of the bed and running his hand teasingly down her thigh.

Don't leave me, she thought. She drew her nightgown over her head and tossed it to the floor. "Marshall Compson," she said, "I am going to eat you up. I am going to nibble you to pieces and devour you so you will always be within me and never be able to leave me."

"Who's leaving?" he asked, unaware of her recent thoughts. "But nibble away."

▼

"I THINK HE HAS PNEUMONIA," HEIDI SAID THE NEXT MORNING.

"How in the world . . . ?"

"Well, he has shortness of breath, and he coughs—though I admit it's mildly—all night long." They took turns looking in on Jack every night. When it was Liliane's turn, she stayed in her old dormitory room. She decided to take another blood test, expecting to see a rise in blood cells, and managed to take the blood while Jack was in a deep sleep, breathing noisily through his mouth.

Puzzlement filled her when she saw, instead of the expected rise in blood cells, a reduction in the white blood cells. She called for Rose. "Look." She pointed to the microscope. "Tell me what you see. I just don't understand."

A frown creased Rose's forehead. "Oh, Lili." Tears were trapped in her eyes. "I don't know."

Liliane had both Heidi and Anoka study the microscopic results. They were in agreement: None of them could decipher it.

"The only thing to do," said Heidi, "is make him take frequent soups and other liquids. Give him aspirin and sponge him off. I don't know what else."

Jack became the center of their conversation and their thoughts.

"It's a mystery," Liliane told Marsh.

"A mystery disease?"

"I guess so. It doesn't react like anything I've seen before."

They heard a rapping from the verandah. It was Heidi. "Lili, I think the end has come."

Liliane followed Heidi through the dark night to Jack's room. Even from outside they could hear his heavy stertorous breathing.

Rose sat holding his hand. His eyes fluttered open and he tried to talk, but his voice was barely a whisper.

"This is it, right?"

Rose squeezed his hand, and Liliane tried to hold back the tears.

"Ladies," he wheezed, "I can't say it hasn't been great. You've been the three finest women I've ever known. I used to think of you all . . ." Rose tried to hush him, but he paid no heed. "I used to think of you, and I knew no women anyplace are more beautiful!"

Rose smiled through her tears and twined her fingers more tightly through his.

"It's been a good life. I never dreamed I'd stay twenty-five years." Whether he was talking to them or to himself didn't matter.

He gave a barklike laugh. "I come to get outa marrying a girl

I got in the family way. Now, isn't that a shame. I wonder if somewhere I got a son or daughter."

No one said anything. Jack opened his eyes. "I hope that don't shock you. I hardly knew her. I told her I wasn't the marrying kind." After a while he continued. "I was just gonna hide out here a year or so, till she forgot all about me. I thought no one could find me here. It's been a good life. I wouldn't've changed it for nothing. And as long as I'm dying, I'm glad I'm surrounded by three angels." He looked very deliberately at each of them.

Rose could no longer control her tears. "Oh, dear Jack," she cried, kissing his hand, then pressing it to her cheek.

They could see the fright in his eyes, hear the rattle in his breathing. Then his eyes blanked, and the rattle stopped. Jack was gone.

CHAPTER 22

▼

ANOTHER $18,428 ARRIVED WHEN THE *OREGON* NEXT BROUGHT THE mail.

"What are we going to do with so much money?" asked Heidi. "We've run out of cigar boxes."

"I think you should bury it," said Marsh. "Bury it where only the three of you know where it is."

Rose laughed. "Our own private bank?"

"So to speak," agreed Marsh. "There are no banks and no way to cash checks. I've been meaning to mention that for ages."

There were also thirteen letters from doctors and nurses in response to the ads for help.

"How will we choose?" Liliane wailed.

Marsh joked, "Tell them all to come."

"Oh, I wish I could! Wouldn't that be wonderful. I really would love to have two doctors right here. And one at the new station. And start two other outposts."

"Where?" Marsh mused.

"Well, they'd all have to be along the river. It would take too long to carry severe cases by travois through the forest paths.

Now," she teased, "I could plan an outpost in the interior if I had a plane to ferry people back and forth. . . ."

Marsh failed to rise to the bait. Instead, he said, "You can ferry patients as well as supplies from one river outpost to another in *My Gal Sal.*"

"Yes." Liliane sobered at the mention of Jack's boat. For a fleeting moment she let her mind dwell on Jack's last kindness; then she returned to the business at hand. "What do I do about these?" she asked, holding out the letters of application.

"Let's look them over." Marsh reached for them.

They held a conference after they'd all read the letters and voted unanimously to invite Dr. Mark Highland from East Lansing, Michigan. He'd written that he had taken as many tropical medicine courses as the University of Michigan offered in the hope of just such an opportunity. He would finish his internship at Chicago's Cook County Hospital in June and could be in the Congo by late September. His enthusiasm overruled his lack of experience. Another strong reason for the choice was that in June he was marrying Estelle Browning, an R.N. They wanted to start their marriage ministering to African natives. Though Presbyterians, they had no burning need to make Presbyterians of the Africans they would serve. They could give no logical, defensible reason why they wanted to come to Africa. It was a dream they had been sharing for the last two years. Seeing Liliane's ad, and having read about her, engendered such excitement in their souls that they were eagerly awaiting a response from her. The references that both Estelle and Mark included were enthusiastic and attested to their integrity, intelligence, and diligence. The coup de grace for Liliane was that one of Mark's references made mention of his sense of humor.

"If all goes as I figure it," said Marsh that evening as he came from telling Carolyn a bedtime story, "they should arrive just about the time I finish the book."

He walked over to Liliane and took the hairbrush from her hand. Standing in back of her, he began brushing her hair.

"If I were a cat," she murmured, "I'd purr." But her contentment was not complete. His book would be finished.

"What then?" she asked, trying to sound more casual than she felt.

"I go to London for a bit." His brushing rhythm soothed her. "Find a publisher, if possible. Stay to rewrite it if there's not too much. If there is, I'll say to hell with it. I've said what I want to say in the way I want to say it."

They had not talked about his book. Marsh was very private about it. She knew he lived in the world of his mind daytimes and entered the active life of Simbayo ambivalently—he resented the time torn from creating; he needed to escape for refreshment.

"Are you pleased with it?" she asked, but her heart beat "London . . . London . . . London."

"I am."

"Does it have a theme?" she asked.

"It's the same theme as most literature through the ages." He sighed. "Man's inhumanity to man."

Liliane looked at him in surprise. "I don't know why that's such a recurrent theme. I really haven't witnessed it all that much."

Marsh took her chin in his hand and kissed her nose. "Lili, my love. You are the most cloistered of women. You've lived so long in an atmosphere of people helping each other that prejudice and greed are alien to you."

"You seem to ignore the fact that I deal with death and disease daily."

"I'll give you that." He looked at her fondly. "But cruelty and sadism have not touched you."

Liliane leaned back. "I'm glad. They're never going to, either."

"Maybe it has to do with civilization. Here in the Congo you don't see cruelty for the sake of cruelty. It may have to do with the African attitude toward the here and now."

"The here and now is all that exists. Most of them can't even plan for tomorrow. And certainly not for six months from now."

"That's what I mean." His hand slid across her breast through the vee of her blouse, touching the softness of her. "Perhaps it takes cunning and learning to be malicious. It takes forethought."

His fingers were gently rubbing her nipples.

"Do you think Anoka and Naldani are mutants?" She bit the palm of his hand.

"They're examples of what education can do. If you knew that tomorrow and the next day and the day after you could find some sort of food, you would never have to save money or plan for the future. If you knew that you would never be without a home, would always be warm, would always have your family around you, if you knew that it took very little work to find meat or grow vegetables or catch fish, you would not have to plan the future, either. That's one of the reasons, I imagine, that life here has not changed in thousands of years. The future will always be exactly like the present.

"However, we educated Anoka and Naldani to our way of thinking. Thinking isn't an engrained process; it's part of education."

"In other words," Liliane said thoughtfully, "thinking as we do jeopardizes the status quo, and there's no reason to shake that when you have a full belly and a roof over your head."

"I can think of a reason. Leopold of Belgium began it. You're lucky, Lili. Here one doesn't see it. But Belgium's colonialism is sadism; it's inhumane. Someday, the natives are going to rise and throw off the yoke."

"What yoke?"

"See? You're not even aware of it here. But certainly you saw evidence of it in Coquilhatville. And even a bit in your beloved Baxter. The white supremacy bit. How would you like to wake up every morning and look in a mirror and think that because your skin's a different color you're inferior and nothing can change that? Hey, what are you doing?"

"Unzipping you. A man's mind gets to me every time." As her tongue wandered over his stomach, the nature of their conversation changed markedly.

While they made love, a gentle breeze rustled through the branches of the palms, the scent of cape jasmine and moonflowers and night-blooming lilies wafted through the air, drums cried into the night. The moon, majestic and huge, moved up the sky, sending its wavering reflection upon the Mombayo, exposing the lacy foliage of the big bokongu tree upon the river's edge.

SEPTEMBER CAME ALL TOO QUICKLY. THE LOGGING CAMP SENT WORD that the infirmary and an office and the living quarters for the Highlands were ready at the new outpost. Liliane did not think much more was needed. But there was no furniture and the radios had not yet arrived.

Heidi suggested it might be wise for the Highlands to remain at Simbayo for at least a month. Anoka had been talked into giving up one of his best helpers, Lombo, so that the Highlands would not be alone at the new outpost.

But Marsh could not wait. His novel was finished.

"Aren't you going to let me read it?" Liliane asked, looking up from the medical journal she was studying.

Marsh glanced up at her. "You know," he said, his voice low, "this is the first time you've asked. Of course you can read it."

"How long do I have?" She suspected he was eager to head to London. She had sensed his growing restlessness. He was not given to a short temper, but his patience had been strained. She had known he was ready to leave.

She was filled with emptiness even before he left.

When they were alone later that night, after Carolyn had been tucked in, Marsh laid a mound of papers on the bed.

She read all night and into the morning.

When she finished the last page, she looked at him, saying nothing. He waited.

Finally she said, "Funny, I thought I knew you so well. I don't know you at all. To think you've had all of this within you. It's not about man's inhumanity to man, as you said. It's about beauty and hope."

He was pleased, she knew, but impatient, too. He reached for Liliane's hand. "You know I have to go, don't you?"

"Oh, darling"—she nuzzled his neck—"you'd have to go even if you didn't have a novel."

Marsh didn't respond.

"I shall miss you and Caro. But I shall stay only as long as it takes to find someone who's interested in this. And then . . ."

"And then?" she murmured.

"Oh, hell, why don't you marry me? Come with me. You and Carolyn. You don't have to devote your whole life to this place, do you? I can't live here forever, Liliane. This goddamn heat does me in. And the jungle gives me claustrophobia. You can't see beyond the edge of it. If we didn't fly a couple of times a week so I could look at distant horizons and know that there's more to this universe than trees that hem me in, I'd go nuts. Don't you ever feel that way? Don't you ever long to leave this heat and dampness, experience civilization again, see more than just these few people? Don't you ever need . . . more?"

No. The center of her whole world was here. Why couldn't his be? Why couldn't he go back to England each time he finished a book, for a few weeks or even months, and get it out of his system? And be content here.

Instead of answering him, she suggested, "Look for a teacher. Or even two." She was telling him she intended Carolyn to grow up here, too.

She heard him sigh.

He turned over on his side to face her, leaning on his elbow, his right hand brushing through her hair. "Do me a favor," he said, looking into her eyes. "The time you've spent with me, spend it with Caro. She needs you." Marsh kissed the end of Liliane's nose. "I know you have to save the world, but Caro is running wild. I've often taken time in the late afternoons to spend with her. But I haven't taken enough time. You and I are so caught up with our dreams that we forget to live in reality."

Oh, that chestnut. "Caro's more loved than most children in the world."

"I'm not denying that. She has playmates, and if you don't give time to her, there's always someone else who will. But don't lose her. Don't let the rest of the camp become her mother. If so, you'll miss something precious that can never be recaptured."

"You know, Baxter warned me about something like that, though he was talking about himself. He said that if you follow a dream, those closest to you will suffer. That you can't give both to them and to your dream."

"I hope he was wrong. Though, admittedly, dreamers do tend to be singleminded. But if we ignore the human aspect in our lives, we are the losers."

"How can you say I ignore the human part? That's what I'm all about—people."

"People, not always persons. Though you are wonderful on an individual basis. These people adore you." He stopped to kiss her. "So do I. But you know what I think? You're not going to like this."

"Wanna bet?" she said, nuzzling his neck.

"I think you're more loved than loving."

Her head snapped back and she pulled away from him. "How can you say that?" Her voice was filled with anger and hurt. "Everything I do is for love of these people."

"Oh, yes, you're a visionary and quite selfless. And I think, if it came to it, you'd probably give your life for these people. But your dream is predominant. You love on a grand scale. It's nice to have me around to touch when you're in the mood, to exchange ideas with. It's nice to have a daughter around and know she's yours. But these you take for granted. You don't need us."

She fought anger. "I suppose you mean because I won't sublimate myself to your dreams like a 'normal' woman would, that I'm sadly lacking."

Marsh was silent for a minute. "I wonder if that *is* what I was saying."

"You want to pursue your dreams, but I shouldn't do the same, isn't that right?"

Marsh stood and walked over to the window. He was quiet for a long time. Liliane's anger began to dissipate.

"You know what, Lili?" He was staring out at the river, talking more to himself than to her. "The very things that drive me crazy about you, that frustrate the hell out of me, are the very things that make me love you. It's because you're not like others that I love you. Yet I want you to be like others and be satisfied to live my life with me. Life is never simple, is it?" He turned to face her, a sad smile on his face. "I wonder if you suddenly said to hell with Simbayo, that you and Carolyn would trail me around the world, if that is what I want. I think it is, but then you wouldn't be you, would you?"

She held her arms out to him, but he didn't come to her. "You know," he continued talking, "we can go along for months or, in this case, years, and be happy together. And then suddenly there's no way I can stay and be happy. I think if it weren't for this damnable climate, I might make it. I honestly think I've reached a point where I'm ready to settle down, but I can't do it here. I can't live forever in a place where my shirt is always damp, where it's never less than eighty-five humid degrees, where the jungle encloses and stifles me. I also find it difficult to do without other people, without variety. But I've never taken you for granted. And I've never felt such a closeness as I feel with Carolyn. You may not be sure who her father is, but I am. I know. My heart nearly bursts when I look at her. There's never been a more beautiful human being in the world. And it rends me to part with her, even if I'll only be gone for three months. I want to hear the new words she says, I want to watch her discover something new about life each day. . . ."

Liliane was thinking, I could stand it if Marsh were gone three months each year. But just three months. And I'd know he'd return. I need to know that. In her heart she did know it. She knew Marsh couldn't leave her even if he had to leave the jungle once in a while.

"You're going tomorrow, aren't you?"

"This sounded like a farewell speech?" He walked slowly over to her.

"Let's make love all night," she said, "over and over. I want to store you up inside me. I want a part of you within me for the next three months. I want to carry you around with me."

"I will always be with you," he murmured into her neck. "There will never be a time in my life that you are not part of me."

And they did make love all night, storing up sweetness and passion that would get them through the time alone.

As dawn broke through the mist, Liliane lay staring out into the morning. Neither of them had slept. She knew she'd feel sorry for herself the moment Marsh left.

I'll go check on the outpost, she thought. That will give me something to do and think about. I'll stop at the logging camp and pay them. I'll take some supplies. If I keep busy, I won't think of Marsh as much.

Carolyn reacted to his leavetaking with equanimity when he explained he would be back soon.

"Stay here, in this house by the river, will you?" he asked Liliane. "This is where I want to think of you. In our home."

He was gone by midmorning. They all walked to the airfield to see him silver into the sunlight, squinting into the sky until they could no longer see the tiny speck that disappeared beyond the trees. Then they returned to the waiting line of patients, to work that always demanded, to duties that never ended.

AT LUNCH TWO WEEKS LATER, LILIANE ASKED, "IS IT ALL RIGHT WITH everyone if I take Lombo and we go to inspect the new outpost? I'll be gone for nearly ten days."

Now that Marsh was gone, Liliane again spent evenings with Carolyn, reading to her, listening to what the little girl had done that day. It was like getting acquainted again. Marsh was right.

She had allowed him to take over, to get close to Carolyn while she ran Simbayo. Now that he was not here, she gave her time to Carolyn and looked with amazement at how the child had grown.

Not just physically, but that, too. She was shooting up in height and was slender as a reed. Her blond hair was nearly white and, unlike Liliane's, was straight. When Carolyn tossed her head, even at barely four, and her hair cascaded like a fan and her fiery eyes lit like aquamarines, she resembled an elfin spirit. She was so at home in the forest that Liliane wondered if her daughter could ever adjust to civilization.

Though Carolyn enjoyed affection, she reacted to it rather than offered it. She liked to be read to, sitting cuddled on a lap or in the crook of an arm; she liked to be hugged, but she never initiated the action.

When Liliane began to read to her, Carolyn crawled into the circle of her arm and leaned against her, her eyes following the dots on the page, her ears and heart listening to the words. Liliane realized what she'd been missing. She was tempted to take Carolyn with her, upriver, but realized that eight or nine days in a canoe would not be pleasurable to the lively little girl.

The next morning she and Lombo took off, with two natives paddling the pirogue. As she sat in the middle of the canoe during the hot muggy days, she had time to think and to wonder: was she doing the right thing? Would it be better for Carolyn to grow up in civilization, in a pretty house surrounded by a garden? And would she herself be happier if she let Marsh shoulder the responsibilities, if she took trips to exotic places with him, if they were never torn apart?

A flock of herons flew into the air, waving their majestic wings above her, and she thought of the wings of Marsh's plane. He is probably in Egypt by now, she thought. And I am going the other way, farther into the heart of Africa. I wonder if Estelle Highland will feel about it as I do. Will their marriage survive such isolation? I shall need to visit them regularly and ask Rose and Heidi to do so. We shall have to expand ourselves as our outposts grow.

They stopped at the logging camp on their way to the outpost. She thought, I won't pay them yet. First, I want to inspect it, see that they've done an adequate job. Three of the men insisted on accompanying her to the site. They obviously took a personal interest in it, though they claimed they just wanted to see what else was required.

When she came to it, her breath caught in her throat. It was beautiful.

They had followed her directions closely. A small house was perched on the incline above the river, its verandah jutting out over the water, able to catch the river breezes and the view up and down the length of the river. When she climbed the bank and stood on the verandah, she could smell honeysuckle in the soft air and look out over the surrounding country to where the soft blue of the sky and the gray-green of the jungle met on the hills on the other side of the river. She had not realized hills were visible from this location.

Envy mingled with delight when she saw what they had done to the inside of this cozy cottage. A rocking chair had been carved of mahogany and sanded until its smoothness gleamed. Liliane ran her hand over its planed curves. Another chair, of lighter wood, was caned with palm leaves and rope. It was surprisingly comfortable to sit in, she discovered. A small round table sat next to it. In the bedroom was a four-poster bed waiting for a mattress, its four posts intricately carved and reflecting pride. A matching chest stood against the wall.

Oh, thought Liliane, how lovely. Her heart swelled with joy. The Highlands would be coming to a home. The generosity of the loggers overwhelmed her. Yet a shudder at the cost of it all ran through her. Would they charge her exorbitantly for all these extras? She had requested just the basics.

In the small dining hall were a gleaming-smooth table and five chairs. Someone had taken great pride in building this furniture.

The infirmary and the office were connected to the dining hall, as they were in Simbayo and as she had drawn for the builders. The whole place was far more comfortable and cozy than Liliane had imagined. Certainly the logging camp could send its patients here more easily than to Simbayo. And it would be the first hospital that this part of the river had ever known.

She turned to the man who was obviously the spokesman for the loggers.

"It's beautiful," she said. "I'm amazed at the professional work. You've done far more than I dreamed."

His grin of satisfaction showed that he was aware of the fact. "It gave us something to do," he said. One of his front teeth was missing.

In a French accent, a second unshaven man said, "It's the only thing we've enjoyed here." Then he pointed to the third man, who stood on one foot and then the other, a silent man with haunted eyes. "Sid's the one who built most of the furniture."

Sid grinned shyly but stared at the floor. "Weren't nothin'," he said.

"Oh, you must know it is. I don't know how to thank you." She knew she shouldn't talk money with them but with the boss at the logging camp.

"Being able to do it," said the first man, "was thanks enough. The rest of life here is like being in jail. Nothing to think about, nothing to do. No one caring."

Liliane held out her hand. She sensed he needed to touch. If I had courage, she thought, I'd put my arms around each one of them. The first man awkwardly stretched out a hand toward hers. Nonsense, she thought. Why does it take courage? She put her arms around him and kissed his cheek.

"Your kindness is overwhelming," she said to the embarrassed man. Turning to the Frenchman, she saw that he was waiting his turn. She hugged him, and her lips brushed him, too.

"Don't touch Sid," he warned. "Sid won't let no woman near him."

Sid shifted from his right foot to his left. But he raised his eyes to the Frenchman and they flashed resentment. "Why the hell don't you mind yer own business?"

Liliane walked over to him and put her arms around him. He was short for a man, just her height. As her arms went around his shoulders, she felt him shake, but no sound escaped him. She kissed his cheek.

How could Marsh say she wasn't loving? She loved these three men. This was what life was all about.

On their way back downriver to the logging camp, Lombo told her he'd decided it was time to get married and bring a wife with him to this lonely outpost. He liked the idea that he could have a dormitory room with windows instead of a hut.

Liliane realized she wasn't surprised when Murphy, the logging boss, told her there was no charge. He was a big man with broad shoulders and biceps that jumped at you. She'd thought he might easily be a bully. He was the boss; there was no doubt about that. "Listen," he said, "the whole time they were building that place, this camp was happy. We didn't have one fight, and they got their work done in jig time so they could go over to that place. And then those three guys built that furniture in their free time. Madami"—it was a name he always called her—"it was a real pleasure. A small way of paying you back for the years of help you've given us."

On the river again, she listened to the water as it flowed with them, taking her home. Home, she thought. Nowhere else in the world could I put down roots as I have here. Noplace else could give me the happiness I find here.

She hoped Marsh would never force her to make a choice.

CHAPTER 23

▼

"DO YOU KNOW," NALDANI ASKED LILIANE, "THAT EVERY YEAR EACH tribe has ceremonies of manhood and womanhood?"

Liliane nodded. She had seen the circumcisions that the men had had and marveled at the neatness of the surgery. She could tell that it had not been done at birth. When the boys were somewhere between twelve and fourteen years old, they were taken from the villages by the old men of the tribe, who kept them sequestered for a month. No one ever told what happened during that time, but when the boys returned, they were men.

For a girl, becoming a woman occurred with her first sexual intercourse. It was never undertaken lightly or impetuously. All girls of thirteen were inducted into womanhood in ritual ceremonies conducted by the old women and attended by all of the unmarried young men of the tribe.

"Each year," Naldani said, "all of the girls who have turned thirteen are taken away by the oldest women. Though it is never to the same place twice, and no one is ever told where it will be, the young men always turn up. Would you like to attend a ceremony?"

"I thought white people were never permitted to attend."

"That is true. But the Mogundas have invited you. I will be your guide, if you like. That is the tribe I come from. It means a two-day trip back into the forest."

Liliane's eyes shone. "Oh, Naldani, I would be honored to go."

"We go alone. No men may accompany us even as far as the village."

She was eager for the adventure. Last month the Highlands had arrived and spent the month at Simbayo. Now they had gone on to the outpost. Liliane felt restless.

Estelle and Mark were a delightful young couple, enthusiastic and capable. They brought with them new ideas from the States, new ways to dress and to wear one's hair, talk of a depression in America, and financial distress the world over. Americans appar-

ently spent their time in movie theaters trying to forget poverty;
the country was alive with hobos; and once-rich men were throwing themselves out of windows in despair. Communism and Nazism loomed on the horizon as world threats; Japan had invaded
China; and someone called Chiang Kai-shek was fighting the Com-
munists rather than the Japanese. No one quite understood what
was happening in the world. Franklin Roosevelt was the most
popular president since the other Roosevelt at the turn of the
century.

While all of this was very interesting, it was so removed from
Simbayo that no one there felt affected by it.

The most extraordinary thing about the Highlands was that
they looked alike. They were both tall and very thin and very
blond. They had pale blue eyes, sharply defined noses, and cleft
chins. They looked mild and colorless and piously conventional,
but in contrast to their appearance, they had dynamic personalities
and verged on irreverence. They laughed often and were exceedingly funny. By the second day Liliane also realized they were both
brilliant. Oh, how lucky she felt.

She had volunteered to go upriver to the outpost with them,
but they wanted to discover it alone, with Lombo and his new wife,
who would cook for them. The radios had still not arrived, but
Mark felt he could handle any medical emergencies that arose.
They would send messages via river travelers and always by way
of the mailboat. So, when the *Oregon* next arrived, they boarded it
with their belongings and supplies of medicine and food, heading
toward their new home and new life.

It seemed quiet after they had gone. They had brought new
zest to Simbayo. Liliane was not ready to settle down to routine;
Naldani's suggested trip into the interior would be a welcome
change. It had been years since she had trekked into the interior,
and she was eager to see native villages again.

She thought, I need another doctor here so that I don't feel
guilty when I do these things.

Before she left, she explained to Carolyn that she would soon
be back.

"That's what Marsh said." The little girl didn't quite pout, but
suspicion was evident.

"I'm going back in the forest with Naldani, to visit her tribe,
and I will be back in seven days. Now I know you can count to
seven. Every day Rose or Heidi will help you to count." She pulled
her daughter close to her and circled her with her arms, looking

into the beautiful blue-green eyes. "Rose is coming over here to sleep with you while I'm gone, and you'll hardly know I'm away. I'll be back before you know it."

Carolyn was so used to security that when it was threatened she didn't know how to handle it. Her mother had, once or twice, gone off—upriver—for a week, and it was true, she had hardly known she was gone. But she didn't like the idea.

"Tell me a story," she said suddenly. "Tell me one of Marsh's stories." Liliane tried to remember one, but they both knew it wasn't nearly as interesting as Marsh's telling.

EARLY THE NEXT AFTERNOON, THE TWO WOMEN SET OFF, FOLLOWING a narrow path that led from the compound into the forest. In all the years that Liliane had been here, she had never taken this path. It was a narrow, age-old path that wound in and out among the trees, wide enough only for the passage of one person. The ground had been worn bare, trodden by thousands of feet over the centuries. The narrow path was immediately swallowed by dense tropical vegetation and became a leaf-carpeted vaulted highway. It's endlessly fascinating, Liliane thought as she followed Naldani into the Congo wilderness. It shuts a person in so completely. This is what Marsh can't stand. It makes him feel small. It's not so much fearsome as awesome.

The decaying musty odor of rotting leaves and logs mingled with the smell of moist greenness. Every branch was hung with green-gray gossamer threads and climbing vines. As they walked along the path, the underbrush thinned, as it always did when deprived of sun. High overhead, shafts of light filtered into the darkness a few feet, but the thick foliage above prevented the light from reaching the ground.

Liliane was aware of how gracefully, regally, Naldani trod along the path. Her back was straight, her pace even and sure-footed. How good it was to be with Naldani again. As soon as Marsh had left, she and Naldani had begun to spend more time together. Love surely monopolized one's time, she realized.

Before dark she and Naldani came to a village of fewer than two dozen huts, made of split reeds tied together to form the walls. As in all villages, whether small or housing a hundred people, there was the same double row of low houses on either side of the path, with the jungle pushing from behind.

The natives insisted that the women stay in the "guest" hut.

Gingerly, they stepped over the dirty sill. The stench was overpowering. Naldani had become so used to cleanliness and windows that even she turned her nose up, despite efforts not to show revulsion.

"I can't sleep in here, Naldani," Liliane whispered.

"You must," said her friend. "You cannot offend the people."

Despite the relative cleanliness of the hut, a chicken roamed around and refused to leave. In a corner a sick-looking dog lay and would not get up. There was paraphernalia lying on the floor and in corners. Liliane longed for the tents she and Marsh had used when they hiked into the wilderness more than five years ago.

Women were preparing dinner in big clay pots. Manioc mixed with greens and palm oil, was boiling over open fires in front of every hut. There was much talk and gaiety.

When dinner was finished, the villagers mingled with each other around the flickering fires and laughter filled the air. This is the romantic hour of the Congo night, thought Liliane. Night breezes rustled the tree branches; the intense heat of the day had dissipated.

But Liliane had great trouble sleeping; the vile smell kept waking her up. Once, back in Buffalo, when she was young, the septic tank had backed up. The smells were similar.

In the morning the sky was light long before the sun rose high enough to peek into the village. Liliane realized these people had never seen a horizon, never seen beyond the encircling rim of trees surrounding the tiny village. Life here seemed so narrow, so restricted. This was how Marsh must feel about the entire continent of Africa. Perhaps she couldn't see much beyond the limited horizon, either. Was she as narrow in her outlook as the natives? No wonder Marsh was restless if this were true. How could he love her when he had all the sophisticated women of the world to choose from?

She had never felt so small.

The next day, about noon, they passed through another village, which was deserted. The men were out hunting and the women and children were tending the gardens. Pots, gourds, and half-dried hunks of meat were suspended from the thatched roofs, collecting flies and emanating odors.

It was nearly dusk when they came to Naldani's village, indistinguishable from the others. But as soon as the villagers recognized Naldani, a cry went up and women who were tending the fires left them and came running to see her. Within minutes, villagers with raw running sores, with limps, with rheumy eyes, with the eternal jiggers between their toes were brought to them.

Kneeling to examine an ill child, Naldani raised her eyes to Liliane in apology. Liliane nodded her head and opened her medical pack. Throughout the evening and early the next morning, she and Naldani attended to the sick—patients who were not so sick that they would have made the two days' walk to Simbayo, but sick enough to be unable to work, to feel defeated, to welcome Mother Lili's attention.

In the morning, as they ministered to the ill, Liliane observed the activity of the small village. The men, as usual, had left the camp shortly after daybreak, but today the women had not gone out to the fields. They scurried around, collecting things and putting them into plaited baskets. The older girls laughed and pointed their fingers at the thirteen-year-olds, who were gathered into a circle, eight or nine of them, already fully developed with trim little waists and beautiful upstanding breasts. They smiled shyly in anticipation, but their eyes were filled with a mixture of pride and fear.

Liliane and Naldani put aside their medical kit when the three oldest women in the tribe walked toward the circle of young girls. Banging pans, the old women marched around the circle. Each girl reached for her basket, and in single file followed the old women into the forest. Naldani and Liliane brought up the rear.

They walked for most of the afternoon. The silence was broken by the giggling and chattering of the girls, but the old women never turned around. At last they came to a large clearing.

"They will build a house," Naldani told Liliane.

"Why?" Liliane asked.

Naldani's eyes narrowed. "You will see."

"What do we do?"

"Nothing. They will feed us, but they will ignore you."

"Do they usually allow observers?"

"Never." Naldani smiled. "I have been asking them for this for the last three years. I told them you couldn't truly become a part of us until you experienced this. I am going to help them build their house, but they will not let you. Only members of the tribe can help, women who have been through this themselves."

"Does each tribe have different practices?"

Naldani shook her head. "All are alike."

The first evening the girls built fires for the evening meal in a small circle in the center of the clearing. Then the oldest woman, wizened and wrinkled, began to talk in sonorous tones. She talked of keeping men happy and of having children, of the need to grow food, and of the need to please.

In the morning, the girls were sent into the forest to gather logs to build a hut and leaves for thatching a roof. It took them all day to build a house that a good breeze could have blown down.

That night, after dinner, another of the old crones walked to the house and invited all of the young girls to enter. The other two old women, Naldani, and Liliane were left outside.

"I cannot tell you what happens in there," Naldani explained. Liliane wondered how nine little girls and one old woman had managed to fit into the small house. There was never a sound from it.

The next morning, however, there was a cacophony of noise. One of the old women had brought a drum and early in the morning began beating on it. For the next two days the drumbeats reverberated throughout the forest until Liliane thought her brain would begin to beat in that staccato rhythm.

The girls built a big fire, which they tended for hours until there was a large bed of ashes. Then one of the old women raked the ashes about and put some into a large baked-clay dish. Another of the old women slowly added water to the ashes, and these were stirred slowly until a white paste was formed.

One by one the girls sat down in front of the old woman, who dipped her fingers into the ash paste and painted designs on the girl's forehead, her nose, her cheeks. She stopped to admire her work, then, taking more of the paste onto her fingers, the old woman reached for the young girl's pointed breasts. Round and round she painted a circle. With her other hand, she massaged the nipple until it became erect. The old woman dotted each nipple with the paint.

Then she told the girl to stand and spread her legs. She painted intricate designs on the inside of her thighs, all the time talking to the girl in a low voice that only the girl could hear.

By the time she had finished, they looked like wild young witch doctors, but Liliane suspected that the old crone had imparted to them more information about their bodies than they had ever known.

In the afternoon, the wildly painted girls and the three old women went off into the woods.

"They will gather liana vines," Naldani told Liliane.

"What for?"

"You will see."

When they returned hours later, the old women cooked dinner, but the girls did not play and giggle. In the evening, around the fire, the old women showed the girls how to fashion their vines into whips. They peeled the vines and whipped them against logs until they became as malleable as ribbons. They then laid them in a circle around the fire. Lilian stared, uncomprehending.

The girls were herded back into the house.

Chimpanzees screeched faraway.

Suddenly, out of the forest, walked nine women. Liliane sensed immediately that they were the mothers of these girls. As they walked from the dark jungle, they began to sing. Forming a semicircle, they joined hands and raised their voices into the night. Liliane felt her heart expand.

Then all hell broke loose.

With whoops and cries, more than a dozen young men swooped out of the forest and ran toward the house.

The mothers, in one instantaneous motion, reached for the liana whips and began beating the males. Their passion built up to a frenzy until Liliane saw blood on the back of one of the young men. The men shouted and the women wailed; no man got near the door of the house.

It was probably no more than twenty minutes, but it seemed like hours to Liliane before the young men withdrew into the forest.

"Won't they come back?" She whispered to Naldani.

"Not tonight."

"Did the women have to beat them?"

She suspected Naldani smiled in the dark. "It is always so. Owning a woman is not easy. Desire is more important than comfort."

"What if the man would rather not be beaten? Or rather nurse his wounds?"

"There are some. But it is shameful. All the young men of the tribe who do not already have a woman come to this. It is expected."

"Do they know what to do any more than the girls do?"

"Oh, yes," Naldani said firmly. "They have been trained in how to initiate girls into womanhood."

Liliane wondered if she would be a witness to that process.

"There are more boys than girls. What happens then?" she asked.

"Some girls will get two turns."

"Is that fair?"

Naldani said into the night, "Do you know of anything that is fair between men and women?"

On the third morning, the girls bathed in a nearby stream and appeared before the three old women for examination. The old women peered into their mouths, jabbed their breasts and their stomachs, and probed between their legs. The young girls stared straight ahead, no emotion visible. Then the oldest one again sat before a clay pot, and this time she painted the girls in different colors. Their arms and legs were circled with bands of blue paint; slashes of yellow were brushed across their abdomens and but-tocks—no two girls were the same. Around their mouths, thin lines of red were daubed; scarlet was circled on the tips of their breasts and on the inside of each thigh. Each girl was given a bracelet of gold that wound around her left arm like a snake. All afternoon they admired themselves.

Before the full moon could rise, they were hustled into the house again. The mothers picked up the liana whips and began lashing out into the empty darkness, crying high-pitched wails, daring the young men to come from the jungle and be beaten.

As if on cue, one young man ran from the forest, through the throng of mothers, hurling himself against the door of the hut that housed the virgins. The women turned on him in apparent fury and lashed at him with their whips. Liliane noted, however, that none of them struck him.

In an instant all was mayhem. Young men ran from the jungle and beat out the fire before throwing themselves against the house.

Above all the shouting, Liliane could hear cries from within the house, high-pitched young girls' voices crying encouragement to the young men. Suddenly the door caved in and several men disappeared inside.

In a minute the young man who had been the first out of the forest returned, carrying a young girl, his arms stretched high, holding her over his head.

All noise ceased.

He carried her to the center of the clearing and all fell back to watch. This was the initiation not only for the young women,

Liliane realized, but for the young men, too. She felt like a voyeur, yet she could not avert her eyes.

Slowly he lowered the girl and stood her opposite him. Naked, gleaming in the moonlight, they faced each other. In the stillness, an old woman brought him a bowl. Putting his hand into it, without ever taking his eyes off his partner, he brushed her forehead with what Liliane instinctively knew was blood.

The girl reached out and took his hands. As though in a practiced ballet, they began to move as gracefully as dancers, swaying to a silent rhythm, touching each other deftly in places designed to fire desire. She pretended to run from him, but he pulled her back with force; she stood still as he bent down and rubbed his mouth across her breasts. Then she slid to the ground, pulling him with her. By the light of the moon, they moved in increasing frenzy; out of the darkness, a drumbeat accompanied the rise and fall of their cadence. Her thin, high voice cried out into the night, the drum was silenced, and only their heavy breathing could be heard as a cloud obscured the moon. In that moment, a low moan escaped him, a shaken sound that trailed along the ground. All was still.

They lay together, unmoving.

Then screams rent the night; men moved toward girls—pulling and carrying them from the house, into the clearing, shouting. The drum reverberated through the forest. Liliane was aware that her own body was taut, wild with desire; she yearned for Marsh. Some force within her wanted release, and she knew that at this moment she might have given in to anyone.

She slept restlessly, dreaming of Baxter and of Marsh—her body alive while her mind dreamt.

In the morning, Naldani said, "The old women and the young people will stay here for three more days. We will return with the mothers."

As she and Naldani walked back to Simbayo, Liliane's mind stayed with young people cavorting in the forest. How the mission society would frown on that, she thought.

THE *OREGON* HAD PASSED THROUGH WHILE THEY WERE GONE. WAITING for her was not only a letter from Marsh, but a short, black-haired man.

His skin was swarthy, his black mustache curved magnificently, his black eyes twinkled with unspoken laughter. Liliane could tell that Heidi and Rose were already taken with him.

He bowed exaggeratedly, introducing himself. "I am Dr. Philippe Dussault, at your service."

He had, he explained, read Marsh's article about her in the Paris edition of the *Herald Tribune.* When he had also seen her ad in the *French Journal of Medicine,* he decided not to take a chance in applying for fear he would be turned down for someone younger. He was an Algerian who had spent ten years as a physician in French Indochina and now found Paris too rich for his tastes. Hot, humid climates appealed to him; out-of-the-way places were lures. He was here to volunteer himself. If he did say so himself, he was an excellent physician and a compassionate man. Liliane looked at his eyes and thought, And often drunk.

But Liliane was not about to turn him away until he proved unfit. He had already moved into Jack's old dormitory room.

She had no time to open Marsh's letter—her first since he'd been gone—until long after dinner, after Carolyn had been listened to and told a bedtime story.

My darling Lili,

It seems impossible that nearly three months have passed since I left you. It is time that has been filled to the brim. I'd forgotten how exciting London can be.

I am being wined and dined rather grandly. The conversation is stimulating but disturbing. A large number of my countrymen sense danger from Germany. A madman (according to my viewpoint) is taking control, and fanatics are rushing to join what he calls Nazism. I see him as a threat to civilization and to life as we know it.

Liliane was having trouble staying awake. Yes, yes, she thought. But when are you coming back?

I shall be staying several more months so that I can read the galleys. Publication is set for September, and my publishers, Davis & Walters, would like me to be around for that. However, I don't think I'll wait; I don't envision staying nine more months. That's too long away from you and Carolyn. I miss you both. London in December is damp, with a biting cold that cuts through one, but I find it invigorating. I used to think I hated cold weather, but now I want to walk *into* the wind.

Christmas is approaching and London is bedecked. I have sent presents for you all but doubt that they will arrive in time. None gives me the pleasure that I received from giving you that jeweled comb that Christmas five years ago, or being able to bring music to Simbayo. No Christmas can ever equal that one.

I had no idea I would be gone so long. I wonder if the Highlands have arrived and if they're what you've hoped for. I have talked to several teachers about going there and am impressed with one woman, who may possibly be on her way by the time you get this. Talking about Simbayo to this splendid, dedicated, and intelligent woman, who found the idea of starting a school in the midst of nowhere intriguing, was like dangling a kitten in front of a wild dog . . . or, more apropos, a carrot in front of a rabbit, because Miss Engle does seem gentle. She does not have your fire, but I suspect she could share your dreams.

Merry Christmas, my darling. Except for missing you, I am happy. But missing you keeps me from happiness. I do love you. Marsh

It was not a satisfactory letter. Tired as she was, Liliane had trouble falling asleep. She was unable to put her finger on what actually disturbed her, but for many days she felt hollow.

Why could Marsh not see that Simbayo was the most exciting world possible?

CHAPTER 24

▼

IT WAS NOT JUST ANOTHER NINE MONTHS BEFORE MARSH RETURNED; it was an entire year.

Philippe Dussault proved to be an excellent doctor with no propensity for alcohol at all. He was amusing, patient, a surgeon par excellence, and he fell in love with Miss Engle on her arrival two months after Marsh's first letter.

She was quiet, mousy almost, at first acquaintance, but Marsh was right—she had drive and boundless energy. By the time she arrived, Simbayo had become a real community. One of the High-lands managed to get downriver once a month from Alpha outpost (Rose had suggested they give the outposts names, beginning alphabetically). Ten months after the Highlands arrived in the Congo, Estelle gave birth to a son, named Paul.

Anoka and Naldani built themselves a western-style house, a small version of Marsh's, and reveled in windows and space. Even with Philippe on hand, they were not able to handle all of the patients easily. Some days there were over two hundred.

The leper island was still a sore spot for Liliane, so with part of the $111,983 they eventually received as a result of Marsh's article, she advertised for a doctor and a nurse to run a leprosar-ium. Dr. Dan Travis wrote from Carville, Louisiana, where the only one in the States existed, volunteering to pioneer a leprosarium with the newest methods. Liliane wondered why her life was pro-ceeding like a magic charm. There should be some problems, she told herself. She should have more trouble getting medical help. They should be less satisfactory, or there should be more tension between the members of their small community. There was next to none.

Liliane was the leader, and that was never questioned. Anoka was her right hand.

Philippe might have been less content if Miss Engle had im-mediately responded to him. Liliane thought that part of the daily excitement for Philippe was trying to gain her attention. It was a drama that amused everyone for a long time.

Deborah Engle had a missionary's zeal about teaching. The idea of bringing education to natives who had never seen a book galvanized her energies and involved all of her powers. It frus-trated but did not defeat her that students would not work hard, that they did not *want* to learn to read, that they saw no connection between education and a better life. Even the idea of a better life was so remote as to seem unreal. Here there was little greed, few prejudices, no haves and have-nots. Everyone was a have-not.

They did not see that education would bring self-rule because they had no concept of being ruled. If the taboos of the tribe were obeyed, all was well. Tribal religion was concerned with the rain-fall, a wedding, an illness. The witch doctors gave immediate an-swers to immediate problems. The Christian concept that there was a life after death, that there was more to life than today, was impossible for these people to grasp.

Deborah Engle had a difficult task ahead of her, but she looked at Naldani and Anoka and knew there could be breakthroughs. She would make her own.

She *was* disturbed by the idea of pythons hanging from the trees, of cobras and puff adders, of deadly ambushes by snakes, but nothing else seemed to threaten her equanimity. The hysterical screams of monkeys swinging through the upper branches delighted her. Seeing her first elephant put her in a state of ecstasy for days. When a poacher collecting animals for a circus went through, she opened a leopard's cage and let it escape into the night.

Marsh's absence became more an irritation than an acute pain. Liliane knew he would return, but she was angry at him for taking so long. If he loved her, he'd be here. If he cared for Carolyn as much as he'd claimed, he'd be here. But she did not allow herself to be consumed by his absence; she was too busy. She immersed herself in Dan Travis's leprosarium plans. He envisioned one of such scope that patients from up and down the river could be sent to it. He thought the island was a perfect place for it but told Liliane he'd need nurses to help. He thought natives in arrested cases of the disease could be trained as aides. His ultimate goal was to have a lab so that he could study the disease in its various stages.

He wanted to research the causes of leprosy; he was convinced a cure was on the way. Father Damien of Molokai was his idol, but he had no intention of incurring the same fate. He was of a more scientific bent of mind and intended this leprosarium to be a milepost in the history of the disease.

His ideas and enthusiasm excited Liliane. But when, one day, he tried to kiss her, she pushed him away.

"It's not you," she told him gently, "but I'm in love already. He'll be back here soon. My heart isn't big enough for another."

"Then find me someone," he said. "I need to share my dream and work."

So, rather calculatedly, they set out to find a nurse who would answer his needs. Dr. Travis and Lisa Bausor were married less than three months after she arrived.

All of this happened in the time that Marsh was gone. His irregular letters informed her that he was working with his publishers and was also outlining a new novel. He had settled into a flat and had even gone so far as to buy furniture; spring (and then summer and another fall) in England was lovely. He had forgotten how beautiful roses were; the air invigorated him. He spent, Liliane thought, an inordinate amount of time writing of the weather.

The week his book was published, he sent her reviews from the leading newspapers and periodicals. One, typical of the others, began "Pearls, pure pearls."

He promised to be back before Christmas.

And he was. But it was not like other Christmases.

The day his plane landed was the last clear day for two weeks. It rained; not the usual dismal dripping, but torrentially. Nothing dried out; the very air quivered with dampness. Sheets on beds were damp; clothes, even though on hangers or in drawers, stayed damp. The air was oppressive. Everyone felt depressed.

Liliane couldn't even greet him with the warmth that over a year's separation warranted; she was angry with him for staying away so long. And he acted as though he weren't sure of his reception. He looked guilty.

With all the other new people who had entered their lives in the past fifteen months, Carolyn's memory of Marsh had dimmed. He was disappointed that he could not immediately resume the close relationship they'd had.

When Marsh and Liliane came together, alone, their love flared larger than life, but their paths had diverged in the last year. The daily problems of life in Simbayo, which were the main topics of conversation, left him bored because he had not been in on the developments. He looked over Dan's leprosarium plans; he motored upriver to the Alpha outpost; he argued politics with Philippe; he glanced appreciatively at Lisa; he hugged Heidi and Rose; he told stories to Carolyn and made love to Liliane.

But after the first two weeks Liliane knew he was not going to stay.

"I can't," he admitted. "I just can't live here."

He walked from the living room out onto the verandah, listening to the river glide by. "It's funny, though. I've missed this place. This house. The water flowing by in the night. The herons on the other side of the river. I've missed the smoothness of life here; I've missed you."

Liliane followed him outside. "But not enough to stay and write your next book here?" A knot formed in her stomach; a churning started in her chest. She'd been so sure of Marsh's love, of his return.

Marsh turned and took her hands in his, looking intently into her eyes. "Lili, I love you. There will never be anyone in my life like you. But our dreams don't mesh. What we want out of life has nothing to do with each other."

He dropped her hands and walked over to the porch railing. Her breathing had stopped. "You're like the tribes in villages." He looked out across the river. "Your world is focused. You never see beyond the trees. You don't see the hills, the valleys, the cities. You don't long for variety and any life other than your own.

"You don't care about the theater, or of conversation except about medicine, or anything that interrupts your vision. You don't want to see snow. The goddamned humidity doesn't do you in. You're hardly aware of it."

"That's not true!" She felt she had to defend herself. "My clothes are always damp. I know I'd have more energy in a temperate climate."

"Liliane, if you had more energy I'd fear for the world. You are going to save this part of the world, you're going to surround yourself with people who share your dreams. But I can't live here and be a part of your dreams any more than you'll come away from here and be a part of my dreams."

"Did England do all this to you?"

"It acted as a catalyst, I'm sure. It gave me back a zest for life that I think had escaped me. It made me see that I was forgetting about myself so that I could be with you. I love you so much that I was willing to make the sacrifice, but . . ."

"But love isn't enough?" Liliane thought she might cry.

"Love isn't enough. Though I know I'll never find a love like ours. I know I'll never stop loving you. But I cannot live life on your terms, and you will not live your life on mine."

Silence filled the night air.

He strode over to her. "Lili. Try it my way. I tried yours for two years. Please. Give us a chance."

When she didn't answer, he pushed on. "You have good people here. They can manage. Your good work won't be lost. Come with me. If Africa's what you need, let's go to Nairobi. Or Cape Town. Let's go where we can look up and see the wide sky. Where we can entertain. Where it's not always hot. Where people get excited about what's happening in the world. Let's go where there's variety. Lili, I don't need to travel endlessly. I want to put roots down. Lili, let's build a house. Let Carolyn find friends, go to school. She'll be five before too long. You can't keep her here forever."

Liliane turned from him, her anger surfacing. "I know I can't." She wanted to pummel him with her fists; instead, she clenched them tightly by her sides. "You've made that clear over the years. But she doesn't have to go yet. What makes you think you know what's better for her than I do? She does have friends here. She has Petelo. She's happy."

"She's growing up to be a female Tarzan," objected Marsh. "A wild creature more at home with monkeys than with her own people."

"Her own people! What do you mean by that? White people? Americans? British? What are her kind of people?" Liliane's voice was raised.

"Come on, Lili, you know what I mean."

"You have no right to judge what's best for her!"

"And you do? You really think you have the right to choose illiteracy—"

"We've started a school."

"Yes, and is Carolyn going to be like all the others here? Able to think only of today? Never to be challenged? Never to be allowed to grow to her potential? Lili, my God. I know you know better."

"What am I supposed to do, lose both of you because I have to live this life?"

He gathered her in his arms, kissing the top of her head as she dampened his shirt with her tears.

"You have to make a choice," he said softly. "You cannot have the people you love and the life you have chosen."

"But I can have the people I love if I give up the life I have chosen?" she sobbed in short bursts.

Marsh didn't answer.

"Then what kind of life is that?" she gasped. She was silent for a moment; then she spoke more calmly. "I've thought if you really loved me, you'd be here with me. But if I really loved you, I'd give this up to be with you, wouldn't I?"

Marsh sat down and pulled her with him. He kept an arm around her.

"We really love each other. So much so that it will ruin us for anyone else. But I think we might stop loving each other if either of us gives up . . . what we need . . . to follow the other. I don't know how to solve it."

They clung to each other.

"What about Caro?" he asked quietly.

Her shoulders shook. "I don't know. I can't face it yet. I can't understand if I'm happy and fulfilled here, why the people I love can't be."

"Maybe Carolyn can be happy here, but how will she feel about it when she's twenty?"

"How can I part with her, Marsh? She's a part of me. I need her."

"And I need you *and* her. But you and she are both going to be denied to me. Lili, you will survive Carolyn's going to school. She'll come home to you summers, for Christmas, and for the mid-winter July break. But you have to give her a chance. You can't create a freak."

Freak? Oh, damn you, Marsh.

"I'll pay for her schooling," he offered. "I want to."

"I can't talk about that yet, Marsh."

"You're going to have to soon. She should go away to school next year."

"No! Let me have her for a couple more years. Deborah will teach her."

"It's not just the basics of reading and writing she needs. She needs to adjust socially."

Liliane jerked her head up. "Marsh, I will not send her away from me to be brought up by strangers until she's at least seven!"

"But you will let me leave you both? You won't come to America with me for a visit? You won't come to a pretty house in Kenya or South Africa? Or Rhodesia, if you'd rather? You won't even try it?"

"If I try it . . . if I leave here for a year, I will never fit in the same way again. You know that."

"I knew before I came. But I had to try once more."

"I have no choice, Marsh. You may think I do, but I don't think so."

"No," he said with resignation. "I don't think you have even as much choice as I do."

"We're trapped, aren't we?" she asked, putting an arm around his neck. She kissed him, her tongue running along his lips, wanting all of him for whatever time she could have him.

WHEN HE LEFT, THREE DAYS LATER, THEY CLUNG TO EACH OTHER AND could not let go.

"Marsh, you know I love you. Life will never be the same. I love you and I can't bear this."

"I know. Life will always be less, Lili. Your face will be in front of me every night. I'll start every time I see short red curls ahead of me on the street or hear a voice that might be yours."

"Oh, Marsh." Tears flooded her eyes. He was leaving her forever.

She began to cry, great, gasping sobs.

"Come with me, Lili," he whispered urgently. "Get Carolyn and run away with me. I need you. You're what gives any meaning or stability to my life."

"I can't," she sobbed. "I can't leave here."

"Good-bye, my love." His voice broke, and a tear ran down his cheek. "I love you. I shall love you forever." He kissed her. "Good-bye."

CHAPTER 25

▼

MARSHALL COMPSON WEDS

May 25, 1937, London: Marshall Compson, 37, one of the western world's more colorful writers, married Dolores Stratton-Leigh, 28, in a small ceremony at the home of the bride's father, the Earl of Saxton of Widbourne Abbey.

Compson, author of *Misdeeds* and, more recently, *Heceta Head,* is famous for his exploits of danger and exploration as well as his two novels.

Misdeeds is currently one of the most successful movies of record, playing to capacity audiences around the world.

This is a second marriage for both the bride and groom. They plan an extended honeymoon in Tahiti and Bali.

It was the first she had heard from Marsh in the months since he had left. The wedding announcement had been roughly torn from the newspaper and glued onto a sheet of stationery. In Marsh's black scrawl, he had written:

I need someone. I was not made to live alone. Forgive me. My heart, though, is yours. You and Carolyn are always with me. I love you. I shall forever.

Liliane laid the letter down and stared at nothing. Then she put her head on her desk and cried. She cried until there were no more tears, great, gasping sobs until her ribs ached. She cried for her loss, and because she had no choice. She cried in self-pity. And she cried as much for Marsh as for herself.

The pain that racked her chest, she knew, was her heart exploding into a thousand shattered fragments.

She was nearly thirty. Not for nearly another thirty years would she weep like this again.

CHAPTER 26

▼

THE PLANE'S ENGINES DRONED ON. CAROLYN LAY ASLEEP, HER HEAD on Liliane's lap. The seven-year-old girl had so grieved at leaving Simbayo that she'd had no energy to enjoy the sights going downriver to Léopoldville. She had smiled at nothing and stared resentfully at her mother at the same time she clung to her. Finally she had cried herself to sleep.

I didn't think my heart could break again, Liliane thought.

Her mind played back the highlights of recent years. Did the satisfaction outweigh the losses? Will I ever know? she wondered.

There were now four outposts up and down the river: Alpha, Bonnie, China, and Detroit. She smiled as she recalled the fun and laughter involved in choosing the names. The last three outposts were staffed by nurses, who rotated every three months with duty at Simbayo so that none would feel the constant isolation. *My Gal Sal* made it possible to bring the most urgent cases to Simbayo. Radios worked effectively and kept the outposts in touch with each other. A second school had even been started down at Detroit, and at the island leprosarium stunning results were in evidence. Though there were no permanent cures, Dan Travis had succeeded in checking many cases and even in improving some. Clergy from the large Catholic mission at Kabugani had come to study it and stayed for several months.

Now, in 1937, there were over fifteen white nurses and doctors connected with Simbayo and its outposts, and scores of native aides. Deborah Engle and the new teacher, Jane Barber, while often at odds about methodology, were both showing that Congolese could be educated. Each had tapped a desire to learn in some students. Deborah even had two candidates she wanted to send abroad for further education.

Despite the success of the school, Liliane knew Marsh had been right. Carolyn's quick mind thrived on challenges and would soon reach the limits that could be offered in the shelter of Simbayo's schools. Petelo had an equally inquisitive mind, but opportunities for seven-year-old African boys in foreign schools were few. Naldani was unwilling to part with Petelo, anyway.

When, at last, Liliane decided the time had come for Carolyn to be educated, she could not bear to send her as far away as America. She wrote to the mission for information about schools. After Marsh's article and its worldwide circulation, they had been extremely helpful to Liliane, sending most of the materials and medicine she'd requested. It seemed that when she had money to pay for supplies on her own, they helped more than when she had to beg. She had never asked the mission to recruit her staff.

The mission informed her that there were three schools in Africa that might be appropriate for Carolyn. As the daughter of the renowned Baxter Hathaway, she would be welcome in any of them. Cairo, Nairobi, and Cape Town. The one in Cairo was, by far, superior, but Cairo seemed too Muslim to Liliane, too foreign. The school in Nairobi couldn't compete scholastically with the other two; Nairobi was a small town with few whites.

Cape Town was nearly three hundred years old; a white enclave in a black continent. She could fly to Cape Town without too much difficulty and Carolyn could fly home for vacations. Liliane told herself the only country that separated them was Rhodesia. Cape Town seemed infinitely nearer than the States and preferable to Cairo. Compared to Simbayo, it would appear to be a modern city. So, Cape Town it would be.

The evening Liliane told Carolyn was a night of terror for the little girl. Liliane explained that she would be starting a wonderful new adventure by flying to a foreign country, that she would be entering a school where all the children were white, where she would learn about the white world in which she would someday live. But Carolyn screamed and cried, wailing into the night, hurling innumerable "whys" at her mother and at fate. She would not leave Petelo, she didn't need to learn anymore, she was happy here, she didn't want to leave Liliane. No No No No No. Her cries were heard throughout the camp.

Liliane wanted to gather her up, to comfort and reassure her, but Carolyn would not let her mother near her. "No, I'll die," she hurled at her. "I won't go. I'll run away."

When, exhausted, Carolyn finally fell into troubled sleep, Liliane lay awake, unable to relax. She held her head between her hands and accused herself. Was her own selfishness destroying the lives of those she most loved?

Should I have gone with Marsh? I send my little girl out into a strange country all alone. I send Marsh to the arms of another woman. I, myself, am harder; I know it. I don't allow myself to feel deeply. To survive, I have shielded myself. Why?

If I really love her, could I send her away? I can't keep her here and make a freak out of her, as Marsh feared I'd do. If I really love her, wouldn't I leave Simbayo and makes a home for her where she could go to school and not be alone?

These questions flashed through her anguished mind; in the end, she knew they were all rhetorical. Whatever the right or wrong, whatever the good or bad, she could not leave Simbayo. She cursed the fates that had brought her to a place in life where she had no choice; but she recognized that she *had* chosen, long ago.

Caro, Marsh, and I may have less personal joy than if we'd all been together, she thought, glancing down at the thousands of miles of trees beneath her, but I can't choose happiness over duty. *Our* lives might have been fuller, but many Congolese would have lesser lives, and I know it. It's the one thing I do know. Three lives with less and thousands of lives with more—maybe eventually a country with much more.

Twice a year she wrote Marsh short formal notes about Carolyn, sending them to his old address at *The Times*. She knew he no longer worked there, yet the letters never came back. He did not answer until she had written to tell him she was following his advice and taking Carolyn to the mission school in Cape

Town for the beginning of the new school year in January. In response to that came a brief note and a check for $1000.

> I told you I wanted to pay for Carolyn's education. Please let me. Not a day goes by that she isn't in my mind. You, too.

Liliane felt a catch in her heart.

So she made plans to leave Simbayo for the first time since she had arrived, ten years ago. At the staff conference held after dinner, everyone agreed that it would be good for Liliane to stay with Carolyn for five or six weeks while the child adjusted to her new way of life. Philippe suggested that Liliane study new medical techniques at the larger hospital in Cape Town and also see what the university could advise in the way of new treatments. This way, he knew, she would feel less guilty about taking time away from Simbayo.

"What if you find out you don't need me?" she asked wistfully.

Philippe reached out and put his hand over hers. His little mustache curled as his eyes crinkled into a smile.

"I will be the first to admit I am a better doctor than you are, though not by very much. But you are the one with vision. You dream the dreams and we go along for the glory."

Deborah said, "I imagine it will seem lonelier here while you're gone. Your going away will make us appreciate you all the more." She still had not given in to Philippe's amorous attentions, but she had grown beautiful in the nearly three years she had been here. Liliane saw them look at each other now and then with that secret look of lovers, but Deborah kept just enough out of his reach to tantalize Philippe, just near enough to give him hope. Liliane wondered if they'd even kissed.

It will be good for me, she realized, to get away. I need a break. I need to see how the rest of the world lives. I need to study a little. I need to be alone with Carolyn.

Yet she was surprised to feel herself afraid. She didn't even know what clothes to wear.

"I'm sure," said Deborah, "that any you have will look ridiculous. As soon as you arrive in Cape Town, you must buy yourself and Carolyn new clothes. Then we can see what styles are in fashion when you return. I want a pretty dress. I think you could buy me a dress, size ten, please."

"Oh"—Heidi was delighted with the idea—"I think you could

buy us all some things. We can all make out lists."

They spent the evening around the dining table, making out their lists, crossing items out and adding others until Liliane said, "I can't bring that many things back on a plane. Limit your lists to five items each." They spent another evening debating and deleting.

When the *Oregon* came downriver the next time, Liliane was ready. Caroline refused to go. She planted her feet firmly on the ground, wound her hands around the porch railing, and cried, "I won't go! I'm not going!"

Liliane and Philippe pried her hands loose, and Philippe carried her, screaming and writhing, to the boat. Petelo stood by helplessly, not understanding that it would be many months before Carolyn would be part of his life again, nor that their relationship would never be the same. Not understanding that the next time he saw Carolyn, they would be strangers to each other.

All the way up to Coquilhatville on the *Oregon* Carolyn was silent. She stared at the river's edge and clutched the arms of her chair, staring at their passage downriver with angry, unseeing eyes. After dinner she lay on her bunk and stared at the ceiling, wide-eyed, until after Liliane fell asleep.

They spent two nights at the hotel in Coquilhatville, waiting for the steamer that would take them to Léopoldville. Carolyn clung to her mother's hand in desperation, her small, thin fingers wound tightly around Liliane's. They made an odd picture on the streets of that town. Liliane, with her curly auburn hair cut in the same short style she had worn for the ten years she had been in Simbayo, in a pale dress that was faded from too many washings and worn from too many years. To a world conditioned to fashion and chic, Liliane would have looked laughable, but in this small town on the equator whose fashions hadn't changed in hundreds of years, she was simply a rare white woman. The few white men in town turned to look at her. The heart-shaped face that had been so pretty in Buffalo had become serenely beautiful, age having etched character into the planes of her face. The still-thick black lashes accented the startling color of her eyes, and her generous mouth suffered nothing from a lack of lipstick. Looking at herself in a mirror, Liliane could see none of this—only the increasing lines around her eyes and the two or three gray hairs that she thought had come far too early to a thirty-one-year-old woman.

As she walked along, holding Carolyn's hand, people stared. Two pairs of such turquoise eyes were rare. Carolyn's flaxen hair hung like silk and framed her tanned face so that her looks, too, were striking. Carolyn did not have her mother's obvious beauty; though she looked like a fragile child, she was really wiry and energetic.

Carolyn looked at the people in the streets and felt strange and frightened. She had never seen multistoried buildings or cars or horses or cows; she had never known a store, or a boat other than *My Gal Sal* and the *Oregon*. She had never seen so many people or heard so much noise. She hoped Cape Town wouldn't be like this. She was terrified.

And she hated her mother, she told herself as she clutched Liliane's hand.

On the trip to Léopoldville, the little girl evidenced more interest, though she wouldn't admit it. Here, the river was often nine miles wide, dotted with hundreds of islands through which the ship wove a tortuously slow path in order to avoid constantly shifting sandbars. Hippos and crocodiles sunned themselves on the wide banks. The boat stopped at nearly every small village, and natives came running to trade with them. They offered coconuts, tangerines, peanuts, pineapples, sugarcane, manioc, bananas. Most of the passengers were natives and had to supply their own food, so the trade with villagers was often brisk. Liliane urged Carolyn to watch the village bartering. Freshly killed monkeys were held high in the natives' hands, and crocodile eggs and even a dressed-out antelope were proffered to the passengers. There was palm oil and live grubs and fresh fish. The passengers built small fires on the deck where they cooked and even did their washing. They slept here, too, and it was a noisy festival time.

Dawns on the big river were constantly shrouded in fog. In the early afternoons, an eerie gloom preceded the wind that sprang up, like clockwork, sweeping the decks with a fine drizzle. One day the boat had to stop before the furious onslaught of a thunderstorm. The captain turned on the spotlights and swept their beams into the torrential downpour where nothing could be seen. He ordered the boat to a standstill for two hours. Liliane and Carolyn sought shelter, but the majority of passengers had paid only for deck space and huddled under blankets or against the walls or stood stalwart in the face of the deluge.

As abruptly as it had begun, it stopped. The gray clouds evaporated and a sapphire sky danced above them. In another hour it was drenched in blood, reflecting orange-red stripes shimmering in the river as the sun set. Birds by the thousands flew from the river into the trees, off beyond the horizon.

Oh, thought Liliane. Marsh would like this; the horizon is limitless. He threaded through her thoughts at odd times.

The jungle began to give way to the high, craggy yellow limestone hills of the Crystal Mountains that rose on either side of the river. The boat slid into Stanley Pool, an expanse of the river that seemed more like a lake—fifteen miles wide and twenty miles long.

The distant roar, Liliane knew, was Livingstone Falls, beyond Léopoldville.

Carolyn's eyes widened in wonder as they pulled into the vibrant dock of the capital. Barges, tugs, steamers, cargo boats, and pier after pier lined the waterfront, and there were shipyards and chandleries and warehouses. All river traffic began and ended in Léopoldville even though it was still three hundred miles from the sea and a thousand feet above it. Even in 1937 more than a million passengers a year passed through the port.

Carolyn and Liliane stayed in the large, bleached-stucco European hotel. They were served by black waiters in white jackets with white linen napkins over their arms; they slept in high, soft beds and took baths in a tub that had clawed feet raising it above the floor. There were curtains at the windows, and the noise of the city drifted up to them on the fourth floor. There were electric lights even in the bathroom. There was an outdoor café where they had breakfast of French croissants and cocoa. At last Carolyn was wide-eyed, her interest awakened despite her unhappiness.

Carolyn had never seen so many people or so many buildings or heard so much noise. There was a comparatively large population of Europeans, mainly Belgian, German, and French. Liliane looked at their clothes and felt out of place in her ten-year-old dress. Yet she could not take the time to shop here.

They had a plane to catch—the first in a series that would take them five days, with luck, to travel two thousand five hundred miles. The first plane would take them south in the Congo to Elisabethville, on the northern border of Rhodesia. From there they would pass through customs and fly to Salisbury, the capital of the country fathered by Cecil Rhodes, then to Johannesburg, and from there to Cape Town.

In less than a week they would arrive at the southernmost tip of this enormous, still unexplored continent.

In the rush and stress of customs procedures, in the strangeness of it all, Liliane gained no sense of the places where they transferred planes. The hotel in Elisabethville was not worthy of the name; Simbayo was cleaner. Salisbury was more cosmopolitan. There were quite a number of white people, and it had a European aura, but Liliane got no clear sense of place.

Johannesburg was just a city in which to change planes. They were there no more than two hours, all of it at the airport. When Carolyn was not staring sullenly out the window, she slept. She had hardly talked since they'd left Simbayo. Liliane was confident she would adjust rapidly—as children do—to school and a new environment, but nevertheless at the moment she felt guilty. One had only to look at the child to sense her pain. Liliane stroked the blond hair fanning over her lap.

Oh, my darling, she thought. How I shall miss you. Miss your questions, and your laughter, and your snuggling close to me early in the mornings. I shall worry about whether you are sick, or if you've wandered away and gotten lost, if you're making friends, and if you've forgiven me. I shall miss reading to you—though in the last year you've taken to reading to me, reversing our roles. They had devoured all of the Winnie the Pooh books Liliane had ordered years ago. And read them over and over again.

The Cape Town hotel clerk smiled when he noticed the outfits Liliane and Carolyn wore. The next morning, before they even saw the ocean, Liliane took them shopping. Carolyn would be wearing uniforms, but she should not arrive at school looking as though she had just come out of the jungle.

Carolyn stared at herself in the mirror and her eyes showed signs of life. Once in a while she had looked in her mother's jade hand mirror, but never in a full-length one. Her new black Mary Janes shone back at her when she glanced down at them, and the pink dress had a full, gathered skirt that she kept trying to push down. Liliane bought her white gloves that were buttoned with pearls and a little straw hat with a ribbon. She also outfitted her with a navy blue blazer and a tartan skirt and some comfortable brown walking shoes. Carolyn preferred them to the pretty patent-leather ones.

They spent two days exploring the city before Liliane contacted the school. She talked to the silent Caroline as they shopped and as they strolled down to the wharf and viewed the ocean. She continued her one-way conversation as they walked beside the solid buildings and as they ate the food that was strange to Carolyn, who left most of it on her plate.

Cape Town was not nearly as large as Liliane had envisioned. It looked more the way she pictured Holland, rather than England. The English spoken here was a mixture—some of it sounded as British as one would hear in London, but most of it sounded like a patois of English combined with Dutch. Only by listening very carefully could Liliane understand it.

Despite her ten years away from civilization, the city did not intimidate her, but neither did it charm her. Its formality, its busyness, its crowds caused her to draw into herself.

I never used to be this way, she thought. In the past, I always found myself in the center of the fun. She felt lost and estranged.

Carolyn's eyes observed it all, but she continued to say little. Nothing would make her admit her excitement now, thought Liliane. She's punishing me for taking her away from her friends. When they did, finally, take a taxi to the school, Liliane was charmed by the countryside.

She was enchanted by the acres of vineyards on the gently rolling hills, the neat white houses, surrounded by sturdy Dutch barns, nestled in the hillsides.

The school compound was encircled by a tall brick wall over which one could not see; wide wrought-iron gates opened at the blast of the car's horn.

There were two brick dormitories, which housed eighty or ninety students, a brick dining hall combined with a recreation room, and a classroom building. The taxi stopped in front of the school.

A middle-aged woman descended the steps and held out her hand as Liliane emerged from the cab.

"I'm Miss Blake." Her voice was like quicksilver.

Liliane shook her hand. "Mrs. Hathaway." She helped the sullen Carolyn from the taxi. "Will you wait?" she asked the driver.

"Don't bother," said Miss Blake, "our car will take you back to the city." She glanced at Carolyn, who was looking at the building and studiously ignoring the woman who would now have charge of her life. Miss Blake stooped down to hug the little girl, who backed away.

She smiled reassuringly at Liliane. "We won't rush her." She led them up the steps, talking to Liliane. "We're honored to have the daughter of Baxter Hathaway and Mother Lili in our school."

"I'd no idea you had heard of me way down here." Liliane's surprise was genuine.

"I imagine much of the world has heard of you." Miss Blake opened the large front door.

In her office, sitting on comfortable chairs with colorful chintz covers, Liliane said, "I plan to stay in Cape Town for a month or so in order to help Carolyn make the transition more easily."

Miss Blake smiled. "That's lovely, though I think it will be easier than you imagine." She turned to Carolyn, who looked at her blankly. She rang a bell and a young woman with braids and dressed in the school uniform appeared.

Miss Blake introduced the woman as her assistant, in charge of the dormitories. "We'll be along in a few minutes, Annie, but you might take Carolyn to her room."

Carolyn turned to Liliane with cold fear in her eyes.

"I'll be along," Liliane tried to reassure her. "Miss Blake and I want to talk for a bit."

Carolyn reached out her hand and stuck it in Liliane's.

"No," she said.

"This is so strange to her," Liliane said. "We've never been apart. She's never been away from Simbayo."

"Well," Miss Blake said with understanding, "why don't we all go to see Carolyn's room. I'm sure you'll be pleased with it."

The four of them crossed a courtyard shaded by two large trees and planted with hundreds of flowers. They entered the dormitory where Carolyn would live for the next three years.

Her room contained two of everything—two narrow beds, two desks, two bureaus, two closets, two straight-backed chairs, two footlockers, and two small bookcases. Two large windows flooded the room with light.

The room surpassed Liliane's expectations.

"Your letters so clearly explained the way Carolyn has been living." Liliane wondered if she imagined vague disapproval in Miss Blake's voice. "So many of our students are the children of missionaries. It is often a difficult transition for them. But we handle it rather well, if I do say so. Carolyn will be rooming with the daughter of missionaries from Nigeria. I expect they'll have much in common. Classes don't start for a week, so they have time to get to know each other and become accustomed to our routine."

Carolyn walked around the room, fingering the bedspread, opening and closing drawers, looking out the windows.

"We have high standards. When your daughter leaves here, she will be academically prepared for any good college and will carry herself with social self-confidence and high moral conduct.

"Though boys and girls share the same classes, they have separate dining halls and, of course"—she laughed lightly—"separate dormitories. There is no need for worry."

Oh, Carolyn, what a narrow viewpoint of the world you'll get, thought Liliane. She sighed aloud.

When neither Liliane nor Carolyn responded, Miss Blake asked, "Can she read yet?"

Carolyn haughtily responded, "Very well."

These were the first words she'd uttered all day.

"And," added Liliane, "she knows her multiplication tables, too. We have a school at Simbayo."

Miss Blake sat down next to Carolyn, taking the child's hand in hers. "Your roommate will be arriving later today. Most of the students will arrive this afternoon and tomorrow. I think you'll enjoy the children here. Annie will show you where everything is, and this afternoon Victoria and you can become acquainted."

Carolyn's gaze continued to be vacant.

"When may I see her again?" Asking permission to see one's own daughter. Maybe I can't stand this any more than Carolyn can.

Desperation filtered from Carolyn's eyes to Liliane's, as though longing for one last chance.

"Oh, let's see. This is Wednesday. How about the weekend? If you'd like, you can come to Saturday lunch."

"Can't I have her with me for the weekend? We've really never been apart."

There was a slight hesitation on Miss Blake's part, but she smiled. "Yes, if you'd like. That would be all right. But keep in mind by then she and Victoria may be inseparable."

Liliane knelt down and put her arms around Carolyn, who stood unmoving within the circle.

"Oh, darling," Liliane whispered. "Just try it. You can't stay in Simbayo forever."

She knew that Carolyn was frightened.

"You are," said Carolyn in an accusing, pinched voice that sounded close to tears.

"When you're grown up, you can, too, if you want. You can become a nurse like I am and come back and help. But without education you won't learn to be a nurse. For now, this is where you need to be." She clutched Carolyn to her. The fact that they would see each other in four days did not make this seem less like a good-bye.

As she rode back to the hotel, Liliane thought, I've lost something precious and important. And it's my own fault because I won't give up Simbayo for my daughter. She buried her head in her hands but could not cry. Her head throbbed as if her unshed tears had formed a blockade that would pound there ceaselessly.

CHAPTER 27

▼

LILIANE FOUND GREAT PLEASURE IN SHOPPING FOR HER FRIENDS. Armed with their lists, she wandered in and out of stores for the next three days, whiling away the time until she could be with Carolyn again. The stores were exciting, filled with luxuries Liliane had long since forgotten about, but her mind was never free of worry. Was Carolyn speaking? Eating? Being friendly? Still blaming her? Adjusting to her new life?

In the evening Liliane wrote letters. They were not letters to anyone in particular; they would never be mailed. Sometimes they were to herself, asking questions that had no answers. Sometimes they were to Marsh, wondering if she were doing the right thing . . . and sometimes asking if he still loved her, if he was happy. One she wrote to her mother, apologizing for leaving home.

> Now that I am leaving my daughter and know of a wrenched heart, I wonder how I could have done that to you. I left you, and now I'm forcing my daughter to leave me. Oh, Mother, what kind of woman am I? I have always said good-bye to the people I've loved the most.
> You forgave me, didn't you? Will Caro ever forgive me?
> Oh, Mother, I wonder if you'd like me now. The world seems to know who I am, and they've made me into some kind of heroine. But I don't think I like the person I've become.
> I wish I could use God as an excuse. To say "I've done all I've done so I could dedicate my life to God. I've given up the man I love and my daughter for God." But I haven't. I've done it for me.
> I wonder how you and Daddy would view the life I've

lived. Here, in Cape Town, in "civilization," I am so aware of what a narrow life I've lived the last ten years, unaware and unconcerned with the outside world, trying to solve the problems of my own little world. I have limited my horizons so greatly.

She stopped writing and stared out the window into the twilight. She'd forgotten there could be lingering twilight and that clouds could gradually change from vermilion to orchid to soft blue and then to gray. That it could take an hour for darkness to descend and that it could be such a slow, magical time.

Night shadowed its way into Cape Town. Liliane thought, I've given up love in all its guises for something that seemed more important. Ironic, she said to herself, when what initially brought me to Simbayo was love: the towering form of Baxter Hathaway, in a Buffalo living room.

What path might my life have taken, she mused, had Baxter not walked into our home eleven years ago? One chance meeting, one casual contact, had changed the whole course of her life and the lives of those who now lived and worked at Simbayo. Had I not followed my heart to Simbayo, she thought, all of these lives would be different.

And what about her own? By giving up the two she loved most, had she lost more than she had gained? Could one ever measure life? Could one ever make up for what was lost?

ON SATURDAY MORNING, WHEN SHE DROVE OUT TO THE SCHOOL, SHE found Carolyn, dressed in her new blazer and plaid skirt, sitting on her bed, her hands folded on her lap.

A small dark girl, her elfin face as winsome as Carolyn's was stern, sat on the windowsill. Neither of them was talking.

When Liliane entered the room, she forced an engaging smile on her face. Carolyn looked up at her but made no move. Liliane threw her arms around her daughter.

"Oh, you look beautiful all dressed up. Are you ready?"

Carolyn slid off the bed and nodded toward her roommate. "This is Victoria."

Liliane walked over to the little girl and knelt down. "How nice to meet you. I hope you and Carolyn will be good friends."

"I hope so, too." Victoria's voice sounded like bells. "I've never had a friend. There are no other white people where we live."

Carolyn's voice came from across the room. "There aren't other white children where I live, either. But I have very good friends."

"My mother won't let me play with the niggers," Victoria said. "It's going to be very nice here. Everyone is white."

As Carolyn and Liliane headed toward the taxi, Liliane took Carolyn's hand. "Would you like Victoria to come with us?"

"No," Carolyn said, and withdrew her hand from Liliane's.

Liliane had thought it would be fun to climb Table Mountain and had talked the hotel into preparing a picnic lunch. At last, a good idea: it was the first time Carolyn had responded with anything akin to enjoyment since leaving Simbayo. She frolicked up the path ahead of Liliane, exploring and running, sometimes skipping. She called back down to Liliane when she saw something interesting, a small flower or a rabbit scurrying away.

"Oh, Mama," cried Carolyn, looking out over the valley. "It's like being on the airplane. How far you can see."

It was a steep climb, so they did not even try to reach the top. But even at this height, Liliane drew in her breath. It was a splendid view. One could easily see the ridges known as Lion's Head, Signal Hill, and Devil's Peak rising like mounds among the surrounding houses. The shores of Table Bay shone with whitecaps, and they could see where the construction of Duncan Dock was beginning. A large ocean liner was in port, the people, from up here, resembled ants scurrying around. From the other direction one could see the low, rambling hills of vineyards, mile upon mile, running out to False Bay. In the distance were the Mountains of Africa, lavender in this light. The ocean stretched interminably; as Carolyn said, "Forever and ever."

It had been worth every inch of the climb. Carolyn was not daunted at all, but Liliane felt her heart pounding in her ears.

Spreading a tablecloth out on a rock, they sat down to chicken sandwiches and deviled eggs. Carolyn again looked like the child Liliane knew. Her eyes were alive.

"Is this how all the rest of the world is?" she asked between bites.

"No," answered Liliane, "much of the world is very ugly and very crowded. This is much prettier than most of the world."

"Is New York bigger than here?"

Liliane laughed. "Oh, New York is a hundred times bigger. And it's very tall. It goes up and up. Some buildings have one hundred floors."

Carolyn tried to imagine this as she nibbled her egg. "Why do Victoria's parents think she shouldn't play with black children?"

"I don't know." Liliane wiped her mouth with a linen napkin. "I really don't. Some people think that because we have white skin we're superior."

Carolyn didn't quite understand. "But why can't she play with them?"

"Maybe you'll have to find out. Maybe you'll have to help Victoria see the world as you do."

"Why did I have to come to a white school? Why can't I learn what Petelo learns?"

"Because someday you may want to leave Simbayo, and you wouldn't know how to live anywhere else. You'd have a very hard time."

Liliane knew none of these answers could satisfy a seven-year-old girl, but Carolyn did skip over to her now and then, on their way down the mountain, and reach for her hand.

At dinner in the hotel dining room that night, Carolyn asked, "If I had always been a good girl, could I have stayed with you?"

"Oh, darling, is that what you think? Do you think I'm punishing you?"

Carolyn looked down at her plate.

Liliane reached across the table and put her hand over Carolyn's. "I love you more than I love anybody in the whole world. I don't want to be away from you. I'm doing this for your sake, so you'll learn things you couldn't learn at Simbayo. So that you will grow into a thinking, intelligent adult. And so that you will be able to make intelligent choices."

"Would intelligent choices have kept my father or Uncle Jack alive?"

Where did she get such thoughts? Liliane didn't even know she thought about Baxter, and Jack had died years ago. Carolyn could hardly have known him.

"Not your father, but maybe Uncle Jack. If we had known just a little more about what disease he had, or why he was dying, maybe we could have helped him. That's one of the things education can do. Help us to find cures for diseases."

"Why couldn't Marsh," Carolyn said, changing the topic, "be

my father? Why did you send him away? To learn more about the world?"

Liliane pushed her plate away. She had lost her appetite.

"No. I didn't send Marsh away," she said, her voice low. "He didn't want to stay."

"Didn't he love us enough?"

Carolyn had never asked any of these questions before; now, Liliane was being barraged with the questions that Carolyn had been storing up.

"I guess not. He didn't want to stay at Simbayo. He said he needed more that the world offered." How in the world could a seven-year-old understand this when she herself had trouble with it? "We don't all want the same things. And love isn't always enough. We each have to search for what we want, and sometimes we hurt the people we love along the way."

"Like you're hurting me?" Carolyn's eyes narrowed.

This is one precocious young girl, thought Liliane.

"I don't mean to cause you pain," Liliane said. "I am doing something to help you, and it hurts us both."

"Whatever it is"—tears formed in Carolyn's eyes—"it hurts a lot."

That night, Liliane and Carolyn shared the same twin bed.

DURING THE NEXT WEEK, LILIANE WENT OVER TO THE GROOTE SCHUUR Hospital and spoke to the administrator there, explaining who she was and asking if she could make use of their library.

The administrator welcomed her in a thick Afrikaans accent. Of course he knew of her work and of her late husband's, and she was welcome to use the library. If she would also like to view some operations . . . anything else . . . So Liliane spent her days at the hospital, which she soon realized was not much more modern than the one at Simbayo. The doctors were no better than Philippe, and certainly not as good as Baxter had been. This hospital was larger and much more crowded, of course. There were, as in all public places in Cape Town, two entrances. Blacks were not allowed into the white part, which was much cleaner, more modern, and less crowded than the dingy native side.

She wondered how any white person of sensibility could live in South Africa, with its natives barred from restaurants and hotels and public restrooms and even buses.

▼

IN THE NEXT TWO WEEKS, LILIANE COULD SEE CAROLYN THAWING A
bit. Though she did not resemble the sunny imp she had been in
Simbayo, she did talk more and even smiled a couple of times. She
even asked if they might take Victoria out to lunch on Saturday.

"She's rather nice," Carolyn admitted. "I don't think I'd want
her around Simbayo, but she isn't silly like a lot of the girls are."

Liliane had thought they seemed like a sober lot. These children had not been brought up in America or England; these
daughters of missionaries had grown up in isolated primitive soci-
eties. Many were returning from their summer holiday and were
accustomed to the school, but few of them behaved like the carefree, sometimes silly schoolchildren Liliane remembered in Buffalo.

She thought it might be fun to introduce Carolyn and Victoria
to the cinema, so after lunch she took them to see Shirley Temple
in *Little Miss Marker.* The two girls were mesmerized by this
method of storytelling. Afterward, however, she heard Victoria
say, "I don't think people really act like that."

Carolyn, who was used to Winnie the Pooh and the realm of
make-believe, enjoyed herself thoroughly.

On the way back to school, Carolyn asked, "That's one of the
reasons I'm here, isn't it?"

"What do you mean?" Liliane ran her hand through Carolyn's
soft hair.

"The movie. That's one of the things I had to come out of
Simbayo for, isn't it?"

"In a way, yes."

Carolyn was silent until they reached the school. As Liliane
walked to the gate with her, she said, "I really liked the movie,
Mother. But it's not worth giving up Petelo for Shirley Temple."
Then she stood on tiptoe, reaching up to kiss Liliane's cheek.
Liliane leaned over and hugged her daughter.

"You don't have to give up anyone. You'll be with all of us in
a few months." Few? Was six months really a few?

IT WAS DIFFICULT FOR LILIANE TO ADJUST TO THE AFFLUENCE AROUND
her. The streets were thronged with purposeful, well-dressed
white people. She found the beds luxurious and realized she had
almost forgotten what the amenities of civilization added to life. In

part, she thought it rank waste and luxury; another part of her basked in it. Hot baths in tubs and heavy pile towels, enough light in a room so that reading did not mean squinting at night, stores that could supply a lifetime of luxury.

She bought herself some fashionable clothes, then wandered into a beauty salon and luxuriated in a stylish haircut and shampoo. She felt decadent when she answered yes to the salon's suggestion of a manicure, but glancing down at her fingers and observing herself in the mirror made her smile with satisfaction. For the first time since she'd left America she felt feminine and pretty.

The theaters changed their programs weekly, and she saw every one. Greta Garbo and Robert Taylor made her weep in *Camille.* She sat through Fred Astaire and Ginger Rogers in *Top Hat* twice, then took Carolyn to see it. She laughed uproariously at Irene Dunne and Gary Grant in *The Awful Truth.* Maybe Marsh was right about Carolyn's being exposed to the world. There was so much that never touched Simbayo!

She was surprised to discover how much she was enjoying herself. Aside from crossing the Atlantic, she had never done anything alone before. There was no hurry or pressure. Occasional bouts of guilt at the frivolous life she was temporarily leading did not interfere with her pleasure. She gradually felt her whole body begin to relax; she had not known that she was so tightly wound up after ten years with no vacation.

She wandered through Cape Town, which was really a rather small city. She was fascinated with the city's history and studied the monuments whenever she discovered them. Jan van Riebeeck's statue on Adderley Street delighted her. She'd had no idea the city was founded in 1652, which was when he had landed. The oldest monument, the Castle of Good Hope, dated from 1666 and was still in fine condition. She visited the Old Supreme Court, which incorporated part of the structure of a slave lodge built in 1680. Slaves even then. What right had one person to dictate to another?

Some of the graceful rounded-gabled homes, dating from the 1700s, reflected Dutch architecture. She'd had no idea white people had colonized this part of Africa so long ago.

She spent a whole day in the National Botanical Gardens on Queen Victoria Street. She had thought the Congo reflected Africa's climate and flora. Now she realized it was but a small part of Africa, not at all typical of the rest of the continent.

Carolyn still smiled infrequently and still continued to express anger and resentment, but her curious mind responded to the teaching the school offered. Victoria's attitude toward the natives of Africa created a barrier for Carolyn, but Victoria, too, was a keen student. Their lively, inquisitive minds bound them together even if their viewpoints kept them from understanding each other.

Carolyn greeted her mother each Friday afternoon with such hugs that Liliane's breath was squeezed from her. Certainly Liliane had never enjoyed Carolyn more. Because, she told herself, I've never given her my undivided attention. And here, too, Carolyn did not have Petelo to divert *her* attention.

On the Friday morning of her third week in Cape Town, Liliane's world exploded. A fire that had lain smoldering burst into flames.

Arriving in the dining room for breakfast, she wended her way through the tables to the one that had become hers; she thought she saw Marsh.

She stopped suddenly and shook her head. No, of course not. It must be her imagination.

But as she neared, he rose in that graceful way of his, stretching to his full height, a smile on his lips and a question in his eyes. "Liliane," he said.

She stood still. Suddenly weak, she felt as though her legs would give out. She put her hand on the nearest chair to steady herself.

His dark eyes stared straight into her. She saw his finely chiseled face in stark relief, as though he had never been away.

He was dressed in a dark suit with a vest and looked more formal than she had ever seen him. The burgundy silk tie accentuated the crisp whiteness of his shirt.

"Marsh."

Her mind had stopped.

"I'd hoped you'd still be here, so I could see both you and Carolyn. Great luck." When she said nothing, he gestured toward an empty chair. "Won't you join me?"

She sank into it.

"You're looking more beautiful than ever." His voice curled itself around her, drawing her in.

"What are you doing here?" she blurted out.

"Oh"—he smiled, but his eyes were hard—"we're on our way to Nairobi. Dolores wants to go big-game hunting, so I promised her a safari after my latest book was finished."

Nairobi by way of Cape Town?

A waiter offered her a menu. She waved it away. She had no appetite.

"Bring her coffee," ordered Marsh.

She sat staring at him, wordless. Her heart sounded like the ocean crashing against a rocky shore. A pulse raced in her right temple.

"You wrote," he said, "that you were bringing Carolyn to school here. As long as I was going to be in Africa, I wanted to see her. See the school. See . . . Oh, there you are." He stood graciously as the most regally dressed woman Liliane had ever seen suddenly stood by the table.

Though not exactly beautiful, she carried herself with such assurance that she commanded attention. A halo of reddish-gold hair framed her oval face. She wore a white sleeveless dress and very high-heeled white shoes. Liliane could tell her clothes were not chosen casually. She felt dumpy in comparison. Dark blue eyes hinted of arrogance, yet her voice was friendly as she seated herself between Marsh and Liliane. "You must be Liliane," she said as she unfolded her napkin. No smile appeared on her face.

Dolores concentrated on the menu and gave her order before raising her eyes to study Liliane. Like a butterfly pinned to the wall, Liliane reacted to this situation as though she were immobilized. Paralysis overcame her. She felt her hands begin to shake and put them in her lap.

"Small world," she forced herself to say. The words, she realized, were inane. "Imagine running into someone I know in Cape Town, when I know so few people in this whole world."

"Not so strange," said Dolores, looking at Marsh and smiling, "when you realize we detoured to Cape Town just to meet you and your daughter."

Dolores was orchestrating the meeting.

"Oh?" Liliane bristled ever so slightly. She disliked feeling manipulated.

"Well," Marsh said, unable to force a smile to his face, "when I heard we'd both be in Africa at the same time, I realized how long it had been since I've seen Carolyn. Far too long."

"Yes," agreed Liliane, matching the casualness of his voice. "What is it, two years, three years?"

Marsh's lips grew thin and rigid. "Some time, anyway. I thought it might be nice—"

"To renew old acquaintances?" Liliane couldn't believe the bitterness she heard in her own voice. Why was he doing this to her, flaunting his wife in her face, dredging up pain? Damn him.

Her coffee arrived and she scalded her tongue with it.

"Where have you been all these years?" It was the sort of conversation people who hadn't seen each other in one year, eight months, and nineteen days would not have.

Dolores examined a long red fingernail. "Marsh makes marriage very exciting. In two years I've seen more of the world than I ever dreamed possible. We hunted elephant in India, and I shot a Bengal tiger there." She smiled with satisfied delight. "Though I think the hunt is more exciting than the actual kill."

She is very different from me, thought Liliane.

"Then why kill?" The hammering in her head would not let up.

"Oh, my dear! The fun of it." Liliane could tell that Dolores thrived on danger. This must be what Marsh desired. One of the reasons Simbayo could not satisfy him. "Now we're heading to lion country. Though what I'd really like is a cape buffalo."

"She's been reading Hemingway," Marsh said as though that explained everything. Marsh was looking at Liliane from across the table. Not staring, just looking, listening to the interchange.

There was a moment's silence as the waiter brought Dolores's breakfast.

"I'd like to see Caro," Marsh said.

Does Dolores know he might be Caro's father? Liliane wondered.

"She's not happy to be here," Liliane said. "She thinks that we don't love her at Simbayo and that she's being punished. She can't understand why she has to leave all she holds dear in order to learn. It doesn't make sense to her."

Did Marsh understand that she, herself, was questioning the wisdom of his idea? Good. He could see what his insistence was doing to Carolyn. He could see that maybe it wasn't the perfect solution. He could see—

"When can I see her?" he asked. His voice sounded faraway.

"I pick her up Friday afternoons at the school," Liliane answered, "and we spend weekends together. I thought it might help if I stayed for a few weeks."

"How long have you been here?" asked Dolores, her azure eyes glancing around the dining room. If she sensed there had been anything between Marsh and Liliane, it did not seem to disturb her.

"Three weeks," Liliane answered. "It's been a hard time for Carolyn."

"What about you?" Marsh asked.

"It's been hard for me, too," she answered. "The hardest part for me is knowing how both Carolyn and I will feel when I leave."

"When is that?" asked Dolores. Was there a sense of condescension in her voice? *I have him; you don't.*

"I'm planning to stay another two weeks," Liliane answered, but it was to Marsh she was speaking.

"May we all have dinner together tonight?" he asked. "Do you think Carolyn would like that?"

"I'd like that," said Dolores. "If we've come two thousand five hundred miles out of our way for a little girl, I want to meet her."

"Yes, of course," answered Liliane, her thoughts frozen. She wanted to reach out and touch Marsh, put her hand in his, feel the warmth of his arms around her, the touch of his lips on hers. She wanted to unveil her eyes so that he could see how she really felt.

Were his eyes masked, too? Is that why he looked like a stranger? Once she'd been able to look at him and know exactly what he was feeling.

Dolores ran a napkin across her scarlet lips. She smiled graciously and said, "If you'll excuse me, I'm going to run. Only because I know I'll see you again tonight. Actually"—she smiled brightly—"I've waited a long time to meet Lili and Caro. You two plan the weekend, and anything's all right with me."

With a flourish, she was gone.

The coffee settled in Liliane's stomach like molten steel.

"May I drive out to the school with you? I'd like to see it. Maybe meet the headmistress." Marsh's hand wound around his coffee cup; the other lay motionless on the table, but she could see its tenseness.

"I guess that's the least . . . since you're paying for it."

A shadow flickered across his eyes.

Liliane pushed back her chair and stood. "The car will be here at three o'clock," she said. "If you want to meet me in the lobby."

Marsh reached a hand across the table. It brushed hers and she jerked her hand away. "Don't go," he urged. "Stay and talk with me."

"I really can't," she said, her voice sounding brittle and false. "I have important things to do. But I'll meet you at three."

She turned and left hurriedly.

The important thing she had to do was to vomit in the gleaming-white porcelain toilet.

CHAPTER 28

▼

"I DREAM OF YOU," HE SAID, "EVEN WHEN I'M AWAKE."

Marsh broke the silence as the car sped toward Litchfield.

Liliane stared straight ahead.

She knew his eyes were riveted on her; she could feel his dark gaze boring into her, trying to see below the surface as he used to. It had been so easy then. Now she refused to allow him past the wall she had erected. She would not permit herself to relive the agony she had experienced; she would not cry like that again.

She would ask for no explanations. Had he been unaware of the pain this reunion would cause her, of the emotions it would awaken in her? Had he no thought for her feelings? If he had to see Carolyn, he could have come at any time during the next nine months.

She had trouble swallowing.

"Dolores knows about us . . . about Carolyn. The past doesn't bother her."

Doesn't it bother you? she kept herself from asking.

She dared not let herself glance over at him, so close to her in the backseat. She mustn't be drawn by the look in his eyes or by his finely chiseled face that she saw in her memory every night of her life. She had learned to handle it in the dark, beside her on the pillow or imprinted on the ceiling. The image had even become an old friend she could turn to, whom she always knew was there. But this Marsh, in person, was another matter.

"This Africa is very different from the Africa I know," Liliane said, her voice impersonal. She felt it float through the air, disembodied, quite separate from her.

"This Africa," said Marsh, "is beautiful and more ordered than the rest of Africa on the outside, but it is cancerous and breeds the seeds of destruction on the inside."

"I would find it difficult to live here." Liliane continued staring straight ahead.

"It's certainly beautiful. I would have to fight the mores, though, if I lived here."

"Ah, but the climate's so invigorating." She was unable to suppress her sarcasm.

Another silence.

Then he asked, "Do you think Caro will recognize me?"

Liliane shrugged her shoulders and glanced out the side window. The vineyards were trim and the houses painted and neat.

"She's vulnerable right now. And very unhappy. She doesn't need any more sadness."

"Are you saying you think seeing me will make her unhappy?"

"Probably no unhappier than she already is. She thinks we're all rejecting her. She may find it difficult to open up to more hurt."

"Is that why you're acting like you are?"

Now she turned to face him. Her voice rose in anger. "What did you expect? Did you want me to throw my arms around you in front of your wife? Did you want me to say how nice it is to see you again?"

"The latter, certainly. Lili, the past is not erased. What we had was beautiful. We both know that. I had to go on. But I also had to see you again."

"Don't you think that's quite like rubbing your tongue into a cavity? Making yourself feel worse? A form of masochism?"

"It's making myself feel better. I *had* to know how you are. What you're doing. How Carolyn is. What she looks like. I want to know if your outposts are successful, how Heidi and Rose are, what Anoka and Naldani are doing." He reached out and took her hand in his.

The touch jolted her, yet she let her hand be surrounded by his. She concentrated on keeping her hand very still and unresponsive.

"Simbayo's a big part of my life," he continued. "Almost as big a part as you are. I can't let go of it."

The big gates loomed ahead of them, and Liliane said, "We're here."

She opened the car door before the driver could get out.

"May I come in with you?" Marsh asked.

"No. Let me prepare her. Let me tell her you're here. We'll just be a few minutes. She'll already be waiting."

Once inside the dormitory, Liliane leaned against the wall. Oh, she thought, can I stand it? Her legs felt weak again.

Marsh. Marsh and his wife.

Supporting herself against the wall with her left hand, she

journeyed down the hall to Carolyn's room. As usual, her daughter waited on the edge of the bed, looking lifeless compared to the Simbayo Carolyn. Victoria was nowhere in sight.

"I'm ready," Carolyn said tonelessly.

Liliane said brightly, "I have a big surprise for you. One you'll like."

"We're going home?" Faint hope arose in Carolyn's blue-green eyes.

"No, darling." Liliane put her arms around Carolyn's thin shoulders. "Doesn't it get any better?"

"It's not home." Carolyn's voice was plaintive.

"Well, someone who loves you very much has come to see you. He's come a long, long way just to see you."

"Petelo?" Happiness tempered with a question showed in Carolyn's face.

"No." Liliane forced herself to smile. "It's Marsh. He's come all the way from Europe to see you."

"Marsh . . . ? Marsh!"

It had been nearly two years since Carolyn had seen Marsh. Of course, she and Liliane had talked of him. She remembered him, but Liliane wondered if Carolyn would even recognize him. Two years was almost half a lifetime to the little girl.

"He's waiting out in the car."

Carolyn's eyes lit up, and she started to run, gathering speed. "Marsh," she cried to the empty halls. She was ahead of Liliane the whole way.

Marsh was standing beside the car, one elbow resting on its hood. He was unprepared for his own reaction. That fairy spirit in the doorway, looking . . . She saw him and screamed, "Marsh!" Then she ran toward him with her face screwed up, laughing and crying at the same time.

His heart tilted. He knelt down and opened his arms, his eyes fogged, too, by emotion.

Carolyn hurled herself into Marsh's outstretched arms. They clung to each other with intensity.

"Let me look at you."

They gazed at each other, laughing through tearstains, and hugged each other again.

Liliane felt a catch in her throat. She heard him say, "How's my girl?"

Carolyn kept repeating, "Oh, Marsh, Marsh, Marsh."

Liliane stood back and watched the tableau. Let Marsh have his moment. In the meantime, she clutched her chest to still the sharp pain.

On the ride back to the hotel, Carolyn showed more animation than she had since they'd left Simbayo.

"I didn't think I'd ever see you again," she said, snuggling into the arm that Marsh put around her.

Maybe, Liliane thought, this will prove to her that the people she loves will never be completely out of her life.

Maybe the people *I* love will never be completely out of my life. . . .

She was able to sit back in the corner and watch the two people she loved most in the world. And the two that she was going to have to learn to live without.

Carolyn was listing the numerous activities of Cape Town, ones which she had shown little interest in while participating in them.

"Oh, movies are such fun," she said gaily to Marsh. "We go to a new one every Saturday. And there are so many things to buy in stores. And have you ever seen the ocean?" She rattled on.

Marsh raised his eyes in amusement and met Liliane's.

"Oh, we're a family again," Carolyn said happily, looking from one to the other. She reached out and took a hand of each in hers, smiling radiantly.

"Can we have dinner together?" Marsh asked Liliane.

"Where are you going?" Carolyn asked. "Can't you just stay with us?"

"I have to meet my wife," he told her, his eyes avoiding Liliane's. "She wants to meet you, too."

Carolyn looked at him questioningly. Then she turned to her mother. "Isn't he going to stay in our room with us?"

Liliane folded her hand over Carolyn's. "Marsh is married now," she said. "He stays with his wife. But we can see them at dinner."

Damn you, Marsh. I don't want to see you at dinner. Don't you know what you're doing to me?

I could handle it, she thought, if he were here and not married. If I were free to reach out and touch him, free to show how I feel, free to rejoice in his presence. If I didn't have to hold back my emotions, my love. If I didn't have to hide the real me.

When they entered the dining room that evening, Liliane heard Carolyn suck in her breath and say "Oh!"

Marsh was waving at them, and as he did so, Dolores stood. Her dress was a bright red chiffon. Its multilayered skirt swirled even as she stood. The neckline plunged nearly to her waist, revealing smooth, evenly tanned skin that glowed from across the room. Long silver earrings spun under the muted overhead lights, and her golden hair haloed her head like a cloud. Silver bracelets climbed her right arm. Her left was bare, the better to accentuate the enormous diamond that shone on her hand. Liliane was sure it had not been there this morning.

She felt dowdy in the tailored, pale green linen dress she had thought such an extravagance. She just knew Dolores's shoes would be fashionably high-heeled and shiny black. Her own were sandals, though new. Everyone in the dining room was admiring Dolores.

Dolores was unself-conscious. She greeted them warmly, paying particular attention to Carolyn. Her manners were impeccable, and she made conversation easily. Liliane and Carolyn had only to follow her lead. She told Carolyn how much Marsh had talked about her and how long she had looked forward to meeting her. She asked questions about the school that drew Carolyn out; she asked Carolyn about Petelo and could "imagine how much you must miss him." She told Carolyn what fun school could be and asked if she'd ever seen elephants or leopards or monkeys.

Liliane could understand how Marsh was attracted to her. She was witty and intelligent and glamorous. She also listened intently; Carolyn had a ready audience. Liliane observed that Carolyn had thawed in no time. But after just three weeks in school, Carolyn was no longer the carefree little girl Liliane had always known. She displayed manners and restraint. She had become civilized all too quickly.

Yet Liliane knew of the wildness beneath the affected exterior.

Despite her own feelings of discomfort, she, too, thawed. Dolores asked questions that had Liliane and Marsh reminiscing and laughing uproariously. She was able, now, to answer Marsh's questions about the outposts, telling him of the success of the four river ones and expressing hope that eventually she could get into the interior; about Heidi and Rose and the others at Simbayo; she could even discuss her pride over the success of the leprosarium. Dolores made it all easy. She found herself liking Dolores even though they had little in common . . . except Marsh.

Carolyn's eyes began to glaze over at about nine o'clock.

Dolores suggested, "Perhaps we can do something together

tomorrow. We'll be here for another two weeks. And certainly"—
she smiled down at Carolyn—"I want to see *you* again."

Carolyn held out a hand to shake. Liliane had never seen her
do that before. In mock solemnity, Dolores shook it, but Marsh
would not settle for that. He kissed Carolyn and said, "It's so good
to see you again."

As Carolyn drifted off to sleep, Liliane heard her ask, "Did
Marsh leave us for Dolores?"

"Not exactly," was the only answer Liliane could give.

THE NEXT DAY THEY WADED IN THE OCEAN, SPLASHING AND SHOUT-
ing. Dolores seemed to enjoy it as much as anyone. They had fish
and chips at a little restaurant down on the beach. Liliane noticed
that only white people populated the beach. It was a world she had
forgotten.

All the time, at every moment, she was aware of Marsh. Aware
of the way he moved and of his laughter. She was conscious of the
way he looked at Carolyn, and at Dolores, and at her. She was
sensitive to that voice of his, which sounded like rusty nails, and
of the graceful way he walked. She noticed the crinkles around his
eyes and mouth when he smiled. She was also aware of an enormous amount of self-control. A hundred times she started to reach
out without thinking, to point something out to him, or to touch
his arm, or to murmur something for just his ears. But she must
not. She felt as though she were encased in a mental straitjacket,
unable to move of her own volition.

She heard Marsh say something to Carolyn about "next weekend." A tight knot formed in her stomach. She didn't think she
could get through weekends like this.

Marsh and Dolores insisted on driving back to the school to
say good-bye to Carolyn. "We'll see you next Friday," assured
Marsh, "and we'll think of something exciting to do. Maybe we'll
rent a car and drive up the coast to Port Elizabeth. Stay there
overnight."

As the three adults drove back into town, Dolores lit a cigarette and said, "You can certainly be proud of her. She's a lovely
little girl." She sounded as though she meant it.

Marsh invited Liliane to dine with them. She pleaded a head-
ache, though it was really her heavy heart that pained her. She had
a light supper in her room and wondered if she could last.

No. She would leave. She would let Marsh have the next two weekends with Carolyn. Let him spend time alone with her. Carolyn seemed to be settling in, and Marsh's presence would ease Liliane's leaving. Marsh, Carolyn, and Dolores could take a holiday up the coast next weekend and Dolores could play stepmother. Liliane would get back to Simbayo as soon as she could. Away from Marsh as soon as possible.

After a restless night with little sleep, she made arrangements at the desk for the next train to Salisbury. The one plane a day was filled for the next five days. From Rhodesia she would figure out how to get back to the Congo, even if it meant detouring by way of Nairobi. Even if part of the way she couldn't get a plane.

"I can book you on the ten-thirty train tomorrow morning," said the hotel clerk.

Liliane made the reservation. Now to tell Caro.

She left the hotel and wandered around the city, wanting to be out of Marsh's reach. In the late afternoon, she took a taxi out to the school, then approached Miss Blake. "I've been called home unexpectedly, so I've come to say good-bye to Carolyn."

Miss Blake clucked sympathetically, adjusted her pince-nez, and suggested that Liliane stay for tea. She and Carolyn could dine at her table.

But Carolyn was in no mood for watercress sandwiches and shortbread after Liliane told her she was leaving. She said nothing, just stared at her mother as though she were seeing through her to the empty air behind her.

Liliane told her that she'd received word that Philippe was ill and she was needed. No one else could operate. "But Marsh will be here for another two weeks," she said in an attempt to comfort her daughter.

Carolyn stared mutely.

At tea she didn't talk and wouldn't listen.

When Liliane was ready to leave, she stooped down to face Carolyn. "Darling, my leaving you doesn't mean I don't love you. I do. I love you more than anything in the world. Someday you'll understand."

"Someday," Carolyn's voice was scathing, "may never come."

"Oh, darling." Liliane threw her arms around the icily controlled little figure. A shiver ran through her. God, what am I doing?

Neither of them cried. Carolyn would not kiss her mother,

though when Liliane looked up at Carolyn's window before she stepped into the taxi, she saw the slender, flaxen-haired figure there, statuelike.

She leaned her head back in the taxi and closed her eyes. How, she wondered, do people ever know if they're doing the right thing?

It was twilight when she entered the hotel. She was drained of energy. Marsh rose from a deep chair in the lobby.

"Oh, there you are." His voice was congenial, but there was anger in his eyes.

Yes, here I am, she thought. But not for long.

"I've been looking for you all day. Thought you might like to dine with us."

"No, sorry. I'm tired. I've been busy all day." She couldn't look him in the eye. As she started to move away from him, he slipped his hand around her wrist.

"Lili." His voice was low.

"Marsh, leave me alone. See Carolyn all you want, but leave me alone."

"Please." His voice was urgent.

"No," she said. "I can't. I can't be with you, Marsh."

"Lili."

She turned to confront him. "Marsh, leave me my memories. Let me remember you as a part of us."

"Oh, Lili . . ."

"Stop saying that." Her voice was sharp with irritation. "She's nice, Marsh. Don't do this to yourself or to her—or to me."

"I can't help it."

"Well, I can."

"What does that mean?"

"I'm leaving tomorrow." As soon as she said it, she could have cut her tongue out. She should not have told him. She should have let him discover it after the fact.

He let go of her wrist.

She walked to the elevator and never looked back.

THOUGH SHE FELL ASLEEP BY TEN, SHE WAS WIDE AWAKE AT MID-night. She lay there for half an hour, eyes wide open, listening to the night sounds. Then she got up. Arms clasped around herself, she stood staring out the window at the city where a few lights twinkled. She heard the crow of a rooster. "Dawn's not for hours," she told it.

I'd thought my life had a magic charm, she thought, and now I don't ever remember being more miserable. I should go get Carolyn and take her on that train with me . . . take her back to Simbayo and life would be the same.

But she knew life would never be the same.

Maybe she and Carolyn should return to the States, find a small house in a small town. Carolyn could go to a good school and make nice friends, and she, herself, could nurse in the local hospital. Find a husband. Live a normal life. That's what she should do.

She heard herself sigh.

There was no way she could do that. It was not even a viable alternative.

She should be brave and stay and face Marsh. She wished she did not feel tempted to touch him. She should forget what they had had and face reality. But that's what she found so hard. She had been able to live with the knowledge that Marsh was never coming back, that he was married now—until she'd seen him—because she'd had her memories. She had had them tucked into her heart and had known that they were sacred to both her and Marsh. But seeing Marsh with a wife, with Dolores, had nearly erased the closeness she still felt. It was just too hard, knowing that they had shared secrets, that Dolores knew about her and Carolyn (just what did she know?), that Marsh and Dolores went to a room where they shared a bed and maybe some laughter and a life.

Her breathing became ragged.

She heard him calling to her, calling across the jungle, across the plains. "Lili . . . Lili . . . Lili."

Damn him. "Lili . . . Lili."

"Goddamn it," she cried into the night. "Stop it!"

Then she heard the knock.

It had not been across the plains. It had not been in her imagination. He was at the door.

As though sleepwalking, she moved in slow motion to meet him.

And there he was. His eyes were bloodshot, and she could tell he'd been drinking. He pushed past her and into the room.

"What the hell do you mean," he blurted out, "you're going?"

She'd never seen him like this before.

She didn't answer.

"I came seven thousand five hundred miles to see you."

"You used to come halfway around the world to Simbayo on impulse, so I'm not impressed." She made her voice cold.

"Jesus, Lili, don't you care anymore?"

He was asking her if she cared?

"Whether I care or not has nothing to do with anything. You're married. You and I are in the past."

He grabbed her arm. "You and I are never in the past," he said. "You haunt me. Every goddamn time I make love to Dolores, you come between us. Every goddamn thing she says, I compare to you."

"Marsh, don't blame me. And you're hurting me. Let go."

"I never intend to let go. I should have made you come with me, made you and Carolyn leave Simbayo."

She could smell the alcohol on his breath.

She wrested her arm from his grip and turned away from him, but his hand grasped her shoulder. He swung her around to face him.

"Don't walk away from me," he said in a voice so low she could scarcely hear it.

His hand touched the strap of her nightgown. "All weekend I've wanted to touch you. I've wanted to kiss you, to hold you. I've wanted . . ."

The fabric screeched as he ripped it off her.

"Marsh . . ." There should be anger in her voice, she knew. She should pick up her torn nightgown, hold it around her, and order him out. Pick up the hotel phone and ask for help. Throw him out.

Instead, she watched as he unbuttoned his shirt furiously.

"Marsh." She hadn't moved.

He reached out and picked her up, moving swiftly to the bed. "Lili." He slid out of the rest of his clothes. "I need you. Oh, God, how I need you."

He tossed her on the bed. She looked up at his hard, lean body and reached her arms up for him. He came to her with such anguish and desire that their lovemaking had a fury about it, an intensity that burned deep inside them. She cried out several times; they made love again and again as much in anger as in lust. Their passion exploded and ignited again . . . and again.

When their fury had spent itself, streaks of dried blood on his back and shoulders were witness to the clawing her nails had done. For days afterward she would treasure the purple blotches that indicated where he had bitten her, where he had grasped too hard, where he had shown how much he still desired her.

It was nearly dawn when they pulled apart, exhausted, passion and anger spent. They had not spoken in all that time.

She lay back, letting the cool morning air wash over her, drained. It was then she felt the gentleness she used to know, felt Marsh's finger trailing over her stomach, gently rubbing her breasts, fluttering down her thigh. She heard him say, "There's never a day or a night you're not with me. I love you beyond any ability to tell you so."

"And I love you."

This time they came together tenderly and gave to each other, murmuring soft words into each other's ears while tasting the honey of each other.

CHAPTER 29

▼

THE TRIP HOME HAD TAKEN EIGHT ARDUOUS DAYS; NO PLANE—NOT one—had been on time. She flew from Salisbury to Simbayo, but it took six days of short hops and long waits in makeshift airports whose only shade was under tin roofs that intensified the heat.

She imagined hell could not be worse. Her leavetaking of both Carolyn and Marsh rendered her nearly catatonic. During her long waits at the numerous small airports across Africa, she sat staring off into space, seeing little, unable to think because of the dull throb that pulsed through her head. She scarcely responded when spoken to.

She had pulled an invisible shield around herself upon her return home. Heidi had gasped, "You are so thin. How did you lose so much weight?" She had lost it all in the last eight days.

"May I broach a touchy subject?" asked Rose as they washed up after a routine surgery.

"Of course," Liliane said. She'd been back in Simbayo for nearly a month, though she had left Cape Town six weeks ago.

"We were all very understanding about how you felt to leave Carolyn so far away. We feel equally bad about it, you know."

Not true. They couldn't possibly understand the depth of her pain. Caro was her own flesh and blood.

"So we've all stepped rather gingerly since your return, but it's become really awfully difficult, Liliane."

What now, she thought. "Well?"

"Well? There! The way you say it. As though I'm interrupting you, meaning get on with it, leave me alone. Lili." Rose reached out and touched Liliane's arm affectionately. "Do you know how short-tempered you've been since you came home?"

"Short-tempered?"

"Liliane, you're ready to bite everyone's head off. Haven't you noticed how we try to stay out of your way? It's not just me. If it were, I wouldn't say anything, but you're making us all miserable. Nothing we do is right, nothing you do is right. You haven't said a kind word since you've returned."

Liliane looked at Rose in amazement. Her friend's face held anguish.

"We know you're mourning," she continued, "and we all miss Carolyn, but life goes on here and it all circles around you. When you're out of sorts, it makes life uncomfortable for us all. People are afraid to approach you about anything for fear you'll act—well, like you've been acting."

Have I really? Liliane wondered.

"Haven't you noticed how we've been the buffer between you and patients? You even frightened several of them with your brusqueness."

"I'm sorry, Rose," Liliane said. "I haven't even been aware of it."

"We know that, Lili. But we've come to the end of *our* patience now. If we can do anything to help you, you've only to let us know."

Liliane sat down and put her head in her hands. "I know that. I've been so sorry for myself that I haven't been aware of how I've been acting." She looked up at the nurse. "From now on, let's have a pact. Point it out to me when it happens."

"I've a feeling it won't happen"—Rose smiled, her gray eyes warm through the thickness of her glasses—"now that we've talked about it."

They finished scrubbing and put away the implements.

"Lili, why don't you move back to your old room? Living in that house all alone may be too lonely."

"Philippe's in my old room," Liliane pointed out.

"Oh, not the office rooms. He's too settled in there. He likes it. I meant your dormitory room. You'll know people are nearby."

I like being alone, Liliane wanted to say. I don't need anyone. But, instead, she answered, "I'll see."

She kept waiting for a letter from Carolyn but received one from Marsh instead. He alluded not at all to their night spent together, but said he and Dolores had taken Carolyn on an expedition to Port Elizabeth and then spent their last weekend together at the beach. Carolyn could not understand why Liliane had left so suddenly. She had been unable to enjoy either weekend and Marsh was worried about her. He had not wanted to leave but had been "very tempted to settle here in Cape Town and take care of our daughter. She is lost and bewildered. I know, I know . . . you're going to tell me it's I who insisted on this. That's true. But I would not leave a seven-year-old alone in a strange land were I able to do otherwise."

He's scolding me, she thought, but I feel the same way. Could I do otherwise, I would. Her heart ached.

She wrote long letters to Carolyn, telling her about Petelo and of her river trips to the outposts. She told her little anecdotes about daily life that would bring Simbayo back to Carolyn. She told Carolyn how much she missed her and that she loved her more than anything in the world.

As she wrote that, she laid her pen down and stared out her window at the river. I don't love her more than anything in the world, do I? I love Simbayo more than anything. She sat, hypnotized, staring at the water flowing by and thought, Maybe I love myself and my dreams more than anything in the world. The thought filled her with infinite sadness.

Everyone had gathered for lunch when the sound of the engine was heard. At first the faint whirring, then the gradual increasing hum of an airplane's engines. Liliane's heart was the first to recognize it; they all stared at each other.

It's Marsh, she thought. He's come back! Pushing her chair from the table, she started to run, nearly bumping into the door. As she ran, she gathered speed; the trees along the path were but a blur to her as she sped toward the landing field. The noise became louder, much louder than Marsh's plane sounded. Her feet flew along the path, and she fantasized that he had brought Carolyn with him.

When the forest suddenly ended and she was propelled into the open meadow, one plane had already landed and a second was just gliding in, its tires touching the ground smoothly. There were two silver Cessnas.

She stopped abruptly, watching an unfamiliar figure emerge from the first plane, a short, helmeted man who jumped from the wing to the ground and looked around. He raised his goggles from his face, pushing them back onto his leather cap, and shook his head.

Liliane walked toward him, puzzled.

The second plane's propellor continued to whir.

The man on the ground shouted above the engines' roar. "Madame Hathaway?"

"Yes." She held out her hand.

Tentatively, the pilot shook it, holding out a key with his other hand.

Liliane looked at it, baffled.

He spoke rapidly in French.

"I can't understand," she said.

"This." He pointed at the plane he had just left. "This is yours."

"Mine?" Marsh, she thought. Marsh has sent me a plane.

The pilot made no other explanation. He walked over to the other plane and climbed into the front cockpit. Liliane watched as it circled around the field and took off.

She stood in the middle of the field, holding on to a key, staring at her new acquisition. She walked over to the shining metallic bird, walked all around it. It was a two-seater and as beautiful as a machine could be. Pulling herself up on the wing, she climbed into the rear cockpit.

There, taped to the wheel, was an envelope with Marsh's undeniable scrawl: "Lili."

She snuggled herself into the seat and turned the envelope over several times, touching it as though it were a dear friend. She held it, unopened, and looked out at the landscape. I want to do this slowly, she thought. I want to savor every second.

She heard herself sigh loudly. Both sadness and joy surged through her.

The letter was brief, but his black scrawl ate into her.

I thought you might like some help. Here's something that will allow you to develop your outposts in the interior.

My love, since you are doing this, and you seem to have no choice in the matter, don't let what might have been poison you. Carolyn is young and will emerge intact, if bowed. I will survive, and that you will, I have no doubt. You are the strongest of the three of us.

Use this in joy. And pleasure. And love. It makes me feel good to be able to send it to you. I have made arrangements for the *Oregon* to bring you gasoline each trip it makes.

I admire the hell out of you.

There was no signature.

WHILE LILIANE FLEW AROUND THE CONGO SEARCHING FOR POSSIBLE outpost locations, Carolyn struggled to adjust to a way of life that was alien to her.

Victoria was as serious and fearful as Carolyn was; it was not their only bond. They escaped the emotional barrenness that had so suddenly been thrust upon them by studying. The girls not only had to learn from books, which Carolyn found relatively easy, thanks to Deborah Engle's tutelage and to her own inquisitive mind; they had to learn new customs and mores. Nothing at Litchfield was casual. Shoes were expected to be polished to a high luster; skirts and dresses were a given; gloves were always worn when they left the school. Once a month they were taken into Cape Town, where they had tea in the hotel dining room after the cinema matinee.

At Litchfield, Carolyn's world was as restricted as at Simbayo. However, Simbayo represented freedom and Litchfield felt like a jail.

When some of the little girls gossiped or played tricks on each other, Carolyn pulled back. She found no pleasure in these pastimes. She would stare out her window, as dusk descended each evening, at the other dormitories and the eight-foot wall—brick after brick—but in her mind's eye she saw the jungle paths along which she and Petelo had raced . . . saw a pale orchid opening under an okoume tree . . . heard the river gurgling as she watched the storks standing in the rapids across the river . . . heard monkeys cry and the beat of drums in the night. She remembered Petelo reaching out for her hand, always ready to protect her. And she sighed.

Rather than sadden herself with the memories that could no longer be part of her life, she opened a book.

"Where's Athens?" Victoria asked. Together they would locate Greece. But it never stopped there. One question led to another and the two little girls explored far more than they were expected to.

"I'm glad we're roommates," Victoria said in the dark one night as they lay in their beds. "And I'm glad you're not silly like Dawn is."

Carolyn didn't approve of many of Victoria's ideas, but she began to like her roommate. Why, she wondered, can't I tell her I like her, too?

She lived for mail.

At first, Marsh wrote every two weeks, from Nairobi and from Istanbul and from Bombay. Carolyn looked them all up on the map and read about them in the encyclopedia. So far away. She kept the letters tied neatly with a pale green ribbon. She imagined him stalking lions, creeping up on Bengal tigers, floating down wide rivers on barges.

Her mother's letters were less frequent, usually one or two a month, but they were always long. Liliane told her how much she was loved, but Carolyn thought these were hollow sentiments.

If she loves me so much, thought the little girl, she wouldn't be happy without me. And Liliane sounded happy. She wrote, with excitement, of her new plane and of flying and of eventually establishing new outposts. She wrote that she thought Deborah Engle would never give in to Philippe's entreaties. She told Carolyn how Petelo was growing and that he was becoming the school's prize pupil. She told her of unusual occurrences and funny little stories. Liliane's letters made Carolyn more homesick than ever.

Her spirit rebelled at the rigidity of life here. Every hour of the day was structured. When other students made friendly overtures, Carolyn, while not overtly rebuffing them, did not respond.

"The ice queen," she heard someone whisper as she passed by.

She never showed her emotions, which had always floated on the surface at Simbayo. If I hide my misery, if I learn my math tables, if I show Mama I'm an excellent student and don't need more schooling, maybe she'll let me come home. Though she could not forgive her mother, she tried exorbitantly to please her. And if pleasing her meant learning the ways of the white world, so be it. Whatever it would take to show her mother that she had learned whatever it was she was supposed to learn, she would do.

She was not the chatterbox she had been at Simbayo. The two little girls across the hall would stick out their tongues and call

"Cat got your tongue?" because Carolyn kept to herself. She practiced civilized manners and learned how to smile and say please when she didn't feel like it.

Only once did she allow her feelings to surface.

At the dinner table one night, she listened to Kathy one time too many. Kathy, who was never silent, expounded at least once a week on the Christian benevolence of whites, who willingly turned their backs on creature comforts and came to Africa to live among savages so that the natives could learn the precepts of Christianity. And the natives repaid them by hardly ever learning. In trying to save these savages, white men were noble martyrs. It showed white superiority.

Carolyn threw down her fork and stood. The clatter of silverware against glass, and her unprecedented standing in the middle of dinner, turned all eyes upon her.

"What makes you think we're superior?" Her voice was frozenly controlled, but everyone in the room heard each word. "When I listen to you night after night saying how wonderful we are, I wonder if you're trying to tell God something he doesn't know. Personally, I think you're disgusting. I don't think you even know what Christianity is!"

She pushed her chair back and tossed her napkin onto it, while Miss Blake stared at her, mouth agape. Carolyn marched from the room, staring straight ahead.

No one ever reprimanded her, but Victoria told her that that was the reason the girls in her hall weren't speaking to her.

I don't care, Carolyn told herself, and was not even aware that the ostracism lasted barely a week. If she had cared, it might have lasted the rest of her school years.

CHAPTER 30

▼

As she stared down at the endless landscape of trees, Carolyn realized the thrill of coming home.

She had made many adjustments, even though she had resisted every effort to acclimatize her to a way of life she had come to so unwillingly. She understood, even at nine years old, that the school had succeeded; she no longer felt herself to be an integral part of Simbayo when she returned for vacations.

Petelo was still playing the same games he had played two years ago. He wanted to include her, as he always had, but an invisible cultural wall had grown between them. No longer did the simple games seem as interesting. Last year it had not been until nearly the end of her holidays that she and Petelo became close again. He had tried to pretend there was no barrier there, he proudly showed her what books he was reading, but he sensed that she had traveled beyond where he could go. Rose and Heidi, and even her mother, acted as though she were no different, going out of their way to include her in everything, but it was not quite the same.

Though Liliane invited her on trips—up or down the river on *My Gal Sal* or flying into the interior to her two new camps—Carolyn was aware she no longer belonged in the way she once had.

Jumping from the modern white world to the primitive black world was not easy for her, nor was being hurled into the impersonal civilized world of Litchfield after nearly three months in the warmth and informality of Simbayo. She did not scream and fight as she had the first time but accepted the inevitable. She still harbored the feeling that she was being sent away because she wasn't quite lovable enough. Her mind knew better, even at this tender age, but that's what it felt like nevertheless.

She knew her mother had arranged to slow down her usual work load when she came home from school so that she had time for Carolyn, but it felt as though Liliane were saying, "All right, Caro. Here I am. Let's be close." There were still moments of incredible warmth that Carolyn tucked in her heart to be brought out at the lonely twilight hour in Cape Town. Moments she forced into her memory as she lay in bed in Litchfield where no one ever kissed her good night, where hugs were few and far between and then only between little girls in a joyous moment, like winning a race.

Yet when she returned to Simbayo, she realized she had left Petelo behind her. She found Simbayans narrow in their interests; they had not changed considerably in the time she had been gone, while she sensed she had grown beyond them. After a few weeks with them, however, she found herself relaxing and enjoying simple things—splashing in the pool, running down the jungle paths and shouting. But she felt she belonged in neither place. She was a visitor in Simbayo now, even though it was the familiar beloved ground, where her roots were deep. Simbayo, Litchfield—each kept her from belonging to the other.

Yet her heart came to life at Simbayo.

She knew there would be additions to the Simbayo family whom she had not yet met. Her mother had written of the outposts in the interior. The outpost called Freedom was staffed by nurses from the United States, women named Ilene and Dickie. Last year she had met Diane and Judy, the nurses at Evangeline outpost, who had arrived from England. So far, no one had left Simbayo. Those who came, stayed.

One of the wonderful things about Simbayo, Carolyn thought, was that people weren't always jealous of each other, as they were in Litchfield. The petty fights, the whispering, the gossip she found so rampant at Litchfield was missing in Simbayo.

And no one in Simbayo paid attention to how they dressed. The girls at school wasted hours considering how they looked, primping. Even girls as young as she. Those hours seemed like a waste of life to Carolyn.

The pilot interrupted her reverie to inform the passengers they would soon be landing in Léopoldville. The small plane had only three other travelers, flying from the copper mines at Elisabethville. Carolyn knew her mother would be waiting for her in the capital. Now that Liliane had her own plane, transportation into Simbayo was much easier. Her classmates were filled with wonder that her mother flew her own plane. But little else of her life in Simbayo amazed them, for nearly all of them went home to similar experiences on their holidays. They were the children of missionaries not only in Victoria's Nigeria, but in Kenya and Tanganyika, in Rhodesia and the Ivory Coast, from Madagascar and Mozambique, and from other parts of the Congo. The twelve children of missionaries in Ethiopia were not going home this summer because of the war there. Someone named Mussolini, who lived in Italy, had decided he wanted to own Ethiopia, so he brought his soldiers there to fight the people who lived there. Now, the country was his. It perplexed Carolyn. How could someone decide to own a country? How could someone just come over and choose to rule, to make the people who had lived there for hundreds or thousands of years suddenly learn to live differently and obey his rules?

Yet wasn't that what she had done at Litchfield? Learned how to live a different life and obey their rules? But it didn't seem quite the same as Mussolini and Ethiopia. What if someone came to

Simbayo and told them how to live? She bet her mother would put up a fight. What if that happened while she was at Litchfield . . . where would she be then? Would she have to stay at school, like the children from Ethiopia, for the whole holiday, and never see the people she loved? Would that mean she might never see her mother again . . . that Simbayo might cease to be?

She didn't understand what a war was supposed to accomplish. She could comprehend fighting to defend the place where you lived, but she couldn't imagine anyone telling you how to live, or wanting to kill people. Or why people took pleasure in hurting someone else. She had seen Gladys at school take pleasure in taunting another girl. She had seen her twist Patricia's arm one day; the look of pain and bewilderment on Patricia's face cut into Carolyn's heart. The other children stood around and watched while Gladys cried, "Say uncle." But even after Patricia whispered, "Uncle," Gladys refused to let go. Only when Carolyn had rushed into the fray and cried, "Stop that this minute!" did Gladys stop.

Had Gladys done that because Patricia was so pretty and popular, because Patricia was always doing kind things for other people? Was Gladys so jealous she would hurt Patricia, when what she really wanted was to be like her?

Her thoughts jarred as she felt the landing gear loosen; she looked out the window to see buildings replacing trees. Léopold-ville's buildings were not the clean, whitewashed structures of Cape Town. Compared to Cape Town, Léopoldville appeared dirty and poor; it seemed much larger than when she had first seen it nearly two years ago.

The concrete of the runway had large broken portions where grass peeked through the cracks. Landing in Léopoldville was never as smooth as at Cape Town's airport. Looking out the window, she realized she was in a different world than she had been two days ago.

The door opened and hot, humid air enveloped her. She forgot how much more energy she had at school. As soon as the blast of heat hit her, she could feel herself slow down, even emotionally.

Her heart quickened, though, when she saw Liliane standing at the edge of the runway.

As she walked toward Liliane, who stood behind the fence, a wide smile on her face, Carolyn thought how beautiful she was. She hadn't met anyone in Cape Town who was as pretty as her mother.

Her copper hair, always worn short to keep the hot dampness off her neck, curled tightly in the humidity. Her mother didn't dress like anyone she'd ever met outside of Simbayo. Liliane stood there, waving to Carolyn, in wrinkled khaki slacks and an open-necked shirt, looking more like the boys who carried her luggage than like the other women.

It's that special something that sets her apart, Carolyn thought, like the fragrance of her. Unlike anyone else, she always smells like the jungle, a faint musty odor tinged with exotic flowers. Carolyn loved the aromas she associated with her mother. When she was little, she could wake in the dark night and feel safe because she could sense her mother nearby. She thought how lovely it would be if she could bottle her mother's scent and take it with her to Litchfield.

"Darling," Liliane cried, "you've grown so tall." Carolyn felt Liliane's arms surround her.

Despite Carolyn's vow never to trust her mother again, Liliane represented safety and warmth and the years of happiness that now eluded Carolyn. She also sensed that for the month she was in Simbayo, she would be loved, cared about, in ways she could never be in Cape Town.

"We're going to stay at the hotel and have a hot bath," Liliane was saying. Carolyn was used to hot baths every night. "We'll head home tomorrow. Oh, don't you look wonderful." Liliane squeezed Carolyn's hand.

Mama doesn't even know I don't trust her, thought Carolyn as they walked to a taxi. She doesn't even know I'm different. She thinks life just goes on in the same way, as it does in Simbayo. Nothing affects her if it doesn't happen there.

I wonder if she knows about wars.

She looked wonderingly at her mother. For the first time, it dawned on her that Liliane had once been an American. She had lived in houses, like Ginger Rogers and Fred Astaire and Shirley Temple did in the movies they had seen together. She had lived where there was snow, and in cities like Cape Town, where most of the people you saw were white. She had lived where there was electricity and running water and radios that told stories and played music, not just static that connected her to one of her outposts. How strange to think of her mother in some place other than Simbayo.

What had made her mother give all that up to come to a

strange country? When she asked Liliane about that, at dinner, Liliane looked across the table at her and smiled, a faraway look in her eyes.

"Love," she answered. "I came to Africa because I fell in love with a giant of a man."

Carolyn wondered how tall he had been. "You mean my father?"

Liliane shook her head as though trying to think. "Yes. Baxter Hathaway."

"Why isn't Marsh my father? I never knew Baxter Hathaway."

"Marsh can be your father if you want." Liliane reached a hand across the table to enfold Carolyn's smaller one. Her turquoise eyes smiled into Carolyn's. "Does it matter so much? Someday I'll explain."

"Maybe it doesn't matter." Carolyn was picking at her dinner. She didn't feel hungry, though Liliane was eating with obvious relish. "Marsh hasn't written to me in so long I'm beginning to forget him."

Liliane looked at her, a serious expression on her face. "Don't you know? He was in Spain."

Carolyn nodded. "He told me he was going there. But he never stays long in any place. I figured he and Dolores were someplace else by now."

Liliane shook her head. "No. He's been covering the Spanish Civil War for *The Times.* I saw his byline in an old newspaper a couple of months ago."

Marsh in a war? Carolyn's heart constricted.

"Why would Marsh fight in a war? Wars are bad."

Liliane was silent for a moment, finishing her dinner. Then she folded her napkin. "Killing is bad, yes. But some wars are necessary. Sometimes bad people have to be killed so that evil can be eradicated."

Carolyn didn't understand what her mother was talking about. "Do good people ever get killed?"

"Unfortunately." Lillian sipped coffee. "Good people die all the time. Yes, bad people kill good people. Sometimes that's why good people have to fight a war."

"Could Marsh get killed?"

"I don't know how near battle he is. He's not fighting. He's writing about it."

"But could he get killed?"

"I guess so. But let's not talk about that. Let's talk about nice things. I want to hear what you've been doing, and what you've been studying, and what new friends you've made."

That's not nice, Carolyn almost said. All the nice things are at Simbayo. Yet she knew that wasn't as true as it had been a year ago.

PETELO WAS WAITING FOR HER. CAROLYN DIDN'T LET HERSELF RUN over and hug him. Petelo looked at her questioningly and then stared at the ground. Then he smiled shyly, scraping his bare feet in the dirt.

Rose acted as though not a moment had passed since their last meeting. This both pleased and irritated Carolyn. She wanted to be welcomed back into the womb of Simbayo and be a part of it, yet she also thought they should immediately notice how much she had changed. She knew she was growing in ways that no one at Simbayo was. As Heidi took a turn hugging her, loneliness washed over Carolyn. She thought to herself, I imagined loneliness would leave me when I came home, but it hasn't.

While she had not quite come to love Philippe, she found herself liking him a great deal. She appreciated his not hugging her when they did not know each other well. She liked the way he always listened when she spoke and the way he treated her as an adult rather than a child. Much of the medical work of Simbayo had shifted to his shoulders while her mother had absorbed more and more administrative work. The outposts were Liliane's babies, and she kept in constant touch with the six.

Without fail, she paddled herself over to the leper island. The Travises, she told Carolyn, worked wonders; they were making medical history. Despite Liliane repeatedly telling Carolyn that she could not catch leprosy, she refused to allow Carolyn to go to the island.

For the first week of Carolyn's vacation, Liliane hardly left her side. Evenings, after they had left the camaraderie of the dining room, Liliane quizzed her about life in Cape Town and shared with Carolyn the things that concerned her. Carolyn knew her mother felt that these were times of real closeness. She knew that Liliane was trying to prove, to herself at least, that nothing between them had changed, that her decision to send her daughter away had not been a wrong one.

But Liliane could not put aside the demands made on her. She could not spend all her time with Carolyn, who turned to her old friends and tried to fit in. But their ribald games seemed wild and childish to her. She couldn't talk with them about wars and ask them the questions that burned within her. She couldn't talk to them of loneliness and isolation. She couldn't talk with them of long division and *The Wind in the Willows.* But she and Petelo sat for hours on the ground, while he asked her how the ocean looked and made her tell over and over again what cities were like. He wanted to hear about civilization even though it was beyond his comprehension. Petelo listened with veiled eyes, studying Carolyn as well as her stories. Losing Carolyn, and never having been able to recapture the person who had been so nearly a part of him, was something he could not fathom.

One afternoon as Liliane and Carolyn headed toward the swimming pool, Liliane said, "I have to make my monthly trip to Freedom tomorrow to deliver the medical and food supplies. I'll probably stay overnight. Would you like to come?"

Carolyn loved going on these overnight expeditions with her mother. She loved flying above the trees, looking down, seeing elephants lumbering along paths where the forest thinned out. She loved the excitement that Liliane generated wherever she traveled, and she basked in the knowledge that Liliane enjoyed her company. Last year Liliane had taken her on two trips; maybe this year she'd include her every time.

"Of course," answered Carolyn.

In the twelve years since Baxter had built the pool, Liliane's enthusiasm for it had never waned. Sometimes she thought it a lifesaver; it renewed her more than a nap ever did. Though the water tower made it possible for them to take showers, nothing revived her like a swim. The only trouble was that now it was used by so many people she never had it to herself as she had in her early years at Simbayo.

"You'll like Dickie and Ilene, I think," Liliane said as they swam across the lagoon. "Ilene is a typical New Yorker and Dickie's a southerner. Their backgrounds are as different as two Americans can be. Ilene should be the worldly one with a sophisticated viewpoint and Dickie the small-town girl with a conventional outlook on life, but it's just the opposite. When they arrived I was sure I'd made a terrible mistake, putting the two of them together without anyone else up at Freedom, but they get along famously. They solve all problems with wonderful senses of humor."

"What makes Americans leave the United States to come over here?" asked Carolyn.

Liliane turned on her back, floating. "We all have different reasons. Some want to serve God. Some want to live in a different land, see the world. Some are driven to help other people. Dickie came because she'd just been jilted."

"What does that mean?" Carolyn was doing the crawl so she could continue to be near her mother.

"The man she was engaged to decided he didn't want to marry her."

That didn't explain anything, Carolyn thought. But her mother continued talking.

"Ilene came because she said she just didn't fit in. She wanted to get as far away from New York as possible and try to live a different way." Liliane turned on her stomach and began to swim. Why did I stay? she wondered. It couldn't have been just to carry on Baxter's dream, even if I thought that at the time.

At that moment, Petelo came rushing to the bank, shouting. He jumped in with a splash, and Carolyn began roughhousing with him. Liliane stayed in the water for a few minutes while the children splashed and giggled, then Carolyn was disappointed to see her emerging from the water, running her hand through her hair and shaking her head so that the water drops shimmered like a thousand diamonds in the sunlight.

I'm like Ilene, thought Carolyn, I don't fit in, either. I don't fit in anywhere. Her thoughts were interrupted as the back of Petelo's hand sliced the water, splashing her. He cried aloud in delight and waited for her to chase him.

She fell back into ancient patterns and did as she was expected.

How they ever found the spot for Freedom Carolyn couldn't guess. Over an hour into the interior, the only sign of anything other than thick impenetrable jungle was a narrow treeless patch scarcely large enough to land in. But Liliane managed.

As they maneuvered the uneven field, jolted by growth that the inhabitants could not keep under control, they saw the nurses standing at the edge of the jungle, waving. As soon as Liliane cut the engine, they came running toward the plane.

They dressed much as Liliane did—one wore wrinkled slacks

and the other had on baggy shorts. Except, thought Carolyn, Mama's shorts never look baggy. She always looks wonderful. As Liliane gracefully jumped onto the wing and lowered herself to the ground, Carolyn saw the three women hug each other. Then her mother turned and raised an arm up, to help her down.

"And here's this darlin' girl we've been hearin' so much about." Dickie's voice curled around Carolyn like a cocoon. It was a funny kind of English, the girl thought. "I'd an idea you'd be this pretty."

"Oh, how nice. We'd no idea your mother would bring you. Isn't this a treat." Ilene's dialect was as difficult to understand as Dickie's. Carolyn noted they each added an *r* to the word *idea*. Ilene's thin body looked like a boy's but it had a toughness to it, a lean hardness.

Dickie reached out and took hold of her hand. There was a softness to Dickie, yet Carolyn could tell, from the way she grasped her hand, that she was strong.

Freedom was not nearly as pretty as the outposts along the river. It was simply a few cottages carved out of the jungle, along a path that had been trodden dusty hundreds of years before. There was the infirmary—just two small rooms. One was an office where patients were treated, and the other had two beds for patients. Not only were the two beds occupied, but three patients lay in pallets on the floor.

"We'd better think of adding another room or two," Liliane said.

"Oh, I don't think so," said Ilene. "Sometimes no one's in here. This isn't usual. Most of ours are outpatients. We call you when there's anything they need to be hospitalized for. And they like company. These people hate being alone. Privacy is a word they don't understand."

Liliane smiled. "How well I know. Even after all my years here, I don't understand that. If I don't have some time alone, I'm ready to scream."

"Yes," agreed Dickie, "but westerners spend time thinking or reading. I can lie on my bed for hours and just think about the world and my feelings and God and—"

"And she does just that." Ilene poked her friend gently in the ribs. "She's the biggest one for thinking I've ever met."

"Well, you paint." Dickie seemed to feel she had to defend herself. "You spend hours and hours off in the forest painting and sketching."

Ilene grinned. "It's true. We never seem to get lonely. Particularly when we're alone."

Funny, Liliane thought. The loneliest time of my life was when Baxter was in it.

Carolyn was thinking, Ilene's right. I'm loneliest when there are other people around that I'm not a part of. I'm not so lonely when I'm alone anymore. Except sometimes right before dark, in that twilight time "between the dark and the daylight, when the night is beginning to lower . . ." she thought, remembering a poem she'd memorized in English class.

"That one came in last night," Dickie said. She pointed to a tall man whose lips moved, whose eyes stared wildly at the ceiling and saw nothing. "He has deliriums now. He must have walked fifteen or twenty miles. He was shivering and could hardly talk. I suspect it's blackwater fever. It would be good for you to look him over."

"Blackwater? And he walked?" Liliane's voice indicated concern. "Oh, dear."

"What's wrong with walking?" Carolyn asked.

"Any movement can kill someone with blackwater fever," answered Liliane.

Liliane walked over to the bed. The patient shivered uncontrollably. She leaned over and heard him murmuring unintelligible sounds.

"His symptoms are malarial," Dickie said. "They usually are. One doesn't know if they're connected or not."

"I thought so"—Liliane continued to study the patient—"when I first came out here. But I've read that sometimes blackwater occurs where malaria isn't present."

"I didn't know there was anyplace in Africa where malaria isn't present," Ilene said.

"It does seem that way," Liliane agreed.

"Why is it called blackwater?" Carolyn wanted to know. For the first time, medical talk interested her. She had usually been too busy playing to bother with talk of sickness.

"Because"—her mother turned toward her and leaned to put an arm around Carolyn's thin shoulders—"that's just what happens. The urine becomes bloody—black."

"Is it dangerous, or can quinine help it?" Carolyn knew that quinine helped malaria. One couldn't have lived at Simbayo for as long as she did and not know that.

She saw her mother and the two other nurses exchange looks.

"It's almost always fatal," her mother answered, futility in her voice.

Fatal? Then this man was going to die? This man she was standing next to, this man she was looking at, this man who was mumbling, whose wild eyes stared blankly, was going to die? She studied him. Where would he go, she wondered, when his body died? When he closed his eyes and stopped breathing, would the spirit that was within him die, too, or would it go someplace?

Couldn't anyone keep him from dying? "What causes black-water fever?" she asked. She knew mosquitoes were the carriers of malaria.

"We don't know," answered her mother. "If only we did. There are so many things we don't have answers to. How many lives we could save if we knew those answers."

Carolyn thought, I'll find answers. I'll keep people alive.

"What's wrong with that man?" She pointed to one on the floor who was asleep.

"Probably the usual jungle rot," Ilene said.

"What's jungle rot?"

Ilene laughed, and it had a deep, rich sound. "Oh, that's what I call anything I've never seen before. And don't know how to cure. It seems bad for the moment, but the patient recovers, and we never know what he recovers from."

"Come on," said Dickie, "I'll tell Mpeci to prepare lunch, and while he's doing that we'll unload the plane."

"I hope he's preparing that dish I like so much."

"He is," assured Dickie. "I told him you were coming."

Lunch was delicious. It had been a long time since Carolyn had tasted banganju, a paste made by hammering palm nuts in a wooden mortar, then mixing the oil with finely pounded cassava leaves. In nearly every home, there was always a big kettle of banganju ready to accompany a meal, but Carolyn had never tasted any as delectable as this. It was served with fish, roast corn, and plaintain cakes.

"I think you ought to bottle this. You could get rich," she said, realizing Congolese food was one of the things she missed most in Cape Town.

"Come, missy," cried one of the native workers to no one in particular. The three nurses jumped from the lunch table as though it were a conditioned reflex.

Though she did not want to stop eating, Carolyn followed them to the door.

Four natives stood by a litter that they had just laid on the ground. On the stretcher was a man whose shoulder had been ripped away; no skin or muscle remained. Blood soaked the litter and made a splattered path indicating where they had come along the ground.

The patient had been clawed by a leopard.

In unison, the three nurses knelt down beside him. The looks they exchanged told Carolyn the man was already dead.

Where his shoulder had been, red meat quivered. What looked like pink worms wound like corkscrews from the open wound.

I can't help that kind of pain, Carolyn thought. But I can help with sickness.

She didn't know how. But she knew she could. She also knew she did not want to be a nurse. Even at nine she sensed she could never compete with her mother, never be as good or as dedicated a nurse as Liliane. She would have to find some other way.

She alone returned to finish her lunch.

CHAPTER 31

▼

WHEN LILIANE AWOKE, HER RIBS ACHED AND HER BACK HURT. Straightening out her knees and arching her back, she moaned softly. Thirty-three is too old to sleep on the floor, she thought.

Her eyes focused on Carolyn, curled against her. Still drugged with sleep, Liliane let her fingers play with the white blondness of the hair fanning out beside her. It was soft and fine and still felt like a baby's. My baby, she thought. Always my baby.

Wouldn't it be terrible—unbearable—if her baby caught one of Africa's diseases? Her mind saw Carolyn thrashing around with a high fever, her urine dark red, weight dropping off her until she looked like a skeleton. She visualized Carolyn without fingers or toes or a nose, a victim of leprosy. She saw Carolyn in an endless coma, suffering from encephalitis.

I'm glad she doesn't stay here all the time; Liliane imagined the brisk air of Cape Town, not laden with the humid, insect-ridden diseases of the equator. She kissed Carolyn's downy hair and heard a car screeching its brakes, too late; she shuddered.

I'm going to miss so much of her life, Liliane thought, hugging Carolyn more closely. Carolyn murmured.

Liliane forced her mind away from these imagined atrocities, to a real one . . . to blackwater fever. Everyone knew you shouldn't move someone who was suffering from it. The disease was almost always fatal, and invariably so if the patient moved. Every movement hastened the destructive forces begun in the liver and kidneys.

Philippe had long been fascinated with the disease. Since patients usually died of it before they could even get to the hospital at Simbayo, they saw few cases. Yet they had seen enough, seen the drawn-out process of dying a bit each day, to interest Philippe in both the cause and a cure.

If this patient was going to die anyhow, mightn't it be helpful to Philippe if she took him back to Simbayo? There was always the chance of saving the patient, too. Moving him from the infirmary to the plane and settling him there so he could not move would be the hard part.

Carolyn stretched and opened one eye. For a moment she was disoriented, but her closeness to her mother reassured her. She felt her mother's even breathing, smelled the wonderful fragrance, knew before she even looked that her mother was smiling at her. She felt soft lips brush her eyelid, and then as she opened her eyes, Liliane stood, saying, "I'm going to call Philippe on the radio." If he agreed, she'd try to move the patient.

It wasn't until late afternoon that Liliane felt free to depart from Freedom. She knew her monthly visits were Dickie's and Ilene's only contact with outside news and with another white person, so she deliberately did not hasten her visit. But she did want to arrive back in Simbayo before dark.

At about four o'clock they readied the unconscious patient for what might be his last trip. The hardest part was trying to get him from the stretcher into the plane. Once that was accomplished, Liliane decided Carolyn would have to sit on her lap, no small feat in the rear cockpit. Settled in, she waved to Ilene, who moved the blocks from under the plane, while Dickie twirled the propellor. The engine revved up until it purred familiarly, and they rolled up the short runway, leaving the ground right before the trees could catch them.

I hope he stays unconscious for the next hour, Liliane thought, so he won't move.

Carolyn pretended she was flying the plane, sitting in front of the controls, watching the switches her mother pulled. It was always invigorating to be flying at five thousand feet, above the humidity. She wondered if the man in the front seat was still alive.

In that time when it would be twilight in Cape Town but was the moment before day became night in the tropics, they sighted the landing field at Simbayo.

"Here," said Liliane, guiding Carolyn's hand and covering it with hers. "We're going to pull the throttle—gently now." The motor changed to a light hum.

"Look outside." Carolyn had to stretch to see over the sides. The earth sped by under them as the wheels of the plane touched the ground. Carolyn saw figures at the edge of the jungle, where she knew the path was. A figure on crutches began to hobble across the field.

Running past him were three others, carrying a stretcher, prepared for their new patient.

One immediately knelt under the plane, placing the wooden blocks that would keep the plane secure. Philippe jumped up on the wing, his slight frame agile and quick.

"You stay here"—Liliane squeezed out from under Carolyn—"until we have him moved. Okay?"

Carolyn nodded. She would pretend to be a pilot while they attended to business.

Lifting the unconscious man out of the plane with a minimum amount of movement was difficult. He was still alive.

"He's dehydrated," Philippe commented.

Liliane was sweating by the time they had accomplished the task. She leaned in the cockpit and said, "Okay. You can climb down now." It was then that Carolyn saw her mother turn pale, a hand at her throat. There was disbelief in Liliane's eyes, and a vein throbbed swiftly at her temple. Her face was white; a plaintive sob escaped her throat.

Without waiting to help Carolyn, Liliane jumped from the wing to the ground, crying out. Carolyn climbed out of the cockpit and looked down from the wing. The man on crutches, whose arms encircled her mother, smiled up at her. Tears made his eyes shine.

Marsh was home.

"I'M BACK FOR GOOD," HE SAID. "I NEVER INTEND TO LEAVE MY women again." He was holding Carolyn's hand but looking into

Liliane's eyes. "I'm home from all the wars I ever want to fight."

Liliane knew he was not referring just to the Spanish Civil War.

He told them of that war, in bits and pieces. He'd spent months in a hospital, undergoing two operations, and would never walk without a limp. "They wanted to keep me in their damned hospital, but I promised I'd put myself under hospital supervision and do as the doctors ordered, so I'm here."

Rose and Heidi welcomed him warmly. Anoka was overjoyed to see him and the rapport they had once known was reestablished immediately. Carolyn curled up in his lap every evening.

Liliane felt at peace with the world.

The long years apart evaporated. It was as though Marsh had never been away. Except he was quieter.

"The trouble was," he told her later, when they lay in bed after making love far more tenderly than they had two years before in Cape Town, "that Dolores wasn't you. No one's you."

A second divorce. It had not been friendly. Liliane put her arms around him.

For days Marsh had to reach out to touch Carolyn or Liliane, to reassure himself that he was here, with them. The haunted look in his eyes would take a long time to leave, Liliane thought. His thinness made his cheekbones stand out prominently, like the young Marsh she had first known. He insisted on keeping a candle burning all night; he could not sleep in darkness. He hovered near her and Carolyn.

Philippe moved the blackwater-fever patient into the office, so he could be near him at night. The man was, in turns, delirious and unconscious. There seemed to be no doubt that he would die. He hovered between life and death for a week, while Philippe dosed him with arsenic, Atabrine, and cinchonine. Gradually his urine turned from dark red to pink, while Philippe pumped gallons of blood into him.

When the patient regained total consciousness, he must have weighed forty pounds less than when Liliane had brought him to Simbayo. Philippe's method then was to flood him with a sea of orange juice, milk, and chicken broth.

Amazingly, the man gained strength if not weight.

The next month Liliane flew him back to Freedom. He was able to walk away from the outpost; they never saw him again.

Pretty soon Marsh was hobbling around on just one crutch and leaving that on the sandbank when Carolyn helped him into the lagoon. He spent many hours a day in the water, where he could maneuver without his crutch. His return restored equilibrium to Liliane's life. It was as though a part had been missing; now she was whole again. There was no strain or awkwardness after nearly five years; there was simply a resumption of where they had left off. But it was obvious they took nothing for granted, cherishing every moment.

"I can breathe evenly again," she told him.

He kissed her eyes.

He kissed her constantly. He kissed her when they were alone, and he kissed her when others were around. He seemed to be verifying his presence by kissing her hand or her neck or an earlobe or her nose. They were just friendly little kisses in public, but they were kisses nevertheless. It soon stopped embarrassing Philippe.

Philippe, however, could not warm up to Marsh. At first Liliane didn't understand; she'd have thought he'd be delighted to have another white man at the compound, a potential friend.

But it was Deborah. Deborah was fascinated by Marsh. She and Marsh argued politics, enjoying the give-and-take of their heated discussions. Liliane could also see Deborah staring at Marsh when she thought no one else was looking. She managed to go swimming more often than she used to.

Liliane felt sad for Deborah and for Philippe. She suspected Philippe's hope for a relationship with Deborah, after all these years, was a futile dream. There were times when Deborah and Philippe seemed on the verge of romance, when they had "in" jokes and smiled secretly at each other, but to Philippe's great frustration, these never lasted.

"I'm going to stop globe-trotting," Marsh told Liliane. "I've had enough of danger and excitement. And enough"—he smiled at her—"of other women. There's never going to be another woman—ever."

"Ever?" Carolyn wanted reassurance. "Just Mama and me?"

"Just you two." Marsh hugged her to him. "Forever and ever. That's a promise."

Then he and Carolyn played Parcheesi. She let him win one of the three games. Carolyn debated whether or not to teach it to Petelo, but she was afraid if she did Marsh wouldn't play with her as much. Marsh could teach him after she returned to Litchfield.

Now that Marsh was here, she had nightmares about returning to Cape Town. The holidays were too brief. She didn't want to leave.

Marsh sensed this and talked with her for hours about the advantages of school. He promised over and over that he would never leave Africa again. "I shall always be near when you want me, darling."

"I want you all the time. I want to live with you. I don't want to leave and be by myself at school. I hate it there."

But when it came time to return to South Africa, Carolyn went without tears, though her heart was tight. Marsh had promised to come see her during the brief July vacation. They would have a holiday together, just the two of them, but only if she promised to write every week. He would do the same.

He stood waving his one crutch as Liliane and Carolyn circled into the air. He would have to do something to make life easier for his daughter, that much he knew.

HE DID GO TO SOUTH AFRICA FOR THE WINTER VACATION. HE AND Carolyn spent the week touring the Karoo, staying in quaint inns, traversing hairpin mountain curves, studying the history of the region. He bought himself a cane and trained himself to rely on that rather than his crutch. He would need that cane for the rest of his life. If it ever bothered him, he did not show it.

When he returned to Simbayo, he started to write again. He had spent the time immediately after his return staring into the river, taking Liliane's plane out and flying around aimlessly. He showed no interest in visiting any of the outposts with Liliane but seemed content to sit on the verandah and stare.

So, when he started writing again, Liliane was pleased. It was not that he brooded; he seemed to be in limbo. Now that he had turned again to his typewriter, life returned to him.

"I have to write about it . . . the war," he explained.

"Why?" Liliane asked.

"I need to write a book that shows the senselessness of war. But, at the same time, I think the world is hurtling toward a war that needs to be fought."

"You mean Hitler?"

"He scares me to death. But so did the war in Spain. I don't know if that had to be fought. But if someone doesn't stop Nazi Germany, a war unlike any we've ever known will affect the whole world."

"Another world war?"

"I suspect that within the next three or four years we'll all be involved."

"Not us here? Not the Congo? Not Simbayo?"

"Oh, dear Lili. You think you'll always be safe and untouched by global problems, don't you? Someday, my love, you, too, will need to fight."

Liliane knew he'd seen too much war, that he could not think rationally about the subject. He thought the whole world would get caught up in a common problem, but she knew there was no way this part of the world would be involved with the rest of the world's crimes.

"Why are people letting Hitler get away with all the evil he does?"

"Ah, the twenty-four-dollar question. Why is Neville Chamberlain talking of 'peace in our time'? Why are Poland and Czechoslovakia not putting up more of a fight? Why are Germans sitting back and letting him annihilate Jews? Is it because as long as they're safe, it's okay?"

"I thought you just said war is senseless."

"Oh, Christ." Marsh ran his hand through his hair, which was beginning to curl over his ears. Liliane liked the looks of it. "I don't know what I think. I saw men dying; I saw their legs blown off; I saw cannon shoot holes clear through their bodies; and I wondered why. I saw boys fighting in a war they didn't understand. And I'd ask why. And there was no reason. Except it seemed right. But is killing ever right?"

"Doesn't one have to weigh the rights?" Liliane asked.

"Exactly," Marsh answered, striding restlessly around the room. "Do you know there was a town in Czechoslovakia, Lidice? It is no more. The Germans rounded up everyone in town and shot them. Just wiped the town off the face of the earth. How can the world stand by and not do anything? Those people died senselessly."

There was silence. Liliane had seldom thought of these things. She did not want to think of them now. She had enough of death and dying around her, enough of sickness and scrabbling for mere existence. She did not want to think of people dying in far-off places, in places like Czechoslovakia when she wasn't even sure where it was.

He never broke his typing rhythm, but always looked up and smiled.

At dinner one night, he said, "I want to announce I'm dedicating this book to Rose. Her thoughtfulness and literal sustenance has made it possible for me to survive to write all day long."

Rose's fork clattered to the floor, and her face flushed pink. Her mouth hung open.

Marsh had not been prepared for Rose's reaction. He had meant for her to know he appreciated her thoughtfulness, but he didn't know how deeply affected she would be.

"Oh, my," she whispered, taking her glasses off so she could wipe her eyes with a napkin. "Oh, dear."

Isn't it wonderful, thought Liliane. What kind of life would this woman have had if she'd remained in England? Certainly she would never have been as loved as she has been in Africa. Jack died holding on to her, telling her she was beautiful, and Marsh shows his love by dedicating a book to her. Liliane looked at Rose's long face, her round gray eyes hidden behind her thick glasses, her stocky, no-nonsense body, her graying hair with its wisps caught carelessly with bobby pins, and she, too, thought Rose was beautiful. She loved Marsh's gesture.

"You know," he said later when they were alone. "I've never dedicated a book to you."

"You don't have to." Liliane smiled in the flickering lamplight. "I know how you feel."

"Did you know I loved you when I left Simbayo, when I married Dolores?"

"Of course. But I know it takes more than love to live together. I know, too, that our time is limited now. I see how you waste in this humidity. I see how your energy lessens the longer you stay. I see how you have to fight to write the long hours that you do."

His dark eyes warmed her. They understood each other so well. "Yet I'm driven to this book as I haven't been to the others."

"War is so gloomy." Liliane sighed. Yet she knew his book would contain much that was hopeful. She knew his writing that well. "You know, I've never even read *Heceta Head*. And you didn't bring a copy, of course."

"I was unhappy when I wrote that. It's bitter. I went through a period when I was very angry with you."

"I know."

"It seemed that all the men I knew had wives who would uproot themselves, would do what the men wanted, would help advance their careers. And my woman wouldn't. I wanted you to give up the life you needed to lead and live mine with me. I wanted you to show that you loved me more than anything else."

"And you wrote *Heceta Head* because you thought I didn't?"

"Yup. The furies of the gods controlled me."

"And now?" She lay back on the pillows, watching him as he undressed. She knew he would not stay in bed but would write later. She fell asleep nights listening to the hammering of the keys. It had begun to lull her to sleep—like the river. Their tempo had become attuned.

She liked to watch him undress by lamplight. She liked to watch the dark hair on his chest and his lean, muscular arms. She even liked to watch the scar on his leg, now a stark white where no hair would grow.

"Now," he said, "I'm able to accept that you don't love me more than anything else in the world, but at least as much as Carolyn and Simbayo."

"I love you more than life itself," she said.

"I know that," he said, lying down beside her.

CHAPTER 32

▼

"EDEN NEVER LASTS, DOES IT?" SADNESS FILLED LILIANE'S VOICE. Though the news was not unexpected.

Marsh had just said to her, "I'm bogged down and I can't finish the book."

She'd nodded. She'd felt it coming for the last two months but hadn't wanted to face it. She'd noticed it particularly since Carolyn was home for the Christmas holidays. Marsh used any excuse to avoid writing. He spent afternoons in the lagoon or sleeping. The usual lethargy that overtook him after months in the tropics was at work. And he'd been here over a year this time, she mused.

The zest with which he'd written for three months had dissipated; it was a pattern she'd seen before. She'd known that despite his intentions and desire he could not stay in the tropics. She saw his health begin to deteriorate, his energy diminish. Carolyn had told her that his limp was less pronounced when he'd visited her in Cape Town. So Liliane knew that the humidity affected his leg as well.

But this time his news wasn't as horrid as last time. He was not leaving forever. And she was confident he would never turn to another woman.

Marsh could no longer bear to think of Carolyn growing up alone, spending her adolescent years without love, without affection, with no one to listen to her questions. He could not abide thinking of her going to sleep without good-night kisses. And, most of all, he could not stand to have her growing up without his knowing her.

"I'm going back to Cape Town with Carolyn," he'd announced. "I'm going to buy a house there, and Carolyn and I are going to live together. We're going to be a family.

"Lili. Can't you give us a couple of months a year? Can't you come to Cape Town twice a year? We'll come here for Carolyn's July holidays, and you can come to Cape Town for her Christmas vacation and perhaps one other time as well . . . keep our lives entwined."

She walked out onto the verandah. Maybe she could.

Sensing her mood, he pressed his advantage. He rose from the chair and followed her. "Your abnormal need to be needed . . ."

She turned swiftly, her eyes afire. "Abnormal?"

"Don't get upset. Maybe I should say your *great* need to be needed can be satisfied by Carolyn and me. There are many people, now, to take care of Simbayo while you're away. Philippe and Anoka can run things. You know that. The hundreds of people who need you *can* be helped by someone else. But the two people who need you the most can never be helped by anyone but you." He put his arms around her. "Lili, we love you. We need you. We've always needed you. Consider our needs for a change, won't you?"

Wasn't it precisely because she had considered Carolyn that she'd sent her so far away?

"C'mon. Break down. Let's get married. I'll buy a house and Carolyn and I will create a home base. You don't have to leave Simbayo. Just come visit us twice a year."

Liliane leaned back against him, enjoying his arms around her. She stared out at the river.

"I'll come visit you," she acquiesced. "Send me some good maps and I'll fly down. That would be fun." To herself, she said, Maybe I haven't been fair. "But I won't marry you."

He hugged her tighter, leaning down to kiss her hair, her back held close to him. "Why not? Aren't you convinced we're going to spend our lives together?"

"I think we stand a chance of it if we don't get married. If we get married, you'll feel you own me and you'll pressure me to leave here and I'll feel guilty and unwifely. It would ruin everything."

"Don't you want to be a family?"

"We are a family."

They were silent, and she felt his breathing, in rhythm with hers. His hands were still locked around her waist.

"Has anyone ever told you you're the most impossible woman in the world?"

"Which may be why you love me."

"Well, it's a standing offer. If you're ever in the mood to make us legal, just let me know."

He sighed and let go of her. "I'm going to find Caro and tell her. Do you think she'll be pleased?"

Liliane couldn't help smiling.

CAROLYN HAD ENJOYED THIS VACATION MORE THAN ANY SINCE SHE'D been sent to Litchfield. Partly it was because Petelo had begun to write to her regularly. She had received a letter from him every month, and sometimes two. When she mentioned a book, he begged her to bring it to him, and when she talked of history or geography, he wanted details. He devoured any information she sent him, and together they explored questions for which neither of them could find answers. He kept her in touch with her roots, and she opened new vistas for him. During the school year, after her homework was finished, she wrote in a journal, thoughts that she wanted to capture before they'd fled. She got in the habit of sending them to Petelo, even though that was not her intention when she wrote them. In the process, he became the only person to know what went on in Carolyn's mind and in her heart. Much he could not understand, because his world was so different.

This year when they met again, it was not as strangers but as the beloved friends they had once been.

Even at nine Carolyn knew the pleasures of teaching. She felt a physical warmth when Petelo understood a new concept and could challenge her thinking. She realized she'd never had a friend like him in her years in Cape Town.

Her renewed closeness with him made it doubly difficult to think about leaving Simbayo. After the first few weeks in Cape Town each year, she adjusted, now that she'd spent three years there, but she was never happy. She seldom smiled and usually kept to herself. She never resembled the happy child who had grown up in Simbayo. She went through the motions of living but felt that life had run out of her. Now, in another month she would again be thrust back into that cold world.

Sitting in a homemade hammock, she swung between two okoume trees. She had just come from swimming and rocked back and forth, looking up at vestiges of the sun through the lacy leaves high above her. The sun was so different here. Seldom did the hazy glare disappear; never were the skies as crystal clear as South Africa's.

She didn't hear Marsh walk up.

He sat down in the middle of the hammock and it nearly sank to the ground. Carolyn slid toward him and laughed.

"How would you feel about leaving Simbayo three weeks early?"

Carolyn's heart pounded. Leave Mama and Petelo and Marsh? She had thought Marsh was the one person who understood.

"Take a trip with me. See the country. We can visit the copper mines at Elisabethville and stop at Victoria Falls, watch giraffes and cape buffalo and lions. See some of this wonderful continent we live on. Would you like that?"

She didn't know. She would have, last year. Now, she didn't want to leave Petelo. Oh, why was life so difficult?

Yet—a trip with Marsh?

He reached out and took her hand, looking into her eyes, a smile hiding in his.

"Something else you might like. Though I don't know." She could tell from his voice that he was teasing. "Do you like the idea of not living at school next year?"

What did he mean?

"I'm going to leave Simbayo," he went on.

"Oh, no!" Her eyes became saucers. "You promised you wouldn't."

Now the smile escaped and covered his face. "No. I promised never to leave you. And I won't." He put an arm around her shoulder, hugging her close. "How would you like me to move to Cape Town?" He gave her a moment to let that sink in. "We'll buy a house, and you can come home every afternoon after school, and

I'll be there with you all the time. Would you like that?"

She stared at him. Her throat closed. She could feel her eyes grow large. She blinked to keep back the tears. Then, uncontrollably, she began to cry and put her arms around him, dampening his shirt with her tears. She felt his hand run through her hair and heard him whisper, "My girl."

She looked up at him. "What about Mama?" she asked.

"Mama has agreed to come visit us. And we will come here every summer, for Christmas holidays."

"Oh, Marsh." She wound her arms around his neck and laid her cheek next to his. "Oh, Marsh."

Now it was Petelo's turn to be unhappy. The person who made his life different was being torn from him. It was as though the big part of his life stopped.

"But we'll write," Carolyn reassured him. She hated leaving him, but Marsh's news had so captivated her mind that she could think of little else.

"Maybe, when I am older, I can come visit you," Petelo said.

Carolyn already knew this was not possible. Not in South Africa. He couldn't even stay in their house. House. Their house. A home of their own, a home where she could feel loved and have someone to talk with, and where she could be alone—not always surrounded by people who made her feel lonely. She would never be lonely or frightened again.

The next month was one that both of them would cherish for the rest of their lives. During the next fifteen years, Carolyn and Marsh would see the pyramids of Egypt, safari out of Nairobi, spend three weeks on the Serengeti Plain in Tanganyika, visit the Etosha Pan in South-West Africa, take the train along Lake Victoria in Uganda where more wildlife abounded than any place else they visited, and even take a steamer to Madagascar, but never would any of those trips have the wonder of this first excursion.

For Carolyn, it was a magical time, and because it was for her, so it became for Marsh. For the first time, she could enjoy traveling, not considering it a punishment—being sent back to school. She was so elated that Marsh was coming with her, that they would make a home, that no longer did she have to live at Litchfield, that everything she saw pleasured her.

After Marsh found maps, Liliane had flown them south three hundred miles to Port Francqui, where they could catch a train to travel the remaining seven hundred miles to Elisabethville. Here they left the equatorial rain forest, rising high into plateau country.

Gorillas stared at the train and elephants lumbered along; zebras striped the horizon as far as the eye could see, and native thatched-hut villages dotted the countryside. As they neared the provincial capital of Elisabethville, an aura of gentility and European culture took over. The result of years of enormous profit from the world's leading copper mines, Elisabethville had broad boulevards with elegant houses surrounded by a profusion of blooming flowers and cultivated lawns.

The train stopped here overnight. In this part of the world, trains seldom traveled at night.

Marsh and Carolyn stayed at the Hotel Le Gare. From their room, Carolyn looked down on the outdoor restaurant and for the first time heard American jazz. She fell asleep to the strains of "Smoke Gets in Your Eyes." After she slept, Marsh wandered downstairs and sat having a gimlet while he listened to the music, wondering if he had ever been more contented. The mellow music wound itself around him in the soft night air, which had little of Simbayo's humidity.

HE WOULD MISS LILIANE EVERY DAY OF HIS LIFE THAT WAS NOT SPENT with her, but living separately was a fact of life they both had to accept. That he could offer Carolyn security and happiness and find it himself, with her, delighted him. He wanted to buy a solid house, an old one, to give physical roots to the place that would be home to them, a place where they could build memories. A place that Carolyn could forever think of as "home." A place where he could spend the rest of his life writing the kind of books he wanted to leave to the world, that would be his path to immortality. The kind of books he hoped might make a difference.

A saxophone wailed through the air, and Marsh smiled. He had last heard music like that in a smoky bar in Greenwich Village.

In the morning, as they resumed their train trip to Victoria Falls in Northern Rhodesia, Carolyn put her hand in his. "Don't you think it would be all right if I call you Papa?"

Marsh swallowed hard. He started to tell her that he would like that very much, but no words came. He settled for pressing her hand and nodding.

"Look," she cried, staring out the window. "You can almost see it become a different country."

I want to show her so much, he thought. I want the world to be hers. And then, Papa. She wants to call me Papa.

They were both impressed with Victoria Falls. Just beyond the town named for David Livingstone, the Zambezi River suddenly plunged over a sheer wall a mile wide. Across the cliff, which was over two hundred feet high, the river plunged, tumbling and spraying into a chasm with a deafening roar.

From their hotel overlooking the river, they saw elephants wading in the river, their long trunks spurting showers over their babies. Farther out in the river, hippos could be seen, their heads sticking above their submerged bulks, their eyes hooded. Carolyn and Marsh watched the long sunset, the bloodred turning to oranges and then bright pinks and faint lavenders.

Walking through the bazaars in every town where they stopped, they listened to the differences in the music and observed each city's different fashion of dressing. No matter what the style, most of them had in common a level of basic poverty: mended shorts on the men, sometimes a belt, but otherwise holding their pants up with safety pins. Now and then, some man proudly wore a top hat or a derby, obviously obtained from an American mission. Once in a while, one wore a tie, tied in some peculiar fashion, with his shorts.

The women wore long, sarong-type clothing; in the cities, their breasts were covered. Most of the young women, their postures erect and regal, carried babies strapped to their backs. Children displayed skinny arms and distended stomachs—the result of malnutrition, Marsh informed Carolyn.

In the marketplaces, heavy slabs of meat, still bloodred, were covered with flies, which also infested the eyelids of most of the children, who ran around seemingly oblivious of them. The meat and the children both smelled putrid.

The marketplaces were colorful with vibrant vermilion, bright gold-yellows, hot pinks, bright purples. Yards of cheap fabric and Woolworth-type jewelry reflected the penchant for bright colors.

"Are you enjoying yourself?" Marsh asked, though he already knew the answer.

Very seriously, Carolyn answered, "I'm having the best time of my life."

AT THE VERY MOMENT MARSH AND CAROLYN STEPPED ONTO THE TRAIN that would take them to Bulawayo—where they would view the desolate grave of Cecil Rhodes—Liliane was sloshing through ankle-deep puddles caused by torrential rains. The path had turned into a slippery quagmire.

Twelve hours earlier, a runner had come into camp, nearly naked and soaking wet. He had been running for a full day and night.

"I want the white mother," he said, in a dialect not quite like the one spoken at Simbayo but understandable, nevertheless.

Liliane and Anoka had been in the midst of setting a broken leg, so the runner had to wait. Heidi bade him dry off and gave him food. His impatience could not be hidden, but he would confide in no one but "the white mother."

He shifted his weight from one foot to the other; he stood wrapped native-style in a blanket Heidi had offered him, drinking hot tea designed to warm him.

Liliane first heard of his presence as she scrubbed after surgery. She sighed. She'd hoped to be able to sleep or at least have some time alone. Since Marsh and Carolyn had left, she had had no time to mourn. She felt a desperate need to be by herself, away from the demands of her daily life.

A towel in her hand and still dressed in her operating uniform, she walked to the dining hall where the tall, thin native awaited her.

"My chief very sick," he explained.

From the description he gave her, combined with his pointing to his groin, Liliane surmised that it was a hernia. And probably a strangulated one at that, as the chief had been unable to come to the camp. If the messenger had been running for twenty-four hours, this probably meant the village was a normal three-day journey. The jittery man was afraid his chief would die. She could see that. Maybe he was already dead.

"What tribe are you?" Anoka asked, having followed Liliane to the dining hall.

The man gave him a blank look. Then he said, pulling himself erect regally, "My chief Nkunda." To him, this explained everything. Nkunda was the most important person in his world.

"I'll go," volunteered Anoka, knowing how tired Liliane was.

"No," the sharp voice of the messenger interrupted. "Nkunda want only the white mother."

"I can't go," Liliane said. "One of the other doctors will do just as well."

"No." He was stubborn. "Only you. I was told not to return if I did not bring the white mother."

Anoka shrugged his shoulders and looked helplessly at Liliane. Thunder rocked the earth. The rain had not let up in three days.

"All right." Liliane sighed. "Give me an hour."

As she was nearly ready to leave, her medical bag in hand and a knapsack thrust over her shoulder, Naldani appeared. "I am coming with you," she announced, already dressed in clothing that would protect her from the downpour.

"You don't need to," Liliane responded.

"Anoka and I talked it over. We are not going to have you go alone on a three days' journey into unknown territory. I know of no births about to occur in the next week, so I am coming. Please do not argue." Her eyes showed that she was ready for a fight.

Liliane smiled. "I'm not going to argue. You're a true friend."

Naldani nodded.

And so, in the stormy half-light of the late afternoon, they started off, following the runner, striding hard to keep up with him. They walked until Liliane thought she would collapse. And then, as if by a miracle, a small hut appeared by the side of the path and the runner indicated they would sleep for a while.

Liliane was asleep before her head hit the hard ground. When they awoke, gray gloom had replaced the inky night, but the rain had not let up. Fortunately, the wind did not kick up until they were close to their destination.

What time it was, Liliane did not know, nor did it matter. She would not have been surprised to learn it was midnight. They had stopped to rest several times but only long enough to eat or to regain their even breathing. Liliane could hear her heart pounding through her eardrums.

The runner led them to the largest hut in the village. Liliane could hear chanting from the hut, a mournful dirge, the same words repeated over and over. She lit her flashlight and nearly gagged as she stepped over the threshold.

The stench was overwhelming. At least twenty people were gathered in the small, windowless thatched-roof hut. These huts always smelled bad, but so many unwashed bodies crowded into this small, airless place was insufferable. Mixed with the sweat and dirt of so many bodies was the fetid odor of disease.

The rain came in gusts, spraying water over everything, whipping the dust from the hut's floor.

Nkunda, the chief, lay on the ground in the center of the hut surrounded by the chanters. He was a splendid specimen of manhood, muscular, with an athletic build. He was naked except for a loincloth and an elaborate headdress studded with shining stones and stuffed with gaily colored feathers. His eyes were closed and Liliane could tell that pain had drained his energy.

She wanted to ask the crowd to leave, but she knew they would not. She wanted to hack a window in the hut and let ventilation take out the foul odor. She fought the urge to vomit from the smell.

Instead, she took off her raincoat; someone grabbed it from her. Kneeling down beside Nkunda, she saw at once that she'd guessed correctly: it was a strangulated hernia. She could imagine how he had managed it over the years. The hernia would be like a balloon poking down from the groin into the sac near the testicle on one side. Straining or coughing would make it worse. He probably found that he could push it back in, maybe keep it in place with some strapping across the abdomen and groin.

Gesturing for Naldani to kneel down next to her, Liliane said, "I can tell what's been happening lately. He's been trying primitive treatments. Probably a week or so ago he began having extra pain in the groin, plus an inability to push the scrotal sac back in. Plus he's probably had several days of nausea, vomiting, worsening pain. They no doubt sent for us when he developed the complication of fever."

The chief's moaning gathered their attention. "I know what I'm going to see," Liliane told Naldani. "He's had intestinal cramping; finally there's been a breakdown of tissues; infected pus has been released into the hernia sac and into the abdomen as well."

Though Naldani was the best midwife Liliane could imagine, she knew little of surgery or other aspects of medicine. Liliane would have to explain so that Naldani could understand and be prepared to help.

"This happens because, in having a strangulated hernia, the arterial blood supply to the portion of the colon that is trapped in the hernia is shut off, so it begins to hurt and break down, causing severe pain. Just like a heart attack—which is a death of heart muscle. It's excruciatingly painful."

Gesturing with both hands, she begged the bystanders to move back. She put her hands on the chief's forehead. He was burning with fever. Opening his eyes with great effort, he focused for a moment on Liliane and smiled weakly. "White mother." His voice held hope.

This is not the type of surgery I should be doing out here,

Liliane thought. It's a life-threatening situation. What happens if he dies?

Time, she knew, was of the essence. "If there's any way to save him," she said to Naldani, "we have to operate quickly. He can't be moved."

A gust of wind and rain swept through the hut, swirling dust but bringing a moment of freshness to the foul atmosphere. Lightning crashed and thunder reverberated until it muffled itself.

"I have to get my lantern," Liliane said, reaching for her knapsack. "Though I don't know if it'll be adequate."

Naldani told the crowd to move back, that the white mother had to have room. There was no place for them to move, so they crowded even closer together and watched as Liliane lit her Coleman lantern and hung it on a hook from the thatched roof. They watched it sway over the sick Nkunda.

"Tell them we must have much water. Tell them to boil it— large quantities of it. That will give some of them something to do. And you and I must wash before I can do anything."

She told Naldani how much chloroform to administer to the chief.

The surgery involved cutting an incision paralleling the groin, though a little bit farther up in the abdominal wall, separating some muscle layers, cutting into the peritoneum, and releasing the tight connective tissue of the hernia sac which was strangulating the bowel.

There was no sound at all from the onlookers, not even the sound of breathing. Once a swish of rain rushed in and the lantern rocked back and forth, but the light held.

Whether talking to herself or to Naldani, Liliane kept up a running commentary. "The normal bowel would appear pink, and when pressed would blanch white and then immediately pink up again. That's in large contrast to this infected, gangrenous bowel, trapped as a little loop—see it?—deep in the hernia." It was bluishblack, swollen, weepy with pus and crusts of pus, and there was a whitish area on the bowel. Liliane had to turn her head away when she smelled the malodorous contents leaking from one or two holes in the bowel.

The stench was overpowering. Even several of the natives made gagging sounds and left the hut for a few minutes. Liliane hoped she would not retch here. She could not take time to see how Naldani was holding up.

Sweat dripped from her forehead into her eyes. She tried to wipe it away with her sleeve.

"I'm not prepared for this," she said aloud.

"You can do it," said Naldani's steady voice.

"I know. But I'm still not prepared. These are not ideal conditions for anything, much less an operation like this. The repair of the bowel will be rather tricky." Essentially, it involved clamping off the infected bowel from the normal bowel on either side. Liliane reached for a clothespin—despite the situation, she couldn't help smiling. Clothespins had served her as well as any medical instrument over the years. She never traveled without a supply of them. She took the two clothespins and placed them firmly on either side of the eight-inch section that looked like rope.

"I'm placing them well into the normal-appearing tissue," she explained to Naldani, "so that I won't be including the infected tissue in reconstruction."

She made a clean cut just on the side of the clamp, then removed the gangrenous segment. With great care, worrying about sterility, she irrigated with water. Slowly, and with multiple small sutures, she attached the ends of the normal bowel together, using an inner stitch of catgut and then outer stitches of silk.

"Imagine," she continued her lesson, "trying to repair a cut hose. You'd have to start at one end and work out to either side and eventually close it over the top."

She kept irrigating it. The major problem facing her now was the infected pus swimming around surrounding the other bowels. "The problem here," she continued, "is that infection can kill the chief more quickly than surgery."

She removed the dead portions of the intestine. "Now for the boiled water." She had given it enough time to cool and hoped that, in the process, it was still sterile. In a relay that Naldani had set up, someone outside the hut, standing there in the still torrential downpour, began to send small bowls of the water into the hut. Naldani carefully poured water into the belly while Liliane drained it out. They poured it in and drained it out, poured it in and drained it out, by soaking it up with cloths passed gently into the wound. Liliane spent much time trying to remove all bacteria and pus.

When she was satisfied, as much as she could be under the circumstances, she said, "Closing the wound will be fairly simple. Watch. I'll repair the hernia sac and then reapproximate the peritoneum fascia and muscle layers." She then sprinkled sulpha powder into the wound. "The wonder of modern science," she murmured.

Naldani and everyone else in the hut watched with silent absorption. Liliane tied some of the layers to the peritoneum to make a strong hernia closure. With satisfaction, she listened to the chief's breathing, felt his pulse to find his heart rate. And relaxed.

Her loud sigh indicated to all that it was over.

She closed her eyes, more exhausted than she could ever remember being.

Now, the natives crowded around them, and two of them leaned down to lift the chief up.

Startled, Liliane cried out, "What are you doing?"

"We take him back to his house."

Standing up, she said in a strident voice, "Out in the rain? You will do no such thing. You will leave him right here. And you will all leave. Not one of you will stay with him tonight or come back here until he can sit up."

They stared at her. No one made a move.

"You have seen the operation. He will be asleep until morning. I say you will leave."

They stared at each other in confusion. Then they crowded out the door.

"Get water," Liliane told one of them, "so that we may wash up."

The thunder sounded farther away this time.

In a minute, one of the natives reentered the hut. He was of medium height and as handsome as the chief. "I am oldest son. The next chief. I stay."

Liliane nodded. One seemed reasonable.

After she and Naldani washed, Naldani said, "You sleep now. I'll sleep when you wake."

She did not wake Liliane until morning, however.

They requested brooms and swept the hut clean. Liliane ordered that blankets be washed in boiling water.

"I will not leave until I am positive he will live."

As the chief regained consciousness, Liliane could see him studying her out of slitted, half-opened eyes. He was a handsome man. His black skin gleamed like velvet, and when he felt Liliane's cool hands washing him, he opened his eyes wide and stared at her.

On the second day, he grabbed her hand and said, "Do not do that. Woman cannot wash man."

"I am not a woman," Liliane suggested. "I am the white

mother, the doctor. You will do as I say, and I say I am going to wash your wound."

He stared at her coldly.

On the fourth day he walked. Just a little bit.

When Liliane and Naldani got ready to leave, after a week, Nkunda was able to laugh without pain.

"I am forever at your service," he said formally.

Liliane gave him instructions for his recuperation and told him not to sleep with his wives for a month.

The night before they left, the villagers celebrated with a big party and gave Liliane and Naldani so many presents that another runner had to accompany them back to Simbayo.

Liliane's present from Nkunda was a small, carved ivory elephant of great delicacy and beauty. He had carved it himself, he told Liliane.

She still had it when she next met him, twenty years later.

PART THREE

▼

1955
TO
1968

CHAPTER 33

▼

LILIANE BECAME THE GUEST. DURING ALL OF THE YEARS THAT Carolyn was growing up, it was Marsh in whom Carolyn confided; it was Marsh with whom she laughed and took long walks. It was Marsh who helped her with her homework and bought dresses *for* her—and, when she was older, *with* her.

It was Marsh who spent hours planning their trips with her, and Marsh who excited her imagination. No problem was too small, no idea too large.

When Liliane arrived for a month each year, it was into a tightly knit relationship that she was welcomed. She envied the closeness of the two people she so loved. Carolyn was on her best behavior; she put on the ladylike airs she had learned so well at Litchfield and consciously aimed to please her mother.

Marsh had talked Liliane into an exchange; one summer they would celebrate Christmas at Simbayo and the next she would spend the vacation in Cape Town. But after only two visits back to Simbayo, Carolyn was restless. The ties she had formed there in her childhood were not strong enough to compete with the life she now lived. Though Marsh could slide back to the slower pace, neither he nor Carolyn managed to become part of the routine of Simbayo. The daily problems did not absorb them; they had broken the rhythm that had once engulfed them. The problems of the outside world elicited only polite listening from Liliane, and from Rose and Heidi and Philippe. They all wanted to hear what Carolyn was learning in school, but after that initial conversation their focus returned to their own world and its daily dilemmas.

Before she reached fourteen, Carolyn realized how small the world of Simbayo was. It was surrounded by jungle; her world now had unlimited horizons. The previous vacation Marsh had taken her and Liliane to Kenya, promising that when the war was over he would take them to Egypt. Carolyn had observed that the world was not all sickness, not all work. And yet she had difficulty relaxing. The Puritan work ethic, inherited from her mother, allowed her little frivolity. When she and Marsh traveled, she did so with intensity. Everything she did had a fierceness about it.

One of the things she and Marsh most loved to do was argue about ideas. Then her eyes would blaze, her thin arms grow tense. When she rejected an idea, she stubbornly crossed her arms across her chest as though keeping the world away.

When Carolyn finished her homework at night, she would stroll into Marsh's study, her favorite room. On winter evenings a fire burned in the big stone fireplace; shadows played across the books that lined the walls. He sat, hunched over his typewriter, pecking it in his two-fingered way. He was never too involved to leave his work when she entered.

Yet her mother's influence was profound. Carolyn already talked of becoming an immunologist; she wanted to study the reasons for diseases and help defeat them. She also wanted to show the world that black people had as much worth as whites. In these aims, Marsh gently urged her on.

She never brought friends home from school, never spent afternoons or weekends at the homes of schoolmates, but she was well liked at school. She was an excellent student and never involved herself in the petty jealousies that abound at every school. She was not so aloof that she wouldn't do homework with a classmate, even help others; she was invariably kind, never rejecting a request for help. She laughed quietly with the other girls at lunchtime or in gym classes, and sometimes, during her teenage years, she would meet girls downtown on Saturday afternoons for a movie. But she never shared private thoughts or invited confidences. Her aloofness caused her classmates to be somewhat in awe of her.

What even she didn't understand was that when she was seven years old, she had determined never to allow herself to love unconditionally. Except for Marsh, she never permitted anyone to know her inner self, including—and perhaps, mainly—her mother. Because Marsh was allowed in, he filled her whole being. As for Marsh, Carolyn contented him. He wrote to Liliane every week, knowing that Carolyn wrote only sporadically. There was never a time, though, when he did not long for Liliane to be in Cape Town with them. He eventually talked her into spending a month with them during the winter also, as well as every summer. When Carolyn was eighteen, she came back for one final time, but other summers, after the war permitted, they traveled, and Carolyn's and Liliane's horizons were broadened. They laughed a lot, the three of them, and talked of things important and things not. But it was

Liliane who hugged Carolyn, who came to her room or her tent to kiss her good-night. Marsh was the only one with whom Carolyn initiated affection.

Marsh lavished affection on both his women. When Liliane was in Cape Town, she felt loved. When she was there, Marsh did not write in his study during the evening, so there were no long talks with Carolyn about God or about apartheid or about stars or about anything that came to mind. Yet, despite her closeness to Marsh, Carolyn never resented Liliane's intrusion into their life; she looked forward to her mother's visits. She wanted to share her accomplishments at school, and when the three of them traveled together, she basked in the joy of their being a family. But she never trusted her mother with her heart.

Her mind was a different matter. Because of Liliane's influence, Carolyn did major in immunology. She did become an early member of the Black Sash movement. These decisions pleased Marsh as well. And when Carolyn graduated from the university, he tried to prepare himself for her leavetaking. But she had no desire to leave. They were both pleased when she was offered a job in the immunology lab at the university, even though for the first few years the job was more of a learning process than one that encouraged creativity.

There were men in Carolyn's life. She had gone to school dances, and at the university she went to parties, the kind where the guests drank white wine and discussed ideas. She had been kissed several times, and even kissed a few of the men back, but as soon as a man's hand wandered beyond the limits she had set for herself, that was the end of that man in her life. Not that she didn't yearn for something more; but none of the men she met seemed to be more than boys. None awakened in her what she was certain lay dormant, waiting to be brought to life.

When men heard of her work in the Black Sash movement, they would smile and say "You can't really believe in that?" "You're just working in the lab until you get married" was another response destined to relegate the speaker to Carolyn's past.

Yet there was also a certain charm to Carolyn. The still flaxen hair shimmered like spun silver. Her blue-green eyes blazed, startlingly colorful and vibrant in her pale face. Her determined chin was softened by the sensuality of her lips; her face had distinctive beauty. So, unlike her mother, Carolyn developed a flair for style, a knack for choosing clothes that lent an air of drama to her.

Though she was aloof, she was never arrogant. She carried her kindly nature into adulthood; her lack of communication was just one way, for she listened well. Strangers on buses confided tales of such intimacy that Carolyn was shocked. People with whom she worked shared details of their marriages, told her of their secret dreams. They seemed to have no need to share Carolyn's soul in return. She listened, gave her frank opinions, and shared the details with Marsh at the dinner table; some eventually found their way into his books.

Carolyn had a warm laugh, though she did not laugh frequently. When she smiled, which *was* often, only Marsh noted that it was not usually with her eyes. In this, she was like him.

Litchfield had done its job well. Carolyn exhibited all of the social graces, and her detached coolness fascinated rather than alienated.

She was not detached in the realm of ideas, fed to her so carefully over the years by Marsh. About some things she was passionate, and with these she involved herself. But they did not supply answers.

Only Marsh sensed that Carolyn's restlessness involved impatience; she wanted life to excite and to challenge her. She wanted her passion to involve not only ideas but also a man. She wanted life to be brighter than the sedate one she knew in Cape Town. It didn't dawn on her that she would have to leave Marsh to make that happen.

He had been trying to prepare himself for her eventual departure for ten years. When it came, it came with no warning.

WHEN ANDREW McCLOUD OPENED THE ENVELOPE, THAT LOVELY FALL afternoon of 1954, he read the name. Then he said it aloud.

"Rhodesia?"

He walked over to the world map tacked to his office wall and, after a brief search, located the place.

Staring at the words on the map for a long time, he broke into a grin. He was thirty-one and eager for adventure. The kind he'd already had was not satisfying. He'd been an RAF bombardier for five years, and though he'd not set foot on foreign soil during the war, he'd flown nightly over Europe in the interests of democracy, dropping death on Nazis and innocent people alike, destroying antiquities never to be replaced.

When the war ended, he had no trouble joining one of London's most prestigious engineering firms. He'd worked there now for nine years, but the work had become plodding, unchallenging, too predictable; he felt limited. His life had a monotony to it.

Three months ago, he had answered an ad in *The Times.* The ad had stated that there was a challenging engineering job available, which included surveying, building, and drawing, and that both government and private work were included. It was "headquartered in a 'garden spot' city," but no specific locale was given other than "British colony." For a month he impatiently waited for the mail. Then, not having heard anything, he forgot about it. Almost.

When, two months later, he received the invitation from Llewellyn Ltd., to come to Salisbury, Rhodesia, he could scarcely contain himself. He carried the letter in his pocket for three days. Then he sat down and wrote an acceptance. After that he went to the library to read about Rhodesia.

He wondered how to tell his mother, with whom he dined every Thursday evening. She had never been possessive, but, still, to have one's only son move seven thousand miles away!

On Thursday Andrew notified his supervisor at work that he'd be leaving within the month, knowing he'd have to break the news to his mother at dinner that night. He broached the subject over dessert.

"Have you ever heard of Rhodesia?" he asked.

She raised her head, a regal, proud head, her hair faintly shot through with gray. They strongly resembled each other: sharp, defiant chins; aquiline noses that made them look as though their profiles should be on ancient Roman coins; high, well-defined cheekbones; broad foreheads under mops of curling red hair. Andrew's dark eyes were brown; eyes that were not as brilliant as his mother's blue ones. He was a large-boned man who dwarfed his mother's slight frame. While her complexion was the famous British peaches-and-cream, his was ruddy and freckled.

In her youth, she had been one of the most beautiful women in England; she was still a handsome woman at fifty-two. Andrew would not have been surprised to learn that she had lovers. Dorothy McCloud looked as though she had been born to wealth and aristocracy, but though she had been born into the latter, she had acquired wealth only by marriage. A fringe benefit, she thought. The husband who had meant more to her than any amount of money had been killed in the escape from Dunkirk.

"Rhodesia? Of course." Her voice was like silken threads drawn across the table. "It's in Africa."

"Know anything else?"

"Let's see. Named after Cecil Rhodes, wasn't it?"

Andrew nodded. Then she surprised him. "I think it's beastly of us. We go visiting other lands and think we've 'discovered' or 'conquered' them and name them for us. Victoria Falls! Victoria, indeed! Rhodesia! Because one white man with his white-supremacy theory decides to get rich there! You know, he really lived in South Africa."

Andrew stared at his mother with astonishment. He'd had no idea she thought that way.

"You don't approve of our civilizing the colonies?"

His mother put down her fork. "Is that really the term?" Andrew had never seen her so agitated over an abstract idea. "Isn't it that we won't rest until they're like us and we've erased their roots, their histories?"

"What," asked Andrew, "about our having introduced God to them?"

"Oh, God," his mother said. "The horrors done over the centuries in the name of Christianity! It's enough to make one an atheist." The clear blue of her eyes darkened.

"Are you one? An atheist?" Andrew asked.

Amusement stole into his mother's voice. "And if I were?"

Andrew looked at her. For the first time, he realized he had taken his mother for granted. "I think I don't know you."

She smiled; it had the look of a Cheshire cat. "I thought you might never want to." Continuing the conversation, she said, "Missionaries and proselytizers of any kind are more interested in their ideas than in humanity. I'll tell you something really heretical."

Andrew waited.

"I don't like Albert Schweitzer. There! I've thought it a dozen times. I'm probably the only person in the whole world who feels that way."

"Tell me why."

"Oh," she replied between bites of beef bourguignon, "I read about him doing his good works for the natives of French Equatorial Africa, and I do like that. But it's the way he does it. He told some visitor not to even try to communicate with the Africans, that they're nothing but mindless children. He devotes his life to a cause but not to a people."

"And you." Andrew tried to sound casual. "How do you feel about colored people?"

His mother smiled grimly. "Colored? What an awful pejorative, as though one is less than human. Well, I like *pink* babies."

Impulsively, Andrew reached his hand across the table and put it over her long, elegant one. "I love you," he said.

His mother went to the sideboard for the decanter of cognac. When she poured his, she asked, "Is there some magic word? If so, I want to keep it ready."

"No." Andrew laughed, accepting the snifter of brandy. "I just wanted to tell you."

Running her fingers through his thick, unruly hair, she kissed the top of his head and returned to her seat across the table from him.

"How did all of this start?" She wanted to know.

"Because, I think"—he had no more hesitation—"I asked you about Rhodesia."

She looked sideways at him. "Then that's the magic word?" She paused for a moment and looked into him. "May I visit you there?"

He stared at her in continued amazement. He had not told her he was going there.

SINCE HE HAD TWO MONTHS BEFORE HE HAD TO REPORT TO THE office in Salisbury, Andrew opted to take a freighter to Cape Town, a slow one that stopped at numerous ports along the Atlantic seaboard. The ship smelled, more of the sickening smell of copra than of anything else, for it was a clean ship with a captain who enjoyed having passengers, who played bridge or chess with them and regaled them with tales of his adventurous years at sea.

When the ship stopped at ports, Andrew stood on the docks and watched the bustle of the loading. Voices cried out to each other; coffee and cocoa and copra and teak were taken on board the ship and European-made goods were left on the docks.

Two of the eleven ship's passengers were young women who eyed him covertly, but he enjoyed roaming around by himself. There was too much to see to limit himself to a shipboard romance. He did play bridge with the young ladies and danced on the deck evenings to the blare of an old Victrola. He talked with them for hours and kissed each of them in the tropical moonlight. He felt happy and expansive toward the whole world.

The long boat trip relaxed him; life was slow, and for the first time in his life he began to unwind. It seemed the most wonderful time in the world. He wished it would never end.

The Captain told Andrew of Table Mountain, the flat-topped Cape Town butte that had served as a landmark for over three hundred years. When it finally came into view, Andrew viewed it with mixed feelings: sorrow to be leaving such a pleasant voyage and excitement to be landing at last near the area that was to be his home.

He sensed the importance of disembarking onto South African soil. Here, in Cape Town, he intended to spend two weeks trying to acclimate himself to, and to absorb, this part of Africa, which he knew would be similar to his Rhodesian destination. He was to report in Salisbury in exactly fifteen days. The timing couldn't have been more perfect. He'd decide later whether to fly or to take the two-day train ride.

The ship pulled into Table Bay, overshadowed on the right by the mountain after which it was named, its flat top usually covered with a tablecloth of round, white clouds that clung to it as though part of it.

Andrew had imagined that all African cities would be but paces from the bush, but Cape Town was even smaller than he had anticipated. He had expected a patina of sophistication in this city founded over three hundred years ago by the Dutch. Certainly it was more sophisticated than Accra had been, but it was nothing like he'd envisioned. Stolid, perhaps, in a Dutch sense, but also outrageously beautiful, caught in the shadow of the mountain and nestled between two bays.

From the harbor and later, from the hotel, he could not see the squatter camps and townships where the blacks lived.

He awoke to his first full day on the continent of Africa and decided to roam around Cape Town, trying to get a sense of what this city was like. He couldn't have been in a more spectacular setting. He could see both the ocean and Table Mountain from his hotel window. Perhaps, he thought, I should have tried to get a job here. He already liked Cape Town.

On the streets, English with a guttural accent was as prevalent as English with a British accent. Perhaps there was a more formal atmosphere than in London, less cosmopolitan, of course, but a lively city. It wasn't large enough to get lost in. There were really only seven streets of any major size.

He spent the morning wandering around the business center of the city, ate lunch in an outdoor café, and sat watching the crowds milling about while he sipped a beer.

It wasn't until later, when he lay in bed trying to remember how it had started, that he realized he must have been staring at the woman, who was as pale as a porcelain doll. Her skin was like alabaster, her hair so blond it shone white. Falling to her shoulders, it draped itself over the red-and-white-flowered silk dress she wore. She sat three tables away from him, writing and erasing on a pad, intent upon her task. When she looked up, staring into the distance, he observed the brightest eyes imaginable. They were like the reflections of the ocean on which he'd seen the sun shining so early that morning. She wore her elegance like a shawl, draped around herself, cool and unemotional, but beautiful—not actually untouchable, but perhaps unresponsive. He had seen women like her all over London; women who wouldn't, perhaps couldn't, communicate. The kind who cared more about her lipstick being in place than in passion.

Not that Andrew had had that much contact with passion. The women he had known seemed superficial, listening to his enthusiasm politely but without real interest. Or they were clingers— seeking dependence on a man. None had seemed to arouse his passion or even an urge to continue seeing them for long. A woman was not really on his list of priorities right now. A new continent and approaching a new way of life were infinitely more in his thoughts than women. But, dammit, this woman was special.

So, when she put her pencil in her purse, tucked her notebook under her arm, and got up, walking briskly to the bus stop, he followed. A breeze was blowing and her silken hair billowed out, shining in the bright sunlight, which was brighter and clearer than Andrew was used to in London. When she got onto the bus and walked to the rear, sitting next to an open window, he followed. She leaned an elbow on the windowsill and rested her chin on her gloved hand.

He sat down next to her. They both stared straight ahead.

After two stops, he had the temerity to ask, "I've no idea where I am or where I'm going. Can you help me?"

She smiled, a smile so dazzling that he felt caught in it.

"You're new here?" she asked, in an accent that sounded as if it were straight from home.

"Yes," he answered. "I just arrived yesterday. Thought I'd go sightseeing, but I don't know where to go."

"Well," she responded, "it rather depends on what you want to see."

"That's just it," he said. "I don't know. What *is* there to see?"

She laughed, and he was sure bells tinkled. "Would you like to see our tigers and lions?"

"I'm not quite that naïve." He smiled. "I've got two weeks to spend here before going to Salisbury, and I want to see everything. I've never really been out of England. Do you have any suggestions?"

Her head tilted to the side, she appraised him. The aloofness he had previously imagined had disappeared. The smoothness of her skin, the unexpectedly dark lashes framing those eyes of turquoise, the straight nose, the determined jaw, the fullness of her lips—everything about her enchanted him. There was an ingenuousness about her that he found appealing.

"Do you want to see pretty things or reality?"

"Can't I see both?"

"Yes, of course, but not at the same time. At least, not here."

"Where are *you* heading?" he asked.

"I'm heading straight into reality," she answered, her voice taking on an edge.

She looked out the window, and he noticed they were coming to a poorer part of the city, filled mainly with blacks, though he knew they couldn't live within the city limits.

"What do you do for a living?" she asked briskly, turning back to him, her eyes examining him.

"I'm an engineer," he said. "Let me introduce myself. Andrew McCloud."

"Scottish?" she asked.

"Way back. But London born and bred. In two weeks, Africa will be my home. I've accepted an engineering job with Llewellyn Ltd. in Salisbury. I'd better find out what's real."

She looked delighted at his answer. Holding out her hand, she smiled. "I'm Carolyn Compson. We get off at the next stop."

CHAPTER 34

▼

FROM THE BUS STOP CAROLYN AND ANDREW WALKED PAST JUST THREE shops. Andrew was about to ask where their destination was when Carolyn ducked into a dark store, and he quickly followed. Inside, the walls were clean, but the cracked green paint was peeling. Sitting on straight-backed chairs were a row of blacks, their eyes old, devoid of hope.

Carolyn turned to look up at Andrew. "When you get bored, you can get the number-six bus across the street. It'll take you back downtown."

He knew he wouldn't be bored.

Another woman, older than Carolyn by about ten years, was seated behind a desk looking distraught.

"Oh, am I glad to see you," she said with a sigh, reaching out to touch Carolyn's arm.

"Troops to the rescue." Carolyn saluted with mockery. "Jane, this is Andrew McCloud," she said, introducing the two.

"Help?" asked Jane.

"No. I picked him up on the bus." Carolyn smiled at him, not quite flirtatiously, and gestured to a chair. "Why don't you sit over there?"

He did.

"Tomorrow," said Jane, brushing dark hair away from her face, "I'm going to try to take care of these three cases." She threw papers across the desk at Carolyn, who glanced through them quickly and drew in her breath audibly.

"Good luck," she said, as though she didn't believe in it.

"Yes, rather."

Rising, stiff with exhaustion, Jane gathered her purse and the papers she'd tossed across the desk and left after waving to Andrew.

"What do you do here?" he asked Carolyn.

"You'll see. This will be quite an awakening for your first day in Cape Town," said Carolyn, finding other papers in a file and looking through them. She was silent for several moments. Then she called, "Mrs. Desai."

A small black woman, dressed in clean faded clothes, got up from one of the chairs and walked slowly, her shoulders slightly humped, to Carolyn. She stood until Carolyn nodded for her to sit.

"What can I do for you?" she asked, and Andrew thought it sounded like the heavenly angels he'd been told about in the church of his youth. Sweetness, warmth, hope—her voice held all of these at once.

"They are going to send me to Soetgrond," Mrs. Desai answered. To Andrew, she had a strange accent, though her English was clear. "My husband died last week. And they tell me I cannot stay here longer. They are going to send me to Soetgrond," she repeated, her voice choking. "They say they send me back to my homeland, but it is not my homeland, and I do not want to go." She enunciated clearly and slowly.

Carolyn's breast heaved. Andrew realized what a lovely body she had. But it was her empathy that caught him more.

"Oh, Mrs. Desai!" cried Carolyn.

Tears welled in the black woman's eyes, which were red from crying, and she nervously twisted a handkerchief in her lap. She was frightened.

"Who did you see?" asked Carolyn, restrained anger obvious in her eyes and her voice.

"Mr. Grossbart." Tears now fell down Mrs. Desai's cheeks; she tried to wipe them away with the crumpled handkerchief. "He tells me he could send me away in seventy-two hours, but that he will give me two weeks to get all my belongings together. I do not even know where Soetgrond is. I will not know anyone there."

With the woman's strange accent, Andrew had to strain to follow the conversation.

She began to cry openly. "If I have to leave, let me go back to my home. I lived there fifty years. I have friends there."

Carolyn got up from her side of the desk and walked over to Mrs. Desai. She pulled the woman from her chair and put her arms around the frail body. Now the woman allowed herself to sob uncontrollably.

"I will go to see Mr. Grossbart tomorrow," Carolyn promised. "I'll tell him I'm willing to hire you. I'll see what can be done. I'll come to your home the day after tomorrow."

Her handkerchief to her nose, Mrs. Desai turned and shuffled away.

Carolyn stared after her and then turned to Andrew.

"Her husband worked here for years. But it's forbidden to bring a wife until requirements are met. So, for twenty-eight years, he saw his wife only about every four years. His children were grown, with children of their own, and he scarcely knew them. Once, a decade passed before he was allowed to visit. Yet, because he worked here and could send them money, he and they lived better than they could have otherwise. He died last week. Now, the house they lived in together for the last five years is no longer available to her. Now, she's what they call a temporary sojourner.

The government wants to resettle her, and others like her, in a shack in the middle of nowhere so that she'll be out of sight and mind. It might just as well be in a different country. And there's no way to earn a living. No stores are allowed. The land is barren; it's practically impossible to grow anything there. One must erect one's own shack, and how can Mrs. Desai do that?"

Andrew didn't know whether his overwhelming feeling of compassion was for Mrs. Desai's situation or for Carolyn's reaction to it.

"She'll die," Carolyn whispered, whether to Andrew or to herself he didn't know. "Or want to."

"Can you do anything?" he asked.

"I can try," she answered with a shrug of her shoulders. The red and white dress seemed strangely out of place now, its vividness too bright for what was happening here.

Carolyn stared at the sheaf of papers on the desk, and her fingers played with the corners of them, before she read the next one and called a tall man who walked from his chair belligerently, hope still alive in his being.

His name was Daniel Mpopo.

Anger blazed from his eyes. "They promised me that after eight years, my wife could come. It's over eight years. Now they say ten."

Andrew noticed that Carolyn didn't ask what the reasons were.

"You have worked for the same employer all these years?" asked Carolyn.

Daniel shook his head. "I been working so hard 'cause they told me when I work eight years my wife and my two children can come live with me and we get a house. A government house." He slurred his words more than Mrs. Desai did, but he talked slowly.

"Was it Mr. Van Hoogeveen who told you this?" Carolyn asked.

Daniel nodded.

"I'll see him this week. And I'll come see you Thursday at work." She reached her hand across the desk and gently touched his fingers, which were gripping the edge of the desk.

When he relived the day later, he thought that perhaps it was at this particular moment that he had fallen in love.

The next man was about forty, an erect, handsome man. He carried his bandaged hand in front of him. He did not sit down but stood in front of Carolyn. His voice boomed. "I won't go!"

"Tell me"—she looked at the paper in front of her, then at the man—"what happened."

Three weeks ago, at the warehouse where he had worked for seven years, a large box fell onto his hand and broke it. "Now they tell me since I haven't worked in three weeks I can't stay here, that I am going to be sent back to my village." He shook his good hand, fire jumping from his eyes. "I stayed here all these years, I put up with being treated like an animal so that I could get a permit to live here, so that I could marry and have a house and start a family. Now, they're going to send me back to where I can't earn a living, where my people are starving, because one of *their* boxes fell on my hand!" he shouted, angry with the injustices of the system and of life.

Carolyn talked with him, promised to see what could be done. She talked with seven people that afternoon and promised to try to help them all.

When the last person had gone, when all of the chairs were empty, Carolyn let her body sag.

There was silence in the store.

She read through papers, wrote some notes, and then began to gather them up. She turned to Andrew.

"How do you feel about what you've seen this afternoon?"

"Sick. Puzzled. Wanting to know more. What can *you* do about it? Why are you here?"

"There are a group of us—all women; we call ourselves the Black Sash Society—who try to help."

She stood. "I'll try to follow through with these cases. Then I don't come again for another two weeks. And I won't succeed with even half of them."

"Why do you do it?"

A bitter smile came onto her face. "Oh, just because you're defeated before you begin is no reason not to try. But it's not hopeless. I'll probably be able to help at least one of them. One week I did something for three. That was an all-time high."

She unscrewed the single light bulb, and they went out into the still bright light. It was five o'clock.

Crossing the street, Carolyn's body began to straighten, vitality crept back into her. Andrew had stared at her all afternoon. He thought that perhaps he'd never seen anyone more beautiful. How could he keep her? How could he stop her from disappearing?

"Allow me to buy you dinner. I want to hear more about this."

"Well," she breathed, a door closing inside her. "I don't want to talk about it right now. But if you want to see the pretty side of Cape Town, I'll take you home to dinner with me. Would you like that?"

Would he!

And he'd been in South Africa just twenty-four hours.

ANDREW AND CAROLYN GOT OFF THE BUS WHERE THEY HAD MET. SHE had become a different person. Until tomorrow she had left today's tragedies alone. She laughed, the still shining sun dancing through her hair, as she led him to her red Ferrari convertible.

Sliding into the driver's seat, she gestured him into the other side, responding to the question in his eyes. "I think it's rather ostentatious, don't you, to drive something like this to that part of town, when I'm trying to give courage to people. But I don't see having to play the martyr—doing without just because they need."

She drove fast, not quite recklessly, but with abandon, as though it excited her to drive fast. Yet she also drove with great care and skill. They were out of the city proper in minutes. They soon approached what looked, to Andrew, to be a farmhouse transposed from the Normandy countryside, surrounded by green lawns, acres of orchards, and miles of vineyards.

Andrew whistled.

"Well, I do admit you told me it was going to be pretty." Brakes screeched as Carolyn went from sixty to nothing in a matter of seconds. She leaped from the car as soon as it stopped, turning, holding out a hand to him. He had certainly not expected this.

As Carolyn led him into the house, he realized that here at last was a woman who had the energy he had, who had the compassion he would like to develop, whose grip on his hand was strong. He felt stirrings in his body unlike any he had ever experienced. He knew they were not all sexual, either. However, looking at her as she walked before him, seeing her hair tossing, her shoulders straight, her long legs moving in her graceful yet determined manner, feeling the warmth of her hand in his, he knew that his feelings, whatever else they were, were not devoid of sexual attraction.

The house was cool while filled with the summer sunshine, still bright at six o'clock. He smiled to himself—sunny and warm in January. Carolyn pulled him into the living room.

Before he could absorb its beauty, its graciousness, he was attracted to the couple there.

Carolyn's mother was even more striking than Carolyn. She must be about the same age as mine, he thought. She was a woman one would stop to look at on a street. He sensed immediately where Carolyn's fire came from, knew where the generous mouth and turquoise eyes originated, though their colorings were dissimilar.

"I found this man on a bus." Carolyn smiled and put a hand through his arm. "He wants to see Cape Town, so I brought him home."

Sitting in the largest chair was a silver-haired, familiar-looking man. "This is my mother and father," Carolyn said.

It dawned on Andrew, then, why Mr. Compson looked so familiar. "I've read all of your books, sir."

"All twelve of them?" Mr. Compson laughed.

"All twelve of them, sir. You were the first person whose writings of Africa I read. I've devoured every novel you've written. I agree with what one critic said of your last book: 'Because of Marshall Compson's novels, the world is a more beautiful place to live in.'"

WHEN HE LAY IN BED MUCH LATER, MOONLIGHT DANCING THROUGH the hotel window, his head pillowed on his arms, staring at the shadows on the ceiling, he knew what had happened to him. The marvel was that it had happened so unexpectedly, so quickly. Before he even had a chance to be warned or forewarned. Before he could even anticipate. And on his first day in South Africa.

Smiling to himself, he wondered if it could possibly have happened before they'd even left the bus. Or if it had happened as he watched her all afternoon giving that quick toss of her head that sent her hair swirling when she was irritated, when he listened to a lone woman trying to beat the system, trying to give hope and help to the hopeless and helpless.

Maybe he'd fallen in love with the whole family at once. Her mother. As he lay in bed reliving the day and exploring his feelings, he realized that Liliane had made him feel as though he were the most important person in her life, that his conversation was scintillating, that they were all fortunate to have had Carolyn discover him. A streak of gray laced out from her left temple, accentuating the auburn of her hair. Her athletic body reflected rigid training or hard work. She was beautiful.

It was not until some time during dinner that he had discovered Carolyn's mother was the famous "Mother Lili" of Simbayo.

"Oh, I don't live here year-round," Mrs. Compson had said. "I'm on one of my semiannual visits."

Certainly he had not expected women like this to be in Africa, the "dark continent."

How he had walked into such a home on his first day in Africa still boggled his mind. All because he had followed a girl in a red-and-white-flowered dress.

He was certain it had happened before Carolyn said, "I'd better take you back to your hotel. It's after midnight." Standing by the car in the curving driveway in the moonlight, he wanted to kiss her.

They stood, staring at each other. And he knew it then.

When she left him off at the hotel, she asked, as he opened the door, "I *am* going to see you again, aren't I?"

"I suspect," he answered, pulling his lanky frame up out of the low car, "that you may see me for the rest of your life."

The sound of her laughter, the delight of that melodious sound, followed him up in the elevator and into his room.

Am I going to marry her? he wondered. A woman I've known for one day? Am I going to spend the rest of my life with a woman I didn't know yesterday?

As he fell asleep, he saw her among the shadows on the wall, and she stayed there all night.

"IT HAPPENED JUST AS QUICKLY FOR ME, TOO, YOU KNOW." Carolyn smiled.

Andrew reached out, putting a hand over hers, and leaned closer to hear her over the sound of the plane's engines. He knew he should be looking out the window, seeing what the rest of South Africa looked like. But he was too entranced with his bride.

"I knew for sure"—Carolyn recollected the exact moment two weeks ago—"when you said 'I suspect that you may see me for the rest of your life.'"

Up until that moment she'd only known that she'd met the first man who totally fascinated her. Except her father, of course. Now and then, comparing the boys and the men who floated through her life, she'd thought, Has my father spoiled me for other men? But she didn't actually believe that.

The last few years she'd been so involved with life that she had stopped wondering about her lack of romance. She was satisfied with the way she lived, even though she knew there was more to life than what she was experiencing. She was doing something for humanity, tiny speck that her work was, though most of her efforts with the Black Sash proved unsuccessful.

And her job, which consumed five days of her week, satisfied her.

At a party she had met one of Cape Town's few psychiatrists, who admitted that after seven years he was pulling up stakes and returning to London. "There's no business here," he told her. "The Afrikaners never have doubts. They know who they are; they know what is right and wrong, and are never driven by larger questions."

"Or inner ones, either, you mean?"

"Exactly. How wonderful to have all the answers and positively know they're the right ones." He sighed; sorry for himself because he was leaving this beautiful land and sorry for people who knew they were right about everything.

But when Andrew followed her and sat looking at what she did all afternoon, Carolyn began to suspect that here was a man unlike any she'd met. Also, he was so handsome!

Those warm brown eyes, alternately like a puppy dog's and a man who knew what he wanted, centered on the petitioners who came to her desk. When she felt the familiar tug of hopelessness, Carolyn would see Andrew's eyes on her, reading her feelings, wanting to help. For the first time in three years at this work, her concentration faltered. She found herself wanting to look at Andrew instead of listening to the people who needed help. Her first reaction was one of irritation at herself and then she thought, Isn't it about time?

And when he talked, the timbre of his voice—a sandpapery sound that was nevertheless appealing—went straight down her backbone. She kept asking him questions so that she could listen to his voice.

She had wanted him to kiss her before he left. Maybe the feeling isn't mutual, she thought, when he made no attempt. Yet she knew he was as aware of the electricity as she was.

It wasn't until he said "I suspect that you may see me for the rest of your life" that she was sure. Of course, she thought as she drove home, concentrating more on the crescent of the moon than the road, that's how it was destined to happen for me.

She slept marvelously well and woke early. She went for a

swim in the pool and burned off some of the energy that was bursting from her.

As she pulled herself up after the last lap, she saw Liliane standing at the pool's edge, laughing. "I told your father we're going to lose you." She didn't seem terribly upset at the idea, Carolyn thought, but maybe that's because she loves me. Besides, it's Papa who will feel lost.

Like a wet dog, Carolyn shook her hair, purposely getting her mother wet. That didn't bother Liliane, either.

"Let's not rush this." Carolyn laughed. "How do we know how he feels?"

Liliane handed her daughter a towel. "I've never known you to be unwilling to work for what you want."

"But I don't always get what I want," Carolyn countered. It seemed that in the Black Sash she hardly ever got what she wanted, what she thought was right. She was beginning to believe there was no such thing as justice.

Ignoring Carolyn's remark, her mother said, "Are you going to see him today?" Even after nearly thirty years in Africa, she still had an American accent.

Carolyn asked aloud what she'd been wondering as she'd raced back and forth across the pool. "Shall I wait by the phone all day, agonizing to find out, or shall I do something about it?"

"How long do you have?" Amusement shone in Liliane's eyes, but her question was serious and Carolyn knew it.

"Two weeks, less a day."

"It seems to me that's your answer."

Wrapping the towel around herself, Carolyn asked, "What do you think? I mean about the whole thing?"

Liliane sat down in a wrought-iron chair by the poolside and stared out at the vineyards. She smiled at Carolyn, a tinge of sadness in her eyes. "I realized last night I've never thought of your leaving Cape Town. I don't know why. When I was twenty-one, I left my parents and traveled eight thousand miles and never saw them again. I should have realized the same could happen to me. It seems only fair."

Walking over to her mother, Carolyn leaned down and, in a rare gesture, put her arms around her. Liliane patted her hand, almost absently.

"And after all," Liliane's voice became bright again, "Rhodesia is not eight thousand miles away."

"You liked him enough?"

"Of course. I knew within half an hour that he was the man for you."

She stood, and they began to walk toward the house. "Darling," Liliane said, "I am excited for you and feel only a little sadness and sense of loss. Marsh will be a different matter. After all, he's been spoiled."

"Here we are, having me married and far away in Rhodesia, and he may not even be thinking of me."

"Wanna bet?" asked Liliane.

CAROLYN COULD TELL BY ANDREW'S VOICE THAT SHE WAS WAKING him.

"I know a wonderful café where you can get croissants and café au lait and watch ships at the dock."

Joyous laughter flooded from him. "Do I get time to shave?"

"It's irrelevant to me. If you feel you must."

"I'll be ready when you get here. How long will it take you to drive in?"

"I'm in the hotel lobby. So hurry up."

"Hey." Warmth emanated from his voice; it became low, intimate. "Good morning."

"Wear comfortable shoes," she said, and hung up. Her whole being tingled. Good morning. He'd said it as though he were saying "I love you."

As he emerged from the elevator, a shyness overcame them both. They smiled like junior–high school students at a dance. And at that moment each knew how the other felt, though it wasn't until late afternoon that they acknowledged it.

Andrew's hand moved across the table at the French café, inching over to Carolyn's, and he formed a gentle fist around hers. The question in his eyes disappeared when he saw the look in hers.

Then they climbed Table Mountain. "Whatever else you do in Cape Town," Carolyn told him, "you must take away the memory of having climbed it."

She had brought a picnic lunch from home, which she carried in a day pack up the mountain. She never thought to ask Andrew how he felt about climbing, whether or not he was the outdoor type, whether he thought the climb would be a welcome experience or too arduous. Some inner part of her knew the answers to these questions. She could not have fallen in love with him so quickly otherwise.

When they reached the top after a four-hour climb, Andrew was far more winded than Carolyn, but exhilaration surged through him.

Carolyn knew how he felt about the view. She hadn't known him for twenty-four hours, yet she knew how he reacted to the sight.

There aren't many views more impressive than the three-hundred-and-sixty-degree panorama from the plateau top of Table Mountain. Robben Island, that infamous prison, lay sparkling in the sunshine far out in the harbor of Table Bay, known locally as the Cold Sea. The water across the peninsula, officially named False Bay, was nicknamed the Warm Sea. The shanty-towns north of Cape Town—Cross Roads, Guguletu, Nyanga, Mitchell's Plain, and Kaputo—lay sleepily in the hot sun; none of the squalor, the pain, the frustration, and the poverty showed from this rarified atmosphere. Verdant vineyards, some established well over two hundred years ago, graced the valley surrounded by water on three sides—water as far as the eye could see. On this summer day in January, it was impossible to think of the winds that could tear across these reaches in the winter and lead to so many shipwrecks.

"Do you believe in reincarnation?" Carolyn asked.

Andrew turned to her and reached for her hands. Looking down at her, he smiled, a craggy smile that lit up his face. "I've never even thought about it. But you are asking, aren't you, because we already know each other so well?"

"Yes." Her answer was a whisper. Weakness flooded through her and she felt dizzy. He knew what she was thinking. She felt that she had known him forever, had stood here before with him, had loved him before. From now on, their lives were inextricably woven together. Did he know that, too?

Andrew raised a hand to her chin, tilting it up toward him, and covered her mouth with his, the warm wetness of their mouths intermingling. She felt his heartbeat drumming against hers, felt him weaving her into his being. The dizziness left her and strength surged through her. She felt stronger and more alive than she had ever been, capable of feats never imagined, a queen, a sorceress, a priestess.

A group of fellow climbers came into view; the spell was broken.

But only briefly.

He came to dinner again that night. Later, they went for a

swim in the darkness, the stars shining brightly, the moon a glowing silver, and felt their bodies next to each other. He leaned down and kissed her breast, and she ran her hand along his leg. He murmured, "Can your parents stand having me for dinner for the next week?"

Her mind far away from her parents or any meal, she lay back in the water, her hair fanned out, feeling again like a priestess, a primal being whose whole body and mind were alive with the wonder of the world. "Why?" she asked, her voice languid, as in a dream.

"I know how it will be for me to take you from them. If you have only a bit more than a week, I'm willing to share you with them every night."

He leaned over and kissed her thigh. Music splashed down her legs as they spread out, and her arms reached up to him.

He pulled her up out of the water and into his arms, sliding her out of her bathing suit, kissing her breasts, holding her close. Her legs encircled his strong body as he stood in the water. He pulled at his own suit, kicking it away, and then entered her, there in the warm water, under the stars. Her blood mingled pinkly with the water. His body surged within hers; his mouth enveloped her breasts; his arms surrounded her. She wanted to hold him within her forever. She raised his head from her breasts, taking his tongue into her mouth, and they rocked back and forth in the warm water of the pool, sensing the wonder that had invaded their lives.

Later, as they lay close together on the grass, as he traced invisible patterns on her neck and her shoulders and her arms, he said, "I knew when I saw the word *Rhodesia* in that letter that my life would never be the same, but I never dreamed it would include a woman like you. I never knew there *was* a woman like you."

He raised his head, and she could see his shadowed face. "On the other hand, maybe I knew all along that you were waiting for me."

"I think it was predestined," she murmured, lying in the warm grass, satiated from lovemaking. Her fingers drifted lightly down his arm.

"You think God planned it?" he asked, levity in his voice.

"No," she answered, "the fates."

COURTNEY WAS CONCEIVED THREE MONTHS LATER IN A TENT ON THE Rhodesian veld, with a lion's roar in the background.

CHAPTER 35

▼

IN 1954, SALISBURY WAS NOT YET THE GARDEN SPOT THAT IT WOULD BECOME, but it was already on its way to being one of the world's prettiest small cities. The shoddy, corrugated tin–roof shacks were being torn down and replaced with trim bungalows, which were surrounded by wide verandahs, and set on large plots of land that enabled the new owners to display well-watered lawns lush with poinsettias, jacaranda, and bougainvillea. Some houses even had swimming pools. Andrew had not expected this. But then he had not expected anything that had happened to him since he left England.

Africa had not been what he had anticipated. It was so different from what he had imagined, either before he arrived or after just a few days here. There was a primal pull to Africa. He thought he had been prepared for culture shock, but war had been easier to assimilate than Africa. Africa was a total surprise to him.

No two days were alike. In Cape Town, he followed Carolyn around as she tied up loose ends before they could leave for Rhodesia.

His sense of surprise and awe was accented by the nights he spent with Carolyn, in such passion and abandon and discovery as neither of them had ever known. They were learning not only about each other but also about themselves. At night, primeval forces were at work in the dark, comparable to the continent's magnetic tug he experienced during the day. It was as though he had been born with Africa as his destiny, yet he had been mostly unaware of it until five and a half months ago.

He and Carolyn had flown to Salisbury an hour after they were married. Fortunately, neither she nor her parents insisted on a large wedding. Carolyn told him the newspapers would be furious and would make a big splash about it the next day, but they would be well away from Cape Town by then. After all, it was not she whom the papers wanted to write about, but her famous parents.

He saw tears in her eyes as the plane began its takeoff at the Jan Smuts Airport. Staring down at the land she loved with the policies she hated, where she had spent most of her life, Carolyn made no effort to control the loss she felt. Andrew's large hand covered hers, and she squeezed it as she said good-bye to all that she knew.

They stayed at the Ambassador Hotel. Darkness was descending as they arrived, so they had no real chance to see the city. They were tired from the rush and excitement of the last week; they were hungry; and they wanted to make love. The hotel restaurant served a bland English menu, but they bought champagne and took it to their room. They laughed and drank and toasted the future, Andrew's job, their life together. They ordered more champagne, and toasted love, happiness, and marriage. They both loved champagne, and they toasted everything probable and impossible, laughing and kissing, over and over again. They fell asleep cradled in each other's arms, contented, even though they did not make love on this, their wedding night.

In the morning Andrew had to report to Llewellyn Ltd. He asked Carolyn not to start looking for a flat until he could accompany her.

Walking out into the clear air, he felt as though he owned the world. He sensed the presence of the bush even if he could not see it; he exulted in the open spaces he knew were there, beyond the city. Adventure with a capital *A*. Romance. Laughing aloud as he strode along, he thought, I could be the star of an adventure movie—Clark Gable or Errol Flynn—for all that's happening to me.

From the sounds echoing around him, he could tell that Salisbury was in the midst of a building boom. Though a small town compared to London, it was more cosmopolitan than he'd imagined. He knew that the copper companies had arrived and were headquartered here; he saw tall buildings with scaffolding and a large department store. Despite what he'd read and what his intellect told him, the Africa of his imagination and old movies had conditioned him to expect native huts, not modern department stores.

On the streets he noticed an intermingling of blacks and whites, unlike Cape Town; the color bar was far less restrictive here, yet it was alive and, he thought, perhaps too well.

Instead of quaint trails winding into the bush, wide boulevards—wider by far than in any city he'd ever seen—were filled with careening cars. Later he learned that Cecil Rhodes had insisted on streets wide enough for a team of eight horses to turn around in. It sounded as though every driver leaned on his or her horn. He'd read that one out of four Europeans in Rhodesia owned cars, and he decided they were all in Salisbury.

On the other hand, he knew from his research that two million black Rhodesians dwelled in arid, dusty, remote reserves eking out a subsistence living by farming. Even in London he had never been in a slum area, though he knew they were there. Never had he been inside a poverty-stricken home; he sensed that would change in this new life. He had always wanted to experience all that was possible. Now it was not only possible, but probable.

Suddenly, around a corner and in front of him was Llewellyn Ltd., an imposing, four-story building with a shiny brass knocker on the door.

What struck Andrew most was that all of the men he met that morning wore shirts and ties—and shorts. At lunch with the engineers who would be his colleagues, he dropped his napkin; when he leaned over to pick it up, he burst out laughing: under the long table were a dozen tanned legs with knee socks. Andrew was delighted; men did not wear shorts in England.

Never did man and company meld more harmoniously than Andrew and Llewellyn Ltd. were destined to. Two months ago exactly, he had left England for the first time. And with a new wife yesterday and a new job today, he suspected that at no time could his life be as fortunate or as full.

"I'll fly you up to Kariba tomorrow," Mr. Reyes said. "A dam's being built up there. They hope to have it finished in five years. It's a godawful place, as you'll see. Weather's rotten. The dam'll supply hydroelectric power for both Northern and Southern Rhodesia for years to come. Maybe forever. But there are unbelievable obstacles."

Andrew leaned back in his chair, enjoying Donald Reyes. He was of medium stature and had a round, mustached face with a hard, muscular body.

He had a gentle voice and serious pale blue eyes. His lips were wide and accentuated his enormous smile, which he did not often display. He wore a light khaki-colored bush jacket, and khaki shorts with long black knee stockings and sandals. When he felt formality was called for, he donned a tie, but otherwise his shirt was always open-necked.

"They've let the contracts. The bloody Italians came in with a low bid on the actual building of the dam. Can you imagine? We just finished fighting them. And everyone knows Italians are never on time. Whoever let them the contract . . . Oh, well. Metropolitan Vickers has the contract for generators; Thomas-Houston will supply the switch gear. Altogether, sixty different contracts have been let.

"We," he continued, his eyes shining with pride, "are going to build the town. Three towns, really. Two temporary ones: one for the Europeans and one for the Africans. And a permanent one. From beginning to end. We must rush to put up temporary housing for ten thousand men and then concentrate on the permanent one. We have five years to complete it."

He looked at Andrew as though he expected a response. His was the keenest mathematical mind in the country, perhaps in Africa, but he lacked the ability to create plans. He had vision in abundance—he knew what was needed for Rhodesia to rush into the twentieth century; he could calculate how to get it there in the realm of engineering; his mental vistas were wide—but he needed someone who could turn his abstractions into real projects. He needed a partner with foresight.

Although there were twenty engineers at Llewellyn, he had hired Andrew with the hope that here, at last, was that man. Every bit of information he had accumulated indicated that Andrew was a practical visionary, the man who could put form and reality to Reyes's grandiose ideas.

He hinted of this as they sat, after lunch, in Reyes's multiwindowed office, on wicker chairs amid yellow walls, with a ceiling fan whirring softly—so unlike the London offices with which Andrew was familiar.

"Where do I fit in, sir?" Andrew asked.

"Sir?" Donald Reyes laughed. "Oh, come, come. It's Donald. We're going to be working together for many years. I'd have thought you understood where you come in. You're going to be in charge of our project there. You're going to build the towns. Decide what's needed, lay them out—the whole kit and caboodle."

Andrew was sure his mouth dropped open.

"You've your work cut out for you, I admit." Donald laughed, tamping down tobacco into his unlit pipe. "We'll fly up tomorrow and look it over. Of course, I've ideas. We'll camp up there for a week. Let you get the lay of the land."

How's Carolyn going to react? wondered Andrew. This isn't what I'd imagined. I promised her Salisbury, not the wild beyond.

"There is a road now; they've just finished it. Called 'the Elephant Path.' " Donald laughed as though at a private joke. "An extraordinary endeavor in itself. The Kariba gorge—it's on the Zambezi River, on the border—was fifty miles from the nearest road and two hundred from the nearest industrial town. As an engineer I'd say that gorge has been crying for a dam. There's a narrow chasm through which the river passes between walls seven hundred feet high. There's a marvelous valley around it. Hot as hell, though.

"When Huggins—he's our prime minister—decided on going ahead with the whole project, he sent engineers to search through a complex mess of hills. It was estimated that a road would cost three million dollars and take a year and a half to build. To show you what Rhodesia's like, Jim Savory, who's head of the Department of Irrigation, spit when he heard that and said, 'I could do it in half the time and half the money.' So Huggins said, 'Do it.' "

Reyes cut himself short. "I'll explain all that as we fly over it tomorrow," he muttered. "It's quite fascinating. You're about to embark on a mission that will change the face of this part of Africa forever." He stood. "Hazel and I hope you'll come to dinner tonight. We've invited a few people. I know you're tired, but bachelors seem to have more stamina than us old married men."

Andrew smiled. "I'm not a bachelor anymore. I brought a wife with me."

"Oh, sorry"—Reyes lit his pipe—"don't know where I got the idea . . ."

"Oh, you were quite right. I just got married yesterday."

A veil fell over Reyes's eyes. "Dash it! This may be a bit muddy."

Andrew waited for an explanation.

Reyes's teeth clamped on his pipe. "How would you have known? You'll be in no-man's-land for five years. One of the things—one of the minor things—that made you good for the job was your being unencumbered by a family."

"Carolyn's a good sport," Andrew said, and wondered whether this was true.

"Well, you can come in from the bush once a month," Reyes was thinking aloud. "Perhaps she won't be too lonely." Then he gave one of his rare smiles. "This calls for a celebration. Hazel will be delighted to think she's having a wedding party. I must call her."

Andrew returned to the hotel by midafternoon, with an intense desire to hold Carolyn, to tell her about his morning, to look into her sea green eyes and see her love reflected there. They'd been married over twenty-four hours and still hadn't made love. He felt his groin come alive, the warmth flowing through him.

But Carolyn was not there.

When she did return, her eyes were sparkling with excitement. "I've had the most delightful day. Salisbury is an absolutely charming town. I had no idea. I've walked every place. I'm going to be quite happy here, I think."

"I'd be happy anywhere with you." Andrew put his arms around her waist.

She leaned up and kissed the end of his nose. "And, Andrew, I don't think I want a flat."

I'm glad, he thought, wondering how she'd react to his news.

"I think I want a house. One with verandahs and surrounded with green lawns. A place to put down roots. Have a family."

"Sit down," he said to her. "And let me tell you."

He had bought a map on his way back to the hotel and had located the Kariba gorge. How would Carolyn react to their being together only once a month?

As he told her of his future duties, her eyes shone. When he finished, she took his hand and said, "This is the most exciting news. I'm glad I didn't know before or you'd have thought I married you for adventure rather than love."

"You don't understand," Andrew said. "It means we'll be apart for most of five years."

"Nonsense!" She shook her head, her blond hair shimmering in the late-afternoon sunlight. "I didn't marry you to be alone. I'm coming along. It's far more exciting than living in a stuffy city. Oh, Andrew, real adventure. How wonderful."

"You can't. You're a woman. Out there?"

"Out where? You don't know a thing about it. Besides, if a man, if ten thousand men can do it, why can't a woman?"

"There won't be anything for you to do. The climate's terrible."

"Then that's my problem, isn't it? I can't imagine being bored." Her eyes blazed into him. "Darling, will it embarrass you? Is that it?"

Andrew lay back on the bed, laughing. And he'd wondered if she'd be a good sport. "Nothing you could do would embarrass me. What it will no doubt do is prove I'm the luckiest man alive."

Carolyn glanced at her watch. "We've two hours before we have to be at the Reyeses'. Want me to prove, Mr. McCloud, that in other ways you're the luckiest man alive?" She moved toward him with feline grace, already unbuttoning her blouse.

"Stay there," she purred. "Let me undress you."

But a part of him was already moving.

CAROLYN WORE A SOFT GREEN DRESS THAT CHANGED HER EYES TO emerald. Andrew wondered if everything she wore made her eyes the focal point. She looked feminine and desirable and infinitely alluring. As she twisted long silver earrings into her ears before the mirror, he stopped tying his tie and went to her. He stood behind her, cupping his hands around her breasts, feeling the warmth of her body, her shape cradled against his, smelling the faint scent of plumeria that emanated from her. He kissed her neck and ran his tongue along her bare shoulder.

HAZEL REYES WAS SHORT, PERHAPS FIVE FOOT TWO, SOMEWHAT pudgy, in her late thirties—typical Helen Hokinson club woman. But only minutes after meeting her, it was obvious that Hazel was one of the most attractive women in the world. Violet eyes shone out of a heart-shaped face framed by glistening black hair already streaked with gray; her full, sensual lips smiled warmly. Though she never touched them, Andrew and Carolyn could have sworn she hugged them into the room.

The room itself was stunning. Part Indian, part Spanish, it was an enormous room with beamed ceilings and walls hung with brilliant tapestries. A stone fireplace dominated one entire wall.

Though Hazel didn't gush, she did announce to her guests that this was a wedding reception, a party to welcome the new couple. There were six other couples there, all connected with Llewellyn Ltd., all originally from England. Carolyn was the only native African. This immediately made her the center of attention, though Andrew thought that no matter where they were, Carolyn was destined to be the center of attention. Her pale, fragile-looking beauty, her passion for life, the warmth she could kindle when she felt at ease, and—like Hazel—her innate intelligence and wit made her charming company. Not for the first or last time Andrew wondered how he had been so lucky. How had someone like Carolyn decided to link her life with his? Maybe there was a God after all.

He grinned at the thought. He didn't even know whether his wife believed in God. He already knew she deplored the fundamentalist religion of the Dutch Reformed Church, which she thought was still back in the seventeenth century. "Take away that God-fearing, Bible-spouting religion and most of your South African problems wouldn't exist," he'd heard her say.

At dinner, he sat next to Hazel. Carolyn was at the other end of the table, next to Donald. He heard her silvery laugh as she responded to something, and it tingled his backbone.

"THERE, YOU CAN SEE WHERE THEY'VE HACKED THE ROAD THROUGH the forest." Donald Reyes pointed to it from the plane. "Savory's surveyors said there was a range of hills where they couldn't find a pass. A road wide enough for heavy equipment was needed, and the forest floor was too thick with trees for a road. Jim knew that elephants make their paths on ridges of hills, so he found an elephant path and followed it. It led him through the hills and not the valleys. Thus the name, Elephant Road."

Carolyn stared down at the jagged topography.

Reyes had been astonished when Carolyn announced at dinner that she planned to accompany Andrew. Conversation had stopped for a moment; everyone stared at her, then Hazel covered nicely, and no one commented. So Donald was prepared for Carolyn's appearance at the airport.

He kept up his running commentary. "No one knows what Kariba means. The gorge was already named when Livingstone walked into the valley in 1860. Until three or four years ago, it remained almost as wild and remote as when he saw it. Couple of missions now, and a district commissioner's been here for years. But for the Tongans—that's the major tribe in the valley—time stood still.

"Now, with force, the twentieth century is going to uproot their way of life."

"Are they going to have to move?" asked Carolyn, peering down.

"Fifty-sixty thousand of 'em," said her husband's boss. "This is an undertaking of gigantic proportions. It'll cost twelve hundred sixty dollars for every white person in Rhodesia, including children."

"I imagine there's some kind of outcry," Carolyn mused, "when you need schools and hospitals to raise the standard of living."

Reyes narrowed his eyes as he studied her. "This will help raise the standard of living. The Tongans have lived a marginal existence. They'll now be offered industrial jobs and a chance for decent housing and enough to eat."

"How much will they be paid?"

Andrew had said Carolyn couldn't embarrass him; he wondered why he found himself fidgeting.

"Very good wages, for Africans. Five cents a day. There, look down there, where they're clearing those trees. That's your town, Andrew. By this time next year, you'll have transformed a forest inhabited by lions and elephants into an English town. Within five years, I want good schools, a hospital, a cinema. And the houses of the officials will be high on that hill so that when the valley there fills with water, their view to the west will be glorious."

"How big a lake is envisioned?" Andrew asked.

"It's going to be one hundred twenty miles long and ten to twenty wide." Reyes's voice held pride. "This is 1955. By 1960, this place won't be recognizable. It's one of the largest engineering undertakings the world's ever seen. It will allow Rhodesia to become an industrial nation."

Carolyn could see that Andrew was excited. She wondered why her prevailing feeling was one of sadness.

CHAPTER 36

▼

SUNRISE WAS THE COLOR OF SPILLED BLOOD, DILUTING ITSELF AS IT spread up from the jagged horizon.

A solitary baobab, with its swollen trunk and absurdly meager crown, shaded Carolyn. Down in the valley, a herd of elephants moved single file toward the river.

The wail of a bird stung the air. Pink and gold shards of light, like fragments of broken glass, threw themselves across the valley.

The day was already hot, and the sun was not even above the horizon. It was cooler up here, on the ridge. She'd climbed the hill as dawn streaked the sky. Andrew was not yet awake, and she wanted to watch the animals as they moved to their watering holes.

From here, she could hear pots and pans rattling down at the campsite. Good. Lobengula and Bildad were getting breakfast. She could get a cup of coffee.

She knew Donald had brought her along with misgivings. Men always thought women couldn't take rugged conditions, couldn't possibly enjoy a primitive life-style. Of course, he didn't know where and how she'd spent her first seven years. Andrew, too, had no knowledge that safari life was second nature to Carolyn. Marsh had taken her on safari numerous times, even teaching her how to shoot.

As she descended the hill, Carolyn saw Lobengula's smile covering his gleaming face as he leaned over the fire, his teeth a glittering white in the midst of the purple-black skin. Before she could reach for it, he handed her a cup of coffee. Bildad, who did not have half the energy of his brother, hummed softly to himself as he heated a frying pan.

Coffee cup in hand, Carolyn looked heavenward, absorbing the sky that had so suddenly lost its colors and become a vibrant dark sapphire. The sun had climbed into the sky and vanquished the blood. Despite yesterday's rain, not a cloud was in sight.

She sipped the best coffee in the world.

The banging of a spoon against a frying pan called everyone to breakfast. Bildad sat on his haunches in that squatting position that white people never seemed able to master, but which so many Asians and Africans preferred.

A month ago, she mused, she'd never heard of Andrew McCloud or the Kariba gorge or the Zambezi River. Now, here she was, married exactly a week and spending her fifth day in the Rhodesian backcountry. The green floor of the valley still looked primeval, even though a mile upriver it had been ripped to pieces by gigantic earth movers. The hills across the river looked blue. One could wade across in the dry season.

She had discovered thorn trees; soon they were replaced by mile after mile of acacias and mopane trees. Now, in early February, the heat in the valley was in the nineties, cooled considerably from the one hundred ten degrees of the October spring. Sometimes, when thunderstorms burst torrents of water over the valley, the steam rising from rank vegetation recalled her childhood.

The valley forest was full of wildlife. One evening, she had taken Andrew by the hand, urging him to be quiet, and from a vantage point on a hillside by a bend in the river, they saw small delicate antelope called klipspringer and the larger impala and kudu antelope. She heard Andrew draw in his breath as he watched elephants cavorting, spraying water on their young, trumpeting loudly with pleasure. There were cape buffalo farther up the valley and strange birds she had never seen before. Rounding a curve in the path, they had come face-to-face with an enormous black-maned lion, who was startled to see them. After a moment, he licked his lips and yawned, emitting a loud, bored moan.

Leopards and rhinoceroses proliferated in the valley, and the river contained the hippos and crocs of her youth, while familiar monkeys and baboons thrust themselves hand over hand along the treetops, chattering endlessly. Up on the hills, which sometimes rose abruptly two thousand feet into the sky, she had found no signs of human habitation, but down in the sweltering heat of the valley bottom, she found a forest path that had been padded bare through the years.

Last night, from a distance, she'd heard the sound of drums and dissonant music.

West of the gorge, in the valley that was destined to be flooded, lived sixty thousand natives in assorted small villages.

She'd investigate them later, after they'd moved up here to stay. Andrew still had not made that clear to Donald, who took it for granted that she would live a lonely, ladylike existence in Salisbury.

"A penny for your thoughts." Donald's voice intruded into her reverie. She looked up to see him reach for coffee.

"I'm just thinking how much there is to explore here. It's so much more exciting than a city. So much more to do."

"I doubt that many would agree with you—" He was interrupted by the thunder of the earth movers going into action, even though they were a mile upriver.

"Perhaps I'll learn the native language," Carolyn mused. "I might be of help." There, that's preparing him.

"You're not thinking of visiting regularly, are you?" Carolyn searched for disapproval in Donald's voice but heard none.

She laughed, sitting down at the table covered with spotless white linen. "Not exactly."

Donald sat down next to her and adopted a paternal attitude. "I do hope you're not planning some romantic claptrap like—"

"Like living up here?" She turned her turquoise gaze on him. "Oh, but I am. I didn't marry Andrew to be a widow for five years."

"But a woman up here—"

"Can live like a man can. I grew up in the Congo jungle, Mr.

Reyes. I'm more at home out here than I ever am in a city."

Andrew exited from their tent, freshly shaved. He's beautiful, thought Carolyn, reaching out a hand to catch his. "Besides, I have no intention of living life without this man of mine."

"Not exactly coy, this wife of mine." Andrew looked at her fondly.

Donald's mild voice asked Andrew, "How d'you feel? One woman up here with ten thousand men? Doesn't that make you nervous?"

As Andrew sat down, breakfast was served.

"Eggs the way you like them." Lobengula passed a platter to her. On it were a wrinkled orange that she knew would be juicier than any she'd ever known, two eggs whose golden yolks looked like the sun's reflections, and biscuits dripping with butter and honey.

Carolyn pressed her leg against Andrew's under the table, even though she couldn't feel him through her jodhpurs and boots.

"One of the men told me the D.C.'s wife lives in a bungalow up at the Boma."

"That's sixty miles away."

"Yes, but she's one woman and there aren't ten thousand men there. And, my dear"—Donald stuck a biscuit in his mouth—"she doesn't look like you."

Carolyn looked directly at the president of Llewellyn Ltd. "Will you fire Andrew if I choose to live here?"

"Of course not. But . . ."

"Then I shall. It's settled. And he shall be far happier than if he were here alone."

They returned to Salisbury the next day and spent a week shopping for supplies and proper clothing. Carolyn insisted on a double cot and that had to be ordered from Nairobi. At the end of another ten days, they left Salisbury, Andrew driving a Land Rover, with two trucks accompanying them.

"I'll be flying out every other week." Donald walked over to Carolyn's side of the jeep. "Take care," he said in his quiet voice. "I disapprove, as you know, but I envy him and admire your intestinal fortitude."

Carolyn smiled. Actually, it took no guts at all.

▼

CERTAINLY NO ONE COULD HAVE HAD A MORE GLORIOUS HONEYMOON than she was having. They had all the time in the world to fall in love with each other and this country.

Carolyn had thought she knew Africa. She was, after all, a native. She had been brought up in the humid equatorial rain forest *and* in the urban environment of the southernmost tip. She had seen the Nile and the Pyramids, the desert, and the mountains of Africa. But never had the land so affected her as Rhodesia did: the high savannah with its thousands of animals, its rolling endless plains, the high escarpments, and the deep valley.

Often, late at night, the faraway roar of a lion penetrated her sleep, and gooseflesh swept down Carolyn's legs—not from fear but exhilaration. She felt a part of the elements, as though she had dug her feet deep into the earth and planted them there. When the roar of a lion or the cough of a leopard awoke them, Andrew's hand reached for hers, not for reassurance but for the joy of sharing such experiences. Inevitably, it led to lovemaking, with such joy and abandon as Carolyn had never imagined. Once in a while, they heard nearly silent padded feet stalking through the camp—maybe felt more than heard—and it never ceased to awaken lust in each of them.

One night, a night neither ever forgot, the intensity of their lovemaking was reflected on the canvas of their tent, where the shadow of a lion danced between their tent and the fire. They heard him growl softly as their primal thrusting built to a climax. As the lovers lay together, spent, still breathing heavily, the lion turned—they could see the shadow of his luxurious mane in the reflection of the flickering light—and padded silently into the night. Later, they both knew that that was the night Courtney was conceived.

It had been a miraculous three months. They had their occasional philosophical differences; it had been a time of getting to know each other, of love growing, love of each other and of the land.

Carolyn would look at Andrew as he returned to the campsite after a day spent mapping out the future town and thought him the most beautiful man she had ever seen. She loved the way his hair curled over his ears now that he'd been away from a barber for three months; she loved the tanned, raw-boned look of him, the way his freckles merged together, and how the skin around his eyes crinkled in the bright glare of the Rhodesian sun. She loved the hair curling on his arms and peeking out of the neck of his open shirt. She loved his belly button and the lean hardness of his leg muscles. She loved the way his stomach muscles tightened when she kissed him there and the way he looked at her in the glow of the evening campfire.

In the evenings, after dinner—when the noise from clanging pots and pans had ended, when the night stillness descended and the stars seemed within reach—they spent hours exploring each other's past, learning about the person with whom they had fallen in love.

"My life can't compare with the adventure and variety of yours," Andrew said. "It was so normal. And I think that's what made me hyperactive. I didn't want normality. I wanted adventure and excitement. I was always restless, always searching, always filled with what my mother called 'divine discontent.' I never have quite figured out what that means, but I always thought it meant I wasn't satisfied with the normalcy of life. The status quo always seemed too little."

"Yet," said Carolyn, "you don't come across as bored."

"No," he said, laughing, "I don't think that's what I felt. I was too busy living every minute to the hilt to be bored. But I always knew there was more; I kept searching for it. And here it was, eight thousand miles from home, waiting for me—thank goodness."

A star shot across the heavens, leaving a trail of light fading behind it. It disappeared.

"But you, what happened after you and Marsh moved to Cape Town? Did your mother visit? Did you return to Simbayo?"

He always wanted to hear about her past. Wanted not only to learn all he could about her, but also to hear all about those places that he had not even known existed. He couldn't imagine he was married to someone born in the Belgian Congo, who had never had a white playmate until she was seven years old. He couldn't believe he was married to the daughter of two such famous parents, whose lives were so diverse from any he had known.

"No, I didn't go back to Simbayo often," she answered. "Papa wanted to show me the world, so he talked Mama into coming on trips with us. It was good for her. She could go back to Simbayo renewed. It helped her get a perspective on her own life, I think. Papa has always been great at that. With me, too.

"Once we had a house, I felt safe again. I've always loved my mother, but it took me years to get over what I perceived as her abandonment of me. I thought if she really loved me she'd never have sent me away. I thought she didn't love me as much as she loved Simbayo."

"Do you still feel that?" Andrew interrupted.

"Yes," Carolyn answered without hesitation, "but I've learned to live with it. However, I'm closer to Papa than I am to her. He has always had time for me. He's married to his writing, but he was never—I mean, never ever—too busy to listen to me. He's always shown me that I come before his writing."

"Do you come before your mother?"

"I think he loves us quite completely. It's not a matter of loving one of us more than the other. I do think I was able to have all his concentration because Mama was with us so little."

"Didn't you ever go back to Simbayo?"

"Oh, yes." Carolyn nodded. "But Papa couldn't take the tropics for long, and I grew away from the people there, even though none of us wanted it. I still feel love for them. Though many are gone, the nurses at the outposts have changed over the years, but Rose and Heidi and Naldani and Anoka are still there. And Philippe. There are new ones I scarcely know, except through Mama's letters."

She was silent, remembering the last time she had seen Rose and Heidi. Seven years ago. It was the summer after her first year at the university and the last time she'd even wanted to return to Simbayo. In the early years, when her whole life had been circumscribed by Simbayo, she'd had four mothers—not only Liliane, but Rose and Heidi and Naldani. Sleeping in Liliane's room made her special to Carolyn, but it was Heidi and Rose who had always taken time to answer her questions, to wash her hands, to read to her—though Heidi's voice always put Carolyn to sleep.

The three of them would play endless games of Go Fish and giggle together. Only once did she ever hear either of them speak harshly, and then their voices were raised against each other. She forgot now what they'd argued about, but Rose burst into tears and Heidi had stomped out of the room, banging the screen door. Funny, after all these years, to remember the one brief time of dissonance.

She wondered what they looked like now. They'd always looked old to her, like grandmothers must look, yet they were barely ten years older than her mother. That must make them in their late fifties now, she thought, maybe sixty. She thought they'd always been sixty.

That same year, when they were both eighteen, she had last

seen Petelo, too. They had looked at each other not as childhood friends but as a man and a woman, and she had been frightened. She had always loved Petelo; other men were never what he was to her. She had looked at him and seen a black prince, a man who might be destined to lead his people out of darkness, a man who shared her birthday, a man who understood her—thanks to letters and summers—as no other man ever had.

She had looked at him and sensed tension in the air—the tension of wanting, of self-consciousness. She knew it could never be. And because of that knowledge, desire flamed brightly and dangerously. She had played with that danger; the night before she left she had taught Petelo how to kiss. "You're going to London to become a doctor," she had said playfully. "You had better learn how to act with the women there." She had drawn his face close to hers and said, "You do this with your lips." And hers had brushed his lightly.

She had known she was playing not only dangerously but unfairly, yet she had been unable to control herself. More than anything in the world, she wanted, just once, to feel his lips against hers, his dark skin against hers.

Just one light brush, she had thought. Just once, our lips touching, but she found her breasts straining against his naked chest, felt his arms surround her, and knew the unfairness of what she was doing.

She pulled away from him and ran away. She did not say good-bye to him or answer any of his letters from England.

She did not tell Andrew about it.

Instead, she told him about the trips she and Mama and Papa had taken, and about the hours—and weeks and years—of philosophical conversation she and Marsh had shared, of how he had helped to shape her thinking and her life. She told Andrew how Marsh had encouraged her love of learning, how he had helped her to disdain the Boers' rigid seventeenth-century Calvinism that led to much of the oppression of the blacks.

She told Andrew that Liliane approved of Carolyn's participation in the Black Sash Society. "Mama never quite comes out and says she disapproves of anything, but you can tell. She thinks we should all be committed to improving others' lives. We should all dedicate ourselves selflessly and endlessly to making life more bearable for others."

Andrew reached over and took her hand. "You sound as though you don't believe it."

Carolyn smiled into the night. "It's a curse I carry with me, an albatross around my neck. Mama has instilled in me her vision of the world, but Papa has shown me that I can still enjoy life and its luxuries and think of myself now and then without being sinful."

"How have they stayed together so long, with such different sets of values?" Andrew stood and stretched.

"Oh, their values aren't so different. My mother puts into action the virtues my father writes about."

"So you do consider him your father then?"

Carolyn stood to face her husband and put her arms around his waist. She leaned her head against his chest. "When I was sixteen, I changed my name to his. He's more father and mother than I've known anywhere. I never knew Baxter Hathaway."

"Yes, but he's such a legendary figure, I'd have thought you might want to carry the Hathaway name around with you."

"Maybe somewhere there's some Hathaway in me. But Compson is what I am. Compson is how I feel. Compson is what I'm proud of. Blood couldn't make me feel any closer to Papa."

"Did your mother mind?"

"No." Carolyn looked up at Andrew, whose face glowed in the fire's reflection. "She said Simbayo was the Hathaway temple. Besides, I think she's always felt guilty that she couldn't give all of herself to Papa and me. Letting us have each other was the least she could do."

"Don't people wonder about her and Marsh living together . . . about your last name?"

"One thing they've both taught me is not to care what others think. It's what I think of myself that is important."

"Oh, lucky you," Andrew murmured into her hair.

"I am now." She raised her lips to his.

"HOLY SHIT!" BREATHED ANDREW.

It was an enormous herd of eland, larger and more spread out than any they'd seen in all their months in the bush.

Carolyn caught her breath. Never had she seen such a large herd. There must be hundreds, she realized, a thrill running through her. She knew they'd have no trouble getting one. She wished one of the natives would do the shooting, but that wasn't how things were done. The eland were grazing, their numbers stretching as far as the eye could see.

This is what Africa's all about, she thought. This is what feeds the soul. It hurt her to think she had to kill one of the beautiful creatures. She wished they could sit and watch for a while before disturbing these graceful animals.

They had driven out in the Land Rover, an hour from camp, because they'd been told the herd was in this direction.

The plain stretched forever, the golden grassland dotted here and there with trees that looked as though their tops had been cut off with a sharp knife. It was this land, and land like it all over the eastern half of Africa, that had attracted hunters for a hundred years—hunters with guns and with cameras. Nothing like it existed anywhere else in the world.

Andrew, who knew nothing about shooting and left it to others, stayed in the jeep as Carolyn and the natives fanned out. Bildad and Lobengula began circling the herd, inching northward; Carolyn headed toward the acacias. Her soul was filled with the beauty of the scene and her heart ached for what was about to happen. She had the urge to run. But, she told herself, they did need meat.

Then she, too, began to walk toward the herd. Long necks arched to the ground, the graceful animals were unaware of danger. The largest of the African antelopes, they were enormous beasts, weighing up to a ton, yet surprisingly agile for their size. The closer she walked, the more she realized she would be killing something she loved. Something symbolic of what all of Africa meant to her.

A slight breeze worked in their favor. Carolyn placed herself beside a tree.

Then, quickly, the animals started to thunder. In one giant motion, they all began to run. Carolyn stood stock-still while they raced in front of her. She could smell the panic emanating from them. Bildad and Lobengula had started the stampede.

She fired a shot; an eland fell.

The thunder of hooves shook the plain.

Black birds began to fly across the sky. The rushing eland galloped away from her, jumping as high as a man's head.

Now, tall clouds of dust in the distance indicated their escape route; still frenzied animals rushed in front of her. In the distance, the heart-shaped derrieres grew smaller as the frightened animals raced to safety, away from the danger they sensed.

Bildad and Lobengula gutted the eland. Carolyn headed back to the jeep.

"What a scene," Andrew said.

Carolyn sat, silent. Her husband looked at her but said nothing.

As though talking to herself, she said aloud, "It's not that I can't eat meat. It's that I can't bear to think of the extinction of what is so dear to me. I've read of what happened to the buffalo in America so long ago, and I know what's been happening in this part of Africa for the last hundred years . . . to the wildlife of this land. My land."

CHAPTER 37

▼

"I HAD A FEELING YOU'D BE HERE SOON." LILIANE LAUGHED.

Marsh looked around. It had been seven years since he'd seen Simbayo. Now that Liliane came to Cape Town once a year, there was no burning need for him to come here, and he'd always hated the thought of leaving Carolyn.

"I'm lonely," he admitted. "It's been fifteen years since I was last alone. I'd forgotten what it was like."

Simbayo had changed dramatically in the twenty-eight years Liliane had been there. There were modern buildings, the operating room was air-conditioned, and another dormitory had been built for the increased staff—two more full-time doctors, three nurses, and four teachers. Another plane and a full-time pilot had been added so that no emergency in the field was ignored.

Liliane had been right. The war that had raged all over the world in the forties had not touched Simbayo. It had made petrol more difficult to obtain, but medical supplies had arrived regularly from the States, and the discovery of penicillin had improved life considerably. Leprosy had been brought under control and was no longer a death sentence; in fact, many patients were now released to lead normal lives. The leprosarium was still a model and had many patients, but it was no longer filled with the hopeless. The outposts caught patients in early stages of the disease and shipped them to the leprosarium, which was able to release patients in remission before the disease became deforming. The Travises, with their three children, had long gone, but a Catholic priest and three nuns had arrived to replace them.

Philippe was still there, his curly dark hair turned silver. He had become philosophical and grandfatherly, resigned to never having children of his own after Deborah Engle had left, twelve years before. But she had established a school that was now able to send not only Petelo but other natives on to get further education. Petelo was still in London; he had completed his interning and was now specializing in tropical medicine. He had been home three times, to the great delight and pride of Naldani and Anoka—to the great delight and pride also of Liliane, Rose, and Heidi.

Heidi still ran the business end of Simbayo and still had a pronounced German accent; it was as though she had come from Berlin but weeks ago. Rose spent her days training native nurses and working in the vegetable garden, supplying the succulent vegetables that still accounted for much of Simbayo's delicious food. She had urged Naldani to try her hand at teaching, too, so Naldani taught the classes in midwifery. Women still would not come to the hospital for delivery, so the native nurses fanned out into the villages, or were called to them, and the rate of survival of both babies and mothers was superior to any other place in the Congo—or perhaps throughout Africa, for all anyone knew.

Although Naldani and Liliane were nearly the same age, Naldani had aged less gracefully. She was far more wrinkled than Liliane, whose complexion still looked like a young girl's except for the lines around her eyes. But Liliane was aware of aging. "I still make out lists of all I want to do during the day; I used to get it all done, but now I'm lucky to get halfway through it," she admitted. She knew she tired more easily, though as Marsh told her, "You accomplish more in a day than most people our age do in a week. It's just not as much as *you* used to accomplish."

"How come," Liliane asked him, "you age more gracefully than I do?"

"You fight it," he answered. "You still want to do as much as you used to. You still see all you want to accomplish and are afraid you won't get it all done. I sit and write. My life is mostly in thoughts. I don't mind getting older. You do."

"Even then," Liliane said with a sigh, "middle-aged men are so much more attractive than middle-aged women. I'm surprised you put up with me when there are all sorts of attractive young women who would love to be with you."

Marsh smiled at her. "You don't even believe I'd look at

anyone else. From the minute I met you, despite Dolores, there's never been anyone else for me, and you know it."

She smiled contentedly. Yes, she did know it. And knowing it had freed her from other emotional involvements to live her life as she had wanted to. Wanted to? Or had to? She often thought she wanted to be with Marsh and Caro in Cape Town, in that beautiful house of Marsh's, smelling the salt air from the sea, gazing out at the acres of vineyards, watching Carolyn grow up, being as much a part of molding Carolyn's character as Marsh was.

On her visits to Cape Town and on the trips Marsh had orchestrated for them, Liliane observed the problems that Carolyn was having socially. She was so serious and studious that Liliane often worried that her daughter lacked a sense of humor. As a child in Cape Town, Carolyn had trouble relating with most people. The attitude toward blacks offended the little girl, whose world had been overwhelmingly black for seven years. Carolyn realized the differences in thinking, in attitudes, and in culture, but she had been a part of the black culture before she was of the white. She never did quite assimilate herself to white "civilization." Partly, Liliane was proud of this; partly, her heart ached for the daughter who didn't quite fit in.

Marsh fed Caro's individuality and her inability to conform. Though he had chosen to live in a country whose apartheid policies offended him, he could not condone them. He had nurtured Carolyn's intellectual bent, spending hours and years talking and arguing and philosophizing.

Liliane watched Carolyn open up to Marsh as she did to no one else. When Carolyn walked into a room, even if she had been away from Marsh only a few hours, she automatically hugged him. She let down her reserve only with him. The wall that had been created when Liliane had sent Carolyn from Simbayo never completely came down, and for this Liliane blamed only herself. She knew her priorities had been misplaced, but she also thought she had had no choice. Though she never felt like an outsider when she visited them in Cape Town, she noticed that the emotional warmth that Marsh and Carolyn provided for and received from each other filled the very air. Liliane knew they both loved her, but their day-to-day living together gave them a natural closeness that was denied to her. She was their guest.

As a teenager, Carolyn had been far more opinionated than Liliane ever was about politics, about what was right and what was not, about religion and its destructive influences as well as its grace.

"Is Caro going to be happy with that young man?" Marsh wondered aloud.

"I think so," Liliane responded. "If any one person can help Caro be happy, I suspect Andrew can."

"I hope so. God, I miss her. Lili, come stay with me. Let Simbayo run itself."

She looked at him with the same expression she always wore when he made that suggestion.

"I THINK I'M INTELLIGENT ENOUGH," CAROLYN SAID AS THEY ATE breakfast outside their spacious tent, "to understand why a dam's necessary, but give it to me in simple layman's language."

Andrew had returned from work for breakfast. He had gotten into the habit of rising before dawn every day so that by the time they breakfasted at eight o'clock he'd already worked a couple of hours. Each morning he awoke supercharged. Never had he imagined life could be so exciting and fulfilling. Each day he was challenged, both by his work and by his wife.

Waving his jam toast, he stood and walked into the tent. He returned and tossed a piece of paper at Carolyn. "Here. Reading this will make it clearer than I can. It was written by David Howarth, who wrote it for just such a purpose—in lay language."

She read.

The principal use of a dam in a hydroelectric plant is to store water in a reservoir so that a constant amount of water can be run through the turbines, and a constant amount of power taken out, however much the flow of the river varies. Rivers in Central Africa vary very much from season to season, because nearly all the rain falls in four months of the year. Small rivers dry up in winter, and the Zambezi itself shrinks to a twentieth of its summer flow; and in some summers the rains themselves are sparse. For this reason a hydroelectric plant in Africa needs a very large store of water: to be on the safe side, enough to last two years. A dam 420 feet high at Kariba would flood nearly the whole of the valley and make a reservoir 175 miles long and up to 20 wide, by far the biggest in the world, and it would produce enough power to carry on the expansion of industry for many years to come, in both Southern and Northern Rhodesia.

She looked up at Andrew. "How are you going to put it in words to explain to people who've never invented the wheel?"

"That's the district commissioner's problem," Andrew answered, wiping crumbs from the mustache he was growing.

"But doesn't it bother you at all?" she asked. "Displacing sixty thousand people who have never known anything beyond this valley?"

"What do you propose?" Andrew asked.

Carolyn shrugged. "I've no answers. But they all have to leave here in four years or be drowned."

Andrew nodded. "It's sixty thousand being moved versus the federation's whole future."

"Ah, progress . . ." Carolyn sighed. "It never takes the individual human factor into consideration, does it?"

"How would you have it?" he asked.

"I don't know," she answered. Looking out at the dry, brown terrain, Carolyn could see how he and so many others thought a dam would be a boon to Rhodesia. So perhaps it would. She had seen the distended stomachs of the children out here in the bush, indicating malnutrition. With luck, these people could learn the ways of farmers to improve and prolong their lives. With the river harnessed and irrigation possible, famine need never be a problem. With water brought to this dusty soil, what might not blossom?

If it were possible to bring only good and not the side effects of civilization, Carolyn could wholeheartedly endorse Andrew's work.

"One of the things that so amazes me," Andrew said during that time that was theirs together, that time after dinner when the valley was dotted with the flickering lights of campfires, "is how little impact people have made on the land even after thousands of years of inhabiting it."

"I think it's because they've never tried to change it," said Carolyn. "They use the land, then they move on. And the land has grown to hide the fact that anyone was ever here."

"Yes, they've had none of our desire to harness nature for our own uses, have they? I mean, they simply fill their water gourds where water is; they've no inclination to push it into flumes and make it work for them."

"Exactly," agreed Carolyn. "They live with nature. Engineers are always looking for ways to turn nature to their own use rather than living in harmony with it."

He glanced down at the fire. They'd argued this way since they'd been married. She'd known she was marrying an engineer. Carolyn wanted life to stay as it should have been; not so much as it was, but as she would like to think of it. Yet she did not feel that way in the medical field. She never ceased to talk of wanting to find cures for the diseases that were rampant here. Couldn't she see that his idea of progress in bringing new technology to Africa was the same as hers medically?

"Africans," she continued, "aren't interested in their surroundings. Oh, yes, they have names for trees and animals, but they think they are part of it all. They never desire to re-create or tame or control the country. They just accept it."

"They have spent thousands of years," offered Andrew, "reacting to life rather than acting upon it."

"Ah," Carolyn's voice showed her interest, "I've never thought of it that way. I think you're right."

"They just leave the land alone; it's not a terraced Chinese hillside or a cultivated English farm, but thousands of miles of savannah and forest. They never own it; it owns them. They all live in fear of the unknown, of the leopard stealing their children at night, of any beast's sudden hunger if there is no other game around, of the evil spirits in the forest."

"Do you think the dam will remove famine from this part of Africa, and superstition, too?" There was skepticism in her voice.

"Well, it will be progress of a sort."

"Of a sort. But I can't really see that as man's true destiny."

"What is?"

"I don't know. I suppose Mama's idea of helping others."

"And you don't think that's what I'm doing?"

Carolyn stood. She walked over to him and took his head in her hands, burying his face against her breast. "I don't know. Sometimes I think I'm out of sync with the world." She kissed the top of his head. "Why don't we go to bed so you can show me I'm synchronized with someone, anyhow."

And that time, intense as it always was, brought them together in ways their words never could.

The next morning at breakfast, Carolyn said, "Andrew, I want to meet these people. Visit their villages. See how they live."

"Darling, you know I can't take time for that."

"I'm not asking you to. Would you mind if I take one of the natives—either Bildad or Lobengula—and go on a week's walk?"

"You can't do that."

Carolyn's spine stiffened. She wanted to respond and say, "Don't tell me what I can't do." But she didn't. Her cool gaze bored into her husband.

"Women don't go knocking about by themselves."

Carolyn laughed. "You forget what stock I come from. My mother always did. Are you afraid I'll get raped?"

"Oh, come on, Carolyn." He paused. "Yes, maybe that's part of it. But there are also leopards and lions and . . . who knows what. You could get lost, too."

"Not if I follow the river. I'll take a rifle. I'd be more afraid of getting raped or lost in an American or European city than I would be out here."

He knew he wouldn't win. He knew she'd go. Yet he couldn't give in gracefully. He didn't want her to go. He wouldn't have a moment's peace until she returned safely.

But he recognized that all of the challenges here were his. His job carried enormous responsibility, required all of his creative energies. His mind was engaged all day and part of the night. He was so involved that he had not taken time to realize that Carolyn would not forever be appeased by daily walks to watch animals and to explore the nearby territory. She, too, needed excitement. He already suspected that if it weren't thrust at her, she'd invent it.

"Do me a favor," he said. "Let me send word to the D.C. and see what the best way would be."

That will do for beginners, she thought.

When the district commissioner himself arrived ten days later, they were surprised.

He was a young man, in his late thirties, tall, slender, tanned. He joined Andrew in trying to talk Carolyn out of it, but when that could not be done, he suggested she join him for a ten-day foray to visit the villages closest to the gorge. It was obvious he was not going to be comfortable carting a woman around with him. "When I take my trips into the valley, my wife goes to Salisbury," he said, puffing on a pipe. "But if you're game . . ."

Carolyn was.

LONG AGO, IT HAD BEEN NAMED THE GWEMBE VALLEY—A WIDE SWATH, verdant in the rainy season, enclosed on the north and the south by steep cliffs that effectively cut it off from Africa's great, high plateau that surrounded it. It was a world unto itself.

No woman, and only a few men, had ever been outside the valley. The great river that plunged through it from west to east did so through a series of chasms that began below the Victoria Falls and escaped from the valley through the Kariba gorge. In October and November, the African spring, some of the valley trees burst into glorious, incandescent color. Along the river, splendid tall African mahogany towered above a plethora of other trees: baobab, mopane, acacia. The valley floor, unlike the plateau above the escarpments, never felt the cooling breezes. From June to September, the African winter, it was hot and dry; when the temperature fell into the seventies, people shivered and the forest browned and became arid. Spring was the hottest of all: two months of one-hundred-twenty-degree temperatures. Even nights were suffocating, and the acrid smell of smoke hung in the air, the result of forest fires. The earth was dusty. December, the harbinger of summer, brought temperatures down to the high nineties. The forest became a jungle and, after the Niagaras of rain, the earth steamed. Thunder rolled through the valley; a whole world of vegetation flourished, grew rank, smelled of decay.

Carolyn learned that aside from the animals she had already seen, there were pigs, enormous ants, poisonous snakes, rabbits, fearsome insects. The forest was so full of life that one could always see some movement. Elephants and lions abounded. The valley people's spears could always supply an antelope, a pig, or a porcupine for dinner. Fish were caught in hundred-year-old nets that were meticulously mended.

The tribes who inhabited land close to the river had winter gardens; when the river overflowed its banks every summer, the river people were forced to retreat to the valley's hills, but the alluvial soil deposited by the floodwaters fertilized the garden plots.

This valley was inhabited by the most primitive people on earth. For fifty years, the British district commissioners had been making annual three-to-four-month walks through the valley, visiting each tribe, so all the natives had seen white men, but civilization had touched them not at all. They lived much as people had lived in this valley since the beginning of time.

The men wore no clothes at all. The women attached six-to-eight-inch strings that gave a fringe effect to the belts they wore around their waists. Unmarried girls wore fringes only in the front;

wives also hung them down the back. They were a people who had not yet connected sexual intercourse with babies, though women recognized a swelling belly as a sign that a child was on the way.

The men were warriors, though not very effective ones. In the past, they had slaughtered and eaten their neighbors, but these customs had died out. Basically, they were neighborly, simple people. The Portuguese slave traders had stopped their marauding and kidnapping at the entrance to the gorge, so the Tonga had no reason not to be friendly to those who trespassed into their wild isolation.

Without exception, the district commissioners had cherished the Tonga. They learned their simple phonetic language and treated them fairly, enjoying their primitive sense of humor and trust. In fifty years, not a single D.C. ever cheated the Tongan tribes or treated them with anything but affection.

Not one of the sixty thousand suspected that their world, and all that they knew, was doomed. And nothing they could do would stop the flood that would disrupt their way of life forever.

Their ancient culture was about to be sacrificed so that factories could bring industrialization to Rhodesia, so that housewives could bake cakes in electric ovens, so that civilization could prove that progress was the god to be worshipped.

Carolyn learned all this during the evenings as she and Michael Carver, the D.C., sipped gin and tonics. She found him to be a sensitive man, invariably polite to the natives they met. He held conferences in each of the villages they visited. On several evenings they even ate with tribes, and the natives' childlike curiosity at seeing a white woman, "especially, I think, with your blond hair," as Carver put it, touched her; she allowed them to touch her arm, prod her stomach, finger her hair.

Here, as in the rest of Africa, it was women who did the work. Men fished and hunted but performed none of the other labor.

Carver, himself, had been here on two consecutive assignments. He had been lonely, so the last time he'd been home he'd married a girl he'd known for years. Now it was she who was lonely. When he visited the villages, she took a flat in Salisbury, but still, he told Carolyn, she didn't have much chance to make friends or to get to know other women. He realized what a lonely life it was for women.

Yes, she thought, if the only thing they do with their lives is please their husbands. She didn't ask him why his wife chose not to take these treks down into the valley with him.

That first sojourn into the valley was a brief one. When she returned, she told Andrew she thought she was pregnant. She'd felt queasy every morning and realized she'd missed her period.

He greeted her news with a whoop; immediately, however, he said, "This means you'll return to Salisbury, of course."

"Whoa," said Carolyn. "Why 'of course'? I've no intention of sitting in a chair for the next eight months, not knowing anyone and having nothing to do. I've been thinking. When Mama learns I'm pregnant, she can arrange to deliver the baby."

Andrew looked aghast.

"Carolyn! You're not thinking of having the baby out here?"

"I don't know why not. I was born in the jungle. I'd like *my* first child to be born in the wilds of Africa, too. My mother has delivered hundreds of babies. She'd like to deliver her grandchild, I think."

Andrew was nervous at the thought, but he was also doubly delighted that Carolyn was as she was and that she had cast her life with his.

Carolyn was ecstatic.

BY JANUARY, THE GORGE WAS CRAWLING WITH PEOPLE. TEN THOUSAND men were crowded onto the hill that would later become the genteel town of Kariba, but now anyone who had ever seen an American western would have recognized the backdrop. Five saloons had sprung up, all of which permitted gambling, none of which permitted blacks. Blacks had to buy their liquor at the back door and take it elsewhere. Four more women had come to town: one was a Eurasian woman, one had a Cockney accent, and two were half-caste coloreds. They lived together in a four-room shack, which was the most frequently visited house in town. Carolyn's only contact with them was a quick smile as they passed on the street. The streets were simply mud in the rainy season and dust the rest of the year.

The temporary huts for the natives were thrown together quickly. They were raised about two feet from the ground, had wooden platforms, and were octagonal; the thatched roofs, which bred insects, were supported by poles. There were no walls to these domiciles, and anywhere from four to six natives slept in them.

The Europeans would have been more comfortable had their

huts not had walls either, but they lived in shacks of hessian that had been sprayed with cement. The huts were insufferably hot, but cooler than the valley bottom, which reached one hundred and twenty degrees in January. Each man had a bucket of water, in which he carried his tools, for they were too hot to handle.

The workday lasted from dawn until dark. And the Italians surprised everyone. They arrived, en masse, in tight, well-fitting shorts, which immediately aroused dormant distrust. For many years, the British had worn shorts in Africa, but they were baggy white or khaki and had no shape or style. The Italians' shorts were brightly colored and fitted snugly. Their olive skins glistened; they were short and swarthy and laughed often. No one at Kariba had any faith in them.

But the Italians' worked at an amazing tempo, at high speed and under high pressure; they were willing to do work that Anglo-Saxons had reserved only for natives. At the end of the day, they could drink their Anglo-Saxon peers under the table, and then awake the next morning filled with zest for their work.

The dam was progressing with astonishing speed.

"It's gonna be 'igher than the cliffs of Dover," one Limey was heard to exclaim. Immense as it was, the arch was also slim and graceful.

Now that the temporary living quarters had been thrown together, Andrew could concentrate on building the permanent town. Though never destined to be beautiful, it was an attractive town that resembled typical suburbia. One of the first buildings was a cinema, which was crowded every Saturday night. The bungalows that would house the people who would be brought here were not ugly, but they had certain similarities. Andrew made sure that no two houses on the same block were alike, nor any two painted the same color. Bathrooms were installed in all of the homes, but none could be connected until the dam was finished and the water supply could be tapped. Then the outhouses could be torn down.

Months ago, Carolyn had said, "I think you've all forgotten something."

Andrew's eyes questioned her.

"You can't wait five years for a hospital, not with ten thousand men," she said with a smile, "and five women."

"You're right," agreed Andrew. "Probably need a jail, too."

With Carolyn's help, he sketched a small hospital. The next time Donald flew in, he told him of Carolyn's suggestion.

Donald looked appreciatively at Carolyn; she felt intense pleasure.

"We'll need a doctor, of course," she said, "and a couple of nurses."

Before he left, Donald drew her aside and asked, "Would you think of how we might recruit medical help? You seem to be more aware of this than any of us."

Carolyn was thrilled. At last something useful to do. She flew to Salisbury twice to talk to the hospital administrator there and wrote asking her mother for suggestions on how to recruit medical personnel.

Before the hospital was finished, a doctor arrived from England, a mild-mannered young man who soon married one of the three nurses who arrived shortly thereafter.

Carolyn had refused to move into one of the new bungalows, preferring her spacious tent, but when the torrential rains began, she gave in; she and Andrew moved their belongings into a small house, surrounded by a wide verandah, that would eventually overlook the lake.

Liliane and Marsh arrived there in the last week of February. An airstrip had been built before Andrew and Carolyn had arrived, so Liliane had no difficulty making a smooth landing. Andrew had worried that they would resent his having brought Carolyn to this remote outpost, but their immediate delight allayed his fears.

"I'm not sure I approve of the dam," Marsh said. "But since it's a fait accompli, let's go on from there."

Carolyn had not seen her parents in nearly a year. The first thing Liliane did was examine Carolyn and pronounce her in perfect health. Carolyn had had an uneventful and happy pregnancy. Her usual restless nature gave way to placidity and contentment. She had never been happier. She loved seeing Andrew excited; she loved feeling his baby kick within her. She appreciated Donald Reyes offering her her own responsibility and took great satisfaction both in the building of the hospital and in hiring its staff. The four newcomers became regular visitors at their dinner table. Carolyn and Andrew delighted in their lively company.

Though Dr. Jefferson had examined her, Carolyn made it clear her mother would be arriving to deliver the baby.

Liliane saw the change in Carolyn and marveled. For the first time, her daughter seemed at peace.

"Next time I come," she said at dinner one night, after hearing of Carolyn's adventures up in the valley, "I'm coming with you."

Marsh looked at her. "There's no reason we can't take a little trip into yesterday by ourselves. Would just a couple of days assuage your yearning?"

Liliane's eyes lit up. "It will probably ignite my curiosity more than assuage it," she said. Turning to Andrew, she asked, "How can it be arranged?"

"Hey," said Carolyn, "I'm the one who's taken three trips up there. He's never even been past the gorge. I'll arrange it for you." Looking at her mother, she wondered if she'd ever grow old. Except for gray at her left temple, Liliane seemed ageless.

Michael Carver arrived to meet the two famous visitors. "I'd have brought my wife, but there's no road between the Boma and here, and it's over one hundred miles," he said. Carolyn and Liliane both wondered why that would have stopped her.

But they had to cancel their planned trip.

At one-thirty in the morning of March 25, 1956, Carolyn awoke with a sharp stab. She waited until she timed the pains. Then she awoke Andrew and said, "Get Mama for me."

Though Carolyn had initiated the hospital, she wanted her baby born at home. Liliane sent Andrew to find clean sheets and Marsh to boil water.

When Liliane suggested anesthesia, Carolyn interrupted her. "No. I want to experience every minute of this. It's going to be all right, isn't it, Mama?" Her hands clasped Liliane's.

"Darling, everything looks normal. The head's in position, and you're dilating nicely."

Marsh was the most nervous. At least a dozen times, he asked, "Is she all right?"

Andrew drank eleven cups of coffee. Walking restlessly in and out of the bedroom, kissing Carolyn's forehead, sweating himself when Carolyn winced with a contraction, he finally told Liliane, "I want to watch. Help if I can." He wondered if he'd be sick.

"Ask Caro," Liliane suggested.

Carolyn loved the idea.

"Wash you hands thoroughly," Liliane instructed.

Carolyn moaned; beads of perspiration covered her face and her hands tensed into knots. A hint of fear accompanied the pain in her eyes and she cried, "Oh, Mama!"

Liliane separated Carolyn's legs and knifed her knees into the air. "Be ready to receive the baby," she told Andrew. He wondered what that meant. Carolyn reached for his hand and screamed. His stomach contracted.

"Push, darling. Take a deep breath, and when the next pain comes, press hard. The pain won't last long," Liliane assured her. "It's what it takes to bring a new life into the world."

Her fingers felt fuzz through the wetness, hair on the baby's head. Andrew stared; his breathing had stopped.

"Now, honey," Liliane soothed. "Take a deep breath and—"

Carolyn cried out.

"Push, push hard." Liliane's skilled hands received the damp head, maneuvering it gently so that her fingers could help first one little shoulder and then the other to slide out. "Once more," she urged. "Just one more big push, darling."

Carolyn gathered all of her reserves of energy, aware of nothing but the searing pain. And pushed. As she did so, Liliane's hands gently pulled the baby girl from her mother's body.

The mucus surrounding her, the blood on the bed, the scrunched-up, red ugliness of this wondrous creature did not sicken Andrew. His exhilaration was boundless.

Carolyn and I, he thought, together we've created new life, this child. His love overflowed.

Liliane cut the umbilical cord and wiped the infant dry, holding her upside down and gently slapping her back until she gurgled a little cough. Then she swaddled her in a cotton receiving blanket she'd bought in Salisbury and handed her to Andrew.

Carolyn's eyes were closed.

"Push again," Liliane said, "and let's get rid of this afterbirth."

The power of blood ties, she thought. No childbirth had ever filled her with such joy. A girl. A granddaughter. "She's perfect," Liliane told them.

After cleaning up, she left Andrew and Carolyn together for a few minutes. He laid the little girl in the crook of Carolyn's arm. Her eyes fluttered open to see her daughter and then met his.

Marsh was waiting in the outer room, sweat pouring off his forehead. "Tell me she's all right."

"She's wonderful." Liliane laughed happily. "I need some coffee. Come to the kitchen with me. And then you can go see her. Leave the three of them together for a few minutes."

Marsh brewed the coffee. "Do you know how wide your smile is?" he asked.

"Wait until you see her." Liliane laughed. "Except for her coloring, she looks exactly like you."

CHAPTER 38

▼

WHEN LILIANE FLEW OFF THREE WEEKS LATER, MARSH STAYED. AND stayed. He had missed Carolyn more than he wanted to admit. He took great delight in holding Courtney, in listening to Andrew talk of his work and the future he saw for Rhodesia. Sitting for hours every day under an acacia tree high on a hill, he watched the dam take shape.

Marsh liked Andrew better and better. He admired his energy and the way he worked with others. He understood his sense of humor. He also understood the chemistry that was set into motion when Carolyn and Andrew were together.

"She's the most unbelievable person I know," said Andrew one night over a campfire. "She has a wildness, as though she's part of this environment . . ." His gesture was meant to include all of the vast empty spaces, the trees, the animals. "Yet she has an intensity about the injustices of the world, and she's not satisfied to let life be."

"Those are inherited characteristics." Marsh grinned. "Her mother and I have tendencies to tilt at windmills."

Carolyn basked in motherhood. She had been brought up in an African society where white women did not keep house. Here she never cooked a meal or cleaned house, and she was satisfied with that, but she thrived on taking care of Courtney. If she had been living in a town, a native nurse would have changed the diapers and even been the wet nurse. Here, Carolyn could tend Courtney herself.

While Courtney suckled at her breast, Carolyn thought fiercely: I shall never leave her. If this dam isn't finished when she needs schooling, I'm going with her.

But Courtney was not enough to soothe her restless spirit.

While pregnant, she had taken two other trips into the interior of the valley. Michael Carver had lent her a Tongan dictionary, and she now spent hours teaching herself new words.

Andrew took it for granted that Carolyn would stay put.

"Whatever for?" she asked. "I've no one to talk with all day long. Nothing to think of, really. I've no intention at all of letting myself atrophy." She turned to Marsh. "You're an old adventurer. Don't you have a penchant for exploring a doomed valley that will exist for only two more years?"

Marsh's irresistible smile lit his face. "Are you inviting me on a safari?"

"That's too sophisticated a word for what I do," Carolyn answered. "Michael tells me one hundred and ninety-three villages lie below the flood line. I've trekked three times up the south side of the river. Now I'm ready to start on the northern side, where there are many more villages. Most of them are small, ramshackle, barely standing. People really only live in their huts during the rainy season. When a village becomes too filthy, they move a few hundred yards and rebuild it. Only the villages close to the river, with winter gardens, are permanent. This time I'd like to go as far as Chisamu, about eighty miles west of the gorge. From there it's about sixty miles to Michael's headquarters, the Boma."

Marsh nodded. "Of course I want to come. That way of life will not exist much longer. Life is so simple when there's no electricity," he mused.

"Yes," agreed Carolyn. "When the sun sinks, there's nothing to do but gossip, or dance to the light of the fires, or go to bed."

"Which, no doubt," Andrew said with a twinkle in his eyes, "is why Africa will populate itself into starvation by the end of this century."

Carolyn looked up at him. "What I'd like to do is teach these people birth control."

"How do you do that with people who don't know how to count to twenty-eight?" Andrew asked.

Carolyn sighed. "I don't know. But I've been giving it thought." She had rigged up a backpack for carrying Courtney and off she and Marsh went, accompanied by natives carrying tents and cooking gear. Both Carolyn and Marsh carried rifles.

Partly, Andrew was jealous. He would have liked to share these journeys, but not a day could be spared from his work, and certainly not the three or four weeks Carolyn planned to be gone this time. He felt lonely when she was not there at night. He didn't sleep as well; he reached out in his sleep for an empty pillow, and the emptiness always awoke him.

He told himself he had stopped worrying about the elements

or wild savages overpowering Carolyn, but he would be uneasy until she returned. He was glad Marsh had gone along.

Marsh and carolyn camped in an open, unforested area by the river. They were waiting for Lobengula's dinner, and Carolyn was suckling Courtney.

In the hazy, almost purple distance, they could see the high escarpment on the Southern Rhodesian side of the valley.

"Water will rise up to there," Marsh said, thinking aloud. Beyond the river, the land rose gently from a level plain over a half mile wide. The forest began again and grew thickly to the ten miles or so to the high cliffs. The Tongan thought these steep hills were the end of the world. They were. Of their world. And that world, the world that had been theirs from time immemorial, was about to end.

"Michael has spent the last year trekking to all of the villages, warning the people that this valley will be inundated, but he says none of them understand. The only kind of flood they understand is the annual one after the rainy season. They leave their villages for the nearby hills, watch the water recede, and return to plant gardens in the fertile soil deposited. They just can't imagine anything else."

"They probably practice ancestor worship," said Marsh. "If so, they won't be willing to leave the buried spirits."

Carolyn buttoned her blouse, burped Courtney, and handed the little girl to Marsh, knowing the pleasure this gave him. "This is a major concern of the government. How do you take away the spiritual needs of a people when there's no way to replace them?"

They were both quiet, thinking—and listening to Courtney's cooing.

"They've always lived a marginal life," Carolyn explained. It was wonderful to be able to share her thoughts with Marsh. Andrew listened, but not with the same sympathy Marsh evidenced. Andrew saw the dam as a vehicle for bringing civilization to primitive people as well as bringing industrialization to Rhodesia. Marsh could appreciate the values of tradition. He could understand that uprooting an entire way of life was a cataclysmic undertaking. What need had those illiterate primitives of civilization?

Carolyn looked into the distance. "In the last few years, with the help of understanding D.C.s, the government has not allowed the Tongans to starve. They bring in grain, despite their thinking that the natives are lazy."

"Who wouldn't be," interrupted Marsh, "in this heat? I don't know how those Italians keep the pace they do on the dam."

"Exactly." Carolyn smiled as Bildad brought them gin and tonics. She sipped hers and grimaced at its warmth. "The government, or so Michael says, sees that the natives do not starve—but just barely."

The next day a Land Rover approached them. Only a four-wheel drive, and then only in winter, could navigate this land just a few miles on either side of the road that connected the Boma—forty miles north—with Chisamu, a river village. Two missions were on the lone road; one run by Catholics, and the other by the American Pilgrim Holiness Church.

Michael Carver jumped out of the jeep. Carolyn had sent him word of their impending visit.

"My wife insists you come for dinner and spend the night. You can fit in the Rover. Leave your natives and equipment here, and I'll return you tomorrow."

Michael and his wife had been waiting for two days for Marsh and Carolyn's appearance since they had few visitors.

On the way up into the northern hills, in the back of the Rover, Carolyn could tell Marsh was having the time of his life. "In traveling all over the world to remote places when you were young," she asked him, "did you ever think you'd be doing it with your daughter and granddaughter?"

"Never." Marsh's eyes danced. "It's too good to be true." He reached over and squeezed Carolyn's hand.

Frances Carver was almost exactly as Carolyn had pictured her. Her hair was curled in a current fashion, her flowered dress of sheer lawn would have been acceptable on the streets of Salisbury or London, her fragile-looking pale hands, which she waved in the air as she spoke, had nails painted a pale pink. She wore stockings and high-heeled pumps.

She was pathetically pleased to have company and immediately begged to hold Courtney, but the meal she served was as bland as though it had been cooked in Yorkshire, and she had long ago given up trying to make the square cubicle they lived in look like a home.

"I told them last year and again this year," Michael told Marsh. "I tell them they have to move and we will help. They have to take all of their property and their animals. I try to make them visualize a lake—water covering the whole valley; everything they've ever known drowned . . . That fishes will swim where birds now fly, that breaking waves will wash against those distant high cliffs, that the towering trees will be covered with water. But they can't visualize it. They listen and nod their heads and go on with their lives."

"I've listened to them, too," added Carolyn. "One girl with a lover on the other side of the river wonders whether to marry him and go with his tribe to new lands far on the other side and never see her family again or give him up and stay with the people she's known all her life. She can no longer have both."

"Some of them must think," Marsh said, "that the river will rush over the wall in flood season and destroy it."

Those who thought that way were partly right.

The Zambezi River behaved as vindictively as though witch doctors had put a spell on it.

As 1956 reached its last days, reports above Victoria Falls indicated that an exceptional flood was building, the worst one in a hundred years, they predicted. Early in 1957, the water rose in the narrow Kariba gorge.

The cavernous underground powerhouse, built of rock hewn inside the hill, resembled nothing so much as Westminster Abbey, so immense was it. On the dam itself, two million yards of concrete had been poured. Above the north bank a quarry had been built where three quarters of a million yards of sand had been dug from what would become the lake's bed. The Italians' work had proceeded far more quickly than even the most optimistic estimates had predicted.

But the river proved that nature, or the witch doctors, held supremacy. After the waters crashed over the falls two hundred miles away, the river poured into the valley, churned through the gorge. All of the machinery that had laboriously come two thousand miles from the sea and had been hand-placed had to be lifted out hurriedly and brought up to one of Kariba's hills.

The water swirled onward and upward. It rose sixty-six feet. It was a hundred-to-one chance, and no one had mathematically taken such odds into consideration. It covered what could be seen of the dam, of the millions of dollars that had already been spent and the tens of thousands of hours invested. When the water subsided, to the great relief of everyone in Kariba, the dam was intact. The workers looked at each other with pride.

The Italians and Africans sweated around the clock in the

sweltering, ovenlike heat of the gorge, while the valley rang with the sound of pneumatic tools, and dust drifted up and down the valley for miles.

The work grew increasingly more dangerous as the dam grew higher. "When the next great flood comes, in another hundred years, the dam will stop it," the men said to each other.

No one dreamed that this very year there would be a flood such as hadn't been seen in a thousand years.

Spring, the hottest time of the year, was drier than any in memory. Half the Tongans, thirty thousand of them, had been moved to new lands; the remaining natives sweltered agonizingly in the heat. Even the Italians slowed. Vegetation withered, animals were lethargic, people nearly comatose. They sat and stared at the faded orange sky, and those who believed in prayer prayed for rain.

By November of 1957, Andrew's streets were completed, and the houses, too; hundreds of rectangular boxes that included the latest electric amenities, which could not be put into operation until the dam was completed. It was not an unattractive town. The hospital was in full operation, and a school was nearing completion; men who knew they'd be here for another two or three years were bringing their families to Kariba. A small hotel was in operation, and at the very highest point in town, the Italians—in their spare moments—were building a delicately beautiful circular church that would have the town's most beautiful view of the lake.

By December, the dam was at its most crucial point in relation to a flood. What had already been built created an enormous obstacle for churning waters to flow through, but was not yet strong enough to halt the water's flow.

The rain didn't begin until mid-December. When the first rainclouds belted into the valley, cries of thanksgiving were heard up and down the trickling Zambezi. Overnight, the desert was painted with color. Rivers that had been dry since fall gushed into life. People stood in the rain, letting it pour over them, their faces raised to the sky. The heat did not abate, so being wet was no discomfort.

Within days, the earth was sodden muck; streams that hadn't existed five days before became rivers.

By the end of January, rumors were rampant that on the Barotse plain, five hundred miles away on the Angolan–Northern Rhodesian border, where the river flowed through marshes of gigantic proportions, a flood was building that would make the Hundred-Year Flood look tame.

Later, it was not only the natives who attributed motives to the great river, which gathered itself like a caged animal and came hurtling down the valley, clawing at the dam as though it were but an insect in its path.

At night, while the bulldozers and other heavy equipment were inside the cofferdam, the river raged. In the morning, the road bridge atop it had disappeared. People watched in stunned silence as the river reached up for the other bridge, a fragile suspension footbridge, built more than a hundred feet above the river.

Nothing could be done. People gathered on the hills, and thousands watched as the river ate away the footbridge and pounded through the cataract created between the two highest towers. Estimates later suggested that six hundred thousand cubic feet of water a second crashed over the dam's foundation.

Michael Carver, all alone, took his motor launch up and down the river, warning those he had not been able to talk into leaving. Move back to the hills, he urged. The river rose so rapidly that a man couldn't run away from it. The tributaries backed up and circled behind hills, ambushing villages that water had never before touched. One day it rose over six feet in six hours.

Then Michael set out in his dinghy, trying to rescue people who had climbed the low hills, already stranded by surrounding water. How many people drowned was never ascertained. Conical thatched-roof huts floated in the flotsam, crocodiles swam through villages, black mamba snakes slithered onto the land.

Relentlessly, the rain continued. Scattered Tongans lived in fear, starvation, and misery.

It was not until March that the boiling water subsided. Remains of villages were exposed, but at Kariba the dam still stood.

In a redoubled effort, the Italians vowed that the dam would be sealed before next winter's floods.

In the rush, three Italians and fourteen Africans plunged from a two-hundred-thirty-foot shaft into wet concrete. It took pneumatic picks to rescue their broken bodies.

But by the winter flood of 1959, the final dam openings had been blocked, and the water was stayed. From then on, the winner of the river race was never in doubt. It was now simply a matter of keeping ahead of the slowly rising lake, which was trapped behind the dam.

▼

MARSH AND LILIANE VISITED OFTEN. THEY FLEW THEMSELVES IN, AND together they stayed three or four weeks. Courtney was Liliane's special delight, but she was interested in everything around her, too. Each year she and Marsh trekked up the valley through the native villages with Carolyn, and in 1959 Andrew went up the valley for two weeks with them. Carolyn seemed to be trying to hang on to a vanishing way of life. Sometimes Andrew thought she was obsessive about it.

That winter of 1959, in July, the valley had been cleared of the last of its people. A few of them had been eager to move, envisioning work in factories, of which they had only been told, but the vast majority felt uprooted, forced to leave the spiritual homeland controlled by their ancestors, which was all they knew of the world.

Fertile lands had been searched out for them, for the D.C. was a man of tender conscience. The government knew that none of its solutions was ideal, but worked to make the new lands acceptable to the various Tongan tribes that were now spread far and wide. Much of the land on which the natives were resettled was far more fertile than the rocky valley; the people had to be taught to garden. Farming was a new way of life for them. Living on these wide plains, even along tributaries of the river, were frightened people who were unaccustomed to open spaces. Now there were no limits to their world, and many of them were forever lost, unable to adjust to a world that was far too complex for them to assimilate. Neighbors had vanished, and each tribe was left isolated, strangers in a strange land.

By the end of 1959, all Tongans, whether because of the new climate or the influence of civilization, were wearing clothes; most of them had learned to covet civilization's newly discovered amenities.

On this last trek into the valley, the last winter it would lie open to the elements before becoming cold, dark, and slimy forever, Carolyn watched the slowly filling valley with a great sense of loss. The river crept inexorably across the land, inundating villages, slowly covering the lonely, forlorn, abandoned huts, surrounding and advancing on treetops that had once towered over the valley.

One afternoon, as she sat on a hillock looking for the last time on this favored valley, Carolyn felt Marsh's hand on her shoulder.

"I know," he said, "what you must be feeling."

"A way of life lost forever."

"There are many," said Andrew, "who would say it wasn't worth preserving. It was a stone-age existence."

"Look!" exclaimed Liliane. In the distance, four small boats were wending their way upriver. Their *putt-putt*ing could be heard in the valley's silence. Rowboats were drawn behind each of the motorboats.

Courtney waved. Liliane, holding Courtney's hand, smiled down at her granddaughter and waved, too. The driver of the lead boat waved in return and shouted something back to his companions. The flotilla changed direction and headed toward the camp.

Marsh smiled. "Shall we go greet our visitors?"

The boaters were all men in their late twenties and early thirties, tanned from prolonged work in the sun. They wore shorts, short-sleeved shirts, and sneakers. The leader, who introduced himself as Sam Elliot, wore an American-style western straw hat. He was a tall, swarthy man with shining black hair and a bushy mustache. His blue eyes looked bleached, as though he had been staring at the sun too long. It was apparent that none of them had shaved recently.

Since it was late afternoon, they invited themselves to share camping space after asking Andrew if he'd mind.

They worked for the Society for the Preservation of Africa's Heritage, partly financed by fees at the game preserves and partly by world-wide donations. Marsh was the only one who had heard of the organization.

Now that the valley was devoid of humanity, Sam Elliot explained, it was time to consider the animals. He and his men were a rescue squad.

Carolyn had taken for granted that, as the river rose, the animals would simply retreat.

"Not so," said Sam. "They're used to safety on hilltops and will gather up there, waiting for the water to recede. But this time it won't. Waiting will mean drowning."

"Can we help?" inquired Marsh.

Sam looked at him, appreciation in his glance. "We feel like the proverbial drop in a bucket. We know four men can't rescue all of the wildlife that will be trapped. Eight can rescue twice as many. We'll welcome any help."

Carolyn felt a charge of adrenaline.

As the two groups shared dinner, the men told of their rescue plans.

"This goddamned dam," said Sam, "is immoral. It's destroying a way of life."

"One really can't hang on to the past," Andrew said defensively. "It *is* 1959. Actually, the standard of living for all of Rhodesia will rise because of this dam."

"What alternatives are there, Mr. Elliot?" Liliane asked. "One can't stop the government once its mind is made up. What do *you* intend to do?"

"You mean after we save the animals here?"

Liliane nodded.

"We've just moved to Salisbury. There's another branch of our organization working out of Nairobi. We can lobby the governments, try to jog their consciences. Failing that, we'll do whatever we can do to make the transitions easier, to save lives and traditions. Personally, I think if the wildlife of Africa becomes extinct, so will our world."

"Let's help," Carolyn suggested, her eyes shining.

"Of course," agreed Andrew. "What can we do?"

Sam Elliot was only too glad to take them up on their offer.

During the rescue operations, one of them stayed on land every day with Courtney. They took turns caring for her, and she was a three-year-old handful when there was so little to do. She couldn't understand why she, too, couldn't ride out in the boats, but the trips to what had once been hills and were now islands were fraught with danger. Debris of all kinds floated swiftly; trees whose tops were barely below the surface were constant hazards, branches of drowned trees jutted upward at crazy angles through the dark water.

Treetops teemed with millions of creeping things, all searching wildly for safety. When the branches were shaken by the boats, snakes slithered out of the dark leaves, crocodiles wallowed under the watery branches.

The gardens of the deserted villages abounded with animals; the next day the gardens were under water. The river crept relentlessly on.

With great care, yet with some danger, they rescued monkeys from trees. In Rhodesia, baboons were on a par with rats; the government paid a bounty for dead ones. Even so, none of the rescuers could let one drown. They captured them in nets and set them free on the shore, where they would run off, to be captured by bounty hunters.

Elephants, stranded on islands, were intelligent and capable enough to swim to shore before the distance became too great, and the other large animals—the lions and leopards—must have had a fifth sense, because only one of them was found stranded. Fortunately, it was a cub, so it was easy to rescue without fear of harm to themselves. Carolyn rigged up a bottle, Liliane found powdered milk, and they let Courtney feed the cub. It amused her for several days.

Many antelopes had allowed themselves to be beached on islands; their rescue was exciting, requiring ingenuity and bravery ("or foolishness," said Marsh) on behalf of the emancipators. Three or four had to capture the frightened animals in nets, truss them so that their legs were shackled, then carry them in the motorboats to shore. By the time these graceful animals were let loose, terror had put them in a state of shock. They stood on the shore like statues, their nerves frayed, minds frozen.

When Liliane and Andrew had to leave, Marsh decided to stay and help with the rescue.

"I'm not surprised." Liliane smiled at his announcement, reaching out to touch his hand. He wrapped it around hers. The tenderness in their eyes, thought Carolyn, it's as though they're newly in love. It's always been that way. Even after nearly thirty years, they still touch each other often, their eyes meeting in open declarations of love.

Carolyn looked at them proudly; they were still a handsome couple. Marsh's silver hair gave him a distinguished appearance, and except for the streak of white that flowed from her left temple, Liliane looked much younger than her fifty-three years. Still slim-waisted, she wore the same clothes she had for the last thirty years, but her shorts were trimmer and better-fitting, and she alternated now between sandals and sneakers. Somehow, her khaki slacks and open-necked sport shirts in no way detracted from the womanliness she projected.

Just recently, she'd complained to Marsh, "I left femininity behind me so long ago that I'm surprised you still think of me as a woman."

He had reached out to stroke her cheek, still like velvet even after all the years of jungle humidity. "You're more woman than anyone I've ever known."

Carolyn sighed with contentment as she looked at her parents together. She could only hope that her own marriage would be as successful as theirs, but already there were tensions at work, always centering on the conflicting views she and Andrew had about the future of Africa.

"Mama," she asked, filled with sudden inspiration, "if I stay, will you and Andrew take Courtney back with you? Sue Ann Kirby will look after her when you leave. I'd like to stay and help, too."

Andrew turned to study her. Carolyn could tell he wanted to tell her she couldn't—or shouldn't—stay. She said, "It'll just be for a week or two. It makes me feel that at last I'm doing something worthwhile."

Andrew said nothing, but his lips tightened into a firm line. Liliane and Marsh sensed the tension charging the air. So did Sam Elliot, who looked from one to the other.

"We'll see she gets back safely," he said. "We can use all the help we can get. We have to return to Kariba in another ten days for more supplies, anyhow."

There was nothing Andrew could say.

CHAPTER 39

▼

BY THE END OF 1959, THE FIRST SUMMER THAT THE NEW DAM WOULD control the Zambezi's raging floodwaters, Carolyn was pregnant again and they were back in Salisbury.

Donald Reyes, who had flown to Kariba every month, had developed great admiration for both McClouds. His decision to hire Andrew had been reaffirmed on each visit. And, as he told Hazel, "That Carolyn's something. She thrives on rugged conditions, leaves him to go out in the bush for weeks at a time, yet their marriage seems more solid—no, that's not the right word—more exciting than others I've seen. She also has the knack of making a house—even a tent—a home. When I visit there, I feel at ease. She creates an atmosphere of coziness, and then just when you're relaxed, she aims for the jugular." He laughed. "She wants to challenge everything. I think she's a bit too—what'll I call it?—too ivory tower. But, by God, it's fun to argue with her."

Hazel turned out the light on her side of the bed. "It sounds like you like her."

"I do. And you will, too, when you get to know her. I admire her." He turned his light out also and threw an arm across his wife. "On the other hand, I couldn't stand to be married to her. She's not—not comfortable, like you are."

"I think I've just been insulted."

Donald kissed her neck. "No, you've just been told you're wonderful."

THE NEXT DAY HAZEL VOLUNTEERED TO HELP CAROLYN FIND A HOUSE. They found it on the first day. Carolyn's heart jumped the minute she saw it.

In an era of so much building, houses were mostly one-story modern bungalows surrounded by a patch of trim lawn and inevitably including a swimming pool in the backyard. Carolyn looked at one of them and shook her head. After the open vistas of the last four years, after growing up in Marsh's vineyard retreat, the new houses, where you could look out the windows into the neighbors' living room, gave her claustrophobia.

So when she saw the big, gray Victorian house at the edge of town, set amid two acres of luxuriant lawn, dotted with lush plantings of poinsettias, bougainvillea, and hibiscus, she fell in love before she even saw the interior.

The large, graceful rooms, one leading into another in a way that lent airy spaciousness, only added to her desire.

I want it, she thought. I want it the way I haven't wanted anything tangible in years.

She told Hazel, "I must phone Andrew immediately."

Andrew left work and met them at the house. His first thought was, Why did Carolyn want such a big house? His second, after looking at her eyes and listening to her voice, was that they could be happy here.

That night, Hazel wonderingly asked her husband, "How can they afford the Thompson place? None of your other engineers could."

"My dear," answered Donald. "Do you know what I pay that young man? And, for four years, they haven't had anyplace to spend it. I've been depositing it in the bank for him, and the only time either of them came to town was when Carolyn wanted to talk with the hospital administrator. I won't be surprised if they pay cash for it."

And so the old Thompson place became the new McCloud

place. Carolyn went on a spree of spending, furnishing their new home with taste if not elegance.

Before all of the rooms were finished, she phoned Michelle Elliot. Except for the Reyeses, she knew no one in the city, and Sam had asked her to introduce herself to his wife. She invited her to tea, though when Michelle arrived, Carolyn had not yet changed her clothes. She had been arranging furniture, playing with Courtney, and overseeing new plantings in the yard and had forgotten it was nearly four o'clock.

She greeted her visitor in a slightly wrinkled blouse that had peat moss sprinkled over it and slacks that were covered with dirt and dog hair, thanks to the newest family member, a large shaggy black dog Andrew had named Othello.

Michelle was not what Carolyn had expected. She had clear, pale skin and soft brown hair that framed her oval face. Her hazel eyes never quite lit up, but they were warm and friendly. She had obviously spent a great deal of time on her makeup, and her long fingernails were a pale coral. There were ruffles on her skirt, which was of fine pastel-flowered lawn. The heels of her shoes were exceedingly high, and she had a habit of running her tapered fingers down one silk-stockinged leg, as though caressing it. Everything about her was muted.

It was obvious that she resented being left alone to raise two young children, ages five and six, and couldn't understand why Sam had to be away from home. "I don't feel really whole without a man around. Of course, no woman does," she said in a soft voice that was more a sigh than anything else. "One isn't invited to parties, and of course I can't go to dances. But I do enjoy gardening. I refuse to have a gardener, no matter how it looks. I like to dig in the dirt."

Africa frightened her a bit; they'd been in Salisbury less than a year.

"Sam's been too busy to join the country club," Michelle explained. "His mind is always on his work. Besides, he's not much for social life. Perhaps when he returns . . ." Her voice trailed off.

Marsh arrived just as she was leaving. He had flown up to see the new house.

"Well, what did you think?" Carolyn asked him.

Marsh eyed her. "No, you tell me first."

"Terribly feminine. One gets the idea that she will do only those things that are traditionally womanly. And she clings to a man—resents Sam for being away. Has no inner resources."

"Sexy," said Marsh. "She oozes sensuality."

Carolyn raised her head. "You think so?" She laughed at him. "That's not what I saw at all."

"You will," he assured her. "Just wait."

"Changing the subject, Papa," Carolyn said, "what would you think if I work for Sam's outfit after the baby's born?"

Marsh sighed and sat down. "Well, at least you'll wait until the baby's born."

"His name is going to be Justin."

The crow's-feet by Marsh's eyes crinkled, but his eyes remained solemn. "You are your mother's daughter," he said.

"I know," Carolyn admitted. "That's why I need to work. And they're trying to do such exciting things!"

"You've always resented Lili for putting Simbayo ahead of you and of me. Are you going to follow in her footsteps?" Marsh's voice was more casual than his question.

"I hope not. I want more than she's allowed herself."

"Have you thought that they may not want you?"

"No." She grinned. "That's never crossed my mind."

DURING THE NEXT YEAR, JUSTIN WAS BORN, COURTNEY NEVER stopped asking questions, and Sam and Michelle Elliot and their children, Saundra and Evan, became regular visitors at the McClouds'. Carolyn began to lay the groundwork for her plan— talking about preserving Africa's heritage, about trying to find things of value to replace those traditions ripped from tribal life, about finding ways to prolong the lives of tribal Africans.

"Someday," Carolyn warned, "I'm going to work with you, Sam."

Andrew never expressed opposition.

Michelle did ask, "Why in the world would you want to go to work when you don't have to?" Her father had sent her a check that enabled them to join the country club, and Michelle enjoyed being the woman whose dance card was always filled. Carolyn remembered what Marsh had said about Michelle, but she only saw the helpless, fragile woman who refused to learn how to work any machine "because they're really men's work, aren't they?"

Michelle didn't pretend to be helpless; she really was. At times this irritated Carolyn, but at other times she enjoyed talking with Michelle about gardens and their children. Michelle remained oblivious to events close at hand, but could talk for hours about events happening far away. She never knew the facts, but she always had an emotional approach to faraway events. She was a political liberal who believed everyone should be treated equally; if a person didn't want to work, the government should support him. Though Carolyn certainly considered herself a liberal, she couldn't go that far, but sometimes it was fun to listen to Michelle's strange perceptions.

She enjoyed Sam enormously. He was a dedicated biologist, intelligent, demanding of himself and his staff, yet, unlike Andrew, he could seldom relax. Because it pleased Michelle and because they could go with Andrew and Carolyn, he did attend the Saturday-night dances at the club, but Michelle could never persuade him to dance. Her soft, doe eyes concentrated on whatever her partner was saying, and in her muted chiffons she looked lovely. Once in a while Sam's eyes followed her, but he left her to her own enjoyments. He sat at the table and talked with Carolyn and Andrew; he walked out onto the verdandah when they danced.

Andrew and Sam had become good friends, but Andrew thought Michelle slightly vapid. She made him appreciate Carolyn all the more.

"Imagine being married to her," he told Carolyn.

"Marsh thinks she's sexy." Carolyn laughed.

"I won't deny that. But she's so damn fragile."

"I'm told that's what many men like. But I don't see what's so sexy about her."

"If you were a man you would."

"Does she appeal to you?" Carolyn teased.

Without answering that question, Andrew said, "Michele expects life to be like the movies of the thirties and forties. She wants a continual romance and she's content to ignore the realities."

Carolyn started to tickle him. "But does she appeal to you?"

Andrew grabbed her hands and pinned her, laughing, on the bed. "No," he said. "No one in the whole world do I lust after but you."

"Prove it," Carolyn whispered as his lips closed on hers.

IN JANUARY 1959, ALL HELL BROKE LOOSE IN THE BELGIAN CONGO. Riots in Léopoldville, whipped by the winds of independence that were sweeping across Africa, culminated in full-scale mayhem in the city. The Belgian colonial authorities were forced to listen.

Patrice Lumumba negotiated with Brussels. The following year, on June 30, 1960, in haste and with no preparation for the transition of authority, independence was abruptly granted, with Belgian authorities formally handing over the reins of government in a public square in Léopoldville, which immediately changed its name to Kinshasa.

Marsh was not particularly worried about Liliane. In her part of the world, they were scarcely conscious that anyone owned the country. They went about their own business and had only harmonious relations with the natives. Liliane had been in Simbayo for almost thirty-two years, Rose and Heidi even longer. Now that freedom had been granted to the natives, they had renamed the country and the river Zaire. Liliane would be pleased, but it could scarcely make a difference to her way of life.

He was finishing his Rhodesian novel, which had been interrupted by a trip to Salisbury to see his new grandson. His stomach tied in a knot when he answered the doorbell to receive a telegram. Lili? Carolyn?

No. There was no way for Lili to send a cable. And Carolyn or Andrew would have phoned him if something was wrong. He tore the yellow envelope open.

"Oh, my God!"

He stared at the black dots on the coarse yellow paper and moved to the sofa. Sitting down with a thud, he looked at the cable again. He stared at it for a long time.

Rising, he moved to his office and picked his glasses up from his desk. He read it a third time.

"I'll be damned," he said to himself as a smile broke over his face.

The telegram was from Stockholm, inviting him to attend the banquet and celebration where they would formally award him the Nobel Prize for Literature.

He removed his glasses and searched for a handkerchief.

"All along I thought it would be Lili," he murmured. "I thought she'd get the Peace Prize."

By the next day reporters were converging on his doorstep and Carolyn phoned to scold him for not telling her immediately. "I'm so proud of you," she said.

"I'm going to Simbayo," he told her. "I have six weeks before I have to be in Sweden. I want Lili to go with me. I want her to share this. The toughest part of living alone is having no one to share your joy."

"Stop here on your way, Papa. You'll have to change planes here, anyhow."

"I'll make reservations for next week. I can rent a plane myself when I get to Coquilhatville and fly to Simbayo from there."

"Haven't you heard? Coquilhatville's now called Mbandaka. You don't pronounce the *M.*"

"I'll never get it straight."

"Papa, we think it's just wonderful. I'm really not surprised. It goes to show some people do have taste."

Marsh hung up the phone. This is what all my life has been leading toward, he thought, and I didn't know it.

The next day's papers acclaimed him as the first long-time African resident to be so honored. It also carried a story that the province of Katanga had seceded from Zaire and civil war had broken out. Two nuns and a priest had been murdered—the two nuns had been raped first. Foreign governments urged all Europeans to leave immediately. A fighting faction was screaming "Death to all whites." Colonialism's backlash had erupted.

CAROLYN MET MARSH AT THE AIRPORT.

"Now, you know nothing's going to happen to Mama," she said with an assurance she didn't feel. "Mama's as much a part of Africa as anyone there. She's worked for them for over thirty years." Cramps had tied her stomach in a knot since she'd heard the news.

Marsh nodded his head. "I know, I know. It's not the people who know Simbayo I'm worried about."

They were walking rapidly toward her car.

"No planes are flying into the Congo," Carolyn told him.

"I know that. I wonder how long that's going to last."

"There are no phone lines working, no railroads. I've checked them all."

"So have I. Maybe if I could get up to Uganda, I could get to Stanleyville, and maybe take a boat down the Congo—"

"Zaire," Carolyn corrected.

"Too many years for me to undo my learning quickly," Marsh said, stepping on the invisible brake on his side of the car.

Carolyn leaned over and patted his knee. "Papa, I'm driving."

Marsh continued with his plan. "If I can get to Stanleyville and hop a ride down the river, it would take about ten to fourteen days—"

"If boats are still moving downriver," said Carolyn.

Marsh went on as if he had not heard her. "And get off at Coquilhatville, or whatever it's called now, and get down the Mombayo—"

"Papa, boats probably aren't even running on that river."

Marsh stared straight ahead.

"Caro, I've got to get to her."

"You may not be able to. All the borders are closed. And you have to get to Sweden next month." She felt torn. Was her mother safe? She'd had terrible nightmares the last three nights, waking in cold sweats; her shivering stopped only after Andrew held her and stroked her damp hair.

"Do you think that matters when Lili may be in danger?"

They had arrived at Carolyn's house. She jumped out first and dragged his luggage from the trunk.

Nothing could happen to Lili. Lili wouldn't let anything bad happen. Carolyn would put her mother up against anyone and know who'd be victorious.

And, even though she believed that, she was scared.

"There's no way to help her, Papa," she said. She didn't want Marsh to see how worried she was. He was in a bad enough state.

Nothing would dissuade him. The next day he flew to Nairobi and from there chartered a plane to the lake region of Uganda. He spent two weeks trying to get through any customs point, going as far south as Lake Tanganyika, all to no avail. The borders were closed.

Then, discouraged, he flew back to Salisbury.

"Papa, it's always harder for those who wait. Andrew's been a wreck each time I've been in labor because he didn't know how easy it was for me. Those who stand and wait are always afraid of the worst. Can you imagine anyone trying to harm Simbayo or Mama?"

Actually, Marsh couldn't.

He waited in Salisbury for another three weeks before flying to Europe. They jumped every time the phone rang; they read the papers; they stayed glued to the radio. Finally, Carolyn convinced him that staying there could not help either Liliane or himself. "Mama would be angry to think you didn't go give a rousing acceptance speech. Go to Sweden and say something immortal, so Mama'll appreciate it when she hears it. No one will let harm come to Mama." She was still having nightmares.

▼

It took weeks for news of the insurrection to reach Simbayo. The change of governments had made no difference to them. Rose had announced, "I quite like the idea of the people governing themselves, but I know so little about it." This was everyone's view.

Drums along the river relayed the message that armed rebels were sweeping through the countryside, annihilating anything that had to do with Belgium or with Europeans.

Liliane thought to herself, but we're Americans, not realizing she was the only American among them. Forgetting she had not seen America in thirty-three years. Not realizing it didn't matter; she was white.

It wasn't until the farthest outpost sent an SOS. It began with a cry—a scream that rent the airwaves—and Anne, one of the nurses there, crying into the microphone, "We're done for. Don't come to help." Then silence. Dead silence. Dead. Liliane and Rose and Heidi stared at each other.

"Oh, dear Gott," Heidi said.

Three days later, the doctor and his wife who were at the Detroit outpost appeared in their pirogue. They were a couple in their early sixties and had found the Congo harder than they had imagined, but they stuck it out for the second year. The doctor's wife stared straight ahead, seeing nothing, hearing nothing.

"They killed every patient we had," he said hoarsely. "They raped them *after* they killed them. Even the men." His voice had no life. "They killed the little children, too."

"Oh, why?" cried Rose. "They're not white. I thought they're only angry at the whites."

"They're out for blood. Marauders with an excuse to kill. They're going to eliminate anything or anyone who's had anything to do with white people. They set fire to the hospital and all of the outbuildings." He sat down on the dock and wept. "We escaped because we'd been out in the field gathering yams for dinner and they didn't see us."

"Should we leave?" asked Rose.

"And go which way?" Liliane asked. "We'd stand no chance in the jungle. Of course I'm not going. Where would you go, Rose?" Her voice was sharp.

"They'll kill all of your help and your patients and anyone who ever helped you or knows you," the doctor said.

Liliane was already trying to figure how to save them. She had to get the natives away from Simbayo. Take the patients with them, be absorbed into the villages.

When the armed rebels arrived, they would find only the whites. And they would take into consideration all that they had done for the natives for over thirty years. They would not kill four white women and two old men. She looked at Heidi. Old women. We are all old, she thought. Heidi and Rose must be sixty-five or more. I'm the youngest of the lot, and I'm fifty-four. It depressed her at the same time she felt reassured. What purpose would it serve to kill people as old as they? The marauders would pass right by Simbayo once they saw there were no patients, no help, just a bunch of old people.

Anoka and Naldani refused to leave.

"Don't be heroic," Liliane pleaded. "It will just be for a short time. Go back to Naldani's village. When this is all over, we will gather again. I'm sure it won't last more than a few weeks. What good will you be to me dead?"

Anoka's grizzled gray hair was the only sign of aging in the still handsome man, but Naldani, once so beautiful, now covered her sagging breasts with blouses sent from America. Her hair was streaked with gray, and wrinkles covered her face. Her walk, however, was still regal and she held herself erect. Liliane was aware that over the years she had slowed more quickly than even Rose and Heidi, who were still marvelously efficient. None of them could attack as much each day as they had years ago, but now they had much more help.

Liliane would have to do something about all of that help. The three teachers, who were young. Oh God, young white women. How could she hide them? How to advise all of the outposts to take cover? And where? Was there any place that was safe?

She could not ask the natives to take white people to the outlying villages with them, could not ask them to hide the whites. If discovered, it meant certain annihilation. She would think of that after all of the patients were dispersed, when only the white people were left.

It took three days and much cajoling to persuade the natives to leave; they had worked and lived at Simbayo for so long they did not belong to tribes anymore. Yet Liliane knew their tribes would always take them back and welcome whomever they brought with them.

By Friday night only the three young teachers, the old doctor and his disoriented wife, and Rose, Heidi, Philippe, and Liliane were left.

"There's nothing to do but wait," observed Philippe, whose

calm gave them all courage. "Perhaps they won't even come here. But if they do, we shall be waiting for them. I do not want to go anywhere else."

"I couldn't stand to hide in the jungle," said Heidi.

"What will we do if they torture us?" Rose asked.

Liliane couldn't imagine that. "They're not going to torture us, Rose," she said, as though speaking to a frightened child. "What would be the purpose?"

The old doctor looked at Liliane.

At noon on Saturday, a band of natives marched out of the forest. There were nearly twenty of them, smeared with yellow, red, and white paint, carrying shields. They halted before the dining hall, where the Simbayans had gathered.

The leader stepped forward. He was a tall man in his late forties with a commanding presence. His arms were covered with bracelets, his ankles surrounded with feathers. His headdress was half again as tall as he, gaudily decorated with stones and brilliant plumage.

Liliane motioned for the others to stay where they were as she walked from the darkened room into the bright sunlight to do battle. She straightened her shoulders and stepped with more confidence than she felt.

The leader crossed his arms and stared at her. "You white mother?"

Liliane nodded, afraid to trust her voice.

"You not look like white mother."

"I am," she said, hoping her voice sounded firm.

"We have come to take you away."

"We're not leaving. This is our home."

"It will be burned. You will be killed. We have come to take you away."

Something dug at Liliane's memory. Then, with a flash of recognition that had been stored in her memory for twenty years, she looked at the headdress.

"You are Nkunda."

A smile warmed the man's face.

"You saved my life once, many years ago. It is my turn to repay you."

She wanted to hug him. Instead, she said, "There are nine of us."

"Hurry. We do not waste time. It is a long journey."

Liliane thought of the old couple. "We have two who can't walk that far."

Nkunda indicated they were prepared for that by gesturing toward two litters.

Liliane packed the few things she thought she might need. Along with her penicillin supply, she packed the carved ivory elephant Nkunda had given her and the jeweled comb from Saigon that Marsh had brought her so many years ago. She also took Baxter's Bible.

She turned and took one last look at the place that had been her home for more than thirty-two years. Would she ever see it again? she wondered. And where was she heading now?

CHAPTER 40

▼

"To survive with dignity is not enough. We owe it to ourselves and to each other to give to life the most of which we are capable."

Carolyn and Andrew sat glued to the television set watching Marsh accept the world's most prestigious literary prize. Andrew reached for Carolyn's hand as he noticed a single tear start down her cheek. She sniffed.

"He's photogenic," Andrew commented.

"I wish Mama could see it." Carolyn's voice was choked. "It was a lovely speech."

"You knew it would be."

"Of course." She squeezed his hand and wiped away the tear, sniffling again. "My father."

Andrew rose from the flowered-chintz couch and flipped the dial. "C'mon, let's get dressed. The Elliots will be here in less than an hour."

"Let me stop in the kitchen and see how dinner's coming."

"What would you do about it if it weren't coming?" Andrew wore an amused smile.

"You're right. It's not my bailiwick, is it? But let me remind Lobengula of the time."

Andrew and Carolyn showered and changed into formal evening clothes, stopped in the children's rooms, and kissed them good night. They were just starting on whiskey sours when the Elliots rang the bell.

Michelle reminds me of a pale rose, thought Carolyn. In her favorite shades of pink, Michelle always looked innocent, always passive. She never tried to be dramatic, talking in her soft, hesitant voice, urging others to do the speaking. When she did interject herself into the conversation, she spoke in non sequiturs, often talking of topics that had nothing to do with the subject at hand or rambling on until the listener had no idea what the subject was. She personalized all topics.

Yet Carolyn enjoyed her. "She's out in left field," she told Andrew. "Yet I find myself fond of her. She doesn't have a mean bone in her body. There's much of the little girl about her."

"You know what the rumors are, don't you?" he asked, tying his tie.

"Do you believe them?" she queried.

"I dunno. One hears them everywhere."

Carolyn nodded to her reflection in the mirror, her wedgwood blue dress turning her eyes dark. "I'm so fond of Sam I hate to think they're true. When would she have time to do . . . those things?"

"Not *those* things," Andrew corrected. "The same thing with so many."

"She only feels worthwhile when she's desired by a man."

"Do you think it matters what man?"

Carolyn pinched his arm playfully. "Going to volunteer? Find out if there's truth to them thar rumors?"

He leaned down and brushed his lips against her cheek. "I have no need to. She can't possibly be as exciting as you. In fact, as sexual as she comes across, I wonder if she *is* exciting."

"Oh, you wonder that, do you?"

"I imagine she's quite conventional."

"You mean only the missionary position?"

Andrew looked at her abruptly, his eyes dancing. "Where in the world do you learn such things?"

"I get around."

THE DRUMS TOLD THEM THAT SOLDIERS WERE BUT ONE DAY BEHIND. Nkunda was impatient at the slowness of the procession. Neither the doctor nor his wife could walk far, and Heidi and Rose could not keep up with the natives. It was all Liliane and Philippe could do to keep pace. The three young teachers were in the best shape, but they were also the most frightened. A trip that twenty years ago had taken Liliane a day and night of hard walking now took three and a half days.

When they finally reached Nkundo's village, he called together the tribal elders. They, along with Liliane, who was the only Simbayan who spoke their language, consulted about what to do now. The oldest man, his hands gnarled so badly they had difficulty opening, said, "I have been thinking of this all day and all night since you left. We shall bury them until the soldiers pass through here."

"Bury?" Liliane shuddered.

He turned to her. "We shall dig trenches where you can hide, then we shall lay branches across the openings and then sod on top of that so it will look as though it is part of the earth. There will be a crack so you can breathe but not be seen. And there will be no trace of you. They will not doubt us."

The men of the village began to dig four square gullies six feet deep, widely separated from each other. It was not an easy job in jungle soil that was crisscrossed with roots everywhere; it took the better part of the day. Gourds of water were lowered into the trenches.

Nkunda told Liliane, "We have guards posted. They will warn us when anyone approaches. You will be safe here. But there must be absolute silence."

Liliane nodded, translating for her fellow Simbayans. She was thinking, What ye sow ye shall reap. This man, Nkunda, whom she hadn't even thought of in twenty years, was endangering not only himself but his whole tribe to help her and her friends.

Nkunda wanted each of the young teachers to be in a different trench. "I am sure you will be safe. But in case there is some mistake and they are found, three young women . . ."

He did not need to elucidate.

So Margaret was assigned to the trench with Dr. and Mrs. Colter. Heidi would go with Rose. Sally and Liliane would be in the third trench. Philippe and Nancy would occupy the fourth.

At dawn the next morning, a runner informed them that a band of soldiers with guns was a two-hour march from the village. To be on the safe side, Nkunda insisted that the Simbayans be lowered into the trenches. As Liliane started to jump into her trench, she heard Heidi, over by the edge of the forest, crying, "I can't do it." She ran over to her friends of thirty-two years.

Rose was looking distraught. Liliane put a hand on her arm. Heidi shook it off.

"I am not scared of the soldiers," Heidi said. "I am afraid of the trench. If they put a top on this, I shall go insane."

Liliane had forgotten about Heidi's claustrophobia.

"Heidi," she whispered, "hold on to Rose. You won't smother in here. You'll be all right."

But the woman began to shake uncontrollably. Not since the day she had heard of Baxter's death had Liliane ever seen Heidi lose her composure.

"I can't help it, Liliane," she said, her teeth chattering. "It is like a disease. I cannot control it."

"Can you stand heights?" Liliane asked.

Heidi nodded affirmatively. "Anything but closed-in places."

Liliane waved from deep inside the trough. Nkunda walked over. "My friend cannot stand to be in here. Could she climb up a tree and hide in the foliage?"

Nkunda looked at Heidi and Liliane, then shook his head back and forth in rapid little shakes.

"Here he is offering to save my life, and I am not gracious enough to accept," Heidi said, between gritted teeth. "I am so ashamed."

"Don't be embarrassed." Liliane put an arm around her friend. She bartered further with the chief. Finally, he reached up an arm and pointed at a tree. Then he gestured for Heidi to follow. Heidi climbed the tree with surprising agility. Liliane turned to Rose. "Do you want to come with Sally and me?"

"No." Rose nodded. "I'll be all right here alone."

Liliane returned to her trench, where Sally sat forlornly, looking up out of the darkness. Liliane climbed in, and two natives laid branches across the opening above her; on top of that, great sods of earth were placed. It was dark, silent, and dank.

"Are you there?" she heard Sally's voice ask.

"Yes."

They sat there, Liliane's arms around her pulled-up knees, her ears straining for any sound. A tiny ray of light sifted through the crack of sod but did not illuminate the pit.

How many hours later it was, she could not tell. But the soldiers came screaming with a lust for blood. They wanted victims.

With difficulty, Liliane unraveled herself from her sitting position, trying to peer out through the narrow crack. At first she could see nothing; then, by squinting her eyes, she could perceive fuzzy outlines.

The soldiers were in dirty and wrinkled khaki uniforms. Rifles and ammunition belts were slung over their shoulders. Around their waists were pistol belts and cartridges. In their hands, they carried knives and machetes. They were bent on destruction.

Fortunately, this village was far enough from Simbayo that there would be no suspicion of white fraternization, thought Liliane.

She could see Nkunda going through the formal gestures of welcome, but even with her furry vision she could tell the soldiers were impatient. Nkunda waved his arms and the women of the tribe brought out calabashes of palm oil wine, signifying hospitality. Staked out around the edge of the village, in positions that gave the appearance of lethargy, were Nkunda's warriors. A few mingled with Nkunda and the soldiers so that nothing would look suspicious.

Before the soldiers could make demands, the women of the village brought out great platters piled high with food. Nkunda seated himself in the center of the village and gestured for the soldiers to follow his example. Satiated with food and drink, they would be sent happily on their way. Oh, what a smart man, Liliane thought, filled with admiration.

"What can you see?" whispered Sally.

"Shh," Liliane answered.

She stared through the crack until her legs could stand no more. Then she sank down, her shoulders rubbing against the damp earth.

Again in the dark, there was no way to gauge the passing of time. But she climbed up against the earth again when she heard shouting. What she saw was terrible to behold.

"Oh, God," she said aloud. Her blood turned to ice water.

A soldier was pulling Heidi into the circle of rebels. One reached up and poked her with a finger. Cheering went up from his compatriots.

Three other soldiers immediately jumped up. Liliane stared in frozen silence as she watched them attach leather thongs to Heidi's arms and wrists.

Heidi did not shout, nor did she writhe, but stood with dignity, and though she could not see clearly, Liliane suspected Heidi was glaring at the soldiers with contempt. One of them kicked at her knees, and she collapsed onto the ground.

Then, amid laughter and shouting, each of the four soldiers backed off, pulling Heidi's limbs in four directions, stretching her out slowly and painfully. Liliane's hand rose to her mouth to keep herself from screaming. Oh, dear God, she thought. Don't let this be happening.

The German woman lay spread-eagled on the ground as the leather thongs grew taut, as first one soldier and then another jerked her arm or her leg, waiting for her to cry out. She remained silent. In unison, they stepped backward, the cords stretching her limbs beyond ordinary human limits.

Then, with a piercing shriek, Rose ran from her hiding place, crying in a thin, high-pitched wail, "Heidi, Heidi!"

As she ran toward her friend, a soldier turned and threw his arm out in front of Rose. She ran straight into his machete; her body propelled itself onward, while her head shot through the air and landed in the lap of a soldier who was drinking palm wine. Then Heidi screamed.

CHAPTER 41

▼

SOMEONE WAS STARING AT HER, SHE KNEW. SHE FOUGHT TO OPEN HER eyes.

Concentrating, she felt her eyelids pulsate weakly.

If I give one gigantic push, she thought, they'll open. Focusing all her energy, she succeeded only in fluttering them erratically.

Closed.

A void.

Maybe she didn't want to open them. Didn't want to see. She lay there, listening.

Soft murmurings. Rustling. The sound skirts make when swishing . . . a woman walking . . .

A woman walking? Skirts swishing? With no effort at all, Liliane's eyes flew open.

A white ceiling.

A black face thrust itself above her, white teeth surrounded by a wide smile.

"Awake, are you?" The eyes like coals came closer . . . peering at her.

Liliane screamed.

The black face jerked back, the wide grin gone.

"Now, now . . ." A reassuring hand was put on her arm.

She felt the scream rather than heard it. Her body rigid, the noise poured from her, a high-pitched bloodcurdling wail.

She waited for the black face to—to what?

Then, a wide-brimmed white hat swept into view, looking ready to fly into the nether regions, taking the pinched, pale face under it up and away. "Shh," said the white face, the gray-green eyes mottled like a dirty sea.

But the black face didn't move. It looked down at Liliane as if in judgment. She heard her own voice still piercing the air.

A sharp jab in her arm. The room began to spin, the black face spiraling crazily in circles until the circles melded together into darkness.

The next time she awoke she knew it was twilight before she even opened her eyes. She lay there listening . . . to the call of a bird, a bright green bird with a purple head, she thought, and a red splash on its elongated tail. She could tell that the sun had sunk low in the heavens, knew that beyond the trees blood brushed the skies, gradually turned bright pink, tinged with heliotrope not yet turned blue. Below the brilliant palette, pale gold tinged the horizon.

It was peaceful. Serene in the cool evening air. There was no dampness or humidity.

Opening her eyes, she turned her head and saw a curtain undulating in a faint breeze.

Where am I? she wondered, without fear this time. Muffled night sounds drifted to her.

I'm in a bed with white sheets and curtains at the windows, she realized. Perhaps I'm safe. Safe from what, she wasn't sure.

"Ah, you are awake." A soft voice with a French accent made her turn her head. This time the tremendous, crisp white hat was held up by a tall, angular woman with dark eyes and a soft smile.

"Where am I?" Liliane was surprised at the weakness of her own voice.

"Bukavu," answered the nun.

The name meant nothing to Liliane.

"How long have I been here?" She stared intently at the kind face.

"Nearly ten days." The woman disappeared, but returned shortly with a cup of tea. Putting an arm under Liliane, she raised her shoulders while plumping her pillow. Then she held the cup to Liliane's lips.

The fresh night air washed over Liliane; she felt bathed in a thousand roses, though she knew roses did not grow in the Congo. Yet attar of roses filled her nostrils.

The woman scraped a chair across the floor and pulled it close to Liliane. Sitting down, she took Liliane's hand in hers and gazed at her.

"Do you know who you are?"

Of course, thought Liliane. Why wouldn't I? "Liliane Hathaway."

The nun continued to stare at her, a benevolent, surprised look in her dark eyes. She shook her head, quick, little back-and-forth movements. Squeezing Liliane's hand, she stood. "I'll be back in a moment."

Liliane watched the window darken as night quickly descended.

An armada of billowing, starched hats sailed gracefully into the room, the dark-clad forms underneath them floating, surrounding Liliane's bed. There were five of them. She had never seen such gigantic headgear. The nuns could not stand close to each other.

The nurse who had just been with her smiled, gesturing as she introduced each of them. "Sister Thérèse, Sister Brigitta, Sister Caterina, Sister Sophia, and I am Sister Marie-Hélène."

The youngest of them whispered, "Oh, madame, we never dreamed Mother Lili was with us."

Another said, "We heard a year ago that you had been killed."

A third said, "Madame, we are honored." A tear fell down her cheek. "You are alive!"

A year ago?

What had happened?

She closed her eyes. Try to think. Why did they imagine you dead? she asked herself.

Then, with rushing intensity, she saw Rose's head hurling through the air and her body running straight ahead before collapsing onto three khaki-clad soldiers, blood spattering onto the dusty leaves of the trees above.

"Oh, God," she cried aloud, her whole body convulsing in great spasmodic jerks.

MOONLIGHT POURED IN THROUGH THE CURTAIN. THE SMELL OF ROSES again surrounded her. Though she knew it could not be true, it was June in Buffalo, New York, and she was seventeen again.

She lay in the dark for a long time, her mind blank, studying the shadows of the night, deliberately trying to keep her mind away from memories. But she kept seeing Rose's head.

The nun had told her that it had happened a year ago. What had happened to her since? Lying on the soft bed between the clean white sheets, in the cool night air, she tried to remember, but nothing came to her. Her mind kept slipping away. She remembered Marsh telling her that someplace in the world "Stardust" was playing every minute of the day or night. His face obliterated all other memories.

Suddenly she realized what had triggered that memory. As though floating across water, she heard the faint strains of an orchestra playing that song, heard a trumpet crooning until it curled around her and sank under her skin. Wherever I may be, wherever Bukavu is, "Stardust" is playing in the middle of the night. She lay there, straining to hear the song. When it faded, there was no noise, none at all. She wondered if she had imagined it.

If I've been here ten days, she asked herself, where was I before that? She cleared her mind of all thought and waited for memory to come to her. And waited.

I wonder where Bukavu is, she thought. If I knew where it was, maybe I'd know how I came here. It's somewhere where they know me, where they know French and English. Someplace where nuns run a hospital.

Try as she could to recapture recent memories, her mind kept turning only to Marsh. "Stardust" had thrust Marsh into her mind. Now he had captured her heart, and she could think of nothing else.

She began to ache with hunger for him. If he were here, she'd be all right, even if she remembered. If Marsh were here, she wouldn't be afraid.

Why have I never married him? she wondered. Now, nothing seemed more important. If I ever get out of here, she thought, if I live . . . if I escape . . . I'll marry Marsh. I'll ask him to take care of me. It's what he's always offered. Why did I spend so many years away from him and Carolyn? Why did I deny myself?

In her imagination, she saw Carolyn as a young girl, sitting on the verandah at Marsh's Cape Town house, doing homework, drinking a glass of milk. Liliane came out of the house with a plate of freshly baked cookies. Carolyn's face lit up with delight, and she grabbed one. Liliane sat down on the rocking chair next to her daughter and together they laughed. Carolyn asked, "What does pi r squared mean?"

Marsh came around the corner of the house. "What's all this laughing?" he asked, waving his cane. "May I join you?" He walked up the three steps, scooped a cookie into his mouth, and, crumbs on lips, put his arms around Liliane and Carolyn. "My girls," he said. "What a family."

Liliane heard herself sigh aloud.

Memories of what might have been were clearer to her than what had been.

She tried to make sense of what she *could* remember. She thought of meeting Baxter, and that was very clear. She tried to remember Jack, and it was as if it were yesterday. She thought of Naldani and Anoka. Of the last time Petelo had been home. She even remembered he was one of only thirty Congolese in a university. She could clearly remember the time she and Marsh and Caro had visited Egypt; she could see the Sphinx and the dark tombs. She remembered how she had felt the day she read her aunt's letter telling of her parents' deaths. She remembered the day Marsh sent her the airplane. She recalled the hernia operation in the dark of a stormy night. Nkunda, that was his name. So many years ago . . . Nkunda, hadn't he appeared at Simbayo to help her?

She turned her attention to the muffled noises she was beginning to hear. Footsteps in the hall, instruments rattling against each other. A rooster crowing. In the distance, a man's voice calling.

In total stillness, her mind blank and receptive, she became part of the dawn. She could not continue to think; her thoughts ultimately led to remembering Heidi spread-eagled in the sun and Rose's head spewing forth blood as it arched over the soldiers.

One of the tremendous white hats swept into her room, and Sister Thérèse—or was it Sister Caterina?—smiled beatifically. "Well, and are we better this morning?" Her voice sounded like the strings of a harp. "Perhaps we can sit up for breakfast this morning." She glided a hand under Liliane's shoulders and, with amazing agility, hoisted her upright. "I imagine we'd like our face washed, wouldn't we?" The nun whipped a washcloth from a basket beside her and Liliane felt cool wetness refresh her. She hadn't yet said anything, though she tried a weak smile.

Sister Thérèse or Caterina plunged another pillow behind her and gently helped her to a sitting position. "There, there, isn't that nice," she fluttered. "Breakfast will be here soon and then we'll be feeling stronger and maybe we can take a little walk later. Wouldn't that be nice?"

Liliane nodded. The thought of walking was more than she could conceive.

The nurse turned to leave, but Liliane said, "Wait. Where am I?"

"Why, we're at the mission hospital of Our Lady of Francesca in Bukavu."

"Where *is* Bukavu?"

"Oh, my." The nun looked at her. "Do you know you're in Africa?"

Liliane nodded. Of course. "But where?"

"We're on Lake Kivu." When she noticed the blank look on Liliane's face, she came back to the bed. "Do you know how you got here?"

Liliane shook her head. "No."

"Lake Kivu is on the eastern border of the Congo. Pardon me, Zaire."

"Zaire?"

"That's what the nationalists have named it. Even the river. Across the lake, to the east, is Rwanda."

What's Rwanda? Liliane wondered. "Why is there no humidity? I don't feel the jungle."

"No." The sister laughed kindly. "Bukavu is nearly a mile high, the days are cool and the nights are chilly. The lake is surrounded by mountains, and the slopes are forested quite like yours in Michigan, which I visited as a child. We're on the south end of the lake, but the north end is ringed by volcanos, and sometimes at night, great, low-lying clouds glow red from the heat smoldering within the great cones. It's quite beautiful.

"Wives and children come to Bukavu from Stanleyville in the rainy season. I'll never learn to call it Kisangani." Her gentle laugh erupted again. "There are a number of lovely resort hotels here, and the swimming and boating is wonderful."

Stanleyville. The name rang a bell, but Liliane didn't recognize it. She thought it was on rapids of the Congo but couldn't remember. And why would she remember rapids? She had never been to eastern Africa.

"Thank you," she said.

The sister turned and glided from the room, her hat looking for all the world like a three-masted schooner.

I'm in eastern Congo, puzzled Liliane. How in the world did I get here? What's happened to me in the past year?

As she asked herself this, her gaze rested on her thin left arm. Large white welts covered it, as though she'd been raked by a wild animal. She looked at the arm impersonally. Certainly, she thought, I should remember how that happened. The nurse in her recognized that whatever had happened to her arm must have been excruciatingly painful. It also had happened enough months ago that it had healed with permanent scars. It had not healed by itself, either, but had been medicated and tended by an expert. She tried, in vain, to remember.

In the afternoon, Sister Marie-Hélène came to her and pulled a chair by the bed. "Would you like to talk a little?" she asked.

"I don't seem to remember what's happened in the last year."

The nun nodded. "That's understandable. I think you've been in shock. You're trying to block out what you don't want to remember."

"Is that it?"

"What's the last thing you remember?"

Liliane told her. The sister grimaced. "I suspect you have had some very bad things happen to you." She gestured to the scars on Liliane's arm. "Perhaps I can help by telling you what's happened to the Congo in the last year and a half. Murder and mayhem. The white people are paying for the way Belgium and the slave traders have treated these people for the last hundred years. What ye sow ye shall reap," she whispered as though to herself. "Africa is a contradiction. Take Stanleyville. It's a delightful modern city, drenched in the scent of jasmine and mimosa. Pastel-colored office and apartment buildings, an aura of sophistication.

"In the villages nearby, and in some of the sections of Stanleyville itself, the practice of witchcraft flourishes, and cannibalism, and ritualistic murder. We suspect that is how your arm . . ." She shrugged her shoulders, her voice fading away.

When she resumed, she said, "There's a society of tribesmen known as the Anyoto, the Leopard Men. They carry out savage, senseless murders at night. No one knows where or why they will strike. Though this has been going on for years, no one knows anything about it. They fasten steel claws to their hands, then, howling like leopards themselves, they fall on children or women or old men—never able-bodied men—and rake them to death."

Liliane shivered. This was not the Congo she knew.

"Since the revolution, it has been even worse. The Simba warriors who have come up from Katanga province pour out of the jungle, devouring everything in their path. It is just a matter of time until they arrive here. A General Olenga leads the Simbas, and anything or anyone connected with white people is doomed. A Congolese who wears glasses is pinned to a stake and left to rot because he is contaminated by the white man's ways."

"Why do you stay?" asked Liliane.

Sister Marie-Hélène shrugged her shoulders, and the hint of a smile played in her eyes. "We did not come just for the better times," she said. "How can *you* ask that? You stayed."

Liliane shook her head. "No, I left. I left Simbayo."

"Before you had to?"

"No, not until the last minute."

"Well, perhaps we will leave then. Or hide. Or cross the border to Rwanda. But General Olenga and his Simbas are not in Bukavu yet. Fortunately, we are likely to be warned. Stanleyville is three hundred miles away over a road that is not conducive to quick travel. For the time being, you—and we—are safe."

Liliane's head rested against the pillow. She felt extraordinarily tired. "How long have you been here?" she asked.

"The mission has been here since the end of the last century," responded the nun. "I have been here for six years. Not nearly as long as you have been out here."

"What year is it?" asked Liliane.

"It is 1962, May 1962."

"I left Simbayo in late 1960, I think," Liliane said. "Or early '61. I don't remember."

"Do you remember anything?"

Liliane closed her eyes. Sister Marie-Hélène sat there even when she wondered if Liliane had fallen asleep.

What Liliane remembered most of all was Marsh. I want to be with him, she thought. I want his arms around me. I want him to tell me everything is all right. I want him to . . .

A skull impaled on a long spike. She saw it clearly, as though her eyes were open and she was there. A human skull with its empty sockets staring at her, some ragged, dried flesh clinging to the blanched bones, the black hair still flopping in the breeze, gigantic ants climbing up the stake, marching across the skull in a straight line, a never-ending cabal of ants disappearing into the cracks of what had once been human. . . .

She felt a soft hand on her scarred arm; the scars felt nothing, dead flesh. But she was aware of the nun's reassuring pressure and realized she was shaking again. Not convulsively, this time, but a tremor that she could not stop.

LILIANE STAYED AT THE MISSION IN BUKAVU FOR SIX WEEKS. Gradually, she regained her strength. She wanted to send a message to Marsh, to let him know she was alive, but no telephone lines worked and the borders were closed. How would she get away? "I want to marry Marsh," she said aloud to herself. If it's the last thing I do, I want that. He can help me through this remembering. When there's something I can't face, he'll help me. He'll hold me in his arms and I'll know I'm safe. No matter what my memories bring to me, I can stand it if Marsh is there to protect me.

She walked through the mission's rose garden and gazed out at the forested slopes of the surrounding mountains. She inhaled deeply of the fresh clear air. She walked down to the shores of the lake and stared across it, seeing the purple mountains of Rwanda in the distance. She watched the ancient wooden boats glide across the water, the fishermen gracefully casting nets, pulling in their catches—a way of life, like all of the Africa she knew, that had continued from the beginning of time. She watched the African women, their turbanned heads bright with color, walking erectly to town, passing the mission with chickens squawking in cages, with jewelry dangling from their ears or encasing their ankles, surrounded by children who ran back and forth across the road in front of them. These African women seemed far more worldly than those she had known in Simbayo.

She had lived in Simbayo for so long she had taken it for granted that all of the Congo was like her small portion of the world.

She ate her meals with the sisters, who were curious about Simbayo. Sister Sophia told Liliane, "When I was a young girl, I read about you. After that, I never dreamed of anything but coming here, following in your footsteps."

"How much of the world you have influenced," murmured Sister Marie-Hélène.

It was not for a long time that Liliane dared to face a mirror. She was dismayed at what she saw. Her hair, its bright auburn now flecked with gray, the ribbon that flowed from her left temple now pure white, hung limply to her shoulders, too long to give life to the curls she knew were still there. She looked emaciated, her cheekbones jutting below sunken eyes that stared back blankly at her. When she said she yearned for a haircut, Sister Brigitta volunteered, and Liliane's short curls reappeared, but she still was not used to seeing herself so gray. The only bright spots of color were her blue-green eyes, still vibrant and startling—even more so in such a pallid face.

"How will I get out of here if the borders are closed?" she asked Sister Marie-Hélène.

"There are ways. I do not think you are strong enough yet. Once you leave here, you will have to walk for many miles, hundreds of miles."

The thought left Liliane exhausted. It was all she could do to walk down to the lake's edge and stare at the blue sky's reflection, now and then watching a cloud scud across the mirror of lake.

Her memories of the last year came back in bits and spurts. When she concentrated on remembering, nothing came to her. Then she thought of Marsh. She thought of him all the time.

But one night, and she never knew whether it was a dream or a memory, she was in Stanleyville. She knew that's where she was because of Sister Marie-Hélène's description of the pastel office buildings and the boulevards lined with palms and mangoes and the number of white people in the city. She was part of a frenzied mob that had gathered in a lovely little park ringed with coconut palms that swayed in the warm tropical breezes. The park was behind the post office, and there was a square in the center surrounded by pretty red flowers.

A tall, fat black man in an ill-fitting uniform dragged a man to the square.

"This man has worked for white men all his life," screamed the man in uniform. "Is he guilty?"

"Guilty," the crowd screamed.

The man in uniform stepped back, and as he did so, the victim's body was riddled with bullets. Liliane saw a squad of Simba warriors in the front line of the crowd. They kept on firing until the body had been shattered to ribbons. The pieces were kicked to the background.

Another victim was hauled before the crowd. His sin was that he had graduated from high school and could read. Blood spurted onto the uniforms of the guards who fired and onto the bloodred flowers.

Liliane watched as this went on, over and over, for an hour or more. The last man had been long recognized for his powerful position. Collapsed was the missionary work of decades, as something as ancient as Africa stirred the crowd into a frenzy; the man in charge took a long knife and pierced the man's side, tearing the liver from his body while he stood there. As the victim collapsed onto the wooden platform, bloody pieces of his liver were snatched up and devoured; triumphant screams rent the air. Now the cannibals had acquired the victim's lost power.

The next morning Liliane was so twisted in her sheets that the nuns had to help extricate her. All morning she sat at the window staring out, seeing a fringe of the lake over the expanse of lawn, wondering if she had really experienced the massacre at Stanleyville.

When she finally became restless, she realized it was time to move on. She could not stay cloistered forever in the cocoon of Our Lady of Francesca.

Sister Marie-Hélène told her, "We have someone who can take you as far as Lake Victoria, which is two hundred miles to the east. But from there we can be of no help. You'll have to cross the lake, and that costs money—walking around would take many weeks longer—and find your way to Nairobi. Once you're in Nairobi, it will cost you more money to eat and to sleep. I don't know how to be of help then. What will you do?"

Liliane didn't have an answer. All she knew was that she had to head toward Marsh. Most of each day was spent thinking about him, remembering the first time she saw him, reminiscing about living in his house on the promontory, listening to his typewriter keys clacking into the night, watching his eyes as they lit on Carolyn, remembering the stories he wrote for the children. Feeling the touch of his hands on her, the security of his arms around her, the excitement of his lips on hers. The way he could look not only at her but into her; the way he used words in the books he wrote; the way shadows flickered across his cheeks under a palm tree; his long, tapering, graceful fingers, his gravelly voice. He had become an obsession.

She knew that when she could get to him, she would be safe. Then she could let herself remember, force herself to face the memories, so that a year of her life would not be obliterated. She dared not let herself recall that year until Marsh was beside her.

She walked out of the mission one predawn morning with Munir, an Arab who spoke a little English, a good deal of French, Swahili, and several lesser dialects. He did not speak Bantu, so their conversation was limited to what he could communicate and understand of English. It was a silent trip that began in an old rowboat while the stars still glittered in a dark sky. By the time he had rowed to an island, it was nearly noon. They hid the boat in a cove and slept under the trees. When the half-moon was high in the night sky, they started out again across the choppy water. It was not until the next evening that they reached Rwanda. The Arab had rowed constantly, never showing signs of tiring, his stern face never smiling, his dark eyes unreadable.

It took them twenty-one days to walk through the mountains of Rwanda and the northern slice of Tanganyika before Liliane beheld the body of water that was called Lake Victoria. Here, Munir arranged for her passage on a motorboat. From here on, Liliane was on her own.

She was far stronger now than when they'd left Bukavu. Tanned from days spent walking through the mountains and across the high savannah, Liliane had gained strength each day. At first, her muscles had hurt so badly she thought she could go no farther. The patient, inscrutable Munir had slowed his pace and the number of miles to be covered each day, and because she never complained, she could see a grudging respect come into their relationship. By the fifth day, though one could never call him loquacious, he began to point out places of interest. With no seeming difficulty, he arrived at villages in time for supper and lodging. No one turned him down. Sometimes nomads made them welcome and served them goat meat and side dishes Liliane could not recognize. There was never enough food to grow fat on, but her muscles grew strong and her stamina increased, and by the time she and Munir parted, he didn't have to slow his pace for her at all.

Though they learned nothing about each other, she grew enormously fond of him. His silence did not offend her but left her free to absorb the scenery and this new experience.

When he paid the captain of the boat from a small purse he pulled from the voluminous folds of his dusty clothing, Munir's eyes flashed warmth for the first time. "Madame"—he bent over in the French fashion and kissed her hand—"it has been a rare pleasure."

CHAPTER 42

▼

TWO THOUSAND SEVEN HUNDRED AND FIFTY MILES AWAY, SHE HEARD the phone ringing. Please, God, she prayed, let him be there.

She heard the purr again. Still no answer.

On the third ring, Marsh answered. At his "Hello," her throat closed. She had thought she'd never hear that wonderful rough sound again. She opened her mouth to speak and nothing came out.

"Hello?" he said again. Static quivered through the telephone lines.

She said, "I'm hoping you're still interested in marriage." She was so overwhelmed with emotion at hearing his voice that she had to sit.

There was no sound from the other end.

Then, "Lili?"

She began to cry. "Oh, Marsh." Tears filled the air, choking sobs hurling themselves to Cape Town.

"Lili. Oh, Lili. My God. Where are you?"

"I'm in Nairobi. The American embassy's put me up in a hotel. How soon can you get here?"

"Lili. Are you all right? I'll be there as soon as I can get a plane. Lili. Tell me. Are you all right?"

"No." Her crying tapered off, though her voice remained jagged. "I'm not all right. I need you. Marsh, all I've thought of for months is that if I got out of there I'd marry you. I want us to spend the rest of our lives together. Oh, Marsh." The tears started again.

"Lili. I'll be there within twenty-four hours."

"Marsh, I look awful. I'm old and gray. I've no clothes to wear and no money to buy any. And Marsh—oh, I need you so badly."

"Darling, I'm coming. As fast as I can. Lili, you're alive!"

"I'm going to bed and sleep. I'm going to sleep until you get here. Hurry, Marsh. Oh, please hurry."

"Lili. My love. I'm coming. I'll take care of you."

You've always wanted to, she thought. "Yes, yes, I want you to. Oh, hurry, Marsh. Come to me."

She placed the phone back on its cradle and collapsed on the bed. It was so soft, so clean. So . . .

She slept for over fourteen hours. When she awoke, the stars were fading from their black background into the pale gold-pink of early morning. She lay motionless, staring out the window, watching the sky. The stars gradually disappeared; the brilliant pink of dawn trumpeted across the heavens, fading into the milky blue of a Kenya summer sky.

Early-morning sounds sent the city up through her open window. Horns began to blare; she heard someone crying out. Rising, she looked down upon Nairobi—for a minute not remembering where she was. Automobiles careened around corners; already carts were being pushed along the streets. Liliane thought it far more dangerous than the jungle. She looked out over the trees at the tall buildings and saw the edge of the city, saw the plain stretching out to where the hills began.

It must be about seven or seven-thirty, she thought, judging from the dawn. She looked at her bed. The sheets were so white. She had slept with her arms curled around one of the soft pillows. Through the walls, she heard the sound of flushing in the next bathroom. Flushing. Running water.

Like a somnambulist, she walked into the bathroom. Porcelain white was reflected from every corner. She ran her hands over the smoothness of the sink. Turned on the faucet. Luxuries she had forgotten. A bath. That's what she'd have. A long, warm bath to get rid of the kinks. To wash away the grime. She'd planned to bathe as soon as she'd spoken to Marsh, but sleep had overcome her. A bath. What a lovely thought.

She immersed herself in the full tub, letting the warm water soak into her. If I were a cat, she thought, I'd purr. Nothing could feel more wonderful than this does. Closing her eyes, she sighed. It had been six weeks since she had left Bukavu.

She knew she should phone Carolyn. I'll do it as soon as I finish bathing, she told herself. She dunked her head under the water to rinse out the soap.

She looked down at her naked body, at its spareness. She was thinner than she'd ever been, yet there was a hard leanness to her; her months of walking had tightened her muscles. I'm skinny, she thought. And old. I'm fifty-six years old, my skin looks like leather, my hands are veined like an ancient crone's, and I'm tired. I'm so tired. In the mirror yesterday she had observed crow's-feet around her eyes; there was a tenseness to her mouth that had never been there in the past. Her cheeks had a sunken look; her eyes were haunted.

And I've just proposed to a man! She laughed at the irony. She imagined Marsh's hands touching her; the warm water lapping at her nipples were like his fingers upon her. She wondered if he would want to touch the body that hers had become. Would he not want to marry her now that she wanted it?

The terry cloth massaged her as she towel-dried herself. Everything *felt* so soft, so luxurious.

She looked at her ragged clothes lying on the chair. Certainly she couldn't walk around Nairobi in them. She hated to put them on next to her clean body. As she ran a hand through her hair, realizing she needed a comb, she heard a knock at the door.

Perhaps it was someone from the embassy; certainly it couldn't be Marsh yet.

But it was.

He stood there, taller and handsomer than ever: his silvered hair elegantly combed; his eyes behind glasses now but still a warm brown that leaped into her; the crinkles around his eyes; his right hand wrapped around his ubiquitous cane—the same one he had carried for over twenty years.

They stood in the doorway, looking into one another, unable to speak. Then their arms reached out, surrounding each other, and Liliane was pulled into him, felt the warmth and strength of Marsh embrace her, savored the brush of his lips against her ear, heard him murmur, "Lili, my Lili," as his lips searched for her. His lips touched hers and Liliane felt twenty-four again, felt a fire kindled within her, felt life seep back into her.

"Oh, Marsh," she whispered.

They stepped back into her room and he kicked the door closed. His hands framed her face as he said in a husky voice, "Let me look at you." He pulled back, searching her face, his hands never leaving her. His voice choking, his head shaking, he told her, "I shall never again doubt God."

She burrowed into him.

"Was it terrible?" he asked.

She nodded. "Don't make me talk about it now. Maybe later." Her body relaxed. The recent past faded. "But now, buy me breakfast."

He laughed out loud. "Oh, my darling. It is you. The first thing you think about is eating. I shall let you eat to your heart's content."

"Even if I get fat and ugly?"

"Even if you get fat. You could never be ugly."

He called room service, and Liliane gorged herself on orange juice, scones dripping with peach jam, scrambled eggs and ham, and three cups of coffee. Marsh joined her but mainly watched her stuff herself.

"Did you mean it last night?" he asked, unable to resist reaching out and brushing her arm lightly.

"I swore that if I ever got out of the jungle, all I wanted to do was spend the rest of my life with you. I want to live a nice normal existence and look up every evening and see you across the dinner table; and go into the library and read and look up and see you in the chair next to me; and never do anything in the whole world that doesn't include you."

Marsh sighed. "I may be thankful for whatever hell you've gone through."

"So you'll marry me?"

"Has there ever been a minute's doubt?"

Liliane smiled at him, loving him in the same way she had for the past thirty years. She leaned over to kiss him, peach jam sticking to his cheek. "Let's phone Caro. Do you want to fly to Salisbury and get married there?"

"I want to do it here. Now. Today. The first moment we can."

"Buy me a dress first," Liliane said through a mouthful of eggs. "In fact, I need a whole wardrobe. And comfortable shoes."

"We'll buy you a trousseau." Marsh laughed.

A trousseau at fifty-six. Liliane smiled. And he doesn't even care how I look.

His hand folded around hers. The look in his eyes told her he thought she was beautiful.

"I may never let you out of my sight again," he said softly.

"That's just where I want to be. Never out of your sight." She sipped the last of her coffee.

"Well, come on." Marsh stood and reached his hand down for her. "Let's go buy you some clothes. Wait. Wait a minute. We really should phone Caro first. Let her know you're safe."

Marsh put through the call.

A servant answered, and he asked for Carolyn. "It's her father."

Carolyn's voice was breathless. She'd been on her way out the door. "Papa?"

"Hello, darling. Wait a minute." He handed the phone to Liliane.

"Caro?"

There was silence. Then Carolyn asked hesitantly, "Mama? Mama, is that you?"

Liliane didn't trust her own voice. "I'm safe," she blurted out.

There was a moment's silence, and then Carolyn burst into tears. "Oh, Mama, you're safe." Carolyn's voice sounded as beautiful as anything she'd ever heard.

Liliane began to cry, too. Marsh reached for her hand and took the phone from her.

"We're getting married, honey."

"Oh, Papa." He could hear Carolyn sniffling. "When?"

"As soon as we can."

"Don't do it until I can get there, please." Then she laughed. "I don't even know where you are."

Marsh smiled. "Nairobi."

Carolyn's voice held incredulity. "How in the world . . . ?"

"We'll tell you when we see you."

"I'll get a plane as soon as I can, Papa. I can't today. Give me until tomorrow, will you?"

Marsh looked down at Liliane, who was sitting on the edge of the bed. "Caro's coming up."

"Don't make me legal until I get there, now, Papa, you hear?" Carolyn's voice crackled over the distance. "Let me speak to Mama again."

Marsh handed the receiver to Liliane.

"Mama, are you all right?"

"I'm fine," answered Liliane, though Carolyn could tell from her voice that this wasn't true. "I'm glad you're coming, Caro."

"Oh, Mama, the world's all right again."

Marsh insisted they go shopping. He bought Liliane far more clothing than she thought necessary. "That's what's fun," he said, pawing through a selection of silk underwear. It didn't embarrass him at all. "Being able to afford more than is necessary. Here, look at this . . . peach color." He brushed the gossamer silk softly against Liliane's cheek.

"I'm not in my twenties anymore." Liliane laughed.

"It's a state of mind," Marsh observed.

"Just two sets of underwear," Liliane said. "I'll buy more in Cape Town."

She would buy only one pair of shoes, sandals like the ones she had grown used to wearing over the years. A tailored skirt and shirtwaist were enough for her, but Marsh insisted on a dress of pale turquoise also. "To match your eyes," he said.

Then they went to learn about how to get married. A two-day wait was required. They filled out the necessary forms, and the young British civil servant, who waited on them, glanced up as soon as he noticed Marsh's name.

"Oh, Mr. Compson, sir, I'm honored, sir." His eyes had grown round. "I've never had anyone famous get married here. Can I help with any arrangements you might want?" He smiled brightly at Liliane.

"We just want whatever is easiest, quickest."

It's going to last forever, thought Liliane. I have already spent too much of forever away from Marsh.

The young man said he would arrange with the judge to perform the ceremony in two days, on Thursday. What time would they like?

Marsh turned to Liliane.

"Make it around ten," she said.

It was now nearly noon.

"I'm tired," Liliane apologized. "I seem to have left my stamina in the jungle."

"We'll go back to the hotel and you can rest. I'll order lunch sent to our room," said Marsh, slipping her hand through the crook of his arm and holding on to it.

After lunch, Liliane fell asleep. When she awoke, Marsh was next to her, leaning on an elbow, gazing at her.

"How can you be so beautiful, when I can but imagine what you've been through and when I know you're fifty-six?"

"Are you still going to marry me?" she asked, her eyes still caught with sleep.

"I am going to marry you," he conceded, "and it will be a long time before I will ever part with you. I don't want the world to share you yet. Soon they're going to have to know you're safe, but I want you to myself for a while."

"Caro's coming," she said, as though he didn't know. "Isn't that nice?"

"It is indeed." He squeezed her arm.

"Tell me about Caro," Liliane said, not even struggling to keep her eyes open.

"She's her mother's daughter." Liliane could hear the smile in Marsh's voice. "She is never happier than when she's working for a cause. She's happy. The children are delightful, though it's still too early to judge much about Justin. But Courtney's a charmer. Bright. Already inheriting your nursing instincts. Takes in all sorts of sick and wounded animals. Andrew's built her a compound near the garage, and you can find birds with splints on their wings, or a cat that's been scarred in a fight, or a baby leopard whose mother was shot."

Liliane felt Marsh's finger feathering across her eyelid. She opened one eye.

He leaned down and ran his tongue across her lips, softly yet urgently kissing her. "You can still drive a man crazy," he whispered into her ear.

In the late afternoon on the high plateau country of Kenya, in the African autumn of 1962, they made love with an urgency they had not known even in their early days together. Liliane felt beautiful again, as Marsh teased her close to a climax but stopped her just short of release. He did this to her over and over again until she was wild with desire, until she wanted him as she could not remember wanting anything in her entire life. Until she was aware again that she was fully alive. Until she felt physically well for the first time in over a year.

They lay wrapped in each other's arms after their long lovemaking. Marsh still had not asked her about her lost year, and Liliane had volunteered nothing. Nothing existed for her except the present. Nothing else could fit into her heart. "What a fool I've been," she murmured against his chest.

His arm around her tightened. "Don't think of the past," he whispered. "We have the rest of our lives. We'll make up for it. I'll keep you safe."

She knew he would.

They dined that night on chateaubriand, and Marsh ordered the most expensive wine to be had in all of Nairobi. Liliane's hungry gaze absorbed the life around her: the well-dressed men and women, the muted atmosphere of the restaurant, the ease of life. She wanted to clutch the evening to her, to live like this the rest of her life. At the same time, it seemed false, hedonistic, and shallow. I'm ready for this now, she thought. When she said it aloud, Marsh laughed.

"Time will tell."

She held out her arms and said, "I don't know if I remember how, but I remember the song. Dance with me?"

"Do you know, in all our years, we've never danced?" Marsh smiled. "I don't know if I remember how, either."

The small orchestra was playing "Stardust."

"I heard this playing in the middle of Africa, in a little town by a lake," she said, her head on his shoulder.

"I told you, this song is playing somewhere in the world every minute of the day or night."

"I can see why," she said as she hummed along with the orchestra.

When they sat down, he said, "Oh, I quite forgot. I've been so happy to see you I'd forgotten anything newsworthy had happened to me."

"You've written another book and it got the usual raves."

"That, too. But I received the Nobel Prize last year."

Liliane's fork clattered to her plate. "Oh, Marsh." Her eyes glistened.

They stared into each other; she knew what this meant to him. But he reached out a hand and put it over hers. "I couldn't enjoy it, Lili. I don't even know what I said there. I was so insane with worry about you." And this time, it was his eyes that held tears. "I tried everything I could to find out where you were. I nearly went crazy."

IT WAS THREE A.M. WHEN SHE STARTED SCREAMING. MARSH WOKE with a jolt, sitting upright. One glance told him she was dreaming. He gathered her in his arms, but her yelling did not stop. Finally, he shook her, and she opened her eyes, her voice dying out in an eerie wail.

There was a knock on the door; she had been heard down the hall. Marsh assured the person next door that Lili had been having a nightmare and made Liliane say something to the man.

Then he sat beside her and put his arms around her again. She stared at the wall for a long time, then began to shake. Just a little at first. Even his warm arms around her could not stop it; she shook so that her teeth rattled, and she could not control a spastic hand. She began to cry, soft, sad sounds that came from unplumbed depths.

He did not try to stop her or to tell her that she'd be all right. He just held her.

After half an hour she spoke. "Marsh, I think I killed a man."

He rocked her back and forth in his arms. "Tell me. Tell me all about it."

WHEN THE PALE ROSE OF DAWN TURNED TO VIBRANT PINK AND THEN to vermilion, Marsh called room service for coffee. By the time Liliane stopped talking, the sun was high in the sky.

Marsh found himself shaking several times. Knots formed in his stomach, and once he thought he might be sick. Liliane stood at times and paced back and forth across the room while she continued her narrative. Her voice became hoarse, but she continued, her eyes gazing out into an unseen distance. At times she talked in a monotone, with no feeling at all. Other times her eyes relived the fright she must have felt. Every now and then she whispered so that Marsh had to lean close to hear her. Terror overcame her when she described how she had killed. She had to spit it all out, he knew.

He stared at her the whole time, mesmerized. How had she survived? he wondered. How could her emotions have stood all that had happened to her? How could she have walked as far as she had? She had walked across the African continent. How was her sanity intact?

She had lost all she had held dear for thirty-three years. Simbayo was gone; he was sure it had been burned. Rose and Heidi . . . Liliane could never erase that scene for as long as she lived, he knew. The only consolation was that nothing worse could happen to her.

When she finished, she turned to look at him. Then she collapsed in a heap on the floor, surrounded by the new pale green satin nightgown he had bought her, and sobbed. She wept uncontrollably. She cried until there were no tears left. He sat on the edge of the bed and let her cry. Now, he knew, she had allowed herself the freedom to mourn. Now, she would have to go through a period of coming to terms with the horror of the last year.

When she looked up at him, her energy spent, he lowered himself to the floor beside her and cradled her in his arms.

"We won't go to Salisbury," he said, his voice muffled in her damp hair. "You need to be alone, to recover. We'll go right to

Cape Town and I'll take care of you. Caro will understand. It'll be just us, my darling."

"Oh, Marsh, you're such a comfort. I knew you would be. All I wanted, all this time, was to be with you again. I never want to leave you."

"It'll take you a while, Lili. But there is life ahead. We'll find something of value together."

"We have something of value," she whispered, "or I'd never have made it this far."

Carolyn phoned in midmorning to say she'd arrive in time for dinner. No, Andrew wasn't coming. Just she, by herself, so there'd be the three of them.

Liliane's heart skipped a beat when she saw her daughter framed in the airliner's door. Carolyn hesitated, her eyes scanning the crowd. Seeing them, she waved, her face breaking into a smile, and headed down the stairs, skipping a little.

Liliane stared at her, so trim, elegant really, in a white linen tailored suit, a sheer smoke-gray blouse peeking out at the neck. Her shoulder-length flaxen silk hair was pulled back from her face, and the sea green eyes looked startled even from a distance. She broke into a run, heading straight into her mother's arms.

Later, while Liliane was still dressing for dinner, Marsh walked across the hall to Carolyn's room. "Don't ask her," he advised, "about the trip." He sat on the edge of Carolyn's bed. "She's still in shock. There's much she can't remember. What she does recall, she can't bear to think about. Let it come out a little at a time, if it ever does at all."

He thought that perhaps what she'd told him last night might be all she'd ever remember. "She acts all right, but she's not yet; she's tremendously fragile right now. She's not herself."

"What about Rose and Heidi and—"

"Dead," answered Marsh.

Carolyn laid down her brush and sat next to him. "Oh, Papa."

"She's made it through all the terror and through the long walk from Rwanda because she hasn't let herself dwell on the horrors of the last year. The will for survival got her through it; now she has to face her subconscious. I'm going to put my Rhodesian book aside and nurse her back to health. I want to help her face the demons." He could be a rock, and he knew it. Lili needed him.

At dinner, Liliane had to hear about Courtney; so clearly she remembered the moment of her granddaughter's birth. Justin wasn't real to her yet.

Carolyn did not mention her own restlessness, her yearning to be doing more with her life. She concentrated on the things that would make her mother happy. But nothing she said erased the haunted look from Liliane's eyes.

This gaunt woman with the odd short haircut, this nearly gray woman whose ribs stuck out and who said nothing about the great white welts on her arm, was scarcely recognizable as the mother she had always known.

Liliane listened and asked questions and laughed at times, but mainly she was sober and silent; Carolyn wasn't sure she was really there at all. She kept reaching out to touch both Marsh and Carolyn every few minutes.

In the morning, Marsh insisted Liliane dress in her new turquoise dress and that they have a wedding breakfast.

"You first proposed to me over thirty years ago." She smiled, for the first time in two days. "I'd never have guessed, then, that you would be such a constant lover."

"And so I shall be for the rest of my life," he promised, adjusting his tie.

Liliane walked to him and put her arms around him. "Marsh, I've always loved you. Even when Baxter was still alive. But never more than I do now."

For breakfast, they had strawberries on crêpes sprinkled with confectioners' sugar and lemon juice. "It's the most wonderful breakfast I've ever eaten." They couldn't keep their eyes off each other. "We're getting married," she told the waiter. Carolyn and Marsh laughed.

"I've wanted this all my life," Carolyn told them. She ran out and found a bouquet of roses and gypsophila for Liliane. Her heart ached for what Liliane must have gone through, but she also felt joyous. At last, she thought, as she raced back to the hotel. At long last.

Carolyn held the rings—simple wide gold bands—and acted as best man, matron of honor, and witness. She wished they would come back to Salisbury with her, even for a week, but Marsh had said, "She's in a state of trauma. I think a little quiet, a little tender loving care is what she needs. She doesn't have enough within her right now to give anything to anyone. The fuss and the family would be more than she can handle right now. We'll fly to Cape Town now, and then either go up to your place in a month or so, or you can fly down to us. Try to understand."

Carolyn was trying.

At 10:11 A.M. Liliane became Liliane Compson, Mrs. Marshall Compson, mother of Carolyn Compson McCloud.

The clerk had told the newspaper, so when they came out of the judge's chambers, a reporter took their picture. Marsh waved away any questions.

"We'll have time for lunch," said Marsh, when they'd returned to the hotel room, "if I pick up the plane tickets now." He put a hand on his wife's shoulder. "We have reservations for the two o'clock flight this afternoon."

Liliane reached up to touch his hand. "What would I do without you." She smiled wanly.

"I hope you never have to find out." He leaned down to kiss her cheek. "I'll be back in an hour. Do you want anything before I leave?"

Carolyn had gone across the room to pick up her suitcase.

"No." Liliane sighed. The past that had so suddenly caught up with her still lingered. In her mind, though, she forced herself to focus on the wide verandah at Cape Town looking out over the vineyards, Table Mountain in the purple distance. She saw herself rocking in a chair, an afghan on her lap, Marsh's orange cat curled on it, purring. She heard the sounds of Marsh's typewriter from inside. And the breeze that came from the ocean was soft and fresh, washing away memories.

She held up her face for a kiss.

When he closed the door behind him, she realized it was the first time they had been separated in three days. She stood and ran to the door, wanting to accompany him, but the elevator doors had closed behind him. I'll watch for him from the window, she thought, unable to bear the thought of not being with him.

She saw the sun shining on his silver hair, saw the erect, still powerful body of her husband waiting at the curb. Fingering her new gold wedding band, she smiled. "Liliane Compson," she said aloud, trying to get used to it.

I want to go with him; I don't want to spend one more minute without him.

Leaning out the window, she saw him step from the curb, and she cried, "Wait! Wait for me!"

She saw him look up, his left hand reaching up to shade the sun's glare from his eyes. He stopped for a second and began to wave at her when the screech of brakes assaulted her ears before she saw him jerk like a puppet and fall to the pavement.

As though from a great distance, she heard someone shouting and a policeman's whistle. Immobile, she watched the crowd gathering around the inert figure and saw Marsh's blood seep onto the asphalt.

CHAPTER 43

▼

LILIANE LAY CURLED IN THE FETAL POSITION FOR OVER THREE WEEKS. Andrew had flown to Nairobi to bring her home, with Carolyn; she hadn't recognized him. She had sat in her hotel room staring vacantly out the window. When he had touched her, she collapsed. He had to take her to Salisbury on a stretcher. Carolyn, too, was in shock, though she was forced to take responsible action. She carried Marsh's ashes in an urn.

For the first week, Andrew received little help from Carolyn, who could not accept her father's death. "He can't be gone," she sobbed over and over. Once she thought, If he hadn't gone to Nairobi . . . If Mama hadn't come out of the jungle at just that time . . . If Mama . . . But she crushed such thoughts. For over a year, she had worried about her mother and would dream sometimes of dreadful things happening to her, like the ones with which the papers were filled daily. Stories of nuns being raped, of people being tossed off the bridge at Stanleyville and soldiers laughing as they watched the crocodiles consume the bodies, limbs first. However, with time, the nightmares lessened and she had told herself her mother was dead.

But Marsh. Gone? She cried until she thought she must turn inside out. She cried until not only tears but emotion were drained. And then she walked. She walked through the streets of Salisbury; then she would take the car and drive into the countryside, walk over the dusty paths, up into the dry hills, and sit overlooking the landscape, seeing nothing. She wondered how she could face life knowing Marsh was not there for her when she needed him. She

loved Andrew, she adored Courtney and Justin, and her mother
. . . though since Liliane had sent her to Litchfield she had never
loved her unreservedly. Respect her, certainly. Admire her, of
course. Love her, to a degree. But she had never loved anyone the
way she loved Marsh.

Andrew put Liliane in the room where Marsh had always
stayed. She lay inert, not moving, not eating. Carolyn hired Eulalie, a black woman, to care for her. The doctor ordered intravenous feeding to keep her alive.

Liliane looked pale and pathetic, lying motionless. It was three
weeks before she opened her eyes; then, she was disoriented. She
opened her mouth when Eulalie or Carolyn fed her, and she
chewed and swallowed, but her empty stare focused on nothing.
She neither saw nor heard Carolyn.

Together, Carolyn and Eulalie dressed her and sat her in a
chair by the window, where she could look out over the green
lawns, where there was shade from the jacaranda, where she could
see—if she saw—the pink and red flowers with which Carolyn had
surrounded the house.

Each afternoon, after school, Courtney tiptoed into her
grandmother's room and sat on the floor, studying her. She
brought Othello with her, and Othello sat and watched Liliane,
too. The little girl had a pixielike quality; her solemn, clear gray
eyes seldom reflected the mischief within. She would barely reach
the top of the stairs before unbuttoning her dress; she threw it on
her bed as she ran into her room and immediately pulled on her
shorts. Left on her own, she invariably went barefoot. High cheekbones, like Marsh; his aquiline nose, sharply defined; the long
black lashes, so much darker than her chestnut curls. They weren't
nearly as tight as Liliane's had been, but they were soft and framed
her lightly freckled face.

Six weeks to the day after Marsh's death, Liliane came back to
life. The first things she saw were Courtney and Othello and a
strange room.

"Who are you?" she asked, as clear as a bell.

Courtney stared at her with round eyes. She had been unprepared to hear her grandmother's voice. Othello perked his floppy
ears.

Courtney stood and walked over to Liliane. "I'm Courtney."

Liliane smiled. "My, how you've grown since I last saw you."

"I'll be right back," said Courtney, dashing from the room,
running down the stairs, shouting, "Mama. Come quick."

Carolyn came bounding up the stairs. When her mother said, "Hello, Caro," Carolyn clasped her and tears ran down her cheeks. Liliane, however, remained stoic. She showed no emotion whatever.

That night, Liliane came down to dinner. She didn't ask how she had gotten there or make any mention of her lost year—or of Marsh. She spoke politely to Andrew and looked at Justin, who was just beginning to walk. She remembered them, apparently, but made no particular mention of anything familiar.

After dinner, she asked, "Will someone show me to my room? I'm quite tired." She walked up the stairs.

Each day she made physical progress, but she still made no mention of the past. Late one morning, Carolyn looked out the window to see her mother swimming in the pool. She watched her for half an hour, while Liliane swam around lazily, obviously enjoying herself. Carolyn gasped aloud, however, when Liliane climbed out of the pool. Her mother was naked.

She ran out to her clutching a large towel, which she threw around Liliane.

"Oh, thank you, dear." Liliane wrapped the towel around her. "It looked so inviting. It reminds me of my pool at Simbayo. The one Baxter built."

It was her first reference to the past.

When she did regain her memory, it stopped with Nkunda's arrival in Simbayo. She remembered nothing beyond that, nothing of her year wandering from tribe to tribe, none of the horrors she had lived through, nothing of Marsh's death, though she fingered the gold ring on her left hand constantly. Carolyn told her that before Marsh's death they had married.

"I'm glad," was Liliane's only reaction.

Liliane was unaware of her surroundings and took no interest in what was happening in the world or in the lives of anyone except Courtney. She and Othello waited patiently but expectantly until Courtney returned from school each afternoon. Then they all went down to Courtney's homemade animal hospital. It was Carolyn, really, who helped the animals to recuperation, but Courtney fed them and gave them her love. She and Liliane and Othello sat out in the area Andrew had enclosed with chicken wire and talked to each other and to the animals that were there.

Otherwise, Liliane's contact with humanity was minimal.

Carolyn and Andrew exerted patience for weeks. And then Carolyn, herself still grief-stricken, said to Andrew, "I wonder if she's ever going to come back. When I talk to her, she listens politely, but I'm not sure she really hears. She never talks of the past and shows no interest in the present or the future. She's a vegetable except for an hour when Courtney comes home. She doesn't even seem to realize Justin's there. She's never held him."

"We may need professional help," said Andrew.

But gradually, a very little at a time, Liliane began to look around and wonder.

When she did ask questions, she made no comments on the answers. She'd ask, "How did I get here?"

"When did you move here?"

"How old is Justin?"

And after many months, she asked, "What year is this?"

The next morning she picked up a newspaper and began to read. In this way she drew herself back into life.

Carolyn was chomping at the bit.

From the moment she and Andrew left Kariba and bought the old Thompson place, Carolyn had been active politically. She'd become part of the small, though influential, group that fought for the right of Africans to be addressed as "Mr." She also belonged to a group that encouraged black women to form women's organizations. But now she yearned to do what she called "real work."

Ever since she'd talked to Marsh about going to work for Sam's group, there had been reasons to delay the move. Now that Justin was nearly three and Liliane was recuperating, she saw no reason to put it off.

"You don't think fighting for racial equality is 'real work'?" asked Andrew. He often found it difficult to understand his wife.

"Of course. Yet I still feel useless. What I'm participating in is important, but I miss something to excite my mind, inflame my curiosity, stir my emotions."

"In other words"—Andrew sighed—"make you feel your life is worthwhile."

"Exactly," she answered. "Please understand I'm happier than I ever dreamed could be possible. I love having our own home; I love motherhood; the excitement of you hasn't worn off." She walked over to him, where he sat in the large overstuffed chair and put her arms around him. He pulled her onto his lap. "But I can play with the children for just so long."

Andrew was not surprised when he learned later that Carolyn had approached Sam the next day.

"You've known for the last three years that I want to work

with your organization," she said. "Now I'm ready."

She stood in the doorway to his office, looking radiant in a green tailored shirtwaist dress. Her blond hair haloed her head. She hadn't even said hello. Sam was bent over a file cabinet and looked around at her.

Straightening up, he said, "Come on in and sit down. Be sociable."

"I'm very good, you know." Her smile was dazzling.

Sam's eyes shone with amusement. He sat down at his desk, tilted his chair back, and looked up at her. "How many words a minute do you type?"

Now she sat down. "I don't even think that's funny. You know perfectly well that's not what I mean."

"What, exactly"—he studied his fingernails before looking back at her—"do you mean?"

"I want a real job."

Sam stood and walked to the streaked window. It looked out on a dingy alley. He stared out, hands clasped behind his back. "Why me? Why this place? We don't even pay all that well."

"Oh, Sam, the money isn't important. I'm not willing to work for nothing, but that's not the reason I want a job, and you know it." She joined him at the window.

He turned to face her. "I've always known this day would come."

"I can do it, Sam. I've a biology background; I'm a trained immunologist."

"I know you can." His voice was kind. "Being a woman isn't always easy, is it?"

Carolyn smiled. "I was brought up to believe that being a woman wouldn't inhibit me from doing what I wanted. My mother always did."

"At what price?" Sam asked.

She looked up at him. He took her hands in his and looked down at her earnestly.

"I suspect at great price, my dear. You have more now than she ever had. You and Andrew are bringing up your children together. You have each other. Your mother and father were denied that all their lives. Until it was too late. Don't do that to yourself, Carolyn. Or to Andrew. Or to your children."

She slid her hands from his and walked back to the chair. She didn't sit. "You're right, Sam, and I've thought about all that. I want what I have. But I also want more. I don't want to live life through my husband and children. I don't want my education to go to waste. I don't want the high point of my week to be Saturday evenings at the club. I want to do something worthwhile. Like you're doing."

"Does Andrew know you've come to see me?"

"Not exactly."

Sam sat down behind his desk again and stretched his legs, putting his booted feet on the desk. "Let me see what I can come up with," he suggested. "It's a shame for a mind and energy like yours to go to waste. I can't promise anything, but let me think about it."

Carolyn's excitement was reflected in her eyes. "I'd appreciate it. I need to feel vital again. I did out in Kariba, you know. Never more so than when we saved those animals. But since we've moved to town . . . Oh, I'm always busy. But not always in satisfying ways. And now that Mama's better, she's talking of going to Cape Town and living in Papa's house. I think she wants more peace and quiet than our house offers. Our way of life doesn't satisfy her needs."

"Or yours, right?"

"Yes." Carolyn picked up her purse. "It's not that I don't love Andrew and the children. I do love them. But Andrew's gone so much, and the children . . . there's always someone to take care of them. I can read just so many books." She paused. "I was reading Thoreau the other day. Do you know who he is?"

Sam's eyes reflected amusement. "Yes, Carolyn. I know who he is."

"He said that when it came time to die he didn't want to know he hadn't lived."

"Or words to that effect." Sam grinned.

"Well, that's what I feel."

Sam stared at her for a long time. Then he stood. "As I said, let me think about it. See if I can come up with anything. I'd like to work with you, Carolyn. You'd help make a strong team."

She reached out her hand. "Thank you, Sam."

THE ONE WHO MISSED LILIANE MOST WHEN SHE LEFT WAS COURTNEY. Liliane had not regained her old joie de vivre or her memory of what had happened after she left Simbayo. She had read Carolyn's treasured newspaper articles about Marsh winning the Nobel Prize, and she had read his speech. But because a year and a half of her memory was missing, she had difficulty realizing he was dead. Not that she expected to see him. She remained strangely calm about both that and the fact that she no longer lived in Simbayo.

"I feel restless," she said, echoing Carolyn's own feeling. "I don't belong here. I want to try Marsh's home. I want to try being Liliane Compson." Her thumb rubbed the ring on the third finger of her left hand. "I want to see if there's life for me yet."

Carolyn did not feel comfortable sending her mother off alone, but she hadn't felt at ease with her here, either. And that made her feel guilty.

"The tension between you and Andrew makes me uncomfortable," Liliane said.

Carolyn looked at her, amazed. "Tension? Mama, Andrew and I—"

"Whatever you may think, there's tension. You think so much of what he does is immoral. You criticize his bridges because they disrupt the way of life of the natives and the habitat of animals."

"Well, that's true."

"I agree with you, but only partly. Andrew feels he is doing something good and right for the future of Africa. Yet you tend to belittle him. You two always find ways to argue."

"Oh, Mama, we don't. I think Andrew's wonderful. I admire him."

"Honey, you can't ignore the twentieth century. Maybe you both have things to contribute. Maybe you're *both* right."

Carolyn looked down at her hands. Maybe she *was* too hard on him at times, but she hadn't been aware of criticizing him. Sometimes she wished his work were more like Sam's—a saving operation rather than bulldozing civilization into the heart of this continent.

"He's a very sensitive man," Liliane added. "More so even than Marsh was at his age. And he's far more sensitive to your needs than you are to his."

"You weren't aware of Papa's needs," Carolyn cut in. What right had her mother to criticize her when she had so flagrantly followed her own path?

"Ah, darling, I was. I just couldn't meet them. I couldn't leave Simbayo. We effected a compromise, eventually. I suggest you and Andrew find a way to compromise, too."

I don't want that, thought Carolyn. Mama's life is nearly over and she's never known what it is really to live happily.

"Maybe," she mused, a hint of desperation in her voice, "the women of our family are too restless ever to find complete happiness."

"Perhaps"—Liliane patted her daughter's hand—"what I want for you is what I couldn't have myself. Love is supposed to be the answer for all women. Without love, life doesn't mean much, but it was never enough for me. And, for that, I'm sorry."

"I don't think it's enough for me, either, Mama. But I don't know what is. I talked with Sam. I'd like to work for his outfit. They're doing research as well as field work."

"I know," said Liliane. "I've known since Kariba."

"So did Papa."

"Yes," said Liliane, and her eyes stared into space. "Your father was a very perceptive man. See if you can't combine what you have with what you need."

Carolyn went into the kitchen to get tea. When she returned, she asked, "You're telling me, aren't you, that it would be nice if I could practice what you preach?"

Liliane smiled, that sad smile that was hers so often lately. "That's one way of putting it. I guess I don't know, were I to live my life over, if I could do it differently. All I know is that I miss knowing your father is somewhere in the world for me when I need him."

"Mama?"

Liliane sipped her tea and looked at her daughter. Their eyes met.

"Mama, could Papa have been . . . ?"

Silence hung in the air. Then Liliane sighed. "I know what you're going to ask. I've been waiting for you to ask it for years."

"Could he have been? I mean, Courtney so often looks like him. It's around the eyes. And her nose. I look at her and think: Could Papa have really been my father?"

Liliane reached out for Carolyn's hand. "I think I've been afraid to tell you I don't know. Afraid of what you'd think of me if I didn't know who the father of my child was."

"Oh, Mama, that doesn't matter. What does is that there's a possibility that Papa was my father. Did he know?"

Liliane's sad smile echoed her voice. "Yes. As far as he was concerned, there was no doubt he was your father."

"And he never told me."

"He didn't need to."

"I wish I'd known when he was alive."

"You couldn't have loved him more, no matter what. He knew

that. All I can tell you is that it's a possibility. Looking at Courtney, it seems more than likely." Liliane stood. "I'm going to his home, Caro. I'm going to live among his things, and I'm going to look out on the view he looked out on for all these years. I'm going to bury his ashes in his beloved rose garden. I need to be there. I need, too late, to live with Marsh."

CHAPTER 44

▼

THREE WEEKS AFTER LILIANE LEFT FOR CAPE TOWN, SAM ELLIOT called Carolyn.

"How about letting me buy you lunch?" he suggested.

She was excited. He must have come up with an idea.

Sam always looked rumpled. He could leave the house in the morning with freshly pressed clothes, but by five o'clock he looked as though he'd slept in them. Unlike the engineers at Llewellyn and much of the rest of professional Rhodesia, he never wore suits. He wore blue jeans or khaki pants to work.

"I wish he'd dress like the rest of the men," Michelle would moan. She'd been complaining of Sam's lack of sartorial style for as long as Carolyn had known her. "How I do love to see a man in a three-piece suit." Very few of the men they knew wore three-piece suits to work. That kind of dress was reserved for Saturday nights at the club, if one wasn't wearing a dinner jacket.

They lunched at a small Indian restaurant, locally famous for its curry and dal. When Carolyn ordered iced tea, the waiter shook his head. "No, may I suggest not. With spicy foods, iced coffee would be better. It will soothe the throat."

"First of all," said Sam, as they waited for their lunch, "let's talk about Andrew."

Carolyn felt herself bristling. "I'll talk about him if you'll talk about Michelle."

He sighed heavily. "Sometimes you're impossible."

Her smile lit her face. "It's one of the things you like about me."

"It's one of the things," he admitted, "everyone loves about you. Why aren't you content," he asked, buttering a roll the waiter had brought, "to be like other women?"

"There must be others like me. I can't imagine I'm unique."

"Oh, but you are." He raised his blue eyes to hers. "You know what I'm afraid of?"

"They won't let you hire a woman?"

"Andrew. I keep thinking how I'd feel if Michelle came home and said she was going to work."

"How *would* you feel?"

Sam hesitated, thinking. Then he said slowly, "I guess I'd feel threatened. That I wasn't giving her what she needed."

"Do you really think one other person can supply anybody's needs?" Carolyn asked. "If you didn't have this job you love so much, but you had Michelle and Saundra and Evan, would that be enough to make you happy?"

"Of course not."

"Then why should it be for a woman?"

Sam leaned back in his chair and looked at her. He didn't answer.

Carolyn concentrated on her chicken before continuing. "The waiter was right," she said. "Iced coffee does soothe the hot taste. Does Michelle think it's unfeminine of *me* to *want* to work?"

Sam kept looking at her as they ate in silence.

She pushed on. "What gives Michelle satisfaction? What makes *her* feel important?"

Sam looked reflective for a moment. "I suppose being a mother. Winning at bridge. Buying new clothes. Having a full dance card at the club. Women aren't supposed to find satisfaction in the same ways men do. What do you want? A chance to be a man?"

"For heaven's sake, Sam. Listen to yourself. No. I don't want to be a *man.*"

"Lower your voice."

She looked around and saw that people were staring at her.

"Next time you want to talk with me, let's do it in a private place," she admonished him. "Did you really invite me to lunch just to talk about how Andrew will feel if I go to work?"

"No, but I had to get that off my chest first." He tilted his chair back. "I may have come up with a job for you. One that would also be of great help to the group."

She listened.

"We're going to be up on the Zambezi where it enters Mozambique, below Kariba. It's elephant country as well as nearly everything else—giraffes, lions, leopards, antelope, zebra, crocs, hippos—one of the largest concentration of game in the country, aside from Wankie. The government's mandated a national wildlife refuge, and that's where we'll be working, doing research, establishing guidelines, and, I suppose, inevitably arguing with one or more government organizations. My crew and I'll be up there most of the time, as I told you. I plan to come home at least monthly. Maybe for several weeks at a time. All our work won't be in the field. We'll have to do research, compile it—which will take hours and weeks. We'll have to analyze and interpret the data.

"That's where you would come in. I refuse to take you in the field. I'm not going to be responsible for ruining your marriage. But you *could* do valuable work analyzing the data, compiling the research. Not as much fun, of course, as being out in the field. Though maybe you could get in a week here and there so you'd understand the lay of the land. It would mean doing your work in the office, staying here.

"I don't think it would be full time. At least not at first. It would mean trying to figure out why some areas are prone to the tsetse fly and no cattle can be grazed, while some territory right next to it has none. It means figuring out how many animals the land can support and what we have to do to help them. It means helping to write rules and regulations."

Carolyn felt a stab of disappointment. Sitting in an office analyzing biological data. That's not what she'd had in mind. She remembered rescuing the animals at Kariba. Yet in her heart she knew Sam was right. She was not willing to leave Andrew and the children for months on end.

"It's important work, Carolyn. If you don't want to do it, I'll have to send to England for someone."

"Don't do that," she said. "Let me give it a stab."

"I'm not doing it just to please you, I want you to know that. I think you'll be a big addition to the team."

"Thanks, Sam. I appreciate it. I really do."

At least, she thought, it won't control my life. I'll never fall in love with it. But I know it's important work. I wonder if Andrew will have a fit.

He did not.

"I won't pretend I'm thrilled. Marsh and I talked about this years ago. Maybe he was preparing me. I'm surprised you held out this long. And I guess I can't say much when I'm out in the field for months each year. And if you have to work for someone and something, I'm glad it's Sam's group."

It was a gradual, slow apprenticeship. There was next to no work to do until the team had gathered data for a few months. Before the work formally began, Sam suggested, "So that you can have a picture of where and what we're doing, how would your family like to join us"—he meant Michelle and the children—"and take a camping trip up there the beginning of summer vacation?"

Andrew arranged to take two weeks off. Even Michelle did not complain too much about living without a bath, about ants, about the lack of amenities. They laughed a lot, and the children—even baby Justin—ran riot.

When they arrived home, a letter from Liliane awaited Carolyn. It begged her to allow Courtney to come spend a month of her July vacation in Cape Town.

This began a routine that Courtney would follow every summer vacation of her school life.

Liliane was lonely. She knew no one in Cape Town and made no move to make friends. The couple who had tended Marsh and his home now took care of her needs. She did sit on his verandah and stare out at the green vineyards and the purple hills, at the cloud tablecloth that so often covered the flat top of Cape Town's signature. She did smell the salt air and listen to the lonesome wail of foghorns.

Away from the jungle humidity, she regained energy. As she rocked back and forth and stroked the orange cat, her memory, in bits and pieces, came back to her, but she would never totally remember the experiences that signaled the end of Simbayo.

Vivid scenes flashed into her consciousness: floating down a river on a raft in the moonlight, natives paddling silently, only the silver ribbon of water visible, dark trees on the banks hiding anything else. Being hidden in a rank-smelling hut, hot poultices placed on her left arm; the only voice a woman's—soft, unintelligible sounds.

And she never completely accepted Marsh's death. She did remember the screeching brakes and the blood on the pavement, but Marsh, in death, accompanied her as he never had in life. He never left her side.

When Liliane wrote to ask if Courtney could visit for a month, she knew she must rally herself so that the little girl would not be bored. She knew she must begin to live again. It was time.

And so she and Courtney together discovered the Cape Town that Liliane had shown Carolyn, so many years ago when they had first come to Litchfield together. Liliane learned to drive Marsh's car; far more difficult, she thought, than learning to fly her old plane. She and Courtney packed the car with picnic lunches and explored the coast; they traveled into the valleys and viewed the old Dutch towns and the neat outlying farmhouses. Together they discovered that South Africa was one of the most beautiful countries of the world.

They also discovered the outskirts of Crossroads and Kaputo, squatter towns surrounded by barbed wire. These were where the blacks lived, in tiny, squalid shacks with little or no plumbing, in conditions that allowed not at all for human dignity. Cape Towners seldom drove by these permanent camps, preferring instead to forget about them. Their consciences were not troubled by them. Life went on, with the local opera and visiting entertainers from America and England. Lawns were watered, and now and then a black man was invited to a cocktail party at a liberal Britisher's, but he had to leave early to meet the curfew.

Liliane did not keep this from Courtney; she discovered it with her. On her visits to Marsh in years past, they had done little exploration, but she had known of the conditions here; years ago she had applauded Carolyn's involvement with the Black Sash Society.

Liliane took Courtney partway up Table Mountain. She could no longer manage to climb as far as the top, not an easy climb at best, but she did take her as far as she had taken Carolyn on their first trip to Litchfield, twenty-seven years before. It was one of the few things that hadn't changed.

"What's that, Grandmama?" Courtney pointed to Robbeineiland, shining far out in Table Bay.

"It's a prison," answered Liliane, "a prison for people who disagree with the government."

Courtney let that sink in. "It looks pretty in the sunlight."

"It's not." Liliane's voice hardened. "It's a miserable testimony to the lack of freedom of speech."

Courtney look up at her, a question in her sober gray eyes. "Do you mean people can't say what they think?"

Liliane reached down and put a hand on Courtney's shoulder.

"Particularly if you're black. Nelson Mandela is there, sentenced to life imprisonment for treason."

"Treason? Did he try to betray the government?"

Liliane smiled. She loved having a precocious granddaughter. "Not in my opinion. But he led protests against apartheid and the government banished him forever to Robben Island. I hate to think what must go on out there. Blacks are not people to this government and it does not allow them to have any dignity."

Courtney stared out into the bay. "Isn't that sort of the way Hitler treated Jews in Germany?"

Liliane squeezed Courtney's shoulder. How did one so young know so much and think so individually? She knelt down beside Courtney and put an arm around her waist.

"I love you," she said, hugging her granddaughter. "You have no idea how much pleasure you give me."

Courtney put an arm around Liliane's neck, still gazing out at the wide expanse of water. "Would love help?" she asked. "Bonnie's grandmother says love cures everything."

"I don't know. Sometimes," answered her grandmother, "love is not enough."

Hand in hand, they walked down the mountain.

What most delighted Courtney that July were her grandmother's reminiscences of life in Simbayo. When she returned to Salisbury after her month in Cape Town that summer and each summer afterward, she would write down all she could remember of her grandmother's stories.

One afternoon of her third year in Cape Town, Liliane was sitting on the porch, an afghan thrown over her, the orange cat, Shiva, on her lap. It was a typical afternoon posture for her. Her actions spoke more of seventy-nine than fifty-nine. Her eyes were closed when she heard steps on the gravel.

She looked up to see a tall, erect, middle-aged man who carried himself like a tribal chieftain. He was ebony black, his hair salt-and-pepper, and he wore a shiny black suit that had seen many years of wear. Bloodshot as his eyes were, Liliane's first thought was that they were the kindest eyes she had ever seen.

"Mother Lili?" he asked.

It had been so long since anyone had called her that.

She nodded her head; part of her was still back in the Congo jungle, staring at the man she had murdered.

"I am Moses Matabane." His deep baritone had a decidedly

British accent. He stood, an old wide-brimmed straw hat in his hand. "You are needed," he said simply.

Liliane sat upright, and Shiva leaped from her lap, running the length of the verandah, jumping into the petunias.

"Who needs me?" she asked, wondering why this stranger did not frighten her.

"Africa needs you."

If I didn't know better, she thought, I'd think it was the voice of God calling to me—the basso profundo, the entreaty rolling like thunder.

"I need you," he said more quietly.

She looked around. He had not, of course, arrived by car. In the distance, at the driveway's entrance, she noticed a bicycle, its fender dented.

"Would you like some lemonade?" she asked. She felt like a character in a play, as though she had no will, as though whatever was happening had been preordained. She knew that could not be true, but there it was, nevertheless. "Come up on the porch and sit down and we'll have some lemonade."

The man smiled. He was the biggest man Liliane had ever seen.

While they waited for their cool drinks, he began. "You know of Kaputo?"

Of course. Everyone knew of Kaputo. It was the second largest native compound on the outskirts of Cape Town. Several years ago, she and Courtney had stared through its barbed wire at the nearly naked children running around, laughing, screaming at some kind of game. They had seen the women, rags wound around their heads, gossiping at the water hydrant; seen the squalor in which these people spent their lives; smelled the omnipresent stench of urine that infested all of these squatter towns. Every day, the people from Kaputo went into Cape Town, some wearing starched white jackets and white gloves, to serve luncheons to their white employers, to tend white babies, to dig ditches, to lay macadam, and to do all the menial, dirty jobs that whites of South Africa would never dream of doing—then returned there every night, by curfew, to rooms that contained twelve people, to sleeping on the floor or taking turns on the one bed, a sheetless bed that had perhaps one dirty blanket. Dirty, because there were no facilities for washing, except the one spigot provided for every fifty shacks, because the only way to heat water was over an open fire and wood was scarce.

Even now, Liliane remembered seeing raw running sores on the legs of children whose stomachs were distended from malnutrition. She had seen the flies clotted on the festered wounds and wondered if the wounds ever healed.

"Yes," she said, "Yes, I know of Kaputo."

"Kaputo needs doctors," he said. His mellow voice wound itself around her like a cocoon.

"I would imagine," responded Liliane, "that Kaputo needs everything."

"I am the only doctor," he explained, "and I am not really a doctor."

Liliane looked at him. He used his enormous hands expressively, gesturing as he talked.

"What are you, then?" she asked.

"I grew up far away to the north, next to a mission. And there I went to school. There was a doctor there, Dr. George Burnham . . ." His eyes glistened as he repeated the name. "He thought we should be trained to help our own people, that we should not have to rely on outsiders, on . . ."

"On white people?" offered Liliane.

Moses Matabane nodded. "For five years I trained with Dr. Burnham until they closed the mission . . . until they herded our tribe onto a reservation far away, where the soil could not be farmed, where there was not enough water, where our people starved to death."

He stared out into the distance; silence hung like dust. Liliane heard a bee; she did not take her eyes from this man with the mellifluous voice. Despite his shiny suit, his tattered hat, and his shirt with the threadbare cuffs, he had a regal air.

"We came to Cape Town. Filthy as the ghettos are, poor as everyone is, it is still better than slowly starving to death. But people die here, too. My first night here I sewed up an arm ripped open in a knife fight and the leg of someone who got caught in the barbed wire." He sighed.

"Your fame must have spread quickly."

He turned to look at her, and a smile lit up his face. "I have a calling," he said simply. "But one person cannot care for so many thousands. And I must have an outside job or my pass will be revoked. We need more doctors." He looked at her.

"But I'm not really a doctor, either. And I'm white," she said. "Will they let me into Kaputo?"

"I have given that much thought," he answered. "I do not

think we could do this if you were just *any* white person. But even the government of South Africa cannot deny Mother Lili. They would not dare that kind of world censure."

The two of them sat rocking in the drowsy afternoon warmth. Shiva came sauntering back onto the porch, jumping with no hesitation onto Moses's lap. He ran his huge hands through her fur, and Liliane could hear the purr. She felt excitement shooting through her.

"Shiva does not accept most people," she commented while her mind raced.

Moses nodded. "I have a way." It was not bragging, she knew, but a statement of fact.

"During the day," Moses said, "I work for Dr. Thomas Bryan. I am a general handyman."

"Doctor?" asked Liliane. "Does he know of your work?"

"He knows and supports us. He helps us. But he would deny that in public. I will not, cannot, tell you the many ways he helps. But he is unable to come into Kaputo. His is to serve us behind the scenes, so to speak. We need help. Ten doctors would not be enough.

"Only recently I heard that you live here. I discovered where you lived and what you do with your life."

"And what," asked Liliane with a faint smile, "have you found that I do with my life?"

"You have been waiting." His eyes bore into her.

He's pulling at me, she realized, like a magnet.

"What am I waiting for?" she asked, suspecting she already knew the answer.

"Me and mine," he answered with self-assurance. "There are sixty thousand people in Kaputo waiting for your help." His eyes never left hers.

Liliane felt her deep breath reach into her diaphragm. Her hand grasped the glass of lemonade so tightly she thought it might break.

"I know you are a woman who does not consider danger. Admittedly, there is danger. But your fame would be your security. Everyone in Kaputo will protect you unto their own death."

"How do you get medicine?"

"There are ways. Not enough, it is true. But we have some."

Liliane's mind was racing.

"And instruments?"

"We will even provide an operating room, though it may not be as elaborate or sterile as you are used to."

Hers at Simbayo had become a model of efficiency.

"Why me?" she asked.

"Because," he answered, "we have been waiting for each other."

It's like climbing a mountain, she reflected. Because it is there; because I am here.

CHAPTER 45

▼

THAT FIRST TIME SHE RETURNED FROM VISITING LILIANE, THAT summer of her eighth year, Courtney took a notebook and a sharp pencil out to the backyard, to the table under the mimosa tree where they usually ate breakfast.

She was determined to set down in writing all that she had learned of Simbayo, of the life her grandmother had lived. She did not realize then that every time she visited her grandmother she would learn more—enough so that each year another notebook would be filled. Enough so that she thought she knew what Simbayo looked like, could feel its texture and hear the monkeys calling from its trees. She saw the coffee-colored Mombayo and felt the heat beat into her in ways she had never experienced in the high, dry lands of Salisbury.

Neither of her parents was home. Although there really was nothing yet for Carolyn to do at Sam's office, she had begun driving down there after lunch. She told herself she could learn what needed to be done when Sam's team finally went out into the field.

Andrew arrived home first. When he saw Courtney sitting under the mimosa, in profusive pink bloom, he came out to her. "Just the person I'm looking for." He smiled as he reached out a hand to tousle her chestnut curls.

She looked up at him with her serious clear gray eyes and put her pencil down. There was little lead left at its stubbed point.

Her father sat down beside her. "How would you like to take

a trip with me?" he asked. "I have to go down south, over in the desert country for two weeks. I thought maybe you'd like to come with me."

"Oh, Daddy, how wonderful! Just you and me?"

"Well"—he grinned at her—"we'll see if either Lobengula or Bildad wants to come with us. There'll also be Mac Howitt; you've met him. He's an engineer, too. Of course, you won't have anyone to play with, but I thought you might enjoy seeing new country."

"Are there going to be lions and elephants?"

"I'm not sure about elephants. But there'll be plenty of wild-life, that's for sure."

THAT JULY, THE WINTER OF 1964, MOLDED COURTNEY'S LIFE forever; her love affair with the bush country began, a love her father shared.

Courtney loved the silence of the open plain. It was like a precious, gift-wrapped package. She was first aware of that silence when the motor of the jeep stopped: The total silence was immense. It only lasted for a moment, then voices broke into the air, ready to set up camp.

She loved the chirruping of crickets and frogs at sundown. After everyone was in bed, when she saw the flickering fire through the canvas of the tent, when Andrew's breathing had become so even as to be silent, Courtney listened to the night.

When the men were busy during the day, the little girl strode by herself over the savannah, always keeping the camp within view. She heard the woof of a startled zebra puncture the air; the silence seemed deeper afterward. She would hear, like a symphonic movement between silences, the distant cowlike grumble of a wildebeest, conveying a warning of a human's presence to other animals. Then ever deeper silence. A bird flying through the air, sensing her presence, would caw. Silence again.

Early in the morning, before breakfast, she would waken her father and, hand in hand, they would venture out into the morning so that they could observe the animals that roamed these plains. One morning she and Andrew drove out in the jeep toward the trees in the distance. A leopard, its tail dangling from the limb of an acacia, looked down at them indolently. It had slung a little Thomson's gazelle over a branch.

"It's the way some women toss their minks over the back of

a chair," observed Andrew. The leopard was too busy with its kill to do more than gaze at them.

Never a day passed that they did not see elephants. Sometimes just ten or fifteen; one day, hundreds. In twenty years they would all be gone.

She would lie by herself, under a tree, watching the sky through gently moving leaves, watching a cloud skitter across the bright azure background, listening to the tinkle of cowbells in the distance, for the tribes here raised cattle. She could feel the hot earth drinking in the sun, baking it inside itself; she could hear the fragile, dry movements of insects in the earth. If she lay there long enough she could even hear the movement of herds of animals in the distance. She became part of the earth.

It was not until their third vacation out on the veld that they ran into nomadic tribes or saw thatched-hut villages, scattered here and there. Gradually, Courtney became aware of the festering sores on the natives' arms and legs, surrounded by flies, the pus thick. The children's faces were old; their frail, skinny bodies, with legs and arms like sticks, and their fat, hard tummies, from malnutrition, the curse of most of Africa.

"Why aren't there any old people?" she asked.

"The average lifespan," Andrew told her, "is thirty-six." By the time she learned this, she was eleven.

"It's funny," she said, thinking of old people. "Grandmama seems to get younger."

THE NEXT JULY, COURTNEY FLEW TO CAPE TOWN THE DAY AFTER school ended. She and Liliane had conspired, via mail, all year. Liliane had flown up to Salisbury for Christmas. The big house seemed to have been made for Christmas. By then, Carolyn was working at the lab every day. "If I'd worked this hard in college," she told Andrew, "I'd have been Phi Beta Kappa."

To her surprise, she loved the lab work. "When I discover something, I feel creative," she said.

"To say nothing of intelligent," he added.

Carolyn grinned. "It's true."

Her job did not upset the household. She was home by four every afternoon and spent that time, until dinner, with Justin. Courtney was usually at a friend's, or some of her friends were upstairs in her big room, or a clutch of little girls was swimming in the pool. Carolyn would hear the high-pitched cries of little girls, listen to them giggling, and smile contentedly. How she envied Courtney's youth, so well adjusted and stable, so happy. Yet, she thought, look how I've ended up. I have love and beautiful children and an exciting job. I have everything . . . except Papa. She still carried his loss within her.

Liliane did not stay long at Christmastime. Carolyn had taken it for granted that her mother would stay at least a month as she usually did, but Liliane left after one week. She had to get back to her work, she said. "I feel guilty that I've taken this much time away from those who need me."

Liliane told them that she was helping to nurse in one of the black squatter towns but gave no details. To her granddaughter, however, though she concealed the horror, she did tell stories of how she helped with breech births and how she set broken arms, and how penicillin, smuggled in, saved many from pneumonia. She did tell her of head lice, of poverty, and of the injustice—inhumanity, she called it—of the way these people were forced to live.

In Kaputo, she told Courtney, life was hard, but winter was especially so. The shacks had no stoves, no heat, no electricity, no plumbing. If children could not reach the filthy, crowded latrine in time to relieve themselves, they did so in the streets. If downpours raged, people wet their beds or the hard-packed dirt floors rather than brave the elements. The smell of excrement invaded the nostrils, and the ubiquitous smell of urine wafted through the air even into the trim, clean suburbs.

Deadly gas, caused by coals burned over braziers indoors, caused infant deaths at night. Shacks—two dingy, small rooms built of zinc and porous brick—overlooked dark, rat-infested, narrow alleys. One outside lavatory and one faucet offering cold water in a thin stream served fifty dwellings—two or three hundred people.

Police raids in the middle of the night or right before dawn were a fact of life at Kaputo. "Anyone, man or woman, who is unable to immediately lay a hand on his or her pass is jailed. If a man doesn't return from his twelve-hour shift, his wife knows he's in jail. No one knows where or for how long. Or why."

"Oh, Grandma," cried the young girl, "why? Why would anyone do that? It's not fair."

"No, darling." Liliane reached out for Courtney's hand. "But I have never found anything in life that is fair."

Liliane could not understand why epidemics were not rampant throughout these squatter townships. Most families had one washcloth and no towels. This rag served to wipe faces, dirty hands, and runny noses; to wash dishes, to cool fevered foreheads. Most children and many women went barefoot. Ragged people huddled around street braziers to keep warm in winter and suffocated in the small, dark shacks in summer. Gaunt men and women ran to catch buses to their jobs in the white world, their eyes fearful, leaving mournful cries issuing from the shacks—the cries of hunger from neglected, hungry children left alone all day behind closed doors or free to roam the dusty or muddy streets of town.

Each day that Liliane entered Kaputo her heart constricted.

It was no wonder, she thought, that so many took their frustrations out in anger and violence—anger that resulted in knife wounds, in wife and child beatings, in abuse of all kinds. Tuberculosis and pneumonia flourished as well as all kinds of venereal diseases.

The clinic she and Moses ran was filled. Deformed children, the result of malnutrition during pregnancy; infants with oversized heads and stomachs due to starvation; victims of burns; people with wounds that bled from chests and heads; people whose fingers were severed or eyes gouged. There was never enough penicillin or disinfectant or bandages. Liliane remembered the early years at Simbayo when they washed and rewashed gauze bandages. There was never enough iodine or alcohol. There was always too much blood and too much coughing, and too little faith. None of the eyes she looked into held hope. Even the children's eyes were haunted.

At the beginning, she arrived at Kaputo six days a week at 8:00 A.M. Head erect and shoulders firm, she walked through the gate that was locked every night at curfew time.

However, by 2:00 in the afternoon, her energy gave out. Her hands would begin to tremble and her eyes could not focus. Much as she fought it, she eventually gave in, if not gracefully, when Moses suggested she leave by midafternoon.

"Harness your energy," he advised. "Do not wear out on us too quickly." And because he needed her so badly, he refused to let her come to Kaputo more than four days a week. Liliane realized the intelligence of this, understanding that at nearly sixty and after all she'd been through, her stamina was not infinite.

On the days when she didn't work at Kaputo, she dug in

Marsh's rose garden, oversaw the cultivation of the vineyards, and rocked on the verandah as she read the pile of books beside her or the letters from Courtney and, more infrequently, from Carolyn.

Every night of her life, she fingered the jeweled comb that along with the carved ivory elephant were the only tangibles that remained from Simbayo, all that she had to show for over thirty-three years in the jungle. She still could not remember what had happened to any of the people who had left Simbayo with her. In her heart she knew they were dead. She knew she would never see them again. But she was biding her time until the rebellion in the Congo died down. Despite the UN's involvement, it had not yet happened.

One day, she told herself, I have to go back and see if it is there. I have to see if Anoka and Naldani are alive and if anything that I built still stands.

When Courtney came to visit, Liliane took her to Kaputo. It was a rude awakening for the young girl, but instead of horrifying her, it added dimension to a life that already had direction.

"If Simbayo still stands," Liliane told Courtney, "I will take you there, too."

"I MISS CAROLYN," ANDREW SAID OUT LOUD TO THE SAVANNAH.

More and more, Andrew found himself away from home. He did not like it. Yet he loved his work. In the years he had been with Llewellyn, he had not only built the towns at Kariba, but bridges over rivers, roads over savannahs, office buildings in Bulawayo, a dam to stay the floods of the narrow Wembasi, railroads that wound through the hills and could bring copper to the capital. He built stations that generated electricity and brought irrigation to arid lands. He spent months at a time in land that had more hippopotamuses than people, more antelope and lion and breath-taking sunsets than most minds could even envision.

But he missed his family. He did not let himself dwell on that when sojourning in the bush, but he carried emptiness around with him. He longed for that smile that told him he and Carolyn shared some intimacy, he missed Justin's "why, Daddy's," he yearned for the endless talks that bound Courtney to him. In the summers, after she returned from her month with Liliane and accompanied him into the bush country, he knew boundless pleasure, but he was aware that some thread was weakened at home when he was away for long stretches at a time. And he missed Carolyn.

At night, as he sat staring into the dark sky after the violent purple-red of the setting sun, he ached for his wife, for the softness of her breasts, for the slender waist he could still encompass with his two large hands, for the way they came to each other with passion that had never lessened, sometimes tearing at their clothes in their eagerness for each other. Staring at the stars as they began to illuminate the sky, he imagined her breath on him, the tip of her tongue darting in his ear, her fingers playing at the inside of his thigh. He envisioned her nipple growing erect in his mouth; remembered what it felt like to have her on top of him, riding down on him as her silver hair flowed like a mane while she pressed him tightly into her, grabbing his hands to her breasts, pushing against him in a driving rhythm, bringing him to a climax as she herself cried out in the night. And then her leg thrown over his while her head rested on his shoulder, his arm around her, and hearing their even breathing as they fell asleep together.

God, how he missed her.

Sometimes he missed her when he was at home, too. When they'd sit around in the evening, watching TV, he'd notice her eyes would leave. She no longer saw what was on the television, didn't hear the words. When he'd ask what she was thinking about, she'd shake her head as though coming out of a daze and say, "These green monkeys we're studying . . . Darwin was right. Those monkeys can teach us so much about ourselves." Or: "I wonder why one field can have tsetse when the adjoining one doesn't. Why can't cattle be raised all over the country?"

At those times he resented her job, despite the realization that this was unfair of him. Certainly there were evenings when his mind, too, wandered, envisioning the bridge that so far was only in his mind, remembering a bend in a river where a dam could be built, seeing the ribbon of tracks wind high through the hills instead of over the plain. Why should he be jealous that Carolyn did the same thing? So far, it had never interfered with the routine of their life, what routine there was to it. Dinner was always on time, the household ran smoothly, on Saturdays there was always company for dinner or they were invited somewhere; often they went to dances at the club. Justin and Courtney both did well in school; in fact, Courtney was always at the head of her class.

But when he remembered long, close talks lately, they were with his daughter, not with Carolyn. When he was home, they spent Saturday afternoons tramping around town or out riding on the veld on horses that belonged to the Reyeses. Some Saturdays they'd all motor to nearby towns, taking picnics and exploring, and Justin would carry Boo Boo, the wooly bear with which he would never part. They laughed a lot. Andrew would be in the driver's seat, the top of the convertible down, Carolyn's pale hair blowing back, and Justin trying to disentangle his mother's hair from Boo Boo. They would picnic on potato salad and deviled eggs and iced tea and chicken sandwiches, and lick the mayonnaise from their fingers.

In Courtney's memory, they always seemed to be laughing. These were golden times.

Years later, Courtney, too, could not remember having long talks with Carolyn. The long talks were always with Andrew. She knew how her mother felt on major issues, because Carolyn pronounced them at the dinner table, but she could not remember asking questions of her mother, the two of them exploring aspects of the universe as she did with Andrew and Liliane. Carolyn was warm and loving, always hugging her children, always asking if they were happy, never looking below the surface when life went smoothly. And for years it did go smoothly.

CHAPTER 46

▼

THE YEAR THAT COURTNEY WAS TWELVE, TWO THINGS OF GREAT importance happened to people she loved dearly. One she knew about; the other she didn't.

For Liliane, the time had come to return to the Congo, to see if Simbayo and the people she loved still lived. Although Zaire was still in great confusion, the rebellion that had reigned for so many years was under control. Whites were still not permitted to live in the country, but they could be issued temporary visitor's visas, and Liliane intended to find out what was real and what was imagined. For six years, nightmares and memory had intertwined; she could not tell what had really happened and what was an illusion. She *knew* she had killed, but it never became clearer than that. Whether she had knifed someone—for that's how she always saw it—in order to save herself or others or in revenge, she did not know.

What mainly mattered was that a year of her life and the fate of her friends remained obliterated.

She would lie in bed at night and wonder if the work begun by Baxter and carried on by her and so many others still continued. She told herself that it did not matter. What mattered was that it had been important at the time. Yet no matter what she told herself, she knew she had to return to Simbayo and find out if it was still there.

Her reflexes were no longer quick enough to enable her to fly a plane; she was aware of that. So she took a commercial flight to Salisbury and stayed for ten days with Carolyn and Andrew before proceeding to the Congo.

Andrew left after her third day there, heading out for three months in the southwest part of the country.

"What about Kaputo?" Courtney asked. "What will they do without you?"

"I'm not going back to stay at Simbayo," explained Liliane. "The government wouldn't let me anyhow. I am going back to see if it's still there."

It was on this brief visit to Salisbury that the years of resentment Carolyn had harbored at last surfaced.

It started one evening when Liliane commented, "You seem to enjoy your work a great deal."

Tersely, Carolyn answered, "It has its rewards."

Liliane had noticed that Carolyn seemed tense and short-tempered; she had barely kissed Andrew good-bye. In the evening, she sat around making polite conversation with Liliane, tapping her nails on the table, wishing she were at work. She was certain that they were on the verge of some great discovery, and having to sit around and listen to her mother talk of returning to Simbayo was not her top priority. It irritated her to watch Courtney's admiring gaze follow her mother's every gesture, listen to Courtney say, "I want to go to Simbayo, too."

Liliane patted her granddaughter's hand. "If it's still in existence, I promise you that one of these years we shall go." She smiled at Carolyn. "You can see where your mother was born and where she grew up."

"I didn't grow up there," Carolyn said sharply. "I was sent away from there when I was seven years old."

Liliane felt a sharp pain in her chest. That's how she's always seen it. She still doesn't understand. She looked at her daughter.

Caro doesn't have much of a sense of humor, Liliane realized.

She's always so serious. Not that she couldn't laugh; she did. But she was so intense, so absorbed in whatever project was consuming her, that she failed to see humor—and certainly she never saw any about herself.

Suddenly, Liliane saw the look in Courtney's eyes—eyes that begged her mother . . . for what? And it dawned on her that in some way Carolyn had left Courtney—maybe Andrew and Justin, too—in a way she herself had never voluntarily left Caro. Caro's mind is not with her family, thought Liliane. Her mind is down at her lab, wondering what those green monkeys should be showing her, wondering what was incubating in her petri dishes, wondering how she might help save African lives.

Courtney looked at Liliane when she heard her sigh. Caro is compounding what I started, thought Liliane, but she doesn't realize it. And if I confront her with that, she'll deny it.

Over the last few years, Carolyn's job had changed dramatically. While Sam and the field group tried to round up the rapidly vanishing elephants of southern Rhodesia and provide havens for them on the wildlife refuges, Carolyn's work had shifted in another direction. It had begun when the group worked on the study of the tsetse fly and why it bred in some fields and not in adjoining ones. Where the tsetse proliferated, cattle could not be raised and tribes starved. The carcasses of dead cattle, victims of the dread encephalitis, littered the countryside. The advent of DDT helped to eliminate the insects, but as time passed and scientists became skeptical of the side effects of the chemical, further studies were needed.

In the process, Carolyn's interest shifted from helping to round up the animals for preservation to the area she had been trained for: immunology. By studying the animals, she hoped to discover what could be determined about the diseases that were peculiar to Africa. Once this was ascertained, she would try to discover a vaccine that could save thousands, if not millions, of lives.

Sam encouraged her. Though Andrew listened to her, his reaction to her, she thought, was the same as hers toward his work. Because they loved each other, they wanted to be interested in each other's work, they listened and asked questions, but it was seldom a sharing, for neither quite understood what the other was doing. And though Andrew always listened to Carolyn with pride, part of him yearned for a woman who would be waiting for him when he returned home from his jaunts. On the other hand, he would not want Carolyn to react as Michelle did. Michelle seemed to stop living when Sam left. Unless the rumors were true. Then she at least came to life nights. When Andrew would dance with Michelle at the club, when Sam sat watching the dancers or was involved with Carolyn in a discussion that lit up their faces, she brushed her legs against his, managed to make him aware of her breasts against his chest. He could imagine how other men, not as devoted to their wives as he was, might react to Michelle. He would tell Carolyn about this and say, "Poor Sam."

Carolyn would add, "I imagine Michelle thinks 'Poor Michelle.' She thinks all relationships with men must be sexual. I once told her that rules out half the world."

Andrew brushed his lips through her hair. "God, you smell good."

"Are you sure it's not formaldehyde?" She laughed.

WITH ANDREW ALREADY GONE FOR SEVERAL MONTHS, LILIANE HEADED back to Simbayo, with the children in school all day, Carolyn was able to throw herself wholeheartedly into her latest project. Green monkeys, which proliferated in so many tribal areas, showed signs of a disease similar to those that mysteriously affected a few people in most of the tribes. It was only after Liliane left that Carolyn thought, I should have asked Mama. It sounds so much like the mystery disease she's been chasing for years, like whatever killed Uncle Jack.

What if it really *was* that mystery disease? What if it's something that's been going on for years, undetected, not quite pinpointed—an undefined disease, something we don't yet understand? Her blood began to race; what were those symptoms of Jack's so many years ago—symptoms that Mama had seen now and then in the natives, too, and felt so frustrated not to understand, not to know how to help?

Even though it was after ten, even though she had been planning to go to bed early, she threw a sweater around her shoulders and dashed out to the garage, trying to start the car without waking the children.

IN THE MEANTIME, LILIANE WAS CHUGGING DOWN THE OLD FAMILIAR Mombayo, her heart churning with both memories and hope. The

Oregon was no longer, but she had been able to book passage on an old, rather small boat whose erratic motor kept the passengers awake nights. It delivered goods to the villages along the river, as the *Oregon* used to. There were no longer logging camps or missions to cater to, and the supplies were meager, but the captain, a tall, rugged black man with eyes that never quite looked at her, assured her that the hospital at Simbayo still operated.

The humidity enervated her as it had in the very beginning, the way it had always affected Marsh. It sapped her energy. She had forgotten the glare of the air in the jungle, after those clear blue skies far from the equator. She had forgotten how damp one's clothes became in only a few minutes. These things had not bothered her during her years in the tropical forest, but now they slammed themselves at her, and the humidity made her tired and queasy.

Yet the incessant buzz of insects, the crocs sliding into the muddy water and gliding along with the boat, the inevitable, indefatigable chatter of monkeys overhead, the deep silence of the jungle all seemed like dear, lost memories to her and she felt, "I'm coming home."

She watched as naked children ran along the banks of the river when the boat pulled up to, and left, small villages. Nothing seemed to have changed. The havoc wrought by the revolution had left no traces here in the heart of the Congo—of Zaire, she corrected herself.

Then suddenly a moment of déjà vu overcame her. The bend in the river—she recalled the first time she had seen it, when Rose's hand had reached out to touch her arm and she had said, "There. Around the next bend. There's Simbayo." And she remembered the happy look in Rose's gray eyes, nearly hidden behind her thick glasses, and she almost waited for Heidi to greet them at the dock. She smiled to herself, remembering her first impression of Heidi, realizing how wrong she'd been and how much she and Heidi had come to love one another.

Love. She had never known love like the love she'd had here. Not just Baxter and Marsh and Caro; all of the people she had worked with she had loved. The thousands of patients, the lepers, Naldani—oh, dear Naldani. True friend. Are you still here? And Anoka? What has happened to you?

Her heart pounded so loudly she did not hear the boat's whistle as they rounded the bend that brought Simbayo into view and back into her heart.

Her hand fluttered to her chest and she felt the deep intake of breath she couldn't control.

Simbayo had not burned.

ON THAT SAME EVENING, THE CONTENTS IN A PETRI DISH ONE thousand five hundred miles to the southeast were about to affect her life—and the lives of Carolyn and Andrew, of Courtney and Justin, of Sam, and of who knows how many others. More than one drama was set in motion that night.

Carolyn sat hunched over a microscope, staring at the slide, sketching what she saw on onionskin paper. She had never seen what she was now observing. It perplexed and excited her.

Damn, she thought, I wish we had facilities to photograph this.

So engrossed was she that she did not hear the door open, did not see Sam staring at her from the doorway, did not hear his silent footsteps, did not sense that another person was with her even when he stood next to her. He did not know how long he stood there, watching her drawing, thinking her hair looked like spun silver under the single lamp she had lit, listening to her murmuring to herself.

When he did say softly, "What the hell are you doing here at this time of night?" she was so startled her hands flew from the microscope, knocking over the petri dish that she had carelessly left uncovered.

"Oh, no," she cried, jumping off the stool, "now we've lost it!"

With dismay, she knelt down, cutting her knee on the jagged edge of the broken glass dish. Looking up at Sam, she said, "Get something to wipe this up." Her first thought was for the loss; her second was for safety.

"I've no idea what's in this," she said, her voice on the verge of tears. "Oh, Sam, I think we're on to something." She did not notice the blood on her knee, but splinters of glass were wedged in her fingers.

"Carolyn, I'm sorry." His voice was filled with apology.

"It's not your fault," she assured him, "though, heaven knows, you scared me. It's my fault for forgetting to put the cover back on."

"Cover or not," Sam said, "the dish would have fallen anyhow. I should have let you know I was here instead of scaring you."

They soaked up the broth as best they could, putting the paper towels in an airtight bag.

"All is not lost," she said. "There's another dish with the same culture." Despite the interruption and the destroyed culture, Carolyn's eyes lit up. "We're on to something, but I'm not sure what. I think it's something big. Something no one's seen before."

Sam took her hand in his, searching for the splinters of glass and brushing them away, dabbing her hand with alcohol. Neither of them saw the blood on her stocking, drying now to a dark red.

"Is that what you're doing here at this hour?" he asked. "It's after midnight."

She shook her head. The hour didn't matter. "I think it's connected with what my mother called her mystery disease," she said. "Can you believe that?" She told Sam about Jack and about her mother's occasional cases for which she could figure no cure and no cause. "She always wished she'd had a tissue of Jack's. Not that it would have helped her then. But we might now be able to define what killed him. And discover what these monkeys have that they pass on to the occasional tribesman."

"Or vice versa," said Sam.

Carolyn looked at him sharply. Sam always made her think of things she had not thought of on her own. His blue eyes were looking at her in a way she had not seen before.

"What are you doing here?" she asked.

"I often come here at night," he answered. "When I can't sleep. When . . ."

He was silent.

"When . . . When what?" she urged him.

He reached out and took her hands in his, their eyes meeting. "When I can't get you out of my mind. When you stay on the ceiling and I see you whether I shut my eyes or not, when I turn over and it's not you there, when I need to be where I can smell you, where I can visualize you hunched over a microscope talking to yourself . . ."

Carolyn stared at him. He leaned down and kissed first the palm of her right hand and then the left. She felt the imprint of his lips wind up her arms, and she shivered. Yet she did not withdraw her hands. She looked into the eyes she thought she knew so well and saw there was much she did not know.

"Sam," she whispered, "don't do this. Don't say these things." Then more loudly, "Don't destroy our friendship."

His blue eyes searched hers; he dropped her hands abruptly.

Turning his back to her, he walked over to the door. He stood there as she stared at his rigid back; then he turned, his lips pulling into a smile that did not touch the rest of his face.

"Hoots is open all night. Want some coffee? I'd like to hear more about this mystery disease."

They were back on their old familiar footing; the only difference was that she still felt the stamp of his lips on the palms of her hands.

WHEN SHE AWOKE IN THE MORNING, SHE LAY THINKING NOT OF HER lab work, not if it were too late to see the children off to school, but of Sam.

Maybe Michelle's right after all, she thought ruefully. Maybe all relationships between the sexes are sexual. Yet she knew that was not true. But she also recognized that in one brief instant, her nine-year relationship with Sam had changed.

Why? she asked herself. Just because he said he thinks of me? Can't we be the same toward each other as we've always been? She knew they might not be able to. She would always be wondering if he were thinking . . .

Tossing the covers aside, she bounded out of bed, headed for the shower. As she shampooed her hair, she wondered if she were afraid. No, she was sure she wasn't. Not even afraid her friendship with Sam would deteriorate. They had too much in common for that to happen. After all, it was Sam to whom she turned when she needed to share a new experiment, Sam with whom she got excited at a mutual discovery; it was Sam—and only Sam—who understood her devotion to her work, who shared her wonder and excitement. It was Sam . . .

She turned off the water and wrapped a towel around her head. Drying herself in front of the mirror, she tried to view herself objectively, tried to see what her thirty-eight-year-old body really looked like, tried to imagine how it would look to Sam.

"Oh, God," she said aloud, realizing where her thoughts had led her. "Dear God."

After throwing on a skirt and a blouse, slipping into sandals, she ran down the stairs. She forced herself to think of what she'd seen under the microscope last night. What if something happened to that other culture? She'd inadvertently destroyed one.

She'd ask Sam—maybe they could go together for just a week—to capture several monkeys. They'd have to go north for that, do experiments to find infected monkeys and bring them back. She'd get cages and keep several at the lab, study them. She shook her head furiously, as though to negate thoughts of caging animals. It was an idea repellent to her, yet she understood that by sacrificing a few monkeys, she might discover a way to save hundreds or thousands of human lives.

As she drove to work, she realized she was playing with fire. What if an infected monkey escaped in an urban area and bit someone? What was she thinking of—a week alone with Sam?

CHAPTER 47

▼

PETELO SAT IN THE OFFICE, IN THE CHAIR BEHIND THE DESK, AND looked up as Liliane appeared in the doorway. She heard the sharp intake of his breath. Neither of them said anything. Then he stood and walked over to her.

He had become a giant in the years since she had last seen him. He wore a neat short-sleeved khaki shirt, open-necked, and trim khaki shorts.

He seemed confused about how to greet her, so Liliane held out both her hands. He clasped them and looked down at her before putting his arms around her and crushing her in a bearlike hug. Closing her eyes, she remembered the very minute he had entered the world. It seemed like yesterday, rather than thirty-eight years ago. Was it really that long ago?

"Let me look at you," she said, taking a step back and placing her hands on his arms. "Your parents, are they . . . ?"

"Only my mother," he answered, not letting go of her. "But she is old . . . not like you. We wondered if you were still alive."

Naldani, he told her, was certain that she was. They knew nothing of the fate of anyone who had been at Simbayo.

"But let us not talk without my mother. She would not forgive me. Come, she is at my house this afternoon."

He led her out of the office, which looked so much like she had left it, through the compound toward Marsh's old cottage where she had lived for so many years. It still stood, bougainvillea entwined around the porch, and she heard the old familiar sound of the rushing river. Automatically, she looked across, expecting to see the flock of white storks above the little rapids and was delighted to see there were more than ever. It hadn't changed.

Sitting on the verandah, with a little boy about four at her knees, in a chair that Marsh had helped Anoka to make, sat a woman who looked indescribably old. She would never have recognized her. Tufts of grizzled gray hair barely covered her head; wrinkles made her face resemble a monkey's; veins stood out on her gnarled hands. Her bare feet tapped to a rhythm that only she could hear. How could she have grown so old in just eight years?

Then Liliane realized that Naldani had passed the average age limit by far. She and Anoka had been old by Congolese standards years ago.

When Petelo said, "Mother, look who I've brought," the old woman turned her head toward him, and Liliane could see that a milky film covered her left eye.

"She's still the best midwife anywhere," Petelo murmured in a low voice. "But women must come to her now."

Naldani stared quizzically at Liliane, so unexpected this late afternoon, so unfamiliar-looking with her own nearly white hair. Then the black woman gasped; her good eye came alive. Pushing herself against the arms of the chair, she rose more quickly than Liliane expected. The frail arms reached out, and she let out a little screech, which sounded more like a sob.

Liliane moved toward her friend. Before they flung their arms around one another, they stood for just a second, their eyes fastened on each other, the past come to life.

"Oh, dear friend," cried Liliane, tears stinging her cheeks as the two women embraced. "I didn't know if I'd ever see you again."

DURING THE WEEKS SHE STAYED AT SIMBAYO, LILIANE LEARNED THAT Anoka had died the year before, three years after Petelo had returned to help run Simbayo. The present government, he told Liliane, had tried to urge him to stay in Kinshasa. He had been afraid they would force him to do so, to run the hospital there, but he had adamantly refused. Someday, he imagined, he'd have no choice—the need for him would be greater in the capital—but he had had to return to Simbayo. Fortunately, the University of Liverpool was willing to pay the present government a great deal of money for Simbayo to be their research center on tropical diseases. Though the university and the government were still negotiating, Petelo felt assured that the grant would go through; soon these woods would be filled with British researchers. He told her with pride in his voice, "I will be in charge of it. That may help keep me away from Kinshasa."

Anoka and Naldani had returned to Simbayo when they heard that the marauders had passed through and would not return. Despite all of their querying over the years, they never discovered what had happened to Liliane or any of the other white people at Simbayo. They did know that there had been a massacre at Nkunda's village.

Liliane told them of Rose and Heidi but confessed to a year's loss of memory. She told them of her trek from Bukavu to Nairobi, and of Marsh, and of Carolyn's children and her work. She told them about Kaputo, which Naldani could not even comprehend. She told them, not in so many words, that her heart had been put on hold, waiting for the day she could return to Simbayo.

"No place else feels like home," she said as beads of perspiration trickled down her cheek.

Liliane met Charmaine, a small, erect woman whose features were Caucasian and whose skin was more tan than black. She was an Algerian nurse whom Petelo had met and married in Paris. Their children were Malia, six, and the little boy she'd seen playing with Naldani, Jean, who was four, the image of his father at the same age.

Petelo invited Liliane to assist him in operations and in the line of patients that still waited each day, but she soon realized he did not really need her; he was being polite.

She saw Simbayo running smoothly—as smoothly as it had run when she and Naldani and Anoka and Heidi and Rose and Philippe were in charge. There were no outposts now, no schools, but Simbayo was a model hospital to which people still traveled many days for help.

Simbayo did not need her. It had its own people. It had Petelo, whom she had delivered into the world and whom she had sent off to study medicine. That it no longer needed her saddened her only a little. What Baxter, and then she, had planted here still flourished. The seeds had taken root. She thought that was enough. She realized also that at her age the tropics took too much out of her.

But she also knew she had to come back again, and soon, next summer, perhaps. Before Naldani died. She had to bring Courtney to Simbayo. Already Liliane knew that the idea of Simbayo burned brightly in Courtney's imagination; she had to share its actuality with the little girl who had become so all-important to her. Even more important than Kaputo, which, Liliane realized, was a place that did still need her.

"Do you feel you've absolved yourself of guilt?" Sam asked as he slammed on the brakes. In the back of the jeep were two captured monkeys. He jumped out of the vehicle and gingerly lifted out one of the cages.

"What is that supposed to mean?" asked Carolyn, trying to heave the other cage to the ground. But it was too heavy for her. In a minute, Sam was beside her, his shoulder brushing against hers as he leaned over and, together, they lifted it out. The monkey screeched in anger.

She had studiously avoided closeness or any personal conversation during the three days they'd been on the Mozambique border. This time, though, Sam stood his ground, not moving away from her.

"Calling to invite Michelle to come along with us." Carolyn couldn't tell whether irritation or amusement was reflected in his voice. "Did you want to assure yourself, or her, that this trip is innocent?"

"Maybe to tell you," she answered, though it sounded more like a question than an answer.

"You knew she wouldn't want to come into the backcountry." His voice smiled along with his eyes.

They had brought no bearers or cooks on this trip. Carolyn had told herself over and over that this was all right, that nothing was going to happen between her and Sam. Each night since she'd suggested the trip, she had lain in bed and reminded herself how much she loved Andrew.

Yet she also admitted how much Sam had come to mean to her over the years. It was Sam with whom she shared what had become the most vital part of her life, Sam with whom she worked at important tasks, Sam who shared her philosophy of life and her attitudes toward the future of Africa. There was never any tension with Sam as there often was with Andrew. Sam viewed dams the same way she did; Sam valued tribal traditions as she did; Sam's priorities to protect animals and their habitat warred with those who wanted to develop the Rhodesias. Sam was as bored with the superficial aspects of Salisbury society as she was. Wasn't he actually more of a soulmate than Andrew?

Such thoughts made her feel unfaithful, if not guilty. There had never been, not once in all of their thirteen years together, a time when she had questioned her love for Andrew. Their times apart, and even their disagreements, added an edge to their relationship; there had been very few dull times. There was tenseness now and then, when she disapproved of Andrew's bringing twentieth-century values to Africa, but she knew Andrew respected and loved the land as she did. Only their visions of how best to use their knowledge clashed. Hers and Sam's never did.

As she and Sam had driven north under the unrelenting sun, she'd studied him. Though his actions that night in the lab had dismayed her, they had also awakened an awareness in her. Maybe she did love him a bit.

Sam failed to hear her sigh as the air whistled past them while he zoomed down the dusty road. She and Andrew were tied together with a passion that had never lessened, with Courtney and Justin, with the shared intimacies—large and small—of thirteen years. But she and Sam were also laced together, not only with a common vision, but with the closeness of working side by side and sharing that work. She always knew how Sam would feel about something; he would feel exactly as she did.

Wasn't that a form of love?

When she and Sam had spent the last three nights sleeping outdoors beside a fire designed to ward off four-legged prowlers, a few feet from each other in their sleeping bags, gazing at the stars like diamonds glittering on a velvet background, Sam had not said a personal word, but she sensed a control on his part. He pointed out constellations, he recited poetry, and he wondered whether or not there was a meaning to the universe. She had not done those things since she'd been a girl with Marsh.

Last night, she had said drowsily what she felt as they lay in the dark. "I like being out here with you. I feel close to you." In the morning, she reflected that perhaps she should not have said it. Sam had not answered her. Had said nothing to her before she fell asleep.

Had she wanted him to make a move? Had it been an invitation?

Now, when he brought up her phone call to Michelle, she had no real answer.

"Wanna talk about us?" he asked, amusement lighting his

eyes though his body was as tense as a coiled spring.

"Us?" she asked. "There's nothing to talk about."

Sam laughed loudly and walked away from her. He knelt down where they had had a fire and reached out to gather tiny dried twigs for kindling. Methodically, he built a base for a new fire.

Carolyn watched him, liking the deliberateness of him, the way he knew exactly what he was doing, the artful manner in which he laid the twigs, one by one. She had always admired the fact that Sam never had to use more than one match to light a fire. He would let the fire build while they drank gin and tonics in the late afternoons and then, as the sky turned violet before streaking itself with vermilion, he would put steaks on the fire. She would flounder through a salad. He would throw a can of vegetables into a frying pan and wave it back and forth over the flames. Simple fare tasted so wonderful out here. By the time they'd finished dinner and sat drinking coffee, only the disappearing rays of the sun would be visible on the horizon and the lemon moon would be partway up the sky in the east; the first star would be visible. The cries of birds heading toward treetops would be the only sound, and then silence would fill the air. Only the crackling of the fire would be heard, and they would sit in silence and become a part of the magnificent night.

But that night, when Sam got up from his camp chair to put another log on the fire, he walked over to her and said, "Stand up." She looked up at him, wondering whether or not to obey. He leaned down and put a hand around her wrist. "Please," he said.

He pulled her to her feet, and by the firelight she could see his blue eyes staring into hers. She could feel his breath, swore she could feel the heat from his body. Still looking down at her, he reached out to take her hands.

When she did not withdraw, when she stood still with her hands in his, he pulled her to him, his mouth on hers hungrily, his tongue pushing her lips apart, driving his passion into her. His arms wound around her, crushing her against him, and with his lips against her ear he moaned, "Oh, God. I've tried not to do this for years." And he kissed her again.

Instead of pushing him away, instead of saying "Sam, stop," she found her tongue meeting his, found herself thrusting forward to meet him, found herself pushing against the hand that found her breast and cradled it.

Then she broke away from him.

"Sam, I can't."

"Why not?" He urged, "You want to. I can feel it."

It was true. Her body wanted him. She wanted her bare breasts against the leanness of his chest; she yearned for the length of their bodies to touch, to feel his legs against hers. She wanted to feel again the warmth of his kisses on her neck, his hands enclosing her breasts.

She wanted also to feel his tongue on her nipples . . . the hardness of him between her legs . . . his hands on her buttocks.

"Oh, God," she cried into the night, moving away from him. "I do want you, but it's wrong. It's wrong, wrong, wrong."

In two long strides he was behind her, his arms encircling her, whispering in her ear, "Right or wrong has nothing to do with this moment. Do you know how painful it is to work in the same room with you, to touch in passing, to sit for hours and talk about our research, to share our ideas, to look at you and not reach for you? Not kiss you? Have you any idea how painful—and how worthwhile—you make my life?"

He pulled her to him. "How often I've hated Andrew. I torture myself at night when he's at home, imagining him making love to you, touching you, kissing you. Listen," he commanded.

A leopard coughed in the distance.

"Listen," he repeated. "Listen to the pounding of your heart. Here, put your hand over your heart. Feel the pulsing." He took her right hand in his and laid it over her heart. "Listen! Hear the blood pumping through your body. Listen—to the wildness we have always shared, ever since Kariba." His hand left hers, sliding down her stomach, pulling her ever closer into him. His breath rushed into her ear.

Kariba? As long ago as that?

His hand slid under the waistband of her skirt, down the silkiness of her underwear, his fingers intensifying her desire.

She fought to keep the image of Andrew in front of her, but his silhouette became fuzzy and indistinct as she felt Sam's hand holding her close, his fingers exploring.

His hand had left her stomach; his fingers were unbuttoning her blouse. She felt disembodied, as though she were floating; his tongue ran lightly across her earlobe, down her neck, across her shoulder. She quivered. Her skirt fell to the ground; slowly, he pulled her blouse off. She hadn't moved.

When she did turn to face him, he stood naked, his legs spread apart, his hands on hips.

What a beautiful body, she thought. Lean, tan, tall, strong.

"*You* take the rest of your clothes off," he said.

She slid out of them.

There was not a sound anywhere except for the spitting of the fire.

"When I am lonely at night—which is most of the time—I call you before me, trying to imagine you naked." His voice cracked as he studied her. "I have seen your breasts and your thighs. I've imagined my fingers on the velvet of your skin and visualized your hair fanning out on the pillow next to me." He paused. "Are you frightened, Carolyn? Afraid of me?"

I don't know, she thought. A soft breeze sprang up and rushed over her.

Sam took three steps and knelt before her, staring up at her. He reached his arms around her waist and hugged her to him, biting her stomach gently, burrowing his head against her.

"I've dreamed," he said in a thick voice, "of how your nipples would taste, of how your tongue would feel on me and whether you would like that. I've wanted to taste of you, to explore you, to be in you. I have wanted all of you that it is possible to get."

He reached up and pulled her to the ground under him. His tongue began at her breast. . . .

CAROLYN STARED AT HER REFLECTION IN THE MIRROR. TOMORROW, Andrew would be home.

She wondered if she looked any different. If he could tell by looking at her.

Guilt and anguish had plagued her for the two months since she and Sam began making love. She didn't want to be unfaithful to Andrew. She loved him. She didn't want to hurt their marriage. Over and over, she had envisioned his confronting her, telling her the marriage was over, that he could no longer live with her. She would then sob herself to sleep on her wet pillow.

When she'd awake in the morning, she would imagine life without Sam; she tried to picture what value her life would have were she not allowed to go to the lab every day, if she could no longer follow the trail of disease that was becoming increasingly visible. She would close her eyes tightly, trying to erase everything but the sense of what it would be like if Sam never touched her again.

Making love with Sam was so different from the way it is with Andrew, Carolyn mused. There's an urgency to it; a sense of danger and excitement. Her body ached when she left him; never more so than when they had spent that week together. They had made love incessantly; they had made love standing up, sideways, upside down, and almost, she smiled at her reflection, inside out. She had always considered Sam one of the gentlest people she knew, but the pent-up emotion that had consumed him for nine years burst forth with an intensity he had no desire to control.

They had caught a total of five monkeys, she remembered, and not even the scratches and bites inflicted on them as they captured the monkeys dissuaded them from the passion neither wanted to restrain. They made love like caged animals themselves. They made love all night long—slowly, erotically, over and over again.

Andrew always played with her in ways designed to excite and titillate her. He would slow himself down to wait for her; Andrew was intent on pleasing her. Andrew played her body as a violinist plays a Stradivarius.

Not Sam. Sam did what he did because he needed to. Yet the fury with which he made love excited her. He didn't ask what pleased her; he did what pleased him. He uses me, she thought, for his own pleasure. But in so doing, he had brought every nerve in her body alive. At times, he hurt her. And she craved it. He hurt her because he could not control his desire, because his passion would not allow him to be gentle. Out there in the savannah he had brought her to climaxes over and over again, building her up until she thought she could not stand it another second, until she thought she might burst from the fire within, from the frayed nerve endings that were raw with desire.

Back in town, they had managed to meet at night, in the lab, several times a week. It was never quick. It was never calm. Their lovemaking possessed the force of a hurricane.

During the day, too, though they didn't touch each other, they made love. When she'd run a white count and find what she'd been sure she'd see, she'd call him over to look. It was just as intense as when their bodies melded.

This afternoon, when they were sure they were alone in the lab, they locked the doors and stripped their clothes off and made love in his office, on the threadbare rug, and on the couch with a sagging spring, and on a chair. They knew this might be the last time they could make love for weeks or months.

They had not talked about it. They both knew that when Andrew came home they would have to stop. Sam knew that Carolyn loved her husband, but he also knew that she loved him. It would have to be enough. At the end she had said, "Love me so deeply you imprint yourself on me and I can carry you with me for all the days and weeks ahead."

She was like a wild woman with Sam.

"Something's got to give," she said to the mirror as she slowly brushed her hair, longer now than when Andrew had left because Sam had asked her to let it grow. He loved to brush it, to wind it around his hand and kiss the ends, to hypnotize her with his brush strokes.

She wondered if she could be as she had always been with Andrew. Was she tarnished now? Would he be able to tell she had been with Sam?

Yet the thought that tomorrow she would see Andrew sent delight through her. She loved him not one bit less because Sam was part of the love she had to give.

She stared soberly into the mirror, saying aloud, "It's too good. I have more than my share. A husband I adore. A lover I love. Children I cherish. A job that makes me feel worthwhile. I know I'm on the edge of something big, something that may change this part of Africa. Something has to be wrong. Something somewhere must be wrong."

It was. It had already gone wrong: When the petri dish broke and neither she nor Sam had noticed the cut on her knee where the blood clotted wine-red, and the bacteria from the dish mingled with the blood that did not congeal. It had gone wrong again when the first monkey they had caught, that week they spent together, clawed her and the scratch was too small for her to bother with.

She was right. It was too good to last.

CHAPTER 48

▼

It's psychosomatic, she told herself. It's guilt eating away at me.

She had told Sam she would allow nothing to interfere with her marriage. "I love Andrew," she'd said.

Sam knew that.

There were stolen kisses in the lab now and then, but Sam put no pressure on Carolyn. She began to share her enthusiasm about her discoveries with Andrew and even with Courtney, whom she'd bring to the lab some Saturday mornings. One of the monkeys had died, and though this saddened Carolyn, she and Sam were able to perform tissue cultures. These indicated that the monkey had died from something indefinable, something they had not seen under a microscope before, a microorganism neither could identify.

"It looks like a virus," Sam had volunteered, doubt in his voice.

Carolyn showed Courtney how to incubate the cultures. "First you put blood or saliva or tissue on a swab, then dip the swab in broth in a test tube. Then you let it incubate for twenty-four to forty-eight hours."

"How do you do that?" asked Courtney, delighted that her mother was taking the time to instruct her. She so often wondered exactly what her mother did in the lab.

"You put the test tube on a rack in this machine; it looks like a refrigerator, but it's an incubator. It keeps a certain heat so the microbe will flourish. After the time you've allotted for incubation, you take it out of the incubator and streak it onto a plate of agar, a jellylike substance, in a petri dish—this thin glass dish with a glass cover—and incubate *that* for another twenty-four to forty-eight hours. Then you look at it under a stereoscope—"

"What's a stereoscope?"

"A little like a microscope but not as high-powered. Anyhow, you observe it and count colonies, or see if they're behaving in what is considered a normal fashion."

Courtney watched, fascinated, even though Carolyn would not permit her to touch any of it. "Let's not take chances," Carolyn told her daughter. "We're not sure exactly what we're incubating here, and I wouldn't want you to . . ."

That didn't frighten Courtney. How could something so innocent-looking—invisible, really—be dangerous?

The three infected monkeys—two now that the first one had died—exhibited symptoms similar to those they'd studied in the Mbela tribe. Carolyn's particular pet, Dee Dee, began to cough and lose weight. As it did, its white blood count went down, down, down.

Carolyn could hardly tear herself away from the lab, but excitement and exhaustion led to flu shortly before Christmas.

Liliane had arrived for a month's visit and insisted Caro stay in bed. "Your bravura will only give everyone else the bug," Liliane insisted. Carolyn gave in almost gracefully, too sick even to enjoy snuggling in the pillows that Liliane plumped up for her. Her fever was so high that all she did was sleep for three days. Then the fever broke and Liliane thought she began to recuperate until a croupy cough signified the onset of pneumonia.

"She needs penicillin," Liliane told Andrew.

That seemed to clear it up, though Carolyn was still pale and weak on Christmas Day. Andrew carried her downstairs and she lay on the couch as presents were opened.

Andrew's gift to her was a sapphire ring. "We never had time for an engagement." He grinned. "This blue is to remind you every day that our love is as deep as the sky—and as endless."

Carolyn winced. How could she do what she had done to Andrew? She loved him so much.

What if he found out? Andrew couldn't handle it, she knew. I shall have to see, she told herself, that he never finds out.

When Carolyn returned to work, after New Year's, Liliane worried that she wasn't recuperating as fast as she should. The cough hung on. Her first day back at work, Carolyn wondered if she would make it through the day. Her head was resting on her desk when Sam entered her office.

In one long step he was beside her. "Darling, what is it? Are you still sick?"

"Oh, Sam, I don't know." She lifted her head and he was aware of her paleness and the listlessness of her turquoise eyes. "I don't know whether I'm really sick or guilt is gnawing at me."

He reached out a hand to touch her hair. "My God, you're soaking wet," he said. "You're going home."

"No." She shook her head. "Not yet. I have things I must do here. Oh, Sam." She burst into tears.

He knelt beside her and gathered her in his arms.

"I feel so shameful. If Andrew ever found out, he'd be so hurt. And," she sobbed, "I love him too much to hurt him."

Her tears dampened his shoulder; he stroked her head, holding her close in an attempt to calm her. He didn't know what to say. Since Andrew's return, they had not made love; they had continued the routine they had established over the years—except for kisses now and then. Should he tell her he wouldn't kiss her again?

"But I love you, too." Her body shook as she tried to get her breath and talk through her tears. "Oh, Sam, I feel so awful. I think I'm making myself sick."

Gently, he lifted her head from his shoulder and looked into her glazed eyes. "Carolyn, flu is not from guilt. You've had a bacterial infection. Don't do this to yourself."

She took a deep breath, steadied by his hands on her shoulders.

"Carolyn, I love you. I would do anything in the world for you. Leave my family, give up my work, even give you up. I can, if you insist, never kiss you again, never touch . . . Oh, God, could I really? Carolyn, love, we promised to do nothing when Andrew's home. I die each night, knowing you may be in his arms, that you may be sleeping with your head on his shoulder. I hear the two of you breathing in unison, and it . . . twists me."

"Oh, Sam." Her bloodshot eyes glistened. "It's not even what we've done. It's that I love you, too. Andrew couldn't stand to know that. Yet I love him as much as I always have."

"If you didn't feel so weak," Sam suggested, "maybe you wouldn't be so upset. Do yourself a favor: go home. Tell me what experiment you were going to conduct today and I'll do it. Go home and go back to bed."

He called Frank, their assistant, and asked him to drive Carolyn home.

Liliane put her back to bed.

"I'm going to work tomorrow," Carolyn said with determination as she fell asleep.

When she awoke in late afternoon, her mother sat in a chair studying her, thinking, She's lost too much weight.

"I'll get you something to eat," she said to Carolyn.

"No, Mama." Carolyn reached out a hand to touch her mother's arm. "Stay with me. I need to talk."

Liliane sat down again, looking fondly at the pale, damp face on the pillow. I don't really know her, she realized.

"Mama." Carolyn put her hand in Liliane's. "Mama, I'm in love with two men."

Liliane heard the intake of her own breath. "Oh, Caro." Her hand tightened around her daughter's.

Carolyn began to talk, telling Liliane everything, telling her about the week she had spent with Sam, about the times they had found to make love in Salisbury before Andrew returned. Her voice was rushed and breathless, and she held on tightly to Liliane's hand. "I think it's making me sick," she concluded.

Liliane moved onto the bed, her cool fingers stroking Carolyn's brow. "Oh, darling." Compassion filled her voice. Her mind blurred as a thirty-nine-year-old memory came to life. She was in the jungle again, and one night it was Marsh's hands that brought her body to life and the next it was Baxter who stroked her.

She heard Carolyn's whisper, "Mama, I understand about you and Papa. I understand . . . why you don't know."

Liliane bent over and put her arms around Caro; together they wept.

"What can I do?" Carolyn asked, but she already knew her mother would have no answer for her.

LILIANE TOOK COURTNEY TO SIMBAYO THAT WINTER. SINCE SHE could no longer fly in, they had to rely on the boat that went downriver. Andrew agreed with Liliane that this was an opportunity Courtney should not miss. "I'm not going on a long trip this year," he told Liliane privately. "I'm worried about Carolyn. I'll fly out to the project and be home weekends." Though Carolyn had gotten over her flu and pneumonia, and her cough had disappeared, she continued to lose weight.

"Everything I do demands such energy," she said to Liliane the night before her mother and daughter took off for two months. Liliane had debated with herself but realized that by staying she could do nothing to help Carolyn. If Carolyn would just get over her feelings of guilt, Liliane thought. I wonder, If Baxter had lived, would I have suffered that way? She dismissed the thought as futile; what's past was past.

And she had to show Simbayo to Courtney. Or show Courtney to Simbayo.

WHEN ANDREW LEFT, SAM MADE NO OVERTURES TO CAROLYN; HE SAW that she was too weak, too thin. If her conscience was doing this to her, he wanted no part in furthering her anguish. They worked closely together; they went out to dinner together or ordered meals sent in. They kissed, but he never went home with her. He never fondled her body. But he looked at her often.

She never stood at her microscope anymore, but always sat.

"My feet feel like they've been smashed. It's painful to walk. D'you think I'm getting arthritis so early in life?" She tried to sound flippant, but he could tell she was worried.

"I've thought and thought about this. Carolyn, I don't think you're imagining this. I don't think guilt is doing this to you. I think something is physically wrong."

"I've been to the doctor. He's done all sorts of tests. He can't find anything."

"I—" He closed his eyes and breathed deeply. "Carolyn, what if it's because there's no test for what you have?"

She stared at him. "You mean, something here?"

He nodded, pain in his eyes.

"But all of the monkeys who have scratched me have scratched you. Wouldn't you have whatever it is, too?" Her eyes pleaded with him.

"I know. I know. Carolyn." He put his arms around her.

But she was thinking, Am I exhibiting some of the same symptoms that the Mbelo have over the years? Some of the same things that Dee Dee had? Dee Dee had died last week. Carolyn wasn't coughing anymore, but she continued to lose weight and she had terrible night sweats several times a week. She told herself that maybe it was early, very early, menopause. Several nights, while Andrew slept, she crept from bed to take her temperature; it was over one hundred and two degrees. Yet by morning it was normal again. Now and then her knees would throb.

Other days she felt fine except that her weight loss affected her energy level.

When Andrew came home weekends, his worry about her intensified. He begged her to stop working, but she claimed it was too important. Though she did say, "Can you take a week off? I want to go to the ocean and walk along the beach."

The next week, with Justin, they headed to the Mozambique beaches. She felt better there, swimming in the salt water, lying in the sunshine, watching the swaying palm trees. Justin had never seen the ocean and was thrilled with the experience. He and Andrew went snorkeling while Carolyn lay on a rubber float in the water. There was hardly anyone else on the beach; a couple walked along hand in hand, their dog running around them.

For the first time in a long while, she felt at peace, rocking rhythmically up and down on the gentle waves. I'm happy, she thought. I'm happy to be here.

She watched a duck bobbing in the water near some rocks. A

large wave washed over it and surprised the duck. Carolyn laughed. The gulls, she noticed, walked right into the waves. They didn't duck under the waves as the ducks did. They didn't seem to have nearly as much fun as the ducks did, either, or the sandpipers that flew in little fleets and hovered above the edge of the waves and then, when the waves rolled out, landed and skittered along the sand and then rose as a chorus line when a new wave arrived.

When they returned home, Carolyn felt much better. "I'm invigorated," she told Andrew. And, indeed, she looked much better. "I think I've even gained some weight," she declared, though her bones still showed sharply.

When Andrew left this time, he felt safer. Carolyn had improved. She tries to do too much, he thought. "I'll fly home in two weeks," he said, kissing her. Skin and bones or not, he thought, she's still the loveliest woman I've ever known. It's just that now she seems fragile, and that was odd for Carolyn.

Before he left, he stopped off at Sam's and asked him to look out for Carolyn. "I'm worried," he said. "She seems better now, but keep an eye on her. It couldn't . . ." He hesitated.

"What?" asked Sam.

"It couldn't be something from the lab, could it? From those damn monkeys?"

Sam sat down, putting his head in his hands. "Do you think I haven't wondered that? But every monkey who's ever scratched or bitten Carolyn has done the same to me. I can't think of anything, any test even, that's been done that we haven't done together. I'm as worried as you are."

Andrew put his hand on Sam's shoulder. "I imagine you are. It's just that I love her so, I can't imagine what I'd do if anything happened to her."

"I love her, too." Sam moaned.

"Everyone does," said Andrew. "She has that about her. You're a good friend, Sam. Take care of her for me, not that she'll let you. Don't let her work too hard." He reached out a hand to shake Sam's. "Thanks."

For the next few weeks, Carolyn improved. Her appetite returned and she gained a few pounds. She slept through the night without waking in cold sweats, and her eyes focused.

But then the weakness returned. Eating hurt her. She began to exist on toast; her energy level fell dramatically. "Dammit, Sam, what can it be?"

"Let me perform a culture—from a tissue, from your blood,

some saliva." She could tell it hurt him to say this. "Let's see if . . ." He didn't finish the sentence. She looked at him, then held out her arm.

After he had drawn blood and put it in a glass vial, he put his hand over hers. Then he leaned over and kissed her. When he sat down next to her, still holding her hand, he said, "I want you to think—think back to when we went out to collect the monkeys. Try to think of every day since then, all the days and months. Has *anything* happened to you that hasn't also happened to me? Think about it. Not right now, but each day."

Carolyn awoke at dawn. She lay awake trying to find some moment unlike others, some time when something could have happened in the lab. She and Sam always wore rubber gloves, always washed before and after an experiment; she never—oh, Jesus Christ! She sat upright.

The night, months ago, when she broke the petri dish!

She got out of bed and pulled on a robe. That broken petri dish. Her throat closed. Oh, dear God, she thought. A rose dawn streaked the sky as she walked down the stairs and into the kitchen. I need water, she thought. She gulped it down greedily. In her mind that night gained momentum . . . the broken petri dish—she and Sam had wiped it up and put all the shards of glass in a bag; Sam had carefully examined her hands for splinters of glass and wiped them all away, disinfecting her hands. But now, for the first time, she remembered taking off her stockings later that night, remembered the caked blood on the knee of her stocking, remembered that when she pulled off her stocking she had pulled the scab loose and covered the tiny wound with a Band-Aid. She had not thought about it again. Had not connected it with the petri dish and its contents. She had forgotten all about it in light of Sam's confession of love that night.

She stared out the window.

"Goddamnit!" Carolyn clenched the glass as she leaned against the countertop. "Goddamnit!"

She squeezed, but it didn't break. She held it up before the window.

Waves broke in the prism of light.

As she breathed in, inhaling deeply, the waves broke against the smooth sand. With exhalation, the wave rolled out, followed by a fleet of sandpipers, the little birds that raced after the waves going out and just ahead of the breakers—never getting caught in the water, hovering over the edge of it.

Carolyn forced herself to breathe deeply. As she pulled air into her lungs, a wave crashed. A sigh escaped her as the ocean rolled out.

With every controlled breath she took, a wave broke. She was willing the ocean into that glass, willing those sandpipers into life.

Hypnotized by the scene, by being able to control the waves with her breathing, she looked into the glass, down the beach. In the distance, under the circling gulls, were two figures and a dog that ran in ever-widening circles around them.

The waves near them were smaller, and she realized her breathing was shallower.

The sky was a milky blue, the ocean had become gray.

The sharp ring of the phone brought her back to reality. She made no move to answer it. It rang and rang. As the sharp staccato noise jarred into her, Carolyn turned the glass upside down.

Very slowly, the ocean poured into the sink, a swirling whirlpool as it went down the drain, circling out of view. The birds had flown away, but the distant couple and their dog were caught in the vortex and disappeared into the dark hole.

"Goddamnit," Carolyn cried, and heard the glass crash as she threw it at the phone. She knew even before the results of Sam's culture were in. "I'm going to die."

BY THE TIME LILIANE AND COURTNEY RETURNED FROM SIMBAYO, Carolyn was bedridden. Sam spent part of every day reading to her; he had a haunted look. Andrew asked that another engineer be assigned to the project he'd started in the southwest and worked out of the home office. Not that he could work; his thoughts never left Carolyn.

That goddamned lab, he thought. But when he had said that, she had responded, "We're on the verge of something really big, Andrew. If we can identify what the microbe is, maybe something can be done about it. Maybe we can save thousands of lives."

But usually she was not so positive. Pain took its toll; morphine alleviated some of it but put her into deep sleeps; when she was conscious, she often seemed to be in a dreamworld where no one could join her. She stared into space.

Over and over, she told herself, This is my penalty—the price I pay—for being unfaithful. Yet when she was fully conscious, she didn't believe that.

When Liliane looked at her emaciated daughter and saw the

sunken eyes, heard the rattled breathing, paralysis struck her. It can't be, she told herself. It's impossible. She asked Sam to do another culture; she wanted to look at it herself. It was all there. The low white blood count, the reduction in lymphocytes, the unidentifiable microbe that behaved like no others.

"It's my mystery disease," she told Sam, tears in her eyes. "I wonder if she caught it so many years ago in Simbayo . . . from Jack, from the two or three others I've seen with this same thing. Oh, dear God."

"I think"—Sam's rage was controlled—"that I'm responsible. I think she caught it right here. If I'd never given her this job, if I'd never—"

Liliane put her arms around him. Together they wept for the person they each loved so dearly. And for themselves.

Andrew sat by Carolyn's bedside, his heart aching for the wasted body. She was unrecognizable as the woman she had been a year ago.

She can't leave me, his heart cried. But he knew that's what she was doing. He knelt on the floor beside the bed, bent over her, his arms flung across the frail body, and cried.

"Darling." He wasn't even sure she was conscious. "Don't leave me. My life began with you. Caro . . ."

Her eyelids fluttered open and she smiled weakly. "Andrew." He had to strain to hear. "Never doubt our love."

"No, darling, I never have. The happiness . . ."

Carolyn's hand touched his arm. "I know. I know. Get Mama."

Andrew rushed downstairs.

Courtney and Sam followed them, standing in the doorway as Andrew and Liliane went to either side of Carolyn's bed.

Carolyn saw them, and a tear inched down her left cheek. Her once silken hair looked like brittle straw; the brilliant blue-green eyes were dulled; the cheekbones sunken. She barely made a dent in the bed. "Mama . . ."

Liliane reached out to enfold her daughter's hand. I wish I'd gone first, she was thinking. Mothers shouldn't outlast daughters.

Carolyn raised her mother's and Andrew's hands to her lips, and there were tears in her eyes.

Standing in the doorway, with Sam's hand on her shoulder, Courtney thought, Mama can't die. Mothers don't die.

When Liliane turned to look over her shoulder, Courtney knew. She burst into tears and ran into her room and cried until her small body was racked with convulsive sobs. Liliane came to her and lay down beside her. They rocked back and forth, cradling each other, until it was dark.

LILIANE WONDERED HOW CAROLYN HAD HAD ENOUGH TIME TO MAKE so many friends. There was standing room only at the funeral. As many blacks attended as whites. Justin was pale and puzzled. Courtney stood rigid and silent. Liliane placed herself between them, holding their hands tightly. Andrew was forced to respond to his fellow mourners, but Liliane saw the pulse in his temple and knew he was using heroic self-restraint. She wanted to tell him he had been a perfect husband, but she didn't. They were all wondering how their lives would go on without Carolyn.

Her eyes red from crying, Michelle sat in the row behind the family. Sam was not there. He was burning down the lab in a fire that spread so quickly it destroyed the whole city block.

PART FOUR

▼

1980
TO
1981

CHAPTER 49

▼

1968

I TOOK THIS JOURNAL WITH ME TO SIMBAYO. BUT I NEVER WROTE A word. At first, I was afraid I'd forget, but every day is burned brightly into my mind.

Lili and I (I've asked her if I may call her that. She said fine.) flew to Mbandaka in commercial planes. Of course, it took seven planes and four days to get there. Nothing was ever on time. We spent more time waiting in hot, tin-roofed buildings than in planes.

Africa is sooo big, and the part we flew over is so green. Mile after mile, day after day, is green trees. Nothing else. Now and then a silver streak of a river. But as far as the horizon it's all green.

At Mbandaka we chartered a little private plane to take us to Simbayo. I was disappointed. I'd been so prepared for the long, lazy trip down the Mombayo, for the turn in the river that would bring me to Simbayo. To the way Lili first saw it. But she said we didn't have time if I was to be back in school in two months.

I'd seen Simbayo before. I knew exactly which building was which and where the dining hall was, and I could tell an okoume from a bokungu tree. I was afraid there would be no drums in the night, but it's still the only way of sending messages from one village to another. It's not quite in the stone age, but not far advanced, except for the hospital, of course. I could tell Lili was watching me, wanting me to see it like she does.

I was ready to love Naldani, but she wasn't the tall, regal princess I'd envisioned. I can't believe she and Lili are almost the same age. She's old and wrinkled. She could hardly see me, but she ran her fingers over my face and through my hair. And, seeing with her fingers, she said to my grandmother, "She looks like Marsh."

"I know." Lili smiled, her hand on my shoulder.

Everyone made a big fuss over us—even all of the British doctors and other scientists who came this last year. Lili had never met any of them. They were proud, they said over and over, to be

▼

part of what she'd helped start so long ago. She kept saying, "Me and Baxter Hathaway."

I remember I used to think Lili was old. But what she really is is beautiful. Something comes out of her to make her beautiful.

She had another bed brought into the little room where we stayed and told me it was the room where she lived her first years at Simbayo.

Petelo—his birthday is the same as my mothers; it made me sad—and his family live in the house my grandfather built. Flowers grow up the verandah posts and cover the roof, flaming reds darting out of the green.

Lili wanted me to see and to feel everything. She tried to make me feel what she felt. We swam in the lagoon she loves, and she told me stories of the past as we lay under the palm trees as parrots flew overhead. I could listen to her forever.

She took me out to the leper island, something she never allowed Mama to do. The buildings there are more modern than the Salisbury hospital, she says. But I looked out and imagined the days long ago when the fingerless natives dug postholes in the ground and peeled bark off logs for the posts. I could hear their voices as they raised a roof and saw people scurrying along thatching palm leaves, people with no toes or fingers. I'd seen it all for years. But there are no people now without noses. Leprosy is what Lili calls "contained."

When we were falling asleep one night and I heard the tomtoms beating faintly, I asked her if she believed in God.

"I believe in something," she answered, "but I'm not sure what. Not the same God I thought I came to Africa for. But something, yes."

I wonder what. I must remember to ask Daddy about it.

I know I've never felt closer to anyone than I did to Lili all summer. I don't mean I love her more than Mama or Daddy, but I sort of felt like part of her was inside me. I felt, as we walked around or sat under the okoume trees, we sometimes were one. I know that's silly, but I felt it anyhow.

She let me do something wonderful. She let me see a baby be born. The midwife thought I was too young, but Lili said, "Nonsense. It's never too early to experience the beautiful and the awesome." Then she turned to me. "This may be as close as I get to understanding God." She held my hand the whole time, and it was like a miracle. I know I can't put it into words. Someday I want to do that. Be part of miracles. When I came home and told Rosalie about it, she said, "Ugh. That would make me sick."

I told Lili I wanted to be a nurse. She said, "Be a doctor." I wonder if I could.

I wish I'd been born many years ago. It's too late for me to create a Simbayo, isn't it? How I envy Lili. She's helped so many people. I think she really knows how to love.

1971

I CAN'T BE FIFTEEN. ONLY YESTERDAY I WAS TWELVE.

Funny, I never write in my journal during the school year. It's when I'm busiest, of course. With school and friends. This year I've also learned how to play tennis, and how to dance, and I fell in love. I think Steven wishes I'd fall in love with him, but I fell in love with biology. Having a good teacher helped, but I knew I was going to love it before the year began. I have to love it if I'm going to be a doctor.

I told Daddy what Lili said about it. And he said, "Honey, you can do whatever you put your mind to." He thinks Mama would be pleased.

He misses Mama a lot. He spends all his time, when he's home, with Justin and me, but he's lonely, I can tell. He still leaves Mama's clothes in her closet even though she's been dead three years. Dead. That's a sad word. A dead word. I wonder why Mama's being dead doesn't make me as lonely as it does Daddy? I guess because of Lili. I get a letter from her every week. And I write to her, a little bit (sometimes a lot) every night before I go to bed and mail it all to her every Saturday. I'd think she'd be bored at all my thoughts and questions, and I even told her about Steven kissing me. I told her bells didn't ring and I thought they were supposed to.

She wrote an answer and though I know she wasn't laughing at me (she'd *never* do that), I could almost *feel* her smiling. She said, "Bells only ring when you're in love. But don't wait to kiss a boy until you're in love. A *little* experience is good for you. Notice I underlined *little*." I can talk with Lili about things that my friends don't even talk about with their mothers.

Justin doesn't know what he's missing. He only went out on the savannah with us one summer and was bored. He wanted to be at home with his friends, playing soccer and riding horses. He wonders why Daddy and I spend hours talking about "such dull things." He never seems to wonder about God, or death, or why the sky is blue, or why some people are black and others white. He just wonders who's going to win a game or how soon he will be able to drive a car. He spends hours and hours with his horse. He wants to play polo and already talks of going to school in England. How can two children in one family be so different? I love him, though. And he can be very funny. He makes me laugh more than anyone I know, but he never wants to go to Cape Town or to travel with Daddy.

Sometimes I think Lili is the most important person in my life. I told Daddy that the other day and he smiled in that wonderful way that lights up his face and makes his freckles dance, and he said, "If you're going to emulate someone, I can't think of anyone better than Lili." (I had to look up emulate.) He said now that Mama's dead, Lili and I are the two most important women in his life. I thought men weren't supposed to like their mothers-in-law.

1975

THIS FALL I'M GOING AWAY TO JOHANNESBURG. OUT ON MY OWN FOR the first time. I get scared. I know how demanding med school will be. Daddy says I'm self-disciplined enough to be able to make it. In fact, he said that I'm self-disciplined to a fault. "In that way," he added, "you remind me of your mother." I asked Lili if I was like Mother. She thought a while and told me I was "softer." And then she looked off in the distance as though she were remembering and said—in a whisper sort of—"I wish Carolyn and I had been as close as you and I are." I thought she and Mama were.

I asked Lili about sex this summer. It took me about two weeks of trying to screw up (no pun intended!) courage. But I didn't think I'd feel comfortable talking about it with Daddy. When I asked her if I should wait till marriage she surprised me by saying, "I didn't." I thought in the old days people only had sex when they were married. A whole new facet of Lili!

Anyhow, we had a good talk, probably because she wasn't at all self-conscious. She asked if I knew about birth control. Always practical. I did, sort of. So she told me about the pill and diaphragms in a scientific way. She suggested I not do it with just anyone. "Make love," she said, "don't just have sex." But she also told me one can love more than once.

▼

COURTNEY FELT NO REGRET AS SHE LEFT FOUR YEARS OF JOHANNES-
burg behind her. She had learned little about the city that the
South Africans fondly called Joburg. The grind of med school had
demanded so much that her social life had been restricted. So
many would-be doctors competing for too few internships.

And she had gotten one of the choicest: Cape Town.

As her plane left the country's largest city, Courtney realized
she had never been happy there. The city was too large; the lines
of demarcation between blacks and whites were sharper than it was
throughout the country. She knew the lines were there in Cape
Town, but Cape Town was a second home for her.

As the plane soared over the mountains, a familiar trip to
Courtney after so many years, she thought, I'm ready for some fun.
She looked forward to parties, to new friends, to beginning her
adult life; she was twenty-four.

The man across the aisle stared at her. She could tell he liked
what he saw. Most men did. With little vanity, Courtney knew that
men responded to her looks. She had inherited her grandmother's
curls, but neither Lili's nor her father's auburn hair had been
passed on to her. Short chestnut curls ringed her face, so like
Marsh's . . . the high cheekbones, the aristocratic nose, the arched
eyebrows. Clear gray eyes, feathered by lashes darker than her
hair. While her eyes lacked innocence, they had a direct gaze and
were open.

Although she had seen much that dismayed her, she considered her own life rich and full. More than anything else, her summers had influenced her. Half of each of her last fifteen summers
had been spent with Lili.

Lili's quick mind, her rapport with the Congolese, her rever-
ence for life, and her infinite capacity for compassion and healing
inspired awe in her granddaughter. At the same time, Courtney
knew that she needed more, for herself, than Lili had had.

She thought a lot about another influence—Andrew's gift, the
high savannah bush country. For her twelfth birthday, he had
presented her with a camera, complete with zoom lens. "This is the
way to hunt animals," he'd said. Certainly her mother would have
approved. Actually it was her mother's as well as her grandmother's ideology, together with Andrew's trips each summer, that
helped shape her life.

As the plane began its descent into Cape Town, Courtney saw

the clouds hovering over Table Top, the ocean's whitecaps dancing in the sunlight. She knew Lili would be waiting for her.

Lili had driven herself to the airport, as Courtney had known she would. The moment Courtney started down the plane's steps, she saw her grandmother and thought, Distinguished, that's how she looks. Her hair, pure white, framed her face. Instead of shrinking, as most older people did, Lili looked taller than ever. Still slim, tanned from work in her rose garden, her still bright turquoise eyes welcomed Courtney across the tarmac. She looked years younger than she had eighteen years ago when she had emerged from the jungle and Marsh had died.

Lili had stayed in Cape Town and not returned to Simbayo after her visit with Courtney. With a jolt, Courtney realized her grandmother was seventy-four. Lili knew her physical limitations. And she was at ease with the thought that Petelo had taken over what she had started. Of course, he was working on a far larger scale than she had ever dreamed. The University of Liverpool had made Simbayo its field center for tropical diseases.

To Courtney's surprise, Lili didn't meet her with the perfectly kept twenty-year-old car that had been Marsh's, but in a metallic blue sports car. Courtney burst out laughing.

"I never thought you'd get rid of that old car," she said as her luggage was loaded into the trunk.

"I haven't," Lili said. "This is yours."

Courtney turned questioning eyes on her grandmother. Lili tossed the keys to her. "Try it out."

It drove like a dream, purring close to the road.

"I was afraid you might have to live at the hospital, and I certainly wasn't going to entrust *my* car to you." She meant Marsh's car. "Besides, I think you need a graduation present and a thank-you for coming here; this is just a way of telling you how pleased I am."

Looking across at her granddaughter, Lili knew that new life had come to her.

"Lili." Courtney smiled. "I swear you look younger every time I see you."

Lili laughed as the wind swept through her hair. "I feel it. Only when I look in a mirror do I realize how old I am."

CAPE TOWN'S HOSPITAL, THOUGH WORLD-RENOWNED AS THE ONE where Jan Hasbrouck performed his famous heart transplant operations, was not a first-class hospital; South Africa was still a Third World country.

Courtney found it invigorating to be able to share her daily life with her grandmother. Lili listened with rapt attention each evening to details of operations, interplay between staff members, anecdotes of patients.

The vicarious pleasure she gained from Courtney's life vitalized her. At seventy-four she had given up not only Simbayo but also her regular work in Kaputo. She did go every Wednesday to the immunization clinic she had organized there, but there was not always enough vaccine to last throughout the day. One week she would vaccinate against smallpox; the next, polio. Once in a great while they would receive measles vaccine. It was not just young children who needed these. Most of the population of the squatter town had never been exposed to decent health care and certainly not to preventive medicine.

There were always one or two young policemen who tried to give her a hard time, but she ignored them. Ridicule bothered her not at all. As long as they didn't retaliate by harming members of the community, Lili didn't mind what jarring comments they made to her. Her world-wide reputation protected her as long as she didn't try to agitate. The South African government certainly did not want to victimize the revered Mother Lili. They generally left her alone. In fact, they cooperated in as much as they supplied Kaputo with a minimal amount of vaccine. The rest was gotten on the black market—Lili never questioned its appearance.

Two black men, without degrees but with a great deal of knowledge, doctored the rest. One, George, had been but a young boy when Lili had started her ministering to the people of his township; he now had a job as a gardener in the white world, so the only time he was available was evenings. His life was so busy he had not yet found time to marry. Moses, too old and infirm to work, would have been sent to a tribal reservation if Lili had not invented work for him. Technically, he was her gardener and watchman; this way, he was permitted to live with her. They spent many hours conversing about medicine and about life. He was a comfort to her.

Lili had discovered that standing on her feet all day two days a week was as much as her energy could muster. Refusing to feel guilty about it, she spent her time cultivating Marsh's rose garden, walking through the vineyards, and reading. "I have so much to catch up with," she told Courtney, "so much I haven't read."

Her life had seemed full to her until Courtney moved in. Then, the camaraderie and sharing that her granddaughter brought to her made life take on new meaning, and Lili realized there had been an empty spot in her life. It had been a long time since Lili had been aware of such happiness.

From the very beginning, Courtney was a social success at the hospital. Nearly every young doctor evidenced interest in her. She was invited to picnics at the beach, to parties every weekend; she never ate a solitary lunch in the commissary. Aside from her ability to laugh easily—at something genuinely funny or at herself—her inherited gifts of humanity and skill became readily evident. Good-looking women doctors with delightful senses of humor were rare, and no young doctor on the staff wanted to miss this opportunity. Days off, there was always a group of associates, both doctors and nurses, ready to swim at False Bay in the summers; every Saturday, someone had a beer party. Courtney found the shoptalk stimulating, and she enjoyed the opportunity for harmless flirtations. She was already proficient at tennis and enjoyed learning to windsurf.

Lili encouraged her. She didn't wish the life-style she'd led on her granddaughter, though she knew that she, herself, could not have lived any other way. Sorrow periodically surged through her—missing Marsh and Carolyn—but she realized that her lost opportunities were being made up with this chance to share in Courtney's life. It's because I'm reaching out to her, because I'm where she needs me to be, she told herself. Because at this point in life I have no driving needs of my own.

There were times when Courtney needed to be alone. She had always needed this kind of time. She had to be able to walk along the beach with no demands on her or sit in her room—the one Lili had always kept just for her, with its faded quilt and four-poster bed and white ruffled curtains at the windows, overlooking the swimming pool and the vineyards, the room that had been her mother's when she was growing up here.

Courtney could never have told why she needed time for herself, or what she did with it, or what thoughts ran through her mind. All she knew was that she felt tension if it were denied her. Puzzles solved themselves in these solitary periods; and, as she said to Lili, "My soul is fed."

She sat on the deserted beach, huddled, arms around her bent knees, staring out at the horizon, the gray sky blending with the stormy ocean. She tasted salt on her lips and felt the barometric excitement of an approaching storm.

"I know it sounds corny"—her reverie was interrupted by a man's voice—"but haven't we met somewhere?"

She turned her head as the breeze riffled her hair; she raised her eyes from the well-worn running shoes, up the trim blue jogging outfit to the neatly bearded face of Dr. David Hamilton.

She knew who he was because she'd seen him at several parties, because she'd watched him operate with the skill and care that had already earned him a reputation. But she really did not want anyone interrupting the drama the wind and ocean currents were promenading before her.

"You're David Hamilton," she said. "I don't know that we've met."

Without asking, he scrunched down next to her.

"It seems to me I should have remembered you." The blue of his eyes accentuated his sandy hair.

"I'm Courtney McCloud," she offered, realizing that was not the way to get rid of him. She was trying to remember what else she'd heard about him aside from his skill as a surgeon. That he was short-tempered when he encountered carelessness, that he was impatient with people not as intelligent or as quick as he, that he was extremely sure of himself.

"Oh, yes." He bounced up and down in his squatting posture. "I've seen you in the commissary, too. You must be a nurse."

"No," she said. "I'm a doctor. I'm interning here."

Amusement crept into his eyes, and he unfolded his long body and sat in the sand next to her.

Deliberately, she asked, "Are you an intern, too?"

"No." His voice was casual. "I've been here for several years."

She knew that.

Courtney watched the ocean waves break roughly. The breeze became a wind. She pulled her windbreaker up around her neck and hugged herself.

"You from South Africa?"

"I've been in med school in Joburg," she answered, "but I'm really from Zimbabwe."

"I still think of it as Rhodesia," he said. "Is it difficult to think of it by its new name?"

"Not at all," she answered. It was a question she'd heard ever since the country had gained its independence from England last year. Andrew had rather easily made the transition of working in a country now run by blacks. Thousands of whites had left, but Andrew had said that it had been his home for twenty-five years.

It did not frighten him to think of blacks as equals.

It was Courtney's home, too, in a way South Africa could never be.

"I'm from London," he announced.

A wind-whipped rain began, pelting down large, slanting drops so heavy and fast that they could hardly see in front of them. David jumped up, holding out a hand to pull Courtney up. They ran toward the parking lot. As she reached her car, fumbling in her pocket for the keys, David put a hand on her arm. "Let me buy you some coffee or tea. There's a roadhouse a mile or so up that way." He pointed.

Courtney was familiar with it. "All right," she said, shaking water off herself as she slid behind the wheel. After all, she had nothing else on the agenda for this Saturday afternoon.

A fire was lit in the stone fireplace and candles burned brightly on the red-and-white-checkered tablecloths. They chose a table close to the fireplace, hoping to dry off. Rain pounded on the roof.

"What makes a woman become a doctor?" he asked, while they waited for their warm drinks.

"I imagine the same things that make a man become one."

"Why not a nurse?"

"Why aren't you a nurse?"

He looked directly at her. "You're one of those women for whom hearth and home is not enough?"

"I am one of those women. And so was my mother. And my grandmother. It's an inherited characteristic." She felt herself bristling.

He laughed, an easy, unself-conscious laugh. "And I'm a chauvinistic pig, right?"

Courtney shrugged, her eyes flitting around the room, staring into the fire.

"I'm not starting off well with you, am I?"

She laughed.

He stood and asked, "More coffee? Or perhaps a beer?"

"Coffee." She nodded.

David walked over to the bar. When he returned, she watched his hands as they closed around his bottle of beer. Their eyes met.

He has the longest eyelashes I've ever seen, she thought. And the bluest eyes. The beer left a white ridge that he brushed away with the back of his hand.

"Why a doctor?" he asked again.

"My father told me I could do whatever I wanted."

"Unusual man," David commented. "But why medicine?"

"My grandmother . . . my mother . . . the people in my country who need me."

Before she realized it, she was telling him about her grandmother and summers on the savannahs with Andrew, about her mother's research and of her death, about seeing the distended stomachs of malnutrition and festered sores and encephalitis, of typhus and tuberculosis and cholera and the myriad diseases rampant due to lack of sanitation and lack of medical facilities. Lack of education.

"I'm going back there," she said, "back to the countryside and help the people save themselves." She was silent for a moment. Then she smiled at him. "Do you like being a doctor?" she asked.

"Do I like it?" David said. "I love it. I can't imagine anything in the world I would rather do; I'm in love with medicine. I love the operating room, the dispensary, and most of the patients. The poorer they are, the more attention I lavish on them. I've been championing the underdog all my life. Not exactly"—he laughed wryly—"a way to get rich."

"What brought you here?" she asked, narrowing her eyes. I like him, she realized.

"Ah, that's a long story." He glanced at his watch. "Want to get a bite to eat and I'll bore you with how I came via Tunbridge Wells to Cape Town?"

Courtney asked, "Is it that late? I can't. I'm sorry. It's my grandmother's birthday, and I promised her I'd be home for dinner."

"Your grandmother?" He laughed loudly. "You live with your grandmother?"

She resented his making her feel young and naïve. "My grandmother is the reason I'm a doctor. My grandmother is the most remarkable person I've ever met." She stood, knocking her empty coffee cup over.

"I don't seem to be saying anything right today, do I?"

But when she thought of him later, what she remembered was those clear blue eyes, the hair that looked like it was meant to be riffled through, the strength emanating from his hands, the feline grace with which he walked. And though his eyes had not left her face, she had the idea that he had been mentally undressing her the whole time.

▼

THE STORM HAD PASSED; THERE WASN'T A CLOUD IN THE SKY. A RARE two days off had made Courtney restless. She and Lili had just sat down to lunch when the doorbell rang.

"I'll get it," Courtney said to Anna, who was putting the salad on the table.

Grinning a cockeyed smile and holding two red roses in front of him, David leaned against the doorjamb.

"One of these is for your grandmother's birthday, and one is a bribe, hoping you'll come for a drive with me."

Courtney couldn't help smiling.

"We're just starting lunch. Come on in. I imagine there's enough for one more."

He followed her into the house, glancing around admiringly.

"Lili," Courtney introduced him, "this is David Hamilton, one of the doctors on the staff. David, my grandmother, Lili Compson. Lili, I've just invited him to lunch."

Lili was delighted to meet one of Courtney's colleagues. She was enchanted with the rose and immediately centered the conversation around their guest.

Today, Courtney was amused to notice, David set out to be charming. There was none of the baiting that had been evident in his voice yesterday.

When Lili asked him what had spurred him on to medicine, he replied, "I don't think I had much choice." His eyes were warm with remembrance. "There were three of us children and all of us . . . My mother took in anything stray. In the middle of the night I can remember the bell ringing—a neighbor bringing a cat about to have kittens. People would bring birds with broken wings to my mother, and bunnies that had been abandoned, a peacock with a torn tail, dogs—"

"Wasn't there a veterinarian in town?" Courtney interjected, feeling left out of the conversation.

"There was. A nasty-tempered old man. He took care of horses and cows, but people didn't want him in their houses. They brought their animals to my mother. Many's the night she sat up with a newborn lamb, trying to force it to drink, or making splints for broken wings. One time we had fifteen cats."

Courtney laughed, trying to envision such a menagerie, liking the sound of his mother. "I'm surprised you didn't become a vet."

"My brother did. I'm too much a people person. I thrive on drama, and people are more dramatic than animals."

"What made you leave England?" Lili asked. "Why come to Cape Town?"

"Actually, it was easy but indirect. When I did finally receive my M.D., I felt burned out. I realized I had spent all my life in school. So I took a year off. I tended bar for six months so I could travel for six months. I hitchhiked my way through France and Italy, spent a couple of months in Rome, took a boat to Athens . . ." His eyes softened, remembering. "Have you ever been to the Greek islands?" he asked, enthusiasm filling his voice. "They're enchantment." Courtney had never heard a man talk like this. "There's something about the Greek sky—it's bluer and deeper than anyplace else on earth. I spent six weeks there and knew I could never again live in the gray English countryside. I did, however, for two more years. But I found the practice of medicine there geriatric and predictable."

"Boring?" asked Lili.

He nodded. "Dull. Dull people and their coughs, bronchitis, sore throats . . . I'd spent my life aiming toward healing people and ended up wiping noses."

Courtney had the feeling that David was courting Lili, telling her things he thought would interest her.

"So you caught the first boat to Cape Town . . ." Lili urged him on.

"Not quite." He smiled at her. "I went back to school to study surgery. While I was there, a classmate and I became friendly, and *he* was from South Africa, Pretoria. The more he told me of the country, the more I wanted to come here. He painted alluring pictures: the scenery, the animals, the climate. So I came. I'd originally wanted Johannesburg or Pretoria, because my friend was from there, but the hospital that offered me a job is here. I haven't been sorry."

"Not geriatric and dull," Lili commented.

"Not at all. In fact, sometimes I feel like a veterinarian. When some of the natives are brought in from the bush on travois and can't speak English, it's quite something to try to figure out what's wrong. They have that peculiar way of clacking, you know, which I can't understand yet, though I'm working on it. I've got to figure out where they hurt and what's wrong."

He must be around thirty, thought Courtney. Quite young to have established such a surgical reputation. He's saying all the things guaranteed to endear him to Lili and me, Courtney thought.

Anna brought in the dessert, a chocolate souffle, at the very same moment Courtney was remembering the story, so often told, of the day her mother and father met, how they each knew from the beginning—right here in this house, in this room—that their destinies would be entwined.

David winked at her but turned his full attention on Lili.

CHAPTER 50

▼

THEY WENT FOR A DRIVE LATE THAT AFTERNOON AFTER THE THREE OF them sat over lunch until 3:30. David invited Liliane to come along, but she demurred.

"That's sweet of you," she said, "but I think not. Perhaps another time?"

David grinned, and Courtney thought, Not many young men would bother to be so charming to a grandmother. Of course, Lili is not just any grandmother.

David didn't talk much as they sped through the countryside. He asked her questions about Zimbabwe and let her do the talking. He was an expert driver and enjoyed tooling along at high speed. He concentrated on his driving. Courtney responded to the green-gold of new spring leaves. October was one of her favorite months.

"Is there a particular man in your life?" David asked.

"No," she answered. She'd been going to say she'd been too busy, but that wasn't exactly true. Except for a few months during her senior year in high school, she'd never been in love. Most of the boys she'd met seemed provincial to her. Few had the urbanity and questioning intelligence she saw in her father; few had traveled more than one hundred miles from where they'd been born. Some of the boys she'd grown up with went "home" to school in England, but when they returned, they seemed awfully stuffy.

Most of the young interns and doctors she'd met here broke that pattern. That's what made Cape Town so exciting. They were fun. Intense while they worked but ready to break loose when allowed to relax. She wasn't ready to limit herself quite yet.

"D'you like Neil Diamond?" he asked, flipping a cassette on the auto tape player. Courtney let the music soak into her.

Twilight worked its magic as Neil Diamond asked if she loved him. She took her eyes from the road to look at David.

Funny, she thought, yesterday I'd have described him as quite average-looking. I couldn't even have told how tall he was if someone had asked. She closed her eyes and leaned her head against the headrest, opened them again as Neil told her she held his heart in her hands. Actually, she thought, turning to look at David again, he's quite good-looking. She even liked his beard. His strong hands and long fingers curled around the steering wheel. She had an urge to put her hand up, touch his beard.

For heaven's sake, she thought.

He must have sensed her staring at him, for, without taking his eyes from the road, he reached over and took her hand in his, completely encircling hers.

Their hands lay entwined on the leather seat between them; she felt a heartbeat in her throat, a pulse throbbing.

Without her realizing it, they were at her front door.

She unlatched the door beside her. Should I invite him in, she wondered.

"Thanks," she said, "it's been—"

He reached across the back of the seat and pulled her to him. Her eyes closed as his lips found hers, kissing her as if all his energy were centered in the kiss, as though in this one action he plumbed her depths, searching for her as no one ever had.

For the first time in her life, she was breathless after a kiss.

"See you" was his only parting; his tires squealed as he rushed off into the night.

When she looked for him at the hospital the next day, he was nowhere in sight. On Tuesday, he walked into the commissary at noon as she was lunching with another doctor and a nurse. He stopped at their table and greeted all three impartially. Their eyes never met.

After a week of hoping to see him around every corner, of rushing to the phone whenever it rang, her hopes dimmed. The following week one of the nurses, Ginny, noticed her staring as David walked past them with no acknowledgment.

"Oh, you, too?" she said, a sigh in her voice. "He's untouchable. No one gets anywhere with him, and we've all tried. Just look at those eyes!"

Courtney looked at her.

Ginny continued, "They're so soft when he's dancing close to you. You keep waiting for him to make a move, and he doesn't."

Better to hear it now, Courtney told herself.

"Drives all of us crazy. But he's a damned good doctor," added Ginny.

By the weekend, Courtney told herself she'd forgotten him and was looking forward to a party three of the single doctors were having on Saturday night.

That morning, Friday, Courtney was to assist in gall-bladder surgery. Anytime she participated in the operating room, her heart beat more rapidly; adrenaline flowed.

Then David walked into the scrub room. "I heard you were assisting me today," he said, lathering up to his elbows, his voice warm but his eyes impersonal. "Ready?"

He *was* a damned good surgeon, an artist. Courtney couldn't help being impressed and found herself blushing with pleasure when he said to her, "Not bad," and smiled.

"What time are you through today?" he asked, throwing his green surgical outfit into a hamper. She added hers to the heap.

"About five," she answered.

He walked through the swinging doors without another word, but he was waiting for her at 5:00.

"Let me buy you a drink?" he asked.

She wanted to say yes.

"Not tonight," she answered without breaking her gait. She walked into a honeysuckle evening and inhaled deeply. As she headed toward the parking lot, she felt his hand under her elbow, guiding her away from her car to his.

"Hey." She stopped. "I just said no."

His hand still on her arm, he said, "Give me a good reason."

She pulled her arm away and turned to look at him. As icily as she could, she said, "I don't have to explain anything to you."

"That's true." His voice became apologetic. "I've been think-ing of you all day . . . You know, your hands have lives of their own. Your surgical skill is—is very good." He stared at her. "And your eyes are beautiful."

I've been thinking of you for two weeks, she thought. She began to walk on. Coffee, she thought. A cup of coffee or a glass of wine won't hurt. When he asks again, I'll give in.

But his voice didn't follow her; she continued slowly to her car and then turned around. With a screech, his car tore out of the parking lot.

Damn, she thought. Whether she was irritated at him or at herself, she couldn't tell.

▼

EVERY TIME THE DOOR OPENED AND NEW GUESTS ARRIVED AT THE
party, Courtney was aware of a stab of disappointment. No David.
There were people here she really liked, yet she realized she wasn't
listening; she was waiting, hoping.

It was nearly midnight. Linda Ronstadt provided mood music;
Tom Redfield was whispering something in her ear. She moved
easily in his arms, enjoying the dancing but not responding to his
suggestions. He lightly brushed her cheek with his lips. Then she
heard him say, "Oh, to hell with it," and put his mouth on hers.

"Cut it out, Tom," she whispered, moving out of his embrace
and into the line of vision of David Hamilton. From across the
room, his eyes, filled with sardonic amusement, met hers. He
waved his hand in the form of a salute and began to thread his way
through the crowd.

He's going to rescue me, she thought, but he smiled engag-
ingly, murmured, "Courtney, Tom," and passed beyond them.

Later, when she walked out on the patio, he did follow her.
His first words were "Let's cut out."

She turned to look at him, dressed in a gray alpaca sweater and
charcoal pants. "How about 'good evening'?" she said. "A friendly
prelude, at least."

"Come on, Courtney. Let's kick this party. Let's go find some
greasy place that's open at this hour and get to know each other."

"My car's out front," she said.

"I saw it. Let's go."

They didn't even say good-bye. David grabbed her hand and
held it tightly as they wound through the group. Without waiting
for the elevator, he hauled her down the stairway. Her high heels
clattered as she tried to keep up with him.

"Where's your car?" she asked.

"I walked. I live two blocks away. You can drive me home
later."

They found just what David had suggested, a greasy place with
oilcloth on the tables, but it was quiet and nearly empty.

"Tell me," David said as they waited for coffee, "all the really
important things."

Courtney laughed. "Like what?"

"Let's start with your mother."

"My mother wanted to eradicate disease from Africa. She was
a complex person, I think. When I was young, she was just Mama.

But since she died, I've learned a lot about her. She wanted to use twentieth-century science to prolong life, but she didn't want that same twentieth century to corrupt Africa."

"Did you love her?"

"Oh, yes. She's part of the reason I'm a doctor. I've often wondered if Mama had lived, would I have been as close to her as I am to Lili?"

"Or," suggested David, "would you be as close to Lili?"

Courtney thought for a moment. "I think so. I was close to her before Mama died. And never more so than when she took me to Simbayo. That was the summer before Mama died. I think even then Lili knew Simbayo would be important to me."

A waitress slapped their coffee on the table and stood waiting for David to pay her.

"So," he said, "you want to do what your grandmother did. Help increase the lifespan from thirty-five to sixty-five. Help natives to live rather than merely exist."

Courtney felt blood rushing to her cheeks. He understood. Excitement lit her eyes. "Yes, exactly. The summer I was fifteen, and out on the savannah, my father and I spent most of the time camped next to a nomadic tribe, the Mbelas. I swore to myself then that I'd return; I'd come back and make them healthy, cure them, teach preventive medicine." Her hands waved with enthusiasm.

"Create your own Simbayo," David murmured.

Courtney looked at him. "Funny. I've never thought of it quite like that. But maybe you're right."

Her smile was soft and faraway.

"I have a feeling," David said, reaching over to touch her hand, "that each of our lives has become more complex than it was before . . ."

She turned her hand over so that her palm touched his. "Before?"

"Before we met each other."

The waitress said, "We're closing."

When they were in Courtney's car, David said, "Confession time. I requested that you assist me in surgery yesterday."

Warmth spread across her chest. "Were you disappointed?"

He didn't answer except to say, "Turn right at the next block."

When they pulled up at his apartment, he said, "I don't suppose I could talk you into coming in?"

"You're right. You can't."

He got out of the car and walked around to her side and

leaned in the open window. "Well, Courtney, my dear. I was not disappointed. You're going to be a far-above-average doctor."

Going to be?

"And I wasn't disappointed tonight, either. I only came to see you." He bent across the open space and his lips lightly brushed her cheek. "Good night." He turned on his heels and started to walk toward the building. In a flash, before she could start the motor, he turned back, opening the door beside her, taking her arm, and pulling her out of the car up to meet him.

His arms encircled her, his beard was soft. His lips melted her; his tongue brushed hers. His kisses rained over her eyelids, down her cheek, on her ear. He whispered, "You must know as well as I do what's happening," and his lips found hers again. She felt herself engulfed with yearning and returned his kisses.

Then he stopped kissing her, holding her tightly. When she saw his face, he was smiling.

"Go," he murmured, his voice tender. "While I still let you."

His kisses lingering over her, she slid into the seat behind the wheel. Driving home, she thought, This must be what being drunk feels like. The car never touched the road; it floated two feet off the ground. The moon raced with her, little clouds hitting it now and then and rushing over its surface.

THE NEXT DAY SHE DIDN'T SEE DAVID, THOUGH SHE KNEW HE WAS IN the hospital. At dinner that night, she told Lili, "I don't know what to make of him. He appears here for lunch and charms us both, then nothing for two weeks. Then this weekend. He requested me for that operation and swept me off my feet at the party. Then . . ."

Lili smiled. "I suspect what's happening to him is more than he knows how to handle."

Courtney shook her head. "No, that can't be. We hardly know each other."

"What has that to do with anything? I've a grand idea. Let's invite him for Christmas dinner. He's far away from his family, and your father will be here."

Justin was at school in London and Courtney had no extra days off. Andrew had volunteered to come to Cape Town to spend Christmas with his two favorite women.

"No," said Courtney. "That seems too pointed. Come meet my father. Join us for a family Christmas."

"Well, how about a Christmas-night buffet for a number of your friends? People shouldn't spend Christmas alone. The three of us will have a family dinner early in the afternoon and we can have a buffet around eight o'clock." Her eyes were alight. "What a lovely idea. And your father will enjoy meeting your friends. I've never had a party here. Invite David first. Let's make sure he'll come before inviting the others."

"You like him, too, I gather."

"I like him, too."

CHAPTER 51

▼

COURTNEY THOUGHT HER FATHER GREW MORE HANDSOME THE OLDER he became. His red hair had darkened and silver had crept into his temples; the constant tan from years spent out in the brush gave him a leathery, outdoor look. When her grandmother had asked why he didn't remarry, he had replied, "I'm too young for you, Lili. And after Carolyn, no woman measures up."

Not all his considerable energies went to helping Zimbabwe meet the twentieth century. True, a good number of the roads throughout the country, a majority of the dams, and many of the municipal buildings in cities and townships—even some of the towns themselves, intelligently laid out before being built—were due to the visionary abilities of Donald Reyes and Andrew McCloud.

Andrew had also become a wildlife photographer. He realized that Carolyn and Sam had been right: Wherever he was going to bring civilization to the wilderness, big game would be forced to evacuate. When surveying a new district, he and Sam would spend months calculating how the least harm could be done to the environment while best advancing the cause of the people. While Sam and his staff prowled the savannah, Andrew photographed a way of life soon to vanish. He and Sam sensed, long before anyone else, that by 1980 there would be very few elephants left in Zimbabwe.

"Aren't you ever lonely, Daddy?" Courtney asked.

"I admit I like it better when you and Justin are around."

Andrew would smile. "But no. No more so than the average person. When I'm lonely, it's for your mother."

More than one woman tried to break his pattern of life, but always in vain. Courtney wondered if there'd been even brief flings since her mother's death. He certainly was attractive.

Andrew, Lili, David, Paul Taggart, and Phil Rice—two of the young specialists whom Courtney admired—were gathered in Marsh's study. The beat of music from the phonograph indicated others at the party were dancing. The dining-room table was laden with food that Lili had had prepared: an enormous roast of beef, a turkey larger than anyone present had ever seen, yams with pineapple and marshmallows, American canned cranberry sauce, salads and coleslaw, cinammon rolls, orange nut bread, French bread and walnut rosemary bread, apple pie with brandy. Guests stood eating and talking; some were cavorting in the pool in the warm evening air. Courtney was pleased.

Everyone she invited had accepted. It was the first time she'd entertained. Courtney saw Lili holding forth in the library, surrounded by the four men. They all looked intense; her father was gesticulating. She wondered if he and David would hit it off. Certainly David could not have discerned that this whole party was an excuse to share Christmas with him, to allow Andrew to meet him.

Maybe, she thought, *my* feelings will have nothing to do with how this relationship progresses. Just because I'm interested in him . . . She laughed. Interested. That was hardly the word for it. His off-and-on attention drove her crazy. She found herself thinking of him constantly. Yet that frightened her. Frightened her because he was the first man she'd met who excited her.

She'd been terribly aware of him all night: his easy smile; the graceful way he walked, like a stalking leopard; the way he used his hands; what happened to his eyes when he looked across a room at her.

She walked toward the library, drawn by the sound of David's voice. "I, for one," she heard him saying, "do think I'm doing something about it. If I were to publicly protest, I could be ordered under house arrest. Any number of well-known people have been forbidden to leave their homes because they have publicly protested. Of what help is that? In our limited way, we"—he turned his head, waving his arm to include everyone—"are doing something to help. I give blacks the exact same treatment I give whites. I treat them with dignity"—and Courtney had witnessed that—"and do what is possible to help them."

Andrew asked, "Do you do the most you possibly can?"

"Does anyone do the most he possibly can about anything?"

"Yes," answered Lili, "I think many do."

Andrew, standing, leaned down and squeezed Lili's shoulder. "Well, you certainly have, my dear."

"Not lately," she said, as though to herself.

They all looked up as Courtney said, "It sounds like very serious conversation in here."

David grabbed her hand and said, "Come dance with me. Christmas is not a time to be so serious."

When he put his arms around her and began to move with the music, he said, "After meeting your father and Lili"—so it was Lili?—"I understand you a bit."

His hand on her back pulled her close to him, and her body moved effortlessly with his. Their legs moved together. "Did you wear those earrings tonight just to drive men crazy?" he asked, close to her ear. "Or don't you even know that every time you laugh and your hair swings out, as those dangling earrings spin, as your eyes light up, other women cease to exist?"

Courtney had always enjoyed flirting. She refused to let herself take him seriously. "Have other women ceased to exist?" She laughed.

He said nothing but pulled her so close she could feel his heart beating.

Pulling his head back, he looked into her eyes. "Do you have any idea how much you matter?" he asked.

Just then someone broke in; David stood where they had stopped dancing as Courtney was whirled away.

IT WAS LONG AFTER MIDNIGHT WHEN THE PARTY BROKE UP. DAVID didn't leave. He was in a corner with Lili and Andrew, a can of beer in his hand, saying, "The government is not only foolish in its attitude toward the natives. It's trying to prove to the world that it's a modern country. The hospital's famous because of Hasbrouck's transplants, so now they're going to build a first-class modern hospital, but we're not a modern, first-class country. Much about us is Third World.

"Our hospital is so proud of itself because it bought a respirator. The damn thing costs fifteen hundred dollars a day to operate. Sure, it can keep a child alive. But usually by the time the child gets to us, it's so far advanced in illness that it has brain damage from lack of oxygen and will never be all right. It's usually a ninth or tenth child from a family that is already on the brink of starvation. Then the government proudly points out that it costs the black family nothing for this treatment. This treatment that I think is, in the long run, inhumane." David's voice contained anger and frustration.

"Would you deny them the use of the respirator?" asked Courtney.

He turned to look at her as she seated herself in front of the fireplace.

"It would be better to spend the same money to immunize the children and the bush populace. Do you know how many millions of people in this country have never been immunized against diseases that are almost extinct in the western world? Or why not spend the money to feed the millions of starving people? Do you know how many people die from starvation in this country every day? How many people live without hope and energy because they are starving? We can easily sit around and wonder why these people aren't better educated, but who the hell can think when they're starving to death?"

"You're saying that if South Africa fed its people, the world would have more respect for them?" Andrew asked.

"Of course," answered David.

Andrew smiled. "That's what I hoped you were saying."

"The frustration," said the man Courtney was afraid she was falling in love with, "is that no matter how much one can humanly helps, the system can't be beaten."

"I don't agree," Lili said softly.

"How do you fight people who *know* they're right?" David challenged. "Take the hospital. The facilities for blacks and for whites are very different, yet the majority of patients are black, young to middle-aged, and sick with diseases such as TB, pneumonia, malaria, rheumatic heart disease, the unbelievable complications of alcohol and cigarettes. The surgical patients offer a fantastic spectrum of trauma—stabbings, assaults, bullet wounds, venereal disease. I far prefer assignment to the black section. The white side is why I left medicine in England—geriatric, chronic. Nothing new there. That, in itself, tells a story, doesn't it?"

Yes. The Boers thought it proved that the natives were more prone to violence, were illiterate, and flagrantly immoral.

Suddenly, David looked at his watch. "Your daughter and I have to be at work in six hours," he told Andrew. "I think I'd better leave if we're both going to be even somewhat alert." He leaned over and kissed Lili's cheek. "I'll see you again, soon," he promised her.

Courtney walked him to the door.

He took her hands in his and gazed at her, there in the doorway. "Thank you," he said, "for making this the first Christmas I've enjoyed in three years."

She waited for him to kiss her.

He didn't.

He let go of her hands and walked out into the still warm night. She heard him whistling.

OBSTETRICS WAS ONE OF COURTNEY'S FAVORITE ASPECTS OF medicine. She had been assigned to the OB unit for the whole month. "I've delivered twenty-three babies this month," she told Lili. "And it's all been so easy."

December twenty-sixth was to prove different.

When she arrived at the hospital shortly after 8:00 for a twelve-hour stint of night duty, the nurse on OB duty, Ellie De Wein, said, "Potential problem in room 231. And not cooperative. She's only here because her mother-in-law, the biggest woman I ever saw in my life, insisted."

Courtney walked down the hall and into room 231. Sitting on the floor in a corner was a barefoot woman with the largest belly she'd ever seen. Sitting on a chair beside her was her husband, who wore a worried expression. Standing in the center of the room was the biggest woman she had ever seen. The mother-in-law was over six feet, certainly; she stood with her legs spread apart, her arms crossed in front of her, and fierceness in her eyes.

Courtney introduced herself.

The tall woman boomed, "My son's wife is having twins and is in labor. She will not push them out."

Courtney looked at the woman huddled on the floor by the radiator.

"How do you know it's twins?" she asked the big woman.

"I know."

Courtney asked the pregnant woman to stand. "She does not understand English," said her mother-in-law. In that strange way so many have of speaking, she shot sharp, staccato sounds at the frightened girl. The young woman stood. Her belly was so immense that it made her swaybacked.

"Her water broke early this morning, but nothing is happening," the older woman said. "We have never had a child born in a hospital. But my son does not want her to die. He would rather lose the children than his wife."

Between the mother and Courtney, they succeeded in persuading the young woman to lie down on the bed. Courtney told the older woman to send her son from the room. Labor had already begun, but nothing was moving, Courtney observed. "We'll have to prep her"—Courtney tried to explain what that meant—"and I think we'll have to use ultrasound. That will tell us if the babies are in the headfirst position."

Courtney immediately suggested that the older woman wash up and come to the operating room so that she could translate to the young woman and alleviate some of her fears.

"I delivered all of my own children," the mother said, "twelve of them. And I have delivered all of the children of my daughters and daughters-in-law, but this one would not cooperate."

"She may have no choice," said Courtney.

Ultrasound showed that the first twin was positioned to come headfirst, but the second would be a breech birth.

"I recommend a C section—a cesarean," said Courtney. "There's a chance of mental retardation with breech birth; there would be considerable pain and risk if we let nature take its course."

The mother spoke to the young woman on the operating table. The young woman's eyes showed fright, and she grabbed the older woman's hand. "No," said the mother-in-law. "No cutting."

"This will be dangerous," said Courtney. "A cesarean will be far safer." She tried to explain the difference and the risk involved. But both women were obdurate. "Your son or your daughter-in-law will have to sign forms saying they are willing to take the risk."

Courtney found her stomach knotting up. Should she dare to try this on her own? No obstetrician was on night duty, though a surgeon was always on call. Should she hazard a breech birth, especially twins? In trying to prove to herself she could do it, would she be endangering the life of the mother and babies?

"Is there a pediatrician on duty?" she asked the nurse.

"None on duty. One's on call. Dr. Rice."

"I'll call him," Courtney volunteered. "You prep the patient. And keep her mother-in-law with her or we'll never communicate."

She walked down to the doctors' lounge. Excitement fluttered through her stomach and down her arms. I feel like I've had three too many cups of coffee, she told herself as she poured herself one.

The door swung open and David walked in. His shoulders sagged, and his eyes were tired. He, too, headed for the coffeepot.

"You working this shift?" he asked with a noted lack of animation.

Courtney nodded. "You look like—"

"Don't tell me. I just amputated a leg for the first time." He swallowed the hot coffee. "Ugh. Is there no place that has good coffee?" He took another gulp. "Do we never get over this? This empathy?"

Courtney couldn't tell whether he was asking her or imploring the gods.

"I'm going home to sleep for sixteen hours," he said as he flopped onto a couch. He stretched out. "Maybe I'll just lie here for sixteen hours. An army marching through couldn't wake me." He closed his eyes.

She picked up the phone and rang Dr. Rice.

"I'll be there directly," he said. "Meanwhile, have the nurses heat two bassinets under warming lights and set them in the operating room."

Should she call an obstetrician, too? She wanted badly to do this delivery herself. She had performed a breech birth. She had delivered a set of twins. But the two together?

David opened one eye. "Chancy case?"

She sighed. "I don't know whether to call an obstetrician."

He raised himself and leaned on an elbow, ready to listen.

Courtney explained her predicament.

"You really want to do it," he stated.

"Oh, yes, I really do. But isn't that selfish? Shouldn't she have the best care possible? I've never handled a case like this."

"Rice coming as pediatrician? He'll be able to advise. He's good."

"I know. But he's not an OB. Or a surgeon."

"Go see how much she's dilated," David said. "When I leave, I'll stick my head in the OR, and if you need an OB, I'll send an SOS to Dr. Kaplan."

Courtney left to scrub up.

When she arrived in the OR, the young woman was already stretched on the table, her eyes wide with fear, her legs in the stirrups. Her mother-in-law held her hand. Am I breaking a rule allowing her in here? Courtney wondered.

Two nurses were in attendance, one standing beside the patient and the other running around. Dr. Johnston, the anesthesiologist, arrived. They conferred and he administered a narcotic in a small dose. Too much and the babies would be sedated; nothing and the mother would be all over the table. Visibly, the patient began to relax.

Courtney said to him, "The girl doesn't understand English. What happens when we send the mother out?"

Dr. Johnston looked over his shoulder at the big woman. "She's scrubbed." He shrugged his shoulders.

Eyes fierce, the woman said, "I shall not leave."

Dr. Johnston smiled his usual disarming smile. "I guess that settles that."

At that moment, Dr. Rice arrived. "Well, I'm ready," he said cheerfully, "for two more citizens of the world."

The patient moaned.

Courtney examined her. Then she looked at Dr. Johnston and nodded briefly. The outer door opened and David entered, dressed in the green uniform for the operating room, exhaustion no longer evident in his eyes.

"I'm here to assist if you need it," he said.

Just then the patient cried out.

David stood in the background, where he could observe but not participate unless needed.

"Push," Courtney instructed the mother-in-law, who spoke to the young woman.

The baby's head jutted through the vagina, the back of the head up and the baby looking toward the floor. "It's occiput anterior," she said aloud. Without haste, ever so slowly, the baby's head came out. With fingers that belied her inner trembling, Courtney turned the head ninety degrees so that the baby faced the side walls. Then, as she pressed down on the head, she instructed the mother-in-law, "Tell her to push hard. *Push.*"

The woman groaned, a long, high wail, as she pushed. The baby's upper shoulder appeared under the pubic bone. With one hand on the baby's head, Courtney accepted with the other hand the bulb syringe that David's hand stretched out to her.

"Tell her to stop pushing," Courtney said, using the suction apparatus to suck out the baby's airway. "Now, a gentle push—just long, easy, not hard." She lifted the baby's hand while a tiny lower shoulder came out through the bottom of the vagina near the rectum.

"Good girl." She heard David murmur the encouragement.

Suctioning again, she allowed the rest of the baby to fall onto her left arm, clamped the cord, and handed the baby to the waiting Dr. Rice.

With a clamp still on the cord, Courtney reached up into the vagina to determine what was coming next—the placenta of the first baby or the second twin.

"It's the second baby . . . in breech position," she said to David. Two tiny feet were starting to poke through the uterus and into the vagina. Courtney straightened the little legs so that one wasn't pinched up in a compressed, awkward position.

I want both legs down, she told herself, not one flexed and one down.

"You're doing fine," David reassured her.

As she felt the baby descend into the vagina, she turned the baby's legs so that its butt faced the ceiling.

It was all happening so quickly. As the baby came closer, Courtney reached in farther, putting her finger in the crease of the elbow. She pulled gently, so the hand and forearm came down and the arm was straight alongside the little body.

She did the same to the other arm.

"Another push," she said. "Not too hard."

The older woman spoke.

Courtney worked the shoulders out, first the top one, then the lower. Holding the baby feet upward toward the ceiling, she gently eased the body out. By pulling almost straight up on the baby's legs, she allowed the second twin to come out. They could see the baby's nose and mouth at the vaginal opening.

David reached over to suck out the mouth with the suction apparatus. Courtney's eyes flickered at him and he nodded his head, understanding her unspoken question. He handed her the forceps and held the baby's body steady. She applied the forceps on either side of the baby's head and eased it out over the rectum and under the pubic bone.

David continued with the suctioning. They heard the first baby cry.

The second twin was sweaty. No wonder.

Dr. Rice reached for the second infant. The young mother lay with her eyes closed, but the mother-in-law appeared vastly relieved.

"Great job," said Dr. Rice. "They're both in fine shape. You made it look like a piece of cake."

Piece of cake? Courtney wanted to cry with relief.

David talked quietly in her ear. "After a delivery like this, the uterus will be overstretched and less likely to clamp down fully to stop the bleeding after delivery of the placentas. So be ready." He turned to the nurse and ordered, "Get IVs ready. Pitocin."

As the nurse turned to get the pitocin, the placentas slid out of the vagina and blood gushed behind them as though a faucet had been turned on. It soaked Courtney in red warmth, sticking to everything. The patient began to scream. The mother-in-law stared in horror.

"Quick," David said to the nurse, "Inject ten units of pitocin and then set up an IV."

Cries rent the air. Blood poured over everything. "I'll have to massage the uterus, won't I?" Courtney asked David, though she already knew the answer. She steeled herself, for she knew what a painful process it was for the patient. Squeezing the uterus between her hands, she put one hand on the abdomen near the umbilicus at the top of the uterus; she jammed the other hand fully into the vagina. The young woman screamed in a mixture of pain and terror. Courtney's chest constricted, but her hands kept massaging and squeezing the uterus.

"An injection of methergine, too," she said. "Zero point two miligrams, and hurry." She saw the saline solution dripping from the bottle and into the patient's arm. It should take effect any minute. One of the nurses had practically thrown herself over the patient's body to keep her from writhing.

Courtney felt what had been a soft, floppy uterus begin to firm up. The massage was beginning to take effect. Between that and the medicine, the uterus would be encouraged to clamp down further and the bleeding would stop. But when? She could tell it had lessened, but the patient's legs were covered with blood; there was blood over the floor, over the patient, over her own face, up her arms, and her hands were wallowing in it.

Oh, this poor woman, Courtney thought, her heart constricted. Fury was in the eyes of the mother-in-law. Her daughter stopped screaming and began to sob, huge, convulsive sobs of agony. But with each drip of the intravenous feeding, the uterus clamped and the pain subsided. Courtney was able to stop the massage, take her hand out of the woman, lessen the torment.

When it was certain the bleeding had stopped, Courtney nodded her head. The nurses began to wheel the new mother out of the OR, carrying the IV along. The young woman sniffled; she was exhausted. The babies had already been taken to the nursery.

Standing in the midst of the slippery gore, Courtney heard David say, "Walk carefully."

She had forgotten about him.

He reached out a clean hand to take hold of her bloody one and helped her. "Kick off your shoes," he said, "or you're likely to fall."

She did as he said. Suddenly, his arms were around her and he steadied her rocking body. "There, there," he said. "You did a beautiful job."

"She was in such pain." Courtney imagined she could still hear those cries.

"You had no choice. You had to massage the uterus. Had you never done it before?"

"No." Courtney's own breath was coming in gasps now that it was all over and she could allow herself the luxury of emotion. "But I saw it done once. Oh, David." She leaned against him, blood clotting now on his uniform, too.

With relief came tears.

When she looked in on her patient four hours later, the woman was asleep and peaceful.

As she drove home, Courtney thought that she had never seen a more beautiful sunrise.

CHAPTER 52

▼

"THERE ARE NEW CASES OF POLIO EVERY DAY," LILIANE SAID. SHE HAD been to Kaputo for three straight days. "It's an epidemic—and just the beginning."

"Do you have enough vaccine?" asked Courtney.

"Of course not. And no way of getting more. They claim there's not enough. If it spreads outside the township . . ."

"Weren't most of the whites vaccinated when they were young?"

"Urban ones," said Lili. "But people go out of Kaputo every

day into the white sector. Vaccine now could save thousands in the whole city."

"Is there no way to get some?"

"If so, I don't know how. We need it to keep the epidemic from spreading and also for those already infected . . ." She remembered how they had dug a hole and buried the little boy for three days so many years ago.

"When do you next get time off?" Liliane asked Courtney.

It was now Wednesday. "I'm still working nights. I do have days free."

"But you'd be too tired to operate and be alert. What nights do you have off?"

"Friday and Sunday," Courtney answered.

"Will you help on Saturday?"

"Of course. I didn't think I could get into Kaputo."

"I'll get you in. There are advantages to a modicum of fame. Being the widow of their only Nobel Prize winner helps. I don't make waves; otherwise, I wouldn't be permitted to do the little I can do. I'm sure I can convince them this emergency will affect people outside the township, too."

Despite her worry, Lili's eyes sparkled. She was never more filled with life than when she felt needed. Courtney thought, She's still beautiful.

The phone rang. "I'll get it," said Courtney.

The voice on the other end didn't introduce itself. "I've never received flowers before," it said. "I like it."

"I didn't know how to thank you." She smiled. "You wanted to sleep for sixteen hours, yet you scrubbed up and came in to rescue me. It was a very nice thing to do."

"Courtney, I shall do many nice things for you, given the chance."

"Try me," she said, wondering if she sounded too eager.

"You're working tonight again, aren't you?"

He knew she was.

"If you're not in the midst of another dramatic delivery, I thought you might like a romantic supper instead of commissary food."

"A romantic supper?" She laughed.

He was smiling, she could tell. "Sure. When you're free for a bit, come to my office. I'll be there waiting. I'll expect you any time after eleven."

"What if I can't make it until later?"

"I'll be there. Just wake me up."

When Lili saw her smile, she asked, "David? I keep wondering when he's going to make his move. It's about time."

"I think he just made one. He's invited me to a 'romantic supper' in his office tonight. He knows I can't leave the hospital. He's not even on night duty."

Courtney had told Lili about David's support during the twins' birth. Everything she told her grandmother made Lili more interested in him.

"I think this is serious, my dear."

"Oh, Lili. You're a romantic."

"I don't think that's an apt description of me," Lili assured her. "And don't forget. I need you. Saturday."

"Lili, I shall love to help. I never dreamed I could."

IT WAS NEARLY MIDNIGHT BEFORE SHE WAS ABLE TO GET TO DAVID'S office. He was sitting behind his desk, reading. He had set up a card table and covered it with a damask tablecloth. A large candelabra glowed with five tall burgundy candles. The carnations she had sent him were arranged in a silver bowl. As soon as she came in, he switched off his desk lamp and leaned over to touch the button on a portable tape recorder. Soft background music filtered into the night.

She stood by the door, looking across the room at him. She was touched and amused. He'd gone to a lot of trouble.

"Sit down." He gestured expansively. "The supper's cold so that it wouldn't matter what time you arrived. May I tell you you look ravishing tonight?"

Courtney couldn't help laughing. No one, in the ill-fitting hospital uniforms, looked ravishing. David, on the other hand, looked casually elegant. A soft cashmere sweater matched his eyes.

He pulled a chair out and seated her at the table, then moved the flickering candles to the side so that nothing should come between them. He had prepared a cold chicken-tarragon rice dish with artichoke hearts, Greek olives, and subtle spices. "Are you going to tell me you cooked this?" asked Courtney. The women of her family were proud of themselves when they boiled an egg correctly.

David sat opposite her; she felt his leg brush hers. "You have no idea of my hidden talents," he said. "And I have decided now is the time to begin to rectify that."

"Sounds exciting."

"I debated about wine, for chicken tarragon should seldom be undertaken without dry white wine. In fact, no dinner should really be contemplated without wine." The way his eyes smiled across the table at her made his words irrelevant. "But I realized you're on duty, and I certainly want you to operate at top efficiency."

The chicken was delicious.

"This was a lovely idea. I must remember to send you flowers again."

"Talking of flowers and the reason you sent them, Courtney, you are one damned fine doctor."

David, telling her she was good?

"Tell me," he urged, "what you think about in those periods when medicine isn't in the forefront of your mind."

"Oh, dear." She sighed. "It's been so intense for so long that I don't know if I have thoughts that aren't connected with medicine. I keep thinking that after my internship I can begin to lead a normal life."

"What do you consider a normal life?"

"Oh, getting back to the bush. Starting a practice. Then I'll have time to listen to people, time to—"

"Courtney," David said sharply, "that's all connected with medicine. Isn't there anything else to your life?"

She looked at him. Did she want something else? "Oh, of course. A family. Children. But that's in the future. I have other things to do first."

"Do you really want to spend your life out in the bush with a bunch of natives? Don't you need friends? Someone to share your thoughts with? Someone to love?"

Their eyes locked. Someone to love. Of course. Wasn't that what life's all about? Someone to touch. Someone to curl next to each night. Someone to share with. Someone to have a child with. Someone to understand.

"Yes," she said softly, "I'd like that."

At that moment, the music ended. "Damn," muttered David, getting up and walking over to his desk. He flipped the tape over and music again filled the air. He put out his arms and Courtney arose and moved into them. It was as though they had danced together forever. She closed her eyes, letting David and the music move her; his hand on her back excited her at the same time it gave her a sense of security. Her head rested on his shoulder and she turned to touch his neck with her lips. His right hand on her back tightened, and he folded his left hand around her right one tightly. His lips brushed her forehead. She thought he might lean down and kiss her, but he didn't. Their bodies moved as one, slowly, and she knew that, some time soon, she and David would make love. She wanted it. He's making love to me now, she thought.

"Dr. McCloud. Paging Dr. McCloud." The loudspeaker blared. "Dr. McCloud, report to room 432."

She dropped his hand and started to move away from him, but he held her close. "Saturday, I know you're free. Let's drive up the coast. Spend the day with me, Courtney."

"I can't," she said. "I promised Lili I'd help her in Kaputo."

David jerked his head back and looked at her. "Kaputo?"

"A polio epidemic is starting. Lili's very worried. They can't get more vaccine, so it'll be out of hand soon. And the stricken need medical attention. She said she'd get me in if I'd go help. I feel I must. No, that's not quite right. I want to."

"Polio? How come we haven't heard of it yet?"

"If it gets out of hand, we'll all hear about it."

"Dr. McCloud, paging Dr. McCloud."

"I've got to go, David. I loved the romantic supper. And it was just that. Thank you."

"See you," he said. Suddenly, she realized his thoughts were not on her; his eyes gazed into the distance. He reached down and brushed his lips across her cheek in a fraternal fashion.

When Courtney arrived home around 7:30, Lili was already up. Her eyes sparkled and she was bustling around.

"Oh, that nice young man of yours," she said.

"What young man of mine?" Courtney asked. She was ready to head for bed.

"David, of course. He arrived at dawn with hundreds of vials of vaccine. Just left them and ran. Said he had to get to work."

Courtney wondered how he had managed to lay hands on five hundred vials so quickly. She knew she could never get the hospital to part with that much.

As she fell asleep with the sun warming her, she thought, Whether he knows it or not, he's continuing to make love to me. For she knew that, emotionally, she responded to gestures like that.

ON SATURDAY MORNING, AS SHE AND LILI READIED THEMSELVES FOR Kaputo, David arrived at the front door. "I'm coming with you," he announced. He brushed past Courtney and walked into the dining room, where Lili was finishing breakfast. "Can you get me in, too?" His body was wired with energy and urgency. "I've brought you another big batch of vaccine."

"More?" Lili rose from the table and threw her arms around him.

Having heard about the living conditions at Kaputo from the time she was twelve, Courtney was better prepared than David for the conditions, but the actuality depressed her severely. The stench of urine, rotting garbage, and filth was nauseating. Children ran around barefoot, cutting themselves on broken bottles, step-ping in excrement. The squalor was unbelievable. The place was monochromatic: gray. There was no beauty, nothing attractive, nothing that didn't depress the spirit. The inhabitants looked at them suspiciously, cowering close to the shacks or hiding in the doorways, until they saw that Courtney and David were with Lili.

Then they were surrounded. "George Mbeka can't get out of bed" and "Martha's leg wouldn't straighten out," or a baby couldn't move.

Within minutes, a crowd had accumulated, following Lili.

"Is it always like this?" asked David.

"No. But they're frightened now. Polio's one of the world's scariest diseases."

"It's been so long since I've even heard of a case," David said.

"You've been among people who can afford to be innoculated or whose government provides it. I'm surprised these squatter townships aren't constantly alive with epidemics."

"You do know the hospital will be open to those who are ill, don't you?" David asked.

"These people are scared to death of the white world. If their loved ones are taken away, they fear that they'll never see them again. Only the very brave and desperate have the gumption to go to the hospitals. Look around you. Does this look like a place where people can think rationally? Where they can learn? Where they can live?"

"Jesus Christ," muttered David. "I had no idea this was even here . . . I mean, I knew intellectually, but . . ."

Lili stopped in front of a shack that looked like all the others. A corrugated tin roof, openings for windows since no one could afford glass, slats tossed together. She opened the door; none had locks. As Courtney and David stepped inside, they could see that this shack was Lili's hospital. There was no light save that which came in from the small, airy window. Lili immediately lit a kerosene lantern. The walls had been whitewashed in an attempt at sterility; the dirt floors were so hardpacked that they had become like smooth rock.

Liliane turned to the crowd following her and said, "Today I want all the children." She turned to David and Courtney. "We'll innoculate the children first. They're most susceptible. If we can control it in the children, maybe it won't spread to the adults. We can't do them all. There are thousands."

"Will they let us do it? Aren't they afraid of needles?"

"No more so than mankind everywhere. They know medicine is in the shots. They trust me. They trust medicine. Here, we'll have them make three lines."

By 4:00 the vaccine was all gone. Courtney thought if she heard another child crying, she would scream. She looked over at Lili. Her grandmother looked tired. She had been working hard for eight hours and she was nearly seventy-five years old.

I hope I can go on as she does, thought Courtney. She seems to have no limits.

Lili brushed away the hair that had fallen onto her forehead. She hoped she wouldn't collapse right here. She closed the door on the line of people still waiting, telling them, "All gone."

"How hard it is to tell them no, no more."

David was straightening everything up, collecting the needles in the sack in which he'd brought them. "Let's go," he said, talking to Courtney but taking hold of Lili's arm.

He opened the door and shouldered his way through the crowd, which was now imploring, "More tomorrow?"

Lili shrugged her shoulders. "I wish I could tell them yes." She let herself be led through the compound and out the iron gates.

David slid behind the wheel of his car and waited for Courtney and Liliane to join him. None of them talked as he sped toward home. "I'd invite you both to dinner if I thought any of us could eat," he said. "But, personally, I can't."

When they arrived home, David made no effort to get out of the car. As soon as Lili and Courtney closed the door, he drove away.

On Sunday, Courtney's shift changed. She began working days again. As she walked out the door into a day that was more beautiful than any she could remember, the air was fresh with the scent of roses, there wasn't a cloud in the sky. It would be a nice day for the beach, she thought. David pulled up in his long, low car. "Tell me Lili hasn't left yet," he called as he approached Courtney.

"No, she wasn't even thinking of going today."

"She will when I show her what I have." He leaned down and kissed Courtney's cheek as though it were something he'd been doing for years. "Where is she?"

"Still in the dining room, I think."

Walking into the house, David called, "Lili?"

Courtney turned around and followed him.

"What in the world are you sitting here reading the papers for?" he cried in great good humor. "You could be saving the world and you're lollygagging, but, as long as you ask, of course I'd be happy to join you in some coffee."

Lili was staring at him openmouthed as he sat down next to her and reached for the coffeepot. "These rolls look good, too. Thank you; I'd be glad to."

He stuffed one into his mouth and poured half the cream into his coffee. Courtney stood in the doorway.

"Lili, will you promise to love me forever?"

"I've no idea what you're up to, but I suspect I have little choice about loving you forever."

He leaned over and brushed her cheek as he had Courtney's. "In the car I have—are you ready?—I have fifteen hundred needles filled with polio vaccine." He leaned back in the chair, looking smug. "See, you have reason to love me forever. But if it took three of us seven hours yesterday, imagine how long it's going to take us today to dispense fifteen hundred shots, which, incidentally, is absolutely all that is available in Cape Town at this minute. So, let's get going." He turned to see Courtney standing in the doorway.

"Excuse me," he said to Lili, bounded out of his chair, and walked to Courtney.

"Aren't you going to be late? But don't rush away without giving me something to fortify me for the day." He reached out and put his arms around her, bending her back as she'd seen men do in grade-B movies, and kissed her. Kissed her long and deep, yet she could tell he was laughing inside. "There, now," he said, his eyes full of humor, "that should hold each of us for the day. Off with you."

Before Courtney could gather her wits, he again turned to Lili and said, "Come on, let's get going."

All day, as she tended her patients, David's face followed

Courtney. Or, rather, was in front of her. It came between her and everyone she talked to. It watched while she sewed up a gashed leg; it smiled at her when she diagnosed appendicitis; it was morose and quiet—relegated to the background—when she came to Mr. Ellerby, a cantankerous eighty-nine-year-old man who'd been in the hospital for over three weeks.

When a nurse started to change his sheets, he waved her away and said to Courtney, "Tell her not to bother. Sit down and talk with me. Hold my hand while I die. It won't take long."

Courtney pulled a chair over and waved Lina away. Mr. Ellerby's hand felt like tissue paper. She gazed directly at him and asked, "What would you like to talk about?"

He wanted to talk of the summer he was thirteen. Courtney listened as he described the swimming hole near his parents' farm and how his father gave him his first colt that summer and . . . In the midst of a sentence, Mr. Ellerby paused and feebly squeezed Courtney's hand. "I'm going to leave," he told her. He closed his eyes, clasping her hand; he moved his lips silently and died.

But David's face was waiting for her out in the hall, and it replaced that of every doctor she met all day. His face sat right in the middle of the steering wheel as she drove home.

Yesterday she had been sure she could not erase Kaputo from her mind; today it was David who refused to be expunged.

Neither he nor Lili had returned when she arrived home. She decided she would not let him drive away so quickly tonight. She told Anna to prepare dinner for three. When she heard David's car drive up a bit after 7:00, she ran out to the driveway. He and Lili both looked exhausted.

"Dinner's ready," said Courtney. She turned to David. "That includes you, too. You have to eat somewhere."

He did not look as depleted as he had yesterday, though his shoulders sagged and it was obvious he was tired, emotionally as well as physically.

"Just wash your hands and come to dinner."

Courtney was the one who made conversation. She saw they were too tired to add much. When, after dinner, she said, "Go into the library and I'll bring you coffee in there," both Lili and David rose silently and headed toward Lili's favorite room. By the time Courtney appeared, David was sound asleep on the couch; Lili was covering him up with a blanket.

"Courtney, he was marvelous. He has a wonderful way with patients. Just took right over and organized it like I've never been able to do." She sighed. "If there'd been one of him when I was young, I could have shared my life with him. Not"—she turned hastily to Courtney—"that I didn't love your grandfather. But someone like David, someone to live with and work with . . . Don't let him out of your life, my dear."

"I have no intention of letting him out of my life." Courtney looked fondly at the sleeping figure.

Lili kissed Courtney. "I'm going to bed. But I do like our young man."

Our young man. Courtney grinned.

As she walked up the stairs, she thought, I've fallen in love, haven't I?

She fell asleep with a smile on her face.

CHAPTER 53

▼

DAVID WAS SILENT AS THE CAR SPED ALONG THE COAST ROAD. LIGHTS twinkled on as twilight descended. In summer it was still light at 8:00, even though they were heading eastward. Courtney was glad he was quiet; she could commune with the Indian Ocean, watch the reflection of the sun's last rays play orange upon the waves.

They had left Cape Town three hours ago, right after work. A soft breeze cooled the warm evening.

"There's the hotel up ahead." David broke the silence.

It hung along the crest of the sand dunes, looking up the length of the wide, sandy beach. The crashing of waves punctuated the air.

Shortly after his forays into Kaputo with Lili, he had asked Courtney, "When do you next have two days off together?"

When she had told him, he said, "Let's see if we can synchronize. I'll try to change my days off with someone. Let's take a weekend up the coast. I think we're ready for a vacation."

She noted he had not asked her. Was he taking her for granted? At the same time he had said, "Your grandmother is the most remarkable woman I've ever known."

"Are we taking her, too?" Courtney had asked.

He had turned his intense look on her and said, "I may love

her, but not *that* much. I think it's time you and I have some time together.''

She agreed. It was about time.

From the beginning, David hadn't treated her as other men had. No real come-ons, though she was well aware that he found her attractive. No sexual innuendos; no playful, superficial flirting. No rush.

She found him exciting, but she also found him comfortable. She didn't feel she had to make conversation with him; he never made her feel ill at ease. She could enjoy being quiet with him. At the hospital, she felt secure when she knew he was around even if she hadn't seen him.

His interests were more wide-ranging than hers, but this troubled her little. He loved the symphony and the theater, for instance; she knew next to nothing about them. He was a voracious reader, as she was, but she'd had little time in the last five years to read much except texts, and certainly her taste in books had never been as eclectic as his. His unbounded curiosity attracted her.

Her thoughts were interrupted as David slammed on the brakes, jolting her as he careened into the circular driveway of the hotel that strongly resembled a Moorish castle with its arched windows and red-tiled roofs. Lush plants surrounded it; a sweet floral aroma filled the night air.

"How's this?" he asked, his eyes alight as he jumped out of the car. Opening the trunk, he grabbed both their bags, though a bellboy appeared as if from nowhere. "I better warn you. I've been extravagant. I've reserved an oceanfront suite."

"A suite?"

"Well, I didn't know how else to get two bedrooms and still be assured you'd be nearby."

She had wondered whether he thought they'd share a room. Relief mingled with disappointment.

The lobby was more luxurious than anything Courtney had ever seen. "It reeks of elegance," she whispered.

"It should," he whispered back.

"Second-floor front." The clerk handed keys to the bellboy.

The bellboy ushered them in. The rooms were enormous: a living room in shades of blue that matched the ocean roaring down the beach in front of their windows. A fireplace had wood neatly stacked beside it. Large bedrooms opened on either side of the living room. In one, muted lighting accentuated the warm creaminess of the walls, the satin of the bedspread, the plush golden chaise longue. Sliding glass doors opened onto a large balcony. The other bedroom was in shades of rust. There was a small kitchen behind the living room and next to it was a bathroom that astonished them: it had a Jacuzzi surrounded by mirrors.

Without thinking, Courtney laughed and said, "Maybe they expect more of us than we can deliver."

David gave her a strange look.

After Courtney had hung up her clothes, David came into her room. "Let's get in a walk before dark," he said. "I feel restless."

They descended the narrow path that wove through flowers Courtney didn't recognize, emerging onto the wide smooth expanse of beach that stretched endlessly in either direction. The eastern horizon was already darkening, though the sky was still golden. Where sea met sky, the outline of a large ship inched slowly along.

"No more perfect evening ever happened," Courtney said. It had been a long time since she'd felt such contentment. She looked up at David, who grabbed hold of her hand. When he noticed her grinning at him, he stopped and stared down at her, his eyes serious. He reached out and pulled her to him, holding her tightly and completely. Without saying anything, he took his arms from around her and again reached for her hand. They walked along, in awe of the shimmering red splashes of sunset that would take at least half an hour to extinguish itself.

Until they returned, as grayness streaked the sky, they'd not felt impelled to talk but had walked along in comfortable, quiet, shared happiness.

"I'm hungry," said David. "Do you realize it's nearly nine-thirty?"

The hotel dining room was uncrowded, and they sat holding hands across the table, an ease flowing between them.

When they returned to their suite, David immediately began to build a fire in the fireplace. "I don't know that we need it," he said, "but it does have romantic connotations." When it was burning brightly, he turned out the lights and they sat on the couch in the reflection of the flames. Shadows danced across the walls. They sat on opposite ends of the couch, looking at each other, only their fingers touching as their hands rested along the top of the couch.

They talked about nothing in particular and let themselves be mesmerized by the crackling fire. "What do you want to do tomorrow?" David asked.

"Relax," she answered, smiling into his eyes.

"That's what we're here for." He moved across the couch and kissed her.

"I don't care what we do," she said. "You decide."

"Okay. I better warn you. I'm an early riser. I shall get you up early so that we can spend every minute together."

Despite not wanting to, Courtney yawned. It had been a long day. David reached for her hand and drew her up and out onto the balcony.

"Look at those stars," he said. They hung like jewels. "I've never seen them so low."

"See that star. Do you know it's the Southern Cross?"

His gaze followed her pointing finger.

"No. I could always identify the North Star, but a different hemisphere still astronomically confuses me."

"Once you find the Southern Cross," she said as they stared at the sky, "you can identify any constellation." Years of camping out on the savannah with Andrew had educated her in the ways of the heavens.

David stood still and stared into the sky. "See that one?" He pointed at a star. "That third one to the left. Is that always in the same position in relationship to the cross?"

"Always."

"Then let's make it our star," he said, putting an arm around her. "Wherever we may be, when we look at the night sky, we can know the other may be looking up into the same heavens and that star will tie us together. It's ours. It belongs to no one else. And it will always be there—for us."

He turned his face to hers. His lips touched hers and Courtney surrendered to the soft urgency of his lips, to the touch of his tongue against hers. His arms crushed her to him and she could feel the tempo of his heartbeat rush with hers, swore the blood pounding through his veins mingled with hers as their bodies touched. He breathed her name.

He kissed her eyes and feathered his kisses down to her neck, running his tongue lightly against her skin. "You know I want to make love, don't you?" he asked.

"I've wondered what's taken you so long." Her eyes were closed.

"But I'm not going to," he said. "I'm going to wait. Until you come to me. Until you make the move. You must know I've fallen in love with you."

Courtney's eyes opened. "No," she said, "I don't know that."

He grinned at her. "Then you're blind as a bat. And when we make love, your coming to me will tell me you feel the same way."

"You won't make love to me if I don't love you?"

"Courtney, I've wanted to make love to you for months. Maybe from the first day. I've tried to tell myself you aren't different. But it's no use. I feel different with you. About you. I tried to stay away. But I finally faced it. Ready for it or not, I've fallen in love. I've wanted every day to reach out and touch you. I've wanted to take you home with me and make love all night long. But I'm not ready to do it casually. You are not just another woman in my life.

"What this weekend is really about is courtship—I propose to court you all weekend. Make you know how irresistible I am. And when you come to me, you will be telling me what I've just told you."

He leaned down and kissed her again, then walked out of the room. He hadn't waited for her to tell him she, too, was in love. She looked at the door he had closed behind him. Should she follow him?

Instead, she went to her room and immediately fell into a deep sleep, lulled by the rhythm of the never-ceasing ocean.

SHE LAY THERE, DISORIENTED, HER EYES STILL CLOSED. SOMEONE'S staring at me, she thought, in that hazy state between sleep and slow awakening. For a moment she had no idea where she was. Then she cocked one eye open.

David stood in the doorway, a cup of coffee in his hand, wearing a gray sweatshirt and rumpled flannel trousers.

"I've wondered what you'd look like when you're asleep," he said in a low voice. He entered the room and walked over to the bed.

"Hmpf," she mumbled into her pillow.

"Not at all," he said as though she had made an intelligible remark. He sat on the edge of the bed and, leaning down, lightly kissed the end of her nose.

She opened an eye again and he proffered the coffee cup to her. Propping herself up on one elbow, she accepted it. "This is the height of luxury."

"Courtney, my darling." David's voice was playful. "It's time for a run on the beach. Do you want to get up, or shall I drag you there?"

"I don't suppose it dawned on you that you could go alone?" Her smile told him she didn't mean it.

"Not for a minute. I don't intend to do anything alone this weekend." He stood and walked to the door. "It was bad enough waking up alone," he said as he left the room. "Five minutes," he called.

Courtney threw on a pair of slacks, her old green sweater, and her jogging shoes. She rinsed her face in cold water, ran a brush through her hair, and glanced in the mirror. Not that great, she thought, then tossed aside thoughts of her looks and went to meet David and the day.

Both were in marvelous form.

There wasn't a shred of morning fog as far as the eye could see. Except for a couple in the distance with two dogs running around them, the beach was deserted. Slowly, Courtney and David began to jog, increasing their pace steadily though neither was aware of it. The air was cool, invigorating. Gulls screeched and swooped low, diving into the waves for food; a fleet of sandpipers kept ahead of the runners, racing from the breakers. A few ducks bobbed on the waves. Early-morning sun danced prisms on the water.

After about twenty minutes, they looked at each other, laughing, and simultaneously turned around, heading back for breakfast.

"D'you think we have to dress for breakfast?" David asked.

"Well, I certainly need a shower," she answered. "You can have one first."

When she heard him leave the bath, she walked in. The room was dense with steam. She turned on the shower; hot water needled her body. I could start every day like this, she thought.

She hummed as she shampooed her hair. Like Nellie Forbush, she thought, I'm in love, I'm in love, I'm . . .

As she opened the glass shower door to emerge into the bathroom, the door to the bedroom was open and David stood there, a towel tied around his waist. They stood immobile, staring at each other. His chest, still damp, gleamed with soft fuzz; his hair hung damply in a comma over his forehead. His eyes, as they so often were, were unreadable. What nice legs, she thought.

Slowly, very slowly, she reached a hand out and found a towel.

Her eyes had not left him. She could see his eyes on her breasts, saw his gaze travel lingeringly down her body. His eyes came back to hers, searching for something he apparently found there. The towel was still in her hand, not around her. He came toward her. Leaning over, with his hands at his sides, he put his mouth over one breast and then the other, his tongue lingering long and wetly over each one. Then he straightened up and, smiling lightly, took the towel from her hand and wrapped it around her.

Gooseflesh raced down her legs.

David pulled his towel more tightly around himself, laughed a lazy laugh, and went to get dressed. Courtney stood there, unabashed at what had happened, aware that their relationship was accelerating.

THEY DIDN'T SPEAK OF IT.

They spent the day being tourists. They laughed a lot and didn't talk of anything serious. They held hands all the time. They drove north and lunched in a hideaway high on a bluff overlooking the ocean and miles of beach, then they spent the afternoon walking through woods almost as thick as jungle, where leaves were immense and lilies were in bloom, until abruptly they heard the ocean breaking and looked down. Almost directly below them was a crescent-shaped beach closed off at high tide at either end by enormous cliffs that jutted far out into the ocean. David and Courtney looked at each other and laughed happily as they ran down the narrow path.

The cove was sheltered and warm. They sat on an enormous log that was barkless, bleached white from years of sitting in the sun and open to the elements. The sea shimmered silver and broke in long, low waves. The late-afternoon sun beat down with warmth. Courtney brushed back her hair and saw David taking off his shoes. "Come on," he said, rolling up his pants legs. Courtney kicked her shoes off, too. The sand felt hot between her toes. They waded in and out of the water, circling back and forth.

"You know," he said, squeezing her hand tightly, "I like being in love. All along, I thought I was running away from it. I made sure I never let it happen. I wasn't running away. I just hadn't found it."

She stopped and stood in front of him. She looked up into his eyes and then put her arms around his neck. "And now?"

His kiss was her answer.

"Now you're all I think of," she whispered to him. "Lili advised me never to let you out of my life."

He grinned. "Do you agree?"

"I'm considering it."

THEY ATE THAT NIGHT AT A RESTAURANT THAT THOUGHT CHARM meant only one candle for light. They could hardly see each other and kept laughing throughout the meal.

"One of your great virtues," she said, "is allowing me to feel like a little girl again." But ever since the shower this morning she'd been aware of his body, of his nearness, of his maleness. Teasingly, she slipped off her shoe and ran her toes up his leg, under his pants. She wound her foot around his calf and met his questioning eyes.

"Do you know what you're doing?" he asked.

She shrugged her shoulders, her eyes teasing him. "Tell me what I'm doing."

He reached down under the table, grabbed her ankle, and held it tightly. A three-piece orchestra began to play an old danceable melody. She had never taken the initiative with a man and was surprised to find herself doing it so easily with David. "Let go of my foot and come put your arms around me and let's dance. I want you to hold me close."

He let out a loud laugh. "My God! I think you're trying to seduce me."

"Shh. Don't let the whole restaurant know."

As she moved into his arms, she said, "It's your fault."

"I hope so," he murmured into her ear.

They danced in silence, their bodies swaying together. She felt his hand on her back move lower until it rested on her waist, pressing her body into his.

When they returned to the table, David ordered coffee.

"I have a wonderful, exciting idea," said Courtney.

Leaning lazily back in his chair, his eyes alive, his mouth curled in a smile, he said, "How about a Jacuzzi?"

"Exactly." She leaned across the table. "Are you a mind reader?"

"I think"—he was amused, his eyes twinkling—"that it has more to do with body language."

She started to stand. "Let's go," she said crisply.

He shook his head. "No. I'm going to finish my coffee and then I'm going to have another cup, and I'm not going to rush a single thing. Sit down and continue to play. This is too much fun to rush any of it."

"Did you know we'd make love this weekend?"

"No. I must admit it was in my mind. It has been ever since I've known you. Since that first day in the rain at the beach."

"Does it frighten you?"

"Courtney"—David leaned over the table—"nothing about you scares me. What I feel I may be doing, in a country that isn't native to me, is coming home."

She could feel warmth start in her breasts and spread outward. It was as though he had already begun to touch her, to run his hands over her body. She looked at his mouth.

It was a sensual mouth: full, not thick lips, nicely curved, often with a sardonic smile. She wanted to lean over and bite him gently, to feel his lips against hers again. She wanted to unfold; she wanted him to do things to her that had never been done to her before. Her body began to move within its skin.

But he finished his coffee. They strolled out after paying the check.

"Ever been in a Jacuzzi before?" he asked as they entered their suite.

"Never."

He walked through to the bathroom, not stopping to kiss her as she'd hoped. Turning on the water, he then returned to the living room.

Courtney stood in the center of the room, beginning to unzip her dress, letting it slowly drop to the floor.

David stood still; he watched as she did a slow striptease, aware of how she was affecting him.

He began to undress, too.

When they both stood naked, he walked over to her and reached his arms around her, pulling their bodies together. Then he put his lips on hers with a passion he had heretofore denied himself. He lifted her and carried her, his mouth still on hers, into the Jacuzzi.

"I'm going to kiss you everywhere. I am going to study you so that by the time we leave, I will remember every part of you; you will be embedded in my memory forever. I will not let you forget what it's like to make love with me." He gently let her into the swooshing water.

The motion of the surging water was like the swirling of hands upon her. David stepped into the tub and sank into the water with her. He put his head underwater and kissed her breasts, his hands moving slowly, the water eddying around them. She reached her hands out to stroke him, to flutter down his legs, but he grabbed her legs and wound them around him, pulling her closer so that his hands enfolded her breasts, brushing his thumbs back and forth rhythmically over her nipples. He pulled her onto him, entering her so quickly and easily that she was almost unaware of the sudden thrust until she felt him within her, exciting her, moving back and forth, up and down; the water warmly whirling around them, pulling them into its primal pool. His body thrust against her with such raw power, such primordial strength that she shivered. Throwing back her head, she saw that the two of them were reflected in the ceiling mirror, saw David's head reach down and cover her breasts. She had never seen lovemaking before. It fascinated her. She clutched her legs tightly around David. His hands let go of her and she floated back in the water, her hair fanning around her head. They still clung together, moving rhythmically with the undulating water. Closing her eyes, she felt herself being pulled down into a whirlpool, drowning, whorls of water shooting through her body. David pulled her to him, sat her hard on top of him, and, with his eyes closed, he moaned.

They sat like that, in the warm water, for a long time, holding each other, enclosed into each other.

Later, David built a fire and poured wine. They lay on a blanket in front of the fire, staring first at the firelight and then at each other, sharing remembrances of childhoods, dreams of futures, funny, little-known parts of themselves.

Hours later, he leaned over and kissed her gently. But as she turned her cheek and their lips met, gentleness turned to yearning and they walked arm in arm to the bedroom and made love again. But this time it was a long, languorous occasion, in slow motion, trying things Courtney had never tried, staying awake half the night experimenting with each other. There was no intense haste, only a dreamlike quality to their passion and lust.

"I guess," Courtney said with a sigh when it was nearly morning, "I must have known somewhere within me that making love with you would be like this."

They fell asleep breathing each other's breath.

It was nearly noon when they awoke. They kissed little kisses and touched each other lightly, pulled back the blankets and looked at each other's nakedness. And with no talking, no prelude, they began to make love again, this time with much laughter and frivolity.

CHAPTER 54

▼

WITHIN TWO DAYS AFTER COURTNEY'S AND DAVID'S RETURN FROM THE coast, it was obvious to the entire hospital staff that they had a love affair on their hands.

The young doctors who had been making overtures to Courtney, and whom she had dated casually, pulled back. The nurses whose hearts David had toyed with were generally gracious now that they saw he could commit himself. The administration softened, gave them the same days off. Courtney and David managed to show up in the commissary at the same hours, wandered into the doctors' lounge together. They reacted with good humor to the kidding their colleagues inflicted upon them.

They managed to brush shoulders as they passed in the halls, to touch legs casually under dining tables, to rub elbows when they sat next to each other. And when they shared the same duty shift, they'd walk out of the hospital together, heading either to his apartment or out to have dinner with Lili.

Courtney was impressed with David's apartment. She had somehow imagined it sloppy, as bachelors' apartments were supposed to be, needing a woman's touch not only to straighten it up but to add charm. It was, instead, like an ad from a magazine. The furniture had been chosen carefully; though spartan by the standards she was used to, it was elegant. Native African carvings were scattered around—no, *scattered* was not the right word—tastefully arranged. The living room was immense, with an eight-foot couch in warm tones of brown and rust dominating the room. A balcony, behind sliding glass doors, overlooked the city; in the distance, a slice of the ocean could be discerned.

When she saw the bedroom, she said, "You must've hired an interior decorator."

"Not at all." He grinned. "I chose what I like." And he pulled her down onto the waterbed, which undulated gently with their actions.

They developed the habit of staying at his apartment several nights a week. When she arrived one evening after work, he surprised her with her own toothbrush. "So you'll have no excuse." He always did the cooking, though he showed Courtney how to make salads as he liked them; together, they would grocery shop. For Courtney, this was a new experience.

"I can't believe you're twenty-four and so totally sheltered," he said. David didn't shop as others did. He felt tomatoes carefully, sniffed pineapples, bought kiwi fruit, papayas, avocados, and made marvelous Hollandaise to accompany the artichokes he steamed to perfect tenderness. Eating David's cooking awakened taste buds Courtney had not known existed. He made an adventure of meals.

Other evenings, they dined with Lili. Courtney was not ready to abandon her grandmother, nor did David have a desire to. He loved spending evenings conversing with her. David would stretch his legs under the table and Courtney would slip one foot out of her shoe and run her toes up his calf. He would lean across the table and hold her hand while in a spirited discussion with Lili.

"He makes me feel so alive," Lili said after he would leave. "When I think how much you two can accomplish together!"

Courtney had finished her obstetrical tour of duty and had been assigned to the emergency room for the first time. It was an exciting—and exhausting—assignment.

She was the only doctor on duty when the big man arrived. He rushed through the swinging doors, past the clerk on duty, and walked straight to Courtney. He was tall—over 6'4" certainly—broad-shouldered, a hulk of a man, though he had a slender waist and walked with grace and urgency. She had been so entranced with his size, with his coal-black hair and bushy mustache, with the hypnotic blue of his eyes, that for a moment she wasn't aware that his right hand held his left, which was wrapped in a white muff through which blood had seeped. Taking the bandage from his left hand in a dramatic gesture, he held it out. What had once been a hand was now only the bones of his fingers and a thumb, the latter still encased with flesh. Partway up his arm, he had clumsily tied a tourniquet that had succeeded in stopping the bleeding.

"I hope you're a doctor," he said, a French accent evident in his melodious voice. "I've just driven eighty-seven miles with this, hoping I wouldn't die."

In spite of herself, Courtney grimaced, just as the man pitched forward, sprawling unconscious on the floor.

She knew David was the surgeon on duty that day. Thank heavens, she thought. A nurse had come running, and Courtney told her to page David. He was there within two minutes. "God almighty," he exclaimed. Courtney and the nurse had not been able to budge the huge man, whose finger bones splayed on the floor beside him.

Though Courtney knew she should remain on emergency-room duty, she asked David, "May I assist?"

He looked down at her as she knelt next to the huge man. "Let's find someone to cover for you here," he said.

In the operating room, David commented, "He saved his life by stopping the bleeding, but nothing can save this skeleton of a hand." Except for the thumb, there wasn't a shred of flesh beyond his wrist. "Jesus, the one operation that gets to me more than others is always amputation."

Courtney could see there was no alternative, no hope even of a skin graft. Muscle, tendons, veins—none remained.

David began to saw.

"OH, THE POOR MAN," COURTNEY SAID WHEN IT WAS OVER, IMAGINing how she'd react to such a thing, thinking how the man would feel when he regained consciousness.

"He'll be in shock," David said.

Courtney returned to the ER, but when her stint of duty was over, she went back to the Frenchman's room. Groggily, he began to emerge from unconsciousness,. He didn't allow himself long to be disoriented, though it took a while for the anesthesia to wear off. "I lost it, didn't I?" he asked, speaking as though cotton were stuffed in his mouth.

David saw to it that the Frenchman was sedated and out of pain for the night, but when he and Courtney again visited him early the next morning, the man's eyes were bright with life. He shoved his right hand out, ready to shake hands. "The whole thing's my own goddamned fault."

He looked at the bandages that covered the place where a hand had once been. "New challenge, huh?" he asked almost as if to himself. "You know what I was doing? Trying to clear rocks out of a river. I've done it a hundred times. I've worked with dynamite for ten, twelve years. Before I could throw it, it went off.

I still don't know what I didn't do right. I felt it explode right in my hand; I looked up and saw bits of my hand flying through the air. The next I knew I was regaining consciousness and there was all this blood around. It was like my wrist had sprung a leak and all my blood was pouring down my arm and out onto the ground. I grabbed some rope that, fortunately, was lying next to me and wrapped it around my arm and pulled myself over to the jeep, which hadn't been touched. I had an extra shirt and wound it around the bloody hand and thought, I've got to get to Cape Town, otherwise I'll bleed to death. I knew then my hand was gone forever. But I didn't want to die. Even with one hand"—he grinned at Courtney—"I knew there's still lots left I want to do. It could have been my legs," he said cheerily. "Or, God forbid, my eyes. I've got to look on it as being lucky." He grinned wickedly at Courtney. "I can still make love. I can still help plow a field. I can still write and eat. I just can't play baseball."

"Have you ever played baseball?" Courtney couldn't help but grin back at him.

"Never." Then he could do everything he had always done. He wasn't going to let it slow him down a bit.

She stopped in to see him every day until he was discharged.

Courtney had never been happier. She enjoyed living with Lili; she found her a closer friend than anyone her own age had ever been. She found her internship challenging and fulfilling. And she was in love, crazy, head over heels in love.

One evening after work, they sat on the front porch with Lili watching the wisps of clouds dissipate over Table Mountain. Lili had just asked, "Can't you almost smell the grapes ripening?" when David said, "There's going to be a staff opening next year."

"What does that mean?" asked Lili.

"Well, Courtney's internship is up in three months. She has to decide what to do. There's only one woman doctor on the staff now. I think the ratio should be increased."

Lili looked at Courtney.

Courtney was thinking, Oh, so soon? Must I decide my life so soon? She had been hoping it could go on like this forever.

When she didn't respond, David let the matter drop. But not for long.

TWO DAYS LATER, AS THEY WENT THROUGH THE CAFETERIA LINE AT noon, he said, "I was talking with Duffy this morning." Duffy was

Douglas Clapp, the medical chief of staff. "As if I didn't know, the powers that be think highly of you, my love."

Don't pressure me, she wanted to say. But she ladled vegetable soup into a bowl and said nothing.

She headed toward a table where two of their friends sat, and the conversation turned impersonal.

David waited until they were at his apartment preparing dinner: tender, two-inch-thick lamb chops; parsleyed potatoes; cole slaw from a recipe of his grandmother's; garlic bread. "Duffy agrees it's time to hire another woman."

"I don't want to be hired just because of my sex," Courtney said sharply.

David glanced up at the tone of her voice. "All I'm saying is that I think you'd have a very good chance. You know you're a good doctor."

He poured two glasses of Chardonnay and offered one to Courtney.

Ever since David had begun to harp on this subject, there'd been tension between them.

"You know Lili would love to have you stay in Cape Town. Most of the doctors in Africa would love to be given a chance to be on the staff here. Where is living more delightful than here?"

Why couldn't she say it aloud? I'm going back to Zimbabwe. I promised my father; I long ago made a pact with the tribes there. I promised myself. That's why I became a doctor. I can't stay here. But the words didn't come out.

David carried the plates from the small kitchen to the faceted-glass dining table. He flipped a switch on his stereo and dance music floated in the background.

Courtney cut into the tender lamb. "If the way to a woman's heart is through her stomach, you hold the key," she said, trying to lighten the mood. "I'll give you excellent references as a cook should you tire of medicine."

"You could eat like this for life," he said, the food on his plate still untouched.

She looked at him. I do love him, she thought.

"Let's get married," he said. "I can't spend my life without you."

"Married?" She tackled the potatoes. "That *does* sound nice."

"Then you've thought about it?"

She smiled at him. "I haven't really *thought* about it." She couldn't imagine life without him now. She hadn't thought beyond this year. And now she realized why: There lay danger.

"What if we get married and I don't get the residency?"

"But you will."

"We don't know that."

He began to eat, but his eyes were on her.

"Courtney, Lili is right. What wonderful things we can accomplish together."

She nodded. It was mutual. "David, I suppose all people who fall in love think they're unique, that nobody else in the whole world ever felt as much love. But they're wrong. I know that you and I are the lucky ones. I know that for the rest of our lives we'll love each other. Of course I want to spend the rest of my life with you. I want to have your children. I want to work with you. I want to share dreams and hopes and a future with you. From now on, every new experience I want to be with you. But I have to think of *how* I want us to live."

"What do you mean, *how*?"

"I don't know if I can live in South Africa, David. I became a doctor to go back to Zimbabwe. For years I've wanted to do for Zimbabwe what Lili did for the Congo.

"If we stayed here, I'd be afraid to have children and let them grow up. They're doomed, the children that come into this part of the world. A time bomb is ticking and we've no way of knowing when it's going to go off."

"We could get out when we saw it coming."

She shook her head. "I'm not sure we could. Maybe in actuality we could, but psychologically? David, won't you come to Zimbabwe with me and see what it's like?"

"I'd love to."

She smiled and raised her glass to touch his, but his sat on the table.

"But you don't want to practice in Harare," he said.

Harare was the new nation's name for Salisbury.

"Of course not. That would be like your practice in England. Like the white half of the hospital here."

"Has it never dawned on you that you could accomplish a great deal here that needs doing? Darling"—he reached out to put his hand over hers—"I can't live my life out in the beyond, out where there are only natives and blue sky. I can't live away from people. I can't exist in a vacuum."

Funny. She could never call what she had experienced during her summers a vacuum.

Later, when they were falling asleep, he whispered, "You can always refuse it. But apply, to be safe. And then make a decision if it's offered to you."

Well, she didn't think that would hurt. That wouldn't be committing herself to anything.

IN THE MORNING, SHE TOLD DAVID SHE WANTED TO SPEND THAT evening alone with Lili. It had been weeks since she'd had an evening alone with her grandmother.

"David's asked me to marry him."

"I'm not surprised. When is the event to take place?"

Courtney shook her head and sighed. "I didn't say yes."

Lili started to say something but thought better of it. Suddenly, she realized that they were alone because Courtney needed to talk.

"You'd like it if I stayed here, wouldn't you?"

Lili knew she had to answer carefully. "Let me answer it this way. I have loved your living here with me." She was silent for a minute. "I like being with you, my dear. Yes, I like that very much."

Courtney noted that her grandmother had not answered her question directly.

"If you were me, knowing why I originally set out to enter medicine, what would you do?"

"Oh, no." Lili's eyes were serious. "Not that trap. 'If I were you.' No one but you can ever be you or answer that for you. And I don't think the way I lived my life would give you the satisfaction it did me. I lived too narrow a life; it wouldn't be right for you."

"Why not?"

Lili shrugged. "We're not the same. I wouldn't wish it on anyone, particularly someone I love as much as I do you. To give up love to go somewhere where there is no hope of any love."

"You did."

"Ah, no. You forget; I went there for love. And you may never find anyone so right for you as David is. You two have a magic about you."

"I know." Courtney's voiced evidenced her anguish. "Lili, he won't even consider working in Zimbabwe. Do you know how wonderful that could be? We could start a hospital, maybe add missions, as you did. I could learn to fly. We could make a difference to thousands of tribespeople. But he thinks his mission is to help people here. He thinks we can make a difference here. What do you think?"

"What I think shouldn't matter."

"But it does."

"If I tell you it's all right to forget your dream and live here with David, be near me, will you feel absolved? Will that make you happier?"

"Yes, of course." But they both knew that wasn't true as soon as she said it. "No. You're telling me I have to make up my own mind, aren't you?"

"I'm not saying that talking it over isn't helpful. Whenever I had your grandfather around, my problems never seemed as insurmountable. I'll give you this much. I can't bear to think of your losing David. Knowing what I do now, after seventy-five years of experience, I'd do almost anything to preserve that. I know I couldn't have done it at the time, but so often I've wished I could have given up Simbayo to be with your grandfather and your mother."

"So it's all your fault? Wasn't it as much his if he couldn't stay with you?"

"No." Lili looked thoughtful. "The tropics would have ruined Marsh's health. Your mother could not have flourished there."

"Why is it always the woman who gives up her dreams for the man?"

"I don't know." Lili laughed softly. "I was brought up to think life wasn't complete without a man. That a woman's job was to take care of a family. I always felt some failure of femininity because I couldn't fit into that mold. But I was luckier than most. Marsh was always there. Maybe thousands of miles away, but there nevertheless."

"What if you'd given up Simbayo and moved here?"

"I might not have survived. Yet I so often wish I had been able to do that."

They were both quiet for several minutes.

"It should be easy, shouldn't it, considering how much I love David. Now that I know him, I can't envision a life without him in it. I want any children I have to be ours; I want to share sunsets and ideas with him. I want us to grow together all our lives. I know I can never love anyone else the way I love him. And my dream . . . Maybe it was just the idealism of youth. Maybe I should settle for helping the blacks of South Africa, do all I can for people here. You have."

"In the long run," Lili said, "I'm not sure we really have choices. Were I to live my life over, I like to think I'd do more for love. Give up some of the things that kept me from Marsh and your mother."

"But you're not *sure* you would?" asked her granddaughter, looking at her, trying to garner some wisdom that might help her now.

"I think I lived my life as I had to while I was living it. Were I in your position—notice I did not say if I were you—I think I would not let David go. I would try to fit the way I could live life with how I could live with him. The alternative is giving him up. You're not ready to do that."

"Must I give up one or the other—David or my dream?"

Lili reached over and put a hand on Courtney's arm. "Darling, dreams are just that. Maybe it's time for a new dream. One the two of you can share."

"I wish I hadn't been brought up by such puritanical people." Courtney sighed. "You and Mama, and even Daddy, have always worked for the good of society."

"But not as martyrs. And I doubt that puritanical is a description of any of the three of us. We all were driven."

They were silent. Then Lili said, "We have to live with our consciences. We have to do what is necessary for ourselves."

"But you're one of the few," said her granddaughter, "who manage to *live* that way. Most people put their consciences on hold."

"I said I was one of the fortunate few."

"How have you managed?"

"Just luck." Lili smiled. "I didn't start out that way. My choices were easy. I regretted some of them, but I always knew they were right for me. Wrong perhaps for Carolyn and Marsh. But not wrong for me."

"But I don't *know* what is right for me." Courtney moaned.

"Imagine a scale. On one side is the life you'd envisioned but without David. On the other is the life David wants for the two of you. Courtney, think about it: both of you working together, sharing. Oh, what I would have given for that. I knew it a little in the early years with Baxter, but not in the way you two can share. Working together, not only in medicine but to make this country a better place . . ." Lili's eyes were alight. "It makes me long to be young again."

"Are you trying to tell me what to do?"

"It sounds that way, doesn't it? But no, I don't want to. I'd like you near me, and I want you to have love in your life, every day."

Courtney reached over and put an arm around her grandmother's shoulder.

"Don't rush this decision," advised Lili. "Take time. And ask David to be patient. Put in an application for the residency. It doesn't commit you."

They were quiet for several minutes. Then Lili asked, "Does David make love nicely?"

Such an unexpected question brought laughter from Courtney. "Oh, Lili, yes. Yes, he makes love just beautifully. I don't know how I could give that up."

"Maybe you won't have to."

CHAPTER 55

▼

"COURTNEY, I SIMPLY DON'T UNDERSTAND. YOU KNOW AS WELL AS I do that this is a rare thing—what you and I have."

"It's true," she said, her face tear-streaked. "I can't bear to think of living without you."

"Then, for God's sake, what in the world is the problem? I mean, what's important?"

"You've never seen people starving to death because of drought; you've never seen people dying because there's no doctor for hundreds of miles. You've never seen people who are old—beyond the average lifespan—at forty."

"How do *you* propose to feed them?" Sarcasm crept into David's voice.

"I don't know. But I know, I have always known, that I can make a difference to them. I can nurse them through meningitis and prevent polio and—"

"You don't have to go on. We've been through this a dozen times. Courtney, you can do the same here."

"But, David, any doctor can do it here. There are scads of doctors willing and anxious to work in Cape Town."

"Of course. It has the civilized amenities; it offers challenges that European cities don't; it makes those of us committed to medicine and humanity feel we're doing something that many doctors of the world don't want to do. We make damn sure that blacks get the same brand of medicine that whites do. You can't tell me that's doing nothing."

"Of course not," she cried. "I think it's fine. But it's not enough, at least for me." She burst into tears again. "Oh, David."

He walked over to where she sat on his couch and knelt down beside her. Putting his arms around her, he let her cry on his shoulder.

"Why does it have to be done your way?" she sobbed.

"Because I can't, Courtney, I really can't live without people, without mental stimulation, without some of the amenities of the civilized world."

"You can live without me more easily?" she asked.

"And you can live without me more easily out there than you could live in Cape Town with both Lili and me here?"

She sniffed into a Kleenex.

The argument had started because Courtney had been offered the residency. For the last two months, she and David had been skirting the issue, toying with it, trying to be philosophical about it, but not really facing it. Now, a decision was necessary.

"Courtney, have you any idea what you'd be turning down if you say no to a residency here?"

She nodded. "Yes."

"God almighty, darling. Do you have to get down to the raw bone to think that life is worthwhile? I sometimes think your value system is skewed—out of whack."

"I don't know if I could spend the rest of my life in a city."

"Fine, we'll move out to the suburbs."

Her eyes flashed at him.

"Courtney, I can't live a year of my life out in the middle of nowhere"—David waved his hand vaguely—"much less contemplate the rest of my life out there. I'd love to go on a safari. I'd love to explore your beloved continent. But you're thinking of going where there are no trees, where the sun beats down on you, where the wind whips the dust around. Where the people are nomads and you'll have to follow them."

"That's not true. You've listened to Lili and me. She thinks that if I build a hospital, the tribes will be able to come to me."

"Sure. And there you'll be in the middle of noplace, relying on airlifts for food and old magazines and books."

"That was back in 1926 when Lili began. Life's not that harsh—well, not always."

"Courtney, I know my reactions in advance. I'd take one look and wonder how soon I could get away. Darling, I'm the product of civilization. I've no desire to go to godforsaken places like Simbayo to spend my life—or even for a vacation."

"Then maybe you'd better find a woman with the same values. A city girl." Courtney spit the words at him.

"Oh, for Christ's sake." David looked at her, then spun on his heels and left the apartment, slamming the door behind him.

Courtney stared at the door and burst into tears again. She'd been crying for the last hour.

Damn, damn, damn.

She waited until she stopped weeping and then sat looking out the window, down on this city where she had been so happy. *Why* was she unable to continue living here?

She reached for the phone and called Lili.

"You've been crying. I can tell by your voice," her grandmother said immediately.

"Oh, Lili, I don't know what to do. I can't leave David."

There was silence on the other end of the phone.

"Well," said Courtney, "are you still there?"

"Yes, of course. I can't answer this for you. I can't decide for you."

"Oh, I know," wailed Courtney. "I just thought . . ."

"That's what you'd better do. Some hard thinking. Go away for a few days. Go up the coast to that hotel you and David liked so much. Walk along the beach. Sit and stare out at the ocean, away from all of us, and decide what you have to do."

Courtney could feel her breathing regulating itself. Dear Lili.

"I have to let the board at the hospital know by next Monday." It was now Wednesday.

"See if they'll let you take several days off."

"I'll be home for dinner," said Courtney.

SHE WALKED OVER TO THE HOSPITAL AND TALKED WITH THE HEAD administrator; then she returned to David's apartment and left a note and was home for dinner by 6:30.

"I've given the matter a great deal of thought," Lili said. "I'm not ready for the responsibility of your decision. So, in order that I won't enter into your plans, and that your decision hinges strictly on David and what you want to do with your life, I'll plan to be in your life *wherever* you are. So you can't use me as an excuse."

Courtney looked at her grandmother, a question in her eyes. "What are you telling me?"

"If you want to stay here and marry David, we can have the wedding out in the garden. That would be very pretty. And you can come out to dinner several times a week and life can continue much as it has all year. And, darling, I have loved this year. Life has come to this house and to this old heart."

"You're not that old, Lili."

"You make me young again, I admit. Well, life could be very pleasant for all of us. On the other hand, if you feel you *must* return to Zimbabwe, I'll come with you. Maybe I could even be of help. I think I could act as an adviser, keep you from some pitfalls, make some worthwhile suggestions. I can give shots and think I can still deliver babies, but I can't stand on my feet all day anymore."

Courtney stared at her grandmother in open-mouthed astonishment.

"I don't mean forever." Lili's voice was thoughtful. "But I've been thinking that if that's the way you choose, it would be fun to start out again, not that I'm promising more than a year. I'd have to see how I took it physically. But there you are."

Courtney inhaled deeply. Lili was either making this terribly simple or incredibly complex for her. "I don't think you're helping me at all."

"I have no intention of helping you to make a decision and then being blamed for it the rest of your life. I do intend to support you no matter what decision you make."

"I talked on the phone with Daddy last night and he's no more help than you are."

"I imagine he'd like you back in Zimbabwe."

"I know he would. But he said that shouldn't be part of it. What he cares most about is that I'm happy."

"Oh, my dear, there are so many degrees of happiness. Personally, I have found that any happiness I achieve is at the expense of something else I hold dear."

"I'm learning that, too." Courtney wondered aloud, "Lili, do you think we'd have been this close if Mama had lived?"

"I like to think so. Actually, I'm far closer to you than your mother and I ever were. I think she always loved me, but she never trusted me after I sent her from Simbayo. Never let herself feel close to me again. She and Marsh . . ." Lili sighed. "Neither of them thought I loved them enough. If I had, I would have given up all else I held dear to be with them."

"And would have been less yourself."

Lili focused her eyes on Courtney and reached over to touch her hand. "Thank you for understanding, my dear." Then she smiled—a sad smile, Courtney thought. "I thought when David entered your life that maybe the two could be combined, that the two of you could do the work you dreamed of doing together, that you wouldn't have to deny yourself one or the other. I dreamed of a doctor for you, one dedicated to the principles David is, but it didn't dawn on me he wouldn't want to live the life you wanted. The question really is, isn't it, whether or not you're willing to live in a city and settle for a life of comfort when you like the picture of yourself being heroic."

"I've never thought of it quite like that."

"Well, do. Maybe it will help to clarify your thinking."

THE HOTEL WAS NEARLY EMPTY, MIDWEEK IN THE OFF-SEASON. AN oceanfront room was almost cheap—almost. Courtney arrived Thursday afternoon and walked north along the beach until her feet were sore. Her mind was a blank. She watched the seagulls circling, calling in that sharp, gull voice, and she delighted in the smooth, graceful arcs they made as they glided into the ocean. Whoever invented the airplane, she thought, must have studied gulls.

The sky was a milky blue streaked with translucent strips of clouds. The sand felt cool to her feet. Under the hazy sky, the ocean was a mottled gray, the white caps choppy. She was glad she'd worn her sweatshirt.

That evening, at dinner, there were only three other diners in the hotel dining room. A middle-aged woman alone; it made Courtney wonder if that were to be her fate. A woman alone in the world. She tried to imagine how the woman felt, if she were self-conscious, if she were lonely. If she felt unloved. Unnecessary.

Wasn't the possibility of family one of the things she should consider? What would moving out to the savannah mean? That she, like Lili, would have to give up any children—send them off to be educated? No. She would not do that. After the children came, she would live the life David wanted to live. But without David, there would be no children. There was no chance of meeting a man out in the veld. She had to face that.

She couldn't envision life with someone other than David.

When the waiter brought her the check, she suddenly noticed that the other diners had left.

The covers on her bed had been turned down; the soft light on the bed table had been lit. The room looked most inviting. Though it was only nine o'clock, Courtney decided to take a hot bath and go to bed. She would get up early and walk again, maybe swim if it wasn't too cold, wade at least. But it was nearly noon when she awoke. She doubted that she'd ever slept that late in her life. Nearly fourteen hours of sleep!

She jogged several miles up the beach before going in to lunch. She felt wonderful. She took a glass of Chablis up to her room and opened the doors to the balcony. It was a bit windy, so she took a blanket from the bed and wrapped it around herself as she sat on the chaise, wineglass in hand, and let herself be hypnotized by the ocean, a bright blue today. High above, a jet left a trail through the bright azure. She wished David were here.

She wanted to be able to look into his eyes and to see that smile of his, the one that indicated they shared a secret, that they were the only two people in the world. She yearned to see the tenderness that filled his eyes when they were together; she even longed to see his eyes when they flashed with impatience, when they were afire with anger. His moods didn't frighten her; she loved his passion, his caring, his ability to show his feelings.

She wanted to hear his voice, listen to him talk—it mattered little of what, she just wanted to hear the timbre of his voice, hear the smoothness, be aware of how her heart quickened when she heard his voice for the first time each day. She wanted to look at his hands, long, slender, capable. She liked watching them when he operated, so sure, so knowledgeable. She liked what they did to her when he touched her. She wanted to feel his hands touch her, to reassure her, to excite her, to thrill her. She liked watching his hands when he stir-fried vegetables, tossing them quickly, knowing just what they were doing. She watched his hands when he shaved in the morning. She'd sit on the edge of the bathtub and look up at him in front of the mirror and admire the way his hand held the razor. Smiling to herself, she remembered how his left hand would surprise her and tweak her nose, getting lather on her. She wondered if his hands would deliver their children. She would like that. That thought brought her out of her reverie.

She wasn't ready for children yet, that she knew. But someday, certainly, she'd always thought . . .

But then again if she took off alone to start a hospital herself, wouldn't that mean no children? No love?

She gulped the rest of her wine.

"Dammit," she cried to the wind, "how the hell do I decide?"

Then, for several hours, she simply stared out at the ocean, bundled up in her blanket under the autumn sun.

SHE FOUND IT IMPOSSIBLE TO SLEEP THAT NIGHT. NO WONDER, SHE thought, after fourteen hours of sleep. She closed her eyes and tried to push the world away. When that didn't work, she tried to think. No thoughts came. Finally she dressed and went down to the lobby. "I'm going for a walk on the beach," she told the sleepy clerk. It was well after midnight.

Diamonds studded the black velvet sky. There, where the Southern Cross pointed, was their star. She knew that wherever she was, for the rest of her life, she would glance up in the night, looking for that star, thinking of David and their love.

What if she stayed on, accepted the residency, married David?

She tried to imagine what that would be like. She and David in his elegant apartment. Windsurfing, maybe golf, jogging together in the early morning; discussing patients, other doctors, politics. Going out to Lili's for dinner. Probably inheriting Lili's house, living out there where her grandfather and her mother had lived for so many years. Having children there. Would she stay home and be a mother, or could she continue practicing medicine? She knew David would not push her either way. She could do both. She wouldn't have to make a choice as Lili had, as so many women over the years had. She could have it all.

Actually, it sounded appealing. Life with David—forever with David. Children with David. Work with David.

But how long could it last in this country that would be torn apart with violent bloodshed, which already was beginning up near Pretoria. In the night, she imagined the yells as bands of natives ran with torches to the big house amid the vineyards; she heard voices crying, "No, Mother Lili has been good to us. Dr. David and Dr. Courtney, they have helped us." But no one listened. Before the house was set afire, the children, two of them, were pulled from their beds. Courtney and David were forced to watch as their bodies were riddled with bullets. Luckily, their own deaths were quicker. The flames grew larger as her vision came to an end.

She shuddered.

There was little doubt in her mind that in her lifetime South Africa's present way of life would disappear after bloodshed, horror, revolution. What would replace it, she had no idea. But she didn't want to be a part of the process. She knew that the natives would not allow her to fight on their side, that hatred for years of subjugation would act as bile, and that reason would be cast aside as all whites were annihilated.

What was the other side of the coin? Returning to that place where she and Andrew had spent a happy summer, where he had built his first dam, where a thatched-hut village had grown up on the small lake his dam created, which became a crossroads for nomadic tribes wandering to waterholes or to fertile land, where she had seen a herd of elephants outlined against the sunset one morning, stretching as far as the eye could see? During all of her years in med school, when the grind of study and self-discipline sometimes were overwhelming, this vision had kept her going. The idea that she, one person, could make a difference. She knew she could. Wasn't that worth something?

How could she settle for a high-rise apartment or a comfortable life when every day she knew people were dying without medical help that could save them; when preventive medicine could be taught so that some of the scourges of Africa could be eradicated before they began?

She fell on her knees in the night on a sandy beach by the Indian Ocean and pummeled the sand with her fists, crying to the gods or the stars or the wind, "What shall I do?"

IT WAS AGAIN NEARLY NOON WHEN SHE AWOKE IN THE HOTEL ROOM. While she was having brunch in the restaurant, David appeared.

His eyes were bloodshot, and he looked haggard despite the usual elegance of his clothes.

He crossed the dining room and sat across from her.

"I know you want to be alone, but I don't. I won't let you make a decision about our lives all alone," he said as he slid into the seat across from her. "Lili told me where you were."

She knew her eyes melted as she looked at him. Life pumped into her; love such as she had never known . . . she wanted to make him happy. She reached out her hand, and he covered it with his. He stood and, in front of everyone, leaned across the table and kissed her. Then he sat down and ordered lunch.

Later that night, after they had made love with an intensity that bordered on frenzy, David said, "Darling, I refuse to live without you."

If he refused to live without her, didn't that mean that whether he agreed now or later, ultimately he would come to Zimbabwe with her?

CHAPTER 56

▼

THE HAUNTED LOOK HAD LEFT COURTNEY'S EYES, BUT LILIANE KNEW hope still reigned in her heart.

Liliane fully recognized that the nine months they had been here, in the hinterlands of Zimbabwe, had been a mixture of accomplishment, challenge, and the heartache of loneliness for Courtney. For herself, during the times when she could ignore the pain reflected in Courtney's eyes or the sag of her shoulders, it had been a time of rebirth, a time of feeling needed again, a time when her mind was again involved to its maximum. In fact, there may never have been a time when she felt so fulfilled.

She was doing all of the things she had most loved doing in her life; her experience at Simbayo made this seem so much easier, and Andrew had helped to accomplish so much, so quickly. The big difference, however, was that this time she was sharing her work with someone she loved, someone who cared as much as she did about what they were doing. Not that Rose and Heidi and Philippe hadn't cared; they had. But now she was sharing it with a part of her own self—a part of her blood, a big part of her heart. Here, she was teaching and leading someone who mattered to her more than anyone else in the world.

How lucky I am, she thought as she sat in the late afternoon under an acacia tree drinking tea.

Of course, Zimbabwe was different from Simbayo. There was not the unyielding humidity. But there also was not the lush greenness of the jungle—instead, except for the relatively small man-made lake, to the east there was brown as far as the eye could see, broken here and there with clumps of acacias, or a solitary baobab looking as though it had been uprooted and was dangling its roots in the air. Herds of animals still moved across the savannah—

giraffe, antelope, zebra—though not nearly as many as ten or twenty years ago. But no elephants.

Up to the very edge of the lake, it was dry. Dry. Dry. When the wind blew, one inhaled dust and felt it coating one's lungs and driving through one's hair. Water had to be conserved; Andrew had built a water tank, a far more impressive one than the one Marsh had built her so many years ago. But then Marsh was a writer and Andrew an engineer.

Andrew had spent his vacation and his own money down here with them, building the hospital and the outbuildings. A grateful government promised help. It would supply medicine, it would try to find nurses, assistants. Who knows, thought Liliane, where a nation could go if it had a healthy, well-fed population. She grinned when she realized this was the same thought she had had over fifty years ago.

"I would hate to think," Andrew had said to Liliane before he left the last time, "that Courtney will never meet a young man out here, never know the love I knew with Carolyn. I would not wish that on anyone."

"Nor would I," Liliane answered. He had voiced her biggest fear.

"But she's barely twenty-five," said Andrew. "You and I won't let her stay out here forever."

"I'm not sure we'll have much to do with it," answered Liliane, though she knew that without her support and Andrew's, Courtney would not be here now. It was as though they had been training her for this since she was twelve. And another support group, of sorts, arrived shortly.

During their second month out here, before the actual hospital had been built, when they were still living in tents, a priest had stopped for several nights. He was young and had that dedicated gleam in his eyes, the spark that could signify sainthood or insanity. For a time Liliane thought it might be the latter. He was walking throughout Zimbabwe alone, keeping notes and planning a report on where tribes lived, what they were like, what was needed, and how the Catholic Church could contribute. He had no map. He wore a flowing white robe that looked like a dirty sheet, explaining that it was far cooler and less restrictive than his priestly robes. He had no sense of humor whatsoever, but he did have a beautiful smile that showed shining white teeth and a tenderness in his eyes.

He hovered behind or above Courtney when she dealt with a

patient, scrutinizing everything she did. He quizzed Liliane for hours, asking about her ideas, her opinions on how to improve the standard of living, her hopes for teaching these people how to take care of themselves. Courtney told him she wished she knew how to get hold of agronomists who understood the soil and might make it come to life. No agronomist came in the months after Father Francis left, but help of another kind arrived one day—at first in the form of a shimmering mirage, a transparent image hovering above the hot brown earth. It came to life, puttering with the energy of a jeep, and two nuns arrived. They did not look like nuns. They looked like slightly disheveled hippies with windblown hair and clothing that resembled Haight-Ashbury in the late sixties. One of them, Sister Mara, had gold wire-rim glasses and a laugh that bubbled up from deep inside her.

"I have no special talents," she said, introducing herself as she stepped down from the driver's seat. "But I can do most anything, if that doesn't sound too immodest. I'm a tinkerer of things mechanical, and I can cook food that'll make you forget the great restaurants of the world and will warm your stomach *and* your hearts. I empty bedpans as well as anyone in this world, and I'm a good shot."

Liliane and Courtney looked at her in open-mouthed astonishment. Before either of them could respond, the other woman, who was pulling bags and camping gear from the back of the jeep, said, "We didn't drop from heaven. Father Francis sent us. I'm Sister Margaret Gail—Gail, I'd prefer. He felt you could use a nurse."

Neither of the women doubted their welcome. Sister Mara, though they immediately made it clear that the titles could be dropped, had been what she called "bumming around this part of Africa for years." Originally she was from Ireland, but "so long ago I forget what green looks like." She was in her late thirties, and had boundless energy.

Gail, on the other hand, had grown up on a farm in Kenya, and after nursing school in England had determined never to leave this continent again. She was not much older than Courtney. When she learned who Lili was, her big hazel eyes filled with admiration. "I didn't know you were still alive," she whispered.

Together and individually, the two nuns had many wonderful qualities, but the one Courtney and Liliane most cherished was that they never proselytized their religion. Neither hardship nor discomfort fazed either one of them.

It was becoming more and more like Simbayo, thought Liliane.

When Andrew flew in, in the company plane, to consult on what kind of buildings they wanted, Liliane asked Courtney if she had anything in mind.

"All I've ever been able to visualize is exactly how Simbayo looked," responded Courtney.

Liliane sat down and sketched the hospital as she remembered it, the row of dormitory rooms, and, finally, Marsh's cottage where she had lived for so many years. There was no bend in the river, no flock of white storks standing in the rapids to be seen from the verandah, but she asked Andrew to nestle a cottage close to the lake so that each evening from the verandah she could watch the flamboyant sunsets that only this part of Africa offered.

She would, she thought, put the slim, now well-worn volume of e. e. cummings poetry that Marsh had sent her over fifty years before on her bureau. And the jeweled comb from Saigon that she had treasured even though she now knew she could be rich by selling it. And Nkunda's ivory elephant. The only possessions she had ever cared about. Not even her wedding ring was as important.

Two old C-119 transport planes thundered into view and spit out two Caterpillar tractors and other earth-moving machines, all sorts of mechanical devices, a load of lumber, and nine muscular young black men in khaki shorts with wide red sashes and berets. Llewellyn Ltd. was donating the buildings and the labor to "the cause," said Andrew with a smile. He did not tell them it was really his own personal contribution.

Within three weeks the buildings were finished, the water tower and generator functioning. Before Andrew and his crew left, Liliane told him, "I've come home. I've been waiting for twenty-one years to come home. And now I have." She reached up to kiss him. He had no visible qualms about leaving four women alone in the midst of nowhere.

Over the years, a road would be worn by thousands of pairs of feet and myriad vehicles, but there was none now. Yet not one of the four women thought of herself as living in an inhospitable landscape. Jagged hills in the distance, to the north and west, broke the evenness of the view to the east. Wild birds by the hundreds flew to the man-made lake, which also served as a watering hole for thousands of animals at its western end, where the river funneled into it.

There were no drums here to send messages through the

night, as there had been in the Congo, so Liliane never discerned how word of their presence spread so quickly. One day there were no human beings within sight, no tribes on the horizon, no nomads to be seen. The next there were dozens of figures moving, singly or in twos and threes, across the savannah, in direct lines to the compound. Within a month, from any vantage point, one could see black dots in the distance. Limping, walking slowly, painfully, being carried, near death, they arrived by the dozens and then by the hundreds. Soon there was a whole compound, a kraal so to speak, of natives in various costumes and speaking in numerous dialects waiting to be seen by the doctor, hoping for recovery, dreaming of what the white man's medicine could do for them.

The first major problem was how to feed them. Mara's hope was that, with irrigation by the slow, tedious way of bucketful by bucketful, by the use of "night soil" to fertilize, this arid land could be made to grow food. But this did not solve the immediate problem of feeding over five hundred people, who sat huddled in their robes, waiting to be cured or waiting for their loved ones to be cured.

Because there were not enough hours in a day to treat so many patients, because there was not enough food to share, the women soon came to the conclusion that only those patients with the most chance of survival could be fed and treated. Courtney and Gail looked at each other in consternation. Choosing between life and death for another?

Liliane said, "I'll do it. I'll perform triage." Her conscience didn't have as many years left to bother her as did Courtney's and Gail's.

"We need more doctors and nurses; we need several tons of rice; we need helpers of all kinds," said Courtney. "I never anticipated this."

"Would you have come?" asked her grandmother.

"Come? Oh, Lili," she said, brushing hair back from her forehead, "the question becomes: How can one ever leave?"

Later that night, Liliane could almost see resolution enter Courtney's eyes. "All day I've been thinking of children. My children. My not having children. Here, I will have hundreds of children." Her eyes shone.

It reminded Liliane of Baxter's saying, "These are all my children."

When Andrew next flew out—and it had become his habit to do so monthly—Courtney told him to "turn around and go find rice. Or something that will nourish this many people." Andrew was their contact with the world. Liliane saw something creeping back into his eyes and into the way he walked that had disappeared from him with Carolyn's death.

After he had flown away, Courtney said, "I should have told him to send me a dozen people to help. We could use another doctor and about half a dozen nurses as well as a handful of willing helpers."

One appeared that very afternoon. She was as ebony as the night, thin and tall, with liquid eyes that shone like stars. Walking out of the savannah, covered in the usual long, dusty sheetlike garment that also wound around her head, she carried a young child of three. She walked past the long line of waiting patients, up to the hospital where Liliane sat dispensing medicine and advice or sending patients on into Courtney or Gail—much as first Baxter and then she had done at Simbayo. The woman ignored the waiting line and walked directly to Liliane and placed the feverish child in her lap. Its eyes did not focus; it couldn't have weighed much over thirty pounds. It burned to the touch.

Liliane took one look at the child and knew that it was doomed. There was no hope. What ailed it, she didn't yet know, but she knew that it was dying. Looking into the mother's eyes, she saw that the woman knew this, too.

"I have walked over fifty miles," said the woman in perfect English with a British accent. "Save my baby."

Ordinarily, Liliane would have been forced to relegate the hopeless to a placebo. But she could not deny the plea in the mother's eyes. She called for Courtney, though she already knew the answer.

After examining the child, Courtney confirmed Lili's suspicion of meningitis. It had but hours to live.

"My husband developed the sickness first. When we heard you were here, we started out. He died on the way." Tears welled in the woman's eyes but did not drop. "I buried him under some rocks."

She buried her child early the next morning.

The following day she was huddled in her clothing outside the hospital door. Her eyes were blank. But her resolve was strong.

Courtney was the first one who saw her.

"You need help here," the woman said. "I can help. I need to help. Let me help."

Her name was Bmena; the *B* was not pronounced. She had

attended a mission school to the north for several years. She could not have been much older than nineteen though she looked to be in her late thirties. She carried herself with dignity, and no job proved too menial or too demanding for her. At night they could hear her crooning to the sickest patients, and when Courtney or Liliane followed the soothing voice, they saw Bmena sponging the sick one with a cool washcloth or stroking the forehead.

"She's an angel of mercy," said Gail.

She's our Naldani, thought Liliane, remembering her friend of so many years ago.

Shortly thereafter, five trucks appeared on the horizon, winding their way over the roadless veld. It was Andrew, with enough rice to feed several armies for a month or more. It's lucky, thought Liliane, that we're not as out of touch here as we were in Simbayo. We'd have starved to death there if it hadn't been so easy to grow our own food.

Within five years, she realized, looking at the intensity with which Mara was pursuing her dream, we can feed many people, but not yet. Then she caught herself up short. Within five years? I promised Courtney one year. I can't leave here, she realized, not after just one year. Maybe never.

That night, Courtney, exhausted, fell on her bed.

"How long are you going to be able to take it?" asked Liliane.

Courtney looked at her with surprise. "How do you go on to anything else when you know how much you're needed here? Never, in any of my dreams, did I know this is what it would be like. I guess I thought of a hospital like yours, with outposts maybe like the ones you created, and enough people to staff it all, and everything sort of orderly. I never dreamed of these hundreds of starving people, of thousands needing medical care. How can I ever leave here and have these people on my conscience?"

Yes, thought Liliane, now you begin to understand. If not for us, what hope would so many of these have?

"But I think of David every night before I fall asleep. I look at Gail and Mara, and even you, and know that one can live without that kind of love. It seems so easy for the three of you. I've a feeling I'll always be aware of its loss."

They had received little mail, and that only when Andrew arrived. But Liliane knew that each time Andrew had left he took with him a letter from Courtney to David. There had never been an answer.

The next time Andrew came, he brought with him two government officials who stayed for three days, talking to the people, asking Courtney and Liliane what was needed, inspecting the hospital. From that day on, once a month one of those old C-119s arrived with food and medical supplies and blankets. One shipment also brought tents to protect the sickest patients from the sun and from the cold nights. Every three months, on a rotation basis, two young nurses from Harare arrived. They were always replaced just as they became accustomed to the conditions here.

"A far different cry from the way South Africa would treat such a hospital," Liliane thought aloud.

"South Africa would not even allow this," Courtney said. "It's one of the reasons I couldn't stay."

Though the new government of Zimbabwe was still troubled, still trying to find its way, it was doing so intelligently. And compassionately. It was not ignoring its thousands of citizens who wandered through the backcountry, who existed in tribal villages. Though it was anything but a wealthy country, it managed to find food and supplies for its people when it could. It recognized that it needed people like Courtney and had full intentions of rewarding her work with aid.

Eventually, Bmena moved into a dormitory room, the first black to become part of the tightly knit enclave.

Every morning, between eleven and noon, they heard a jet streak across the sky, heading toward Johannesburg. When they looked heavenward, they saw only the streak it left, a thin, white, ruffled trail. It had become a joke. Every day a plane left Harare or Nairobi, or wherever, heading south. Every day, seven days a week, at not quite noon, it passed overhead.

"Do you think these planes go south and just disappear?" asked Mara jokingly. For they never heard planes going north.

So it was with excitement that, late one afternoon, they heard the drone of a single-engine plane. Liliane hadn't heard such a sound since Simbayo. Her heart quickened in remembrance.

Courtney came running out of the hospital, her eyes afire. She hopes it's David, thought Lili. The sun caught the streak of silver against a sky so blue that it must have no end.

The plane circled several times. Before it touched the ground Courtney was running toward it, waving at it. Liliane watched the tableaux from her chair under the trees.

It was a bumpy landing before the small plane's motor stopped. Its door opened by the time Courtney reached it, her arm still raised in the air; her father jumped out of the cockpit.

Liliane watched Courtney throw her arms around Andrew, saw him gesturing, saw Courtney climb up on the wing, bend over into the rear cockpit. Oh, Marsh, she thought. So many years ago.

Andrew's visits always bolstered them. They were used to expecting him, however, every fourth weekend. They would begin to look for a dust puff on the horizon, the sign that his Land Rover was eating up the hard-packed soil. He brought not only a breath of the outside world but food and medicines that always added brightness to their lives.

When he left the last time, he had promised, "A surprise for you next time." But he always brought surprises.

No one else was with him this time.

Lili could see Courtney practically dancing as they came toward her, their arms wound around each other's waists.

So he's learned to fly, Lili thought, smiling. That's the surprise.

"I figured," Andrew told them at dinner, "that I think and plan as much about this place as I do about my own work. By the time two weekends go by, I'm itching to get out here again. So I bought this little Cessna and have been learning to fly."

He beamed, proud of his surprise and of himself. He looked at Lili. "You get the first ride," he said. "Tomorrow right after breakfast. Maybe it'll seem like old times."

And, despite the fanciness of the instrument panel, she still recognized the altimeter, the turn and bank indicator, the magnetic compass. . . . She ran her hands over the wheel, across the instruments. They used to come alive at her touch. Funny, she thought, how one can feel emotional about a machine. But she did. Old familiar feelings came surging back.

"It's been over twenty years," she told Andrew.

"I know." His voice was soft as he looked at her. "Remember when you and Marsh flew to Kariba to deliver Courtney?"

Lili felt a lump in her throat as she looked at her granddaughter's shining eyes, remembering Carolyn.

"Oh, Daddy, it's exciting. It opens up all sorts of possibilities."

Andrew's eyes twinkled. "You may get sick of me. I figure I could take off work early Friday afternoons and be here for dinner."

"Bringing steaks?" suggested Courtney.

Andrew laughed.

"Flying's fun." He turned to Lili. "You never told me what pure joy it evokes."

"It does that," Liliane agreed.

"Come on," Andrew invited. "Let's go, Lili."

When they were airborne, he shouted, "Okay, you take over. See what you can remember."

"Andrew." A tremor of fear started. Stopped. "It's been over twenty years."

"It's like riding a bike. Once you know how . . ."

He's sweet, she thought. The nicest thing Caro ever gave me was Andrew. He's got guts, too. Guts right where his heart is. I'm seventy-five years old. My reflexes have slowed. And he tells me to fly.

Well. fly I will.

Her hand shifted; she felt powerful as she always did when she commanded a plane. She didn't feel old or infirm. I'll show him, she thought, laughing to herself, and turned the plane on a roll.

But she didn't trust herself to land it smoothly. She insisted Andrew do that.

Courtney stood waiting for her turn.

Andrew jumped out and reached to help Lili. He was laughing. "God, Lili, you're like no other woman at all. A roll!"

"At seventy-five years old," she said with great pleasure.

"Talking of age," he murmured, lowering his voice. "You do remember today is March twenty-fifth?"

Courtney's birthday. No, she had not remembered. Days here on the savannah melded together and she hadn't even realized it was March, much less the twenty-fifth.

"I brought a cake," whispered Andrew as Courtney was climbing into the front seat. "And candles."

While Andrew took Courtney out for a spin, Liliane wondered what to give Courtney.

She's given me so much.

She's given me the future.

And suddenly she knew what she should give her. A part of her past. The jeweled comb from Saigon. The rubies and emeralds that Marsh would want his granddaughter to have. The comb he had bought so long ago, with a love that had never died.

Tears stung Liliane's eyes as she went into her spartan bedroom, where the one thing of beauty lay shimmering on her bureau. Love that never dies.

She wished she had tissue paper and a ribbon.

At dinner they sang to Courtney, Andrew and Lili and Mara and Gail. Bmena watched, unsure of what to do.

Gail had found a trinket among her belongings, and Mara offered a Willie Nelson tape she treasured. Only Lili smiled at its title. "Stardust." All these years later. Threads continued to wind through her life, threads that had begun so long ago but had no end.

When she held out the jeweled comb, Courtney was mute. "Here," Lili said. But Courtney could not reach for it. She sat staring at Lili, not at the comb.

I'd have left it to her anyhow, Lili thought, when I die. But she's not letting me die. She's allowing me to go on. She makes me forget how old I am. "Take it," she begged. "I want you to have it."

Courtney reached out a slender hand, a hand that already evidenced the hard work she had done during these past months. "Oh, Lili." Her voice broke as she leaned across the table and kissed her grandmother, her hand caressing the smoothness of the stones. "Thank you."

"Thank *you.*" Lili's voice was a whisper.

Andrew waited for the emotion to dissipate, for a few moments to pass.

"Mine will be a letdown after this," he said. But they could tell by the way he said it that he did not really think so.

"It dawned on me that you're dependent on me, or someone from the government, bringing you supplies. So far, you haven't had an emergency where you've needed to contact the outside world. And, besides, I got a really good buy. Getting two at once put me in a good bargaining position."

Lili knew immediately, though Courtney looked puzzled.

Andrew turned to Lili. "You can manage, can't you, for a couple of weeks while I whisk her away for lessons?"

Courtney felt at a loss. "What does Lili have to manage?"

"Why"—Andrew was about to burst—"I bought two of these little Cessnas. And though I know Lili can help when you have problems, I really think you need some flying lessons. At least enough to fly it out here. How about it, Lili?"

"It's a lovely idea," she said. She looked at Gail and Mara. "Of course we can manage."

"It'll only be two weeks," he said. "I've already made arrangements. Then you and I can take over and teach her the rest."

1980 TO 1981 / 569

"Oh, Daddy." Courtney jumped up and ran over to him, flinging her arms around him. "A plane of my own." She turned to Lili. "See, I'm going to be just like you."

Just like me, thought Lili.

"This must be the best birthday anyone every had," said Courtney, her eyes like stars. "My twenty-fifth birthday. Life couldn't possibly be more wonderful."

In the morning, Courtney kept asking Lili for assurance. "Are you sure you can manage?"

Andrew and Courtney both kissed her, and Andrew said, "You know, I'll be back more often now. This place is becoming part of me, too."

"You know," Lili said as she walked them to the plane, "how much I love you, Andrew."

"I've known from the very beginning." He had her hand tucked through his arm and held it tightly. "And you know how happy I am you came back here with Courtney. I only hope it will be enough for her."

"It can fill one to overflowing," said Lili.

Courtney was already in the plane, waving to Lili. "I promise not to crash. Remember Mrs. Mbula should be due about now, and Safartha's fever needs to be checked, and—"

The roar of the propeller drowned out her voice.

Lili backed away as the wind whipped the dirt, watching as the plane taxied down the field, turned directly into the sun, was silhouetted in front of it, and rose abruptly from the ground, heading north.

For just a second she felt alone. Lonely. A feeling to which she was unaccustomed.

But she's coming back, Lili told herself, her eyes on the dot that was no longer there. Two weeks. She's coming back in her own plane. And she's going to make a difference.

To Zimbabwe.

To Africa.

She walked back toward the hospital. Mrs. Mbula would have her baby today, she knew. It was going to be a breech birth, and if I were not here, she mused, Mrs. Mbula and her baby might die.

But I *am* here.

So Mrs. Mbula will be fine, and her baby will be fine.

And I still make a difference.

AFTERWORD

▼

THIS BOOK IS A MIXTURE OF FACT AND FICTION.

The story and the characters are my own; the places, times, and historical events are true.

In the Congo, all places and dates are real; the exception is Simbayo, a figment of my imagination based on several missions that flourished in that part of the Congo during the years I write about. The events that took place in Zaire after independence are based on historical fact. The Stanleyville Massacre actually occurred in 1964, but I have taken the liberty of changing the date, for my purposes, to 1962.

The events and dates surrounding the building of the dam at Kariba are faithful. Actually, the British firm of Costain received the contract of $9.8 million for building the two towns at Kariba. The events described did take place. A number of conscientious, hardworking district commissioners and aides really did the work I ascribe to Michael Carver and Sam Elliot. The floods actually happened as I have described them.

I have used the names of leaders of countries and government officials (Lumumba and General Olenga in Zaire and Huggins and Savory in Rhodesia), but, aside from these, none of my characters is anything but a fictional person. The places and the times are true; the characters' interpretations of the realities are mine.

Though there are many black squatter townships outside all of South Africa's cities, Kaputo is not an actual one. It is an amalgamation of those I've read about.

In Cape Town, babies are not delivered in hospitals but in birthing centers. For the sake of my story, I have ignored this so that Courtney could deliver babies in her hospital job.

ABOUT THE AUTHOR

A long-time New Yorker now living in Eugene, Oregon, Barbara Bickmore taught English for twenty years, raised three children, and recently spent two months journeying 3600 miles through China. *East of the Sun* is the author's first novel.